More Praise for Lee Killough's Bridling Chaos

Killough has become an author whose every new book is a treat.
—SF Chronicle

This is a grittily realistic police procedural, set in 21st-century Kansas. I enjoyed it, and I recommend it to you heartily. Don't miss this one. You'll enjoy it.
—Analog

Police procedural SF is rare—that makes Ms. Killough's fun romp all the more appreciated. The characters, plot, indeed the whole future society, are very well developed in this novel.
—SF Review 34

Like many procedurals, the novel's strength rests as much in the personalities of the cops as in the solving of the crime, and Brill and Maxwell make an entertaining pair.
—Locus

SF and mysteries a double treat.
—Milwaukee Sentinel

For Dave & Helen
Best wishes at Buccaneer
Lee Killough

Bridling Chaos

by

Lee Killough

This is a work of fiction. All the characters and events portrayed in this book are fictitious. Any resemblance to real people or events is purely coincidental.

The Doppelgänger Gambit © 1979 by Lee Killough
Spider Play © 1986 by Lee Killough
Dragon's Teeth © 1990 by Lee Killough
Foreword © 1998 by Lee Killough

All rights reserved by the publisher. This book may not be reproduced, in whole or in part, without the written permission of the publisher, except for the purpose of reviews.

BRIDLING CHAOS

An MM Publishing Book
Published by Meisha Merlin Publishing, Inc.
PO Box 7
Decatur, GA 30031

Editing & interior layout by Stephen Pagel
Copyediting & proofreading by Teddi Stransky
Cover art by Michael Harring
Cover design by Neil Seltzer

ISBN: 0-9658345-3-0

http://www.angelfire.com/biz/MeishaMerlin

First MM Publishing edition: May 1998

Printed in the United States of America
0 9 8 7 6 5 4 3 2 1

Table of Contents

Foreword

As with *BloodWalk,* my previous book from Meisha Merlin, I'm delighted to have more of my novels back in print...this time the three featuring my twenty-first century police detectives Janna Brill and Mama Maxwell.

I've always loved mysteries as much as I do science fiction. Possibly because I discovered both genres about the same time, but also because both satisfy a desire for order. They open with chaos—destructive threads threaten Pern, a rich young woman is murdered during a cruise up the Nile—but through the application of science and reason, the danger is averted, the murder solved, order restored.

Nor do I appear alone in this dual passion. Mystery and SF readerships overlap substantially, and a number of authors write in both fields. And a few of us satisfy both loves simultaneously by writing SF mysteries. In particular, law enforcement officers populate my novels and short stories: ghost cops, vampire cops, werewolf cops...and future cops like Brill and Maxwell.

Creating an SF mystery presents an interesting paradox. On the one hand it challenges the writer, but at the same time it offers freedom. It challenges the writer first to produce a genuine mystery with an integral, essential SF element, and then to play fair with the reader. Part of the fun in a mystery comes with trying to solve the crime before the detective does. But in order to have a fair chance, the reader must be aware of the possible motives and methods for murder. So the SF mystery writer needs to familiarize the reader with the setting and culture along with presenting the crime and clues...and then stick to the rules laid down, not to pull some SF macguffin in at the last minute to solve the crime.

On the other hand, the SF mystery frees the writer from the constraints of only crime possible in our world and time. In the best tradition of hybrid vigor, mystery provides a framework for the SF story and the SF elements enliven the mystery. The writer may create new poisons, new weepons, even unique motives. Law enforcement can take new forms. In my book *Deadly Silents*, the police had to hunt evidence for the defense as well as the prosecution.

Dopplegänger Gambit, the first book featuring Brill and Maxwell, started as a short story. For years I considered myself strictly a short story writer. True, I had managed to write one novel, *A Voice Out of Ramah*, but I preferred the quicker gratification of short story writing. However, when I reached page fifteen and had only just begun the story, I realized I needed to write another novel.

Janna Brill and Mama Maxwell developed partly through deliberate choice, but also with a generous portion of surprises sprung by the left side of my brain. I chose to create a female cop, but as I started working out her character, she grabbed control to become an officer not just dedicated but tough, able and willing to break heads, definitely not a nurturer. She rejected any hobbies I tried to give her, and insisted on living in an apartment whose starkness, bare of the personal clutter most of us accumulate, made it a bivouac rather than a home. Her male partner turned out to be the nurturer and nest builder, the lover of arts and hobbies. Mama began with my memory of the manic detective Lou Gossett Jr. played in *The Laughing Detective*. But only began. From his name—he was always "Mama," without explanation, leaving me to make up an origin for his nickname—to his personality, he evolved as his own person. I wanted an odd-couple partnership, but Mama emerged as almost Janna's opposite, flamboyant to her conservatism, intuitive where she relies on logic, unorthodox where she goes by the book, a personality forever preferring to color outside the lines.

It sounds peculiar to talk about losing control of my characters, because, after all I *am* the author. No one but me types the words. Yet every author tells stories of characters declaring independence. And however disconcerted or frustrated by it, most of us also take a certain pride in that independence, because it means we have constructed living characters, not mere puppets. So it has been a delight through *Dopplegänger Gambit*, *Spider Play*, and *Dragon's Teeth* to observe Janna and Mama at work, and watch the interplay as they learn to work together and to appreciate each other's strength. Though such appreciation comes slower to Janna.

Fans have asked me what makes Mama click...whether he is borderline wacky or just pretends to be. I always plead ignorance. I can climb into Jana's head but I never looked inside Mama's. I think I prefer not to. Would we find Sherlock Homes as fascinating if we saw how all the wheels work? Perhaps, to paraphrase George Patton, it is not important that we know how crazy Mama is, it is only important that he knows.

Along with the fun of observing the characters has been playing the SF game of "what if:"—what if our society became totally cashless and we paid for *everything* with a credit card, thereby leaving a trail that would let the police pinpoint our location at any particular time? How could someone commit a murder under those circumstances? Could a murderer use the system to help him commit murders? What if political fund raisers had security as tight as that of Fort Knox? How could someone slip through to commit murder and escape again?—then using the SF elements to construct mysteries peculiar to the story's milieu, mysteries that could not occur this way in our time.

I would like to credit a reader for the title of this edition. The title comes from a piece of poetry Mr. Charles R. Stone, once of San Francisco, sent me in 1979 along with very kind compliments on *Dopplegänger Gambit*. Short and almost haiku in form, the poem has stuck with me and it came to mind again when I started wracking my brain for a title. Although mad digging through past correspondence located Mr. Stone's letter, unfortunately the man himself appears to have moved since 1979 and I have not been able to locate him to ask permission to reprint his poem. So I'll quote only the last lines:

"Someone has to bridle chaos
and ride it into exhaustion."

Thank you again, Mr. Stone, for your letter and poetry, and thank you for the title it inspired all these years later. If you happen to read this, I hope you enjoy Janna and Mama just as much the second time around. As I hope all readers find just as much pleasure reading the books as I did writing them, whether re-reading them or coming to them for the first time.

—Lee Killough October 1997

Doppelgänger Gambit

1

The whole world mourned the *Invictus*. People everywhere paused at any news of her, and those who believed in gods and miracles prayed. She was an American-built ramjet, carrying American colonists, but messages from the ships Earth had launched toward the stars over the past twenty years were rare and therefore international events. The *Invictus* became an international tragedy.

The newscanner in the squadroom of the Shawnee County Police Department's Crimes Against Persons squad had been there for so long, no one remembered the set's origin, whether it had been donated or abandoned there or was recovered stolen property someone had "forgotten" to turn in to the property room. It was usually a little-attended but familiar part of the background, and leos—law enforcement officers—on all three watches tossed spare vending tokens into the cup on Lieutenant Hari Vradel's desk so that once a month the burly squad commander could redeem the tokens and have the bankcredit transferred to Newservice, Inc. for the subscription. This morning, however, every eye in the squadroom stared at the set, morning and day watches alike. The only sound in the room was the voice of KTNB's voice-over announcer reading the text that rolled across the screen.

"Her name is the *Invictus*, and in the eternal night of space that covers her, she may be dying. No one aboard knows why. She is a Boeing Starmaster modified 800 ramjet and she was launched from the Glenn Space Platform ten years ago, carrying the nine hundred members of the Laheli Colonial Company. She was bound for a planet seventy-three light-years away. No one expected to hear from her until she sent her tachyon courier capsule to tell Earth she had arrived safely at her destination; however, yesterday the capsule was recovered by workers from the Vladikov Space Platform at 2:53 PM Greenwich time, with this voice-only message inside."

The announcer's voice was replaced by another, a calm voice, but one heavy with weariness. "This is Jaes Laurent of the Laheli Company's ramjet *Invictus*. Over the past two weeks, ship's time, we have experienced repeated breakdowns and failures in the life support systems of our sleeper sections. The onboard computer has been able to instruct us how to make only temporary repairs. We have now lost four hundred of our sleepers and face the possibility of losing more. All ten crewmembers are awake and working to repair failures as they occur, but we don't know how well we'll succeed. We realize there's no possibility of you on Earth being able to help us. This message is not a distress call. We just want someone to know what happened to us, and perhaps bring a problem to attention that may save the lives of future colonists."

The voice of the announcer resumed. "When contacted, representatives of Boeing refused to speculate—"

Lieutenant Vradel reached up and turned off the sound. "I'm sorry to interrupt, leos, but the time is now eight thirty on what promises to be another firecracker July day, and a few light years closer to home, in our very own Topeka, murderers and thieves whose activities we just discussed at rollcall deserve our attention as law enforcement officers."

Someone at the back of the room muttered, "Crap."

Vradel regarded the squad with mock solemnity. "No, Crimes Against Property is the crap squad, not Crimes Against Persons." He became serious. "Morning watch, you're all late for debriefing. Dismissed. Day watch, get to work. Everyone in the drugstore stakeout come to this end of the room."

He gave them a few more minutes to sort themselves out. While he waited for the stakeout teams to gather around him, he looked them over, mentally reviewing the assignments. In addition to his own personnel, he had four teams from Crimes Against Property and eight plainjane teams on loan from the Gage division—those sixteen men and women hoping to impress Vradel enough to be permanently promoted to Investigator I. He chewed on his mustache. Twenty teams made an expensive operation. He hoped the stakeout would produce more results today than it had the past week.

His eyes fell on a dark bulldog of a man standing next to a tall smoky-blonde. Sergeant Wim Kiest wore a worried frown. Vradel supposed the *Invictus* touched some sharp nerves in him.

Vradel smiled. "Be optimistic, Kiest. That doesn't happen to every colony ship. Yours will be all right."

Beside him, Sergeant Janna Brill hissed. "Don't say that. I've been trying for months to talk him out of this colonial insanity. You see how it's affecting him." She plucked at the sleeve of his shirt, one of the currently popular "neo-pioneer homespun" styles. "It's driven him right off his tick. Don't spoil the best case against his leaving I've found yet."

If Wim Kiest was a bulldog, Janna Brill was a greyhound, one hundred eighty-three centimeters of whipcord sinew. The sleeveless blue romper and matching hip boots she wore set off her pale coloring so well Vradel reflected that with some more meat on her, she could be a very flash bibi. Why did she stay so bony thin?

He glanced at the chrono again. The digital readout said, redly: 8:35. "All right, lions and she-lions; we do it like before, one team at each drugstore in a shopping mall. Same assignments. The computer analog profile of our two jons says they'll continue to hit the Gage area and will prefer to strike soon after opening. Be careful. These deeks are carrying shooters, remember."

"Yes, Daddy," someone called.

One of the janes grimaced. "I wish they'd hit the Highland division for a change, or work evenings so it would be the night watch's problem."

His partner shook her head. "Don't wish it. When the computer starts missing, where will we be?"

Vradel pointed to the door. "Sail. I want to see those deeks' heads here on pikes by high noon."

Another Gage jane tapped Janna Brill's arm. "Did your supervisor take an extra degree, say in dramatics?"

Brill looked back wide-eyed. "I thought Criminal Justice *was* a dramatics degree."

"Sail!" Vradel ordered.

Outside the squadroom, Wim Kiest and Janna Brill separated quickly from the other teams and wound their way down through the three floors and two basement levels of the Capitol Division station toward the parking garage. The station sprawled over an entire city block. They passed clerks, investigators from other squads, a few civilians—looking lost and apprehensive—and uniformed officers from the beta squad coming in off the morning watch. At one point Wim and Janna found themselves surrounded by helmeted and booted leos in iron-gray jumpsuits sidestriped with red from collar to the ends of the short summer sleeves and underarms to boottops. The group swirled around them, yawning and wisecracking, on their way to showers and debriefing, that tick talk session where, supposedly, they discharged the emotional charge of the job stress before heading home. The alpha squad would have come in a little after eight and already be in debriefing.

In the garage, the partners passed rows of watchcars waiting for the day watch beta squad. "Bullet on the half shell" some wit had called the floatcar design, for the way the sleek fiberplastic body poised in the middle of the airfoil's spreading skirt. The vehicles were conspicuously marked with white tops, black bodies, and a light-reflecting red stripe circling the body just below the windows. Wim and Janna passed jane cars, too, unmarked by police insignia but still obviously police vehicles by virtue of being Datsun-Ford Monitors. Everyone knew the Shawnee County PD used D-F's almost exclusively.

Their own car was also a Monitor, painted a bright green. They stepped on the airfoil skirt and climbed in, Wim under the wheel, Janna on the rider side. She switched on the car radio and screwed her personal radio button into her left ear. She activated it with a tap of her finger.

"Indian Thirty to control, requesting a T-check."

"Roger, Indian Thirty." The dispatcher's voice came from both the car radio and her ear button. "T-check positive for three."

For good or ill, the transponders built into the car and their ear buttons were registering on the division map.

Janna looked at Wim. "Your button receiving all right?"

He nodded. He switched on the Monitor. The electric motor hummed. Wim activated the airfoil fans. They whined as they wound up. The car shimmied a moment, then lifted off its parking rollers and rose clear of the floor. Wim floated it backward out of its parking slot and reversed to head for the exit ramp.

Janna relaxed in her seat. "I keep finding myself surprised someone should be jacking drugstores in Gage. I could understand it in Oakland where the government doesn't hand out drug coupons to the poor and needy. Do you suppose the jons are street dealers looking for a way to cut their overhead?"

The car sailed up Van Buren and around the corner onto Sixth Street.

"Would you do it?" Wim asked.

Janna blinked. "Do what? Steal drugs or hand out coupons for drugs like the ones for food and housing?"

"Would you really keep talking about the *Invictus* to scare me out of traveling on a ramjet?"

"I'm thinking about it." She trailed her arm out the window of the car. The air felt stifling already. It was going to be one of those days when she wished she had gills to help her breathe. Dear Kansas sauna summers. Then she noticed that Wim's knuckles had turned white around the wheel. She sighed. "Hey, partner, I wouldn't really do it. You ought to know I wouldn't try to keep you from something you want as much as you want to go to Champaign. I just don't understand why you want to go. What in god's name is so attractive about grubbing around on some alien world?"

His hands relaxed. He smiled. "Maybe I have a sense of adventure? Or maybe I just like grubbing."

They had been through this routine dozens of times in the past year. It was like a record. Once the conversation started, it proceeded exactly as the time before, and the time before that.

"I like being outside. I liked being on patrol. I didn't mind Juve and Vice. Since we made Investigator, though..." He shook his head.

"You're a good investigator. We're a good team."

"But so much of it is desk work. I want to be outside."

"You've always said you left that farm you grew up on because you were tired of freezing your ass feeding cattle in the winter and being broiled on a tractor all summer."

He shrugged. "I know I said that, but every spring I find myself out digging up the yard for a garden. That reminds me, can you use tomatoes?"

She rolled her eyes. "The August tomato glut is starting."

The radio crackled and muttered in her ear. She noted the calls with one part of her mind, but for the most part she ignored any announcement not preceded by "Indian Thirty."

She and Wim had been partners a long time. They started in an Oakland division watchcar five years before. They had made Sergeant together. Three years ago they had been promoted to Investigator I and been transferred to the Capitol division. Five years working together—there were marriage contracts that did not last that long. She knew he was serious about leaving when he would not take the Investigator II test with her. How could he give up five years for something he had never seen before? She could not imagine working with anyone else.

"Wim." It was almost a wail. "I'll miss you like hell."

"Yeah." He reached over to pat her thigh. "I'll miss you, too, partner."

They rode out Topeka Avenue in silence. Janna watched the traffic glumly. There were few pedestrians as yet. Most of the traffic consisted of bicycles, and tiny runabouts that danced like motes on their air cushions: GMC Vestas and D-F Fireflies, AMC-Renault Sols, some Hitachi Bonsais and Smith Sundowners. The fans of the big transit buses and trailer trucks thrummed deafeningly and left smaller vehicles shuddering in their wakes. There were a scattering of road cars, too—D-F Monitors and Kodiacs, GMC Titans, and the whole pride of Leyland International cats: Jaguars, Panthers, and Cheetahs.

Janna counted twenty-three moving violations. She would have loved to go after one Sundowner. The driver ducked in and out of every traffic lane, including the commercial lane and the bicycle lane. Farther ahead a big Kenworth was trying to crowd runabouts off the road.

"Look at them," she said in disgust. "Who's monitoring the traffic along here? There's never a lion around when you need one."

Past the Expocentre, Wim signaled for a right turn and slid the car sideways. They turned west down Twenty-first Street toward their stakeout assignment at the Fairlawn Plaza. Janna watched more traffic. After counting ten pedestrian violations and fifteen more moving violations, she gave up and watched the passing neighborhoods instead.

It felt almost like coming home. She had known these particular streets well when she attended Washburn University. She had come to know the streets to the south even better. They were in the Highland Park division, where she spent her probation year. It was a pleasant residential area with a few modern semisunken and earth-covered houses, but more featured older architecture, twentieth-century one- and two-floor aboveground houses of stone and wood frame. Many had large windows. Most of the streets remained still in good condition, though they were beginning to show some age—potholes and shoots of green coming up around brick and through paving. Airfoils did not need a smooth surface to operate, so street repairs tended to be sporadic. Even so, the streets here were still better than their broken, weed-choked counterparts in Oakland.

At the Washburn View Mall, Janna waved to Investigators Leah Calabrese and Dan Roth. They were just settling themselves with caff, notebook computers, and bookchip viewers at the little tables outside a small caff shop next to the drugstore, trying hard to look like students studying for summer school finals.

Wim grinned. "They'll lose their cover if we don't strap these jons before finals are over."

"I wonder if they're learning anything."

They passed the Seabrook Mall. Cardarella and Witt, one of the jane teams, did not appear to have arrived yet. When they reached Fairlawn, Wim set the car down on its parking rollers opposite the drugstore and took out an antique book of bound paper pages. Janna stared at it a minute—Wim had some of the most unexpected possessions—then climbed out of the car and went up to rap on the drugstore window.

The clerk inside nodded in recognition and came to let her in. "You look less like a police officer in those clothes than you did in the jumpsuit yesterday," he said.

She decided to treat his remark as a compliment. "Thank you." She slipped on the smock he handed her and prepared to play clerk again. She pitied Wim. The small store smelled of the strange mixed odor of drugs, but it was cool in here. He would cook in the car.

"Isn't it terrible about that colony ship?" the clerk asked. A small newscanner screen hung on the wall behind the counter. He punched it on and switched to one of the stations that rolled text to the accompaniment of background music. "Several years ago the woman I was married to wanted us to join a colonial company. I considered doing so, but—I don't know. I have a nice house and neighbors I think I can trust. I'm thinking of buying a runabout so I won't be dependent on the bus schedule to get to work. That's a lot to give up for—for something unknown. Now after hearing about that colony ship, I don't think I could ever bring myself to get on one, let alone allow someone to put me to sleep for a year or two."

He did not seem to require return comments from her, or even encouragement, so Janna just smiled the way she had been taught and nodded once in a while and tuned him out. She wondered what effect the *Invictus*'s disaster might have on her father. He was a designer for Boeing. Maybe she should give him a call tonight.

The newscanner was rolling a story about another demonstration by the Arabs For a Free Middle East—this time at the United World building in Zurich—against the Israeli domination of Egypt and Syria. *Halt Zionist Imperialism*, their signs read.

She also listened, as always, to the police calls whispering in her ear. Most of them were Gage division calls, with only a few of the Highland Park calls reaching her.

"Beta Gage Twenty, see the woman, 1102 Prairie Road, domestic disturbance."

At nine-thirty, the clerk unlocked the door. The first customer, an attractive young woman, seemed embarrassed as she handed Janna a prescription slip for prostaglandin suppositories. Janna wondered whether the woman was embarrassed about having become pregnant or was sufficiently influenced by Lifest and Bible cultist propaganda to feel guilty about aborting herself.

Janna handed the prescription on to the clerk, who brought a box up from a back shelf.

The woman handed over her card. The Scib Card was a citizen's most important piece of plastic. It was a social care card, ID, and bankcard in one, a universal credit card. The clerk fed the piece of plastic into the credit register and typed in the purchase and price. The woman pressed her left thumb to the ID window of the register and signed her name across the window with a light scriber. The register hummed as it recorded the purchase and relayed the information to her bank's computers. After a minute it spat back the card. The clerk returned it to the woman along with her prescription and purchase receipt.

The woman left. On her way out, she passed Wim coming in. Wim was grinning.

"I just had an idea, Jan. Why don't *you* come out to Champaign with us?"

Janna stared at him. "Come *with* you? Oh, no." She backed away, shaking her head. "I'm a city girl. I need pollution to survive. Even divisions like Soldier Creek seem back of beyond to me. Besides, even if every passenger aboard your ship weren't already planned for, I couldn't raise the credit for a share in only one month."

"Another ship will be coming out in a year or two. That one isn't full yet."

She rolled her eyes. "Go read your book. I like to look at waving fields of grain, but I'm quite content to let someone else grow them."

Wim headed for the door. "Think about it. There's only so far you can go here. You'll have to get a law degree if you want more rank than Lieutenant. On Champaign you can be anything."

"I can be eaten by a six-legged green wolf." But the door had closed behind him and he did not hear her last remark. She saw the clerk staring at her. "I think it's a fever," she said, "something like Bible cultists' evangelism. Colonists want everyone else to come out and grub in the mud with them."

The clerk looked as if he were unsure whether to laugh at that remark or not. *Toad*, she thought.

"Alpha Highland Thirteen, Alpha Highland Five, accident on 470 bypass at Gage exit. Two trucks involved."

Go out to that planet with them? Wim was one of her favorite people in this world, but that had to be the most brain bereft suggestion she had ever heard. Janna and Wim's wife Vada were good friends, but she somehow doubted Vada had ever considered taking Wim's partner to the stars with them. Vada was not the group marriage kind.

"Alpha Gage One, meet Alpha Gage Ten, at 1017 Randolph."

The call raised Janna's curiosity. Alpha Gage One would be the alpha squad sergeant. Being asked simply to meet a unit meant the unit was involved in a situation it could not leave and did not care to mention over the radio.

Two young men wandered into the drugstore. Janna smiled at them while she looked them over, checking for weapons bulges.

"What kinds of hallucinogens do you have?" one asked.

"All of them," the clerk replied. "Mescaline, psilocybin, LSD, STP, MDT, ALR."

The jons exchanged looks. "Well, we were looking for something stronger." The first speaker hesitated.

His companion said, "A lot stronger...something with a *real* boost."

This time Janna and the clerk exchanged looks. Janna wondered if that were a guilty flush there around the back of the clerk's neck. Could he be doing a little subcounter dealing?

"Trick is illegal," she said.

The two tried to look innocent. "Oh, we certainly didn't mean we wanted any trick."

"It'll cross-wire your brain. Synesthesia. A milligram or two too much will scramble your tick for good. At worst your brain can forget how to make you breathe. Why don't you use something safe, like dreamtime?"

"*Dreamtime*." Their scorn rasped like a file. "That's just a sleep substitute."

"The hyperdreaming can give a good boost, and better, a safe trip."

"No, thanks."

They turned and left the store.

The clerk was trying hard not to frown. "Sergeant." He said it hesitantly. "I would prefer that—you let me handle the sales."

Janna looked at him. "The penalty for selling trick can be heavy. Some dealers go up on manslaughter charges."

The clerk swallowed visibly.

"Alpha Gage Eleven, investigate an abandoned vehicle, Tenth and Fairlawn."

A girl came in. Janna looked her over but quickly decided she could not be one of the deeks they were waiting for. The paint on her depilated head had smeared with age. The scars of a thousand launchings tracked her arms. She was a long-time ulysses making odysseying a lifetime pursuit, the hard way.

She presented her addict's identification and Scib Card to the clerk. The purchase was recorded. The ulysses left hurriedly, clutching her week's ration of heroin.

"Beta Gage Twelve, see the man, neighborhood disturbance, twenty-six hundred block Arrowhead Street."

Janna wished she could hear the replies but the duplex system put replies on a different frequency than the dispatch broadcasts, which was all her ear button received.

"Attention all units, armed robbery in progress, Seabrook Mall."

Janna raced for the door, tearing off the smock. "You can relax," she called back to the clerk. "They picked someone else today."

Wim had the Monitor's fans rapping. Janna dived into her seat and slid the door closed behind her. "We're just a straight shot down Twenty-first. Let's sail."

Wim revved the fans. The car bucked up onto its air cushion. Janna slapped the pop-on cherry on the dash and hit the siren. The car shot forward.

"Attention all units," the dispatcher's voice said in her ear. "Suspects are two males, twenty to twenty-five years old, one Caucasian, one hundred seventy centimeters, eighty kilos, brown hair shoulder length, wearing an orange jumpsuit with sleeves and pantlegs cut off; other suspect is afroam, one hundred eighty centimeters, seventy-five kilos, wearing gray pioneer-style shirt and trousers. Suspects are on foot headed west on Twenty first Street."

"They're coming our way. Kick her, Wim!"

The fans screamed as the car lunged ahead. The traffic scattered before the *whew-whew-whew* of their siren as if pushed aside by an invisible plow. The siren became a hoarse howl as they rocketed through an intersection.

The radio said, "Suspects have turned north on McAlister."

They had almost reached McAlister. Wim wrenched the wheel, and the car banked so sharply it heeled over halfway on its side. For one fearful moment it seemed they might roll and be driven top first into the ground by the fans, but then the car slewed around and straightened. They flew up McAlister.

They saw Cardarella and Witt almost immediately, on foot and running. About a block beyond them were two more runners.

"There they are."

Wim passed the Gage janes and started slowing. Opposite the two suspects, he shut off the fans. Then they kicked the doors forward and bailed out of the car before it had even settled to its parking rollers, abandoning it in the middle of the street.

The suspects looked back. Seeing Wim and Janna, one abruptly ducked sideways through a yard. The other cut across the street into another yard.

"I'll take the afroam." Janna charged after him.

The man was fast, she gave him that, and he jumped like a deer. These blocks had no alleys in them. The yards sat back to back, separated by fences. The black man cleared the barrier in one bound and landed racing through the yard beyond. Janna vaulted after him.

Her choice of clothes for the day had been bad after all, she decided. They were all wrong for running an obstacle course. The romper was fine, but the hip boots were hot and cumbersome. Sweat was already running down her legs inside them. Her gun, holstered down inside one boot, began digging into her thigh.

Damn, that deek is fast. Though one of the top runners in the department, she was barely gaining on her man. He leaped over another fence, through another yard. He almost ran over a small child playing in a sandbox. The child's mother screamed. The afroam leaped the fence on the far side.

Following him, Janna found herself in a group of children. One had been knocked down by the fleeing man.

Janna's hands itched to pull her gun. A needle would stop that deek fast enough. She could not draw here, though. If she missed, she would either have to come back looking for the spent needle, or trust to luck none of these children found it. A child playing with a needle could prick himself and inject the fifteen milligrams of percurare inside. Fifteen milligrams was enough to paralyze the muscles of an average adult. The drug would paralyze everything in a child, including the diaphragm. Such things had happened before.

So she left the Starke in her boot and cursed herself for not bringing the shotgun from the car.

They pounded across a street and between two houses. There was an alley through the middle of this block and the afroam turned up it. Finally she found herself gaining on him.

They reached the end of the alley. Her quarry crossed the street with Janna close behind. A passing runabout came so close she felt it clip her hip as the driver screamed curses at her. She stumbled but did not go down. In another stride she had the pace back. She was only meters behind her quarry, now. She had a clear, easy shot at him.

She reached for her gun.

He turned around suddenly, a shooter in his hand. "I'll kill you!"

She let go of the Starke. No sense needling him now. The four to ten seconds the percurare took to work was time enough for him to empty the shooter at her. Instead she dived to the left as the shooter went off. His aim was bad enough that the bullet came nowhere near her, but it sent a bolt of terror through her, nevertheless. Where, oh, where was that much-rumored stungun R and D kept promising police departments?

The man cocked the hammer for another shot.

Janna dodged again. This time she heard the bullet, a deadly *zit* near her right ear, just audible under the flat popcorn sound of the shot. Before he could fire again, she dived for him. He brought the barrel of the shooter down toward her head. She jerked to the side, then grabbed a handful of his crotch and squeezed with all her strength.

He screamed. As he started to double, she locked on to his shooting arm. She went under it and back, taking the arm with her. She twisted the shooter hard against his thumb. The thumb gave with an audible *pop* and the afroam screamed again.

Janna felt a ripple of resistance building in him, but before he could translate it into action, she shoved him toward a power pole. Her hand reached inside her boot for her wrap strap. She put a little more pressure on his arm to keep him moving and slammed him against the pole, snapping the wrap strap with a practiced flick of her wrist. The strap circled pole and suspect's neck in one loop and adhered to itself. Janna made sure it was tight, then let go and stepped back, panting hard.

The afroam pulled, but the strap pinned him against the pole. He spat obscenities at her.

Then reaction set in. Janna started shaking. This deek tried to kill her! She hefted the shooter in a trembling hand, fighting a desire to lay the barrel across his jungled scalp. "Shut up, toad." She tapped her ear button. Between gulps of air, she said, "Indian Thirty beta to Gage control."

"Go ahead Indian Thirty."

"I have one of the armed robbery suspects in custody. My location unknown."

"Your T's on the board, Indian Thirty. Wait for a mobile unit."

The unit arrived in two minutes, a watchcar driven by a pair of young leos whose uniforms somehow managed to look trim and neat despite the humid heat. Briefly, Janna envied them. Sweat plastered her romper to her and the thick curls of her lion's mane lay sodden on her forehead and the back of her neck.

"What about the other suspect?" she asked.

"Beta Gage Seventeen picked him up a few minutes ago. Needled him."

She grinned. The last of her shakes disappeared. That was good news. Vradel would be pleased. Riding back to her own car crowded into the front seat with the Gage leos, she was jubilant.

The mood did not last long. She had expected to find Wim waiting for her by Indian Thirty with Beta Gage Seventeen. He was not there. She frowned at the officers from Beta Gage Seventeen.

"Wasn't my partner behind this jon?" She pointed at the man sprawled motionless on one of the lengthwise seats in the back of the watchcar, head pushed against the laminated wire and plastic screen that separated the control and prisoner sections, feet at the rear door.

The leos shook their heads. "He was all alone when we needled him."

Cardarella and Witt had not seen Wim since he bailed out of Indian Thirty, nor had several other teams loitering in the area.

Janna tapped her ear button. "Indian Thirty beta to Gage control, requesting a T-check on Indian Thirty alpha."

The dispatcher came back. "Indian Thirty alpha's T north and west of you and stationary."

Janna's stomach flipped and tightened in a cold knot. The transponders were often despised for betraying officers' whereabouts to supervisors. The "breakage" rate on them was phenomenal. At times they could be useful, though. Like now.

The Gage dispatcher directed the search for Wim, watching all their transponders on the board and guiding them toward Wim's. Babra Cardarella found him first. Her shout brought the rest of them running.

Wim lay in a pool of blood between two abutting backyard storage sheds. He was unconscious but still alive. It looked as if someone had tried to take off the top of his skull. A deep laceration circled his head, amputating the tops of his ears, cutting through the scalp to bone, and sawing through the bridge of his nose so far even his eyelids and eyes were cut.

Janna swore. "Someone get an ambulance. I swear I'll cancel the deek who did this to him."

One of the leos from Beta Gage Seventeen cleared her throat. "We took a monofilament garrote off our man when we searched him."

Garrote! Janna's mouth tightened. The deek must have tried to use it on Wim. Wim saw him and ducked, but not fast enough. She felt sick. He was lucky to be alive. Around his throat, the fine wire would have sliced through to his spine before he even knew what happened.

She wiped the blood from his face. It was a mistake. Clearing the old blood only let her see new blood and fluid leaking out of his slashed eyes.

"Oh, god," someone whispered.

Janna swore. Wim had just two weeks left before he resigned, only a month before his ship left. What a hell of a thing to have happen to him now—a goddam-it-to-hell bitch. That damn deek. That skink toad. Just as well he was locked in the back of the watchcar. She would have gone ahead and canceled him, given a chance, or at the very least broken him in half one bone at a time.

She moved so her shadow fell across Wim, shading him from the sun. Moisture dropped on him. Her sweat? She wiped at her face. She discovered with surprise that the moisture was on her cheeks, flowing from her eyes. She let the tears come. What a rotten job this could be sometimes.

2

From the doorway of Jorge Hazlett's office, Andrew Kellener asked, "Did you see the broadcast about the *Invictus*?"

Jorge looked up from the printout he was pretending to read. Indeed he had seen the broadcast. In fact, he had had his newscanner on "replay" and watched the broadcast six times, teetering on the edge of panic. Calm returned, however, as he reviewed his precautions for bad luck like this. He had not lost the game initiative, was not even threatened yet. There was the chance of attack, yes, but if anything, that possibility was exhilarating. Danger made the game more interesting.

"I saw it just a few minutes ago," he lied to Andy. "It's too bad, a real tragedy."

"Just too bad?" Andy walked over and sat down in the chair across the desk from Jorge. "Aren't you more concerned than that? Those colonists were our clients. We contracted with Boeing for that ship."

Jorge widened his eyes. "*Our* clients?" He reached for his computer keyboard and brought up the client file list, then clicked on the Laheli Company.

"I tried that a little earlier," Andy said. "The computer wouldn't give me anything."

Sure enough, across the screen appeared: *What's the password?*

Jorge raised brows at Andy. "What's this?"

"I was going to ask you. You handled the account. You must have coded the records in. Don't you remember?"

Jorge pretended to think hard. "No, I can't." He opened desk drawers and shuffled through the contents. "I must have written the code down here somewhere, though."

Andy's mouth tightened. "I hope you find it. There'll be a government inquiry, of course. We'll have to have our records ready for inspection."

Andy was aging, Jorge thought. He still wore his hair a fashionable shoulder length, but the fiery mop of their law school days grew thinner and paler every year. It was a washed-out copper now. Jorge took pride in the fact that he had only some gray at the temples to mark his age. Those brown and gray paisley jumpsuits Andy wore were the height of conservatism, too. Something in the line of Jorge's dusty rose and yellow stripes would have been much more modish. Yes, Andy was definitely aging.

"Jorge." Andy's voice sharpened. "Are you listening to me?"

Jorge focused on him again. "Of course. Don't worry. The records will be in order and ready for anyone who wants to see them."

That was no lie, anyway. When the two of them gave up starving in law practice to take up colonial contracting, they had fallen into a feast. Jorge was not about to place himself in a position of having to return to starvation or give up the luxuries for which he had acquired a taste over the years. The records would indeed be in perfect order for any inquiry.

He kept pawing through his desk. "It will probably be a routine inquiry, just to see if Boeing can be blamed."

"I hope four hundred deaths will rate more than an opportunity for some congressional committee to target-shoot at a corporation."

Jorge paused in his search, then resumed pawing. He frowned. Andy's zealot button had been pushed.

"Are you sure you will be able to remember the password?" Andy sounded impatient.

Jorge lifted his head and made his smile encouraging. "Of course. I'll have myself hypnotized to get it if necessary. Don't worry. I'll have a printout by tomorrow, or Friday at the latest."

He continued smiling as Andy rose and left. His mouth tightened the moment the door closed behind his partner. Jorge spun his chair back to the computer terminal and typed: RUY LOPEZ.

The name of the chess opening cleared the query from the screen. The Laheli account promptly appeared on the screen. Jorge read through the file. Everything had been typed or scanned in: initial communications between the Laheli board of directors and Hazlett and Kellener, the application to the U. S. Colonial Agency for a charter, approval and granting of the charter, contracts with Boeing in Wichita for the ramjet, permits from Forbes Aerospace Center south of Topeka and Schilling in Salina to launch the ramjet sections for assembly in orbit off the Glenn platform, reservations for shuttle lifting of colonists and supplies.

All that was in order. What would raise brows were letters from Boeing expressing doubt over the performance of the modified 800's life-support systems, and the casual replies to those letters. Someone might also wonder when they checked Laheli bank records and found the company had paid for a Starmaster 1000 instead of a modified 800.

The firm, of course, took its six percent from the price of the colonial package based on the modified 800. Jorge took the rest.

Six percent. The amount rasped at Jorge even though he collected far more than that his own way. Because of that paltry charge he had to resort to fraud. The normal fee for colonial contracting was ten percent. Andy had to be the altruist, had to give the clients every advantage. Whenever Jorge felt a twinge of guilt about his activities, he reminded himself that Andy had driven him to it.

What bothered him most was not the fraud itself—if the colonists were blind enough to let themselves be cheated, it was their fault—but the prospect of being caught. A case like this would not be prosecuted as a simple fraud. With the knowing and deceitful endangering of human lives involved, a prosecutor could invoke the Tescott Act. Under it, actual death resulting from actions like Jorge's made the offense a Class A felony, carrying a mandatory death sentence. Jorge was enraged at the idea of the state of Kansas giving him a lethal injection just because one man considered colonialism a holy mission and clients did not double-check to make sure they were getting what they needed and paid for.

Jorge cleared the screen and pushed away the keyboard. He walked to the window and stared out over the tops of the buildings across the street toward the green dome of the Statehouse beyond, rising into the heat-bleached sky. Frowning, he considered his situation.

He had game plans to be initiated if there were a danger of being caught, but of course he hoped he never had to use them. Best not to come under suspicion at all. All would be well if Andy helped him cover alterations in the records.

Twenty years ago there would have been no question of that. Back then Andy had been every bit the gamesman Jorge was. Until he developed this obsession with colonialism. If anything, that put Andy on the side of the opposition. Jorge would have to counter the check by himself.

There were three ways to answer a check: move the king, capture the attacking piece, or interpose another piece. Jorge had no intention of running away, and trying to do something about the government investigation was of course out of the question. The remaining choice was to move Andy into the line of attack.

There lay the problem. Whatever the threat of being caught at fraud, there was even more risk in offering Andy as a sacrifice in his place. A living Andy could protest, could possibly defend himself with success. Yet the alternative to that was almost unthinkable. How could he kill a man who had been his friend for nearly thirty years? Besides, it would be almost impossible to do so without being traced to the time and place of the murder.

He pulled his card case out of a breast pocket and took out his Scib Card. For all its benefits in social care and financial transactions, the card was a curse. In the process of eliminating cash from society, personal freedom had been strangled. By checking bank records, investigators could learn where any particular person had been at a given time. Purchase records were a fatal giveaway.

He slipped his card back into its case and shoved it into his pocket. How could he get around the damned card? No purchases meant no record, but that also left a blank which investigators would hunt for ways to fill. No, he needed a record of purchases, but in an area of town away from where he actually was. Jorge smiled wryly. What he needed was to be able to be in two places at the same time. That, unfortunately, was—

Wait a minute. He sat up straight. There was something in the back of his head about being in two places at once, something he had heard. He remembered thinking at the time that he should remember it for the future. Where had he heard it?

He searched his memory. A party. He remembered a crowd. He doubled his fist and tapped it against his forehead. A party...Lawrence! That was it. It had been at the mix-and-match party Colla Hayden gave last year.

There had been a man there, tall and elegant, with a very flash red-haired girl under one arm and a nearly identical boy under the other. Jorge had spent most of the party looking at the women—most wore nothing but their body paint, where even the most liberal clubs in Topeka required that pubic hair and female breasts be covered—but he remembered hearing the man talking to a couple of handsome homosexuals, who also wore nothing but body paint.

"Would you believe I'm in two places at once?" He had asked.

The hos had not believed. One of them tugged at the hand of his boyfriend and started to leave.

The man was a bit toxy from liquor or drugs. He seemed to be trying to impress his companions and the hos. "My wife, my very devout Bible cultist wife, thinks I'm in Omaha at a home furnishings show. She's worried I might try to count coup on my assistant, who's with me." He grinned. "She'd never speak to me again if she knew who I'm really counting coup with." He gave the beautiful couple a squeeze.

The couple giggled. "We feel sorry for your poor assistant up there all alone."

The man looked righteous. "Not alone. I'm there. When the bank records come in, the purchase record will prove it."

It was at that point Jorge had started paying close attention. To his disappointment, however, the man changed the subject and drifted off with his beautiful companions.

Jorge had gone straight to Colla. "Who's that man?"

Colla was preoccupied with two male friends. "What man? I don't know. I'll find out later."

He had never gotten back to her about it. Now he could kick himself for not doing so. Why had he let himself be so distracted by that blonde creature—whose most obvious charm was that she wore nothing at all but her glorious hair—that he forgot to find out who the man was?

He returned to the desk in long, determined strides, fishing in his pockets for his memo book. Numbers like Colla's he kept with him. She would be at work now. He looked up her business number, a local one, and punched it into the phone.

Colla answered formally, but broke into a genuine smile when she saw his face on her screen. "Jorgie, honey. How are you?" Her afroam accent made the greeting warm and intimate.

"Never better. When are you going to have another mix-and-match party?"

"When the neighbors stop complaining about the last one. Lonely? You don't need a party to take care of that. I'll be glad to look after you myself."

"And a nova job you'd do, too."

He flirted with her a bit while he considered how best to ask about the man. He did not want to seem too eager. Most of all, if there should be an inquiry at some future time, he did not want her remembering that he asked for a man's name. After they had exchanged several propositions and innuendoes, he brought the conversation gradually back to parties.

"I particularly remember the one in May."

She blinked. "I didn't hold one in May this year."

"*Last* May."

Her eyes went wide. "My, that must have been special. *I* can hardly remember any back that far."

"Do you remember who comes to which parties?"

She laughed. "Don't joke. Among all the people who come, and the friends who bring friends? I just worry about running out of alcohol and junk."

That meant he would have to work hard at jogging her memory about the man he wanted. He could not ask directly, then. He would have to do it roundabout.

"There was a couple I remember seeing at that party. I've seen them several times since, too. They look like twins: red-haired, blue-eyed, not terribly intellectual. They like to wear star body decals."

"That sounds like Michal and Michael Taber."

"Who?"

She spelled the names. "You aren't interested in them, are you? They're bi's. They like threesomes, especially with people who get a boost out of incest. They aren't really twins, though. They just pretend to be. Actually, they're married."

"I've never thought of them for sex. I just think they're interesting to watch. Are they from Lawrence?"

"No, from Topeka, like most of the people who come to my parties. You know how it goes. The Topekaens come to Lawrence to orgy. Lawrence people go to Kansas City. I don't know where K. C.'s hedonists go."

He had what he needed. Without seeming too hasty, he closed the conversation and punched off. He turned to his computer keyboard and typed in a request for the phone directory, for the Taber number. It promptly appeared on the screen. He was starting to punch the number into the phone when he caught himself. He could always justify calling Colla. She was a friend. It might be harder to give investigators a reason for calling strangers.

He glanced at the chrono. It was almost noon. He punched the intercom. "I'm going out for lunch, Nina."

"Yes, sir," his secretary's reply came back.

He left the office casually, waving to the receptionist as he walked past the young Hispanic's desk. Robert smiled and waved back.

Jorge took the elevator down to the ground level. Outside the entrance of the Sunflower Federal Bank and near the elevators in the lobby stood a bank of public phones. Jorge crossed to it and used one to call the Taber number.

The red-haired girl who answered was the one he had seen under the arm of the man he wanted. She gave Jorge a polite, vacuous smile. "Yes?"

Jorge introduced himself.

Her smile became more animated. "A friend of Colla? Well, welcome. What can I do for you?"

He wasted no time on social small talk. "Last year in May you were at one of Colla's mix-and-match parties. You and your…brother Michael were with a tall, brown-haired man in a peacock blue velvet suit."

She thought a moment, then nodded. "Yes, I remember him. Nova body. A tongue that could send anyone into orbit."

"This will sound foolish, but I met him, too, and now I've forgotten his name. It's driving me off my tick trying to remember. Can you help?"

Her blue eyes went wide enough to swim in. "Oh, I wish I could, but I don't remember his name either."

Jorge scowled. "How can you not remember his name if he was such a memorable performer?"

She giggled. "Suns, who cares about *names* at a time like *that?* That is, he did say who he was, but, honestly, I don't remember it. I'm terrible about things like that. I've seen him at other parties, but we haven't put three with him since, so I've just never had another chance to hear what his name was."

Jorge wanted to reach into the phone and shake her. He dug his nails into the palms of his hands. "If he said his name once, maybe you can remember at least a part of it. This thing is annoying me to death."

"Suns, I know how you feel, but—" He would have thought it was impossible, but her eyes went wider yet. "I *do* remember something. I have a little trick I use sometimes, if I want to remember something particularly. I think up an association and make a picture of it in my mind, you know? I remember I wanted to keep that jon's name because he was so good. The picture is a taxi floating on the ocean between Italy and Greece, an Adriatic taxi." She grinned.

He stifled a grimace. "Adriatic taxi?" What kind of name generated a picture like that?

"That's right." She beamed with pride at her cleverness. "And he owns a business in Topeka. He mentioned that. Does that help?"

Not a bit. Still, he had as much as he could learn from her. Time to ring off before the conversation became memorable. He made himself smile. "It helps a great deal. You've jogged my memory and made me remember the name. Thank you so very much."

He punched off before she could ask him what the name was. Adriatic taxi. Disappointment stabbed him. An Adriatic taxi who owned a business in Topeka.

He thought about it while he ate a sandwich at a cafe down the street. He could not see that what she told him could help at all. Going back to the office, he had to force himself to smile at Robert on the reception desk and at his secretary. Lunch's sandwich lay like lead in his stomach.

It was only when he was behind the closed door of his office that he relaxed control of his face. He kicked the wastebasket and swore passionately. That man at the party could be the key to everything. Jorge felt it. Yet there seemed to be no way to reach him…no way. All because a bibi with an overactive libido and a featherweight brain could not remember names. Adriatic taxi! There must be something more useful than that. There had to be!

He sat down and chewed on a knuckle. Perhaps something the man had said would help. Jorge went over the conversation as he remembered it, playing it back sentence by sentence. *Would you believe I'm in two places at once?* Nothing helpful there. *My wife, my very devout Bible cultist wife thinks I'm*—Jorge sat up straight—*in Omaha at a home furnishings show.* Home furnishings show! The man had told the Tabers he owned his own business. Now what business would send a man to a home furnishings show?

Jorge reached for the computer keyboard. He typed a request for the phone listings of all the furniture dealers in the city. Dutifully, the computer put the list on the screen and printed out a sheet. It was a long list.

Jorge went over it. Some could be eliminated right away. Used furniture dealers, for example. That still left quite a number. He sighed and started punching numbers into the phone.

He made up a speech while the first number rang. "Hello, this is the chamber of commerce. We're surveying for the new city directory. Who is the owner of your business?"

The gambit worked. The employee who answered the phone gave him the owner's name. It did not remotely resemble anything that would suggest the image of an Adriatic taxi. Jorge punched off and went on to the next number…and the next…and the next. As he progressed down the list, Jorge felt a knot growing in his stomach. Damn that bibi. This calling was endless, and it might all be in vain. He contemplated giving up only briefly, though. The man was his key to saving himself from a Tescott prosecution. He had to find that man.

He reached the last name without having any luck. Cursing, he punched the intercom. "Nina, bring me some caff."

She had a cup on his desk almost immediately. Setting it down, she noticed the list of furniture dealers. "Is that something I can help with?"

He shook his head. "I'm just trying to find a chair to match one in my study at home."

"And you're calling everywhere yourself? Why not do it the easy way?" she asked.

He looked up. "What easy way?"

"Call one of the decorating firms. Ask them to find the chair for you."

He stared at her. Decorating firms? Lord. He had completely overlooked decorators. They bought furniture, too.

"I'll call one if you like," Ms. Abram offered.

"No, that isn't necessary." He smiled to soften the refusal. He must not seem adamant about doing it himself. "Thank you for the suggestion, though."

She smiled back. "Anything I can do to help."

He asked the computer for a list of decorators. The computer printed it out.

He noticed Ms. Abram still hovering around the desk. "That's all, Nina."

She sighed. "Yes, sir." She left in a soft sway of hips and swish of ankle-length skirt. The door closed behind her.

He punched the first decorator's number. A young woman answered. He used the same speech on her that he had on the furniture dealers, and it worked just as well. From American Interiors he moved through Contemporary Homes and Humble Abode down the list to The Kastle Keep. None of the faces answering looked familiar. None of the names suggested an Adriatic Taxi. Many Mansions came next.

The woman who answered had a tempting pouty mouth and impossibly blue eyes, all framed by a magnificent mane of chestnut hair. "Many Mansions, Marca Laclede speaking."

Jorge smiled. "I'm from the chamber of commerce. We're surveying for the new city directory. May I ask the name of your firm's owner?"

"Mr. Adrian Cabot is chief decorator of Many Mansions," the woman replied.

The name jabbed him like a pin. "Adrian Cabot?" Adrian…Adriatic? That could be, but…taxi? Then it came to him…taxi on the water, a cab boat…Cabot.

His heart pounded, but he tried not to let himself hope too much. "Excuse me, but I think Mr. Cabot and I may have met before. Is he a tall man with a brown lion's mane hair style, a very elegant-looking man?"

The pouty lips parted to show small white teeth. The mouth smiled invitingly. "That sounds like Mr. Cabot."

Jorge took a long breath. "This is really fortunate. I'm trying to locate a certain type of chair for my study. Do you suppose Mr. Cabot would have time this afternoon to talk about it?"

"Just a minute." She put him on hold. In a couple of minutes she came back. "He's free at the moment. I'll put him on the line."

That would never do. He could not talk about what he needed over the phone. "May I come over instead?" He checked the address. Highland Village shopping center. A straight shot down Kansas Avenue. "I can be there in fifteen minutes. I'll bring a photograph of the chair."

"I suppose that will be all right. What is your name, please?"

"Jorge Hazlett."

"We'll be expecting you, Mr. Hazlett."

He punched off and touched the intercom. "Nina, I found a decorator who can help me, but I have to take him a picture of the chair. I'm going over."

"Don't forget you have an appointment with Mr. Schlegel of the Citadel Company at two o'clock."

He checked the chrono. *Damn!* It was ten to two now. "Give my apologies to the gentleman and entertain him until I get back."

"Yes, sir."

She sounded astonished. He could not blame her. Clients were supposed to come before everything else at Hazlett and Kellener. It must certainly seem strange to give a mere chair precedence. The incident might also seem suspicious looking back on it later.

He made himself chuckle. "It's brainbent to be so obsessed with a chair, I suppose, but I've been trying to find this match for some time. Don't tell Andy I put it before the client."

"No, I won't."

He could count on her loyalty, he felt sure. "You're priceless, Nina. I'll be back as soon as I can."

As usual traffic ran heavy out Kansas Avenue. Jorge threaded his Mercedes Vulcan through it as fast as he dared without tripping the automatic speed monitors along the way. At Highland Village, Many Mansion's section of the strip mall had been faced in black glass. On the door an etched outline of a castle glittered diamond bright under the buisness name and over the legend: *Superior Interior Designs to Make Any Castle a Home*. The door, and an inner one, whispered aside to admit him to a large reception room with a floor that looked like marble but gave with the soft resiliency of carpet. Around the room sat chairs in a dozen styles and materials: molded plastic, plastic foam, tip-overs, colloidal plastics, and Coruboard, a heavy cardboard laminate. In the center of the floor lay a piece of carpet. At least Jorge assumed it was carpet; its color, dead black, swallowed all the light, making it look like a gaping hole.

Jorge tested it, cautiously, with a toe. It felt solid. Still, he could not quite bring himself to walk on it. He skirted the area.

"You're very prompt, Mr. Hazlett."

He looked up to see Marca Laclede in the doorway of an inner room. Her body looked as desirable as he had imagined, certainly desirable draped in a half dress. Its skirt swept her ankles, but above that it became difficult to tell what was fabric and what merely painted on her skin. No wonder Cabot's wife worried about her husband counting coup on his assistant. Jorge would not have minded counting coup on her himself.

Marca Laclede looked back at him with equal interest, running the tip of a silver-nailed finger along her full lower lip. After a minute, she turned away, and made the most of the motion in swinging hips and swishing hair.

"Mr. Cabot is this way, Mr. Hazlett."

Jorge enjoyed the delicious motion of her back as she led the way. He was sorry when she stopped in the doorway of a room and made him go in alone.

Adrian Cabot stood up behind his desk, a massive structure of chrome and Lucite. He extended a hand. "Sit down, Mr. Hazlett. What can I do for you?"

Cabot looked as elegant as Jorge remembered. His suit this time, though, was as black as the carpet in the reception area. It made his head and hands look disembodied. He sat down when Jorge did.

"What's this chair you need?"

Jorge cleared his throat. "Actually, there's no chair. It's a personal matter and I felt you would want discretion."

Cabot's brows rose a millimeter.

"I attended a party Colla Hayden gave in Lawrence a year ago May. I saw you there and—"

Cabot's face congealed into the immobility of a mannequin's. "You're mistaken. I don't ever recall being at a party in Lawrence. In fact, the only time I left town that May was to go to—"

"Omaha, to a furniture show. You told that story to people at the party. You also said you were managing to be in two places at one time. I find I need to know that trick."

"I repeat," Cabot said, "you're mistaken. I don't know what you're talking about. I don't know any Colla Hayden. Now, I'm a busy man, Mr. Hazlett, so you must excuse me."

Jorge stood up. Some people pushing could break; others merely became more stubborn. Jorge judged Cabot to be the latter. The man was terrified. Damn him. Gambit denied. "Of course."

Jorge masked his anger in a smile and backed toward the door. Damn the man! So close, and still Jorge was being denied the knowledge he needed.

He almost ran over the assistant outside the door. "Look at me," she said. Before he realized it, she had taken his picture with a small camera. "I heard," she said.

Jorge waited. Anger began draining away, replaced by hope. "Do you make a habit of listening at doors?"

"Sometimes, when it seems like the thing to do." She regarded the silver perfection of her nails with intense concentration. "I have a friend who looks remarkably like Mr. Cabot. This friend and I went to Omaha with Mr. Cabot's Scib Card." She looked down at the picture extruding from the camera. "If my friend can find someone who looks like you, I can help you, Mr. Hazlett." She smiled up at him.

He felt like a bishop with a long, clear diagonal to his opponent's king. He refrained from cheering, though. "What will the price be?"

"Let's not talk about that until I'm sure I can help you. I'll call you when I know, Mr. Hazlett."

"It's important that I arrange this matter soon…this week, if possible."

"I'll try, Mr. Hazlett."

She saw him to the door and watched him leave with great satisfaction. Another potential client. Colonial contractors made good credit. If Tarl could find a match, Mr. Jorge Hazlett should be able to pay well for a doppelgänger.

Marca put the camera back in her desk and dropped the 2-D photograph in her purse. She strapped the purse around her waist, then leaned in through the door of Adrian Cabot's office.

"I have some important errands to run, Adrian. May I leave early?"

Adrian looked gray. "That man saw me at a mix-and-match party. I had better quit going to parties so close to home."

Marca sighed. "I doubt he plans to publish what he knows. Your wife will never hear about it. Good night, Adrian."

He was so busy muttering and wringing his hands, he never saw her go.

The man was a fool, she thought. He either ought to confess his bi preference to his wife or accept the monogamous sacramental marriage he had made with her. How ridiculous for anyone in this permissive time to allow himself to be hagridden by guilt over sexual needs. When she found out what a toad Karel was, she had not sat around gnashing her teeth; she had dissolved the marriage contract at light-speed. She had taken only his name—Laclede was infinitely preferable to, immeasurably more elegant than, Dolitsky—and run. He could have been as rich as Adrian's wife; she would have done the same.

She would have let Adrian stew in his own cowardice but it had been such a shame not to take advantage of that surprising likeness between him and her old cohab of college days. It was so profitable. She also loved the feeling of power it gave her to manipulate the supposedly foolproof bankcard system.

Outside she climbed into her little bubble-shaped VW Moth, switching on the motor and the fans. The Moth trembled, then lifted clear of the ground. Pulling out of the parking lot, she headed north, then east.

Crossing the Sixth Street Bridge over Interstate-70, she could hear the hiss of the occasional passing cars below. A hundred years ago, there had been solid strings of traffic on cross country highways, most of the traffic privately-owned road cars. That was before energy rationing, of course, and before metal became earmarked for building ships to go to the Moon and Mars and the stars, and building cities on the Moon and Mars, instead of being wasted on earthbound vehicles.

Marca revved the fans to full speed. The Moth leaped ahead at its maximum of thirty kph. The speed limit being a crawling twenty five, she checked her mirrors to make sure no prowling lions had seen her, then headed toward the area of town called Oakland.

Tarl worked at a market on Sardou Street. She pulled into the cracked, trashy parking area and set the Moth down on its parking rollers. While she climbed out of the runabout, she steeled herself to go into the market. If only there were a way to contact Tarl without coming down here to see him. This was the only part of their arrangement she hated. The decay in Oakland and especially this market disgusted her.

She pushed through the door. Grime seemed everywhere, from the permanently gray floor to the cans and boxes on the shelves that looked as if they had been sitting there for decades. The place smelled of dust, unwashed humanity, and overripe vegetables. Marca kept her arms at her sides, holding up her skirt, trying to avoid touching anything.

"Where's Tarl?" she asked the Hispanic girl at the checkout counter.

Even the girl looked grimy. Her dark eyes swept Marca. "I don' know any Tarl."

Marca sighed. Did they have to go through this every time? "Of course you do. He's the sligh who works in the back."

"Then why don' you try lookin' in the back?"

Marca twitched away from her. She was careful, making her way back through the dirty aisles, to keep clear of the occasional shopper.

She found Tarl in the rear section of the store, opening cartons. He nodded as she pushed through the swinging doors. "I'll be finished in a few minutes."

She looked around for a place to sit but saw nowhere tolerable. She remained standing. How could Tarl bear working here day after day? He had done the same kind of thing in college. She thought he would change when she brought him to Topeka to introduce him to Adrian and help her in the business Adrian's likeness to him had inspired.

Not that they were *really* alike. They resembled each other only physically. Tarl had none of Adrian's polish, and Adrian had never felt the inner anger that leaked out in everything Tarl said and did. Tarl had a backbone, too.

She frowned. She wished she could understand slighs. Tarl was one of many she met in college. Her group had considered it kicky to mix with the holdouts of society, to give them bed space and food, and help them drop in on classes. Marca went along, but she never understood why the slighs did what they did. She even shared her quarters with Tarl for over a year in an effort to understand, but this hatred of even the most innocuous government regulation or documentation was incomprehensible. How could anyone find identation such an abhorrent invasion of privacy that he would refuse to enroll in social care, that he would refuse to take out a Scib Card and lose all its benefits, just to remain unrecorded by the government? She had never minded the fingerprinting when she started school, nor the fingerprinting and photographs of her retinal patterns when she enrolled in social care.

Look what slighs missed by not having a card: medical care, unemployment benefits, food and housing coupons when there was no income for such things, old age care, bankcredit. They had to live by barter. Tarl would be given a few cans of food and some meat or produce when he left today, items the manager could mark off his inventory as "damaged" goods. He worked somewhere else to earn a bed.

"Is it really worth it?" she asked.

He glanced around. There was no need for him to ask what she meant. She had asked the same question for years.

"Yes!" he came back. "It's worth it because in spite of everything, it's freedom…complete personal freedom."

That was what made him incomprehensible. Marca never felt a lack of freedom. If anything, he had less freedom than she because he had no bankcard and no bankcredit.

Tarl finished unpacking the carton and came over to her, wiping his hands on an already filthy apron. "Does Cabot want to slip his leash again, or is it one of the others this time?"

"I have a new one."

He frowned. "Don't you have enough clients already?"

She sighed in exasperation. "Tarl, there can be very big credit in this if we let ourselves grow."

He shook his head, sharply, emphatically. "There can be very big trouble. The half dozen pairs we have now are good. They use us regularly and keep their mouths shut. Get too many and we'll end up with one-timers who won't be so careful. Either a sligh or a citizen will talk and eventually the lions will hear about it. We have a nice little thing here; don't spoil it with ambition." Then he sighed. "Do you have a picture?"

She brought it out of her purse. "He wants it arranged this week if possible."

Tarl studied the photograph, frowning. "He's in a hurry? I don't like that."

"It's probably a business deal. Tarl, he's a colonial contractor. He can afford to pay well, and I'll check him out before I commit us to anything."

"All right." He put the photograph in a sleeve pocket. "I'll start looking for a match this evening."

3

Janna hardly recognized Wim. In two days the man she knew as well as the face she saw in her mirror every day had become a stranger in a hospital bed, his head helmeted in bandages. Not much more than his mouth and the end of his nose were visible, and she had never seen that thin, grim set of his lips before. He lay with unnatural stillness, hands folded across his stomach. It gave the box created around him by the wood-grain ends and raised side panels of the bed a disturbing likeness to a coffin. Only the rise and fall of his chest and the green LED readings of the vitals signs indicators in the side of the bed reassured her he was still alive. She recognized him mostly because Vada Kiest sat beside the bed in a molded foam chair, reading a pamphlet on organic gardening.

Vada looked up as the door closed behind Janna. She adored her husband. She was one of the few women Janna knew who had adopted her husband's name even though they had just the standard marriage contract. Vada was suffering for Wim, Janna could see. The Dresden perfection of her face looked ready to crack and shatter. When she saw Janna, it did crack. She rose out of the chair and buried her face against Janna's chest.

In the bed, Wim rolled his bandaged head toward them. "You don't have to be quiet; I'm not asleep. That you, Jan?"

Janna held on to Vada. Silent sobs wracked the body of the smaller woman as if tearing it apart. "It's me. How are you feeling?"

He paused before answering. "The doctors decided about my eyes this morning."

She held Vada tighter. "I heard."

The SCPD director's office checked every day on officers wounded in the line of duty. This morning Director Thomas Paget himself had called Lieutenant Vradel to report on Wim. Pass-the-Word Morello, the squad clerk, whose name was nothing if not well earned, had overheard. By midmorning it had been common knowledge throughout the Capitol division that Wim Kiest's eyes had irreparable damage due to the lacerations. The scar tissue would leave him blind.

"Can't they give you transplants?" she asked.

With the genoadaptive vaccines solving the rejection problem, the medicos claimed they could rebuild anyone.

"We asked about transplants." Vada pulled away from Janna. Bitterness edged her voice. "They can't replace eyes."

"The problem is in the optic nerve and ciliary muscles, they tell me." Wim spoke with the careful precision he used in court. "Nerves are hard to connect." He paused. "I'm going to a new world but I'll never be able to see it."

Janna felt totally helpless. What could she say? She reached out to touch him on the shoulder. "Luck is a bitch."

His fingers came up and locked around her wrist. "I was careless. I was running a straight chase, never thinking about lion traps."

"We weren't in Oakland, after all, and even there we made mistakes. Remember that time I fell into the ankle snare?"

Oakland was the lion trap capital of the county, the war zone. Any leo careless enough to leave a watchcar without a helmet was asking for someone on a rooftop to trephine his skull with a brick or bottle. The vacant lots were full of pits to break legs and snares to trap the unwary. The snare Janna tripped had been made of monofilament wire. The jerk of hitting it cut clean through her boot. They found a shallow laceration on her skin when they worked her foot free of the boot. If she had happened to jerk at the snare, the wire would have gone to the bone. She might have lost her foot.

"It was just luck I didn't cripple myself then."

She saw Vada develop the wistful frown she so often did when Janna and Wim started referring to some common experience she could never really understand because she had not shared it with them.

Wim sighed. "Deeks are deeks everywhere. As soon as I lost sight of him I should have started watching for him over my shoulder. I forgot to, and now I'm paying hard card for it."

"It's a rotten, terrible job," Vada said. "I should have listened to Grandma and made you quit years ago.

Wim's head rolled toward her. "Your grandfather belonged to another generation of police work."

"Did he? So they call you law enforcement officers now instead of cops and you have to have college degrees to make rank, and you have to visit the department psychiatrist every month to remain stable. What else has changed? Grandma warned me I'd sit home worried sick wondering whether you were going to come home after your watch. She said there are people out there who hate you and will kill you if you let them. She said your supervisors know that and still send you out into the street. You can't even carry guns to protect yourselves now."

"We carry guns," Janna said. "We just don't carry shooters, except for the shotguns in the cars."

"You can't protect yourselves. I think the tick tech is braintraining you on those visits, to keep you on the job even when it makes you risk your lives." Vada stared up at Janna with an intensity that startled the taller woman. "Quit, Jan. Wim told me he invited you to come out to Champaign with us. Please do it. You're like a sister to me. Quit before some madman kills or maims you, too." She reached out for Janna's hands.

Janna evaded her. "Vada, I can't—Wim...?

"You'll like it on Champaign," he said. "People out there don't wait for someone else to do everything for them. They know they have to depend on themselves. I've met most of the others who will be on our ship and they're all fine people. We'll be building something new and clean. Come out and be a part of it."

Janna felt as if she were being backed into a corner. "How am I going to raise that kind of credit? A share costs fifty thousand, you told me. I can't find that much in time to join the ship leaving next year."

"I have a pension coming to me, but since I won't be here, I won't need it. I'll have the department make a lump settlement and I'll give it to you. That should buy you a share."

"I—" She could not take it. How could she? "I'll think about it." She started for the door. "I'd better go. I'm just on my lunch break. Vradel expects me to keep working for my bankcredit. I'll drop by this evening."

"All the pictures sent back by the probe show Champaign is a lovely world," Vada said.

Janna nodded.

Leaving the hospital, she looked up toward the heat-bleached sky. She had no desire to leave Earth. Still, what might it be like living under a different sky?. Did Champaign have cooler summers? Climbing into Indian Thirty to drive back down to the station, she wondered whether she ought to think about Wim's offer, and if not, how was she going to tell him no?

About the time Janna returned to work, Marca Laclede had Tarl on the phone. "I have a match," he said.

Satisfaction warmed her. "A good one?"

"He's a bit thinner, otherwise they look like twins. His name is—"

Marca cut him off. "I don't care who he is. Does he understand what we want him to do?"

"He understands."

"He's agreed?"

"Absolutely. He grew up as a sligh, going to illegal schools with one eye on the teacher and the other watching for Juvenile leos coming through the door on a raid. He's never had a chance like this and he wants it."

"Can he be trusted not to talk?"

There was a pause on the other end of the line. Marca frowned at her blank screen. She wished she had an image, to see Tarl's expression. He was calling from an Oakland public phone, though, so it probably had a broken screen.

"I don't know him personally," Tarl said at last. "I do know slighs, though, and I don't believe this one is a Mouth. He's waiting for me to tell him when and where to meet your client."

"I'll have to talk to the man first. Meet me at the Lion's Den at five o'clock. I'll bring everything our doppelgänger will need."

The pause at the other end was longer this time, followed by an audible hiss. "Woman, you're off your tick. That bar is two blocks from the police station. It's a lion watering hole. At five o'clock it'll be filled with lions. Forget whatever boost putting your head in the lion's mouth gives you; choose another place."

"Now, Tarl." She made her voice a persuasive purr. "They'll be busy talking shop and drinking. They'll never notice us."

He laughed, a short, sharp bark without amusement. "Everyone notices you. You'd be furious if they didn't. We'll be lucky if one of them doesn't take you for a girl from the Doll's House and try arguing you into a free trip upstairs."

"Everything will be all right, Tarl. The Lion's Den, at five. Be there."

She punched off the phone. After the connection broke, Marca sat contemplating the mirror finish of her nails and thinking about Mr. Jorge Hazlett, wealthy and successful colonial contractor. She had spent most of Thursday and some of this morning checking on him. She had told Adrian she was hunting some paintings for a client, then driven her Moth to Hazlett's house…a luxury sunken townhouse on Brentwood, out near the governor's mansion. She had stopped and struck up a conversation with a man doing yardwork. According to the yardman, Hazlett let his last marriage contract lapse years ago. Now a succession of houseguests the yardman described as "flash bibis" rotated through the master bedroom. Hazlett owned a car, not a runabout or pedal car but a real road car, a Mercedes Vulcan sportster that he drove to work every day. The yardman was obviously impressed.

That impressed Marca, too. She rubbed at a tiny flaw in the finish of her left thumbnail. Mr. Jorge Hazlett could well afford any price she might care to ask for her services. It was best not to be too greedy, of course; she wanted him to come back for more. Steady clients were the real creditmakers.

She punched the phone on and punched in Hazlett and Kellener's number. "Mr. Hazlett, please," she told the beautiful Hispanic young man who answered. "This is Marca Laclede of Many Mansions."

Jorge had clients in his office, four members of the board of a forming colonial company. He was explaining to them why they did not want to have Lockheed build their ramjet—why, with two other builders right here in Kansas—and why they did not want Beech-Cessna's custom-built ship.

"It's true the B-C Pilgrim will be tailored specifically to meet your needs, but that kind of special service is expensive. You can buy one of the standard Boeing Starmaster models for less money and have some extra space in case you find people who want to buy shares at the last minute."

The colonials looked over the literature he spread before them. They frowned thoughtfully.

The intercom chimed. "A Marca Laclede of Many Mansions for you, Mr. Hazlett."

Jorge's pulse leaped. So soon! Wonderful! "Just a moment," he told the clients. He punched on the phone. "Hello, Ms. Laclede. I have clients here so I have only a minute or two." He did not want her saying anything incriminating when someone could hear.

Laclede's impossibly blue eyes smiled back at him from the phone's screen. "I've found that duplicate you wanted. Can you come over soon to discuss placement and price?"

He glanced at the clients and at the chrono readout on his computer. "I'll be right there."

Punching off, he turned back to his clients. He handed them the ramjet specifications literature. "Here. Take these and look them over. Talk about them with your company if you have a meeting before your next appointment here. We'll make a decision on the ship the next time." He eased them toward the door, talking all the way. "I certainly don't want to force you into anything, nor make you feel your arm is being twisted." He accompanied them through the reception room. "Our objective is to send you to your destination planet as inexpensively and yet as safely as possible. You are the future of the human race." He looked at the receptionist. "I'm walking our clients to the elevator, Robert. I'll be right back."

He walked them to the elevator. They looked pleased with all the personal attention. He had no trouble getting on the elevator and riding down. At street level, he shook hands with them, letting the doors close behind him. He walked them through the lobby to the front door. Instead of returning upstairs when they were gone, he lingered a moment or two, then hurried for the parking lot behind the bank and gunned the Vulcan out Kansas Avenue.

When he came back he would tell Robert and Nina that the colonial company had kept him in the lobby talking. He might even embellish the story with some invented bits of conversation. That should account for the length of his absence.

Hazlett was certainly eager, Marca reflected. She welcomed him to her office and made him comfortable in a colloid plastic chair. Its hard surface softened at contact and molded itself to his hips and back. Every movement he made was accompanied by a slight shift of the chair, so that it always fit perfectly. Marca sat informally on the transparent top of her desk.

She went straight to business.

"As I said on the phone, Mr. Hazlett, we have a doppelgänger for you. All I need to know now is when you want to use him and if you're willing to pay for the service."

"How much are you asking and exactly what kind of service do I get for my credit?" He could be as blunt as she.

She smiled. She crossed legs sheathed in skintight hip boots. What there was of her romper had a waistline that pushed her breasts high, almost out over the neckline. She leaned forward, threatening the neckline still more. "What you get, Mr. Hazlett, is freedom for as long as you desire. You can't purchase anything, of course, but you can move around unrecorded. Meanwhile, your doppelgänger will be busy elsewhere, making purchases in your name and establishing your location as there, rather than where you actually are. The charge depends on how long you use the doppelgänger, and on how risky his impersonation is. If he has to fool someone who knows you, for instance, that takes time and education and is, naturally, more expensive."

"He can go anywhere he wants as long as it isn't anywhere I'm known. I'll give you a list of places for him to avoid. I need him for just one evening, three or four hours at most."

Marca uncrossed her legs and recrossed them the other direction. "Five thousand, then."

Jorge rubbed his nose. Five thousand. Not cheap. Still, a bargain for what he needed. "How do I pay you without giving myself away?"

"The doppelgänger makes purchases worth five thousand on your card. Most of it will be jewelry. You can always explain the purchases away, if you need to, as gifts for your various houseguests."

He nodded. Gems, gold, and silver were the few portable credit equivalents. Nothing could be bought directly with them, unfortunately, but they could be sold at any time for bankcredit.

Marca handed him a card and pen. "I need your signature, and that list of places to avoid." She picked up what looked like a powder compact but when she opened it, Jorge saw that a jellylke substance filled the bottom. She passed the compact to him. "You have to press your thumb against this. How soon do you want to use the doppelgänger?"

Jorge lifted his brows. "This evening?"

She shook her head. "That's too soon. He'll need time to practice your signature. How about tomorrow night? The stores are open late on Saturday; he'll have time to make the necessary purchases."

"Tomorrow, then." Still much sooner than he had dared hope. "How do we do it?"

"You'll meet the doppelgänger at a time and place no one is likely to notice you. You'll turn over your card to him. He can't drive, I'm sure, so you'll have to find an excuse for not using your car."

That was easy enough. Jorge felt excitement rise in him. The game had opened. Pawn to King three.

"You should also have a reason for your signature not being quite the same. People don't become expert forgers in one day. I suggest a slight sprain of the wrist. Wear a bandage Sunday and Monday. It may be needless preparation, but..."

But one should always plan ahead, should be covered in case the need arose. Jorge understood that very well. He could have taught this young thing a lesson or two about planning ahead. "How do I get my card back?"

"You'll meet again at the end of the evening. He'll return your card and give you the purchase receipts, then you both go home." Marca smiled. "Any more questions?"

"How does he counterfeit my thumbprint?"

"I'd rather not explain that. It can be done, though."

"One more thing. I don't know anything about this person you've found to double for me, but he'll know me. What's to prevent him from blackmailing me later?"

Her eyes widened. She considered the question for a moment. It was a possibility she had not thought of before. Blackmail was unthinkable with a steady customer, of course, but there might be a time when it could be used on a one-timer. She blinked, a bit shocked at herself. What was she thinking about? Blackmail was dishonest. "This is a sligh, an Undocumented. The last thing he wants is for the government to identify and document him. I don't think he'll try to make trouble, but if he does, call me. I know how to reach him and I'll see he's dealt with. Where and when do you want to meet him?"

They spent several more minutes setting up a time and location. He signed the card and listed the places the doppelgänger must not visit. Then Jorge headed back for his office.

Marca opened a desk drawer and took out two small bottles of clear fluid. She poured a little from each into a watch glass. She swirled them together, then poured the liquid over the jelly in the compact. She swirled it once there, too, and poured the excess into her wastebasket.

In a few minutes the liquid had become an elastic film. She peeled what was left from the watch glass and threw it away. Glass and bottles went back in her desk drawer. With more care, she lifted the sheet in the compact clear of the jelly. She held it to the light and squinted through it. Using small scissors, she carefully trimmed the plastic down to the edge of the thumbprint.

She regarded the result with satisfaction. In her palm lay a copy of Hazlett's thumbprint in a clear, porous plastic that could be glued to the doppelgänger's thumb. It would let the natural oils through so the whorls would print naturally on the register.

The plastic was the invention of another college friend of hers. He had developed it to be painted on the body to cover and protect the wearer so he or she could appear nude and yet be warm even in cold weather. Its porous nature was designed to keep the wearer from cooking to death inside.

Marca thought she was one of the few people to know of the plastic's existence. Luke had not yet found a manufacturer to produce it. Her supply came from hand-mixed batches she had persuaded Luke to make up for her, claiming she needed it for personal use.

At times she pondered the coincidence of finding herself with a boss who looked like one friend and having another friend who invented the plastic that made forging thumbprints possible. Amazing. Without Luke's invention, she could never have made the doppelgängers work.

Sometimes Marca thought it had to be more than coincidence. She was no Bible cultist, but she did wonder about Fate, and if something very big and special was intended for her.

She slipped the thumbprint cast and Hazlett's signature card into an envelope and dropped it in her purse.

The Lion's Den was located on the ground floor of the building officially designated on city maps as the "New Hotel Jayhawk." That was for the benefit of strangers and the active—and vocal—local Bible cultists; everyone in Topeka knew the building was really the Doll's House. The bar was owned and operated by an ex-leo named Vernon Tuckwiller, who encouraged officers from the Capitol division to use his place for informal tick talks and to defuse any stress left over from the official debriefings at the station. He kept expendable glasses, and chairs and tables of Coruboard—cheap to replace, nonlethal when used as bludgeons. He tolerated almost any disorder short of a full riot, leaving the leos to referee themselves. There were just two unbreakable rules in Tuck's place; no uniforms and no rank—he treated Director Paget himself no better than the rawest rookie—and any damage had to be paid for before the officers involved left. As a result Tuck's had become one of the city's favorite lion bars, and around watch change experienced citizens found somewhere else to drink.

The Den started filling up after four-thirty, as debriefing ended. The leos drifted up from the station in twos and threes. The lion buffs came out of the woodwork, women and a few men who loved the company of anything wearing a badge. The noise level increased exponentially with every new arrival. By the time Lieutenant Hari Vradel and Janna Brill came in just before five, anyone without a good set of lungs might as well be content just to sit and watch.

During the walk up from the station Janna kept wondering why Vradel asked her to join him. She had been to the Den often before, but not usually with Vradel, except as part of a group celebrating something. Vradel liked to mother his squad, though, and he had not really spoken to her since Wim's injury. He must have brought her here to comfort her.

In the Den, Tuck himself stood behind the bar. Janna could well believe he had worked Vice. He was built for kicking down the doors of unlicensed and after-hours bars and gambling parlors. In fact, she thought he looked as if he could take out a door just by casually leaning against it. It amazed her that a man his size could turn around behind the bar without wiping out the entire stock of glasses.

"What'll it be?" Without any visible strain, Tuck managed to make his voice clearly audible.

Janna could not hear Vradel order. Tuck, though, either had excellent hearing or read lips. He set up a glass of iced tea and a noxious blue drink the Ares I crew had invented those first bleak months on Mars, known now as a Martian Cow. Vradel handed over his card, signaling he was paying for both drinks. While he pressed his thumb to the register screen, Janna picked up her tea. As they started to turn away from the bar, Tuck handed Vradel a grease pencil. "Use this, will you? Ink doesn't come out of the tabletops."

Vradel grinned sheepishly.

He pointed toward the back of the room and plunged into the crowd. Janna followed, staying close, holding her glass above the arms that gesticulated with abandon while their owners talked shop or sex or argued whether a Jewish President would be able to get tough enough with Israel, and if mining the asteroids, as the people in the Mars colony proposed, could really break Africa's stranglehold on the mineral market.

At the back sat a row of booths. Several of them remained unoccupied. Vradel slid in one side of the end booth. Janna sat down across from him. The colloid plastic of the bench molded to her hips.

Vradel took a sip of his Martian Cow and set it down. He started toying with the grease pencil. Above the roar of voices around them he bellowed, "I want you to know I'm sorry about Kiest. He was a fine investigator. It's a damned shame that had to happen so close to his resignation."

Janna nodded. She watched her knuckles whiten around her glass.

The grease pencil dipped inevitably toward the tabletop. Janna wondered if it were true the edges of the citations Vradel issued as a traffic officer had been adorned with caricatures of the cited individual, doodled there while Vradel talked to the citizen. She was inclined to believe it, accepting for fact the story that in one case where the identity of the citee came into question, it had been settled by comparing the individual who presented himself in court with the sketches on the citation.

Wim's face emerged from the tangle of lines Vradel made on the tabletop. "Times like these I regret not being able to be personal friends with every officer in my squad. Then maybe I'd know better things to say. Sometimes partners aren't friends. Sometimes they don't even like each other. Morello tells me you and Kiest were close, though. Is there anything I can do?"

"He isn't dead, lieutenant."

Vradel looked up. His mustache twitched. "Blind, though—" He bent his head over his sketch. After a minute, he looked up again. "What are you doing with yourself these days, Brill? Taking any classes at Washburn? Still cohabiting with that assistant medical examiner?"

It felt strange to be holding casual conversation at the top of her lungs, but Janna answered, "I'm not taking any classes but yes, I'm still cohabs with Sid Chesney."

"Thinking of making a marriage contract with him?"

"With Sid?" She grinned and shook her head. "I'm the wrong sex for Sid. I don't believe in marriage for leos anyway. The job is a hellish anxiety for a spouse. Sid, now, doesn't get frantic if I'm late and we can talk to each other about our days without being shocked. He doesn't compete with me for dates the way a female roommate would. We're comfortable together. How many police marriages can make the same claim?"

Now it was Vradel who smiled. "Oh, there are a few." He drew another face. It was a woman's, round and gentle. Janna had seen him draw that face often and with great affection. "Hilly and I have been renewing for twenty years." He smiled at the sketch, then looked up at Janna. "I ought to find you another partner. Is there anyone you—"

He broke off as a disturbance rippled through the bar. At first Janna thought it might be a fight, but the source became evident in a moment. Out of the jam of leos came a man and a woman. The woman was pure flash…rich mahogany-red hair, silver hip boots, shreds of a romper that matched her improbably blue eyes. A path opened for her like Moses passing through the Red Sea. The sound of falling jaws and dripping saliva marked her wake.

"A new girl of Risa's, do you suppose, or a lion buff?" Vradel said.

Janna eyed the couple. They took a booth at the far end of the line. "A kind of buff. She flirts, and always wears something to raise the blood pressure. The sligh with her is new, though."

Vradel looked past Janna at them. "He is a sligh, isn't he? I wonder what he's doing in here."

Exactly what marked the sligh, Janna could not say. There was nothing unusual about his hair or clothing, but then, slighs were usually careful to blend in. Probably it was the studied indifference of his walk, as if he wanted to be invisible, but lacking that, was fighting the urge to bolt or dive under the nearest table. She, too, wondered what a sligh was doing walking into a bar full of lions.

Vradel began sketching the man. "I'm curious. How do you feel about Undocumenteds?"

"They're brainbent, but there's nothing illegal in being unidented. I say let them live the way they want to. In Oakland I had a number of sligh friends. I always hated raiding schools."

Vradel grunted. "Anyone except a rock jock hates strapping schools."

The slithyschools were illegal because they were uninspected and unlicensed. Licensing, after all, required identation of all students. It was only a misdemeanor to run a school, though, or to send children to one. That made it dirty work holding a bunch of kids just to force their parents to come in and plead guilty to a misdemeanor. In Janna's opinion, raiding schools was an underhanded ruse to ident sligh kids and their parents.

"What?" She realized belatedly that Vradel was talking to her again.

"Is there anyone you'd like to team with? Anyone you'd rather *not?"*

She gave his question some thought, then shook her head. Most of the squad were good leos. The toads and timesliders all had partners already.

"Any objection to taking a new man? I have one coming in Monday from the Soldier Creek division."

Janna smiled. "I'll bet he's glad to be joining civilization."

Vradel put down his pencil and took a long swallow of his drink. After a moment of thought, he took another. "He's been other places besides Soldier Creek. He's been everywhere, one time or another, including Capitol."

Janna had a sudden feeling she would regret not naming someone she wanted to team with. "What's this leo's name?"

"Sergeant Mahlon Maxwell."

Janna clutched her tea. "Oh, god."

Vradel looked unhappy. "You've met him?"

"I've run into his reputation. He left Oakland just a few months before I transferred in. Mama Maxwell has been with the department for twelve years. He has a law degree, but he's still a sergeant. In Oakland he's infamous for the Night of the Caged Lion."

Vradel chewed on the end of his mustache. "His jacket doesn't list offenses by title, I'm afraid. What's the Night of the Caged Lion?"

Janna leaned back. The colloid of the bench flowed with her. "Once upon a very quiet and boring morning watch, Mama Maxwell and his partner decided that since nothing else was happening, they would entertain themselves with a little flatdancing. They climbed into the back of their watchcar, being very careful to wedge the door open, and started putting to. Along came one of the local citizens on the way home after the bars had closed. The citizen evidently saw them and kicked out the wedge."

"Christ." Vradel reached for his Martian Cow.

"Wait. The best is yet to come. They were parked in their favorite hole and since they didn't want the squad sergeant to learn about it, they disconnected the car's transponder and their button transponders. So when they didn't roger their next call, the dispatcher couldn't find them on the map. She notified their sergeant, and every car in the division was put to work looking for them. The hunt lasted over two hours and eventually included not only the alpha and beta squad sergeants but also the watch supervisor."

Vradel finished his drink. "And the rest is recorded in the disciplinary action in his jacket. He was suspended for six months, then sent to Cullen Village division. His partner resigned."

"How did you happen to get stuck with him?" asked Janna.

"He's been doing good work in Soldier Creek, apparently. His present supervisors recommended promotion to Investigator I." Vradel chewed on his mustache. "He's collected a number of commendations over the years and he's been using his law degree to defend officers against charges brought by Internal Affairs. He's won more cases than he's lost. Brill, he can't be too bad; will you team with him?"

She grimaced. "Why me?"

"You need a partner. Besides, maybe you'll be a good influence on him."

Her lip curled.

"Take him at least until you find someone else you want to work with. I'd make it an order but this is Tuck's place. No rank. I'll just say please."

Today was her day for being pushed into corners, it seemed. She sighed. "All right." She paused, shaking her head. "Mama Maxwell? Lord." She sighed again. "I can hardly wait until Monday."

Maybe it was time to give Wim's offer serious thought.

4

Jorge spent Saturday vacillating between excitement and depression, between the high he felt in a game when his opponent was making all the moves Jorge wanted, and the cold, sweaty certainty that the Laclede woman was wrong, that the sligh could never successfully pass for him. The sligh would be caught, and start the entire domino row going down. He was tempted to call the woman and cancel everything. Perhaps there would be no trouble convincing Andy to help falsify the records. About the time he thought that, though, Jorge also started thinking what would happen if Andy refused to help. That brought on the cold sweat again.

By evening, he had decided that no matter how risky the gambit, he had to use it. The doppelgänger was insurance, just in case.

Jorge dressed for the evening with care, a simple gold and blue jumpsuit and dark blue ankle boots. He wrapped his right wrist in a support bandage. He could claim he sprained it in a fall or during calisthenics. He glanced at the chrono on his dresser top. Six-thirty. Half an hour until met the doppelgänger.

He went to his study. After a momentary hesitation, he pulled open the top drawer of his desk. A .22 revolver lay inside. He regarded the weapon for a moment, licking his lips, then shook his head and closed the drawer. A gun was not only noisy, but this particular one could be traced to him. As part of maintaining a license on it, he had to leave a new test bullet with the police department every fifty firings or every six months. The image of any bullet removed from a body was routinely run through the ballistics computer, he knew, and compared to the images of the test bullets stored in its memory. No, he could not use the gun.

Then he turned around to the planetscape on the wall behind his desk, swung it aside and spun the three concentric rings on the lock of the safe concealed behind the painting. When the three rings were in their proper relationship, the lock clicked. He pulled open the door, reached in and took out a small amber plastic pill bottle.

The lid twisted open hard. Jorge struggled with it for a minute before it gave. The bottle was about half full of a talcum-fine, herbal-scented brown powder—trichlorlysergic something-or-other. Trick. Jorge shook the bottle. It made colors that tasted and sounds that had scent. It was the ultimate trip, some said, and it could be a one-way ticket.

He recapped the bottle and pushed it into a thigh pocket. He had taken this particular sample away from a weekend guest, who brought it hoping to make sex a new experience. Jorge preferred the old variety to a *new* that could become a *last*. He understood his reasons for taking the stuff from Serena, but until now he had sometimes wondered why he had kept it. He should have thrown it away. Perhaps he had been subconsciously thinking even then that the day might come when he would need something deadly that could not be traced to him.

Jorge glanced at the study chrono. Six thirty-five.

He crossed to the phone and punched in Andy's number. It buzzed twice and then the elegant face of Liann Seaton, Andy's wife, appeared on the screen.

She smiled. "Hello, Jorge."

He smiled back. "Hi, you gorgeous creature. Let's run away together."

"I'm busy tonight. How about next week? Do you want Andy?"

"As long as you're busy, yes."

The screen went white as she put him on hold.

Jorge waited, and found himself drumming his fingers in nervous anticipation. He forced himself to stop as soon as he realized what he was doing. Surely there was no need to be nervous. He could manipulate Andy. The trick was persuading Andy to leave the house without Liann learning where he was going.

Andy's face appeared on the screen. "What is it, Jorge?"

"Are you alone there?"

Andy's brows rose. "You mean here at the phone? Yes. Why?"

"I was going over the Laheli records late this afternoon and—" He broke off.

Andy's raised brows pulled toward each other in a concerned frown. "And?" he prompted.

Jorge pretended to debate. After a moment he said, "I don't think I better talk about it over the phone. I'd better show you. Are you free this evening?"

His partner's frown deepened. "I promised Liann and the kids we'd go to the cinaround."

"We really ought to go over this matter before Monday. We don't know when the government will start its inquiry. What I've found could make or break the firm."

Now it was Andy's turn to debate. He did it with obvious effort.

"It won't take long," Jorge added persuasively. "You'll be back in time to take them to a late showing."

Andy gave in. "All right. Shall I come to the office?"

"Yes." Now came the hard part. "Would you mind not telling Liann that I'm the one dragging you away? I don't want her mad at me for spoiling your evening."

"She won't be. You know she has the disposition of a saint."

"I don't want to spoil that disposition, either. Please."

Andy nodded. "All right, I'll make up some excuse that has nothing to do with you. See you at the office in half an hour."

Jorge punched off the line. He headed for the door smiling in satisfaction. Now if the sligh could only carry off *his* part, the gambit just might work.

Owan Desfosses spent Saturday sick with fear. This scheme would never work. He could not hope to pass as this Jorge Hazlett, no matter what Tarl said. He was an Undocumented, a social truant. He had lived his life avoiding those places and activities a citizen accepted as everyday normals. Who was this Tarl anyway? Owan did not know him. Maybe Tarl was a leo, setting a slithytove trap.

Even while he sweated and his stomach churned, Owan sat in his room preparing for the job. First, he cut his hair to shoulder length and curled it to match the lion's mane of the man in the 2-D photograph Tarl had given him. Then he practiced copying the signature on the card and memorized the list of places he must not visit. Owan wrote the name over and over, laboriously at first, then with increasing ease as the day progressed. He covered both sides of sheet after sheet of paper. After he filled each sheet, he destroyed it, tearing it into pieces so small no one would ever be able to tell what he had written.

Watching the signature come closer and closer to matching the one on the card, Owan's fear quieted. He even began to feel a touch of excitement. This just might work. If it did—if it did work, he could enjoy the life of a citizen for an entire evening.

Owan had envied citizens as long as he could remember. They could go anywhere, live anywhere. They never had to cross the street to avoid a leo or take abuse from a store owner who made them work long hours for little compensation. He was not quite sure why he remained a sligh, except that it was the only life he knew. His parents had raised him as a sligh.

Combing his hair, he thought about the times he had considered applying for a Scib Card. Once he had even asked for the application at a Social Care office, but he had never been able to make himself fill out the form. Something in him curdled at the idea of committing facts about himself to paper.

He looked at the clock on his dresser. It was an old thing the apartment manager had given him so he would not be late for work, an antique with a round face and hands. It read twenty minutes to seven.

He took one last look at himself in the mirror and compared the image to the photograph. It was a strange sensation to see a stranger looking up at him with his own face.

Owan opened the envelope lying beside the picture. He shook it. A small tube of glue and an oval of transparent plastic fell out into his hand.

His hands started to sweat. He put everything down while he dried them, then opened the tube and dropped some of the liquid onto the center of his left thumb, spreading it around to the edges of the ridged area. Carefully, he picked up the piece of plastic. He held it obliquely to the light to make sure which was the smooth side and that he had the correct end toward his thumbnail, then he pressed the plastic onto his thumb. He smoothed it down, smoothed the edges.

He waited a minute to make sure the plastic had set, and while it finished drying, tossed envelope, glue, and picture into the top drawer of his dresser. Then he studied his thumb. He could hardly tell the plastic was on it.

Owan took a deep breath. Time to begin.

He left his room and climbed the stairs to the ground floor. Outside, he unlocked his bicycle and backed it out of the rack. He was proud of the bike. He had built it himself of parts he acquired one way or another while he worked at a bike shop. He felt the result was a bike every bit as good as a commercially built machine. At the very least it freed him from having to find ways of earning transport tokens for buses. Except in bad weather, he could travel almost as fast by bike as he could have in a runabout or pedal car.

He swung onto the bike and headed it toward the downtown area. The evening felt unbearably hot and humid. How many days had the temperature been over thirty-five Celsius now? It seemed like weeks. It had to be nearly forty degrees tonight. In no time his forehead was running sweat and his pioneer-style shirt sticking to his back. He did not slow down, though. The time had to be close to seven o'clock and he did not want to be late.

Every red light was an irritant, a demoniacal plot to delay him. What was the actual time? If he were late would this Hazlett wait?

Just over the Interstate, he hit a yellow light. It would be a long red, he knew. He pedaled hard and raced through.

Behind him, a siren burped once. Owan froze.

The black-and-white bullet-on-a-plate shape of a watchcar drifted up beside him and slowed to hover. A she-lion leaned out, folded arms on the edge of the window.

"You can get hurt racing yellows," she said.

Owan could feel the air kicked out by the car's fans. It was hot against his ankles. The rest of him, sweat or not, felt wrapped in ice. His stomach knotted. He swallowed. "Yes, officer."

"A bicycle will lose a contest with a car or runabout every time."

She did not necessarily recognize him as a sligh, he told himself. She was probably not trophy hunting. He gripped the handlebars tighter to keep his hands from shaking. "I know, officer."

She looked him over with narrowed eyes. "Something wrong, jon?"

His stomach lurched. When they started calling someone "jon" they were smelling lion meat.

He made himself smile. "Nothing wrong except I'm late for work."

He thought he said it smoothly but she sat up. Her voice sharpened. "What's your name, jon?"

Traffic was swinging around them. People in the runabouts and cars stared. Owan wanted to run. "Tris." Never, ever give a real name to a lion.

"No last name? Let's see your card, jon."

"I—" His smile widened. "I don't have one."

The she-lion's brows went up. She grinned. "Hey, Cade," she said to her partner at the wheel, "we have a sligh. How'd you get your bike licensed, jon? Do you suppose he stole it, Cade? We better take him in and check on it."

A trophy hunter. Owan could have wept. They could not take him in, not now, of all times…not *now*. "It's registered to a friend," he said desperately. "Clio de Garza."

"Well, we'll just see." She touched the radio. "Alpha Cap Eleven to control, stolen property check. Hey, Cade, do you suppose he'll resist arrest?"

"Let him go," the lion at the wheel said. He sounded tired. "It's too hot for games."

The she-lion frowned, then pulled back into the car. "Alpha Cap Eleven to control, cancel the call." Her eyes bored holes in Owan. "Watch yourself in traffic after this, jon."

The watchcar's fans revved and it pulled away from him.

Owan did not have time to be relieved. He leaned on the pedals and raced for downtown.

At the Sunco parking lot on Jackson Street Owan lifted the bike over the entrance gate and hurriedly parked and locked it in the bicycle section. The lot served workers in the office buildings nearby. At this time of evening it was almost deserted. Owan looked around. He did not see anyone who seemed to be waiting. Could Hazlett have left already?

Then he heard a voice coming from the direction of the public phones. "...and the fans started to sound strange. I'll leave the car parked here. Have someone look at it as soon as possible, please. The address again is the Sunco parking lot. Thirteenth and Jackson."

Owan headed for the voice.

The man punched the phone off and turned around.

Owan felt as if he had been kicked in the stomach. A chill crawled up his spine. Even the photograph had not prepared him for the shock of meeting himself face to face.

Jorge Hazlett stared back. His eyes were coldly appraising. "You're late."

Under that withering stare, no excuse seemed justified enough to give. "I'm sorry." His voice sounded thin in his ears.

"You understand exactly what you're supposed to do?"

Owan nodded.

The man reached into the breast pocket of his jumpsuit and took out a card case. He handed over the Scib Card in it. "Five thousand bankcredits worth of merchandise, no more. Try to spend more and I'll hang both you and the woman."

Owan wondered what woman. He had met no one but Tarl.

"Be back here no later than ten o'clock, and don't forget the purchase receipts. Don't go near the places on that list I wrote out." His tone said that Owan could not hope to fool anyone who knew Jorge Hazlett at all.

"Ten o'clock. I'll bring the receipts. I won't go to any of those places." He would not have had the nerve in any case. Clubs and game parlors like those were places slighs saw only from the kitchen.

Owan left the lot as quickly as he could without seeming to be running away. Hazlett made him nervous. He was glad the likeness between them was only physical.

He wished he could use his bike, but Tarl had told him he must act as Hazlett would and Hazlett had no bicycle. Owan stood at the bus stop for several minutes before he realized he had no transport tokens. There was a token machine in the lobby of the building behind the bus stop. Owan stared at it, licking his lips. His palms started to sweat. Well, there was no time like now to find out if this crazy switch would work.

To his amazement, it worked. The machine accepted the thumb-print and signature and coughed out half a dozen tokens. Owan climbed on the next bus feeling giddy. Two of the tokens clattered into the bus's hopper. He could fool a machine at least.

He was aboard the bus for five minutes before he happened to wonder where it was going. He checked the next street marker it passed. Twenty-third and Kansas Avenue. The bus was going to south Topeka.

For a moment he was jubilant—he could visit Clio and Tesha—but his pleasure faded almost immediately. He was supposed to be Jorge Hazlett. Hazlett would have no reason to visit Clio and Tesha. Owan had things Tarl had ordered him to buy, too. The Granada Mall out this way by the Aerospace center was the kind of place Hazlett probably went.

What he could and did do was to buy some vending tokens at the mall and use a public phone to call Clio.

He had cohabited with Clio de Garza for nearly three years some eight years before. There was no marriage contract because contracts required registration and identification. The arrangement might have lasted indefinitely except Clio became pregnant. Understandably, she wanted to raise the child with all the benefits of full citizenship. Clio herself was a citizen. When Owan could not bring himself to be idented so they could marry, Clio finally moved out. Owan did not hold that against her. He found it miraculous that a woman as beautiful as she and some twenty years his junior could have found him worth living with for even three years. They remained friends.

Clio's face appeared on the screen, Hispanic, darkly beautiful. She looked surprised but pleased to see him. "You're in south Topeka? Are you coming to visit?"

He shook his head, sighing. "I can't. That's why I called. Is Tesha still up?"

"She was on her way to bed, but I'll go get her."

Moments later he saw the olive face of his daughter on the screen. Tesha was the real miracle of the time with Clio. Every time Owan saw her he marveled that he could have been part of producing this exquisite creature. Watching her grow up was the joy of his life. He lived every week for the Sunday afternoon visit with her.

"How are you, *chiquita?*" he asked.

She launched into an enthusiastic description of what she had learned at school that week. It was a real school. No illegal schools for Tesha, no fearful waiting for police raids.

Clio interrupted finally. "That's enough for tonight. You can tell him the rest tomorrow. You will be here tomorrow, won't you?"

"Of course. And I'll have a surprise for you, *chiquita*."

Tesha's eyes widened. "What kind of surprise?"

"If I told you, it wouldn't be a surprise, would it? Good night."

She blew him a kiss.

Clio did, too. "Collect the real one, and more, tomorrow."

After he punched off he rode the sidewalks through the dizzying sprawl of the mall, trying to decide what to buy first. Five hundred of the five thousand bankcredits were his to spend on whatever he wanted. What did he want? There was so much to choose from.

He saw a toy shop. Tesha's surprise ought to be the first order of business.

As he entered the toy shop, he wondered if it were wise when he saw the polished perfection of the clerk. He knew enough about places like this to know clerks like that sold merchandise that cost dearly. Still, he had five hundred to play with.

"I'm looking for something for a very bright seven-year-old girl."

The clerk smiled. "This way, sir."

Sir. As if he were a citizen. Owan felt a meter taller.

The selection of toys dazzled him. He had never dreamed such things existed. They had certainly never been part of a sligh child's world. The toys crowded the shelves around him: dolls, educational put-togethers, toys to develop learning skills, toys to exercise the imagination, toys to develop physical dexterity, toys to cuddle, role-practice toys.

It took him twenty minutes, but out of them all he finally chose two: a small computer which the clerk assured him would be an invaluable school aid, and a Dyan Pennock doll. Owan had never heard the name before but the dark beauty of the doll attracted him. Until he read the biographical booklet that came with the doll, he had not known that the most famous shuttlejocky in the world was a black woman.

The computer proved awkward to carry. He had to set it down several times to try for a better hold. The clerk had offered to have it delivered, but he could not risk that.

As he struggled with the package, he found himself standing in front of a clothing shop. The two jumpsuits on display almost made him forget Tesha's computer. The colors were soft but glowing. They shifted subtly as the light on them changed. He reached out to touch one, drawn almost magnetically. He had never felt anything in his life that soft and light. What a rich feeling it would be to own and wear a suit like that.

Owan picked up his packages and walked into the shop.

Even with the doppelgänger late to the meeting, Jorge still reached the office before Andy. He left the lights off and sat in the reception room letting the air-conditioning cool him off.

He had been disappointed by the doppelgänger. Did the Laclede woman really think that rabbit looked like him? A poor expression of judgment, if so. Still, if the fool stayed away from the places on the list, the substitution might work. Card photos were always so bad that the doppelgänger came close enough to matching the one on Jorge's card.

The office door hummed. Jorge sat up. Someone had pressed a palm to the capacitant plate of the lock. In a few moments the information on the size, shape, and salt content of the hand on the plate relayed through the computer and the computer satisfied itself that the hand belonged to someone who had access rights. The lock opened with a click.

Andy came in, wiping his forehead. "Terrible heat outside, isn't it? Murderous. I wonder how many people it will drive to murder this weekend." He plucked at his jumpsuit, pulling it away from his body. "The air-conditioning was out on my bus, too. Now, what is it you need to show me?"

"Let's go to your office."

If someone came by, such as the building security guard, Jorge wanted lights nowhere in the suite but Andy's office.

Andy pressed his hand to the plate of his office door. The door hummed, consulting the computer again, and clicked open. The room was still bright with light coming through the window strips. Andy did not bother turning on any lamps.

Like Jorge's office, Andy's was dominated by his big L-shaped desk. The chairs in the room faced it, except for several grouped around a low table near the door. Where Jorge covered his walls with pictures of ramjets and photographs of distant worlds taken from orbit by tachyon bioprobes, Andy decorated his with matted and framed cartoons of lawyers, part of his legal humor collection. Behind Andy's desk hung a large brush and-ink drawing of Justice peeping, winking, from under her blindfold.

Andy sat in his desk chair and leaned back, raising expectant brows at Jorge. "Now what did you need me to see?"

Jorge came around the desk to the computer outlet. He punched it on. "I finally found the code for retrieving the Laheli records."

He punched in the request for the records.

The computer screen said: WHAT'S THE PASSWORD?

Jorge typed: RUY LOPEZ, then clicked on the printer icon.

The printer hummed. Facsimile pages began dropping one after the other into the tray.

"I need help, Andy." Jorge made it a plea.

"You said this could ruin the firm?"

"It can. Read that."

Andy picked up the pages and began reading. At first his eyes raced down the sheet quickly, then with an almost audible roar of reversing fans, he stopped. He went back and began rereading, this time with slow care. After several pages, he looked up at Jorge in horror.

"Good god, Jorge. What have you done? *Why?*"

Jorge shrugged. "I don't know. I have the house and those flash girlfriends who like expensive presents. I—I didn't think anyone would be hurt."

"Not *hurt?* Jorge, those letters from Boeing say it all. Where is it?" He flipped back through the printout sheets. "Here. 'We cannot guarantee the continued function of these systems without constant, expert maintenance.' *Constant, expert* maintenance, Jorge. You surely couldn't have thought the colonists were going to be able to become expert in life-support systems maintenance with the crash course they take." He stared at Jorge in disbelief. "You had to know how dangerous it was. I can't believe any of this. Those people's lives were dependent on those systems. There's no walking home from a ramjet. Yet you let them—" He broke off and dropped the sheets on his desk as if they were burning his hands. "Lord. You know what this means, don't you? If a government investigator sees this, he'll invoke the Tescott Act. You willfully and deceitfully jeopardized those people's lives."

"Not willfully, I swear." Jorge leaned toward Andy. "That's why you have to help me alter the records."

Andy stiffened. "Alter the records?"

"We're partners, remember. We're both liable. You wouldn't want Liann or the kids dragged into anything as nasty as a Tescott prosecution."

The worry frown cleared off Andy's face. His mouth thinned. "We're partners, yes. That makes the partnership liable in a civil suit; but the Tescott Act is a criminal prosecution. I'm *not* liable in a criminal action. I won't make myself a party by becoming an accessory. Jorge—" Andy ran both hands through his hair. He sighed. "I don't understand what in god's name you thought you were doing. We're dedicated to helping colonists build new worlds and new lives. To send them off in what's essentially a leaky rowboat is a total contradiction of our goals."

Andy's goals, maybe. Irritation rose in Jorge. He tried to keep it under control and look frantic instead. "We certainly can't help colonists if we're out of business. Help me straighten this Laheli thing out."

Jorge still hoped Andy would cooperate. They had been friends and partners a long time. They had shared an apartment during their senior year at law school, sweated out their exams and then the bar exams together, counted coup on the same girls. They had comforted each other in their starvation those early years trying to develop a law practice. He hoped Andy would not be a fool and force him into a corner.

Andy's eyes dropped to the computer pages. "We can't cover this up. I ought to let you face it alone. After all, you got into it alone. You ought to be responsible for your own actions."

Jorge almost hissed. Lord, a sermon. If this turned into a recitation of Libertarian cant, he was going to strangle Andy.

"But we're friends," Andy said.

Jorge felt a wash of relief.

"Maybe we can avoid the Tescott Act." Andy picked up the printout again. "I wish your answers to Boeing had been less arrogant. 'I have explained the situation to my clients. They say they understand perfectly and are prepared to cope with any possible problem. They would not have ordered this particular ship if it were not what they wanted.'" He looked up, frowning. "You hadn't talked to them, had you? You never warned them at all. You let them think crewing the ship would be just a matter of following the computer's orders and feeding in new programs when required."

"I didn't think there was any need to warn them."

Andy shook his head as if being bitten by something he wanted to shake off. "You, the chess player, the master of alternatives and planner of seven moves ahead—you didn't consider what might happen to them? I can't believe that." He flipped through the sheets.

Jorge waited, very still. He had a sudden fear what Andy was about to do. He hoped he was wrong.

Andy regarded him thoughtfully. His mouth thinned. "I think you did know they ought to be warned. I think you knew very well what might happen. You always have a good idea how everything you do will turn out. You just didn't *care* what happened to those people."

His voice was so calmly unemotional Jorge felt panic grab him. A calm Andy meant a thinking Andy. A thinking Andy was dangerous. Jorge met the accusation with an unwavering gaze. "I would never consciously do anything to harm a client."

Andy threw down the printout. "Crap. When you're playing games, other people are just pawns. You treat them all as expendable. You were that way in the moot court in law school. You were that way with the clients we had in law practice." He stopped. His face grayed.

Jorge wondered if Andy were considering that the Laheli Company might not be the first client Jorge defrauded.

"Jorge, I need to know something. Be honest with me. Is this the first time you've put clients aboard a ship that's too small and too crowded?"

Jorge was ready for him. He let his jaw drop as though in dismay. "Andy, what do you think I am? Of course this is the first time it's happened. I swear."

Andy smiled, but Jorge saw steel under it. "Then you won't mind going over the records of all our past clients, will you?"

Silently, Jorge cursed his partner. The fool. He had to back Jorge into a corner. He had given Andy a chance to help, but Andy would not take it. God only knew what Andy would do when he saw the other records. At the least he would denounce Jorge to the Colonial Agency and the U. S. District Attorney. It was a check, and the easiest counter this time was to remove the attacking piece.

Jorge smiled back. "Of course I don't mind. That's going to take a while, though. I think I'd like some caff to drink while we work. How about you?"

Andy nodded. "Good idea."

"I'll have it ready in a minute."

Jorge knew where the office staff kept the cups and caff and tea mixes. He took the ingredients out of their cabinet and mixed two cups of caff with hot water from the suite washroom. He dropped a tablet of sweetener and a cube of lightener powder into his drink. Two sweetener tabs and no lightener went into Andy's. Jorge glanced toward Andy's office door to make sure he was not being observed, then reached into his pocket for the tube of trick. He had tried everything to avoid this. He had given Andy every opportunity to cooperate. The consequences were Andy's fault.

He poured a third of the powder into Andy's caff. A swirl with a stirrer dissolved it. He carried the steaming cups back to Andy's office.

His partner was watching the computer print out a list of their clients. Andy accepted the mug with a murmur of thanks and sipped it. After the first swallow, he drew back and frowned at the cup.

"Something wrong?" Jorge asked.

"It tastes a little different. Did you put in two sweetener tabs?"

"Yes."

Andy took another swallow.

The list finished printing out. Each client had a code number ending in either *K* or *H*, indicating which of the partners handled them. Andy started down the list with a red pen and, between sips of caff, circled all the H numbers.

He paused over one. "Strange."

Jorge lifted a brow. "What is?"

"I don't remember handling an Outreach Company, but it has a K number."

He would be doubly shocked, and perhaps realize what was happening, when he saw the Laheli Company had a K number, too. Jorge hoped the trick worked before then.

"Curiouser and curiouser," Andy murmured. He circled another number. "When I move the pen, I hear a chiming sound." He looked up and around him with surprise. "When I talk, the air is filled with a minty scent." He sniffed the caff. "It isn't the caff. That smells rich purple." He took a large swallow. "It tastes green, though. It—"

Andy stared into the cup in horror. Suddenly he whipped around and threw it across the room. Caff splashed on the wall. "You put something in it, Jorge. What are gray and greeb iffing snoways for?" The horror overwhelmed his eyes. He put both hands over his mouth. "I didn't creech the say and yoder meaning."

Jorge finished his own caff . He went to pick up Andy's cup. "I don't suppose you did, Andy, but you can't help yourself. Your brain's working on new directions. Enjoy them while you can."

Andy lunged for him, but the trick's cross-wiring effect caused different sets of muscles to react to the brain's orders. He jerked backward and fell flat. Then the convulsions started.

Jorge turned his back. He wiped the wall clean. He set Andy's cup on the desk. He picked up all the printout sheets and cleared the computer. He recoded access to the Laheli records with a new password: WRITE ME A VERBAL CONTRACT.

He heard Andy gasp, looked around. His partner's mouth gasped as he struggled to breathe, but his diaphragm had forgotten how to work. Andy turned blue.

Jorge carried his own cup to the washroom and cleaned it. After drying it carefully, he put it away. Finally, he closed the door of Andy's office. It locked with a soft click.

Jorge regarded the closed door for a moment. He sighed. Why did Andy have to be so difficult? Jorge hoped this would not be too hard on Liann and the kids.

He left the suite, letting the outer door lock behind him, and walked down the firestairs into the hot street.

5

Monday morning no unfamiliar faces appeared at rollcall, but Pass-the-Word Morello read the crimes list in Vradel's place. Janna noticed her colleagues eyeing her with expressions ranging from amused through sympathetic to pitying. That was not very encouraging, particularly after what Wim had told her over the weekend.

Though she had had to work both Saturday and Sunday, she managed to spend the evenings at the hospital. Watching Wim start the painful process of learning to live with blindness, she had wondered how he was ever going to be able to cope with an entirely alien world. Even while Wim struggled with the problem of feeding himself, however, his voiced worries had all been for her.

"You ought to come along with us. It would be much better than putting up with Mama Maxwell." He shook his bandaged head. "You should have refused to team with him. He's a lunatic. He'll pull you into things you'd never do on your own."

"Like counting coup in the back seat of a watchcar?"

"Yes, like counting coup in the back seat of a watchcar." He chased peas around his plate with his fork. "I think dieticians are sadists." He captured a single pea. "He had me lying to two sergeants, a lieutenant, the division captain, and an I. A. peep, to keep them from learning he carried a shooter walking his beat one night."

Janna stared. "He carried a *shooter?*" She could just bet the man did not want his superiors to know about that. "Why were you in on it?"

"I was driving his mobile back-up. The shooter was a beautiful weapon, an old Colt .38 revolver he'd taken off some suspect and never turned in. He must have had it in his runabout and switched it for his Starke after rollcall inspection. I never asked him and he never volunteered that information. What I know for certain is that I got a call from him about three o'clock one morning to pick up a breaker he'd caught going into the back of one of the stores on Stuart Street. I found him in the alley behind the store. The place reeked of gunpowder. The prisoner was a greaser turned albino with fear. He kept screeching that Maxwell had tried to kill him. That fool Maxwell had not only carried the shooter, he'd fired a warning shot at the breaker with it. The ammunition in that shooter was hot-loaded. It must have sounded like a cannon going off. No wonder the breaker was scared shitless."

Janna felt chill. Shooters and warning shots were both against regulations. "Did he tell the booking officer about being shot at?"

Wim snorted. "He told everyone in the station about it. The booking officer had to report it to the sergeant and lieutenant, of course. It went up the line clear to Internal Affairs. Maxwell and I swore there'd never been a shooter. We said the breaker was just trying to make trouble because after his prior list of convictions, he was in big trouble. I'd switched weapons with Maxwell driving in so when the breaker started wailing and weeping about having been put in fear of his life, Maxwell had an innocent Starke to show. Let me tell you, I sweated blood until the furor died. Facing the peeps I was sorry I'd ever agreed to help Maxwell."

"Why did you?"

"Hell, I don't know. I guess because being mobile back-up is almost like being partners. Damn!" The peas kept evading him. With a hiss, he gave up formality and started trapping them against his fork with his fingers. "If the man isn't off his tick, he's at least brainbent, running on a bugged program."

Janna sucked her lower lip. "Vradel says he has commendations."

"He never earned one while I worked with him. I think they promoted him from a walker to car patrol because he talked Irin Vadose into asking for him. That ruined her career." He quit eating and turned his head toward her. "Jan, he can get you in trouble. Worse, he can get you killed. Shed him as fast as you can."

Not a good thought to be taking to work with her. Now the squad looked at her as if she were a sacrificial lamb. Pass-the-Word Morello had been talking, of course. The question in Janna's mind was what had he been telling everyone? After rollcall she caught the squad clerk's eye and crooked a finger at him. "Morello, I'd like to talk to you."

"Your new partner's waiting for you in Vradel's office. The lieutenant said to send you right in after rollcall."

Janna took a deep breath and turned toward Vradel's door, pausing a moment to gather courage before knocking. She felt the eyes of the entire squad on her and squared her shoulders. As senior partner surely she could keep control of him. She knocked.

"Come in."

Vradel sat behind his desk, sketching on his memo pad. He looked up. "Morning, Brill." His voice was brisk. He pointed his pencil from Janna to the man across the desk from him. "Brill, Mahlon Maxwell. Maxwell, Janna Brill."

Janna hardly heard the introduction. She stared in dismay at the man who unfolded from the chair, pushing at heavy-rimmed glasses sliding down his nose. Now she understood the pitying looks outside. Mahlon Maxwell was a freak! He stood even taller and thinner than she, a fact emphasized by the narrow cut of his green and purple jumpsuit. Light gleamed on a head as bald as an egg—a Dutch-chocolate egg. He looked grotesque, like some child's drawing of a black stickman.

"Just call me Mama," he said in a deep, resonant voice. He held out his hand.

She shook it gingerly. She could already hear the wisecracks the other squadmembers would make, comments on the partnership's being like night and day, or salt and pepper. They had other black/white teams, of course, but none with the partners so well matched in height and build they could be considered almost a positive and negative of each other. Christ. She wanted to get sick and go home. "Good morning, Sergeant Maxwell."

How did he get away with that head? The hair regs forbid lengths and styles that could obscure vision, but the rules had never been intended to encourage officers to go skinhead, like trippers. Maxwell had to realize how unprofessional it looked. If his baldness were natural, he ought to have a hair transplant.

The glasses puzzled her, too. The only people she knew who wore window frames in preference to contact lenses were those like Sid Chesney who hoped glasses would add maturity to his babyish face. Why did Maxwell wear his?

"I now pronounce you partners." Vradel picked up a stack of papers. "Put him to work, Brill."

Janna stood looking at him but Vradel kept his head bent over the papers. Sighing, she led the way out into the squadroom. "Have you ever done investigative work before?"

"I've been Investigator I twice." He pushed his glasses up his nose.

"And was demoted back to patrol both times?" The words were out before she realized it, and with an acid edge she never intended.

He followed her to her desk without responding. Pass-the-Word Morello had left a pile of complaint sheets in the middle. Maxwell picked them up and began tapping the edges even. "I take it you don't much like the idea of teaming with me."

"No." Her squadmates still covertly watched her. She kept her voice down so only Maxwell could hear. "I agreed because I lost my partner and I'm a sucker when the lieutenant says please."

He replaced the complaint sheets in the exact center of the desk, squared with the edges. "Lost your partner. Oh." He looked up. The sharpness of the move sent his glasses down his nose. He pushed them back up. "Wim Kiest was your partner? Hell of a thing." He took the pencils and pens out of the cup she used as a holder and began replacing them writing tip down, pencils leaning to her right, pens to her left. "I once worked with Kiest myself."

"He told me."

His eyebrows lifted. She did not need telepathy to know what he was thinking. He had to be remembering the shooter incident, and maybe others when Wim had covered for him. He must be wondering how much Wim had told her. Let him wonder.

The newscanner murmured that employee shortages were increasing. The number of unfilled jobs in the U. S. had reached four-point-two percent.

"Maxwell, I'm not hard to live with. I have a good record as Investigator II, and I intend to make Investigator III. Just remember that. If you follow the rules and don't try any of your lightwit stunts with me, we'll get along fine." She sorted through the complaint sheets. "Now, we have six assaults, including one ADW and three batteries, to investigate. If you're done housecleaning, let's get started."

She was turning away when the phone buzzed. A glance around the squadroom found everyone buried in papers or away from their desks.

The phone sounded like an angry insect.

"Someone get that," Morello said.

No one moved.

"Brill," Morello said.

She glared at him. "No, damn it." She waved the complaint sheets. "I have a day's work already."

Vradel's head came out of his office. "That better not ring a fourth time."

Janna stabbed the phone on. "Crimes Against Persons, Sergeant Brill."

It was the basset-faced civil servant on the 911 desk. "We have a report of a body in the Sunflower Federal Bank Building. Suite ten-oh-three. They don't know if it's homicide, suicide, or accident."

Janna grimaced. A deader. A fine start for the week. "Send a forensic team and notify the medical examiner. Someone from here will be on the way in a minute." She punched the phone off. "You want me to take it, lieutenant?"

"Go ahead." His head disappeared back into his office. Morello went back to paper shuffling.

Janna looked at Mama Maxwell. "Let's sail."

A watchcar was parked at the curb outside the Sunflower Federal Bank Building's main door. Janna stopped Indian Thirty just behind it and let the Monitor settle to its parking rollers. The guard on duty at the bank door watched them curiously and waved as they came into the lobby.

"Have you seen the team from that watch unit?" Janna asked the guard.

"They went upstairs."

She and Mama took the elevator up to the tenth floor. She found the mobile team waiting by the door of Suite 1003. She knew them by sight though not by name.

"Morning," she said.

They nodded to her. "Morning, sergeant."

Janna read the lettering on the door. *Hazlett and Kellener, Colonial Contractors.* "What do we have?"

"The body of a Mr. Andrew Hamilton Kellener, according to the people inside," one of the watchcar team said. "Maggie—that's Margaret Pfeiffer, the local walker—is inside with them."

Janna went in, Mama Maxwell following. The expensive simplicity of the reception room made Officer Pfeiffer's uniform look as out of place as a cannon at a flower show, but the two men and one woman with her clustered around the walker's sturdy form.

Janna showed them her identification. "I'm Sergeant Brill from Crimes Against Persons. This is Sergeant Maxwell."

Their eyes regarded him skeptically. The walker looked as if she were straining to keep a straight face. This is a lion? their expressions said.

Janna returned her ID to a sleeve pocket. As she did, she tapped on the flat little microcorder she kept there. "Will someone please tell me who all of you are and what's happened?"

A wispy-haired man with a face like two profiles glued together said in a shaky voice, "I'm Nels Peddicord."

"He's Mr. Kellener's secretary," Officer Pfeiffer said. She pointed to a beautiful Hispanic man and a plump girl whose hand he held. "This is Robert Sandoz, the receptionist, and Lilla Zontine, the files librarian. The body is in that office. Mr. Peddicord found it."

The secretary ran nervous hands through what remained of his hair. "It? That's Mr. Kellener, not an it. I wish he were an it. I hardly recognized him."

Janna and Mama crossed to the indicated door.

"Christ," Mama muttered. "Poor devil."

His had not been an easy death. Andrew Kellener's body lay on its side on the floor beside a big desk. His face was pulled awry and colored dark blue around the lips. His arms and legs twisted directions human limbs were never designed to bend. He looked as if some giant had practiced knot-tying with him. Making the situation all the more bizarre, cartoons hung on the walls all around.

Janna did not go in. She eyed the office from the doorway, briefly studied the door itself, then came back to Pfeiffer and the office staff.

"How did you happen to find him?"

Peddicord clasped his hands together. The fingers twined, came apart, retwined. "I went in to get some papers I knew were on Mr. Kellener's desk."

Janna lifted her brows. "That's a biolock on the door. Was it programmed for you or was it unlocked?"

The secretary's eyes widened. "Neither. When it appeared Mr. Kellener was going to be late, I had Lilla override the lock."

"Override?"

The plump girl spoke. "As files librarian all functions of the computer are my responsibility. Since the lock is programmed through the computer, too, Mr. Kellener had an override command put in, for use in emergencies. We never thought the emergency would be something like—" She clutched the hand of the receptionist. "I'm the only one who knows the command, aside from Mr. Kellener and Mr. Hazlett."

Close to Janna's ear, Mama murmured, "I hadn't noticed it was a biolock."

Janna felt a flash of satisfaction. She saved it to enjoy later. Right now she checked the reception room chrono. "It's eight thirty-five. If Mr. Kellener were late at—" She paused.

Peddicord filled in the time. "Eight fifteen."

"Thank you. If he were late at eight fifteen, what time did he normally come in?"

"A bit before eight."

"You open that early?"

Peddicord nodded. "Many of our clients are working hard to pay for their ships. We open early and close late so they can see us without losing work time. Mr. Kellener worked from eight until about three, or later. Mr. Hazlett and his secretary Ms. Abram work from eleven until six."

Janna heard footsteps in the hall. The team from Forensics arrived towing an equipment case on a leash. The case moved with near floating silence on its glide bearings.

"In there." Janna pointed.

The team opened the case and began removing holo cameras. They carried them into Kellener's office.

"When did you last see Mr. Kellener alive?"

"Saturday afternoon when I left work." Peddicord's eyes followed the forensic team. "When I opened that door and saw him there this morning—what could do that to a man?"

"We'll try to find out. Do you keep any poisons in the office?"

"No."

"Do you know who his enemies were?" Mama asked.

Peddicord looked shocked. The receptionist and librarian started, too. Janna wished she had a gag to use on Mama. He could have started with gentler questions.

"I can't believe anyone hated Mr. Kellener," Peddicord said. "He was a loved and respected man."

As long as they were covering all possibilities, Janna brought up one they would probably like even less than murder. "What had his mood been like lately?"

Now Peddicord stiffened in outrage. "You can't mean you think he killed himself? Impossible. Mr. Kellener wasn't that kind of person. His mood had been fine."

"I thought he was worried about something." It was the first thing the receptionist had said.

Peddicord glared at him.

Janna smiled encouragement. "How long had he acted worried?"

"Since Wednesday."

Janna reflected that it must have been a bad day all round. First the message came in from the *Invictus*, then Wim was assaulted, and finally something happened to upset Mr. Andrew Hamilton Kellener.

"When you found Mr. Kellener, did you touch anything?"

"Just Mr. Kellener." The secretary swallowed. "I felt for a pulse. When I realized he was cold, I came right back out and called nine-one-one from Robert's phone."

That ought to take care of the preliminaries. Janna tapped her sleeve pocket to shut off the microcorder. She headed back for the door of Kellener's office. The forensic team was holotaping the body.

One of them looked around from bagging the cup on the desk. "IR scan didn't show anything, not even the body. He's room temperature. You can take a look at him now. Don't touch anything. We're starting to dust for prints."

"Be sure to check the floor and wastebasket. Look for anything that seems out of place and may relate to poison." Where was the medical examiner?

As if summoned by her thought, Dr. Sid Chesney walked into the reception room, followed by two aides and a gliding stretcher. Janna smiled at the sight of his earnest, boyish face with its wire-rimmed glasses and struggling attempt at a mustache. His insistence on looking mature always amused her. What did his patients care about how old and wise he looked?

"Did you draw us, Sid, or volunteer?"

"I volunteered when I heard you were the investigating officer." He sent a glance toward Mama Maxwell. "Is that your new—"

Janna nodded. "The body is in here."

Passing her, Sid whispered, "Doesn't look much like a lion, does he? He's beautiful. Invite him dancing with us some night."

"Treece would scratch my eyes out, love." Mama Maxwell beautiful? Janna squinted at him, trying to see something she might have missed before. She shook her head; she did not see it.

Inside the office, Sid became totally professional. He knelt beside the body and opened his case. "Shut the door, will you?" The next events were not for the eyes of civilians.

Sid opened a pack and took out half a dozen sensor probes. He pushed the sharp needles into the body to the hub, into thorax, abdomen, neck, and extremities. He clipped leads from the medicorder to the probe hubs and began fiddling with the dials. "Temperature twenty-one degrees

Celsius, same as the air temperature." He switched modes and flexed the limbs. "No rigor." He pulled out the probes and cleaned them off. "Dead probably between thirty and forty hours, at a rough estimation." He fiddled with the medicorder. "My little black box here narrows it down to thirty-six hours, give an hour or so each way. The postmortem exam of stomach contents may help narrow the time some more."

Sid straightened the body, palpating each limb as he moved it. "Crepitation in the left radius and ulna, and in the right femur. He has some broken bones, it would seem." He sniffed the dead man's mouth. He peeled back the half-closed lids to check the eyes.

He studied the arms, turning them this way and that in the light. His hands probed the skull. With the aides' help he rolled the body onto its side and stripped down the jumpsuit. Bruise-like markes darkened the skin on his buttocks and the back of his shoulders. "Homeostasis indicates he died in the position he was found. Cyanosis of the lips and fingers. No contusions, no blood visible. No external signs of trauma."

Mama pushed his glasses up his nose. "You can't mean he just lay there and let someone do that to him. Or do you mean you think he did it to himself?"

Sid looked up with raised brows. "It depends on what you mean by doing it to himself. If you find a cow dead in a field after a storm and she has both femurs broken, what killed her?"

Mama stared at him. "What does that have to do with this?"

"Think about it. What actually killed this citizen was suffocation. The cyanosis is definite indication of anoxia. What caused the anoxia, however…" He shrugged.

"Come on, Sid. You must have some idea."

Sid smoothed the hair on his upper lip. "Well, when you see his spouse, spouses, or cohab, you might ask if he ever tripped, particularly on hallucinogens."

Janna blinked. "Hallucinogens?" She stared at the body. "Trick?"

"Sure," Mama said. "It must be."

Sid frowned. "He shows anoxia and convulsions. It *could* be. Let me do my post before jumping to conclusions, please, sergeant. Okay," he said to the aides. "Package him."

They lifted the body onto the stretcher and zipped the cover over it. Mama opened the door for them. They were gliding the stretcher across the reception room when Janna noticed a new addition to the group, a woman as quietly elegant as the room itself. She stared at the stretcher with an expression so controlled Janna wondered what storms lay beneath.

She lifted her eyes and looked at Janna. "I'm Liann Seaton, Andrew Kellener's wife."

Peddicord said, "I called her after I called you."

"May I see him?"

The aides looked at Janna. She nodded. The body would have to be formally identified and if not here, at the morgue. It was better done here. They unzipped the cover just enough to expose the face.

The woman flinched once, then looked hard at the face. "Yes, that's Andy." She sat down abruptly in the nearest chair.

Sid motioned his people out. They disappeared with the stretcher. Janna reached for her pocket to tap on the microcorder again.

"When did you last see your husband, Ms. Seaton?"

She did not answer immediately. Her mouth was pressed in a trembling line. Her breathing came quick and ragged. Janna waited. After several minutes, Liann Seaton said with careful deliberation, "He's been missing since Saturday evening at fifteen minutes to seven. He said he had an errand here at the office and would be back in time to take the children and me to the late showing of a cinaround show. Yesterday I reported him missing to the Gage division police."

"What kind of errand, did he say?"

"No."

"Had anything happened immediately prior to the time he left that might suggest what the errand was?"

"He had a call from his partner Jorge Hazlett."

Janna exchanged glances with Mama and Officer Pfeiffer. "Do you think he was meeting Hazlett here?"

"I asked him that. But he said Jorge was not involved in his coming down here. He was emphatic about it, said the call had been about something else and talking to Jorge just happened to remind him of something he'd forgotten to do."

The phone chimed. The low volume kept Janna from hearing the party on the other end. The receptionist listened, then said, "I'll tell him." He glanced up at the leos. "That was Mr. Hazlett's garage service. I'm supposed to tell him they checked out his car and can't find anything wrong."

"You say Mr. Hazlett comes in about eleven?" Janna asked Peddicord.

"And his secretary."

"Call him for me now, will you, please?"

The receptionist picked a card out of a file and fed it into the phone. Janna moved over by the screen.

The image that came on the screen was that of a modish-looking man approaching middle age. "Mr. Jorge Hazlett, I'm Sergeant Janna Brill of the Shawnee County Police. There's been an accident at your office. Will you come down right away, please?"

Jorge allowed himself some surprise, some concern, nothing more. He met the eyes of the bony, smoky-haired she-lion with what he hoped looked like candor. "Accident? What kind? Is my partner there?"

"He isn't at the moment."

Jorge admired her smooth lie. It made the game more honorable to play against people who were also playing. "I'll be down as soon as I catch a bus."

He punched off feeling hot and cold simultaneously. The game had truly begun now. Did the she-lion want to break the news to him gently, or with a shock, to see how he would react? Was he already a suspect? He would not know until he reached the office.

While they waited for Hazlett, Janna watched the forensic team finish and pack. Every so often her eyes returned to a drawing of winking Justice.

"What's that for?" she finally asked.

Liann Seaton came to the office door. "Judicial humor is my—*was* my husband's hobby. He collected books and poems and cartoons that involved lawyers and the law. I had that Justice drawn for him as a birthday present last year."

Janna toured the office, reading the captions on the cartoons. They were yellowed, ancient things, now sealed in plastic to preserve them from further deterioration. She thought one of the truest ones was the lawyer saying to his client, "You have a pretty good case, Mr. Pitkin; how much justice can you afford?"

Without warning, Mama Maxwell said, "Did your husband trip?"

The woman stiffened. "Never. Andy believed a person should be responsible for his actions. He never took more than one mildly alcoholic drink in an evening and he never used any drugs except dreamtime."

"Never used hallucinogens?" Janna asked.

"Especially not hallucinogens." She was emphatic.

"Did you hear any of the conversation between your husband and his partner Saturday night?"

She shook her head. "Andy took the call in his study."

"Had your husband been worried about anything lately?"

"You don't have to answer that, Ms. Seaton," Peddicord said.

She raised her brows at him. "Why shouldn't I? He had some problem, yes. He'd been preoccupied since Wednesday. I asked him about it but he said it was nothing serious yet, and he wasn't ready to talk about it. I left it at that. He has always talked to me when he needed to." She frowned. "You're thinking about suicide? I assure you, whatever the problem, it was nowhere near that serious."

Janna went over the situation with the office staff, but they seemed to feel the same way—even Peddicord, once he finally admitted he had also noticed Kellener worrying. Whatever had been bothering Kellener had been affecting him no more than problems with clients' accounts usually did.

When Jorge Hazlett arrived, nattily dressed in a pioneer gingham jumpsuit, she felt like a recording loop as she prepared to go over everything again. Hazlett was shocked by the news. He held out his arms to Liann Seaton. "Liann, I can't believe. I talked to him just Saturday evening. I'm so sorry. Is there anything I can do?"

She took his hands and squeezed them. "You're a dear, Jorge. I'll let you know. Thank you for asking."

Mama took the offensive. "For openers, you can tell us about your phone call to Kellener and what went on when you met him later."

Janna bit her lip. The query could have been made with more diplomacy.

Hazlett blinked. "We didn't meet later. There was just the call. That didn't amount to much, either." He dropped Liann Seaton's hands. "There was a client's account I needed to go over with him. I asked him to pull up the file this morning so we could review it when I came in."

"Sergeant." Liann Seaton turned to Janna. "There will be an inquest, of course. Do you know when?"

Janna shook her head. "As soon as the medical examiner can schedule it—two or three days. You'll be contacted."

"I don't suppose I can have my husband's body until after that."

"The morgue will release it once the autopsy findings are complete. That could be as early as tomorrow."

The widow looked relieved. "Thank you. Is there anything else you need me for?"

"You may go."

"If anything does come up, I'll be at home."

She left.

Mama looked after her with admiration. "That is one nova bibi. Past pluto."

Peddicord bristled. "That is a *lady*, sergeant."

Mama turned and looked down at Hazlett. "You say you went out for the evening. Where?"

Hazlett frowned at the blunt, accusing tone. "Shopping at the Granada Mall. I bought a few things, had dinner at Peron's there, and caught a bus home."

"You ride the bus?" Mama sounded skeptical.

"When something is wrong with my car, yes. Saturday the fans sounded strange. I parked the car in a lot and rode the bus."

Janna remembered the call from his service garage. "Your garage says they didn't find anything wrong."

Hazlett looked pleased. "That's good. I'll drive it home tonight, then. I really prefer the Vulcan to a bus."

A Mercedes? Janna was impressed.

"What happened to your wrist?" Mama asked.

Hazlett's mouth thinned. "I sprained it pushing the car into a parking slot. I don't think I like your tone, officer. Do you suspect me of something? Check my bank records if you don't believe where I was."

Mama pushed his glasses up his nose. "We will, jon."

Janna interrupted. "Thank you for answering our questions, Mr. Hazlett." She edged toward the door. "We may have more questions later. If not, we'll see you at the inquest."

She sent Pfeiffer back to her beat and the watchcar leos on their way. Mama she backed into a corner of the lobby. "Just what the hell are you trying to do, Maxwell?"

"He killed his partner."

"What?" She stared at him. "Where in the wild blue yonder did you find that idea? There's nothing yet to suggest anyone *killed* Kellener at all."

Mama shrugged. "Not yet, but there will be. Bibi, I've never seen such walking lion meat. Hazlett reeked of killing the moment he walked into the office."

"Smelled like a killer?" Janna snorted.

"Yes. After twelve years on the force I get these feelings about people. I'm not usually wrong. You know investigative work is an art, not a science. Intuition is a valid and valuable tool."

"Which has to be backed up by scientific method to gather evidence." She spoke carefully, as if to a retarded child. "You have a law degree. You ought to know the rules of evidence. Right now anything we take or hope to take to court has to be impeccable. This is an election year. John Dias to be D. A. for another term before he moves on to higher government office. He isn't prosecuting any cases these days that don't guarantee him a conviction. If we could take him something like the San Francisco Terrorist prosecutions that put Dannel Lippe on the road to the White House, he'd love us. You take him a *feeling*, though, a gut reaction, and your next transfer won't be to Cullen Village; it'll be to Silver Lake or Pauline."

"You recorded the interviews, of course. At least we can check Hazlett's voice for stress and take a look at his bank records to see just how good his alibi is."

"Take a look at—christ." Janna grimaced in disgust. "What do you intend to list as probable cause? Forget it; the authorization request will never pass Lieutenant Vradel. We'll check the stress indicators in the voices, if you want, but first we're going to look for the security guards on duty in this building Saturday and Sunday and find out what they know, if anything."

The light from the bright street outside reflected off his scalp. A skinhead leo. He had started to show his peculiarities of thinking already. With a chill, she remembered Wim's words. *He can get you in trouble. Worse, he can get you killed.* Now she believed it. She suddenly felt as if she were strapped to a time bomb. She crossed her fingers, hoping she would be able to break loose before it went off.

6

Jorge Hazlett had no thoughts of time bombs. He felt exuberant. It was a struggle to keep a solemn face. Thanks to Andy's philanthropies, he and Andy were well known in the city. Within an hour after the police left, newscanner station reporters started calling. They came by to see the death scene and to interview him. They taped him in Andy's office. The incongruity of the winking Justice fascinated them.

"No, we don't know how it happened yet," he told them. "It's a great shock. Andy and I have been like brothers since law school. His death leaves a hole in my life that won't soon be filled."

"No, I'm not closing the office. We have people depending on us. Andy was vitally concerned about the hopes and aspirations of our clients. He considered colonial contracting almost a holy mission, a service to people in whom the pioneer spirit still burns. I think remaining open is a more fitting tribute and memorial than closing in mourning."

By afternoon, he had the pleasure of seeing himself on the newscanner channels. He watched the broadcasts with satisfaction. He had photographed well. The views shown all flattered him. He thought his words sounded elegant.

Marca Laclede felt satisfaction, too. She and Tarl met in the back of the store where he worked to divide the jewelry Tarl collected from the doppelgänger Sunday morning. She let herself be talked out of the Lion's Den for the meeting. Even she had to concede that any lions hanging around the Den this time of day were likely to be curious about a pile of jewelry.

She tried on a sapphire bracelet and held it up to the light. "I must say the sligh followed instructions well enough. He bought what we ordered him to and wasn't distracted by the flash baubles. What did he buy for himself, do you know? Food and clothes, as usual?"

"He said he had dinner at Peron's and bought two novalon suits."

Her brows went up. "He treated himself better than most."

"He bought some toys for his kid, too."

"Toys?" She laughed. "I wonder what Mr. Jorge Hazlett will think of finding purchase receipts for toys. I'd like to hear his explanation for them."

Tarl smiled dryly. "He's going with younger girls these days?"

Marca shrieked in delight. "Tarl, that's beautifully wicked. I wish you'd joke more often, the way you used to when I was in college."

"Things have changed since college." His head bent over the jewelry.

She looked around at the filthy storeroom, thinking of the places he had worked then. "Not all that much. Why do you still work this way? With what we've made off the doppelgängers, you could afford not to work for a while at all."

"Restaurants don't take barter, and even if they did, how would they make change?"

"What *do* you do with your share?"

He held up a pearl pendant. "I'm saving to buy a colonial share."

She stared at him. "Share? You can't really want to leave Earth. There's no way of knowing what's out there."

"Freedom is out there." He dropped the pendant in his pocket.

"Freedom?" She sniffed.

He shrugged. "I don't expect you to understand. Just let me know when you need another doppelgänger."

Owan wore one of his new suits to work. Since he ran the dishcleaning machine for the Pioneer's Pleasure, his finery came in for some kidding. The other club employees raised brows.

"Now we know; you aren't a sligh at all. You're a rich eccentric. No sligh can afford novalon."

Owan answered the kidding with a smile. Some days the sarcasm of the legitimate employees stung, but today it was as if the blue of the suit formed a force field insulating him from their slings and arrows.

"Where did you get it? Did you steal it?" The bartender was curious.

After the question had been asked several times, in different ways, Owan said, "I have a friend who gave it to me."

With a glow of pleasure, he remembered the previous afternoon. Tesha had been ecstatic about the computer and the doll, particularly the doll.

"It's just what I've wanted, Daddy!"

A faint line had appeared between Clio's brows.

"Where did you get those, Owan? No store owner ever gives away merchandise like that."

Her suspicions almost spoiled the afternoon. He had been hoping she would not ask that question. He never lied to Clio. They were proud their relationship was an honest one. There were so few people a sligh could trust completely and be completely honest with. He tried to find an answer that was not a lie.

"I did a favor for someone. He let me put a few items on his card in return."

"A few items? Owan these things have to be worth several hundred bankcredits. What kind of favor was it?"

He bit his lip in anguish. "I can't tell you that."

Her eyes widened in horror. "It was illegal, wasn't it? Oh, Owan…you earned toys for Tesha by doing something illegal?"

"It wasn't very illegal. I wouldn't get involved in something really serious."

"If it isn't serious, why can't you tell me about it?"

He sighed. "Because I promised I wouldn't say anything to anyone. Clio, I won't get in trouble. Please let Tesha keep the toys."

He had suffered agonies while she debated, but finally she gave in. After that, she had not pressed him about how he earned the toys, either. The rest of the afternoon had been a delight. He had not even minded the heat. He had worn the yellow suit and felt as if it were made of gold. When they went out to dinner, which Clio paid for, he felt almost like the head of a real family with a marriage contract and everything. He sat with his head up. It was even better than dinner at Peron's had been, where the waiters had bowed and *sir'd* him until he felt like a real citizen. The yellow novalon suit had impressed them, too.

The bartender of the Pioneer's Pleasure interrupted Owan's daydreaming. He called into the kitchen, "Hey, sligh, you're on the newscanner."

All pleasure disappeared. Owan's heart and stomach turned to ice. On the newscanner? How? His body wanted to bolt out the door, but he fought to resist the urge. Pushing reluctant feet, he forced himself to leave the kitchen and go watch the newscanner.

"It isn't really you," the bartender said when he appeared. "But it's some jon who looks enough like you to be your twin. Weird, isn't it? Just think, you could probably go change places with him, like in *The Prince and the Pauper*. How would you like that?"

Owan's tongue froze in his mouth. The novalon suit felt as if it were constricting around him, suffocating him. His hands sweated. "No, thank you." His voice emerged as a ragged squeak.

He lifted his eyes to the newscanner set above the bar. The man on the tape was Jorge Hazlett. Owan did not listen to the story at first. He was too busy wondering how many people would see it and think how much alike this man and a sligh named Owan were. Would Clio see it?

"...a more fitting tribute and memorial than closing in mourning," Hazlett said.

Mourning? Owan started listening.

The voice-over announcer continued. "Post-mortem examination is expected to be performed this afternoon but until it is finished, officials in the medical examiner's office refuse to speculate on the cause of death."

"Whose death?" Owan asked.

"A jon named Andrew Kellener. He and that fellow who looks like you were partners—colonial contractors. I met that dead one once. He contracted for the ship my sister emigrated in."

Owan reached up and tapped the replay button. The story started again. He watched it through, ice creeping out from his heart to his hands and feet. He had trouble breathing. He used a citizen's card and that same night the citizen's partner died mysteriously. Maybe it was just a coincidence, but—Owan swallowed—what if it were not?

He crept back to the kitchen on legs that shook. His stomach churned. He wanted to throw up. Could he have helped murder a man?

The autopsy on Andrew Kellener was over by three o'clock. Sid called up to the squadroom to tell Janna.

"Thanks, Sid. We'll be right down."

She tapped Mama on the shoulder. He stood watching Jorge Hazlett on the newscanner. "Sanctimonious bastard. Look at him, bibi. Grief-stricken, indeed."

"Come on." She tugged at him.

He came, still grumbling. "He kills his partner and now he's parading all over the newscanner channels shedding crocodile tears. Makes me sick."

Janna tried to ignore him. "Did you read the report on the analysis of the contents of that cup found on Kellener's desk?"

That distracted him momentarily. "No. What did it say?"

They passed the medical examiner himself, Dr. Sandor Kolb, shuffling along the hall muttering to himself. As he had every time Janna had ever seen him, he wore a nondescript jumpsuit that draped around him in great wrinkles.

"Does he really spend his nights here, like they say, sleeping in the cooler drawers?" Mama whispered.

"I always heard it was the autopsy tables." He certainly looked as if he did.

"I don't understand how he keeps his job. He looks senile."

"Not always," Janna said.

They found Sid fiddling with gas chromatographs and electron microscopes in the laboratory. He peered over the tops of his glasses at them. "It was trick, all right. Massive overdose. Ingested, probably."

"Put in his food?" Mama asked.

Sid shook his head. "He'd eaten about an hour before he died but he couldn't have gotten the trick that way. The stuff is absorbed too fast. At most he would have had to take it within five or ten minutes of the time he died. A dose that big would have hit him hard and fast. The convulsions were so severe they broke his bones."

Mama pushed his glasses up his nose. "*Oh!* Like the cow. She was hit by lightning and the muscle contractions broke her legs."

Sid arched his brows. "Right. Very good." He stacked up several graphs. "Other findings are what I expected. There were hemorrhages in the mucous membrane of the trachea and on the pericardium. It confirms that what actually killed him was anoxia, like all trick OD's. Now all you have to find out is how he got the trick."

"Easy," Janna said. "Forensics says there were traces of trick in the cup we found on the desk."

Sid considered that. "So the next question—answering a question just changes the question, doesn't it—is who put it in the caff?"

"Hazlett did," Mama said.

Sid peered over his glasses at Mama. He looked at Janna, lifting a brow.

She shook her head. "The reasoning process by which he arrived at that conclusion is called fantasizing."

"I'm not fantasizing." Mama's voice climbed toward falsetto. "The man reeks of murder. If we check his bank records, I'm betting we'll find they don't support his alibi."

Janna rolled her eyes. Christ. He certainly was stubborn.

"Well..."

The long syllable was Sid's. Janna looked sharply at him.

Sid smiled a cringing dog smile. "Why would a man take that much by himself? If he wanted to trip, he would have to be stupid to use a dose that size. Even if he wanted to kill himself, he wouldn't have had to take anywhere near that amount, not if he understood the drug. Becoming a pretzel is a painful way to go, and most suicides don't like pain. He was probably dosed by someone else."

"Thanks, Judas."

Sid winced at the acid in her voice. "Maybe he took it by accident," he added.

Mama sniffed. "Of course. There was a big jar of it in the cabinet with the caff supplies and he thought it was brown sugar."

Janna made a try at introducing scientific method into the conversation. "None of the security guards saw Hazlett in the building Saturday."

"What does that prove? None of them saw Kellener either. We need to look at Hazlett's bank records, I tell you."

Janna gritted her teeth. "Maxwell, what we need to do is clear six assaults. Let's not look for more work. Thanks, Sid. I'll see you this evening...if I get caught up here."

It was too late to visit the complainants in person, so she called each by phone. That cleared a couple in a hurry. One of the simple assaults now declined to press charges, and the rape victim also wanted to drop his complaint.

She tried to talk the ADW out of prosecuting. The case was very poor.

The complainant insisted. “He had a knife. I want that son of a bitch put away.”

“Yes, ma’am.” Janna punched off with a sigh. “We’ll follow it up, collect our points for the squad, then Dias or one of his assistants will refuse to take it to court.”

She could not reach the other simple assault. She did reach the other batteries, however, and both men wanted to prosecute.

Punching off after the last call, Janna totaled it up. “Two cleared. That leaves us one simple, the ADW, and two batteries to work on tomorrow, plus your obsession with Hazlett, and whatever new complaints Morello gives us. After that, all we have is half a kilo of paperwork—my very favorite part of police work. Did you ever stop to think how many billions of words police departments turn out each year?”

Mama shuddered.

Janna started on the day’s paperwork. She would go visit Wim, she decided, and cry on his shoulder a bit. Did colonists have miserable days or did they find endless satisfaction in digging their toes and fingers in the soil and making things grow?

She slid a side glance at Mama Maxwell. He was fussing with the pens and pencils again, and shaking papers into perfect stacks. She rolled her eyes. Maybe she should ask for a special appointment with the tick tech. She did not know if her sanity would last the two weeks until her regular visit.

Owan tried to rationalize away the fear the news story started. As he washed glasses, he used every argument he could think of. The death of the man’s partner was a coincidence—no concern of his. No one knew who he was, except Tarl. Not even Tarl knew where to find him. If anything should come of it, he was safe. No matter how nearly he convinced himself of his own safety, however, he could not avoid the thought that he might have helped kill a man. If nothing else mattered, that fact would continue to gnaw at him. Along with a fear of identation, his parents had instilled in him a fervent belief in the sacredness of life.

He was not sure quite when he first considered asking Jorge Hazlett about it. He did not like the idea—memory of the citizen’s cold eyes tied his stomach in knots—but he needed reassurance that the death had no connection to his using Hazlett’s card. All else was secondary. Only Hazlett could give him that reassurance.

Owan asked the bartender for a vending token.

"You have to call someone now?" The bartender waved at the customers starting to come into the club for after work drinks and early dinner. "We need you running the washer." He gave Owan the token. "Make it quick."

Owan looked up Hazlett's business number. On the newscanner Hazlett had said something about keeping the office open the usual hours because his partner would have wanted it that way. He implied that meant working much later than most people.

It suddenly occurred to Owan that it might be bad if anyone else saw how much he looked like Hazlett. He put his hand over the screen just as a willowy, dark-haired woman answered the phone. "Jorge Hazlett, please."

"Who may I say is calling?"

What could he say? Hazlett did not know his name. Owan could not very well announce himself as a doppelgänger. "I met Mr. Hazlett Saturday night. He'll remember me."

Jorge was clearing up his desk in preparation for closing the office when Nina Abram announced the call. "A very mysterious man," she said. "He says you met him Saturday night. He wants to talk to you."

Fury surged up through Jorge. There was only one person it could be. So the sligh would be no trouble? In only two days the sligh was already after him. He would tell the Laclede woman to take care of him and take care of him fast. This was not supposed to happen. The Pawn was not supposed to move like this.

He might as well see what the creature wanted, though.

He stabbed on the phone. It was the sligh all right, looking overdressed in a novalon suit. "How dare you call me!"

The sligh quaked visibly on the screen. "I'm sorry." His voice was little more than a whisper. "I don't want to cause trouble, but—"

Here it came. "But—" Jorge prompted.

The sligh took a breath. "I saw the news story about your partner. That didn't have anything to do with—with you know, did it? I've been worrying about that. I don't want to be a party to—to—"

Well thank god he was not blurting out everything over the phone. "No, of course it didn't have anything to do with Andy. That was just coincidence."

The sligh chewed his lip. "You're sure."

What a miserable piece of humanity the creature was. "Of course I'm sure!"

The sligh flinched again. "Yes, of course."

Belatedly, Jorge started thinking. The rabbit was frightened. He wanted to be comforted. Without that comfort, no telling what erratic behavior might result. The man was therefore dangerous to him. Another threatened check. Again, he had three ways to deal with it.

Jorge swallowed his anger and made himself smile. "I can see you're upset. Naturally. I'm upset myself. That's why I'm snapping at you. I tell you what I'll do. Just for your peace of mind, I'll meet you again, same place, ten o'clock. I'll show you what I did that evening. Will that help?"

The sligh grinned in relief. "Yes." His forehead creased in concern again. "It won't inconvenience you or ruin something for you to show me, will it?"

What a question. Jorge lied. "Quite the contrary. Now you just relax and I'll see you later."

He stabbed the phone off with a violence that scooted it halfway across the desk. He wanted to slam his fist through the desk top. That unmitigated fool! Jorge would tell Laclede just what he thought of her blithe promises about troubleless slighs. Before he touched the phone, however, he caught himself. No, he had better not tell her. All the rabbit wanted was a clean conscience. The woman would be the one to see the possibilities in blackmail. Jorge would deal with the sligh by himself.

He considered what method to use. With no doppelgänger for an alibi this time, he would have to make himself as invisible as possible. Transportation could be by his car. Vulcan sportsters were not common, though; he would have to disguise the car somehow.

Changing the color was impossible, nor could he hide the fact it was a Vulcan. If only he could think of a way to change the license number.

He studied the plates on vehicles in the parking lot as he walked through. Some numbers had the same basic shape. Eights and threes, for starters. He squinted at his own license. Perhaps the numbers could be altered.

On the way home he stopped and bought a roll of plastic tape the same color as the plate background.

At home he went through his closet and dressed in his oldest, most nondescript clothes. He hunted up a pocket flask and half filled it with his best whiskey. Then he went to his wall safe again. Half the remaining trick went into the flask. He capped the flask and shook it.

While Janna Brill sat in a hospital room across the city listening to Wim Kiest extol the virtues of a planet named Champaign and Owan Desfosses ran tableware through the sonics of the dishcleaner and Marca Laclede hummed a jivaqueme tune while she painted lace on her arms and legs, preparing to go dancing, Jorge Hazlett paced his house, waiting for nine thirty.

The wait seemed eternal. The seconds crawled by like hours. He almost cheered when the chrono finally read half past the hour.

He took the steps to the garage two at a time and vaulted over the door into the cockpit of the Vulcan, just missing the center bar of the safety frame. He backed the car out across the lawn to the street. The fans purred like some great cat.

Jorge forced himself to drive slowly, obeying all traffic regulations. The car felt impatient under his hands. He was impatient, too. He wanted to wrap up the fans and sail, to meet the sligh and deal with him, to get it over with. Instead, he restrained himself. Tonight was no time to be cited for traffic violations.

He passed several police cars on the way. The reflective stripes on their sides flared brilliantly red as his lights caught them. He smiled and waved at the leos in them.

He swung into the Sunco lot a full ten minutes before the sligh was supposed to meet him. So far, so good. He climbed out of the car and, picking up a hand light, squatted down on his heels behind the Vulcan. He tore pieces of tape from the roll, which he carefully pressed over part of the numbers on his license plate. An *H* became an *I*, a four became a one, and an eight, three. He worked quickly, with an ear alert for any approaching footsteps. It would not do to be seen doing this.

No one came. He sat back to admire his handiwork. License SHH 418 had become SHI 113. The alteration would not fool anyone on close inspection. He hoped it would pass casual observation, though.

He had just time enough to tape the front plate and stow the tape and hand light in the car when he saw someone stop at the entry gate and lift a bicycle over the barrier. The newcomer slid around the end of the barrier and picked up his bike.

"Mr. Hazlett?" It was the voice of the sligh.

"Yes." Jorge made his voice hearty. "Welcome."

The sligh chained the bicycle to a rack. "I'm really grateful to you for doing this."

"Think nothing of it. I might need to use your services again, so I want us to be friends. Get in the car. I'll show you where I spent my recess time."

Owan climbed over the airfoil skirt into the cockpit. He sank into the deep seat with a thrill of pleasure. He had never even dreamed of riding in a car like this. It looked designed for interstellar flight, not ground travel. "Beautiful."

"It is," Jorge agreed. "The solar batteries give the car an almost unlimited range. Instead of mirrors, it has a screen for a hundred and eighty view to the rear and sides, adjustable for normal or magnified viewing. Vibration is minimal."

Jorge switched on the fans. Owan felt the car tremble, then float upward, off its parking rollers. What a world of difference there was between a car like this and Clio's runabout.

Jorge guided the Vulcan toward the street. "I was as shocked as anyone to learn about my partner this morning. I'm so ashamed. While I was out enjoying myself, Andy was dying. What a terrible thought."

Owan ran his hand down the interior paneling of the door and over the dash. He caressed the seats. They were real leather. "Do you know how your partner died?"

"A drug overdose, they think." Jorge shook his head. "I never thought Andy was a ulysses. I guess people never know about their friends. They have secret inner lives we never touch."

The night was close and hot, but the air rushing into the open cockpit of the sportster felt cool. Owan reveled in it.

Jorge headed the car across I-70 into east Topeka and down into the Oakland area. He pulled the flask from his pocket. "Care for a drink?"

Owan shook his head. "No, thank you."

Jorge would not let himself frown. "It's fine whiskey." He uncapped it with one hand and tilted it up, pretending to drink. Not one drop passed the tight seal of his mouth. He lowered the flask and passed it to Owan. "Try just a sip."

Owan took the flask. He looked at it. He never drank much; alcohol and drugs were luxuries for slighs. Here he was in a fine suit, though, riding in one of the best cars made, being offered a drink by a rich citizen. Why not enjoy the experience while it lasted?

"Thanks." He tilted up the flask.

The liquor tasted delicious. He hardly noticed it until halfway down his throat, then a low heat spread up and down his throat and out of his stomach through his body. He took a few more swallows and passed the flask back to his new good friend and twin Jorge Hazlett.

Jorge pretended to drink and passed the flask back. "We're almost there."

Owan had another drink. "You were down *here* on Saturday? Why?"

"I'm helping some sligh friends set up a school." The lie came easily. "I come down and teach law every few weeks. Lately, though, I've been afraid the lions have heard about the school. I didn't want them tracking me, so I decided to seem to be somewhere else."

Owan began experiencing some of the strangest sensations of his life. The night filled with a riot of color, and his nose drank in smells of indescribable deliciousness. He tried to tell Jorge about them but the words would not come out right. He giggled. So this was what it was like to be drunk. No wonder citizens liked to drink.

Then without warning the night filled with excruciating pain. His body wrenched.

As soon as the sligh started babbling nonsense, Jorge looked for a place to dump him. He turned the Vulcan up Jacquot Street.

What had possessed the city officials to give the name of that most elegant of Presidents to this derelict street, Jorge could not begin to imagine. The ghost of the man must shudder to see his memorial. Weeds grew up through cracked and tilted paving, so high they scraped the bottom of the car. On either side, twentieth-century wood frame houses moldered in tanglewood yards.

Jorge eyed the houses. An empty one would be a good dumping place. Most of them along here looked empty, but he had no way of telling in passing which were unoccupied and which merely without lights.

He bit his lip. The sligh's convulsions were becoming louder and more violent. Jorge had to find an empty place soon.

Ahead, he saw a boarded-up store on a corner. Jorge stopped the car and vaulted out even before it finished settling to the ground in the trash choked area that had once been the store's parking area. He dragged the sligh out and around the back of the building. Hopefully there would be a back door he could force open.

It had a back door. Even better, the door was already open. Jorge hauled the sligh inside.

The air assaulted him like a kick in the stomach. Jorge gagged. Neighborhood trippers and winos evidently used the building for a latrine. In the stifling hot interior, the stench of drugs and alcohol mixed thickly with the reek of urine, excrement, and vomit. Jorge dropped his burden on the floor and bolted back into the outside air.

He stood for several minutes waiting for his stomach to settle back in place before he made himself edge close enough to the door to pull it closed. He was careful to scrape his ankle boots thoroughly clean before climbing back in the car.

Going home he used the same care he had driving down to the Sunco lot. He checked each street for no police cars before driving that way. He drove through to Sardou and headed west over the Kansas River into north Topeka. There he stopped at an all-night automatic car wash where he stripped off the tape over his license numbers and scrubbed the Oakland dust from the Vulcan. From there he went to a bar for a drink. It took three to clear the stench of the building from his memory. When he felt clean again, he drove home.

The flask he rinsed out thoroughly and put away. His clothes went into the laundry. Only then did he let himself relax. With relaxation came exultation. The check had been successfully countered, a dangerous Pawn captured. Now there remained only the inquest and the government inquiry to face.

7

Lieutenant Vradel leaned out of his office and pointed at Janna. He crooked his finger. "Brill, in here."

Janna picked up the complaint sheets and wound her way between the desks toward his door. Mama was late. He had not been at rollcall. Maybe she had gotten lucky. Maybe he resigned during the night.

She closed Vradel's door behind her. "Yes, sir?"

Vradel held up a sheet of paper. Above it, his eyes had the glitter of winter sun on ice. "What's this?"

She leaned forward and peered at it. Oh, god. A request to examine Jorge Hazlett's bank records. Mama must have submitted it after she left yesterday. She looked to see what he had given as "Probable cause."

"Subject is under suspicion for murder. It is necessary to verify his whereabouts during the time period involving the commission of the crime."

She winced.

"Do you know what this is about?"

Janna grimaced. "Unfortunately, yes." She told him about Mama Maxwell's opinion of Hazlett.

Vradel listened in silence. He chewed on his mustache and doodled on his memo pad.

"Lieutenant, I'm sorry about that request. I didn't know he was going to submit it. It looks like I can't control him. Maybe you'd better team me with someone else."

Vradel raised a brow. "I know he must be frustrating after Kiest."

That was an understatement.

"All new partnerships need time to shake down. One day is hardly a fair trial of a team. Maxwell has turned in some brilliant police work during his yo-yo career. That's why he hasn't been fired. The brass want us to encourage street officers to be innovative and imaginative."

"Maxwell is imaginative, all right."

Vradel's mustache twitched. "A bit more so than Paget ever intended, probably, but some of his best work has come out of intuitive leaps. What he needs to do is learn to follow up his inspirations with solid evidence. Now you turn in careful investigative work that follows procedure, spirit and letter. I'm hoping the two of you will mesh well."

Her stomach felt somewhere in the vicinity of her knees. "So I'm stuck with him?"

"For a while."

Even five minutes would be an eternity. She pointed at the request. "What about that?"

Vradel wrote across it. "Denied. Make him produce a good reason, a documentable reason, for suspecting Hazlett, then I'll okay a bank check. All right; that's all."

She went back into the squadroom feeling ill. So the lieutenant wanted to make a permanent team of them.

The newscanner was running a press conference held by President Lippe the day before. Smiling, he fended off questions about his plans for dealing with Israeli aggression in the Middle East.

Mama Maxwell was still nowhere in sight.

"Have you seen my black rack of a partner?" Janna asked Maro Desch.

Desch's replied with a wordless snarl.

Janna backed off. "Sorry. I didn't know Maxwell had made such fierce enemies already."

"It isn't your partner," Desch said. "It's atropine. I have a suspect in there." He pointed at the interview room. "He knows his pupil response to questions about a certain armed robbery is going to convict him so he took atropine before coming down. His pupils look like this." He made a circle with his thumb and forefinger. "But I'll fix him." He chuckled. "The deek can just sit in there until the atropine wears off. Then I'll ask my questions."

Mama Maxwell banged through the squadroom door. Janna winced. His suit this morning was orange and green paisley. A strip of graph tape hung from his hand.

"Stress, bibi," he said triumphantly. He came between the desks like a broken-field runner to thrust the tape at her. "That's a stress recording of Hazlett's voice. This section is his answer about the phone call Saturday night. It's full of stress. He was lying through his teeth."

Janna glanced at the tape, then looked at a bulge in the breast pocket of his jumpsuit. "Did you have Forensics run the other voices, too?"

Mama frowned. "Yes, but—"

She held out her hand. "Give them to me."

His frown deepened, but he opened the pocket and handed over three cylinders of rolled paper

Janna unrolled the one marked "Seaton." She looked at it. "Stress, Mama. Did Liann Seaton also murder her husband?"

Mama shrugged. "Well, she's grief stricken."

"You know for an absolute fact that the stress in Hazlett's voice comes from lying. Crap. The stress alone proves nothing."

"I watched his pupil response while you talked to him and—"

She tossed the tapes on their desks. "You know as well as I do that pupil responses count only when we have Hazlett videotaped so the experts can read him."

"Then let's bring him down for an interview."

"Forget it!"

Every eye in the squadroom turned on her.

"Need a referee?" Desch asked.

"No, thanks." She lowered her voice to a hiss. "We have six assaults to work on today. Let's go."

"Just a minute. I have to see the lieutenant about—"

"He saw me," she interrupted. "Your request is denied. *Denied!*" It gave her pleasure to say it. She pointed to the door. "Sail."

Two hours later she wished they had stayed at the office and interviewed Jorge Hazlett. She crouched behind a watchcar in the furnace sun with sweat soaking her jumpsuit. Bullets kicked up dust beyond her. It was her fault, too. She should have known better than to let Mama drive the car. She should have anticipated that something like the "man with a firearm" report on the radio would prove too much for him to resist.

As he had revved the fans and slewed Indian Thirty around in the middle of the street, she protested. "We're not a watchcar or jane unit. It isn't our job to answer calls. Do you know how much more paperwork this will make for us?"

He had not been listening. The car shot ahead and she could only hold on, swearing. Though no Bible cultist, she prayed a little, too. Mama did not so much drive as pilot the Monitor.

"Slow down, damn it!" she yelled at him. "We don't have to go this fast. Are you so afraid of missing the excitement? *Maxwell.*"

He ignored her.

They plowed through traffic with runabouts and bicycles fleeing before their siren. One runabout cut aside too sharply. The blast of its fans caught a bicycle. The bike wavered and tipped, throwing the rider into the Monitor's path. They had no time to stop or swerve around him. Janna prayed he possessed the sense to stay flat.

The Monitor skimmed over him. When Janna looked back, he was scrambling for his bike. Janna started breathing again.

The car rocketed on.

The man with the firearm was in one of the new apartment complexes in the lower end of the Highland Park division. Three black-and-whites and two jane units had reached the scene ahead of them, pulled up in front of one building. Janna saw a flash in a third-floor window. Mama parked the Monitor out of range around the corner of the next building and they climbed out to join a jane team and uniformed team standing with two frightened-looking women.

One of the women was the apartment manager. The other cohabed with the gunman. "He isn't a criminal; he's just tripping," she said, obviously afraid for him. "He was having a good flight and all of a sudden it went bad. He started yelling that someone was after him. He grabbed a rifle and started shooting out the window, saying he'd never let himself be taken. I slipped out the door and called a doctor. Why did you come instead?"

"Tripping on what?" one of the uniformed leos asked.

The girl bit her lip. "Dust."

A jane sighed. "With everything that's legal, why do people still use the forbidden junk?"

"Where did he get the shooter?" Janna asked.

"Roy collects guns. He has all kinds of antiques clear from World War I."

"I suppose he keeps them all in working condition and has ammunition for them."

The girl nodded. She chewed her lower lip.

The leos exchanged grim glances. "So much for sitting under cover until he runs out of bullets."

"Has anyone tried talking him down?" Mama asked. "Dusters are suggestible."

"We tried. We tried using his cohab here, and none—"

A shot and a yell of pain interrupted the uniformed officer. As one, the leos spun toward the sound. A uniformed leo collapsed behind one of the watchcars and huddled groaning, holding his shoulder. Beneath his fingers, the iron gray of his uniform turned rusty red.

His partner hit her ear button, yelling for an ambulance. Keeping down, she reached into their car for the shotgun racked there. In another minute everyone had brought out shotguns and were moving up behind the cover cars.

The girl screamed. "Don't kill him! He doesn't mean to hurt anyone!"

"Don't damage the building," the manager called.

"Shit," the partner of the wounded leo spat in disgust.

"Isn't it wonderful?" someone muttered. "The public demands aggressive law enforcement and then expects us to ask for a national referendum before we can shoot back at some deek who's trying his best to kill us."

A bullet whined off the street behind them.

"How about gas?"

No one had any pellets, only some canisters of K-12. They peered up at the window. It was one of the new building designs. Instead of one single expanse of glass, the windows consisted of four vertical strips separated by sections of stone, perfect for firing out through, terrible for hitting from the outside.

"How about going in the back and kicking in his door?" Janna asked.

"No back door," came the answer.

None of them could slide through those window slits.

"There's some cover under the balconies," Mama said. "I could get up on that first balcony and go through that apartment, then on up the stairs."

"Alone?"

"One leo is a smaller target than two. Give me a K-12 canister to take with me."

Janna snapped, "You'll get yourself killed."

He ignored her. He settled his glasses, took a can of gas, and raced toward the building on an erratic course. A bullet kicked up dust near his feet. Janna pumped a shell into the breech of her shotgun and fired at the window.

Masonry chips flew. Somewhere off to the side of them the manager called angrily and the girlfriend screamed, "Roy!"

"Is your partner a rock jock or trying to be a hero?"

"He's brainbent." She pumped in another shell and kept her sights on the window. "The old Wyatt Earp syndrome."

Mama flattened against the building. The balcony was between him and the tripper. He leaped for the railing. His fingers locked around the uprights. Grunting, he pulled himself up and over the edge.

The balcony door must be locked. Janna saw him trying it without success. A bullet struck the metal railing near him. The shot was answered by four shotgun blasts and screams from the manager and girlfriend.

Mama put a booted foot through the glass. In another minute he opened the door and disappeared inside.

The leos crouched behind the watchcars, waiting. More units arrived. It looked like rollcall at the station. The beta squad sergeant rolled in. The uniformed leos in her squad filled her in on the situation. The ambulance sailed in. With the rest of them covering him, the wounded officer was helped over to it.

Janna frowned at the building. What was Mama doing that took so long?

A shooter went off three times in rapid succession. Janna stiffened. No bullets came their way. They must all have been fired inside.

The sergeant slapped four leos on the shoulder. "Go."

They raced for the door, shotguns in hand. Janna pounded right behind them. She could hear the girlfriend still pleading with them not to shoot her cohab and the manager shrilly forbidding them to cause any more damage. They scrambled up the stairs.

On the third floor the apartment door was open, its lock smashed. Mama Maxwell huddled on hands and knees in the opening, gasping hoarsely. His glasses lay on the floor beside him. The sergeant hauled him backward by the seat of his jumpsuit. He landed rolling and stopped against the wall, clutching at his throat. She stepped over him into the apartment.

"Mama!" Janna crouched beside him. Was he hit? She saw no blood. What was wrong with him? "Are you hurt?"

He just lay with his eyes squeezed shut, gasping as though strangling. Janna tore at the collar of his suit. Had his larynx been crushed?

"Mama, what happened?"

The sergeant came back out of the apartment. "The gas got him. Bring him out."

Two leos moved in. They reappeared with a tightly curled, whimpering knot of humanity who was trying to pull away from their grip and crawl into himself. They carried him down the stairs.

"Good old K-12," the sergeant said. "Replaces fight with fright." She knelt beside Janna. "Here. I'll help you with him."

Janna picked up Mama's glasses. They pulled his arms around their necks and, between them, carried him down the stairs to the ambulance. The medic took one look and slapped the oxygen mask over Mama's face.

The apartment manager rapped on the door of the ambulance. "I want to talk to someone in authority."

The sergeant swore under her breath, but she put on a smile and climbed down out of the ambulance. "Yes, ma'am. What can I do for you?"

Mama whispered something. Janna could not hear, but the medic nodded and reached into a drawer for a hypo.

"Look at that building. The stonework around the window is ruined. I don't know how something like that can be repaired," the manager said. "The balcony door and the one up in the hall will be expensive to replace. I want to know who's going to pay for this damage. I have to answer to the owners of the complex, you know."

The hypo hissed against the skin of Mama's arm.

"What's that?" Janna asked.

"Antihistamine. Your partner will be fine now."

What? Mama was dying one minute and would be fine the next? Before long though she saw Mama begin breathing easier. In a few more minutes he took off the oxygen mask and grinned at her. His eyes were red and puffy but otherwise he seemed almost normal.

"May I have my glasses?"

She handed them to him. "What was wrong with you?"

He held out his right arm. Two long red lines crossed the wrist. "There were cats in the downstairs apartment. One of them scratched me when I put them in a bedroom so they wouldn't get out through the broken door to the balcony. I'm allergic to cats."

She did not know whether to laugh or be exasperated at the idea of taking time from stopping a dangerous tripper with a shooter to shoo cats into a bedroom. Several seconds later the last sentence registered. She blinked. "Allergic to cats?"

His grin was rueful. "And milk and weeds and dust and half the rest of what makes up the world. That's why I don't wear contact lenses and can't take a hair transplant."

"All that choking came from just an allergy?"

Suddenly she was furious. She had worried about him. She had been afraid the tripper hurt him. What a waste of time. It was only an allergic reaction!

Outside, the manager's voice shrilled. "Someone has to pay for the repairs. Your trigger-happy storm troopers did it all. I think the city ought to be responsible."

Janna swung out of the ambulance and stalked to Indian Thirty. An *allergy*. She passed the sergeant, listening to the manager with a polite smile, her knuckles white around the shotgun she still carried. Janna slid under the wheel of the Monitor. In a few minutes Mama climbed in the other side. They watched the ambulance sail out with the wounded leo.

Janna glanced from the ambulance to the sergeant and complaining manager, then to Mama. "What a bitch of a day,"

Mama regarded her with a thoughtful expression. "You're very tense, bibi. Do you realize that? It comes from trying so hard to stick to the book. You should let your imagination loose, work by gut feel for a while."

She kept her eyes on the street ahead. "I'll think about it." Would using the shotgun on him be justifiable homicide?

When they went back to the office, she was going to throw herself at the lieutenant's feet and plead with him to take this albatross off her neck. She had a clean record. Was there something wrong in keeping it that way? Why did Wim have to be blinded and leave her at fate's mercy?

The radio murmured, "Indian Thirty, return to the station."

Janna tapped the broadcast button on the car speaker. "Indian Thirty, *roger*."

Pass-the-Word Morello greeted them as they came into the squadroom. He jerked a thumb toward Vradel's office. "The lieutenant wants to see you."

Vradel had company...a paunchy man who blinked as if he wore irritating contact lenses. "Brill, Maxwell," Vradel said, "this is Agent Milo Talous, Department of Justice."

Department of Justice? Janna and Mama glanced at each other with raised brows.

Agent Talous eyed them…raising brows at Mama, then turning his attention to Janna. "I understand you're investigating the death of Mr. Andrew Kellener."

Janna nodded. "Why does that interest the Department of Justice?"

"Kellener's firm handled the colonial contracting for the Laheli Company."

Janna stared at him. "The one on the *Invictus?"*

"Exactly." The government agent looked like a bookkeeper but he sounded authoritative. "It's my job to find out why the *Invictus* broke down. I thought you might like to be along when I interview the surviving partner."

"I sure would," Janna said. Kellener had been upset since Wednesday, the day the news of the *Invictus* was broadcast. That shed brand new light on Kellener's death.

She made herself the last out the door. Before she left, she caught Vradel's sleeve. "When we come back, I have to talk to you. The partnership isn't shaking down; I'm being shaken up."

Morello came up behind her. "There's been a woman calling for you. A Grania Huston. She wants you to call her back. She says it's important."

Janna barely listened to him. Her eyes fixed on Vradel. "I'll call her, Morello. Lieutenant, give me some time, please."

Vradel patted her shoulder. Small comfort to take with her to Hazlett's office.

Jorge examined Milo Talous' identification and extended a cordial hand. "Welcome to our hotbox city, Mr. Talous." His pulse hammered in his throat. End of opening moves. The middle game had begun.

"Washington is worse, I assure you." Talous glanced past Jorge at a chessboard image on the computer monitor. "You're a player?"

"Addict, actually. I find it relaxing." He cleared the screen. "I've been expecting you, sir."

"Then perhaps we can go straight to examining your records of the Laheli Company."

Jorge rubbed his nose. "Unfortunately, it isn't that easy. The account was my partner's and when I try to retrieve the records, this is what I find."

He typed on his keyboard.

The screen printed: WHAT'S THE PASSWORD?

"Andy and I were going to go over the records yesterday morning, but…" He sighed.

Talous frowned at the screen. "Did your partner always password protect his files?"

"Never before in my knowledge."

The smoky-haired she-lion behind Talous said, "Is this the matter you called your partner about Saturday night?"

"Yes.

The she-lion sucked her lower lip. "There's an override command on the door locks. Might there be one on record retrieval?"

Jorge frowned, pretending to think. "I don't know of one, but then, I never use passwords with my files. Andy may have set one up with our librarian." He touched the intercom button on the phone. "Lilla, we need the records on the Laheli Company but Andy seems to have protected retrieval of them. Do you have an override command?"

The plump librarian shook her head. "I didn't know any of the records even had passwords."

Jorge grimaced. "Maybe Andy left a note with the password in his desk somewhere. Thank you, Lilla."

He led the way to Andy's office.

Mama murmured in Janna's ear. "He's lying. He knows how to get the records. Watch his pupil response."

She watched, but only so she would have evidence from her own observation to refute him. Watching Hazlett was hard. She kept being distracted by motions of his hands and the surroundings...like the Justice winking down at them from the wall. She could see why the experts wanted interviews taped, so they could study them at leisure and without distractions.

"What kind of passwords might your partner use?" Talous asked.

"I've no idea." Hazlett's pupils dilated.

Janna looked quickly at Mama. He smirked in satisfaction.

Hazlett bent over the desk and began searching through it. Talous and the leos helped, each taking a drawer. They combed through, paper by paper. Every list was scrutinized, and promising ones tried on the computer. What appeared to be a grocery list proved to be just that. The computer did not respond to it in any way. The maddening WHAT'S THE PASSWORD? remained on the screen.

Janna found the list. It had been pushed to the rear of the top drawer, beneath a tray of paperclips and rubber bands. The paper had two columns. One was names: Rondeau, Novaterra, Sans souci, De novo, and, about midway down, Laheli. Down the other side of the paper were typed cryptic phrases: Wiersma v. Long Beach, Bardell v. Pickwick, write me a verbal contract, the laughing fox.

"Do these references have any special meaning?" Talous asked.

Hazlett studied the list. "Some are obviously legal references, though they aren't cases I'm familiar with. Wait a minute." He looked up. "Laughing fox. That's the name Andy gave Pearson versus Post when we studied it in law school. It's a landmark case that always attracted Andy because of the comic aspects of it. Now I can remember some of these other cases, too. Wiersma versus Long Beach is a humorous case involving the question of whether wrestlers are humans or dangerous animals. Every one of these references is to legal humor of some kind."

"Legal humor was Mr. Kellener's hobby, wasn't it?" Janna said. She eyed the winking Justice.

Hazlett nodded. He looked down the list and his finger crossed the page from Laheli to "write me a verbal contract." Turning to the computer, he typed in the phrase, and as the file opened, clicked on the printer icon.

The printer hummed. It began feeding out facsimile pages.

Talous picked them up and read them as they dropped out. For a long while his face remained expressionless, then he stiffened. His nostrils flared. Janna wanted to snatch away the sheets to see what they said.

"You say Mr. Kellener handled the account?" Talous said.

"That's right."

"Then why do all these papers have your signature?"

Janna watched Hazlett's pupils dilate, contract, dilate again. "*My* signature?" He took the sheet Talous offered him. He peered at it. "I don't understand. That's my name but I don't remember signing—" He looked up at Talous. "That isn't my signature. I'll show you." He took a pen from Kellener's desk and signed his name on a memo sheet. Then pulling his Scib card, he handed both to Talous.

Janna and Mama edged over to where they too could see. The signature on the card and memo pad looked similar to those on the records but on close examination the letter formations looked larger and more ornate on the Scib card. The Laheli records showed signatures with tighter loops and squarer comers.

Talous studied the signatures with pursed lips. "Do you have anything signed by your partner?"

Jorge punched on the computer's keyboard. In a few moments it kicked out another facsimile sheet, this one signed by Andrew Kellener. The signature was different but they could all see that the loops were small and neat and the letters generally angular.

"Would you like our handwriting people to go over those?" Janna asked.

"Our people will examine them...but I'll see you're given a copy of the report." Talous put several of the Laheli records in his pocket and returned Hazlett's card.

"I can't imagine why Andy would sign my name to the papers."

"Can't you?" Mama muttered so only Janna could hear.

"Read these letters from Boeing." Talous handed them to Hazlett.

Hazlett read them over. "So? Colonists can be remarkably pig-headed and foolhardy. They can ignore all common sense in trying to save credit."

"But the Laheli bank records show they paid not for a modified 800 but a Starmaster 1000."

Hazlett's jaw dropped. His pupils dilated.

"What do you think?" Mama whispered.

"My god." Hazlett leaned on the desk. He seemed stunned. "My *god.* I can't believe this."

Talous's mouth tightened into a single slash of lip. "I'd like to see the records on these other clients, too."

They were all similar. The groups had ordered Starmasters smaller than the size they needed and had the ships modified to carry more. In each case Boeing had cautioned about the function of the life-support systems and in each case been reassured that the customer was ordering exactly what it wanted.

"This is incredible," Hazlett kept saying. "I can't believe Andy would do anything like this."

Once Mama straightened up and opened his mouth, but Janna kicked him in the ankle. "Don't you dare," she muttered.

They called in Nels Peddicord. "Does Mr. Kellener have a newscanner here at the office?" Talous asked.

The secretary looked wary. "Yes." He slid open a wall panel. A set hung behind it. "He always watched daily briefs first thing in the morning and when he had time throughout the day."

"He became depressed on Wednesday, according to the police reports."

Peddicord stiffened. "Mr. Kellener was not depressed, only preoccupied and concerned about something."

Without knowing why, Janna glanced at Jorge Hazlett, and suddenly knew what Mama meant by someone smelling guilty. Eight years on the force had taught her all the body English people used. She had learned to differentiate between the nervousness of guilt and that of merely having to talk to a police officer. She could tell when a casual saunter was *too* casual, when a citizen's tears were faked. Hazlett showed none of the signs she knew and could identify. He was doing nothing except watching Milo Talous with apparently genuine bewilderment and concern, yet Janna had the overwhelming urge to wind him up in her wrap strap.

She shuddered. Oh, god; Mama was infectious. She was catching his lunacy.

With Mama and Talous, Janna headed for the office determined to corner Vradel, determined to plead her case so convincingly he would free her from Mama. She turned the Monitor down the ramp to the station garage.

"Do you really think Kellener killed himself when he realized he could be charged under the Tescott Act?" Mama asked Milo Talous. "Why save the state the trouble of executing him?"

From the rear seat of the car, Talous said, "Perhaps he was thinking of the effect of the disgrace on his family. We'll see how the coroner's jury feels about suicide at the inquest Friday."

"Another thing—why should he kill himself when he went to all the trouble of signing Hazlett's name to everything so his partner would be blamed?"

Talous had no immediate answer for that.

Janna parked the car. It settled to the concrete in a dying whine of fans. She pushed her door forward and swung out over the airfoil skirt. Let Talous and Mama argue if they wanted; she was going upstairs. She pushed into the squadroom, aiming for Vradel's door.

Morello intercepted her. "Brill, that Huston woman has called three more times for you."

Janna tried to circle him. "Put the number on my table. I'll call her as soon as I've talked to the lieutenant."

"You might as well call her now. The lieutenant's busy."

Damn. Bloody damn it to hell. She scowled. "All right. I'll call the woman. What's her number?"

Mama came into the squadroom while she was punching the number into the phone. He sat down on the edge of the desk. "That Talous is a mule. He's convinced Kellener committed suicide because of the *Invictus*."

Janna did not look up. "Strange how some people fix on an idea and can't see anything else, isn't it?"

A man appeared on the screen. "Hough's Department Store, Publicity Department."

"Ms. Grania Huston, please."

The screen flickered. Shortly a square-faced woman came on. Her expression became grave at Janna's introduction. "Thank you for calling. The newscanner said you're the officer in charge of investigating the death of that man in the Sunflower Federal Bank Building."

"Yes, ma'am."

"Do you know yet how he died?"

"Why do you ask, ma'am?"

Ms. Huston chewed her lip. "Well, I saw something Saturday night. I don't know whether it had anything to do with that or not, but at the risk of seeming like a fool, I thought I ought to tell you about it."

Janna could feel Mama breathing down her neck. She elbowed him back. "Please do tell me."

"I saw a man leaving that building in what I can only describe as a very furtive manner. He kept looking around, as if he were afraid someone was going to see him, and he walked very fast."

Over Janna's shoulder, Mama asked, "What time was this?"

"A quarter past eight. I made a point of looking at the time."

Mama's breath felt hot on Janna's neck. "Praise Mouths from whom great blessings flow," he murmured in her ear.

Janna pursed her lips. "How did you happen to see him?"

"I'm a window designer for Hough's. I worked late Saturday to have a window ready for Monday morning. I looked out every so often, just to see what might be going on, and on one look out, I saw the man leaving the bank building."

"Can you describe him?"

Ms. Huston frowned in thought. "I couldn't see him really well. The trees in the sidewalk planters were a little in the way, and it was night. I think he was about medium height, and weight. I don't remember anything special about his hair. I do remember his clothes, though."

"Describe them, please."

"He wore tank pants with flared trouser legs and a tank top cut low so that a lot of his chest showed. He wasn't wearing a shirt under it. The color was dark, blue or green, I think, and it had a lighter stripe crossing the trouser legs diagonally from the hip to the inseam at the cuff."

"Sounds like the kind of thing Hazlett would wear," Mama murmured.

Janna said, "Ms. Huston, do you think you could identify him if you saw him again?"

"I don't know. I'd be willing to try."

"Thank you. If you'll arrange to be free about ten tomorrow morning, we'll bring you down and let you look at some people."

"I'll be ready. Good-bye, sergeant."

Janna punched off.

An incandescent grin split the darkness of Mama's face. "Jackpot. The description fits old Jorge."

Janna frowned. "And half the male population of Topeka. Don't count your ID's before they're made."

"You're just annoyed because it might very well be Hazlett, and if we place him in that building, it might mean he's guilty and I'm right."

She looked at him coldly. "I'm not looking forward to having to admit that you're right, but that won't stop me from following up the lead." She stood. "Excuse me. I have to see the lieutenant."

Vradel stepped out of his office and headed for the door.

"Lieutenant..."

"Sorry, Brill." He kept moving. "I have an appointment with the deputy director and then I have to leave right away. There's a Commander's Exchange this evening."

The door slammed behind him, leaving Janna staring impotently. Commander's Exchange? If he had stayed to listen a few minutes she could have given him a beautiful problem to take to his fellow commanders. He could have shared the further escapades of Mahlon Maxwell.

She dropped back into her chair, swearing a string of profanities that raised the brows of her colleagues and reddened the face of the one civilian woman in the room. Janna broke off, muttering an apology, and headed for the dictyper.

8

Liann Seaton descended on the Crimes Against Persons squadroom like a tornado...a controlled, elegant tornado, but a devastating storm all the same.

"I'm sorry," she told Lieutenant Vradel, "but this is impossible. It's ridiculous. My husband could not possibly have had anything to do with the deaths of those people on the *Invictus*." Her voice was quiet, but very firm.

She sat across his desk from him, in his office's most comfortable chair, looking polished and sophisticated even in her gingham pioneer dress. She regarded Vradel with unwavering eyes. Occasionally she lifted her head to look at Janna Brill and Mama Maxwell, standing behind Vradel, but her gaze always came back down to the lieutenant.

That she had shaken him was evident. He toyed with a pencil but had not made a single mark on his memo pad with it. He was not even chewing on his mustache.

"Ma'am, we're not accusing Andrew Kellener of any such thing."

"Mr. Peddicord made it quite clear when he called me yesterday afternoon. You believe the records prove my husband perpetrated a fraud on those poor colonists, that he deceived them into buying a ship that was inadequate, and that because he was about to be exposed, he killed himself. An Agent Talous of the Department of Justice visited me last night. He believes Andy made a practice of under-equipping colonists. He spoke of something called the Tescott Act which it appears he regrets not being able to invoke. Lieutenant, I totally reject all your claims and assumptions."

Vradel ran his fingers up and down his pencil. Janna could see the sketching itch tingling his fingers, but he could not look away from Liann Seaton long enough to draw. "Ma'am, we merely gather evidence. The cause of death will be determined by the coroner's jury Friday and any guilt regarding the colonists is up to the Department of Justice."

"But you and that Mr. Talous are gathering the evidence. If you're biased, the evidence could be, too."

"Ms. Seaton—"

"I want you to know something about my husband. I want to make it clear to you why he could not have committed suicide and why he could not have been responsible for the harm done to those Colonists."

Vradel still did not chew his mustache, but he smoothed it with the fingers of his left hand. "Very well. Do you mind if we record this?"

"No, certainly not."

Vradel took a microcorder out of a desk drawer and set it on top. He tapped it on.

"My husband," Liann Seaton said, "was a Libertarian. You can check his record. He was very active in campaigning for Libertarian party candidates in local and national elections. He believed that every person should be in control of his own life and totally responsible for it. He didn't approve of the womb-to-tomb care our society gives people. He believed it robs people of individualism, of initiative, and of pride. I suppose he might have become a sligh except that since slighs don't vote, they can hardly help shape or change society.

"What Andy did approve of, heartily, was colonization. Colonists, he would tell me, are people who take responsibility for themselves. They're going where there is no one to look after them but themselves."

It was almost an exact echo of Wim's words, Janna thought.

"Andrew Kellener wanted to help send everyone possible to the stars. He worked slave hours and inconvenienced himself in order to be available to clients. He and Jorge Hazlett charged just six percent instead of the usual ten percent commission for their services, so colonists would have to spend less to leave. Lieutenant, he wanted every one of his clients to arrive on his chosen world with the very best possible chance of survival. He would have done nothing"—she leaned forward and an elegant doubled fist came down emphatically on the top of Vradel's desk—"*nothing* to have jeopardized the lives of his clients in *any* way." She took a breath. "He spent his own credit to ensure that the supplies and ship of every client met better than minimum standards. I can show you records that prove it. Andy earned a great deal of credit as a colonial contractor, but he spent most of it on colonists and contributing toward shares when deserving people could not quite buy them on their own. We live in an apartment instead of a house. Andy rode the bus to work. Our one runabout is an economy model. If he cheated the colonists as Mr. Talous claims, he would have accumulated much more credit. Where is it, lieutenant?"

If Liann Seaton had been pleading a case in court, Janna would have found for her client.

The woman stood up, extending her hand to Vradel. "I've taken enough of your time. Thank you for hearing me out. If you're interested in Andy's funeral, it's at two o'clock this afternoon."

Vradel shook her hand. She turned and left, closing the door quietly behind her.

Vradel slumped back in his chair. "That is what in my youth would have been called a hot apple."

Janna and Mama came around to the front of the desk. Mama picked up a stack of papers on one corner and started tapping them into line. "She's a fine bibi, and bright, but I'm surprised she missed mentioning that Hazlett spreads a lot of credit around. I checked on him. He has a luxury townhouse in addition to the Vulcan, and lots of very flash friends who take frequent weekend party trips to distant cities."

A winter glint came into Vradel's eyes. "And that makes him a murderer? The governor has a nice house and several road cars. She also travels on weekends and attends expensive parties. Available evidence says Hazlett is a respectable member of the community. What do you have that refutes that?"

"How many murderers and thieves have you known who were *respectable* people?"

"Not one who didn't have evidence against him."

Janna silently cheered. Go, Hari.

Mama turned the stack to shake it down the other way. "We have evidence against Hazlett, skipper. Like I told Agent Talous, why should Kellener kill himself if he planned to have his partner blamed for the frauds? And how did he bring the trick to the office?"

Both Vradel and Janna blinked.

Mama set the papers down and picked up another group. "We didn't find any kind of container in his pocket or the trash, not a bottle or an envelope."

Vradel frowned. "We could have been careless and not searched every wastebasket in the office. Kellener may have disposed of a container out where he mixed up the caff."

Mama sniffed.

Janna said, "He may have brought it in a gelatin capsule."

Vradel nodded in satisfaction. "That's a distinct possibility."

Mama turned on Janna. "How about you, bibi? You were watching Hazlett when we went over there with Talous. You saw his reactions." He tapped the papers on the desk top. "You saw how guilty he is."

"I saw his reactions." She remembered her irrational urge to strap Hazlett. It sent a cold flush of guilt through her. "I saw nothing that proves he's guilty of anything."

"Your pupils are dilating. You're lying to me."

Vradel suddenly stood and leaned across the desk to snatch the papers away from Mama. "Will you stop that? When I need you to keep house for me, I'll see that it's added to your job description. Now, I like to encourage intuitive thinking in my officers, but I want more than that. Morello put a stack of complaint sheets on your table twenty minutes ago. Go take care of them. Don't bother me about Jorge Hazlett again until you can bring me documented, court-admissible evidence against him."

"Sign the authorization to look at his bank records. I'll bring you documented proof."

"Give me just cause first. Now both of you get to work. *Sail!*"

They left. Mama breathed hard down Janna's neck. "You know he's guilty, bibi. You just won't let yourself admit it. By-the-book Brill." He sounded scathingly pitying. "You're so tied to procedure by all the braintraining the department's forced on you that you can't believe good intuition. Look at it, bibi. Admit to it and believe in it."

He was never going to let this thing alone. She ground her teeth. There was only one thing to do. She scooped the complaint sheets from their table and thrust them at him. "Take these and go down to the car, unless you want to be the second partner I've ever hit."

Leos nearby looked around sharply.

"I'll join you in a bit. Sit on the rider side. *I'll* drive today."

Janna waited for him to leave the squadroom. The newscanner reported Bible cultists picketing the Statehouse today, insisting on revocation of taxes on church property. Farmers were counter-protesting, claiming reducing taxes anywhere else would drive farm taxes up.

When Mama had left, she went back to Vradel's office. "Sir, may I have another minute?"

He sighed. "Brill, I know he's difficult, but he hasn't really done anything yet to justify bouncing him out of here."

"I wasn't going to ask for that."

His brows went up. His mustache twitched.

Janna took a breath. "If he were convinced Hazlett had an alibi, maybe he would lose this obsession and start being more productive. On the other hand, if this Huston woman identifies Hazlett as the man she saw leaving the Sunflower Federal Building, we'll need to check his bank records anyway. So, lieutenant, sir, as a favor to me, will you please okay the authorization for the check on Hazlett's bank records?"

Vradel frowned. His pencil stroked his memo pad. A woman's face emerged, smiling up at him. He contemplated the drawing for a minute, then looked up. "All right. Go try to clear a few of those complaints. See if your witness recognizes Hazlett. The authorization will be waiting here for you when you get back."

Janna blew him a kiss. "Thanks, skipper."

If the heat had been broken by a long, cool rainstorm she could not have felt better. She felt so good she slapped Morello on the rump as she left and hummed a jivaqueme tune while driving Indian Thirty to their first call.

Mama eyed her with suspicion. "You've gone happy all of a sudden. Did you talk the lieutenant into demoting me to patrol again?"

"No."

"You just wish you could have."

She stopped humming and sighed. "I'd like to like you, Mama, but you make it hard. What are you? Where do you come from?"

He pushed his glasses up his nose. "Ulysses, Kansas."

"I've never heard of it."

"It's east of the sun and west of the moon, back of beyond. We were one of two afroam families in the town. They're so conservative out there they still vote Republican."

"How'd you end up here?"

"I used to spend my summers in Dodge City with an aunt, working in Front Street. I played one of the bad guys in the shootout enactments. I learned how to fall off a running horse and off the top of a building. I thought that gave me a calling to be an actor, so after high school I went to Kansas City to study acting. I fell in love with a girl in the UMKC Criminal Justice Course and switched curriculums to be near her. The relationship didn't last but I found I liked being a leo."

"So why didn't you go to work for the KCPD?"

He rolled his eyes. "The year I graduated, they were sniping lions all over K. C. I didn't need that. I applied several other places. They finally accepted me here."

The radio murmured, "Alpha Highland Three, a naked man in the intersection of Thirty-first Terrace and Burlingame."

"What about you, bibi?"

"I grew up in Wichita. My father is a designer for Boeing."

"Seeing all those ships getting ready to go to the stars didn't make you want to be a colonist?"

She shrugged. "Off and on it did, but mostly I wanted to be a lawyer. I was a year through the Washburn course when I realized what I really wanted to do was police work. I switched curriculums, too. Here's our first complainant. Possible kidnapping, complaint filed by a Mr. Ross Borel."

Mr. Borel was a portly man in his fifties, well dressed, well housed. His business partner had been kidnapped. "I think some government took him to steal his invention."

"What invention is that?" Mama asked.

"A new space drive that will make ramjets obsolete. Sol—that's Sol Thoday—left for Wichita last week to arrange for an experimental model to be built. He said he'd call me this week, but he hasn't. That's why I think something's happened to him."

"What's this space drive like?" Janna asked.

When Borel explained she could hardly keep from wincing. It was the Dean Drive. That old skin again.

"When you paid your share of the partnership I don't suppose you used bankcredit?"

Borel shook his head. "I bought jewelry and gave that to Sol. He was afraid if I used bankcredit, the wrong people would learn about his invention and steal it. Looks like they learned about it anyway."

Mama said, "I don't think he was kidnapped."

They told him what had really happened to his partner. While he was still recovering from the shock, they took down the facts of his meetings with the skinner and a description of the skinner himself. They invited Borel down to the station at his convenience to look at pictures.

They climbed back into Indian Thirty and marked the complaint for referral to Crimes Against Property.

Janna checked the car's chrono. "It's nearly ten. Let's go pick up our Ms. Huston."

"How do you want to handle it?"

"By secret show-up, of course."

She could not see bringing Hazlett down to the station for a formal show-up, and if they just marched Hazlett in to her and asked if he were the man, every defense attorney in the world could demolish a positive identification in court. They had to present Hazlett in such a way he did not know what was happening and she was not being influenced.

Grania Huston was waiting for them at the entrance of Hough's. Instead of opening a rear door for her, however, Janna set the car on its parking rollers at the curb, illegally, and they climbed out.

"Before we take you down to the station we have to run across the street to the bank building," Janna said. "Come on along. We won't be a minute."

Ms. Huston's eyes brightened. "All right." She followed them willingly, even eagerly.

They took the elevator to the tenth floor and strolled into the Hazlett/Kellener suite. The receptionist looked up and smiled politely. "Good morning, sergeants."

"Buenos días," Janna said. "Is Mr. Hazlett in?"

"Yes, but he is with a client."

"We don't want to disturb him, then. Would you just ask him to come out for a moment?"

The receptionist considered. He punched a button and murmured into the intercom.

Moments later Jorge Hazlett came out into the reception area. He smiled at them. "Good morning. What can I do for you?" Inside he wondered what the hell they were up to. The leos wore expressions so carefully polite they almost alarmed him. And who was that avid-faced little woman with them?

The she-lion drew Jorge to one end of the reception room while her black partner remained by the door with the little woman. "Your partner's wife was in visiting us this morning." She repeated Liann Seaton's remarks to him. "Is what she says about Kellener true?"

Jorge relaxed. "I would have said so before Monday morning. That's how he's always acted like he believed, but now..." He shrugged. "How could he believe in the holiness of colonials and still cheat them?"

"You think he did?"

"Someone did, and I know I wasn't the guilty party."

Janna watched him as Hazlett answered. He looked back without flinching. His eyes dilated slightly, however. She noted it for future consideration. "Well, I won't take more of your time. Thank you, Mr. Hazlett."

They left. Riding down in the elevator, Janna asked Ms. Huston, "Have you seen either of those men before?"

Ms. Huston's eyes went wide. "You mean one of them might have been the man I saw?" She frowned. "I don't think they were. The young man was more slender than the one I saw and Mr. Hazlett didn't walk the same way the man I saw did."

Above her head, Janna and Mama exchanged glances. Mama was obviously disappointed. Janna had to admit to feeling that way too. An ID would have settled something, at least. This settled nothing. It raised questions, in fact. If Hazlett were not the man, who was?

They stepped off the elevator. The bank guard nodded to them. As one, Janna and Mama stopped cold. They looked at each other. The guard's uniform was dark green. The flared trousers had a gold stripe crossing each pantleg diagonally from hip to inseam at the cuff.

"Was the man wearing something like that?" Janna asked.

Ms. Huston studied the guard. "The trousers took right, but he didn't have that kind of jacket."

Mama strolled over to the guard. He reached out to finger one sleeve of the jacket. "That's nice material and a nice cut. It almost looks good enough for street wear. What are the pants like under the jacket?"

"They have a tank top," the guard replied.

"Do you wear a shirt under it?"

"In this weather? No. You really like this?" He looked down at the uniform with surprise.

"The color is too conservative, though. Have a good day."

They ushered Ms. Huston out to the street. Janna smiled at her. "I don't think we'll need you to identify the man after all. Thank you for calling. If it turns out we need you again, we'll reach you."

"I'm always happy to help the police. How else are the streets going to be made safe?"

They watched her cross the street and disappear into Hough's. Janna asked, "Do you still have the names of the security people on duty Saturday night?"

He pulled a notebook out of a thigh pocket. "Right here."

First on the list came Mr. Klim Hightower. Guard Hightower was not happy to see them. "This is the second time you've waked me up. What is it, more questions about Saturday? I already told you all I know."

Mama pushed his glasses up his nose. "Except which of the guards left in the middle of the shift Saturday night."

The guard stared at them. "Left? None of us left during the shift."

Janna shook her head. "Wrong. He was seen leaving. He took off his jacket so he wouldn't seem to be wearing a uniform." She paused. "Was it you?"

"No!" His face set. "I don't know what anyone thought they saw, but it wasn't one of us leaving. We all three stayed the entire shift. Maybe your witness saw someone disguised as a guard."

They could not move him from that. They headed for the next name on the list.

"He has a point," Mama said. "Maybe Hazlett thought he could fool a possible witness that way."

"You don't really believe that."

Mama looked wistful, then shook his head. "No. He would have worn the entire uniform. The guard's lying."

"They all may, and stick to it."

"We'll shake them."

She raised a brow at him. "The peeps couldn't make you and Wim change your minds about denying you carried a shooter on duty."

His eyes slid toward her. "So he told you about that."

"He wanted to warn me what your partners can find themselves involved in."

Mama opened his mouth as though to start a protest, then closed it again and sat back, shrugging. "I didn't ask him to lie for me. Wim was good back-up."

The second guard also denied that anyone had left duty, but as he did, his pupils dilated. They smelled fear in him.

"Well, that's too bad," Janna said with a sigh. "We didn't want to bring your employers at the bank into this, but—"

"We'll have to," Mama interrupted. "It'll probably mean all three of you will be fired." He turned as though to leave.

The guard went gray. "Wait."

Mama stopped.

"There's no point getting the others in trouble. They're just covering for me. I'm the one who left."

"Why?"

"It had nothing to do with that business upstairs. There was trouble here at home, a fight between my wives. I had to stop it." Sweat beaded his upper lip. "Don't tell the bank. I wasn't gone more than an hour."

"When did you leave?"

"A little after eight."

The two leos exchanged looks.

"All right," Janna said. "We won't mention it to the bank, but if you have to come to court, don't perjure yourself."

They headed back for the car.

"So much for our eyewitness, Mama, and so much for Hazlett being in the building. If he were there, Ms. Huston would probably have seen him leave."

"She couldn't have been looking out the window every minute." He pushed his glasses up his nose. "We need to see his bank records."

Bank records. "So you say. Let's go back to the office."

His brows went up. "We haven't finished clearing these complaints yet."

"Let's go anyway."

Morello was waiting for them in the squadroom. "The lieutenant said to give you this."

It was the authorization, as promised. Mama stared at it incredulously for a long minute, then whooped and threw both arms around Janna. He would have danced her across the squadroom except that she broke his hold and dumped him flat on his back on the floor, much to the amusement of the entire squad.

Mama seemed undisturbed at being dropped. He stood up grinning. "Bibi, I knew you could feel Hazlett's guilt, too. Count him lion meat as of now."

Janna did not like being her colleagues' entertainment. She towed Mama after her out of the squadroom. "I *don't* believe he's guilty," she snapped. "I'm just hoping this will prove his noninvolvement to you."

Mama's grin never wavered. He grinned all the way to the National Bank Central. As they parked and went into the bank, she said, "You're certainly stubborn."

"It makes me a good leo, bibi."

She rolled her eyes.

They presented the authorization to a teller. She took them to the manager. He handed them over to the computer librarian. She punched in Jorge Hazlett's number. In five minutes they sat studying Hazlett's purchase record for Saturday, July 30.

The first glance through the printout, Janna held her breath. All during being shuffled through the bank, the fear had grown that the record would prove nothing. What she saw on reading relieved her. Purchases recorded for the evening included transport tokens at nineteen-fifteen hours from a vending machine on Kansas Avenue to dinner at Peron's in the Granada Mall, which had been paid for at twenty-one-forty. The records included a number of purchases from shops, also all in the Granada Mall.

Janna tried not to sound smug but some of it leaked into her voice anyway. "It looks like Hazlett was at the other end of town all evening."

Mama's disappointment lasted only a minute. "He could have killed Kellener before."

Janna closed her eyes. Give her strength. She opened them again. "Not possible. Kellener left home at a quarter to seven. The bus trip downtown had to take at least twenty minutes. I don't think that gives Hazlett time to meet him at the office, kill him, and run down the street to the vending machine by seven fifteen."

Mama pushed his glasses up his nose. "Then he faked the record, somehow."

"Faked the record?" She kept her voice down so the librarian would not hear. "Maxwell, you are afflicted with the tightest tunnel vision I've ever seen! Fake a bank record? You've lost all your chips."

Mama shrugged. "I know it's supposed to be impossible, but I also know this deek killed his partner. I feel it in my bones. So the record has to be wrong."

She felt like pounding her head into a wall. "Christ."

"There's one way to find out. We'll check to see if his car was really in the parking lot, and we'll talk to his neighbors to see when he came home. We can also ask him to produce those things he bought." Mama frowned at the printout. "Buying this much jewelry suggests he was making a quiet payment to someone for something."

"The child's computer and doll don't fall into that category. And what about the meal and suits?"

"He was bound to buy some personal items. Or maybe we need to learn who helped him. Someone had to help him, I'm sure. Maybe by finding who helped him, we can strap Hazlett."

Janna sighed. "You have the philosophy of investigation wrong, Mama. We're supposed to look at all the evidence, form a hypothesis based on what we've found, then prove or disprove the hypothesis. We don't randomly pick someone to be 'it' and look for evidence against him."

Mama took off his glasses and polished the lenses on his trouser leg. "My hypothesis is Hazlett did it, so let's prove it. Now, he said his car broke down and that's why he took the bus. Let's see if that's true." He put his glasses back on.

Janna considered. It would be good to have all the corroboration possible of Hazlett's alibi. It might even discourage Mama. "We'll check the parking lot records, but if we don't find anything there to suggest he's guilty, we're going to drop it and follow up these other complaints. Understood?"

"We'll find something."

Janna rolled her eyes.

They ate a quick sandwich for lunch, then drove to the central office of the Sunco Corporation.

Sunco's gates issued tickets to all incoming vehicles and required the return of that ticket plus enough tokens to pay for the parking time before the exit gate would open. Unknown to most people, the company recorded all entries and exits from its lots. The visual record was what interested Janna and Mama.

"We do it because the bicycles cheat," the tape librarian said as she hunted up the video clips they needed. "The riders lift the bikes over the gate. By recording, we can see them and have warrants issued on the license numbers."

"We're just interested in cars."

She ran the Saturday night clip for them. According to DMV, Hazlett's car was a bright blue Mercedes Vulcan (official color name of Peacock), license number SHH 418. The tape recorded the rear end of a vehicle with the license SHH 418 entering the lot at Thirteenth and Jackson at nineteen hundred hours. The entire rear end of the vehicle could not be seen in the frame but enough was visible to determine the make and color of the car.

They had the librarian run the tape forward until the computer recognized the number again and froze the image. According to the time indicator on the tape, SHH 418 had left the Sunco lot at eighteen-twenty Monday evening.

"It looks like he didn't drive anywhere Saturday night," Mama conceded.

"So let's forget it and follow up complaints."

"Just one more stop, bibi. I want to check with Hazlett's neighbors."

"Maxwell, this is enough!"

He widened his eyes. "But we haven't found anything yet that either proves or disproves my hypothesis."

She must be brainbent, she decided, for continuing to go along with this madness, but... "We'll see the neighbors, then, but that's absolutely the last call we make on this case today. Absolutely."

"Unless we find evidence against Hazlett."

They knocked on the doors of the townhouses around Hazlett's. At most, there was no answer and among the few people they did find home, questioning established that people in the area either went to bed early or were immovably planted in front of the holo-v until they retired. However, across the street from Hazlett's townhouse, they found a woman who had seen him come home.

"It was a little after ten thirty. He came walking up from the bus stop. I called to him and asked him where his car was because I'd seen him drive out earlier. He told me one of the fans went bad and that he'd had to leave the car parked downtown. He said he couldn't understand how people managed to shop and ride the bus. He found it awkward riding and carrying packages."

"He was carrying packages?" Janna sent Mama a triumphant look. If Hazlett brought purchases home, there was a good chance he had bought them in the first place. Her relief vanished at the neighbor's next words.

"He wasn't when I saw him, no. He said after he'd ridden halfway back from south Topeka with them, he decided to leave what he'd bought locked in his car and bring them home later."

He could very well have done that. The child's computer would have been a particularly awkward thing to handle on a bus. It also occurred to her that if he had never bought the items, he might still give the neighbor that story to explain why he had no packages.

But of course he *had* bought the items. The bank records said so. No matter what wild blue yonder notion had stuck in the glue that served Mahlon Maxwell for a brain, bank records could not be faked. The computer checked the signature on the register plate against that on the card. It checked the thumbprints. Prints were certainly impossible to forge.

She led the way back to the car. "That's it, Mama. Now we start clearing other cases. Nothing we've learned out here suggests Hazlett is guilty of either tampering with a bank record or with his partner's life."

"Nothing suggests he didn't, either."

"You forget, *guilt* has to be proven. Lacking that, a party is assumed innocent." She climbed over the airfoil skirt into the Monitor and started the engine.

Mama swung in, too. "How do you think Kellener got that trick?"

"I'll leave that for the coroner's jury to decide."

"For god's *sake*, Brill!"

The shrill exclamation lifted Janna almost out of her seat. She whirled on him.

He stared at her, eyes burning behind the glasses. "There are times to say to *hell* with the book! Bibi, this deek is guilty as sin. I *know* it! Somewhere there's evidence, and if I don't have a try at finding it, I'm going to be wondering the rest of my life if there's a murderer free because I didn't try hard enough to strap him."

She stared at him. That sounded like some idealistic rookie just out of college. He must know, as she did, that there were thousands of guilty deeks walking around who had caused police officers to lose sleep and gain ulcers looking for admissible evidence against them. It was a harsh and hated fact no one wanted to accept, but somewhere around the third or fourth year on the force, leos interested in keeping their stomachs and sanity gave up torturing themselves over hopeless chases.

Having survived twelve years on the force, Mama must have learned that lesson, too, yet here he was in full cry after what looked like a wild goose. It disturbed her. Was it indicative of a pathologic process, or was his conviction really that strong?

Even more disturbing, however, part of her wanted to run with him. She distrusted intuition on principle, as emotional and therefore unreliable. Still, she had felt that one urge to strap Hazlett and even now something about the case bothered her enough that she could not quite bring herself to choke Mama down.

She considered what they had. If she were to ignore the evidence of the bank records, everything else was equivocal. It did not suggest guilt nor confirm innocence. It all left loose ends. She sucked her lower lip. She hated loose ends.

"All right, we'll give it an honest try…at least until the inquest. After that, the decision will be official and the case will be out of our hands."

"But that gives us just the rest of today and tomorrow," he protested.

"That's right. If you'll agree to that limit, we'll go on. If you can't, I'll insist we drop it right now. I can go to Lieutenant Vradel for back-up enforcement if I have to."

He sighed, a gusty hiss of disgust and surrender. "Okay. After the inquest, it's closed. I'll forget about Hazlett."

She switched on the fans. "Then let's get busy tracking him."

9

"Do you mind telling me who we're looking for, Mama? It's almost the end of the watch." They were cruising all the streets around the Statehouse. Mama called the turns at each corner.

"That trick had to come from somewhere. I'm looking for an Ear who can give us names of street dealers who might have sold the junk to Hazlett."

Janna looked away from her driving long enough to glance at him. "You amaze me. You've just come in from Soldier Creek. How can you have any contacts in Capitol division?"

"I've been in Capitol twice before. I still remember people from then."

Oh, yes…his two other stints as Investigator I. She had forgotten.

"What does this Ear look like?"

"Very female. She always works the streets around the Statehouse, catering to the legislators and their staffs."

Janna clucked in disapproval. "I don't understand why the boys and girls work the street when they have perfectly legal houses to work out of. If they're caught, the fines are worse than the house fees they're avoiding, not to mention the working time lost in jail."

"Why does a sligh give up social care? I don't know. People are perverse."

Janna swung the car onto Jackson and started gliding along the east side of the Statehouse grounds. "Speaking of perversity, why were you broken back to uniform from Investigator those other times?"

"One was a crock. I called a supervisor an asshole in debriefing and he wouldn't forget it. He gave me a poor rating in my next evaluation."

There were commanders like that, despite the fact debriefing was supposed to have free speech with no penalties attached.

"What about the other time?"

He shrugged. "I pushed a suspect a little and some citizens happened to see him bleeding. There she is." He pointed ahead.

They were coming up on a girl in a scarlet romper and matching hip boots sauntering along the pavement. Her round posterior swayed invitingly. Mama leaned out the window of the Monitor.

"Sit on it or give it away, bibi, but move it off the street before you try selling it."

The prostitute turned. Her face betrayed the fact that she was older than she had looked from the rear. She stopped with her hands on her hips. "Well, well, look who's back."

Janna eased the Monitor to the curb and set it down.

Mama grinned at the prostitute. "Come tell Mama what you've been doing with yourself."

"Working with my back to the wall as usual." She waltzed over to the car, swinging her hips. "Are you working in the neighborhood again or just passing through?"

"Working, and about to offer you a chance to earn credit without adding to the calluses on your gluteus."

"You want me to play Ear for you? What do I get in return?"

"The usual: reasonable credit, my help keeping you out of jail, and a bonus if you want it." He leered. "I'm older and better this time 'round, bibi."

She sniffed. "That's what they all say. I've yet to tell the difference between you with my eyes closed. What do you need to know?"

He pushed his glasses up his nose. "The names of street dealers a local businessman might buy illegal drugs from."

"I can think of five to start with. I saw one of them in a bar down the street not five minutes ago."

Mama pushed the car door forward. "Show me where." He looked back at Janna. "If that jewelry is part of a payment, the payee will be wanting to turn it into credit. Why don't you go on back to the station and have the jewelry descriptions sent out to all the local gem people? I'll talk to this dealer."

He swung out and headed back up Jackson with the prostitute. Janna revved the fans and sent the Monitor coasting toward the station.

Getting descriptions of the jewelry took some twenty-five minutes longer than she anticipated, in phone calls to the jewelers who sold the pieces and in waiting for them to look up descriptions in their records.

It was after four thirty before she could fill out the description forms in Communications. Mama had still not returned when she finished. She wondered whether he was talking to the dealer or had convinced the prostitute to let him give her a bonus.

She punched on the intradepartment phone and put in the number of the stolen property computer.

"Wait, please," came the throaty voice of the computer.

No one knew whose voice had been recorded for the computer but Janna had heard a number of het male leos and some ho she-lions say they would give anything to find out. Throughout the SCPD it was fondly called The Voice. She knew one investigator who claimed he had transferred to Crimes Against Property just so he would have an excuse to call The Voice several times a day and arouse himself listening to it.

"Go ahead," purred The Voice.

"Sergeant Janna Brill, Capitol division, badge number one-four-five-five, requesting a watchdog program."

There was a heartbeat before The Voice came back breathily, "State length of program and items to be included, please."

"Program begins now, retroactive to nine o'clock A.M., Monday, August first. Program to end twelve o'clock noon, Friday, August fifth. Items are: numbers one and two, novalon suits made by Stellar Fashions; number three, Dyan Pennock action doll made by Mattel; number four, Eduvac Junior computer made by Battershell Electronics; number five..." One by one, she described each item of jewelry.

When she finished The Voice said, "Thank you. Wait, please, for a memory check."

While the computer reviewed its activity back to Monday, Janna reached for a pencil and note pad, in case the computer found anything. Presently The Voice came back on the line.

"There have been three incidents of activity involving items described in program. Number one: seven novalon suits made by Stellar Fashions were among twenty recovered in a raid at 917 West Seventeenth Street at twenty-hundred hours, Monday, August first. Number two: one novalon suit made by Stellar Fashions, one Dyan Pennock action doll made by Mattel, one Eduvac Junior computer made by Battershell Electronics were listed in a stolen property query made at nine forty-three hours, Tuesday, August second. Number three: two novalon suits made by Stellar Fashions were included in a stolen property query on items found in the car of Mr. Frederick Weltmann at two ten hours, Wednesday, August third."

Janna wrote fast. "Who made the stolen property query in activity number two?"

"The stolen property query number two was made by Officer Niall Cushman, Highland Park division."

"Thank you." She knew the computer did not need any expression of gratitude, but she always thanked it anyway. She could not bring herself simply to punch off, not even with a computer—certainly not with one that sounded so human.

She leaned against the Communications counter, her finger traveling down the list. Number two looked very promising, but there was no point in trying to follow up on it now. Officer Cushman was probably on his way home, as she should be, and he was not likely to welcome being called tonight. The matter was not that urgent anyway. Tomorrow would be soon enough.

She considered whether or not to go down and see if debriefing were still going. Missing it was likely to bring Schnauzer Venn around asking why, twitching the heavy brows and mustache that had earned the tick tech his nickname. The doc was a personable man, easy to talk to, but he could be a troublesome mother hen if an officer showed signs of changing a behavior pattern.

Mama stuck his head into the room. "There you are. Come on, bibi."

"Where?"

"We have dealers to visit." He caught her arm and pulled her down the hall.

She freed herself with one deft twist. "Tonight?"

"If I have just until Friday to strap Hazlett, I intend to use every possible minute. You didn't have anything better to do, did you?"

"As a matter of fact, I was going to a concert at the university with Sid and Treece. An air-conditioned concert," she added, "where I won't feel in imminent danger of heat stroke."

"I'll treat you to dinner at the coldest club in town when Hazlett is locked up."

"How can I refuse an offer like that?"

If he heard the irony in her voice, he chose to ignore it. He put a hand between her shoulders and propelled her toward the garage.

"Indian Thirty is checked in. What car are we going to use, or are we going to double on my bicycle?" she asked.

"We'll use my runabout."

There was one thing to be said for a runabout, she reflected as she climbed into the passenger side of his D-F Firefly: it could not be driven over a safe speed and was virtually impossible to tip over. "Where first?"

"Kay says we can find Roan Kinnis at or around the Carousel Club. Let me go in first and try to intersect, then you come along. If I haven't found him, we'll see who wants to bolt when you come in."

The Carousel was on Quincy, near Seventh. Mama went in with the head bobbing, sliding walk affected by trippers, as if he were moving in time to jivaqueme music. Janna sat in the Firefly and counted off five minutes, then she followed him.

Mama sat in a rear booth talking to a small man in a pink and purple jumpsuit. She walked up to the bar. The Carousel's clientele were business people. A number of them, male and female, looked her over as she came in, some with casual interest, some with speculation. The man with Mama, however, suddenly became very relaxed. He pretended not to notice her at all.

She moved to his table. "Am I spoiling a transaction, Kinnis?" She sat down beside him, trapping him between Mama and her.

The street dealer raked her with his eyes. "I don't know what you're talking about, leo."

"She's talking about the trick you were going to sell me," Mama said.

Kinnis tried to look innocent but the attempt did not quite succeed. He looked from one to the other and clutched at the edge of the table as if considering trying to leap over it. "So you're a lion, too. When did they start pinning badges on skinheads?" His contempt could not conceal the nervous quiver in his voice. "He's lying about me selling trick. He can't prove anything I said," he told Janna.

"Want to hear the playback on my microcorder, jon?"

Kinnis looked gray even in the Carousel's dusky rose lighting. "Bastard!"

"Peace," Janna said. "We aren't Vice. We won't strap you…not this time." She was for damn sure going to pass his name on to Vice, though. "We just want to ask you a few questions. If we like the answers, then we'll just stand up and walk away, and you can go back to peddling your cut-rate happiness pills to these sterling citizens."

Kinnis chewed his lip. "What do you want to know?"

Janna pushed down the contempt that wanted to curl her lip. He was an amateur. It must be soft working downtown with middle and upper class citizens. One of the dealers from Oakland or a similar area would never have surrendered so fast.

"Have you ever sold any trick to this man?" Mama pulled a picture of Hazlett out of a hip pocket.

Kinnis looked it over. "No, I don't think so."

"You aren't sure?"

He shrugged. "I transact my business in places like this. The light's never bright. People's faces look strange. I don't think I've dealt with him, but I can't be sure."

"Does the name Hazlett sound familiar?"

"They don't tell me their names."

"You learn them anyway, don't you?" Janna said. "You check on them?"

He chewed his lip. "I never checked on anyone whose name turned out to be Hazlett."

"How about Kellener?"

Mama's eyes widened for one surprised moment.

Janna lifted a brow at him. "Let's not be too one-track, Mama."

"I don't know that name either," Kinnis said.

Janna described Kellener. Kinnis kept shaking his head. "That could be any one of a hundred jons I've met, but none of them was named Kellener."

Janna caught Mama's eye and looked toward the door. They had all they were going to get out of this toad. In unison, they stood.

"The answers could have been better, jon, but we'll accept them for now. Don't take any bad card."

They left him shaking and pale.

Theresa Olivera came next. She proved more streetwise than Kinnis, harder to find and harder to corner. The effort of making her talk proved equally unrewarding. She had nothing more useful to say than Kinnis had. They could not find Joe Luther at all, nor Fran DiMartin.

Janna was hoping Mama would quit and take her home. She was tired. Her jumpsuit, wringing wet with sweat, had plastered itself to her chest and back.

"This isn't my favorite way to spend my free time, you know, Mama."

"I just want to talk to one more jon."

The jon was a bear of a man with hands large enough to sit in. They found him in a computer games arcade, toxy on narcotics.

Janna eyed him. "Another of your contacts?"

"Let me talk to him alone."

Janna shrugged and went back to the Firefly. She leaned against the side of it, spreading herself to catch the slightest breeze.

Mama came out of the arcade in a few minutes, jubilant. "He gave me the names of some dealers operating in Hazlett's neighborhood. He even gave the name of one in Kellener's apartment area. You can't accuse me of having tunnel vision now."

Janna sighed. "I suppose you want to talk to them tonight?"

"Of course. It won't take long."

They found just one of the three dealers supposedly operating in the Brentwood area. The one they found swore he had never heard of either Hazlett or Kellener, nor sold either of them trick.

"I've never sold anyone trick."

Janna felt he was lying about that. However, his denials about selling to Hazlett and Kellener had the ring of truth. They dropped him off on a corner of his choosing.

Watching the dealer disappear up the street, Mama sighed. "I give up for the night. Let's hunt the rest tomorrow."

Some perverse impulse spurred Janna. "So soon? It's barely past seven-thirty."

He stared at her. "I thought you wanted to quit."

"I did, until you stopped short of looking up the Kellener neighborhood dealer. Now I want to find her, too."

He frowned. "Bibi, I never thought you'd be that kind of woman."

"I'm just asking for equality for all the suspects."

He shook his head but lifted the Firefly off its parking rollers and turned it toward west Tenth.

The address they had been given belonged to an ordinary house in a quiet residential neighborhood. The woman who peered out through the door's security peep could have been anyone's mother or wife.

Mama checked the address again. "Bez Hilos?" he asked.

She nodded, smiling. "May I help you?"

Janna showed her ID and badge. "May we come in?"

Ms. Hilos led them to a comfortable living room. Janna watched her closely. The woman seemed completely at ease. Too much so? Most people were a little disturbed by the appearance of police officers on their doorsteps.

"What can I do for you, officers?"

Janna watched the woman's eyes. "Does the name Kellener mean anything to you?"

"Why, no. Should it?" Her pupils dilated as she said it.

"You've never sold drugs to anyone by that name?"

"Drugs?" Her eyes widened in astonishment, "I don't know anything about drugs. I've never sold any to anyone."

"According to our sources you do a bonanza business among housewives and adolescents," Mama said.

Her eyes were innocent. "I don't know who your sources are, but they aren't reliable. I ask you, do I look like a street dealer?"

"Do I look like a leo?"

She stared at him a moment, then laughed. "All right, appearances don't count. I'm no dealer, but if I were, what would you want with me?"

"Just some information," Janna said.

"Are you Vice?"

"No, Crimes Against Persons."

Janna watched the circuits hum in the woman's head. In her way, Hilos seemed as tough and street-wise as any dealer. Being a housewife working out of her home did not make her an amateur. The woman was in control of herself and appeared to suffer from no pangs of guilt.

She said, "Why are you interested in this Kellener?"

"We need to know if you've ever sold him drugs."

"Him?"

The exclamation slipped out before Hilos stopped herself. Janna and Mama exchanged quick glances.

"You mean it's Kellener's wife Liann Seaton who's been your customer?" Janna asked.

Hilos considered for a long minute, then nodded.

"What do you sell her?" Mama asked.

"A few hallucinogens and some boosts and tranks…the usual housewives' medley."

"Have you ever sold her any trick?"

Hilos snapped around to glare up at Janna. "Certainly not," she snapped. "I like my customers in condition to remain my customers. I wouldn't sell trick to my biggest competitor, or even to a lion."

"Has Seaton ever asked where she might buy trick?"

The dealer's mouth set in a thin slash of lip. "No, and I wouldn't have told her if she had. If I knew anyone selling illegals, I'd have made a call to Vice long ago. Someone who sells trick or dust is as good as an executioner and ought to be locked away for life, or better yet, given their own junk."

Janna bit her lip to hide a smile. The dealer's outrage tickled her. Criminals could be so self-righteous about other criminals and other crimes.

Mama grinned outright. "Very civic-spirited of you."

His sarcasm did not endear them to her. Hilos pointed at the door. "I think that's enough. I'll bid you good night, leos. I don't want you here when my husband brings the kids back from the park."

They let her throw them out.

Climbing into the runabout, Janna said, "Well, what do you think?"

"You can't be thinking she killed him?"

"Why not? She's a tripper. She knows drugs and has access to them. You know how many spouses murder each other every year?"

He frowned. "I suppose you want to talk to her."

"Of course."

He started the Firefly's fans and sailed the runabout the few short blocks to the Kellener apartment.

Liann Seaton's smile was puzzled as she opened the door to let them in. "What brings you out at this time of night?"

Janna listened to every nuance of the question. There was curiosity in it, and hesitant hope, but not a single note of fear that Janna could detect.

"May I bring you anything? Caff? Tea? Liquor?"

"No, thank you."

Janna was tempted to sit in a deep chair that reminded her of one her grandfather used to have. In it, one felt surrounded, almost hidden. She turned away from it to choose a straight and hard one.

"We've just been talking to Bez Hilos, Ms. Seaton."

The lovely face froze. "Bez." Her voice sounded strangled.

"How long have you been a tripper?"

"Since—since college. I've never seen any harm in it if done in moderation," she said defensively.

Mama regarded her keenly. "Your husband didn't approve of drugs, though."

She looked away. "No."

"Is that why you went to a street dealer, so you wouldn't have narcotics purchases on your bank record?"

"What business is it of yours, may I ask?"

"Your husband died of a trick overdose."

She snapped around to stare at him, then at Janna. "Trick?" Her breath caught and her face bleached. "No. You can't think that I—I adored him."

"You never fought over your use of drugs?" Janna asked.

"He never knew. I was very careful never to boost around him. Sergeant." Her voice was intense. "I've never used illegals. *Never.* I don't have the slightest idea where to buy them."

Janna had to admire her. She was obviously terrified, but she was not giving in to panic. She remained as controlled as she had been the day her husband was found. Too controlled, maybe?

"Still," Mama said, "it's interesting that he should be an OD when you're the tripper."

"I was here with my children the entire evening."

Mama's shrug dismissed her children as witnesses.

Liann Seaton looked from him to Janna. Tension twitched muscles in her jaw. "Did you come here to arrest me?"

"No, we're just investigating all possibilities, Ms. Seaton."

"If you're looking for someone who trips, you won't have any shortage of suspects." She paused. "Does this mean you don't think he committed suicide, or that he had anything to do with those poor people on the *Invictus?"*

Even when she seemed to be a suspect for murder, she wanted her husband's name clean. Extraordinary woman. Janna said, "As I said, we're investigating all possibilities."

"What did you mean, we won't have any shortage of suspects if we're looking for a tripper?"

She shrugged at Mama. "Doesn't almost everyone use some drugs?"

"Does Jorge Hazlett?"

She thought. "I don't know. Sometimes when we've seen him socially he's seemed a bit toxy, but whether from drugs or alcohol, I'm sure I couldn't say. I hope you don't suspect Jorge of anything. He can't be responsible. He's been a real rock for me these past few days and he and Andy were always like brothers."

"Siblings kill each other as often as spouses do."

"If Jorge has any aggressions, he takes them out on a chess-board. Have you considered that perhaps Andy died by accident? Maybe one of his office staff left some trick and Andy took it by mistake."

"We've considered that," Janna said.

"And rejected it?"

"We're taking everything to the coroner's jury on Friday."

She became very still. "Including the possibility that I killed him? Why would I have wanted him dead?"

"He made a great deal of credit and gave it away. Without him you could be a rich widow. Or perhaps he caught you boosting and was planning to dissolve the marriage contract. There could be a dozen reasons." Janna grimaced. "I've seen wives kill because the husband wouldn't carry the trash cans to the street on collection day."

The widow laced her hands together in her lap...so tightly the fingers went white. "You have a very unpleasant job, but I suppose it has to be done. I swear to you, I didn't buy any trick, nor did I give any to my husband. I was here all Saturday evening. I can bring in my children to tell you that if necessary. If you won't believe them, arrest me and let me contact my attorney."

Janna felt dirty and sweaty. She wanted to go home and take a bath. If she went to Champaign with Wim, she would not have to spend her life harassing widows with accusations and innuendoes.

She stood up. "It won't be necessary to call your children. Just answer one more question. Could your husband possibly have bought the trick himself, for any reason at all, even an outrageous one?"

Seaton shook her head. "Absolutely not. Andy would have sooner cut off his hands than contaminate them with any kind of narcotics. Andy would never ever have bought that trick."

"I think that's all we need for now. I'm sorry to have bothered you so late. Good night."

Janna made Mama take her back to the station to pick up her bicycle. She pedaled hard for home, trying to outrun the feeling of being unclean. The woman was right. It could be a very unpleasant job. She considered Wim's offer some more.

Not until she was stripping for a bath and heard the crackle of paper in her hip pocket did she remember the computer's response to the watchdog program. She took the list of computer activity out of the pocket and smoothed it on the bathroom countertop. Her finger traced the items listed under number two. They might find who sold someone near Kellener some trick, but the odds were long. This track looked much more promising. In the morning she would have to call Officer Niall Cushman in Highland Park and ask him why he was interested in a novalon suit, a doll, and a child's computer.

10

Mama strolled into the squadroom looking ready to sail. He shifted impatiently in his chair during rollcall and raced through dictyping the reports on yesterday's work. Then he pushed at Janna. "Come on, bibi. We have those dealers to find."

She brought out the list the watchdog had produced. "We have these to check out, too."

He grimaced in indecision. "You just haven't given me enough time. How about another day?"

She shook her head. "The inquest stops it."

"Then we'll have to split up. I'll hunt down the dealers. I can probably pose as a tripper and find them faster anyway. You check out these."

Janna frowned. Did she dare trust him loose on his own? On the other hand, if he flamed, she could use that to rid herself of him.

"All right. But watch it, okay?. Don't push any of them too hard."

"Yes, Mother." He blew her a kiss and hurried out the door of the squadroom.

Janna punched the Highland Park division number into the phone. "Niall Cushman, please," she told the officer who answered. "Sergeant Janna Brill of Crimes Against Persons calling."

"Just a minute."

She waited more like ten, and when the screen went off hold, the face on the screen was the answering officer's. "Cushman's left the station already. I'll have the dispatcher tell him to call you."

She gave him her number and extension and punched off.

A shadow fell across her. She looked up at Morello. He held a stack of complaints. "Happy unbirthday. It's gift time."

She grimaced. "Take those away. I still have all these." She pointed to a stack on her table.

"You haven't cleared very many cases the past couple of days, have you?"

"This Kellener case is time-consuming."

His brows went up. "I thought it was pretty clearly a suicide."

She shuffled through some reports. "There's nothing very clear about it."

Morello regarded her speculatively. "You sure you're not letting Maxwell run away with the investigation?"

She was not at all sure, but she would sooner cut out her tongue than admit that to Morello. "I'm sure. I'm senior partner; I'm running it."

The phone buzzed. She stabbed the on button. "Crimes Against Persons, Sergeant Brill."

The screen brightened into the image of a stocky, freckle-faced man in civilian clothes but with the unmistakable look of leo about him. Jane, she thought.

"I'm Niall Cushman. The dispatcher said you wanted me to call you."

"Yes. Tuesday you made a stolen property query on a novalon suit, a Dyan Pennock doll, and an Eduvac Junior computer. Those items, or ones like them, are part of an investigation. May I ask why you made the query?"

"One of my neighbors asked me to." His forehead creased in concern. "What investigation?"

"The Kellener death. The items in your query turned up on a bank record. Tell me about this neighbor of yours."

"Her name is Clio de Garza." He spelled it out. "She's lived down the street from us for four or five years. We're casual friends. Her daughter and ours play together. Monday evening she came over looking very worried. She pretended nothing was wrong but after jibbing around for fifteen minutes or so she asked if there were a way she could find out whether or not something was stolen without attracting official attention and getting someone in trouble."

"Did she say why she wanted to know?"

"No." Cushman rubbed his nose. "But I can guess. Tuesday afternoon her daughter was over at our house when I came home from work. She had a brand new Dyan Pennock doll. There's a sligh who visits them every Sunday. Clio once told my wife he's Tesha's father. I'd say he brought her the doll on his last visit and Clio was afraid a toy that expensive must be stolen. She certainly seemed relieved when the computer didn't ID anything."

His guesswork sounded good to Janna. "Where can I reach this de Garza woman?"

"She's a teacher. I think she's teaching half days in the summer session at Highland Park High School and doing special tutoring the rest of the day." He paused. "Do you think her sligh friend is involved in this Kellener's death?"

Janna shrugged. "We're looking for leads and following them out. In case I can't find de Garza, what time does she usually get home?"

"About suppertime."

"Have you ever met the sligh?"

Cushman shook his head. "I've only seen him at a distance. I asked about meeting him once, because I was curious, but Clio said it was impossible. He's lion shy."

Janna thanked him for his help and punched off. She sat staring at the blank screen. De Garza taught half days in the high school summer session. The summer semester at Janna's high school in Wichita had run from seven o'clock to noon, letting out before the heat of the day made the building unbearable. Perhaps Shawnee County school officials did the same thing.

She punched the directory button and asked for the Highland Park High School number. It printed across the screen. She copied it down, returned the phone to the call mode, and put in the number.

"Ms. Clio de Garza," she said to the woman who answered.

The woman that request brought to the phone was a young and attractive Hispanic. "I'm Ms. de Garza. What may I do for you?"

Janna introduced herself. Something wary came into de Garza's eyes. The woman appeared a bit lion-shy herself.

"I'm calling in reference to the stolen property query you asked Officer Niall Cushman to make."

The wariness grew more pronounced. "Are those things stolen after all?"

"I don't know. I'm interested in the query because the bank record of an individual involved in a current investigation lists, among other items, the purchase of two novalon suits, and a Dyan Pennock doll and child's computer."

The Hispanic woman's face smoothed into the bland mask of rigid control. Her eyes betrayed fear, however. Janna considered how to proceed. She did not want to frighten the woman into silence.

"Please understand that I'm not accusing you of anything, nor am I trying to trap you, but I must ask why you were concerned about identical items."

"Coincidence, sergeant?" de Garza suggested.

"I doubt it. I'm aware your daughter has a new Dyan Pennock doll. Did your sligh friend bring it to her, and a child's computer, too?"

Her eyes narrowed. "I thought Niall was a friend."

"He had very little choice but to tell me, Ms. de Garza. Please, this is very important. Did the items come from your friend?"

Her hand moved as though wanting to stab the off button. It hovered near the edge of the screen for a long time, trembling, then slowly lowered. "Yes."

"What about the novalon suit?"

"He…was wearing one."

"Do you know how he happened to come by these things?"

She pressed her fingers to her forehead, rubbing at the creases between her eyes. "He said a friend bought them for him in return for a favor."

"You didn't believe him?"

De Garza straightened. "Of course I believed him. We have complete trust in one another. We never lie to each other."

"Yet you asked Officer Cushman to see if they were stolen."

"Because—" She sighed. "The other person could have been lying to my friend. I've seen suits like that in shop windows. I know how much they cost. The toys are expensive, as well. I couldn't believe someone would give them away."

"It might depend on the kind of favor your friend did. Do you happen to know what it was?"

De Garza looked away. Her fingers went to her mouth, then her forehead, rubbing at the skin between her eyes. She looked several shades paler.

"Ms. de Garza?" Janna prompted gently.

She continued to look away. "He—" Her hand went back to her mouth. She spoke through the bars her fingers made across her lips. "All he would tell me was that it was something illegal."

An electric shock trickled up Janna's spine. "Do you know who he did the favor for?"

"He wouldn't say."

From here on the questioning became harder—much harder. "Ms. de Garza." Janna waited until the woman looked at her again before going on. "I'll have to see your friend and talk to him."

"Oh, no." Her body swayed backward. "He won't let you anywhere near him."

"I have to talk to him. Surely you can see that. If he won't agree to an informal meeting, we'll have to bring him in. You say the two of you trust each other completely. If you arrange a meeting and come to it with me, if you assure him that I'm less interested in him than in the man he did the favor for, do you think he might be willing to see me?"

"*Are* you more interested in the other man than in Ow—my friend?"

"Yes. My business is hunting wolves, not field mice. Tell your friend I need his help. Promise him that the three of us will be the only ones there."

The woman rubbed her forehead again. "I don't know. I can trust Niall Cushman because he's a neighbor, but…most of my experiences with the leos haven't been pleasant. I've been arrested six times for teaching in unlicensed schools."

Her special tutoring, no doubt. That was a break. If de Garza was a sligh sympathizer, it gave Janna a chance with her.

"I used to work the Oakland division. The slighs there knew me as a friendly lion. Ask some of them about me. Ask Quicksilver. Call me back at the Crimes Against Persons squad when you've decided you can trust me and have arranged a meeting with your friend."

De Garza thought it over. "If I don't call you back?"

"I still have to talk to your friend, one way or another."

The woman sighed. "I'll see what I can do."

As soon as the screen went dark, Janna went to tell Vradel what she had.

Vradel frowned. "I don't like the idea of your going out alone. If he panics, we have no way of knowing what he might do."

"I'll have my Starke and I can take some K-12 spray. I'll be wearing my ear button."

"All right." His grunt indicated consent against his better judgment. "Be careful. You get hurt and I'll break your arm."

"Yes, sir."

He looked past her. "Where's your shadow?"

"Out hunting the street dealer who sold Hazlett or Kellener or whoever the trick that killed Kellener."

The lieutenant grunted. "I know holding him back isn't easy. All right, that's all." He picked up papers.

Janna returned to her desk. A new stack of papers lay there. She sorted through quickly. They were all reports from Forensics and Pathology. Under the reports lay the sheet with the activity list the watchdog program had located. There were still two items to check out. She laid the reports aside to read later.

Item number one: the group of suits recovered in a raid were part of the goods found with a fence. She talked about it with an investigator in Crimes Against Property. The Stellar Fashions suits had all born the store mark of a Westridge Mall shop. She crossed that item off the list.

The suits found in Mr. Frederick Weltmann's D-F Kodiac were used clothing. They no longer had store marks in them. They were, however, items described in a burglary complaint made on July twentieth. Other items in the complaint—a newscanner, a microfiche viewer, and a holovision set—were also found in the Kodiac. Mr. Weltmann was currently being held in the county jail on a charge of receiving stolen property. The fact the suits were old enough for the store marks to have worn off disqualified them from Janna's interest. She crossed Mr. Weltmann's suits off her list, too.

Mama checked in just before noon and threw himself in a chair with a sigh of disgust. "I've found about half the dealers and none of them has ever seen Hazlett, or Kellener—except on the newscanner." He closed his eyes. "Maybe we can find the rest of them this afternoon."

"Maybe the computer has a better lead than street dealers."

Mama sat up and opened his eyes. He pushed his glasses up his nose. "What lead?"

She told him about de Garza and her sligh friend.

He rubbed his hands together in satisfaction. "When and where are we meeting the sligh?"

"She hasn't called back yet. *You* aren't going in any case."

He frowned.

"Don't pout, Mama. I made a promise."

He shrugged.

They spent the afternoon hunting street dealers while Janna listened to her ear button, waiting for de Garza's call. They found all but one of the dealers they wanted, for what good it did them. The dealers flatly denied selling either Kellener or Hazlett, or Liann Seaton, any trick. They did not recognize the names or pictures of any of Kellener's office staff. It was hot, sweaty, discouraging work. Janna was starting to feel dizzy from the fumes of alcohol and narcotics filling the bars where all of the dealers seemed to hang out.

Janna's ear button murmured, "Indian Thirty, call the station."

At last! Janna tapped the button. "Indian Thirty, roger." She dug a vending token out of a thigh pocket and headed for the nearest phone.

From the station, Pass-the-Word Morello said, "You had a call from a Ms. Clio de Garza. She wants you to call her right back at this number." He read it off.

"Thanks." She punched off and fed in another token. She punched the number Morello had given her.

De Garza answered on the first ring. The background behind her suggested she was using the public phone in a bar.

"Will your friend talk to me?" Janna asked.

"I can't find him. I'm in the place he works, but they say he hasn't been here for days. Sergeant, that worries me. Owan is a very dependable man. This is where he eats his meal every day. I'm about to go check his room."

The sligh was missing? That set off alarms in Janna, too. "Don't leave yet. Where are you? I'd like to talk to the people there."

"I'm at the Pioneer's Pleasure on East Seventh Street."

"I know where it is. Wait for me. I'll be right there."

She had Mama drive her back to the station to pick up her bicycle and a spray tube of K-12.

"Are you sure you don't want me along?" Mama asked as she shoved the K-12 in a thigh pocket.

"Two leos would look like an interrogation team. If I need you, I'll whistle." She pointed to her ear button.

She found de Garza waiting for her just inside the door of the Pioneer's Pleasure. "They say Owan hasn't been in since Monday."

Janna looked around. "Exactly who says?"

"Alyn, the bartender."

Janna headed for the bar. "Hello, Alyn. I'm a friend of Owan. May I ask you a few questions about him?"

Alyn looked her over. "Sure, leo. What do you want to know?"

Leo. Why did people always smell lion when she walked in the door, no matter what she wore? "When did you last see Owan?"

"Monday night, like I told the other woman. He was supposed to work until the club closed but he got someone to come in for him about nine thirty and he left. He said he'd be in at the usual time Tuesday but he never showed up. He ran the dishcleaning machine. The manager was pissed about having to find a substitute at the last minute, too, I'll tell you."

The sligh disappeared the day Kellener's body was discovered. Could there be a link? "Tell me, did he work Saturday night?" The answer to that might help establish if the sligh were somehow tied to the night Kellener died.

"No, he didn't work all day Saturday."

"Was it a regular day off?"

"Day off?" Alyn shook his head. "Owan almost never took a day off."

"Then it was unusual for him to be gone Saturday and leave early Monday?"

"Like snow in July."

Janna smelled lion meat. Somehow the sligh was involved in Kellener's death. He had been free the night Kellener died and he had items charged to Hazlett's bank account. He exhibited unusual behavior on two separate days, both days important in the case.

"Do you have any idea why he left early Monday night?"

The bartender shook his head. "He made a phone call late in the afternoon. After that he said he had to leave and would find someone to cover the last few hours for him."

"Do you know who he called?"

"No. It seemed to calm him down, though. He'd been spooky until then."

Spooky? "From the time he came to work?"

"Not that early. He was fine when he came in. The fool had a fancy new blue suit and went daydreaming around like he was in a world of his own. He didn't go nervy until I called him up to the bar to see that news story about the guy who died."

Her nerve endings buzzed. She kept her voice level. "Guy who died?"

"The colonial contractor who was found dead in his office. The news interviewed his partner. Strange thing; he looked like Owan's twin. I called Owan up to see. You'd have thought Owan saw a ghost, he went so pale. Everyone has a double somewhere, they say, but I suppose it can be a bit of a shock meeting yours."

Janna drew in a long breath. Christ. She felt de Garza looking at her. After thanking the bartender she hurried for the door.

De Garza followed. "What is it you think Owan's done? He's a gentle man. He'd never kill anyone. He told me that what he was involved in wasn't serious."

"I don't believe your friend killed anyone." He would not have panicked seeing Hazlett on the newscanner if he had been knowingly involved in the killing. "It looks now as if he may be involved in the fraudulent use of a Scib Card. Now we need to check out where he lives."

De Garza's face closed. "I don't want to get him in trouble."

Janna snapped, "Talking to him is the only way I can keep him *out* of trouble. I told you, I'm hunting a wolf, not field mice."

As much as it pained her to admit it, it looked more and more as if that lunatic Mama was right. She wanted to establish a definite connection between Hazlett and Owan before she laid this in front of Vradel and the rest of the squad, though.

"I didn't get the reputation of being a friendly lion by strapping slighs."

De Garza debated, her face in a tense grimace. Finally: "All right. I'll take you there."

She drove her runabout and Janna followed by bicycle to a seedy apartment complex on the southern edge of the Oakland area. De Garza showed her to a room in a corner of the basement in the main building. There was no reply to their knock.

"He may not be here. I didn't see his bike outside."

Janna looked around the building until she found the manager. "Do you know where Owan is?"

The manager had no idea. "I haven't seen him since Monday. I'm about ready to rent his room to someone else. If he won't do the chores, he hasn't earned the space."

Another kind-hearted benefactor of slithyfolk. Janna kept her face expressionless. "Do you have a key to his room?"

She did. After some persuasion and a look at Janna's badge, she gave it to them. "What kind of trouble is he in?"

"No trouble," Janna said. She refused to give the manager an excuse to throw the sligh out. "We think he's the missing heir to the fortune of a western Kansas land baron. We're looking for proof of it."

They left the manager staring wide-eyed after them.

Janna unlocked the door. The room was small, little more than a cell, with only one window high in the wall, and a bed, desk, and dresser that would have been spurned in a prison.

De Garza looked around, shuddering. "I don't know why he couldn't bring himself to be idented. Imagine living like this all your life."

Janna preferred not to imagine it. She opened the closet. It held only three suits. Two were what she expected in a sligh's closet, a worn pioneer style shirt and trousers and a near-new but cheaply made jumpsuit. The third suit was a novalon jumpsuit glowing in yellow glory.

"That's what he wore Sunday."

The bartender at the Pioneer's Pleasure said Owan had worn a blue suit Monday. Hazlett's purchase record showed two suits of identical price. One yellow and one blue, perhaps?

She riffled through the desk. There was nothing in it but paper and writing instruments. The wastebasket, however, had a thick layer of small paper scraps in the bottom. Janna picked out several larger pieces. Both sides of each bore writing, but no more than one or two letters each, too little to tell what had been written. One piece had a clear *ge*. On another was *zl*.

"Is it all right for you to do this without a search warrant?" de Garza asked.

"Technically, it's trespassing. Owan can raise hell if he catches us here." She dropped the pieces of paper back in the wastebasket. "But I'm not acting as a police officer," she said righteously. "I'm a concerned friend."

She opened the top drawer of the dresser. Lying on the few pair of socks inside were an envelope of the type sold by the hundreds, a small plastic tube of glue, a white card signed with Jorge Hazlett's signature, and a 2-D photograph of Hazlett, looking surprised.

"That looks almost like Owan, except Owan's hair used to be longer and tied back. Now his hair looks like that," de Garza said.

Janna returned the photograph to the drawer. Ask and ye shall receive. She had her connection between the two men. It was enough, anyway, to take to Vradel. She drew a long, slow breath and closed the drawer. "Let's go."

After locking the room she returned the key to the manager. She could see the avid questions in the woman's eyes but only gave her a card. "Call me when Owan comes back, please."

If he came back. He could have been encouraged to take a long vacation out of town.

"I'd like you to call me, too, if you see him, Ms. de Garza," she said as they left the building.

De Garza sighed. "I feel guilty about this. I hope I've done the right thing."

Without her Janna might never have discovered the possible bank record deception. "You've done the right thing." She watched de Garza climb into her runabout. "You said Owan has a bicycle. Will you describe it for me? What make and year is it?"

"No make or year. He built it himself out of Gitane and Antonioni parts, I think. He used to work at a bicycle shop. It's a ten-speed with dropped handlebars, painted gray and black. Owan said they were good colors for a sligh."

"It isn't registered and licensed, I suppose."

"Yes, as a matter of fact, it is...to me, but I don't remember the number."

"I can look it up. Thank you."

Janna let her go and swung onto her own bicycle, but rather than go back to the station, she rode north to Seward Street, to the Oakland division police station.

11

It was like dropping three years out of her life. Stepping off her bicycle in front of the old Sacred Heart School, Janna felt as if she had never been away. Like calling the division station the Sacred Heart School. Even that came back like reflex. The concrete plaque on the front of the building had said *Oakland Division Police Station* for over fifty years but everyone in the division, leos and residents alike, still called it by its former name. The old building, bricks turned from red to black by time and grime, clung to its identity so tenaciously, it even affected the local slang. Around Oakland, going to the station or bringing someone in was "going to school."

She climbed the concrete steps worn to a sag in the middle by generations of children's and leo's feet. Her own feet remembered every step. She walked in past empty wall niches and thought, once more, of the irony of a bankrupt church school sold for taxes becoming a police station. Its convent, perhaps less ironically, was now the cell block.

It was not like losing the years, she decided after all; it was more like coming home. Sergeant Paul Davila was still the day desk officer. An old warmth woke in her at the sight of him.

"Hello, Paolo."

His head snapped up from his paperwork. His dark eyes lighted. "Welcome back, *chiquita*. Are you homesick for the war zone or just come slumming to wave your Investigator II promotion around?"

"Perhaps I came to see you."

He shook his head. "Don't tease, *querida*. The Phoenix is a mythical bird."

"Sorry. I need a man picked up."

He handed her a form and tilted his head around so he could read while she wrote. "A sligh? That'll make it harder. What's the charge?"

"He's a witness in a homicide case. Make this an APB, will you, and stress that I need him just as fast as possible? I know the watch doesn't have anything else to do."

Paul grinned. "We appreciate your efforts to keep us from being bored. Anything else I can do for you?"

His tone remained light, casual, but something serious touched his eyes. They looked squarely at each other, and for a moment Janna felt that in the midst of the people streaming around them and the incessant buzzing of telephones, they were alone. Wistful regret lay between them, and ghosts of might-have-beens. *Have you changed?* she wanted to ask, *or do you still insist the only proper relationship is in a sacramental marriage?*

Then someone at the far end of the desk called, "Davila," and Paul turned to reply to the officer's request. The moment disappeared. When he came back to her, she said, "I could use a phone with privacy."

"The lieutenant's out at the moment. Use his office."

She stepped around the corner to what had probably been one of the school administration offices long ago. She punched the Crimes Against Persons number into the phone. Maro Desch answered.

"Let me speak to Vradel," Janna said.

"I'll get him."

Lieutenant Vradel came on the screen with raised brows. "What have you found?"

As concisely as possible, she told him about her conversation with the bartender in the Pioneer's Pleasure and what she discovered in Owan's room. Vradel listened in silence, but as she talked, his face became granite and he started chewing his mustache. When she finished, he sat a minute, mustache twitching, before he spoke. "Have you put out a pick-up order on this sligh?"

"Yes, sir."

"Where are you now?"

"The Sacred—the Oakland division station. I thought I'd visit some of the sligh hangouts I know and talk to a few old friends. They may be able to find Owan faster than our people."

"*If* they will." He sighed. "I'd better call Kolb and have him postpone the inquest. Why are you grimacing, Brill?"

"Sir, if we do that, it may alert Hazlett. Right now he must think his alibi is perfect. He'll be relaxed."

"Until we talk to the sligh, we'd better consider his alibi as perfect, too." Vradel chewed one end of his mustache. "You're right about making him suspicious, but we can't very well let the inquest go ahead and risk having the jury return a verdict of suicide."

Janna thought hard. What could delay an inquest that would not alarm Hazlett? A witness not able to be there was one possibility, but none so far were vital enough to delay the inquest for. "Lieutenant, what if we had a street dealer who said he'd sold someone in the firm some trick? We could ask for a delay while we checked out his story."

"You don't think that will alarm Hazlett?"

"It might cause him anxiety, but it won't seem that we're after him specifically. There's always the bank record to protect him."

"All right. We'll handle it that way. Good luck hunting the sligh." He paused a moment. "What I said about being careful goes double now."

She smiled. "Yes, sir. Thank you,"

She punched off and sat for several minutes mentally reviewing the sligh hangouts she remembered, planning her route. She hoped they were still there. Like jobs and living quarters, recreation locations were ephemeral things in slithyland. Three years was a long time.

She went back to the desk. "Thanks for the use of the phone."

He nodded. "I suppose you're going to rush off now. Stay long enough for a cup of caff, why don't you?"

"So we can stir the ashes? I thought you don't believe in the Phoenix."

"I believe in friendship. Let me buy you dinner some night."

"That would be nice." She blew him a kiss as she left.

She came down the steps in long bounds and swung onto her bike. One place she felt sure had not changed was the Buenas Noches just down the street on the edge of Oakland's shopping district. It had been a favorite local bar for three generations and would probably still be serving on doomsday. The Santos family owned it. Jesus Santos, grandson of the original buyer, ran it now. Jesus ran it clean, with some gambling tables and a few girls and boys upstairs, all properly licensed and all closed for business by three A.M. Jesus deviated only in that he took barter, not just bankcredit. That way even locals on government food and housing coupons could entertain themselves. Slighs could, too.

She rode down the street, steering between the potholes and trash. From the outside, neither the faded lettering on the windows nor the begrimed, fly specked windows of the bar seemed to have changed since she used to patrol past here. Stepping inside, she found the place had not changed, either. The wall-mounted phone near the door still had a smashed screen. The floor was still thick with peanut shells. Narcotic haze hung heavy and blue in the dimly-lighted air. A holo player cast a weak image of a jivaqueme band at the far end, playing their music on the lower threshold of perception.

The music was current, though, she noticed. It grabbed her by her biorhythms. Its flutes sang in her blood and the beat pulled her pulse into time with it. It made her want to move into the middle of the floor with the two or three people already there and dance until she folded.

Two men in earnest head-to-head conversation at a table near the door looked up as she came in. They both stiffened, then leaned back casually and pretended to listen to the music. Janna recognized them for street dealers. She knew they recognized her, too, from the time she had worked Vice.

"Still cutting your junk with rat poison, Hilding?" she asked as she passed them.

The street dealer sneered, but as soon as she was past, stood and scuttled out. She hoped she had spoiled a transaction.

Jesus' sister Dolores was tending bar. Janna ordered iced tea and turned around so she could lean her back to the bar while she looked around. The bar was almost empty. Most of the patrons would not begin coming in until after six.

Dolores brought her tea. She paid for it and carried it to a table with a good view of the door. For the next two hours she sat sipping and listening to the music of the player. Gradually the room started to fill. Some of the faces she knew. They returned her gaze with a smile or a sneer. She heard a couple of *miaows* after people had passed and were behind her.

One man called, "Hey, puss."

She ignored the taunt and let her eyes slide past the citizens; she needed slighs. The several who came in all sat at the far back. As she expected, most were strangers. Three had been friends, though. One, Quicksilver, looked sallow and thin as ever. Quicksilver was something of a hero among slighs. He had run a school for fifteen years and never once had it raided.

She caught his eye and beckoned. He unfolded from his chair and made his way toward her, shuffle-walking in time to the music. She was pleased to note he did not hurry. Most slighs came to a leo in cringing-dog eagerness, if they had to come, in order not to take the chance of irritating the lion.

Quicksilver nodded. "Buenas noches. I was talking to someone about you just today, a Ms. Clio de Garza." He paused. "I gave you a recommendation."

"I appreciate it. Q, I'm calling in favors tonight."

His brows went up. "I owe for the warnings you passed on school raids. You hunting?"

"Not really. One of your people is a witness I need. His name is Owan. Late forties, a hundred seventy-five centimeters, medium build, brown hair graying at the temples, worn tied back or in a lion's mane, brown eyes. He may be wearing a blue jumpsuit of novalon."

Quicksilver pursed his lips. "Fine seams. It's a big favor, hunting one of my own, leo."

"I don't want to strap him, just talk to him. Have I ever lied to you before?" She made her voice velvet.

The sligh's smile was thin. "Not that I ever learned. All right. I'll take you around. Most of the places have changed since you moved downtown."

She nodded.

"Let me tell my friends over there that I'm going. I don't want them to worry about me."

Janna went on outside. Her head was spinning from the narcotic smoke and her body pulsed to the jivaqueme rhythm. She leaned against a wall, breathing slowly, waiting for the reverberations in her bones to fade.

Quicksilver came out of the Buenas Noches. He eyed her. "The people who know you aren't going to run away, but there are new people who will take one look and fade into the woodwork. Is there something you can do to make yourself look less like a lion?"

"I don't want anyone to think I'm trying to fool them. I have nothing to hide. I just want to talk to a witness."

"All right. We'll go as you are."

Quicksilver had no bicycle. Janna walked beside him, pushing hers. They passed a 24-hour market.

"You don't sit around in the back of that place anymore?"

He shook his head. "There's a new owner who *no es simpático*."

They continued walking. On down Seward he went around the back of a little cafe and rapped on the rear door. A woman opened it and looked out.

She stared hard at Janna. "A friend of yours?"

When Quicksilver vouched for Janna, the woman let them in. They found themselves in the cafe's smoky little kitchen. It had no dishcleaning machine, just a sink. A man she remembered vaguely was up to his elbows in water and suds. Around a table near the sink sat half a dozen more slighs, playing cards and talking to the dishwasher. Conversation stopped with the suddenness of a cut throat as Janna and Quicksilver walked in. Everyone stared at Janna.

"Davo," Quicksilver said to the dishwasher, "you remember Sergeant Brill. She caught your kid snatching in the Tiggy store and let him go with a warning."

The dishwasher nodded. Some of the wariness faded from his eyes. "What can I do for you, sergeant?"

"Forget rank; I'm off duty."

"One of our people is a witness she needs. She promises no trouble for him; she just wants to talk to him. He's named Owan." He gave them Owan's description. "Anyone know him?"

The entire group shook their heads. "Never heard of a sligh like that. Where would one of us get a novalon suit?"

"Pay for a job," Janna said.

"No one gives slighs that kind of job."

Across the table from the woman who spoke, a man stiffened. His eyes fixed hard on his cards. "Are we playing or talking?" He spun a square of plastic into the middle of the table.

Quicksilver moved toward the door. "Let's go."

Outside, Janna looked back toward the door and sighed. "I don't know that they would have told me if they *had* seen Owan."

"You've been away a long time, slithytime, leo."

"You're sure *you've* never heard of Owan?"

Quicksilver shook his head. "I know his girlfriend from her teaching. That's all. We aren't an organized underground. You ought to know that. Organizations eventually attract official notice and we like to avoid being seen. We're mostly little islands unto ourselves, clumping together when we find other friendly islands, then drifting off alone again. Come on, there are other people to see."

The islands clumped in the kitchens of cafes, in the dimmer recesses of a few bars, and on the grass of parks. There were children in the groupings in parks. They played, running and shouting, while their parents listened to Quicksilver ask about Owan. Say what he would about slighs drifting alone, most of them knew and respected the sallow Quicksilver. It was one of the reasons Janna had cultivated him when she worked down here. The other slighs talked to him even when it was obvious they did not care to say anything in Janna's presence.

As she had times meeting slighs before, Janna noticed that eating was not part of sligh social contacts as it was in the rest of society. They talked, they sang, they complained or argued; but they never ate together. People living on the bare subsistence level did not have food enough to use it socially. Even the bar groups were few, and fewer of them were drinking anything but water. There was more likely to be food in the cafes, where the "host" sligh could feel free to offer something belonging to the boss.

They found a few slighs who knew Owan. "He's a quiet, hard-working man. What do you want him for, leo?" was the usual reaction.

Her insistence that she only wanted to talk to him, that he was a witness, they received skeptically. Even the people who knew Owan had not seen him recently, not since Thursday or Friday.

After stopping in the parks, Quicksilver started on rounds of homes. He would not let Janna come in with him, but insisted on going in alone at each stop. "They'd never forgive me if I brought you in."

Homes were too personal to show to even a friendly lion. Janna had been in a few slighs' houses before, though. They made Owan's room look palatial. Most squatted in empty houses, with virtually no furniture, usually with no electricity or running water. Janna could not understand how they preferred that abject poverty to having their names and life facts recorded in a few computers. It was insane.

At one stop Janna could hear the people inside arguing hotly. Whether they should keep on trying to be invisible or fight the *de facto* illegality imposed on them.

Then the voices quieted. Quicksilver appeared at the door and beckoned to Janna. She went down the steps into the dim, candlelit basement. The room was as bare as she expected, but it was pleasantly cool. The debaters huddled in one corner. The sligh Quicksilver wanted her to see sat in a basket chair, a thin man, bent and twisted into crippled immobility, most likely by a childhood disease like poliomyelitis that a citizen's child would have been immunized against. He had eyes like bruised circles.

"I saw Owan Friday evening. He came by for a few minutes after he finished work. He was excited and nervous about something."

Janna said, "Did he say anything about where he was going or what he was going to be doing?"

"No. He'd only say that the thing he was going to do would earn him enough to start saving for a share."

Janna did not need to ask what share. If slighs had another favorite topic besides how unfair the government was, it was talking about the imagined paradise of a colony world. The dream of almost every sligh she knew was to somehow, miraculously, come into enough property to trade in for a colonial share.

Janna asked a few more questions, but the bruise-eyed man had no answers for them. She left.

None of the calls they made after that provided any more information. Finally Quicksilver said, "Everyone will be going to bed soon. We all have to work tomorrow, and most of us have to start early. I'll keep asking, and if I hear something, I'll let you know."

He began fading into the shadows of the street even as she thanked him.

Janna swung on her bike and started pedaling for home. She was disappointed not to have found Owan, but not surprised. If Owan had put things together after hearing about Hazlett's partner, and if he'd panicked, he was hardly likely to be walking around socializing. The abandoned houses and stores all over the Oakland area afforded countless hiding places, if Owan were still in town. It would take a while to check them all.

She found a working public phone and called the squadroom. No messages had come in for her from either Owan's landlady or Clio de Garza. She was about to remount her bike when a watchcar drifted to a stop and hovered beside her.

"Let's see your card, bibi."

The voice was a familiar one. She turned, grinning, to face Rina Hallard and Moses Kobuzky. "So you two are still on the street together. I'd have thought that by this time the brass would realize they need at least one officer in a team who can see out over the dash of the car."

Hallard and Kobuzky were the two shortest leos in the division.

Hallard regarded her coldly. "Your wit hasn't improved a bit being downtown. For your information, they've issued us toddler seats, so both of us can see out of the car now."

"Have either of you seen the sligh I issued the APB for?"

They shook their heads. "No."

"Give us something easy, like a needle in a hay-stack."

"You can ride with us and help search derelict houses if you like."

Janna eyed the rear compartment. "Not unless you let me ride in front, too."

"I don't know what your objection is. Only two winos have thrown up in it tonight," Hallard said.

"Three," Kobuzky corrected.

"One wasn't a wino, just a ulysses."

"Details, details."

The air from the fans felt hot against Janna's ankles. She moved the bike away from the watchcar. "What street did you have in mind?"

"How about a few blocks of Jacquot? There can't be more than forty empties along there."

Those crumbling houses, at night, in this heat? They were probably joking. She was not about to bite on one of their stunts. "I'll pass. I think I'll go home. I've given the company more than its share of my time today."

She did turn the bike down Jacquot on her way, though. She peered at the houses in passing, when she could spare attention from steering around holes and weeds. Some of them would make good hiding places. For that matter, so would the houses along a dozen other streets.

She passed a boarded-up corner building that had once been a 24-hour shopper when she worked the area. So that place was gone now, too. Had the owner, a friendly man who always had free tea and caff for leos, made enough to buy the colonial company share he was always talking about—or had he been robbed so often he just gave up and closed?

Everyone wanted to go out to a colony, it seemed. Only some of them could ever manage the price. She sighed. She was being given the chance to buy a share. She could leave this jungle any time she wanted. She would even have friends waiting for her when she arrived on the new world. Might she be smart to grab the opportunity?

She must decide just as soon as this case wrapped up. This case. What a headache. She rode home thinking about it. It bothered her that not only had no one admitted to seeing Owan since Saturday, no one appeared to be lying when they said they had not seen him. No one she had talked to seemed to be helping hide him. He might have left town, of course. On the other hand, something worse might have happened. A man who would kill once could certainly kill again.

Janna sucked her lower lip. She hoped they found Owan soon, and found him in good health.

12

Janna appeared in the squadroom early to write up her reports on the evening's work before rollcall. As she talked into the dictyper's mike, the machine's laser mechanism silently printed her words onto the report form.

Mama banged in as she was finishing. "There's a notice on the M.E.'s hearing room. Kellener's inquest has been postponed pending new evidence."

Janna picked the report out of the dictyper's tray. "That's right."

"What new evidence? What have I missed?"

"Nothing. We're just buying time by telling people we have the dealer who sold the trick used."

His eyes lighted behind his glasses. "Buying time? Then there really is new evidence. What did that sligh tell you yesterday?"

"I didn't see him." She handed her reports to Morello.

He handed her another in return. "This just came in."

She glanced through it. It was from Agent Talous, the handwriting analysis on the signatures. The discussion of slant, loops, and stroke pressure would take close reading to decode what the report actually said. She dropped the report on her desk to read later.

The room was filling with the day watch. The investigators lounged in the chairs, yawning and exchanging friendly insults. Some held cups of caff and tea. Vradel walked in as the wall chrono read: 8:00. Conversation and the scraping of chairs died away.

Vradel nodded at them. "Good morning, leos."

"Roar," someone in the back said.

Vradel studied the notes in his hands. "It was a night of fun and games, as usual. You may all take a moment to mourn the passing of that illustrious fence Jet Horlas."

There was light applause.

"Some unhappy supplier or customer helped Jet beat the heat by ventilating him with a knife. Too bad we can't award a medal."

The list went on. It was long. It always was in extended periods of hot weather. Janna took notes, but scarcely paid attention to what she heard or wrote. Her mind was busy trying to think of places a sligh might hide, or something that might flush him out. Surely a sligh in a novalon suit would be a combination easy to notice. There was the possibility, of course, that in the suit, Owan no longer looked like a sligh.

"Here's a beauty," Vradel said. "Last night three pedestrians had legs broken just below the knees where they were struck by the airfoil skirt of a late-model red Hitachi Bonsai. The runabout was reportedly driven by a Caucasian female. She didn't stop, of course. In fact, she missed the third victim on her first try and had to come back for a second run at him. Let's find this bibi.

"The weather report for today is continued hot with temperatures in the mid to upper thirties. There's a chance of cooling and showers tonight. Keep your fingers crossed. All right, let's sail."

Morello said, "Call for you, lieutenant."

"I'll take it in my office. Brill and Maxwell, I want you in my office too."

Janna and Mama followed him and closed the door behind them.

Liann Seaton's face appeared on the phone screen. "Someone from the medical examiner's office called me just now and said Andy's inquest has been postponed. Something about new evidence. Will this help prove my husband didn't kill himself?"

Vradel did not look directly at the screen. "We don't know, ma'am."

"Well, I feel confident that this new witness or evidence will not only show Andy didn't kill himself, but clear him of the charge he was responsible for these poor people on the *Invictus*. Thank you, lieutenant." The screen went blank.

Mama sighed. "I envy that Kellener. None of my wives ever had that kind of faith in me."

Vradel glanced up at him. "They didn't? Strange. Don't start rearranging my desk, Maxwell!"

Mama jerked back the hand reaching for an untidy stack of papers on one corner.

Vradel looked at Janna. "Have you told him about the sligh?"

The phone buzzed. A moment later Morello stuck his head into the office. "It's for Brill."

She punched on. Jorge Hazlett appeared on the screen. "The medical examiner's office called, sergeant. It is true the inquest has been postponed?"

Janna kept her face expressionless. "Yes, Mr. Hazlett. We have a witness who may be able to help us locate the source of the trick that killed your partner."

Jorge felt a hot-cold wash of excitement and fear. Had Serena suddenly remembered the drug he took away from her? Had she told someone else? The game was becoming more serious—more serious and consequently more worth playing. That she-lion was so careful to keep a neutal expression it must mean she thought they had something important. Still, whatever they had, it should not be able to implicate him. He had his bank record alibi.

"I'm glad to hear that, sergeant. Good luck with the witness." He could not keep the mocking note out of his voice. He wondered if she noticed it.

Janna noticed. She punched off with a stab of her finger and scowled at the blank screen. "That bastard is laughing at us, lieutenant."

Mama stiffened. His head snapped toward her. He pushed his glasses up his nose. "Hey, bibi, does this mean—"

"It means," Vradel said, "that we're exploring the *possibility* that Hazlett somehow used the bank records to build himself an alibi. If you let loose that whoop I see in your eyes, Maxwell, I'll suspend you!"

Mama dropped into a chair and sat with fingers laced tightly together. "So you realize I'm right."

Vradel's eyes glinted icily. "We have evidence to that effect now, yes. Note that, Maxwell...*evidence*." He told Mama what they had.

Mama's mouth kept opening, as if he had comments, but Vradel gave him no chance to speak. "Just listen, Maxwell. You had an inspiration, or made a lucky guess. It wouldn't mean a thing without facts to support it. We have some facts now. Unfortunately we need more." He picked up his pencil and started sketching on his memo pad. "I want to know how Hazlett found himself a double. If he did it, so can others. Think what that will do to the reliability of bank records as evidence of whereabouts."

Janna had a worse thought. What if others already had? There was no way ever to find out. It made her feel dizzy and insecure. "Maybe the two of them have known each other for years."

"We can always hope. If they have, some of Hazlett's other friends must be aware of it. Talk to them."

"Except," Mama said, "that Hazlett's a chess player. He thinks a long way ahead. If he thought he might use the sligh this way some day, he would probably have kept the acquaintance a secret."

Vradel frowned. "Can't you contain that imagination for a while? In any case, if what that sligh in Oakland had to say about Owan's behavior Friday is correct, Hazlett set everything up then. Check out his calls for that day. Find out where he went and who he saw." He stopped sketching and toyed with the pencil. "This scares the hell out of me. Investigation can be hard enough without having one of our best information sources taken away from us. So until this is settled, until we know for certain whether Hazlett did or did not use a double—and how he managed it—I'm taking you off all other casework. Live, eat, and sleep with this. Bring me back irrefutable evidence. Pretend I'm the D. A. and make me a case that will look so good in court, I'll be sure to be reelected in November." He laid down the pencil and picked up some papers.

It was obviously a dismissal. Janna and Mama filed out. It gave her great satisfaction to pick up the complaint sheets from her desk and return them to Pass-the-Word Morello. Then the two of them headed down to the garage.

"We don't need it for court, but it would be nice to establish a good motive for killing Kellener," Janna said.

"We have one, bibi. Hazlett killed him to put the blame for the *Invictus* and the other frauds on him."

"You're forgetting the papers weren't signed by Hazlett."

"Hazlett could have forged them so they'd look like Kellener did it."

She stopped to stare at him. "Forged his own signature to look like someone else forged his? That's pretty convoluted. One time I might be able to believe, but those records go back almost twenty years."

"I told you chess players think a long way ahead. I think complexity ought to be expected, too."

She snorted and walked on. "We'll see what the handwriting analysis has to say about the signatures. This is real life, not a holo-v program."

"All right, we'll just see what the handwriting experts have to say, but wouldn't you think that in twenty years, Kellener would have learned to forge his partner's signature better?"

They had almost reached the garage when she remembered that the handwriting analysis lay on their desk right now. She would have to be sure to read it when they returned.

The Sunflower Federal building was the first stop.

Riding up in the elevator, Mama said, "Let's have a chat with Hazlett. Let's ask him what he's done with everything he bought Saturday night, and see what he says."

Janna sighed. "Let's not. I'd still like to avoid making him aware his alibi isn't as secure as he thinks."

"He's going to wonder when that prettyboy receptionist of his tells him we wanted to know all the calls and visits he made on Friday."

She sucked her lower lip. Mama did have a point. The solution occured to her as they walked into the reception room.

She asked the receptionist for all *Kellener's* calls between Wednesday and Saturday.

She had no chance to warn Mama ahead of time, but if her request startled him, he hid it well. He added, "If he left the office during working hours, we'd like to know where he went, too."

"I have the phone log, but you'll have to ask Mr. Peddicord about meetings."

The receptionist pulled the log book from under his desk and opened it to the printout of the previous week's calls. The outgoing calls did not differentiate between callers, simply listed every number called. Janna wrote down the numbers for Friday. Then she had a thought. The news about the *Invictus* came Wednesday. She wrote down Wednesday's and Thursday's numbers, too. The incoming calls were differentiated so she could list only those coming in to Hazlett.

"Robert, close that book," a crisp voice said.

Janna quickly copied down the last number before the log snapped shut, then looked around at the thin secretary. "Good morning, Mr. Peddicord."

"You will be good enough to obtain a warrant before trying to look at any more of our records. You won't find us willingly helping you and that government agent make Mr. Kellener into a villain."

Mama pushed his glasses up his nose. "Hey, jon, we're not trying to make anyone a villain; we're just gathering evidence."

Peddicord switched his icy stare to Mama. "Is that so? Agent Talous made his position quite clear. He's passed judgment and all he wants is enough evidence to convince a hearing committee of his opinion."

"Well, we aren't Department of Justice agents and we aren't working for—"

Janna stepped between them. "We're doing our best to be impartial, Mr. Peddicord. It might help if we were to know all Mr. Kellener's movements the four days before he died."

"I've had to tell Agent Talous. Ask him." He swung on his toe and marched out of the reception room. They heard his door shut firmly.

The receptionist smiled in apology. "Mr. Peddicord worshipped Mr. Kellener."

Janna nodded. Several people had, apparently. "What about Mr. Hazlett's meetings on Friday? May we speak to his secretary?"

"Ms. Abram isn't here today, but I can tell you that Mr. Hazlett had just two meetings on Friday, both with clients."

"Did he leave the office at any time during the day?"

"Yes, once for lunch and once about two o'clock."

"Was he gone long?"

"About forty-five minutes, I think. He came back in plenty of time for his three o'clock appointment."

"Do you have any idea where he went?"

"He walked some clients to the elevator. They kept him there answering more questions." The receptionist smiled. "He acted out the more comical parts for us when he got back. He's a very good mimic, you know."

Janna thanked him and they went back to the car.

"He could have been setting up Saturday with the sligh in that fourty-five minutes," Mama said. "He could have just said he was talking to the clients when he was actually using the public phones downstairs to call the Pioneer's Pleasure."

That was a distinct possibility. They needed to ask the Pioneer's Pleasure's bartender if Owan had taken a call Friday afternoon. "Will you do me a favor, Mama? After this, if you can't say something polite, act strong and silent. You didn't help the department's public relations any by that scene with Peddicord."

"Am I supposed to let him be abusive? You'd think Kellener was a saint we're accusing of being in league with the devil."

Who was to say Andrew Kellener might not be as close as mortals came to sainthood? There were a few genuinely fine people in the world. Not everyone was a deek or a toad, though it did seem that the few nice people she met were always victims of the normal representatives of society. Wim and Kellener had been victimized by the deeks, and though she knew little about the sligh Owan, from his girlfriend's regard for him, Janna thought he was probably another nice jon used destructively. Thinking about the class of people she usually saw, she could understand why Wim wanted to go off to a new world. Maybe the good people would be in the majority in the colonies.

They headed back for the squadroom. There they divided the phone log between them, and started making calls.

"This is Sergeant Janna Brill of the Shawnee County Police. You received a call from Hazlett and Kellener, Colonial Contractors, on Wednesday, July twenty-seventh. May I inquire the nature of that call, please?"

She repeated the message over and over, varying only the day of the call. Usually she received a prompt reply. The call was to arrange for colonial supplies, or to set up medical examinations for colonists traveling in the sleeper sections of their ship. One call Wednesday went to a club where Hazlett made dinner reservations for two on Friday evening.

"Did you see Mr. Hazlett when he came in that evening?"

"No, but the book is marked *reservation used.*"

"Would there be any way to learn who his companion was?"

"I suggest you ask Mr. Hazlett, sergeant."

If Hazlett had come in with a double, some word of it would have spread around. She really doubted Hazlett would have allowed himself to be seen in public with a double, but the question had been worth trying.

The newscanner murmured a public service announcement, urging citizens to buy drugs only from licensed drug stores. "Street drugs are cheaper, but they are not government-inspected. They can be contaminated or below quality."

Janna called the next number. A handsome afroam woman answered. "Lambeth Rentals."

Janna introduced herself. She asked her question.

The woman replied, "I didn't get a call from Hazlett and Kellener as such. Jorgie called me, though."

"May I ask why? This may be relevant to an investigation we're conducting."

"Into why his partner died? I don't think this has anything to do with that. Jorgie and I are friends. It was just a social call."

"Your name, please?"

"Colla Hayden."

"What did you talk about, Ms. Hayden?"

Hayden looked surprised. "On a social call? Nothing in particular. We traded sexual innuendoes and chatted about some of my past parties."

He had called her up at work in the middle of the day just for that? Alarms rang in Janna's head. "He didn't have a reason for calling you?"

"No." She frowned. "Is there something wrong with that?"

Yes, Janna thought. As Mama would no doubt have expressed it: it smelled wrong. "No, I suppose not. Does he often call like that?"

"Not often." Hayden's reply was short.

Janna tried to think of a question whose answer might explain the incongruity. Her mind was blank. She thanked Hayden and punched off before the woman's irritation could become hostility.

The next number was a furniture store. The person answering could not recall having talked to Hazlett or Kellener, nor could anyone else around the store at that moment. The number after that also reached a furniture store, and they did not remember Hazlett or Kellener, either.

After the sixth furniture store Janna wondered what was going on. Which of the partners had made these particular calls and why? This puzzle did not quite replace the question of why Hazlett made a purely social call in the middle of the day, but it pushed it down to a deeper stream of thought.

"Are you getting a lot of furniture stores, Mama?"

He nodded. "Looks like whoever it was, was calling every one in the city. I've also reached one interior decorator. Do you suppose some colonial company wanted its crew quarters decorated in Victorian Revival or Fifties Depression?" Janna rolled her eyes. "I wouldn't put it past them."

Her next number was answered by a pouting beauty of a woman with chestnut hair and sapphire eyes. "Many Mansions, Marca Laclede speaking."

The woman looked familiar. Halfway through the conversation, Janna placed her. Laclede was the buff who had been in Tuck's place Friday with the sligh jon.

"Hazlett and Kellener?" Laclede said. She looked thoughtful. "Yes, we had a call from them. Rather, I talked to a Mr. Jorge Hazlett."

At last! "What about, please?"

"We're interior decorators. Mr. Hazlett wanted a chair to match one he has in his study at home."

Disappointment stabbed Janna. That would explain all the calls to furniture stores. "Did you find it for him?"

"Oh, yes. There was no trouble at all. I had it by Friday."

Janna held back a sigh. So much for that call. She thanked the decorator.

Laclede smiled. "Any time, sergeant."

Mama craned his neck to see her screen as she punched off. "From the sound of the voice, I wish I'd gotten that one."

"I had the impression she would have adored helping a he-lion," Janna said dryly. "All of which is interesting but no help regarding Kellener's murder. Do you have anything?"

"Nothing."

The phone buzzed. Janna punched it on.

Clio de Garza appeared on the screen, looking upset. "Look what came in the mail today." She held an official-looking letter in front of the screen. Janna could read nothing of it but the Traffic Division letterhead. "It says I illegally parked a bicycle in the Sunco lot at Thirteenth and Jackson. The bicycle has been impounded and if I want it back, I have to pay the parking fee, impounding charges, and a recovery fine."

Bicycle? Janna straightened. "The one Owan had registered to you?"

The notice came down from the screen. De Garza nodded. "Sergeant, what was Owan's bike doing in a downtown lot?"

Particularly *that* lot. "The impoundment number should be given in the notice. What is it?"

De Garza read the number.

Janna wrote it down. "We'll check on it. Thank you for calling." She punched out and came up out of her chair heading for the door. "Mama, forget those calls for a while."

Impounded bicycles were held in a warehouse in north Topeka, just across the Kansas River in the Soldier Creek division. At the warehouse, Janna showed her badge to the attendants and read off the number Clio de Garza had given her. They were shown to the bicycle.

It was as de Garza had described it, custom-built of Gitane and Antonioni parts. A beautiful machine. It did not look cobbled together at all. Owan obviously spent time caring for the bike, too. The gray and black paint had the patina of careful waxing and painstaking hand rubbing.

"When did it come in?" Janna asked.

The attendant checked the tag wired to the handlebars. "It came in Tuesday morning."

"Tuesday? This is Friday. Why did it take three days to notify the registrant?"

The attendant shrugged. "Don't blame me. We just keep them here. Traffic's computer is supposed to print out the notices and after that it's up to the post office to deliver them. Complain to the turtle express."

Mama ran a finger over a gleaming fender. "Would he have abandoned a machine like this, do you think?"

"Not if he could take it with him. Hey, don't auction off this bike," she told the attendant. "If it isn't claimed, here's my card. Call me. I'll pay the fees on it." As they left she cocked a brow at Mama. "Interesting it should be in the Sunco lot. Let's pay their librarian another visit."

Sunco's librarian smiled at them. "You're becoming familiar faces. What can I show you this time?"

"Monday night, late. Start about twenty-two hundred."

She ran the tape. Owan's bike appeared on the tape at twenty-two-oh-six. Owan himself, or his back, at least, was also visible.

"How about Saturday night, too?" Mama asked.

"Right. Give us Saturday night, keyed to the bike's number."

On the Saturday tape, Owan's bike came in at nineteen-oh-nine.

"Nine minutes after Hazlett sailed in," Mama said. "When does he leave?"

The tape showed no bike of that number leaving by the *Out* ramp.

"He may have lifted the bike back over the *In* gate. I wonder if he knows about the monitor. We can have summonses issued only on bikes whose numbers we actually record," the librarian said.

"The *In* monitor won't catch him going out?"

"No. It's triggered by weight outside the gate, so by the time the monitor is activated, the bike is already out of camera range."

Janna sucked her lower lip. "Then there should be a space in the tape where the camera runs but there's no vehicle. Run it from about twenty-one fourty-five on through twenty-two thirty."

At twenty-two-oh-five the tape recorded no vehicle in its frame, only empty *In* ramp.

"That's it, bibi. It must be. He got back in time to return the card so Hazlett could catch the bus and be home by ten thirty."

Janna rubbed a crease between her eyebrows. "What was Owan doing back Monday night? Run Monday again, will you, only start twenty minutes earlier?"

At twenty-one fifty a road car with the license number SHH 418 entered the Sunco lot.

Mama pushed his glasses up his nose. "Hazlett!"

"Together again." Janna said it lightly but she did not feel light-hearted. Something cold and uncomfortable tweaked her stomach. "Show us when he left, please."

The tape ran…and ran.

The librarian frowned. "The car doesn't seem to have left Monday night."

"Run Tuesday."

They ran Tuesday, and Wednesday. At no place along either tape did the computer recognize the Vulcan's license plate and stop the tape.

"I don't understand this," the librarian said. "Could he still have his car there?"

One phone call to the attendant at that lot established that no Vulcans were on the lot, and had not been in the attendant's memory. She would have noticed and remembered a Vulcan, she assured them.

Janna sighed. "Too bad you don't have attendants in the evening, too."

"It's the worker shortage, sergeant. We just don't have enough people to keep someone around the clock."

"Just run the entire Monday night tape, then," Mama said. "Let's see every vehicle that leaves."

They ran the tape three times. It showed no SHH 418 on the *Out* ramp.

Janna raked her fingers through her hair. Damn. What had happened to Hazlett? "Would it have been possible for him to have left by the *In* ramp, say if someone triggered the gate from the outside?"

"A car can't move fast enough to beat the camera activation," the librarian said. "We'd catch at least part of the car."

They ran the tape once more just to be sure. It had no sections showing a vehicle approaching the *In* ramp camera. They gave up the search for the time being and went to lunch at the Lion's Den.

"What do you think, bibi?"

Janna took a bite of sandwich and washed it down with iced tea. "I don't like it, Mama. He tricked his way out of that lot somehow. If he went to that much trouble—"

"His game is more than chess, and it stinks clear to Port Bradbury."

"How could he get out of the lot? He had to pay his parking fee before the *Out* gate would open. If he went out that way, the monitor should have seen him. Now we can use one of your blue sky inspirations."

"The oracle doesn't work in the presence of unbelievers."

Janna was searching for a suitably sharp retort when Fleur Vientos, manager of the Doll's House, stuck her head into the Lion's Den. "Hey, she-lion, I could use you upstairs for a few minutes, and your skinhead friend, if he can help toss an obnoxious customer."

Mama sat up straighter. "Come on, bibi. Let's give the lady a hand and earn ourselves some hospitality."

"You can have mine." She finished her sandwich in two big bites. "Let's hope the customer is only unruly, not mean."

He proved both unruly and mean. He was holding a boy prisoner in one of the bedrooms, his thick arm a vise around the boy's throat. The boy, a ho about Janna's age—in his profession he would be a "boy" until he retired—was crying. Both his eyes had been blackened and an ugly bruise had formed on his jaw.

"I'll kill him if you don't let me out," the customer yelled.

"You shouldn't have touched him in the first place, jon," Mama said. "Bruising the merchandise doesn't come with the price of admission."

"He's unclean! Possessed by the devil! I was trying to drive the demon out of him."

"Oh, god, not another." Fleur's mouth tightened. "That's the second Bible cultist this month. I wish they'd content themselves with just praying for our souls. Get rid of that animal. I'm preferring charges against him!"

Janna stepped back out of sight and pulled the Starke out of her thigh boot.

The jon was a big man. One needle might not be enough. Give him two, then.

She leaned around the door and depressed the trigger. The red dot of the laser sight appeared on the man's forearm, where it came around the boy's throat. Janna fired twice and started counting. She hoped the percurare worked fast on this deek.

The jon stiffened in shock, then his eyes flamed in outrage. "I warned you!" His arm tightened on the boy's neck.

Then, as if he were a marionette whose strings had been cut, he collapsed in his tracks. He also quit breathing.

"Damn!" Now she would have to breathe for him. "Call an ambulance! Tell them we have percurare apnea."

She pulled the boy loose from the paralyzed man. Rolling the jon over on his back, she caught the life mask Mama tossed her, spread it across the jon's mouth and began blowing into it. "Don't panic, jon. You'll be all right." He could not move, but he could still feel and hear everything. She continued breathing for him until the ambulance medico arrived.

The medico measured the jon with her eyes. "How many needles?"

"Two."

The medico injected the percurare antagonist with a hiss of hypodermic spray. In a few minutes the jon not only resumed breathing normally, he had regained control of his muscles. He glared accusingly at Janna. "You tried to kill me."

Tried to kill him? The stupid deek. "I thought about letting you suffocate. Maybe I should have." She turned away, disgusted by the sight of him.

"You'll burn in hell for this!" He shouted after her. "The Lord will strike you down!"

He was still ranting as the ambulance attendants wheeled him out. He was going to be even more unhappy when he not only found himself riding to the hospital with Fleur's boy but discovered that the next stop after Stormont Vail's emergency room was the county correctional facility.

"I only hope he doesn't call Internal Affairs. That's all I need, the peeps slithering around trying to find a punishable offense in this." She hissed through her teeth. That grubby planet of Wim's was beginning to look like heaven itself. Could he really buy her a share with his pension?

"If the peeps show up here, every boy and girl in the Doll's House will testify to what happened," Fleur said.

Janna grinned. "Wouldn't that make the hall here a little crowd—"

She broke off, staring. Fleur stood against the open door, her head obscuring most of the room number. Only the last half of the final number was visible.

"Are you all right, leo?"

"Don't move, please, Fleur. Mama, tell me what number that is."

He looked at it, then regarded her with tolerant amusement. "A three."

"All right, Fleur, now you can move away."

She did. The room number was four eighteen.

Mama's dark eyes met Janna's in shock. "My god. Hazlett's license."

"Yes. Let's go back to Sunco."

13

Hazlett's car had to be license SHI113. The number could be made by covering parts of SHH418 and, according to the gate monitor tape, no vehicle with the license SHI113 had ever entered the lot. But license SHI113 had left the Sunco lot at twenty-two ten. Janna and Mama left the Sunco offices deep in thought.

"Four minutes after Owan arrived," Janna said.

"I wish we could have seen enough of the car to tell whether there were one or two people in it when it left."

"I'm betting there were two. The question is whether Owan met him for blackmail, to ask for help getting out of town, or—something else."

"Let's bring Hazlett downtown and ask him."

Janna frowned. It was tempting. "Is that your answer to everything, drag Hazlett in for interrogation? This isn't the twentieth century, you know. You can't harass respectable citizens. Besides, no one ever laid an effective ambush by taking shots at someone over the next hill. Wait until you can see the whites of his eyes."

Mama pushed his glasses up his nose. "You can't clear cases by waiting for nothing but blue-ribbon, tied-with-bows evidence, either. I know this kind of snake, bibi. You have to kick over his rock and drive him out into the sunlight."

The metaphors were thick today. Janna allowed herself just one more. "What if he only finds a deeper hole? No, we don't bring him in. We don't go near him until we know enough of the answers to ask the most uncomfortable questions."

Mama jerked off his glasses and began polishing them on the pantleg of his jumpsuit. "They really have you braintrained, don't they?

You investigate like John Dias prosecutes. When you let your gut lead yesterday, look what you accomplished. Now you're right back in your old set."

She rolled her eyes. He was back in his obnoxious set, too, and just when she had been starting to feel she could get along with him. She noticed clouds building up in the west. She hoped they held rain. Something needed to break this heat.

They went back to the station and resumed checking phone calls. It was discouraging work. Most of the calls dealt with equipping and preparing colonists. There were a few miscellaneous calls, one to a girlfriend of the receptionist, who begged Janna not to tell anyone "Roberto" had made personal calls during business hours.

"Roberto's boss doesn't approve of personal calls," the girl said.

"Which boss, Mr. Hazlett or Mr. Kellener?"

The girl did not know. It would be interesting if the disapproving boss were Hazlett, in light of his call to Colla Hayden. Janna wondered again why Hazlett made that call.

At another number she reached the woman Hazlett took to dinner Friday evening. That finished her half the list. Janna punched off with a sigh. Not one number could be tied to the sligh Owan.

She started on the incoming calls. Without surprise she found one on Friday afternoon from Many Mansions. The Laclede woman had said they located the chair Hazlett wanted by Friday. The call was probably to tell him about it. Nevertheless, Janna punched Many Mansions's number.

Laclede appeared on the screen with a mechanical smile. "Hello, you've reached Many Mansions interior decorations. I'm Marca Laclede. Mr. Adrian Cabot and I are out of the office just now, but if you'll leave your name and number at the tone, we'll call you back as soon as we return."

A recording. Before the tone sounded, Janna disconnected. She grimaced. That was the lot, outgoing and incoming alike, and none of them seemed to be connected with the sligh. The only call she could at all construe as suspicious was the one to Hayden. That one gnawed at her. People did not usually punch up other people at work for casual chatter. Hazlett must have had some reason for calling. What could it have been?

She voiced the question to Mama.

He squinted through his glasses at her. "Ah. Are you intuiting something?"

She scowled back. "No, I'm not intuiting. I have a sound reason for wondering about that call."

"Then don't just sit there wondering; investigate."

Janna reached for the phone one more time.

Colla Hayden blinked on seeing her again, then frowned. "You're still asking about Jorge's call? I told you everything."

"Ms. Hayden, this may be important," Janna said patiently. "Try to remember *exactly* what you said."

Hayden sighed. "It was nothing, just chatter. He asked me when I was going to have another party. I told him he didn't need a party, that I'd party with him. We made sexual jokes and after a bit, he punched off."

"Before you said you talked about past parties. What about them?"

Hayden shrugged. "Really, sergeant, I can't remember. It was just *talk*." She ran a hand through her kinky mane of hair, grimacing. "I think we may have talked about some of the people who come."

Janna pounced on that. "What people would those be?"

"Just people. I think the Tabers' name came up."

"Who are the Tabers?"

"A bi couple who are married but pretend to be twins so people will think they're committing incest. Michael and Michal Taber." She spelled the names.

Janna wrote them down. "Did you talk about anyone else?"

The other woman scowled in thought, then shook her head. "Not that I can remember."

"Do you have the Tabers' phone number?"

"Yes." She disappeared from the screen for a few minutes and reappeared with an address book. She read off the number. It was a local exchange.

"Did Hazlett ask you for the number?"

Her eyes widened in puzzlement. "Of course not. I told you, they're bi. Jorge is strictly het."

"Can you think of anything else you may have talked about? Anything at all?"

Hayden could not. In addition, she started looking at someone or something beyond the range of the screen. "I'm talking to the police," she said. After that she displayed an eagerness to end the conversation.

Janna let her go. She took the number Hayden had given her and compared it to those on the outgoing call list from Hazlett's office. There was no match. She sat back in her chair and stared at the number, lips pursed.

"Are you going to call it?" Mama asked.

"Would you?"

He grinned. "Sure, but I'm brainbent. What excuse would you have?"

She smiled grimly. "I'm desperate for something to connect Hazlett to Owan." She punched the number.

The red-haired young man who answered reminded Janna of the boys at the Doll's House, flawlessly handsome as a store mannequin. His eyes widened as she introduced herself. "Police? Suns. What do you want with me?"

He sounded as intelligent as a mannequin, too. "A week ago Wednesday did you have a call from Mr. Jorge Hazlett?"

The mannequin shook his head. "I was out of town all last week, but maybe my sister talked to him. Michal!" he yelled.

He was joined by a young woman just as red-haired and beautiful. Janna could see why they passed as twins. Michal Taber's eyes widened as Michael's had at Janna's introduction. "Suns," she said.

Obviously an intellectual match for Michael, too. Janna tried to keep her question in words of one syllable. "A week ago Wednesday, did you have a phone call from a Mr. Jorge Hazlett?"

"A week ago Wednesday." Her eyes wandered as she thought. "Hazlett? Oh, *Hazlett*. Here I thought his name was Walnut."

Janna fought to keep a straight face. She ignored Mama's gleeful grin.

"Yes, he called. He wondered if I knew the name of a man at one of Colla Hayden's parties last year. Do you know Colla?"

"I've met her." Odd, Hazlett had not asked Colla. Or suspicious. This man sounded more promising than anything else she had heard today. "Did you know the man's name?"

"Not exactly." Michal Taber grimaced. "I'm terrible about names. What do they matter when you're putting three with beautiful bodies?"

Personally, Janna liked to know who she was bending the mattress with. "So you didn't exactly remember the name. Does that mean you remembered something of it?"

"I remembered what it was *like*. It was something like Adriatic taxi." She paused. "Why are you asking? It wasn't important, just one of those nagging things that drives you off your tick until you remember."

"Adriatic taxi," Janna repeated.

Across the desks, Mama's grin broadened.

"Was Hazlett satisfied after you told him that?"

The bibi shrugged. "Well…no. He wanted the name, after all, but I told him everything else I could remember, like the man had a body past pluto and his tongue was nova!"

Mama slithered down in his chair, laughing soundlessly.

"And he had a furniture fetish," Michael Taber said. "Don't forget that."

Mama started making wheezing sounds. Janna threw a pencil at him. "Furniture fetish, sir?"

"He knew the style names of every chair and lamp and table."

Better not let him wander too far off the subject. "Did Hazlett seem anxious to find this man?"

"He didn't want the *man,* just the *name.*" The bibi's voice dripped scorn. "He remembered it just before he punched off."

"Did he tell you what it was?"

"No, just that he remembered it."

Janna sat for several minutes, after the screen went blank, listening to Mama giggle but hearing the couple's words repeating in her head. Adriatic taxi with a furniture fetish. Adriatic taxi. There was no way that could suggest Owan's name. Furniture fetish. She must not forget the furniture fetish.

"Well, that wasn't very relevant, but it was entertaining," Mama said.

Janna sucked her lower lip. "Not relevant? When Hazlett spent a good part of the day calling furniture stores?"

He stopped laughing. "He was looking for the Adriatic taxi, you think?"

"One of the decorators at Many Mansions is named Adrian Cabot." She paused. "Cab boat."

He stared at her. "I'll be damned. Maybe we should talk to Mr. Adrian Cabot."

"That's what I think."

She punched Many Mansions' number.

Laclede answered, in the flesh this time. She was showing a good deal of it, too. Off to the side, out of view of the screen, Mama drooled.

Laclede smiled at Janna. Her eyes brightened. "Back so soon?"

The undercurrent of excitement in the woman's voice made Janna wonder if Laclede were tripping. "I'm afraid so. Did you call Hazlett Friday afternoon?"

She nodded. "I wanted to tell him I'd found the chair."

"Did he come over to see it?"

Laclede wrinkled her nose. "No, as it happened. He decided the chair cost too much."

Janna wrote on a memo sheet: *Call Hazlett's office and see if Roberto will give you the name of the client Hazlett supposedly walked to the elevator.* She shoved it at Mama.

He read it and nodded.

"I wonder if I might speak to Mr. Cabot for a moment."

The improbably blue eyes widened in surprise but Laclede said, "Of course. I'll get him."

The screen blanked as she put Janna on hold. When it came back on, Janna felt as if someone had planted a foot under her diaphragm. The man on the screen looked at first like the sligh she saw with Laclede on Friday, but a moment later Janna realized this man was too elegant. But otherwise they could have been twins.

"Yes, may I help you?" Cabot said.

Janna held up her badge to the screen. "Have you ever met a Mr. Jorge Hazlett, or a Colla Hayden, or a couple named Michal and Michael Taber?"

The bluntness of the question worked. Cabot's face went gray. Panic flooded his eyes. "No, no, I haven't. Never. I'm sorry I can't help you. Now excuse me; I'm very busy."

Abruptly, the screen went blank. Janna did not care that he had punched off on her because she was already running for Vradel's office. She pounded once on his door and burst in.

Vradel looked up in annoyance from his conference with an assistant district attorney. "Brill, when that door is closed—"

"I'm sorry," she apologized hastily, "but this is important, sir. Do you remember the civilian couple we saw in the Den on Friday?"

Vradel nodded. "It would be hard to forget a woman like that."

"Do you remember the sligh with her?"

"Yes." He frowned and his mustache twitched. "What's this about?"

"I just saw her on the phone. She called Hazlett Friday afternoon and, lieutenant, that sligh and her boss are doubles."

Vradel came half out of his chair. "The link to Owan?"

She felt breath on her neck. Behind her, Mama said, "Sorry but I couldn't get Hazlett's client's name."

"One sligh double might be able to find other sligh doubles," Janna said. "Sir, can you make me a sketch of that sligh in the Den?"

Vradel tore off the top sheet of his memo pad. On the clean sheet he sketched in short, quick strokes.

The assistant D. A.'s brows hovered near his hairline. "Sligh doubles? What are you talking about?"

"Nothing to do with you or Dias for a while." Vradel handed the sheet to Janna. "Will that do?"

It was amazing to Janna that a few lines could convey so much. The sligh's angry face looked up at her from the paper with startling vividness. "It'll do beautifully. Thank you, sir. Sorry to have interrupted you."

"It's all right." His forehead furrowed. "Do you think she's making a business of this kind of arrangement?"

"It would certainly explain how Hazlett found what he needed so fast, wouldn't it?"

Vradel shuddered. "If she is, strap her, Brill…fast."

"Yes, sir." She backed out, closing the door. "Well, Mama, now we need to find out if Laclede and her sligh friend are indeed providing doubles for citizens."

"Let's send someone around to Many Mansions to apply for her services."

She nodded. Good idea. "Why not go yourself? You don't look like a leo. Morello can set you up with one of the false identities in the undercover file."

His mouth quirked. "You'll trust me off your leash? Or will you be on the other end of the wire?"

"No." She folded the sketch lengthwise and slipped it in a breast pocket of her romper. "I want to look up some friends in Oakland and see what they know about Mr. Adrian Cabot's alter ego."

Marca Laclede felt as if the afroam towered a kilometer over her. He had to be one of the tallest, thinnest people she had ever met, but he wore an outré suit with electric blue and lavender stripes and he was a simply lovely Dutch chocolate color. His bare scalp shone with the gloss of wax. She was fascinated. "Won't you sit down?"

Once he folded himself into the chair on the other side of her desk, she could talk to him without straining her neck. She smiled at him. "What can I do for you?"

He smiled back at her. It was dazzling in the darkness of his face. "I looked around my apartment the other day and thought it had to be the worst example of twenty-first century drab I've ever seen. My last wife decorated it. I want to do it over, make it more my style."

She loved his voice. It pulled at her blood almost like jivaqueme music. She noticed he studied her with interest through the transparent top of the desk, counting every square centimeter of skin not covered by her romper. She wore body paint to fill in gaps, of course, but she had the feeling he could tell exactly where cloth ended and paint began. She also noticed he made no pretense of not being interested. She leaned forward to give him a better view of her cleavage.

"Exactly what do you feel your style *is,* Mr.—?"

He paused a moment before answering. "Maxwell...Mahlon Maxwell. Everyone calls me Mama, though. My style is...unconventional. Show me something you think might interest me."

He rested his arm on the desk. She leaned across and put her arm beside his. "I see you surrounded by ivory. I'd paint your walls ivory, hang ivory curtains, furnish in molded foam covered with ivory plush. I'd finish by laying an ivory and brown fur rug so thick you could get tangled in it. Don't you think ivory would look good next to you?"

He moved his arm until it touched hers. His skin felt as warm as its color. "I think you're right, bibi."

She sat back and reached into a desk drawer for a pad of forms. "Before we go any farther, we ought to talk price. Many Mansions can create you a fine decor, but our services cost what they're worth."

He nodded. "Of course. I expect to pay well for any service you provide."

She enjoyed the warmth the sound of his voice and his words sent down her back into her thighs. She crossed her legs, and watched him watch her cross them. She smiled. "What do you do for your bankcredit, Mama?"

He looked up. "I'm a police officer."

The warmth changed to a sharp tingle, something of the same feeling she got making arrangements with Tarl under lion noses in the Lion's Den. She crossed her legs the other direction, letting the romper ride higher as she did so. "You can afford Many Mansions?"

He smiled. "A police officer can develop useful connections so he doesn't have to live on what the taxpayers allow him. You could be one of the useful connections, bibi, and it could be to both our advantage."

The air around him lighted red with danger signs. The tingle in her sharpened. "A decorator's assistant can be useful? How?"

He leaned forward on the desk. His voice dropped. "I'm not talking about a decorator's assistant. I'm talking about sligh doubles."

She felt a spasm of fear so intense it was almost ecstasy. "What do you mean?"

"Your business is small-time now. With my connections, you could develop an empire. Why go for small card when you could be collecting megacredits?"

"How—" Her breath felt short. "How did you find out?"

"I told you, bibi...a lion can develop connections." He smiled. "Don't worry. No one else knows. Your secret is safe with Mama."

Some of her breathlessness subsided. She started thinking. Marca stood and went over to the door. One push shut and locked it.

She turned to him. "Strip down."

He stared at her. "What?"

She made her voice hard. "Strip down. I'm not saying one word more to you until you prove to me you're not broadcasting."

His surprise changed to amusement. He grinned. "Whatever you say, bibi."

He pulled at the pressclose of his suit. The strips parted with a tearing sound. Marca felt foolish. Anyone who agreed to a search that willingly was either carrying a radio so well hidden he knew she would never find it or else he was clean. She did not feel she could back away, though. She let him strip to the skin and as he handed her his clothes, examined each piece carefully. When he had stripped to his skin, he pirouetted in front of her, flexing his sinewy muscles.

Marca quit feeling foolish and started enjoying herself. How many people could make a lion strip naked in a public building? She handed him back his clothes. "All right. I don't find anything. You can get dressed."

He made a show of it. She enjoyed watching. As soon as the game ended, though, she came back to business.

"What are you claiming you can do for me?"

"I'll expand your clientele. What do you have now: ordinary people, citizens with an illegal kink, maybe, or guilty consciences, men with wives they don't want to lose but who won't let them play away from home, women with similar problems. You collect, say, a couple of thousand from each for setting them free." He sniffed, passing off the amount as a trifle. "Bibi, I know people who really need alibis, alibis they're willing to pay handsomely for."

Criminals, he meant. She thought about that. Yes, they probably could pay. The possibilities made her lick her lips. Visions of riches shone in the air before her. She smiled at him. "I'd like to hear more. Come back when I get off work. Five o'clock. Take me to dinner and dancing. Talk to me, and we'll see what happens."

Janna could not find Quicksilver, but was not surprised. He would be teaching and the best Juvenile officers in the department had never been able to find Quicksilver's school. She checked stockrooms and the backs of Oakland's stores until she found other slighs she knew.

One was an Oriental-Hispanic who called himself Amber. He did not freeze up at the sight of her, but he did eye her boots as if checking them for a gun and strap. He did not stop attaching price tags to shirts either. "Are you still looking for that Owan?"

"Yes, but that isn't why I'm here today. I need to know if you've seen this man around."

She pulled out Vradel's sketch of Marca Laclede's companion.

Amber paused long enough to study it. Inscrutable eyes looked up from it to her. "I've seen him. I don't know his name, though, or anything about him."

"What has he been doing when you've seen him?"

"Talking to people." He went back to tagging. "What else would he be doing?"

"Oh, maybe looking for someone. Maybe he gives a description or shows a photograph and asks where he can find a person who looks like that."

Amber bent his head over his work. "No, I don't recall that he ever did anything like that."

She regarded him in silence. He was lying, she felt sure. How much was the question. It would be hard to find out. Accusing him of lying would accomplish nothing useful. In the slithy world, leos and other officials of government and society were meant to be lied to—whatever it took to preserve the anonymity of slighs.

She thanked him for his help, her voice heavy with irony, and left.

Visits to other slighs yielded much the same results. It was frustrating. Many of those people used to be valuable Eyes and Ears. She had been away too long. She could see by their faces that they recognized the sketch. Some even admitted having seen the sligh around Oakland. Beyond that, she found little help.

No one would specify a length of time he had been living there and no one would give her a name.

In two slighs, one a man, one a woman, the sketch provoked a marked pupil response. Those two flatly denied ever having seen him anywhere before. The vigor of their denials suggested that the sligh had approached them with a proposition like the one Owan accepted. If only she could find someone who would talk to her about it.

She finally located Quicksilver in Ripley Park. He sat on the grass in the shade of a tree, surrounded by a circle of children. In the rising wind—Janna hoped it was not spawning tornadoes—Quicksilver was pointing out trees and birds to them, naming each and telling something about them. Seeing Janna, he sighed and stood up.

"You hunt for four-leafed clovers, kids." He came to meet Janna. "I haven't found Owan yet."

"I think this man may be able to help me." She handed him the sketch.

He studied it. "He does seem to move around enough to have met every sligh in Oakland, perhaps even all of Topeka."

"What can you tell me about him? Do you know his name? Where he lives? Where he works?"

Quicksilver frowned. "I smell blood. You're hunting, aren't you?"

"It's important I find this man. Have you ever seen him behaving...oddly?"

The sligh looked past her. "You're using up all your favor credit, leo. Behaving oddly how?"

"Does he spend much time looking for one person or another?"

"Sergeant, of course he asks for people. We all do. I wish I could help you more than that, but—"

"Come on, Q; don't go polite on me! Help me! Believe this, what he may be involved in could hurt slithytown. It could bring legislation against slighs."

Quicksilver's frown deepened. "How? You want me to trust you, leo, try trusting me. Tell me what's happening. How can he hurt us?"

Janna debated. Perhaps he ought to know. As briefly as possible, she told him what they thought Owan had done, and what Marca Laclede and her sligh friend might be doing. "We don't know how they do it, though. That's why I have to talk to some of the other slighs who may have done what Owan did."

Ouicksilver's mouth tightened. "Lightwits! I can see their point. It sounds like a chance to make a fool of the System, but exposing themselves to prosecution that way...stupid. You're right; this business could hurt every sligh. I can see the high muckies in the Statehouse panicking and passing legislation making identation mandatory, just so no one can double for another citizen without leaving a noticeable gap in records somewhere." He looked around at the children combing through the grass for clover. "His name is Tarl. I don't know the rest. He doesn't spend much time looking for people. Usually he asks for them by name when he does. He spends most of his time socializing, just drifting around meeting everyone possible. Doesn't talk about himself and of course no one asks. I don't have any idea where he works. Maybe he doesn't. He must collect something for hunting doubles."

Janna thought of the jewelry Owan had bought. If Marca Laclede and Tarl had found Owan for Hazlett, they would have asked a price. How much of that jewelry went to them?

"Do you remember the names of any people he's asked for?"

"Yes, but I won't tell you. You'd want to know who they were and most of them are terrified of leos. They'd never talk to you."

"Tell me this: are there many of them?"

He shook his head. "Not many."

That was something of a relief. There would be just a few falsified bank records around, then. Perhaps none of the others had involved criminal activity. She could always hope.

"Do you suppose some of the children might know where he works?" Children had a way of knowing things no adults did. Children were a great underutilized source of information.

Quicksilver's mouth quirked. "You can ask them."

Janna took the sketch to the group. "This man's name is Tarl. Can anyone tell me where he works?"

They eyed her in silence. She reached into her pocket for a handful of vending tokens. "These to anyone who can tell me."

A girl said, "I'm very sorry, officer, but I've never seen that man before. I can't help you. I wish I could."

Janna swallowed a grin. Said like a true sligh, so polite, so earnest she could not be accused of being uncooperative, but giving no information. She heard Quicksilver chuckle behind her and turned around to roll her eyes at him. "You've taught them well."

He bowed with elaborate courtesy.

It was almost sixteen hundred hours.

She headed back across the park to Indian Thirty and then downtown to the station. Into the usual organized turmoil of changing watches. Mama Maxwell had not come back yet, but Pass-the-Word Morello gave her a message from him: *I'm counting coup on the doppelgänger queen tonight. I'll give you the prurient details later.*

Janna gnashed her teeth. What was he up to now? "What identity did Maxwell check out of the undercover file?"

Morello blinked at her. "He didn't check out any identity. Was he supposed to?"

"Damn!" She crumpled the slip and hurled it to the floor. "Double damn."

Whether she cursed Mama or herself she was not sure. Why, *why* was it impossible for him to do anything the established way? She must have been an idiot to let him go out to decoy Laclede. It gave her hot flashes and cold chills just trying to think what a strange mind like his might be planning. If he stunted around and bombed this case, so help her she would needle him and inflict long, painful tortures on his paralyzed body.

She retrieved the message slip to throw it in the trash, then stalked down to debriefing. Just let Schnauzer Venn ask her what was bothering her tonight.

As it happened, he did not ask. Too many others volunteered complaints and problems. A couple of rookies were seriously disturbed by the discovery that good, "law-abiding" citizens resented them. They were upset at what they saw supposedly civilized people doing to each other. It gave Janna no chance to talk. She left debriefing looking for a shoulder to cry on.

Wim, she thought…but as soon as she walked into his room at the hospital she could tell she made a poor choice. His shoulder did not stay still long enough to be cried on. The doctors had taken off his bandages that afternoon and removed any tissue staples which had not been absorbed. It sent Wim high as a tripper. There remained just the splint across his nose, protecting the nasal bones while they healed. Just a thin scar remained around his head, and as soon as his hair finished growing back in, it would be almost invisible. Only his eyes looked strange, banded horizontally in red.

"The doctors tell me I can leave in a few days. They just want to make sure I'll be ready to cope with the world out there."

"How are your rehab lessons coming?"

He grinned. "I can find peas with my fork now. And look at this."

He made a wide circle around the room. Janna held her breath, waiting for him to collide with the beds or chairs. He avoided every obstacle, though. Every time he went around something, Vada smiled proudly. Finally Wim stopped and dropped into a chair with no more than a backward feel with his leg to locate it. "Janna, you'd have to go through this to know what it's like. I never knew the world was so full of sounds and smells. Everyone smells different. I think I could almost tell where you and Vada are by tracking with my nose. I'm turning into a bloodhound. Just think, on Champaign there will be a whole new catalogue of smells and sounds. I can hardly wait to learn what they all are."

He seemed to be adjusting to his handicap very well. Janna knew she should be relieved and pleased, but it gave her a strange feeling—something like loneliness, or being shut out. For the first time, she was able to appreciate how Vada must have felt all these years as she listened to Wim and Janna talk about the alien world of their work.

She tried to bring the conversation back to something she knew. "I wish this Kellener case were going as well as your rehab."

"How *is* it doing?"

She thought he would never ask. She started to tell him.

After a few sentences, Vada said, "Our company almost went to that firm." She shuddered. "I'm glad now they didn't."

"I knew it was only a matter of time before someone found a way to beat the bankcard system," Wim said. "It's a war and the escalation never stops. Are you about ready to resign, Jan?"

Outside, thunder boomed. Wim stopped, head tilted, listening. "I knew it was going to rain today. I could feel a difference in the air of the sunroom. My teacher says it's due to static electricity. It's going to pour tonight, but it doesn't quite feel like a tornado breeder. I wonder if the air will change the same way on Champaign." His scarred eyes gazed dreamily into nothingness.

After a minute he shook himself and turned his face toward Janna. "Oh, I talked to the pension office. They say they can't give me a lump sum. The pension comes from tax payments and there's just so much budgeted per year. However, they referred me to the bank. I called the main branch of Topeka National and they'll loan me as much as I want, then take over the pension until the loan is repaid."

Janna stared at him. "Wim, you didn't need to—I mean, not already. I haven't decided yet."

"You have to soon. Our ship leaves in a little over two weeks. I know you want to come. You've been telling me how miserable the job's been lately. Come on and join the future."

"It isn't always bad. Sometimes I almost like Mama, but then—" Then he went off blue skying. What *was* he doing with Laclede tonight?

"If this Laclede woman really has found a way to counterfeit a thumbprint, it's going to play hell with investigations. She'll have wiped out the usefulness of bank records and fingerprinting in one chop. A lion's life will be no fun anymore."

Janna appealed to Vada. "Help. Your husband is twisting my arm hard tonight."

"I'll help him if he wants me to—whatever it takes to convince you to come along with us."

"Enough," Wim said. "The arm-twisting is over for now. Listen. It's starting to rain."

The first tentative drops hit the windows. Janna peered out. The clouds roiled, sagging low and purple. Beneath them the sunlight had a peculiarly luminous quality, making the colors of the city almost fluorescent. With a sharp crack of thunder, the deluge began. The light and world disappeared beyond sheeting rain.

"Let me tell you what I learned about sound today, Jan. Did you realize that a human can't tell if a sound is directly in front, behind, or overhead? A dog can distinguish many separate points of sound origin. So to compensate, a person has to—"

Janna heard him repeat the tricks for localizing sound, but she did not actually listen. Mixed emotions churned in her. She had come wanting to talk, not listen, but Wim wanted to talk, too, and for the first time in their association, neither was interested in what the other had to say. Their interests had become a barrier between them rather than the unifying force they used to be. That realization hurt. Janna did not like it at all. If she were to go out to Champaign, they would be sharing experiences again.

She made an effort to listen to Wim, but could not. Her mind kept sliding back to Mama Maxwell, wondering where he was and what he was doing.

She stood up. "I ought to go. I have to find Mama."

"Let him flame himself. If you're not around at the time, you won't be burned, too."

"I don't care if he flames himself, but it does concern me what he might be doing to our case."

"You can't go yet," Vada objected. "It's pouring."

Janna lied. "I came in Sid's runabout."

Riding in the rain was not bad. By the light of street lamps coming on, Janna could see the hot pavement steam where the rain struck it. The cars and runabouts appeared to be riding on a cushion of smoke. Janna made sure she stayed well inside the bicycle lanes, out of the path of larger vehicles.

She had no destination in mind. No telling where Mama might be. She just wanted to ride, to enjoy the coolness of the rain and forget everything else. It was with some surprise, then, that she found herself swinging down the ramp into the Capitol division's garage. She started to turn around, then shrugged and rode on down to the bike racks. As long as she was here she might as well see what was going on. She wrung out her romper and hair in the locker room before walking up to the squadroom.

Crimes Against Persons seemed quiet. The night watch supervisor Lieutenant Chris Candarian and three investigators stood drinking caff and watching the newscanner. A candidate for Congress was delivering her carefully polished pitch for votes.

Candarian's brows rose as she saw Janna. "Overtime? Vradel didn't tell me he'd authorized any."

Janna shook her head. "I'm on my own time, not wrecking the budget. Just passing by."

One of the investigators glanced toward the window slit. "How is it out?"

"Wonderfully wet. You're looking empty. Everyone on the street tonight?"

"Here and there," Candarian said. "That bibi in the red Bonsai broke four more pedestrians' legs this evening. She's getting skillful." Her eyes narrowed. "What are you tracking? I can't believe you came in just to dry off and you're no rock jock rookie."

"Has Sergeant Maxwell called in since the watch change?" Of course that was what brought her here, she realized all at once.

The lieutenant shook her head. "Is he out on something dangerous without back-up?"

"He isn't supposed to be."

The phone buzzed. Candarian punched the button. "Crimes Against Persons, Lieutenant Candarian."

The screen carried the image of a uniformed officer with sergeant's bars on his collar. "I'm looking for Sergeant Janna Brill. It's important."

Candarian looked up at Janna with arched brows. "It is luck or are you prescient, sergeant?"

Janna moved up to the screen. "I'm Brill. What is it?"

"Hallard and Kobuzky asked me to get in touch with you. They're at Atchison and Jacquot. They think they may have found your sligh."

14

Jacquot Street looked even more depressing than usual in the rain. The downpour absorbed what little glow came from its few operational streetlights, leaving it a black tunnel. The headlights of the jane car Janna had borrowed from the station lighted sodden, drooping weeds growing up through the steaming pavement ahead of her and reflected off turbulent pools made by trash damming the gutter streams. Beyond the reach of her headlights, the houses squatted dark and derelict in the dripping tangle of their yards. The only visible life on the street was at the intersection with Atchison, where it looked like a carnival in progress.

Police cars parked in a cluster before the boarded-up store on the corner in a light show. Red, white, and blue bands chased each other around the light rails atop three watchcars, and the pop-on cherry of a jane car flashed in a ruby strobe inside the front window of the car. The play of lights caught rain-slickered leos moving around the building and intermittently illuminated the Forensics insignia on a fifth car.

Janna's lights crossed one officer as she swung in to the curb, marking the leo with fire where they hit the reflective stripes on the slicker. Janna ran down a window a crack. "I'm looking for Hallard and Kobuzky."

The leo looked around. "Hi, Brill." It was Rina Hallard.

Janna set the jane car down on its parking rollers and pulled on the slicker she had brought from her locker at the station. Sliding out over the airfoil skirt, she sank in half an inch of mud, but she hardly noticed, her attention riveted on the abandoned store.

"He's in there?" She hoped not.

"Yeah."

She grimaced. Even without the strained note in Hallard's voice, Janna's stomach would have lurched An old store made an unlikely place to hide. They were too often launching pads for winos and trippers, too public for good hiding. If Owan had been found here, he had not been found alive.

Hallard leaned against a watchcar. The rain streamed down her helmet and slicker in rivulets alternately red, white, and blue. She leaned her head on her arms. "I never thought I got that Criminal Justice degree just to wade through shit falling over deaders. I could have used it to qualify for the Moon colony, or Mars."

In quadrasonic sound, the radios of the watchcars and jane car murmured of screaming women and traffic accidents and bar disturbances. Janna regarded Hallard with a tired sigh. "How did you happen to find him?"

Hallard did not raise her head from her folded arms. "Usual body count of the known abandoned buildings." Her voice was muffled.

Body counts comprised one of the less loved parts of patrolling in Oakland. But...they could either check the buildings or wait until the stench or some nervous citizen announced the demise of winos and trippers.

"It was my turn to walk tonight. I knew I had one the moment I got near the door. A few more days and we'd have been able to smell him halfway down the block. Christ." She swallowed audibly.

Bloody damn it to hell. Owan had been Janna's witness. Despite all her fears and pessimism, she had been counting on him for testimony against Hazlett. "What makes you think it's my sligh?"

Hallard lifted her head. "How many people down here wear blue novalon suits?"

Janna eyed at the building. "Mose inside?"

"Around back, helping secure the area until the forensic team finishes. Secure the area." Hallard snorted. "What hasn't washed away by this time will be fun picking out of that filth inside."

Janna sighed again. "I'd better go take a look."

"Excuse me for not joining you."

She circled the building. A she-lion from one of the other watchcars shined a light in her eyes. "You must be Brill. What's your interest in this case?"

The faintly this-is-not-your-division-what-are-you-doing-here attitude annoyed Janna. "The man's dead, isn't he?"

"First time I ever saw Crimes Against Persons come out for an OD."

Janna regarded her a moment in silence. "What makes you think it's an OD?"

"Hey, I saw the body. Trick OD's are hard to mistake."

Trick! Janna plunged past her on around the building.

The stench of death hit her about the corner, even in the downpour. She set her jaw and started breathing through her teeth.

Moses Kobuzky and several other leos stood outside the open rear door of the store, watching the forensics team finish holotaping the door and interior of the building. Kobuzky waved at her. "Sorry we had to find your sligh this way."

One of the forensics techs played a light over the ground around the door and shook his head. "No way of picking up prints from that. It was like concrete before, but now the only footprints are those of the officer who found him."

"Any footprints inside?" Janna asked.

"Smeared ones. Can't help sliding in that stuff. It's the local public latrine."

Janna eyed the door with distaste. "Do you have another mask? I need to go in when I can."

"You can go now. We're about finished." He pulled a crumpled paper mask out of his pocket and handed it to Janna.

She slipped the elastic over her head and settled the cup over her mouth and nose. The material looked thin but it did its job well. The air reaching her through the mask was almost odorless.

She went into the building.

Most of the interior disappeared in the shadows beyond the small pool of Forensic's lights, but the prime exhibit was brightly illuminated. The deader lay in the middle of the light pool, twisted and bloated. Janna fought her stomach. Rats had been chewing on the exposed face and hands. It made the half face that remained unrecognizable. No mistaking the jumpsuit he wore, though. By some bizarre irony, the rats had not touched it.

One of the advertising claims for novalon was that the material resisted soiling and wrinkling, so that however hectic, however long the day, clothing made of novalon remained fresh-looking. For once, the commercial propaganda seemed accurate, though Janna doubted the manufacturers would appreciate hearing of this particular example. In the midst of the building's filth, the suit sheathed the contorted limbs of the corpse in clean, unwrinkled, gloriously iridescent blue.

Janna could see why the she-lion outside had called this an OD. The position of the body looked almost identical to Kellener's.

"Is he your sligh?" Kobuzky called from the doorway.

Janna shrugged. The deader had brown hair with gray at the temples. The remaining eye was brown. He had a medium build. He might bear a resemblance to Jorge Hazlett, but in his state she could not be certain. That suit though. It looked right. It also made her nerves twitch seeing a human turned into a pretzel while his clothes remained as neat as if just taken from a closet.

The twitch reached her stomach. She retreated outside and stood with her hood back, letting the rain pour down over her head, while she breathed deeply. The rain made her feel cleaner.

Kobuzky grinned at her. "Glad you're downtown out of the body-counting business?"

Someone said, "Here comes the M. E."

A figure shuffled around the end of the building. Janna's brows went up. They had drawn Dr. Sandor Kolb himself, looking even worse than usual. Now his hair and suit were wet as well as unkempt.

He looked around with a vaguely surprised expression, as if bewildered by where he found himself.

"Good evening, Dr. Kolb," Janna said. "Are you working nights now?"

He peered at her as if she were an alien speaking an unintelligible language. Suddenly he straightened and ran his hands through his hair. The wrinkles disappeared from his jumpsuit. His eyes focused. "Good evening. Sergeant Brill, isn't it? No, I just happened to be in the office and since it was clear everyone wanted to let someone else come out, I volunteered." He swung toward the door of the building. "Well, show me what you have."

Janna shook her head in wonder. In two motions, he went from being the Mad Doctor of Shawnee to Mister Medical Examiner. She had seen the transformation many times, in the field, at inquests, and in court, but it never failed to amaze her. The man who reputedly slept on autopsy tables and forgot to eat or go home became a distinguished professional who remembered the name of every police officer he ever met, every corpse he ever examined, and the names and signs of countless causes of sudden death.

Kolb entered the building without a mask. From the doorway, Janna watched him squat beside the body and go over it with the same careful attention Sid had given Andrew Kellener's body. Kolb peered, probed, and straightened limbs. He appeared not to notice the filth around him or the odor and decomposition of the corpse.

"Fractured left humerus, left tibia and fibula, and right radius and ulna. Cyanosis indicative of anoxia." He looked up at Janna. "You've had a couple of trick deaths now, haven't you?"

"That's your judgment of the cause of death?"

"Oh, certainly, certainly. Couldn't be much else. That's unofficial, of course." He lifted a brow. "Your interest must indicate you don't think it's a simple OD."

"No." She pressed her lips into a thin line.

Kolb cocked his head. "Ugly way to commit a murder. It's a less traceable weapon than a knife or shooter, though, I suppose."

"Did he die here or was he brought in afterward?"

"Judging by the postmortem lividity, he died in this position. Those could have been caused by an agonal struggle." He pointed to smears in the filth on the floor.

"How long do you think he's been dead?"

Kolb shook his head. "I wouldn't care to speculate. The heat in here will have speeded putrefaction. I'll have to see what he looks like on the table. Oh, and I'll let the computer give me a guess, too."

"Could he have died Monday night?"

"Monday?" He considered with his forehead furrowed in a thoughtful frown. "That's within the limits, I'd say."

Which meant he could have died Sunday, or Tuesday. Janna sighed. "I'd like that suit as soon as you get him out of it."

"Pick it up at the office any time. Come on, come on." He beckoned to ambulance attendants. "He's not going to bite. Let's wrap him up."

The attendants hung back, obviously unhappy at being soaked by the rain outside but equally unhappy at having to come inside. Kolb came out and dragged them in. Janna moved aside to give them room.

As she moved outside, she found Rina Hallard beside her looking up. "What do you want to do now?"

Janna considered the building. She looked up the black street. "I need to knock on doors, I'm afraid. The locals aren't going to be happy, but if I wait until tomorrow, no one may be home. Want to go back on patrol or would you like to help me do some real police work?"

"Help interview a population of blind deaf-mutes?" Hallard snorted. "That's masochism, not police work."

She and Kobuzky helped anyway. They took one side of the street while Janna covered the other. They knocked on every door of the blocks stretching up Jacquot and Atchison from the store's intersection. The houses behind many of the doors proved empty. Others might just as well have been. The residents had no interest in being helpful. They resented being visited by the police so late at night.

"Do you know what time it is? Come back in the morning."

In a country club district Janna would have smiled politely and begun every statement with "sir" or "ma'am." Here she leaned on the door to keep them from shutting it and said, "We can talk here or at the station. It's a long trip for just one question. Did you see or hear anything sometime after ten o'clock Monday night, perhaps near the old store on the corner?"

They were Hallard's blind deaf-mutes. They had never in their lives seen or heard anything unusual, certainly not at night, most emphatically not on Atchison or Jacquot Streets. Monday night was a complete blank in their minds.

Janna toyed wistfully with daydreams of picking up a few of them and bouncing them off walls. She also envisioned the glee of the peeps in Internal Affairs when citizens reported a leo playing heavy in the middle of the night over routine questions. She contented herself with leaning on the doors.

She stepped up on another porch shaking rain off her slicker, and knocked on another door. Her second knock brought a man stripped down to undershorts, taking full advantage of the cooler temperature brought by the rain. He regarded her suspiciously through the crack the guard chain permitted the door to open.

Janna held up her badge and ID. "I know the hour is inconvenient but there's been some trouble at that abandoned store on the corner. Are the people in this house the same as those who were in it Monday evening?"

He hesitated. From behind him came the sound of a scuffle, then a muffled giggle. The man said quickly, "Yes…me."

For the twelfth time that evening, Janna asked, "Did you see or hear anything unusual in the street or near the old store after ten o'clock on Monday night?"

He did not even stop to think. "No."

Another muffled giggle behind him.

Janna put a hand against the door. "May I come in so we can talk about it?"

"I didn't hear anything, I tell you."

"Did you see or hear anything at all different from the usual neighborhood routine?"

"Just the car."

Electric shock shot up her spine. She eased her hand to her pocket and tapped on the microcorder. "You say you saw a car on the street Monday night?"

Beyond the crack, the female giggle sharpened. The man started to shut the door. "No, there was no car. Good night."

Janna shoved her weight against the door. "Jon," she said easily, "I don't know what you have going in there and if you satisfy me with answers to questions about Monday night, I won't care."

He stopped trying to close the door. "I don't have anything

going, but I'll answer your questions because I'm a conscientious citizen. Yes, I saw a car Monday night."

Janna smiled at him. "What time did you see it? Can you tell me the make and color? Could you read the license number?"

"Read the license number?" His laugh came in a short, sharp bark. "By what light? I couldn't even see the car well enough to tell you what it was. I think it was a road car, though, a sportster model."

"Why are you so sure of that?"

"Its fans had that whine that sportsters do. It came by about ten thirty, I guess."

"This is very helpful. Is there anything else you remember about the car?"

The man considered, frowning. "Yeah. There was some jon in it yelling."

"Yelling what?"

He shrugged. "I couldn't tell. It didn't make any sense."

Someone with his tongue trick-tangled, perhaps?

She tapped off the microcorder. "Thank you very much, sir. I appreciate your cooperation. Good night. Have an enjoyable evening."

She had two more houses to visit. One seemed empty. She heard sounds of human occupancy in the last, but no one came to the door and when she circled the house, stumbling through the wet tangle of weeds around it, the one gleam of light inside disappeared. They were probably squatters, in which case they would never even talk to her, let alone admit anything which would indicate they had been in this house Monday night.

She walked back to the old store. The carnival had shut down. Forensics and the jane car were gone. All the watchcars but Kobuzky and Hallard's had left, too. The two leos sat in their car waiting for her.

"We found a couple of people who heard some shouting about ten-thirty Monday," said Kobuzky. He reached out through the car's window and handed Janna a microcorder chip and a notebook page with two names and addresses. "One of them even lives near a functional street light. She doesn't know car makes but she's sure it was a road car, not a runabout. It was small. The light wasn't bright enough to see the color well. It looked 'darkish' to her."

Peacock blue would look dark in poor light. Janna slipped the chip and notebook page inside her slicker before the rain could soak the paper. "Thanks, Mose, Rina. I appreciate this."

"Well, it's a change from carrying drunks and toxy trippers home and breaking up fights," he said.

Hallard added, "Next time you're ready to ridicule our size, just remember that if you're nice to the little people, they'll be kind to you."

Janna slipped the chip into her microcorder and listened to it while she drove back downtown. The two witnesses Hallard and Kobuzky interviewed said substantially the same thing as the man Janna had questioned. There was a road car on Jacquot street Monday night. It was probably a sportster. A Vulcan? No one had seen the license number. It was all suggestive, but not very definite, not what she could call real evidence.

She parked the jane car in the garage and went around to the morgue section of the building. She found the forensic and medical personnel taking fingerprints from the fingers the rats had not bitten off. That gave them a thumb and the little finger of the right hand and the last three fingers of the left hand. The corpse lay stripped and draped on a plastic alloy cart. His clothes sat folded on a nearby table.

Janna waited outside in the corridor before entering, peering in through the windows until the cart had been wheeled off to the coolers. Even so, her stomach flipped and churned. The stench of decomposition remained strong in the room. In particular, it clung to the clothes. She grimaced as she reached for the jumpsuit.

A technician grinned. "Don't you know that real lions, the four-legged African kind, like their meat a bit ripe?"

"Just run those prints through the computer, will you?" Janna shook out the suit and checked for the label. The suit had been made by Stellar Fashions. She laid it aside and picked up the other pieces of clothing. In contrast to the suit, the underclothes, socks, and shoes were of cheap manufacture. The soles of the shoes had worn thin and the plastic uppers were starting to crack.

She sucked her lower lip as she put down the shoes and picked up the suit again. She handed it to a forensics tech. "Let's see what the label looks like under UV. There may be a store marking."

The technician held up a small blacklight. "I already checked it. There is a store marking. It looks like this." She handed Janna a notepage that bore a reproduction of what looked like a square capital A, but with the top bar extending beyond the second leg and the lower crossbar not quite reaching the second upright.

Janna returned the page to the tech. "Let's see who uses that mark."

She washed her hands thoroughly before approaching the computer keyboard in Forensics with the technician. The tech drew the symbol on the screen with a light scriber and typed in a search command. The answer came back in seconds. Janna read the screen with a sigh.

The store marking belonged to Fine Threads in the Grenada Mall. She realized she had been hoping the deader would turn out not to be Owan. If the deader wore Owan's suit, though, he was probably Owan. Damn.

She had one more chance, though. What if the fingerprints belonged to someone else? She trotted down the corridor to the fingerprint computer.

The technician there presented her with a printout. "There you are, hot out of the printer."

The prints that had been fed in matched those of a child idented forty years ago in the Oakland division following a school raid. The owner of the prints had never applied for or been issued a Scib Card, however. The name given at the time of the school raid was Owan Desfosses. Still applicable to the physical description were brown hair and brown eyes.

She handed back the printout. "See it gets to me tomorrow, will you?" Damn and double damn. They had found Owen. She sighed. "I'm going home."

The rain had settled to a steady drizzle but water still ran heavy in the bike lanes. Janna took the bus home, dragging the bike aboard with her.

She and Sid shared the second floor of a twentieth-century stone house near the west side of the division. Sid sat reading a medical journal when she sloshed in. He peered over his glasses as she peeled out of her slicker. "You look like you've been soaked and wrung out."

"At least a couple of times." She dumped the slicker over a dining room chair. "Make me some hot tea, will you? I have a hard call to make."

She punched Clio de Garza's number on the phone.

De Garza obviously suspected something wrong the moment she came on the screen. While Janna wondered how to begin, the Hispanic woman said. "You've found Owan, haven't you?"

Janna nodded. "And he—"

"And he's dead." De Garza's mouth trembled. "All day I've had a feeling of dread. Now I know why. How did it happen?"

In as brief and unemotional sentences as possible, Janna told her. De Garza's face reminded her of Liann Seaton's. Both held their grief. Both controlled their faces until they looked like porcelain masks.

"I'm sorry," Janna said.

Something bleak blew through de Garza's eyes. "So am I, sergeant. Thank you for calling me."

Janna punched off. "God, I hate making calls like that."

She turned to find Sid with a bath towel. "I'm heating the tea water now and a bath is running. Go climb in. I'll bring the tea when it's ready."

She hugged him. "People wonder why I live with you. You're the best, Sid."

The bath felt wonderful. She soaked in the water, sipping tea, and Sid sat on the edge of the tub listening to her talk. She reflected that she should have come home to him for that shoulder to cry on, instead of going to Wim. Sid nodded, encouraged, and commiserated in all the right places.

"That's rotten luck to have your most valuable witness killed. What will you do now?"

Janna shrugged. "Dig for physical evidence." She drained the last of the tea and handed him the empty cup. "I wonder if I can talk a judge into giving me a search warrant to go over Hazlett's car and clothes. All I need is some matching soil, a weed, some threads…something to tie him to that building."

"Would you like your back scrubbed?"

"I love you, Sid." She leaned forward and let him scrub. "I want to strap this deek. Lord, how I want him. What kind of person just stands by and watches two other human beings die that way?"

"What kind of man puts lye in his wife's douche? That's what happened to one of my customers today. We've both had enough experience to know there's no limit to what people will do to one another. How come we're surprised when a new cruelty turns up?"

"I suppose we keep thinking we've seen the limit. Hand me that towel, will you?"

She climbed out of the tub. Sid dried her back for her. She smiled over her shoulder at him. "You make a great mother, you know that?"

"Speaking of mothers, where do you think your partner is?"

She sighed. "I haven't the faintest idea."

"Do you think you ought to ask the watch units to look for him?"

"After the Night of the Caged Lion?" She grimaced. "No. Worrying about Mama is probably as pointless now as it was when he went into that apartment house after the sniper. He's thoughtless enough not to call in. I'll wait and see if he shows up for rollcall in the morning." She yawned. "I'm going to bed."

She was asleep almost before she finished crawling under the sheet. A pounding dragged her back to consciousness some unguessable time later. She struggled up through the fog of sleep groping for orientation. What was happening? It took a couple of minutes to register that she had someone at the front door.

In one blink she came fully awake. She swung out of bed, reaching for both a robe and the .32 shooter in her bed table. She padded to the front door on silent, bare feet.

"Who is it?" She stood to the side of the door with the shooter ready.

"Let me in, bibi."

Mama! She peered at a table chrono. "It's three o'clock!"

"I know." His voice reverberated with rich, self-satisfied tones. "This can't wait. Let me in."

She dropped the shooter in her robe pocket and unlocked the door.

Mama pranced in wearing copper knee boots and a sleeveless copper foil suit that looked sprayed on. Gold and silver star appliqués spangled his arms. A cloud of narcotic fumes followed him. "It is a splendid night, bibi." He stumbled into an easy chair.

Janna rolled her eyes. "You're toxy."

He dropped into the chair and lay back, giggling, arms and legs outflung. "Mostly I'm blind. I'm not wearing my glasses, you'll notice. And I'm toxy, too, yes, I admit. The Laclede bibi likes her pleasures and I had to keep up with her." He closed his eyes. "It wasn't easy, especially when she wanted to finish off with some of the most strenuous mattress bending I've ever been a party to."

"But you rose to the occasion."

Her dry tone opened one of his eyes. He peered myopically at her and giggled. "I'm a hardy soul." He closed the eye again and started singing. *"Let's you and me put two, bibi/Let's count coup.* On her stomach she had: *Feel safe tonight; sleep with a leo.* Let's *do* put two, bibi, and both feel safe tonight." He giggled again.

"Do you want help throwing him out?"

Janna looked around to see Sid in the hallway leading to the bedrooms. Sleep had turned his round face pink and cherubic. He blinked at her through his glasses. She smiled at him. "I'll see. Mama, haven't you had enough of mixing partners and passion? What makes you think I'm even interested in you as a sexual encounter?"

With obvious effort, Mama opened both eyes. "This isn't passion, bibi; it's celebration."

"What are we celebrating?"

Mama giggled. "What Laclede told me." He made a weak effort to sit up straighter. "Do you have some caff, bibi? I'm so far in orbit I can't keep my mind going one direction for more than a minute at a time."

She sighed and headed for the kitchen. "I think I can handle this. You go back to bed, Sid."

She made the caff strong and managed to pour six cups of it into Mama, forcing him to walk up and down the living room between cups. Finally his steps steadied and he stopped giggling. Only then did she let him sit down again.

They stayed in the kitchen, where Janna could pour him more caff. Mama propped his elbows on the tabletop and leaned his head in his hands. "Thanks, bibi."

She sat down opposite him. "You can thank me by telling me about Laclede. You contacted her this afternoon?"

"I contacted her."

"You told her you wanted to use her services?"

"Not exactly."

She poured him another cup of caff. "What did you tell her?"

"I told her I was a police officer."

"You *what?"* Janna came up out of her chair.

He extended a long arm and caught at her elbow. He pulled her down in her chair again. "Don't get excited. I knew what I was doing. This bibi is brainbent. You said she took her sligh friend to Tuck's place at a time when they must have been arranging for Owan to meet Hazlett. So it seemed to me she gets a boost out of playing with fire. I went to Many Mansions pretending I wanted to redecorate my apartment. She was advertising herself every minute. I took a chance and told her who I was. That really lit her fuse. When I told her I wanted to go into business with her, that almost short-circuited her."

Janna poured some caff for herself and took a big swallow. "And then?"

He told her about being searched. He told her in some detail.

She raised a brow. "Laclede lit your fuse, too, didn't she?"

Mama grinned. "A man ought to enjoy his work. When she saw I was clean, she invited me to take her out this evening and talk about what we could do for each other. So I did. I wined and dined and danced her at the Ad Astra Club. Then we danced some more. I think we visited every place in the city with a jivaqueme band."

"Where you drank and smoked as well as danced, further enjoying your work."

He peered at her with reproach. "I sacrificed for this. I left my glasses home so I wouldn't keep playing with them. I had to pay a fortune in taxi fares because I couldn't see well enough to drive and I spent an entire evening with one of the flashiest bibis in the city without ever really being able to see her."

"I'm bleeding for you. What did you do after the dancing?"

"She took me to her apartment and counted coup on me. Lord! That bibi is high voltage. It was worth it, though."

"I'm beginning to doubt letting you in here was worth it."

He leaned toward her. "It was worth it because then she told me how she works the doppelgängers. That's what she calls the sligh doubles…doppelgängers."

At last, something relevant. "Are you able to remember what she said?"

He winced at her sarcasm. "I'm not that toxy. Furthermore—" He reached into his pocket and pulled out a microcorder. "—this evening I was *not* clean. I have everything she said recorded."

He tapped the corder on. Marca Laclede's voice said, "Reveal all my secrets to a lion, even if he is a partner? I couldn't do that."

"Can't you tell me something about the set-up? You ought to trust your partner. Talk to Mama. How do you find your doppelgängers?"

"I can tell you that. I have a sligh friend who hunts them for me. Oh." Her gasp was sharp, ecstatic. "That's nice. Do some more of that."

Janna regarded Mama speculatively. "Do what?"

"Hush and listen."

Janna listened. As she did, a reluctant admiration blossomed for Mama. In half an hour, between groans and cries of delight and much heavy breathing, he had wheedled every detail of the doppelgänger operation out of her.

"Do I dare ask where, in that outfit, you carried the corder?"

"In a boot, but with a remote control and mike taped to the inside of my wrist chrono."

"Clever."

He preened himself. "It was, wasn't it?"

She rolled her eyes.

The explanation of faking the thumbprints left Janna with a chill. It was a frightening thing to hear. She had always believed in the infallibility of fingerprints. This was like giving a Bible cultist irrefutable proof of God's death.

"Did I read her right, bibi?"

"You read her right. Nice work."

"Will your sligh object to having another partner?" Mama's voice asked on the tape.

"Tarl has no ambition, no sense of destiny." Laclede's voice purred of satisfaction. "Telling him about you will only disturb him. Let's let you be my secret."

Janna rolled her eyes. "She's incredible." She tapped the corder off. "Let's make sure Vradel hears this right after rollcall. Then maybe we can start wrapping this case."

15

Marca Laclede took her time dressing. Let Adrian complain if she came in late. Soon she would be quitting to set up her own decorating business. She did not plan to do much decoration, but it would make a good front for her real business.

She lingered in her bath and afterward paused frequently, while slipping star and planet appliqués on her arms and legs, to look around her and imagine her apartment as one of those semiunderground townhouses out near the governor's mansion. She wanted one like Jorge Hazlett had. Soon the clothes in her closet would be only the most modish and made of the finest materials. Thanks to the clients Maxwell brought her, she would be able to afford anything she wanted. The afroam was going to be useful, just as he claimed. He made a good bounce, too.

Marca inspected the appliqués critically in the mirror. Were there too many? Not enough? She did not like the bare patch on her left shoulder blade. Contorting, she added a quarter moon and a tiny star. That looked better.

She wiggled into a pair of hose and her dress. It bared her left shoulder and hung to her ankles in steamers. Every movement revealed the entire length of her legs. She checked herself in the mirror and blew the image a kiss. Nice.

She was putting in her contact lenses when the doorbell chimed. Marca's brows rose. She glanced at her dressing table chrono. It read: 9:10. Who could be coming to see her at this hour?

A check of the security screen found a Dutch-chocolate face grinning up at her.

Marca opened the door. "Well, hello, Mama. Back again al—"

She broke off as she saw the lean, smoky-haired woman with Maxwell. That woman was a lion, too, Marca remembered...the officer who had called her yesterday afternoon, and the she-lion was *not* smiling. Sudden fear, unalleviated by any excitement this time, washed through Marca. She started to slam the door.

Maxwell's arm came out and caught the edge. "Sorry, bibi." The she-lion put a paper in his other hand. He held it up before Marca. "We have a warrant for your arrest, for solicitation and conspiracy to fraudulently use a Scib Card."

"I beg your pardon. Did you say solicitation?" Despite her fear, she was able to keep her voice icy. "What nonsense."

"Solicitation," the she-lion said, "is the counseling, procuring, or hiring of another person to commit a crime."

Marca's fingers went bloodless on the edge of the door. "You have no evidence against me."

The two leos exchanged glances. Maxwell said, "I have a recording I made in your bedroom last night."

Imagining everything on that recording was too much. Tearing the door open all the way, Marca launched herself fingernails first for Maxwell's face and eyes. "You goddam filthy fucking motherbouncer!"

Janna caught her before she managed to rake Mama's face more than once. A jerk sent the smaller woman flying across the corridor, to bounce off the wall and onto her knees on the floor. Before Laclede could recover, Janna had both the woman's hands behind her back and a wrap strap around her wrists. She used the bound wrists to haul Laclede to her feet.

"That isn't a nice way to treat Mama."

"Bitch!" Laclede spat at her. She turned on Mama with her lip curled in contempt. "You, too. I should have known any afroam who is such a stinking bounce couldn't be a real man. He'd have to be a pussy."

Mama straightened his glasses and wiped at his cheek. A few flecks of blood came away on his fingers. "You have the right to remain silent. If you give up the right to remain silent, anything you say can and will be used against you in a court of law. You have the right to an attorney. If you want an attorney and cannot afford one, the court will appoint one for you. Do you understand what I've said?"

"Go count coup on your mother again!"

"Do you understand?" Janna repeated. "We can go over it again, until you do."

Sullenly, Laclede nodded.

"Say it aloud, please."

She glared. "I understand my rights!"

"Good girl." Janna shoved Laclede ahead of her into the apartment. She pointed her at a tip-over style chair. "Sit and stay. Where do you want to start, Mama?"

"How about the bedroom?"

"You can't search my apartment!"

Janna pulled the search warrant out of her thigh pocket and waved it at Laclede. "I'll take this room."

Janna found nothing significant in the living room. Mama found some jewelry in the bedroom. They compared it to the list of purchases on Hazlett's bank record.

"That recording last night is worthless," Laclede said from her chair. "I was just playing a game. I don't know any sligh named Tarl."

Janna looked around at her. "Then how did I happen to see you with him in the Lion's Den last week? He looks just like your boss, only without that elegant polish."

"He's just a friend. He could never pass for Adrian."

None of the jewelry in the bedroom matched anything on Hazlett's bank record.

"I'll try the bathroom," Mama said.

Janna headed for the kitchen. On impulse, and prompted by a vague memory of something heard during one of her courses, she opened the freezer. Through the open door of the kitchen she saw Laclede half rise from the chair, then sit back, biting her lip. Janna sorted trough the plastic-wrapped packages. Most felt solid, but one seemed to be made of small, moving pieces. She took it out and broke the seal.

Laclede screamed.

Janna returned to the living room where she tipped over another chair, turning it into a small table. Onto it she poured the contents of the package. "Mama, come look at this."

While Laclede swore at her, Janna compared the jewelry she had found to their list. A sapphire bracelet, some diamond earrings, and a jade pendant appeared to match.

Janna held them up before the other woman. "How did you come by these?"

Laclede glared. "I want a lawyer."

Mama came in from the bathroom with two small bottles. "These aren't marked but look what happens when you mix a little from each." He gave Janna a small oval of soft, rubbery material.

He also carried a pair of shoes. He handed the bottles to Janna and knelt to put the shoes on Laclede. A foot lashed at his chin. Mama ducked just in time to avoid contact.

"Bitch!" His hand drew back.

Janna caught his wrist. "That sidewalk out there is heating up. Let her go without shoes and burn her feet."

Mama dropped his hand. Laclede glared, then jammed her feet into the shoes, launching a few more choice profanities at both of them.

Marca Laclede had not always been such a flash bibi, Janna reflected. That language spoke of more inelegant beginnings.

They did not take her directly downtown. They stopped at Highland Village first. Janna stayed in the car with their prisoner while Mama went into Many Mansions. He came back ten minutes later with two more little bottles, a compact with a jelly substance in the bottom, and an address book. Under the names and addresses of each entry were stars. Adrian Cabot's name had seven. Jorge Hazlett's entry had one. By holding the compact at an angle to the light, Janna could just see a fingerprint in the jelly.

"Nice." She scratched her identifying mark on the compact and returned it to Mama.

Laclede looked pale enough to faint.

Then they took her on to the station.

Lieutenant Vradel had an interview room ready for them when they brought her after booking her and tagging the evidence. Marca Laclede sat in the straight coruboard chair at the coruboard table and rubbed her wrists as if still feeling the wrap strap around them. She stared tight-lipped at the jewelry, compact, and bottles set on the far edge of the table. She also stared at two jumpsuits, a white card, and a photograph of Jorge Hazlett lying beside them.

"The rights the arresting officers repeated to you still apply," Vradel said.

A gleam came in her eyes. "Rights? They didn't tell me any rights."

Janna took out her microcorder and tapped it on. Mama's recorded voice delivered the words repeated to every arrested citizen since the famous Miranda decision more than a hundred years before, and Marca's voice shouted, "I understand my rights!"

"Bitch," Laclede spat at Janna.

Janna tapped off the corder.

Vradel said, "Have you called an attorney yet, Ms. Laclede?"

Her face looked hard in the lights of the interview room. She glared up at Vradel, not knowing the leos stood so she would have to look up, not knowing she faced straight into a hidden camera taping the entire interrogation. When the questioning ended, experts would go over the tape, measuring stress in her voice, noting pupil response to the questions asked, determining when she was telling the truth and when she was lying. The experts' thoughts would not be admissible evidence in court; but they could determine the course of any subsequent investigation of her case.

Unknowing, Laclede said sullenly, "I don't need a lawyer. I haven't done anything wrong."

"Then you'll answer some questions? You don't have to answer any you don't want to."

"You're so kind." Her mouth pouted more so than ever.

"Where can we find your friend Tarl?"

"I don't know any—" She broke off, scowling at Janna. "He's just a friend. He hasn't done anything either."

"Do you know where we can find him?" Janna repeated.

"No." She said in a tone of satisfaction "Slighs never stay still for long."

"You're going to be prosecuted," Mama said. "Do you want to go to trial and maybe jail alone, while Tarl is free to spend what he's made, and maybe set up a new business with someone else? He's the one who finds the doppelgängers. He doesn't need you to find citizen customers. Any ambitious, unscrupulous person can do that for him."

She started to spit at Mama, but stopped. Janna watched the relays close in her head. The room fell silent while they let Laclede think. After a few minutes, their prisoner smiled. It was a thin, malicious smile. "Tarl works at the Goodway Market on Sardou Street, in the back."

Vradel glanced at Janna and jerked his head toward the door. Janna fingered the warrant for Tarl in her thigh pocket. She and Mama left the interview room. They opened the door of the watchbox next to the interview room. Assistant District Attorney Ward Prior sat watching the room next door on a screen leading off the video camera.

"Interesting case."

"You will prosecute, won't you?" Janna said.

"I'll see what you have after the lieutenant finishes interrogating the suspect."

Mama wrinkled his scalp. "You be careful now. Don't make any impulsive decisions." He closed the door of the watchbox, grimacing. "A Dias clone."

They headed for the garage.

They found the Goodway Market without difficulty. In its parking area, they climbed out of Indian Thirty and stood studying the clouded windows papered with bargain notices. The air felt sauna-like, humidity so high it created a visible haze. Janna felt as if she were being steamed.

"Do you want to go in or watch the back?" Mama asked.

"I'll watch the back. You may be able to walk right up to him without him smelling lion."

She watched Mama start in the front, then she circled the building. In sight of the market's freight door she stopped and stood with her hand on her gun, ready to draw and shoot if Tarl came out the back. With her other hand she lifted the hair off her neck. Last night's rain had only made the weather worse, not better. Her jumpsuit had started sticking to her and she could feel sweat trickling down between her breasts.

Then inside the market, a man yelled. A moment later a woman screamed. Janna started running even before the sound quit. She raced for the front of the market.

The sligh she had seen with Marca Laclede came hurtled out of the market as Janna came around the building. He saw her and bolted across the street. Janna pulled her gun.

"Halt! Police!"

He only ran faster. She fired after him. The needle missed. She saw it hit the ground and skid into a crack in the paving. She aimed again but Tarl ran such a bobbing, erratic course that she could not keep the laser sight on him. Swearing, she jammed the Starke back into her thigh boot and launched after the sligh.

She did not like the choice. There could be something exhilarating in running down a suspect, but not here in Oakland. She always listened to what the watch officers at Department Exchanges had to say about local conditions, but hearing did not equal experiencing. Practically speaking, she was three years out of touch with the streets down here, three years out of field experience with the lion traps being set. She had to spend almost as much time watching where she put her feet and checking the space ahead of her for neck wires as she did focusing on her quarry. Too, she kept wondering uneasily what had happened to Mama.

Tarl cut across a lot where the scattered pieces of a razed house made an obstacle course. She followed using exactly the same path he took. With each step she gained on him. Her main worry was not whether she could catch him but if she could do it before she drowned in the saturated air.

Only a few meters ahead of her now, he cut around the end of a crumbling wall. Another few strides and she would have him! She vaulted the wall. And into freefall.

"Oh, shit!"

The wall had been part of the foundation of the house which once stood there. Below her gaped the basement, turned into a pond by last night's rain. Janna plunged into the muddy water.

Tarl had long since disappeared by the time she found a corner where she could climb out. She stared the direction she had last seen him heading, swearing at him and at herself, before heading back to the market.

Mama leaned against Indian Thirty, brushing at dirt on his red and yellow suit. Looking up, he gaped at her. "If that's all due to sweat, it must have been one hell of a chase. Where's the sligh?"

"In Lawrence by this time." She shook her head in disgust, then eyed him. "What, may I ask, happened in there?"

He jiggled his glasses, pretending to adjust the temple pieces behind his ears, and focused somewhere on infinity. "He dropped me."

"How?"

He shrugged. "When I told him who I was, he acted resigned. He came right along, all cringing smiles and careful sligh politeness—you know the pattern. When almost reached the door, though, he came around with a yell and kicked me in the groin. I've spent the last ten minutes getting up off that floor in there." He rubbed at a stain.

Janna raked her fingers through her wet mane. "For a couple of Oakland veterans, we've made a damned poor showing today, Mama."

The manager came out of the market. "My girls just told me what happened. I'm terribly sorry." He almost bowed in his obsequiousness, but a mocking note lay under it. "I want you to know I never realized that sligh was involved in anything illegal. I just gave him a bit of work from time to time because I feel sorry for those people."

The manager had given Tarl work to save himself money and paperwork and they all knew that, but Janna did not call him on it. "We don't know that he is involved in anything illegal. We just want to talk to him."

"You wouldn't know where he lives, by any chance?"

The manager shook his head.

Janna said, "You let us know if he happens to come back here."

"Certainly. Where can I reach you?"

Janna reached into a sleeve pocket for one of her cards. Out came a soggy clump.

Mama handed one of his cards to the manager. "Contact either Brill or Maxwell."

The manager nodded.

All the way back downtown Janna kept berating herself for vaulting the wall when Tarl went around it. She ought to have known better than that. She supposed—hoped—Mama was similarly flagellating himself for accepting Tarl's surrender at face value and not putting a wrap strap on him. He appeared chagrined as they explained to Lieutenant Vradel how they happened to let the sligh escape.

The lieutenant listened in pained silence, his mustache twitching. At the end he sighed. It had a bone-weary sound. "Have you put out an APB on him?"

They nodded.

"Didn't put a strap on him." Vradel sighed again.

The next sigh and criticism must be directed at her. Janna changed the subject. "How did Laclede's interrogation go?"

"She's made a complete statement. She doesn't want to be an accessory to murder, so she's being very cooperative. She told us she arranged for that sligh to double for Hazlett, and told us where and when they met to switch."

Mama whooped. "When do we get a warrant for Hazlett, then?"

"We don't." Vradel's mustache twitched. "Laclede's statement gives Hazlett opportunity, but there's still no evidence placing him in the Sunflower Federal Building Saturday night, or in that abandoned store in Oakland, either."

"Oh, come *on,* skipper. We can at least hold him on conspiracy to commit bank card fraud."

"Keep digging. The DA wants him for murder."

Mama looked thoughtful. "Maybe there's another way. The British have a polite term for it. Let's invite Hazlett down to *assist* us with our inquiries."

Vradel sketched Hazlett's face on a corner of his memo pad. "What exactly do you have in mind?"

"Asking him some nasty questions and seeing how he reacts."

"Hoping he'll give something away?"

Mama nodded.

Vradel doodled meaningless faces while he considered the plan. He drew a pair of frowning eyes. "Do it."

Janna looked up Hazlett's office number. Mama punched it into the phone. He was wearing his most charming smile when the receptionist put him through to Hazlett.

Hazlett nodded courteously. "Good morning, Sergeant Maxwell. How is your investigation going? Have you found that witness yet?"

"The investigation is almost over." Mama's voice was smooth and deep. "There are just a couple of points to be cleared up. I don't want to impose, but I wonder, Mr. Hazlett, can you come down and help us settle some details?"

Across the desk from Mama, out of sight of the phone's screen, Janna smiled and nodded approval.

Hazlett looked doubtful. "I have a very busy schedule today."

"We need half an hour of your time…no more."

"Well." Hazlett shrugged. "I can give you half an hour. I'll come early this afternoon."

"Thank you very much, sir."

He punched off. "Cross your fingers, bibi."

They bought sandwiches in the snackbar and chased down the postmortem report on Owan while they waited for Hazlett. Janna read the report with a frown.

"Trick killed him, too, and it was a massive dose, like Kellener's. Kolb thinks it was administered in some Scotch whiskey." She looked up at Mama. "The whiskey, according to the good doctor, was bottled gold, not the kind a sligh is likely to be drinking."

"I don't suppose he offered any opinion on the brand and year."

Janna sucked at her lower lip. "If we had a search warrant for Hazlett's house, we could compare the stuff found in Owan's stomach with what Hazlett has in his liquor cabinet."

"I like your thinking, bibi."

"Let's hope Hazlett helps us get the warrant."

Circumstances had an air of conclusion about them, Jorge reflected, definitely an end-game feeling. When that afroam lion started being polite it had to come from the realization that he was no longer in a position to be impolite and get away with it. Jorge walked into the Crimes Against Persons squadroom feeling expansive and generous.

"I'm only too glad to do what I can to help settle this," he told the smoky haired she-lion. "This has been very upsetting for everyone, especially for Andy's wife and children."

"Naturally," Brill said. She held open a door for him.

Jorge's good humor faded. It was the interview room. His eyes narrowed. They wanted him to help them clear a few points by talking to him in the interview room? The end game suddenly had a new feel about it, less certainty. He felt the throb of his pulse in his throat, half fear, half excitement.

"Am I being arrested?" He made the question casual.

Brill's eyes widened in surprise. "Why should we arrest you?"

"Then why are we talking in here?"

She smiled. "Just routine. Please sit down."

He sat down in the chair. His eyes moved past her to the perforated acoustical tiles on the wall behind her. The lens of a camera aimed at him through one hole.

"I'm familiar with police procedure, sergeant. The interview room is used for interrogating suspects." He carefully kept all alarm out of his voice; he left in a slight indignation.

"Not always," Brill said.

Behind her, the afraom polished his glasses on a trouser leg. He blinked myopically at Jorge. "You don't have a guilty conscience, do you?"

Brill frowned around at him then turned back to Jorge. "I'm sorry if this makes you feel threatened." Her voice was earnest, apologetic. "We just need to ask a few questions and I thought it might be more comfortable in here, away from the general confusion. Would you feel better outside?"

Jorge made himself meet her eyes. "It isn't important. This is fine. I just like to know what's going on. What questions do you need to ask?"

"Well, to start with, I need to have you look at something." She pulled a carton from under the table and began piling its contents on the table. "It's in here somewhere."

Jorge sat back in his chair and made his body relax. That last sentence rang flat in his ears. Its note of absentmindedness seemed at complete variance with everything else he had seen in the she-lion. She was trying some new gambit on him. He had better take his time and study it.

The pile on the table included two beautiful suits that begged to be fingered, some jewelry, and a metal compact. Jorge allowed himself to touch one of the suits, as anyone might.

Brill flipped a square piece of stiff paper onto the table. Jorge stared at it. It looked like a 2-D photograph, but lay face down. His fingers pricked with the urge to turn it over. For one moment as the she-lion removed it from the carton, Jorge caught a glimpse of the front. He thought he spotted his face. Could it be the instant photo the Laclede woman took of him? If it were, they must have found out about the doppelgänger, and they were not likely to have done that without investigating him.

Brill grimaced. "It isn't here, Mama. Do you know where it is?"

"Not if it isn't in the box, I don't."

She sighed. "Damn. I'm sorry, Mr. Hazlett. I can't seem to find what I need."

"Find what?"

"It doesn't matter, I guess."

The photograph lay so close to him. One touch would turn it over.

"Perhaps you can answer me this. Do you know where all the merchandise you bought Saturday night is?"

They must know. Why else ask that kind of question? He felt the eye of the camera on him, felt his pupil responses and words being recorded for later scrutiny of experts. He casually removed his hands from the top of the table where they lay folded and used them to rub his eyes as he feigned a stretch.

"Why do you ask?" He kept the question casual, innocently curious.

"Well, some of it—"

"Some of it's turning up strange places," Maxwell interrupted.

They had been checking his bank records! They *did* suspect him, then.

Brill said, again apologetically, "We've checked the bank records of everyone connected with your partner."

Indecision prickled at him. If they had been investigating him with the idea of finding evidence against him and found out about the doppelgänger, why should the she-lion bother apologizing for the investigation? Maybe they did not know after all. He dropped his eyes to the study of his fingernails. "Of course." If only he could see the face on the photograph. That would tell him whether they knew or not. If only—but he dared not touch it. He avoided even looking at it.

Brill repeated, "Do you know where your merchandise is?"

He could not tell the truth, obviously, but lying would be worse. He kept his eyes down, away from the gaze of the camera. "I don't understand what that can have to do with deciding why Andy died." He kept his voice low.

"Would you mind speaking louder, Mr. Hazlett? I can hardly hear you."

She, or the recorder?

"I know these questions don't seem relevant to your partner's death, but…it's just one of those little things that turned up and we felt we needed to settle it."

Her tone seemed almost slighlike in its anxiety not to offend. If he were sure they suspected him of killing Andy, he could simply refuse to answer any questions without an attorney present; but if they did not know anything, refusing to answer would be suspicious. Her manner did not help him. If only he could see the photograph!

She sighed. "If only I could find that—" She turned away. "Maybe Morello took it out. Mama, let's go ask him. Would you mind waiting here a few minutes, Mr. Hazlett? We'll be right back."

They left the interview room, closing the door behind them.

The muscles in Jorge's hand ached with the urge to reach out for the photograph. He felt the gaze of the camera, however. Someone would be monitoring it. They may have left him, but not alone.

With everything in him screaming to look at the photograph, Jorge made himself sit back in the chair with arms folded behind his head and stare at the ceiling, yawning now and then in pretended boredom. He closed his eyes.

In the watchbox Janna looked from the monitor screen to Assistant D. A. Prior and Lieutenant Vradel. She shook her head. "He isn't going for the skin. Come on, deek, look at the photograph, damn you."

"I don't think he needs to," Mama said. "An innocent person would be curious enough to take a look. He's being too careful to ignore. And you notice the other things haven't affected him that way. He's just glanced at them, obviously not recognizing any of the stuff. Which means he never bought it."

Prior brushed at a spot on the brown paisley of one knee. "That goes toward proving fraudulent use of a Scib Card, nothing more." He stood and picked up his briefcase.

Mama frowned. "Skipper, did you show him everything we have so far? Did you tell him about the Sunco tapes and the sligh's murder?"

Vradel's mustache twitched. "I told him."

"I can't see that you can even establish the sligh was murdered, let alone that this man had anything to do with it. The physical evidence indicates nothing more than a simple OD," Prior said.

"Oh, come *on,*" Mama protested.

Prior's eyes were cold. "Come on where, sergeant? You have a law degree. You know what constitutes evidence. I admit that circumstantial evidence suggests Hazlett killed his partner, and possibly the sligh, too, but there's nothing a competent trial lawyer can't demolish in court in five minutes. I'll talk to Dias. We may have to settle for prosecuting him on conspiracy and fraud along with the Laclede woman."

Mama rolled his eyes. "Which will earn him what, a relative slap on the wrist?"

Prior stood up.. "Bring me *anything* that places him at the scene of the murders and we'll be happy to go for a murder indictment. Without that though..." He spread his hands.

The door closed behind him.

Vradel chewed a corner of his mustache. "Well, what do you think?"

Janna eyed the man on the watchbox screen. He sat motionless where they left him, apparently dozing. "He's an iceman. He isn't going to give us anything. I don't know if we can touch him."

"We can try, bibi."

She looked up at Mama. He had successfully defended a number of leos against charges brought by Internal Affairs. Maybe he could do something with their suspect, too. Janna freely admitted that the idea of letting Hazlett go stuck in her throat. It violated her sense of justice.

"All right, let's try."

Jorge allowed himself a look at his wrist chrono. The leos had been gone a long time. What, exactly, was their gambit? The debate started in his head all over again. How much did they know? About the doppelgänger? About the murder? Both of them? Or did they know anything at all? Perhaps they just knew about the doppelgänger. In which case they might be trying to see if it related to Andy's death. They might just be fishing for anything suspicious. He saw so many possibilities, and each needed a different response. If he only knew where he stood. If only he dared turn over the photograph.

The door opened and the two leos stepped back in. Brill seemed sullen. "Well, we seem to have brought you down on a wild goose chase. I can't find what I wanted to show you. You're free to go."

Suspicion vied with exultation in Jorge. Had he successfully countered their move, or did this constitute a different stage of their gambit? He stood up. "If you find this thing, feel free to contact me again."

"We will," Maxwell said. Steel edged his voice. "Because we will find it. Believe that. We won't give up until we do."

What was this...threats? Were they trying to rattle him? Jorge bit back a grin. Clearly they had nothing but suspicion. Well, let them threaten all they liked. "Good luck, sergent."

He pushed past them out the door of the interview room. As he crossed the squadroom, he longed to turn and see their expressions. Depression? Frustration? Rage? But looking back was a fatal flaw of humans. Look what happened to Lot's wife, and that harpist of Greek mythology as he led his girlfriend out of Hades. Jorge determinedly kept his eyes front. Inside, he laughed.

Janna frowned after him. "He's laughing at us, Mama."

"Of course. He thinks he's beating us. That's what we want him to think."

She stared at the untouched photograph. "Are you sure he isn't? I'm not confident this is going to work on him, the cold arrogant bastard."

Mama wrapped an arm around her shoulders. "Cold blooded like a snake. And do you remember what Mama told you about how to catch snakes?"

She turned to meet his eyes, her own narrowing. "Drive them out into the sun."

"And are you ready to listen to Mama now?"

She gave him a smile. "Let's go kick over some rocks."

16

Jorge thought this had to be one of the most satisfying days of his life. No matter that the air steamed and the air-conditioning in his offices could barely keep the temperature at a reasonable level. He did not care that the Sunchild Company's ramjet was far behind schedule at Beach-Cessna and over half the Aurora Company still had not taken their physicals with launch just a month and a half away. Jorge felt wrapped in a cloud of euphoria, girded in sweet triumph. They had not arrested him because they could not. Whatever they might suspect, they had no hard evidence. They had wanted him to say something that would help them find the evidence they needed, but he had not.

He took pride in knowing he had given them nothing. If only criminals would realize it, lying was the second worst response to a police question, surpassed only by the danger of truthful responses. Any admission, true or false, could be used by the leos. Statistics showed that suspects who refused to say anything at all were very rarely convicted. The police made most of their cases on damaging admissions by the defendant himself. Silence was not only golden, it constituted sanctuary.

It would be interesting to know exactly how much they suspected, but not vital. Jorge sailed peacefully through the afternoon. When the problems of the office began threatening to spoil his mood, he cut the day short. Leaving the office about three o'clock he visited a local bar for a leisurely drink before climbing into the Vulcan to drive home. He mentally reviewed his favorite girlfriends. He felt like company. He would call Senta. She made a good companion for celebrating.

Not until he was halfway home did he realize a bright green Monitor had been visible on his rearview screen for some time. He turned up the magnification on the screen until he could see the driver. It was that afroam leo Maxwell. Brill was in the car, too. Jorge returned the screen to normal scan. What could they want? He did not for a moment believe coincidence put them behind him. For a heartbeat, fear surged in him. Had they found some definite evidence and come to arrest him?

Jorge slowed the Vulcan. The Monitor slowed, too, maintaining the same distance behind him. Jorge speeded up again. The other car did likewise. Jorge's fear evaporated, replaced by annoyance. They just wanted to follow him. Moreover, they must want him to see them doing so, or they would not be so obvious about it. Well, that at least answered one question. They must certainly suspect him of killing Andy.

When he turned in at his house and floated the Vulcan across the yard into the garage, the Monitor pulled up across the street and settled to its parking rollers. Jorge paused at the top of his steps to look across at them. Maxwell waved. That confirmed it; they wanted him to know they were there.

He hurried down the steps into the house. Did they think following him would unnerve him to the point of self incrimination? Probably. The police mind worked that way. He smiled thinly. Very well, if they wanted to think that, let them. They would see whose nerves went first.

The top half of his windows extended above ground level. He looked out twice over the next hour. The Monitor remained across the street.

Jorge decided to show them how little they affected him. He climbed the steps and crossed to the police car.

"Good afternoon, sergeants. It must be uncomfortable out here. May I offer you something cold to drink?"

Brill smiled. "No, thank you. That would be fraternizing with the enemy. We can't do that."

Jorge stopped his frown before it appeared. He made himself shrug instead. "You're the ones sitting in the sun. I'm just trying to be civil."

Maxwell slouched in his seat with his head leaned against the back, with his eyes closed. "Sure, just like when you offered that sligh your whiskey Monday night. I don't like the additives in your drinks, jon."

Jorge returned to the house chuckling. They really thought they could panic him by telling him how much they suspected. He did not give a damn, except as it sweetened his triumph of knowing how helpless they were.

He glanced out the window again about five o'clock. The Monitor was still there. He frowned in annoyance. Surely they did not intend to sit there all night? They must be off duty by now. He would be leaving to pick up Senta in just an hour. He did not at all welcome the idea of having leos in attendance at dinner and wherever else he and Senta decided to go this evening. He crossed the street again. Brill poked her sleeping partner. Maxwell sat up and the two regarded him quizzically.

"May we help you, Mr. Hazlett?"

"Is it fraternizing with the enemy to come inside my house for a few minutes? I'd like to talk to you."

The two exchanged glances. Brill said, "We're always willing to talk to you."

They followed him back to the house. He took them to the study. There he sat down behind his desk and stared up at them. That put them all in almost the same relative positions as in the interview room. What a difference in circumstance, though. He had command of this interview.

"Just what, may I ask, do you two want?"

Maxwell grinned, his teeth bright in the darkness of his face. "You, Mr. Hazlett."

Brill did not smile. "You murdered two men, jon, and we don't think that's very civil. We think you ought to be punished for it."

"Two men? Who was the second?"

"Don't play innocent, jon. You know it was the sligh who doubled for you Saturday night."

He leaned back and smiled. "You're dreaming. Do you have evidence of this?"

"No," Brill admitted.

"Not yet." Maxwell made it a grim promise.

Jorge lifted his brows. "You expect to find some?"

Maxwell nodded. "You think you're safe, that you've gotten away with it, but the truth is, you're human, jon, and humans make mistakes. Even the perfect murderer slips sooner or later."

"We plan to be here when you slip, Mr. Hazlett."

Jorge chuckled. "How? By camping on my doorstep? I doubt your superiors would approve, even if it were physically possible to follow me twenty-four hours a day. It will all be in vain anyway. Surely you realize two Knights alone can never capture a King."

Janna regretted having come. They did not seem to be driving Hazlett out into the sun. On the contrary, he appeared to be enjoying himself immensely, at their expense. His smile made her hand itch for a night stick. One could inflict a fair amount of pain without leaving a mark. But, they were here to rattle Hazlett, not assault him. "Our superiors have no love for unpunished murderers, either, Mr. Hazlett."

The infuriating, arrogant smile did not waver. "I may call them and ask about that."

In Janna's ear, the Capitol dispatcher's voice whispered, "Indian Thirty, call the station."

Mama's eyes flicked toward her. One brow hopped. She understood the unspoken request. He wanted her to roger the call. She tapped her ear button.

"Indian Thirty roger. Excuse me, Mr. Hazlett, do you have another phone I can use?" She did not want to use the one on his desk.

"There's one in the kitchen. Down the hall to the left."

"Thank you."

She started to leave, then stopped, feeling suddenly uneasy. Mama was eyeing Hazlett so intently. Was it wise to leave him with the suspect?.

"Mama."

He looked at her.

"Keep Mr. Hazlett in good health while I'm gone."

She did not like Mama's answering smile. Still, she walked out, hunting for the kitchen.

She found the phone and punched the squadroom's number. Lieutenant Candarian came on the screen. "Don't you two ever go off duty?"

"We're tracking down new evidence."

"I feel sorry for Vradel having to justify all this overtime."

Janna sighed. "Lieutenant, I'm on a hot lead that may go cold if I don't chase it fast."

"A Milo Talous has been looking for you most of the afternoon, or so he tells me."

"Talous?" For a moment, she could not remember anyone of that name.

"Of the Department of Justice. Surely you haven't forgotten the Feds involved in your case."

Janna felt foolish. Of course. Talous. "What does he want?"

"Does that mean you haven't kept him up to date on the investigation? Maybe that's what he wants. He left a number for you to call: 233-4111."

Janna wrote it down on a pad by the phone. "Thank you."

"Any time." Candarian smiled. "Good luck with the new lead."

Jorge wished the she-lion had not left. The door closing behind Brill appeared to be some kind of release for Maxwell. He flexed his shoulders and seemed to grow even taller. Jorge found him towering over the desk, and smiling very unpleasantly.

"Well, jon, it's just you and me. Let's have a real exchange."

Jorge maintained his smile. "Man to man, as it were?"

"It'd only be man to man if you were, but you aren't, jon. You're a toad. We'll have a man to toad exchange."

Jorge felt his face freeze. Anger flared in him. Just who did Maxwell think he was! "We won't talk at all, sergeant. I find your tone insulting."

The leo snorted. "I haven't even started. My partner is very polite. She's a conscientious officer who's going to make Investigator III and even Lieutenant some day. She works by the book. I'm different, though, so let me put it my way now." Maxwell leaned across the desk toward Jorge. "We're going to live with you, toad. You're not going to be able to breathe without us counting your respirations. You won't be able to entertain your ladyfriends without our company. You might as well make us partners in your business, toad, because we're going to be there for every transaction."

Jorge forced himself to a wintry smile. "That's called harassment. I can bring charges against you for that."

"Harassment?" Maxwell snorted in contempt. "You don't even know the meaning of the word, toad. Harassment is a cold shoulder compared to what we're going to do to you. You're going to find us sticking to you tighter than ticks. Our faces are never going to be out of your sight. It isn't going to be harassment; it's going to be like becoming a Siamese triplet."

Jorge started shaking with fury. He stood up. "I've tolerated enough of this. You have one minute to leave my house before I call—"

"The police?" Maxwell sneered.

"Get out of my house!"

"Not until we prove you murdered your partner and that sligh. When we go, we intend to take you with us. After that it won't be long before some prison doctor draws up a syringe of T-61 and in the name of the State of Kansas, shoots it into your veins to send you on the longest odyssey of them all."

Red haze clouded Jorge's vision. He could hear his pulse thundering in his ears. This—this…creature could not do this! People ordered out were supposed to go. The game was over—and he, Jorge, had beaten them. How dare Maxwell not obey the rules!

Janna met Milo Talous's tired clerk's eyes sheepishly. "I'm sorry we forgot to keep you informed. We've been busy with our line of investigation and it didn't seem to have much to do with yours."

The Justice agent frowned. "Information ought to be shared routinely between different agencies as well as between different departments in the same agency. For all you know, I might have had information that could help you."

"Yes, sir. Now, what can I do for you?"

"You can help me arrest Jorge Hazlett."

Jorge yanked open the desk drawer and pulled out the .22 revolver there. He pointed it at Maxwell. "I said get out of my house! I refuse to be subjected to any more of this abuse. You've lost! There is no evidence I killed anyone. There never will be. You've lost…*lost*!"

Maxwell eyed the .22. "I know: two Knights alone can never capture a King. But what if one of them isn't a Knight? What if one is a Rook?"

Jorge stared at him. He caught the pun. A rook was also a black, crowlike bird. Could a Rook and a Knight capture a King? Any end game implied that each side had at least a King left, and of course it was possible to checkmate with a King and a Rook.

His mind snapped back to attention just in time to find Maxwell launching across the desk after the pistol shooter.

Janna stared at Talous. "Arrest Hazlett? I'd love to, but what for?"

Talous winced. "My god, you not only don't talk to people you need to; you don't even read the reports I've sent you. The handwriting analysis—"

The handwriting analysis! She thought of the report lying on her desk right now, the one she had never quite had time to read.

"—indicates Hazlett signed the contracting papers for the Laheli Company account and ten others. This afternoon the U. S. District Attorney handed me a warrant for—"

The flat crack of a gunshot interrupted him.

Janna whirled. The sound had come from the direction of the study! She charged out of the kitchen.

The shot sounded nothing like the thunderous explosion on holo-v programs, but in the confined area of the study, it sounded to Jorge like the thunderclap announcing the end of the world. He had not intended to pull the trigger. In horror he watched Maxwell collapsing across the desk.

Panic overwhelmed him. He had shot a police officer! He dropped the .22 and bolted from the room. He heard the she-lion shout at him, but did not pause. He dived for the front door, jerked it open, and flung himself up the steps.

Behind him, Janna felt wrenched two ways at once. She needed to stop the fugitive but fear pulled her toward the study. She debated in the last few steps before coming even with the study door. At the last minute she wheeled into the study.

Mama was slowly sliding off the desk onto the floor, clutching at his chest. Crimson stained the bright yellow of his shirt.

"Mama!"

She caught him and helped ease him the last few centimeters to the floor.

"Mama, what happened?"

He coughed and whispered, "Got him on attempted murder."

She tried to yell at him that they did not need another charge. They could get him on Tescott violations. Her throat had tightened to much for yelling, though. Her vision seemed to be blurred, too. Surely she could not be crying, not for Mahlon Maxwell.

He closed his eyes with a soft sigh.

Outside, a sportster's fans wound up.

Janna came onto her feet. She tore out of the house and across the street toward Indian Thirty. Rapping her ear button. "Indian Thirty, Capitol. Officers in need of assistance! One officer down! Brentwood and Danbury."

She reached into the car through the open window and jerked the shotgun from its rack. Pumping a shell into the breech, she spun and raced back for the house. One arm scrubbed her eyes clear.

The Vulcan was backing across the lawn toward the street. It turned as it backed, ready to leap forward at the first possible moment. Janna fired into the nearest fan vent in the airfoil skirt. She pumped another shell into the breech and fired again. The fiberplastic of the skirt shattered.

The fans' whine flattened in sound. As it did, the right rear quarter of the car dropped. The skirt plowed into the lawn. The fans screaming, the Vulcan bucked in anguish. It struggled to stabilize and move, but could only pivot around the damaged fans.

Janna pumped in another shell and circled the Vulcan to the front. "Set her down, Hazlett!" She aimed the shotgun at the open window of the driver's side, straight into Jorge Hazlett's white face. "Checkmate. The game's over. Now climb out of the car...slowly. Make one move I consider too fast and you'll be a candidate for total thoracic transplant."

In the distance, she heard the *whew-whew-whew* of police sirens.

Hazlett climbed out of the Vulcan with infinite care.

17

The waiting room outside surgery was well appointed with comfortable chairs and numerous microbooks and current periodicals. Janna sat down in none of the chairs and read none of the books or magazines. Like some great cat, she paced the carpeted area in endless circles and on each round, paused to stare at the surgery doors. She cursed herself. What a stupid waste the shooting was. If she and Mama had held back...if she had read the damned handwriting analysis when it arrived on her desk...if she had not left Mama alone with Hazlett while she called the station. The "ifs" went on endlessly. She blamed herself. She was the senior partner and By-the-Book Brill. She knew procedure. She had to bend it, though, had to agree to go stick pins in Hazlett. The lapse might cost Mama his life.

She had certainly flamed eight years in one bloody spectacle. The only thing that kept her from writing out her resignation now was the knowledge that the peeps would probably take care of her dismissal. Well, there was always Champaign. Wim might be able to find something constructive for her to do out there.

From the doorway of the waiting room, Vradel said, "He's still in there? How long has it been?"

She could not bring herself to look at him. She kept pacing. "Three hours."

"You look like you think it's your fault."

She twitched her shoulders.

"So what happened?"

Now she really could not look at him. "It's as I told Candarian."

"Hazlett resisted arrest, you told her. Do you know what Hazlett says? He says you two were threatening him and he shot Maxwell in self-defense."

She made herself turn around and stare straight into the lieutenant's eyes. "Mama never threatened him. I could hear every word they were saying while I was on the phone."

Vradel chewed his mustache. "You'll swear to that in court, and to the peeps?"

She swallowed. Look at her. She was doing just what Wim had warned her about. Every lying word jeopardized her career still more. And for what? Maxwell. Why did she do it? She had no idea.

"Of course I'll swear to it."

He regarded her speculatively. "You have a good record. They may believe you."

She started pacing again. He walked with her. They both stopped to stare at the surgery door.

"There's no trace of that sligh Tarl yet."

She shrugged. No surprise there.

They paced another circuit.

"I can assign you a new partner now, if you still want one."

She found herself staring at him, trying to understand the sudden confusion in her, when Wim and Vada Kiest walked into the waiting area.

"Wim."

He came toward the sound of her voice and put his arms around her. "One of the nurses told me what happened. You're sure having bad luck with partners lately."

She leaned her cheek against his forehead. "Luck is a bitch."

"You're looking well, though, Kiest," Vradel said.

"They're letting me out tomorrow." He let Janna go and stepped back to reach for Vada's hand. "It won't be long before we'll be leaving Earth. Which reminds me, Jan. The *Invictus* incident scared a number of people on our ship. They're looking for people to buy out their shares. We could set up the loan and you could come out on this ship. We could all go together."

Go now? If fate ever spoke, it must be like this. It sounded like a fine idea. So why did she have this hollow in her gut? "Leave in two weeks? Is that possible?"

"Sure. All you have to do is buy the share and get your physical."

Vradel's mustache twitched. He said conversationally, "I'm putting together a special squad to find that banzai Bonsai. People aren't safe on the street until we strap that bibi."

Janna looked at him. "The hit-and-run driver?" It was about time they concentrated on her.

Win hissed through his teeth. "Don't let him skin you, Jan! Don't forget that could just as easily be you in there being put back together. It's a bad job. You can do better."

She sucked on her lower lip. The world was full of Hazletts and Lacledes preying on the Kelleners and Owans. Leos stood between the two and the crossfire could be deadly. She thought of the jon who shot at her the day Wim was injured. She had been only millimeters from death then. There had been the sniper, too. Who needed that for twenty years?

The surgery doors opened. Mauve-clad OR personnel guided out a gliding gurney. Mama lay on it, tubes running from his chest to bags hanging over the edge of the gurney. Other tubes ran from bags of solutions down into his arms. Still others led from an oxygen tank to his nose. The life-function indicators on the side of the gurney registered a muddy color.

Janna touched Mama's hand. He did not open his eyes. She looked at the nearest person in scrubs. "Will he be all right?"

"You'll have to ask Dr. Teeter that."

Janna searched their faces. "Where is Dr. Teeter?"

Dr. Teeter stood behind the stretcher, a handsome woman in her fifties. "Are you a relative?" she asked.

A moment later she shook herself. Her eyes went from Mama's Dutch-chocolate color to Janna's smoky hair and fair skin. She sighed. "Excuse me. It's been a long night."

"She's closer than a relative," Vradel said. "She's his partner."

A smile touched the tired face. "I understand. His condition is serious, but it's stabilizing, I think. The next few hours are the most critical. Fortunately the bullet was a small caliber and only nicked the aorta or he would most certainly be dead. I'd say his chances of surviving are fair. Now, excuse us, please. We need to get him to Intensive Care."

They pushed the gurney on down the corridor.

Janna stared after it. "If he dies, what has it all been for? We could have strapped Hazlett anyway."

Vradel said, "Could we? Hazlett has an attorney who's been demanding that a handwriting expert of his own examine the signatures on those records. If Hazlett were arrested for the Tescott violations alone, he could be out on bail. As it is, the judge has set bail so high, your snake is in lock-up. He might beat the Tescott conviction, but he'll have a much harder time convincing a jury he didn't shoot or was justified in shooting Maxwell."

"It still seems useless," Vada said. "I'm glad you're going to get out and come with us, Jan."

The gurney neared the corner. Janna did not take her eyes from it. Strange. She felt a piece of herself going with it.

Maybe not so strange. She took a close look at her feelings. A piece of her *was* with him. He was her partner…but it involved more than that, too. Different as she and Mama were, they shared something of the same soul. Vradel shared it, too. "No, I'm not coming."

Vada caught her breath. "Oh, Jan!"

"Why not?" Wim demanded.

"Not everyone can leave. Someone has to stand between the sheep and wolves or there really won't be any hope for this planet."

"It doesn't have to be you standing between. Don't be noble."

She smiled at him, as if he could still see her expression. "I'm not noble. I'm a leo, Wim, blood and bone. Rotten as it can be, I love the job. I gave up law school for it, and maybe a husband and family. I'm doing what I want to do."

Vradel grinned.

She sighed. "I couldn't be a farmer, never in this world or any other. I'm glad you're getting what you want, and I wish ramjets weren't one-way trips so I could come visit you after you're settled." How strange to think they might be just arriving on Champaign when she was an old, dying woman. "I wish you both the best of luck." She looked around at Vradel. "Is there room for me on that special squad?"

"I expect so. I need something to keep you busy until your partner heals up."

"Thank you, sir." She turned back in the direction the gurney had disappeared. "I'll see you all later. Will you excuse me right now? I'd like to see if they'll let me sit by his bed until he wakes up."

Spider Play

PROLOGUE

The device bore little physical resemblance to a real spider. The long, flat, mechanical body on the monitor screen looked more like some gigantic centipede as it crawled in a spiral path around a suspended cylindrical frame, an embryo centipede trying to avoid entanglement in its umbilical cord. Laboratory lights reflected dully off matte surfaced plastic and ceramic. It acted like a spider, though. Dark strands flowed out behind the body, strands that wove together into a continuous sheet, clothing the framework in midnight. The watcher before the monitor stood with arms folded, fascinated.

It obviously fascinated the coverall-clad technicians around it, too. They circled the construct, holding onto the frame's guy wires for stability as they made notes on their clipboards and chattered back and forth. One young woman reached down to run exploratory fingers over the spider's produce, leaving her pen drifting in the air beside her, but smoothly retrieved it before the air currents carried it out of reach. None of them looked toward the camera. Naturally. The watcher grinned. None of them knew it was there.

"You aren't the only spinner of webs here," the watcher whispered at the spider on the monitor. "Only, mine are bigger than yours. Soon the whole solar system will feel the effects of them."

The watcher carefully deactivated the secret camera, returning the monitor to normal surveillance before floating off to tend the newest strand of that web.

1

Wednesday, January 24. 10:00:00 hours

The web grew across the corner of the Shawnee County Police Department's Crimes Against Persons squadroom. Picking her way delicately along the strands already laid, the spider added more filaments, filling in the pattern of gray gossamer stretching from the newscanner control box on the shelf above the caff urn up to the screen hanging on the wall broadcasting its images of the world to oblivious leos—law enforcement officers. The spider's work had not escaped notice, however.

Sergeant Mahlon Maxwell, better known as "Mama" by his colleagues, said dreamily, "Isn't it exquisite?"

Staring from the web to her partner, Sergeant Janna Brill hissed in exasperation. "*This* is why you've been standing here for ten minutes while I worked on reports alone?"

To think she had been concerned about him when she realized how long he had been gone and looked around from the dictyper to see him standing in a trance with his hand on the tap of the caff urn. He looked like a statue...or rather, she had reflected, some impressionistic representation of a human sculpted in dutch chocolate and drawn out to grotesquely lanky proportions surpassing even her sinewy-lean hundred and eighty-three centimeters. She frowned. Lately he had been unusually quiet and distant. What was wrong...woman trouble again, or could he be flashing back? She had never seen Mama use recreational drugs, not even those accepted by the most conservative leos, but...perhaps there had been something used beyond safe limits in the past?

"Mama?" She pitched her voice to carry above the din of buzzing phones and overlapping conversations between investigators and citizens in varying stages of irritation or anxiety.

He did not appear to hear. The pattern of light reflection did not change on his egg-bald scalp. No fold shifted in the fluorescent red and orange jumpsuit. Janna pushed away from the row of dictypers to hurry across the room. "Mama!" She touched his shoulder.

He finally moved...pushing his glasses up his nose. "Look, bibi." He pointed out the spider web.

All Janna's concern evaporated with his remark on the esthetic value of the spider's creation. Exquisite? she thought. *He* would look exquisite...on the floor with the soles of her thigh boots in his face.

How could she ever have forgotten that her partner was brainbent, wickers, totally over the brainbow? Twice before he had made Investigator and twice been busted back to uniform, and in between using his night-school law degree to defend other officers against disciplinary actions, had been shuffled through every division in the county for such infamous escapades of his own as switching his duty weapon for an old-fashioned, forbidden firearm and managing to lock himself and a female partner in the back of their patrol unit when they climbed in for a game of Grope and Tumble.

"Mahlon Sumner Maxwell," she hissed, "being partners means we share the work of this job, in case you've forgotten, and that includes *all* of it, including the paperwork, not just 'the thrill of the chase.'"

His eyes rolled. "You've certainly gotten bitchy since Sid married the man of his dreams and moved out."

A spasm of guilt momentarily overwhelmed her anger. Had she? Well, maybe, but damn it, she and the assistant medical examiner had cohabed for nearly six years and been like sisters. The apartment felt desolate without his warmth and humor...without someone who cared whether she came home or not.

Then anger hissed back through her. "I'm going to be even bitchier if I have to keep talking at that damn dictyper alone. While we've got this little piece of the arctic,"—she waved toward the swirl of white beyond the window slits—"keeping Topeka's deeks off the street for a change, let's make the most of it, huh? You can admire nature on your own time!" She reached out to brush away the web.

A chocolate hand caught her wrist. "Hey, bibi, she's not doing any harm, just looking for a place out of the cold, like everyone with sense."

"Except them." Janna nodded toward the newscanner screen, where Pennsylvania's Governor John Granville Hershey wore a presidential hopeful's smile amid the drifts of New Hampshire.

"Everyone with sense, I said."

Janna had to grin.

"President Lipp's African policy is a disaster," Hershey's resonant voice said, "utterly failing to recognize that we are no longer dealing with a tribal mentality. The Union of African Nations represents a unity beyond even nationalism, and without delicate handling, the UAN could become to the export of African resources what OPEC was to Mideast oil in the last century."

Mama straightened the containers of stirrers and sugar and cream substitutes into an even line beside the urn, then pushed his glasses up his nose, grimacing. "Much as I hate to agree with any politician, he's right. According to the *Wall Street Journal*, eighty-three per cent of the mining companies on the African continent are owned by a single corporation, Uwezo—which means 'power' in Swahili—and its officers are high officials in a dozen different African governments."

Surprise wiped away the last of Janna's irritation. When did Mama find time for the *Wall Street Journal?* He must watch the *Journal* channel of his newscanner while he ate breakfast and prepared for bed.

"It's nice some of have slack time," a voice said behind Janna.

She swore silently as she recognized the voice, Pass-the-Word Morello, the squad clerk. Was he looking for an idle investigator to hand a new assignment? Why had she ever left the dictyper? "It isn't slack time," she said, turning to look down at him. "It's just a caff break. We still have a mountain of reports to finish."

Morello's foxy face twisted in a smirk. "Crimes Against Property is still out on the street accumulating report material, though. Not all the criminal element are huddling inside by heaters."

Suddenly Janna understood the smirk and the gleam in Morello's eyes. He had a story he was dying to tell. Sometimes she wondered what Morello's home life was like. Station house chop said he and his wife lived with his wife's mother and two sisters. Did he talk so much here in compensation for not being able to put a word in there, or was home one endless, ecstatic gossip session, with a chance to repeat and embellish all the stories from here for a whole circle of listeners?

"All right, I'll bite. What's Crimes Against Property involved in?" she asked.

Morello grinned. "A hearse hijacking."

Mama spun away from the spider and the half-frozen but determined smiles of the candidates on the newscanner. "What!"

The foxy grin broadened. "Driven by Ms. Beta Nafsinger from the Nafsinger Mortuary. You've probably seen their TV ads."

Janna had. A family business, the smoothly solemn man sitting amid his circle of five solemn daughters with Greek alphabet names.

"Nafsinger was on south Topeka Avenue yesterday morning and while she idled at a light, four members of a street gang jerked open the door, pushed her out, and sailed off with the hearse."

Mama glanced toward the window slit and pushed his glasses up his nose, frowning. "In this weather? Which gang?"

"They wore stars painted around their eyes."

That would be the Orions, then, though south Topeka Avenue was a bit out of their Oakland territory. Which concerned Janna less than the sudden white-rimmed gleam of Mama's eyes. That look always preceded a wild leap over the brainbow. Thank god the Hijacked Hearse belonged to Crimes Against Property and not this squad. "Interesting. You let us know how the case comes out."

Morello smirked again. "You tell me. Lieutenant Vradel wants to see you in his office."

Janna glared at him. "Damn you, Morello. How can this hearse possibly have anything to do with Crimes Against Persons?"

Morello shrugged, grinning.

Hissing, Janna turned away and stalked across the room toward Hari Vradel's office.

The burly squad commander had company. Lieutenant Dominic Applegate from Crimes Against Property sat in one of the chairs by the desk, with two of his investigators leaning against the wall behind him, Galen Quist and Teda "Teddybear" Roos. The nickname came from that blue-eyed, freckled, cuddly look, though Lowell Danner from Juvenile reported that Roos could rip a man's head off if she wanted. Rumor had she and her partner spending all their time together, on and off duty, but not counting coup. According to Pass-the-Word Morello, they had tried sleeping together but found each other such poor lovers that they stuck to what they really wanted to do anyway, tinker with Quist's motorcycle.

Applegate and the two investigators stared as she and Mama came in.

A reaction Janna had grown used to. People not around Mama all the time tended to be startled anew at every meeting by his taste in clothes and by his gleaming scalp, which except for the lack of paint or tattoos made him look more like a tripper who had blundered down the hall from Narcotics than like a leo. Everyone else in the room had chosen a more conservative appearance, jumpsuits or tabard-over-bodysuit combinations in subdued checks and diagonal stripes, with the men sporting mustaches and the whole group wearing full heads of hair curled in the tight mop used so often by leos meeting the requirement for hair that would not interfere with their vision that the style had become known as a "lion's mane." And of course, her smoky blondness contrasted so sharply with Mama's darkness.

"You know Sergeant Brill and Sergeant Maxwell, of course" Vradel said.

"Oh, yes." Applegate's grimace at Mama indicated he knew Janna's partner far better than he wanted to. "Still looking at the world through windows, I see."

Mama smiled easily. "I still can't tolerate contact lenses."

"Both Brill and Maxwell have experience with the Oakland area and its gangs," Vradel said. "Brill, Maxwell...Lieutenant Applegate would like our help locating the Orions who jacked the hearse yesterday. I'm assuming that with Morello outside, you're already aware what hearse." He leaned across the desk to hand them a report form, then picked up a pencil and began sketching idly on his blotter. "That's the stolen vehicle report filed by the victim."

Janna read through it quickly with Mama breathing down her neck. The report went into details of the appearance and conversation of the three males and one female who had taken the hearse, but that only confirmed their identity as Orions and told her nothing new. "Why is Crimes Against Persons being brought into this? The driver wasn't hurt." The tone of Nafsinger's statement indicated more outrage than pain.

Mama took the report from her and laid it on the corner of the desk, meticulously lining the pages up parallel to and at equal distances from both sides of the corner. "Maybe it has to do with who else was in the hearse, bibi."

Oh, god, no, she thought with an inward groan, but a quick glance at Vradel found the squad commander nodding. The outline of a space shuttle grew under the point of his pencil. "Perhaps you ought to explain, Dom."

Applegate picked up his report from the desk. "Nafsinger states she was on her way back from Forbes Field, but in her zeal to remember exactly what her assailants looked like, she forgot to mention that she had been to Forbes to collect a body—the corpse of one John Paul Chenoweth, an employee of the Lanour-Tenning Corporation—from their space platform. He died Saturday when his pressure suit ripped while working on construction of an addition to the station. His body was to be left at the Nafsinger Mortuary until his family made more formal arrangements for it."

Janna lifted a brow. "I take it this particular information comes from sources other than Ms. Nafsinger, then."

Applegate tugged at the drooping ends of his handlebar mustache. Behind him, Quist and Roos exchanged glances and grinned. "The information comes from Mr. Leonard Fontana, director of the Lanour platform. Mr. Fontana apparently feels very serious about his responsibility to Lanour's employees, living and dead. He called the mortuary from the platform this morning to see if the Chenoweth family had contacted them yet."

"And wasn't at all happy to find Chenoweth had...gone astray," Roos murmured.

Applegate pretended not to hear. "After talking to the mortuary, Fontana made a second call...to *our* director, and Paget called me. He suggested we make this a multisquad investigation." He frowned toward Mama. "I don't really expect to accomplish any more than Quist and Roos could alone, but it'll look like a good faith effort to the brass, and Lanour."

The face Vradel was sketching developed a scowl, but he said only, "Oh, I think we can do better than that, Dom. Four pairs of legs always cover more ground than two."

Mama murmured in Janna's ear, "I didn't know Lanour carried this much clout way out here in Kansas."

"I still don't understand why we should be excited." She glanced from Applegate to Vradel. "The Orions will dump the hearse as soon as they've had their fun and Nafsinger will have it and the body back, though the hearse will probably be stripped." They all ought to know that.

"They hadn't abandoned it by evening that we could find," Quist said sourly.

Vradel laid down the pencil to chew on a corner of his mustache. "If it's in a snowbank, we might not find it until this junk melts, which could be late March the way the weather bureau is talking." He paused. "Some kinds of heat don't warm up a winter at all."

A glint in his eyes, like sunlight shining on ice, told Janna that he would have said something quite different if they had been alone, like: "Stop arguing and go wrap those Orions. Find that body!" But he would not chew on them in front of visiting troops any more than he would openly criticize a fellow lieutenant's snide crack in the hearing of subordinate officers.

Janna did not wait for stronger phrasing. Digging into the sleeve pocket of her jumpsuit for vending tokens, she tossed a couple into the cup on the corner of Vradel's desk and headed out the door with Mama. Like everyone in the squad, she rarely paid attention to the newscanner and could not even remember where it came from, whether it had been a gift, abandoned, or recovered stolen property "forgotten" to be turned into the property room, but along with everyone else she contributed tokens Vradel could redeem for credit to pay Newservices, Inc. for the subscription.

Quist and Roos followed her out of Vradel's office.

Outside, the scanner was still covering presidential candidates. Senator Scott Early frowned gravely into the camera. "Part of this nation's metal shortage must be attributed to the colonial movement. How can we who choose to remain loyal to Earth rather than abandon her in her difficulties to flee to the stars possibly built a fleet to mine the asteroids when the colonists take so much metal with them in the form of tractors, choppers, and ships' hulls? It should be the sacred duty of the next President to institute a moratorium on colony ship building until such time as the people of this nation have enough metal from asteroid or sea bottom mining that we need no longer depend on African resources."

Mama's eyes gleamed. "Bibi, this hearse—" he began.

Janna tried to head him off. "Just what kind of trouble did you have with Applegate?"

Roos said, "The lieutenant told us that when he was a uniformed sergeant in the Gage division Maxwell put static-adhesive plastic over the solar receptors on his patrol car." She grinned wickedly. "He didn't say so but I got the impression what really popped him was cursing and the kicking the car for ten or fifteen minutes before it occurred to him to switch to battery power."

Janna grinned, too, but Mama protested indignantly, "*I* didn't do it!" His expression went thoughtful. "But that explains some things. I didn't think he would stay so mad about the shotgun."

"Shotgun?" Quist said.

Mama nodded. "I happened to trigger my shotgun in the course of checking it one time. Unfortunately, being in the watch car, it blew a hole in the roof and took off part of the light rail. The sound startled my partner so much she ran the car into a power pole and wrecked it. We happened to be going rather fast at the time, chasing some deeks who'd just boosted a jewelry store." Mama pushed his glasses up his nose. "But this hearse... It's damn strange, a street gang joy riding in this weather. It's even stranger that they'd take a *hearse*. I'd expect them to go after something more like a Vulcan or Cheetah." He shook his head. "Something's wrong here. The whole thing smells. It stinks clear to the orbit of the Lanour platform."

Janna had to agree that the Orions were not behaving very characteristically, but the orbit she worried about was the one Mama seemed about to go into...and drag her with him.

2

Wednesday, January 24. 10:30:00 hours

"God, I hate going out in this shit again." The garage gave Quist's voice a hollow boom. "Sometimes I wonder why I ever became a leo."

"You wanted a legal way to race a Harley down city streets." Roos lifted her brows at Janna and Mama. "Well, how shall we divide Oakland?"

"What did you cover yesterday?" Janna asked.

"Nafsinger said the bibi called one of the jons 'Pluto,' so we went looking for Kiel Jerrett."

Janna nodded, Jerrett being the Orion leader and Pluto his street name.

"We checked his girlfriend's apartment, and his mother's. We checked Orion hangouts. No Pluto. No Orions at all."

Quist grimaced. "They'd all crawled down their roach holes."

Roos did not look at him. "So, suggestions anyone?"

"I say check the salvage yards," Quist said. "In case Jerrett is selling the parts from the hearse."

Mama pursed his lips. "He's not light-witted enough to do that. Let's hit all the obvious places again. He may figure you won't be back. I'd go for the bibi first." He grinned. "Weather like this, if I weren't working, I'd be warding off the cold with shared bodily warmth."

Roos glanced inquiringly at her partner.

He frowned. "I don't know about all of us going to one place. We'll have better have a better chance if we spread out and hit all his holes at once."

"The trouble with Jerrett isn't finding him; it's *keeping* the slippery deek," Mama said.

Quist considered, then nodded. "Sunny Kriegh lives at 520 North Twiss."

They headed for their cars, both Datsun-Ford Monitors like all the others in the row, though Mama had somehow managed to locate and gain assignment of a prussian-red vehicle among the collection of tans, blues, and greens. Quist and Roos eyed the car with envy as Janna and Mama slid into it across the spreading airfoil skirt that gave the car a shape some department wit had dubbed "bullet on the half shell."

"See you in Oakland," Ross said.

One thing about floatcars, Janna reflected as the Monitor lifted off its parking rollers and sailed up the garage ramp onto Van Buren, they did not have to wait for snow plows to clear the streets after a winter storm. The air cushions created by the fans just carried them over the drifts.

Once out of the dim garage, Mama switched from batteries to direct sun power and turned south toward Sixth Avenue, grimacing as the car bucked in the wind.

Janna switched on the car radio and tapped her button radio as she plugged it into her left ear. "Indian Thirty, Capitol. We're activating."

"I have your Twenty on the board, Indian Thirty," the dispatcher's flat voice replied in stereo from the car radio and ear button.

Janna also keyed in the Oakland division frequency before settling back in her seat. She and Mama might lose track of each other in a chase or canvassing Oakland, but if they ran into trouble, the transponders in the car and ear buttons that broadcast their locations to Dispatch's board would let help find them fast. The transponders would locate them even when they did not care to be found.

The voices of dispatchers from both divisions murmured in her ear, sometimes overlapping. Because of the duplex system, however, she could not hear the officers' replies.

"Beta Oakland Twelve, see the woman, Galaxy Lane, the brown house." After a pause, the dispatcher continued, "Brown house is all the description she gave. Check the area. She said she would be there waiting."

Mama turned the car onto Sixth Avenue, heading east past the downtown area and over I-70 into Oakland. Twentieth Century buildings of age-darkened brick with old-fashioned rectangular windows stood between newer structures of buff-colored native sandstone with windows of the energy-efficient slit design in one, two, and three slit groupings. But even the oldest buildings' roofs sported a row of the honeycomb-looking solar panels made up of the solar conversion cells Mr. Edward Lamar Simon had perfected forty years ago, turning light into a truly efficient energy source.

Mama said, "You miss Sid, don't you?"

Janna grimaced. For all the times her partner seemed totally oblivious to everyone beyond himself, other times he read her very well indeed. She did not feel like baring her soul to him, however. "What about you? What's your problem these days?"

"Alpha Oakland Eighteen, report your Twenty. Your transponders do not register on the board. Do you have a malfunction I should report to the supervisor?" After a pause, the dispatcher continued, "Disregard last signal. You're now activated."

Mama chuckled. "Isn't it amazing how fast a 'malfunctioning' transponder is cured with a threat to notify the supervisor?"

So he did not want to talk, either. Janna sucked in her lower lip. Maybe both of them were due for a chat with Schnauzer Venn, the department tick tech.

In Oakland the streets looked untouched since the last snowfall. A few cars sat with only their airfoil skirts covered, but mounds marked where other cars with no garage to protect them had been incapacitated by the bitter cold earlier in the month and now sat buried, waiting for a thaw before their owners made another try at starting them. If even warm weather would help. The tanglewood yards and turn-of-the-century houses bore testimony to oppressive poverty…roofs sagging, plastic siding warped and cracked. Under the snow, the cars were probably sagging and rusting, too.

Back in the early part of the century, some city council had tried to fight back at the Oakland decline by putting up module townhouses along North Twiss. Once the staggered rows with their slit windows and angular roofs topped with panels of Simon panels must have looked stylish. Now, however, many of the solar had panels cracked. Seams between the modules gaped, many of the window slits had been boarded up, and wood-grained plastic railings on second-floor balconies sagged broken. The spray-on plastic siding hung peeling in long, faded strips that rustled in the wind like dead leaves. Not even the alpine charm of the snow and icicles could hide the sad ugliness.

Mama parked the Monitor behind Quist and Roos near the end of the block, well away from 520's window slits. Climbing out, the four of them huddled with backs to the sting of the north wind. "Who goes to the door?"

"Since you and Quist came yesterday, why don't one of you knock today?" Janna said. "The other can go around to the back door." She turned enough to eye the row of balconies stretching down the length of the building. "Mama and I will cover the ends."

Behind his glasses, Mama's eyes regarded her with reproach. "Do we draw straws to see who takes the north side?"

Janna grinned. "Let the Oakland dispatcher decide. If the next call is for an even-number car, the north end is yours, partner."

And the voice of the Oakland dispatcher promptly murmured in her ear, "Beta Oakland Eleven, see the woman, 202 South Lime, the apartment in back. A co-wife is refusing to vacate after cancellation of the marriage contract."

"Damn!"

Janna trudged north well ahead of Roos, huddling deep in her jacket, hands jammed into her pockets. One problem with not plowing streets was that it left nowhere good to walk when the residents felt unmoved to shovel their walks. She waded through knee-deep snow all the way up the block and across the lawn area to the end of the building, circling wide so her tracks would not be immediately obvious to someone on the end balcony. Around the corner, she stood shivering, keeping the hood pulled closed around her face. The wind leaked in through the opening to sting her nose and cheeks anyway.

"Beta Oakland Three, your 10-28 is on a 2072 Volkswagen Moth, registered to an Erica Friesen-Yager and Dara Yager-Friesen of 1715 Downs Road."

Oh, to be back on patrol right now, snug in the warmth of a watch car, Janna thought with longing, or anywhere but here with cold seeping through the soles of her boots. She stamped her feet, swearing silently. How long did it take Roos to knock on the door anyway? If something did not happen soon, she would freeze solid. The department swatbots searched buildings and defused bombs. One ought to be programmed to wait in snowdrifts with a microfilament-mesh net for throwing over rabbiting fugitives.

"Alpha Oakland Twenty, contact management, Drug World, Belmont Mall, reference individual attempting to obtain heroin with an expired addict card."

Then around the front of the building someone swore, and feet thudded on a balcony floor. A split second later Mama's voice shouted, "Police! Stop!"

Janna peeked around the corner. She could not see the person on the balconies, but Mama plowed through the drifts in front of the building, gun in hand, the long, thin barrel of the needler aimed upward.

Janna jerked back out of sight. She easily imagined what had happened. Jerrett, thinking to leave the apartment by the route Janna anticipated, climbing from balcony to balcony, had been headed toward the south end when something either made him suspicious or Mama looked around the corner at the wrong moment. Jerrett had reversed and was now coming her direction.

The thud of leaping feet and plop of snow and icicles knocked from railings marked his progress. Janna forgot the cold in a fiery wash of adrenaline. Was he armed? She felt down the top of her thigh boot for her own gun holstered there.

Snow fell just around the corner, followed by the drop of something heavier, then a figure hurtled past her, a male with his face and depilated head brightly covered. A bare chest showed under the half-opened jacket.

Janna raised the needler. "Freeze, Pluto."

Awareness of the snowball came an instant too late. His arm swung and the handful of snow he must have scooped up along the way struck her square in the face.

Instinctive reflexes snapped her eyes shut just in time to protect them, but training sent her diving blind toward the last location she had seen Jerrett. Slick synthetic slid under her hands. She grabbed at it, throwing her arms around the form, and her momentum carried both of them down to land rolling in the snow. Jerrett writhed. An arm jerked. With another surge of adrenaline, Janna heard the hissing *snick* of a switch blade opening. She used their roll to carry him under her, pinning his knife arm, then released her grip with her arms and jackknifed to land with knees between his shoulder blades and in the small of his back and the muzzle of the Starke against his neck.

"Relax, jon." She wiped her eyes clear.

"Or you'll shoot me full of percurare and leave me paralyzed here in the snow to catch pneumonia?" He snorted. "That's the only way you can hang on to me, isn't it, puss?"

Mama waded up to them. "Are you so sure she's carrying percurare? We've had explosive needles okayed as ammunition now, too."

If only, Janna reflected wistfully, but Jerrett went very still and craned his neck around to peer up at her and the needler, his eyes white-rimmed in the center of four-pointed scarlet stars. "Explosive needles? You're off your tick."

"No, no," Mama said. "*I'm* the one off his tick. She's just a mean bitch of a she-lion." As Janna backed off Jerrett and hauled him to his feet by the collar of his jacket, Mama patted Jerrett down, and took not only the knife but a spool of fine wire he found in one jacket pocket.

Microfilament! Anger flared in Janna. Strung across an opening where someone would hit it, say a leo on a chase, the wire could cut legs, or a throat, to the bone before its victim realized what was happening. Her previous partner had been blinded by microfilament. She hated it, and anyone who used it. Her finger tightened on the Starke's trigger with longing to put a few too many needles into Jerrett and leave him with chest muscles paralyzed, suffocating.

Mama's eyes flashed, too, but he said nothing, only stepped back, pocketed the wire, and began cleaning his nails with the knife. He looked nonchalant, though his hands must be freezing. "That's a nice jacket, Pluto. One of the new no-weight, superinsulating mountaineering/ski models, isn't it. I wish I were underprivileged so the government would give me coupons for clothes like that."

"Or did you pay for it with the profits from moonlight requisitioning?" Janna snapped.

"I don't know what the hell you're talking about, puss." The chatter of Jerrett's teeth spoiled the sneer, though.

"Stripped parts, and in particular, parts stripped from a hearse."

"You ain't making any sense at all." A shiver wracked his body. "It must be the temperature…you know, like lizards and snakes slow down in the cold? Maybe if we go inside, your brains will warm up and start working again."

"Why thank you," Mama said. "See, bibi; I told you he'd be a gracious host. Lead the way, Mr. Jerrett."

Quist met them at the door. Behind him lay a living room furnished with tip-over occasional table/chairs and molded-foam easy chairs covered in fake fur. Roos sat on a scarlet couch with a young woman whose face and head—depilated except for a long blonde horsetail on top—carried the same colorful star designs as Jerrett's. Sullen eyes watched the investigators from red stars surrounded by wide borders of yellow, then blue. The painted-on fit of Kriegh's canary body suit left little of her anatomy to the imagination, but it was not transparent enough to tell whether her torso also carried the planet and comet tattoos the open jacket revealed on Jerrett's chest.

"Tell us what you've done with the hearse, Jerrett," Quist said.

Jerrett's lip curled. "You got frostbite of the brain, too? I don't know nothin' about any hearse."

"Who has the frostbite?" Janna said. Reaching inside her jacket, she tapped on the microcorder in the breast pocket of her jumpsuit. "Yesterday morning, Tuesday, January twenty-third, your people jacked a hearse, license number RSN 405, on south Topeka Avenue. The driver described you exactly and heard your fem friend call you by name. You're lion meat, Jerrett."

Jerrett flung up his garish head. "Not me, leo. I was here all day, wasn't I, star?" he asked Kriegh.

"All day, Pluto." She glared defiantly at the leos.

"Maybe I did hear something yesterday about a hearse, but what would I be doing jacking anything in this weather? I like my fun in the sun, and...a hearse? Shit, I got a whole lot better taste than that. If I take a car, I want something top dink, like a Vulcan or Jaguar. I don't go downstreet."

Mama sent Janna a didn't-I-tell-you smirk.

"Someone else took the hearse and just wants me blamed for it."

"Why?" Roos demanded. "Who?"

Jerrett shrugged. "Anyone. Everyone envies the Orions."

"It can't be the Bolos," Quist said. "They couldn't paint over their faces heavy enough to cover up their rivet and steel-plate tattoos."

"It couldn't be the Simbas or Samurais, either," Janna said. "The jackers were Caucasian."

"Check the Toros," Kriegh said. "Wearing paint, the taco squad could almost pass as human."

Jerrett smirked. "That's good, star. I'll have to remember that. Did you ever think it might be the Pirates? South Topeka runs through their turf. How should I know who might have done it? You're the great detectives. It's your job to track down criminals and find who's trying to frame innocent citizens."

"Innocent," Quist snorted. "We'll see how innocent you are. Put on a shirt and let's go downtown where some people can look at you."

Jerrett frowned. "I want a lawyer."

"Sure," Janna said, "though I don't know why. We aren't arresting you. Aren't you just being a good citizen and proving your innocence by assisting us with our inquiries?"

He smiled thinly. "Oh, of course, puss...but I want counsel."

A public defender met them in the Crimes Against Persons squadroom at headquarters, a new woman Janna had never met before. She looked like all the others, though, a savior-to-mankind gleam in her eyes, wearing a conservative lavender paisley tabard-and-body suit she had probably spent half a month's salary on because she wanted to look like a lawyer someone paid for. Frowning, she fussed around the squadroom overseeing the painting of the clerks and investigators drafted for the show-up. "You may not have formally arrested my client, but that doesn't absolve you from the responsibility of following proper procedure."

Roos looked up from the phone where she sat calling Beta Nafsinger and bared her teeth in a wolfish grin. "Oh, we'll follow procedure, councilor...to the letter."

Across the squadroom, the newscanner murmured and flickered, and for a moment, her attention caught by the word *sligh,* Janna turned to watch debate on a proposed state bill to make Identation mandatory. "Of course this is a free state in a free country," a legislator was saying, "but can we really give credence to the claim of these Undocumented persons we call 'slighs' that Identation restricts their freedom? Doesn't it endanger the freedom of us all, instead? We have proven examples that a large number of them turn to criminal activity to survive, and when they commit crimes, they are untraceable and untrackable. Worse, the honest among them are being robbed by their lack of Identation of necessities all civilized people should share, like good education by licensed teachers, sufficient food, medical care, and decent housing. For their own good and for the protection of all Kansans, every citizen *must* become Idented."

Janna turned away in disgust. Self-righteous bastard. Slighs were brainbent, of course; they had to be to prefer their bartering, scraping existence to Documented life, where the Social Care and Identification Bank Card ensured everything one needed and as a credit card, also bought almost anything else desired. Most slighs in her experience were not criminals, though, only quiet people desperately playing invisible to escape notice. Why legislate against their lifestyle, especially when almost every other had been legitimized?

Watching the clerks and investigators make up to look like Orions, Mama shook his head. "It's a waste of time. Nafsinger won't be able to put the nod on Jerrett."

Janna frowned. "You don't mean you actually *believe* the deek when he says he wasn't responsible for the hearse?"

"The crime and the time just don't match him, bibi."

"Oh, come on. He got cabin fever and went looking for a new thrill. It certainly doesn't figure that someone would jack the hearse to make trouble for the Orions, because it wouldn't, not worth mentioning. Not even if the hearse is stripped. Jerrett can handle a GTA sentence with his hands tied. The prison in Hutchinson is practically a second home to him."

"No," Mama agreed, "it doesn't figure."

"So Jerrett has to be guilty."

She expected him to argue, but Mama just pushed his glasses up his nose, regarded her thoughtfully through them for a moment, then turned away. His silence left her itching with sudden disquiet. Could he be right? But…if Jerrett were not involved in taking the hearse and body after all, and nothing would be gained by framing the Orions for it, then what the hell was going on?

3

Wednesday, January 24. 13:00:00 hours

When she and her father arrived at headquarters, Beta Nafsinger in person bore little resemblance to herself as she appeared in the TV commercial. Janna found herself shaking hands with a strapping young woman who looked like she should be on a farm tossing hay bales instead of tending corpses. Janna liked her on sight. Mama, Quist, and other investigators around the Crimes Against Persons squadroom also eyed her appreciatively. Cornflower blue eyes snapped with fierce satisfaction in the middle of a painted butterfly spreading blue and gold wings across her face.

"So you caught the sons of bitches. Good work. Where are the bloody bastards?"

Janna liked her even better.

"Beta, please. Your language." A crinkle of William Nafsinger's eyes and a twitch at the corner of his mouth belied his protest. Then the inner laughter vanished as he looked past his daughter to Roos and Quist. "Have you found Mr. Chenoweth?"

Janna winced inwardly. Mama studied his nails.

Roos gave both Nafsingers a bland smile. "Not just yet, I'm afraid. Will you come this way please?" She led the way out of the squadroom and down the corridor toward the show-up room.

Nafsinger sighed. "Leonard Fontana called me from the Lanour platform again this morning. He's very concerned."

They circled around three officers—two in the tight gray, red-sidestriped uniform jumpsuits and the third plainclothed—scowling at a thin, pale woman with the vacant expression of a tripper and a flower-tattooed scalp.

Beta Nafsinger eyed the pilgrim disapprovingly. "We're concerned, too. Mr. Fontana entrusted us with Mr. Chenoweth and we don't like betraying that trust."

Quist said, "Identification of these people we're about to show you may convince them to be more cooperative."

Roos pushed open the show-up room door. Nafsinger glanced curiously at the public defender already in the room waiting for them, but when no introductions were offered, she took a chair facing the screen wall and sat poised on the edge of it.

Expectancy became dismay, however, as Quist tapped the activation switch on the controls by the door and the wall screen lighted to reveal a line of four men and four women standing before a wall marked in height graduations. "They all look alike!"

Jerrett and Kriegh did almost vanish among the others, especially with everyone wearing jackets and hiding both hair and bare scalps under stocking caps like those Nafsinger described the jackers as wearing. The public defender smirked at the results of her fussing.

Nafsinger's father touched her arm. "Just relax and look them all over. Take your time. There are bound to be differences between them. Remember your trick of reading a deck of cards by minute differences on the backs?"

Nafsinger sent him a grateful smile.

Watching the affection between father and daughter, Janna felt a sudden sharp pang of homesickness for her own father. She ought to call him tonight. It might make the apartment bearable.

Nafsinger leaned forward again, studying the line of men and women on the screen as manipulation of the controls focused on each in turn and filled the screen with them from the waist up. "I don't know. They look like the people who pulled me out of the hearse, but...I just don't know. Something's wrong."

The public defender's smirk broadened.

"Wrong?" Roos frowned.

Quist smiled tautly. "Look closer." The view on the screen started to shift. "What about the jon wearing—"

The public defender snapped, "Officer Quist, that's leading the witness! Just pull back and let her see everyone."

Scowling, Quist snapped the screen back to the original view.

Nafsinger bit her lip. "When the bastard the girl called Pluto started pushing me out of the hearse, I quit fighting and concentrated on memorizing what they looked like so I could give a good description and identify them, but maybe I didn't look close enough." She sighed with a note of distress. "I don't recognize any of these people."

Her father patted her hand.

Mama moved to the chair beside her and gave her what Janna

recognized as his Reassuring smile. "You said something about them is wrong. Can you tell us what?"

"Well..." Nafsinger stared hard at the four men and four women, grimacing with the effort of concentration. "They look...neater. Take that one." She pointed at Jerrett's image. "His jacket looks new. The gang members I saw wore older clothes. Pluto's jacket had patches."

"Patches." Mama glanced toward Janna.

She swore silently. Jerrett might have worn another jacket yesterday, but she doubted it, not a patched one. A gang leader did not have to dress like a fashion plate or someone from a castlerow section of town, but he had to look as though he knew how to obtain from life what he wanted.

Mama smiled encouragingly. "That's good. Go on. Anything else?"

Nafsinger's forehead furrowed more deeply. "Yes, but I can't quite—" She broke off, closing her eyes for a minute. "Oh, I know...the stars." Her eyes reopened, wide with relief. "The stars aren't painted the same."

"What do you mean?" Quist tapped the controls. The eye of one clerk expended to fill the entire screen.

"The people I saw had red stars around their eyes like these people, but the borders were blue, then yellow on the outside."

Janna sat bolt upright. The wrong color sequence!

"You say the stars were painted?" Mama leaned toward Nafsinger. "You're sure they weren't tattoos?"

Nafsinger thought, then nodded. "The girl's anyway. The star point above her left eye was smeared."

She had looked close, all right, Janna reflected, a *hell* of a lot closer than most victims or witnesses ever thought or managed to.

The public defender stood up. "I don't see any further need for detaining my clients, do you?"

Quist punched the screen off and spoke into a speaker. "Turn them loose, Ed."

They filed out of the show-up room.

Mama caught Janna's eye. "I guess we'd better get back on the street and start asking who could profit by masquerading as Orions." He sounded infuriatingly close to an I-told-you-so.

"Isn't looking for the people first the long way around?" Beta Nafsinger asked. "Wouldn't the hearse be easier to find?"

Roos's smile froze into the professional politeness toward an outsider. "I know it would seem so, ma'am, but our county-wide bulletin on it hasn't found anything so far. It may be hidden somewhere."

"You mean the bastards who took it want it for something, like to use in a robbery?"

A bolt of shock jolted Janna. That was something she had not considered. She swore silently. It just might be the answer. Someone taking it for a purpose like that would want to lay a false trail which would send the leos hunting the wrong quarry.

"There's another possibility we might consider, too," Mama said. "Can either of you think of someone with a grudge against members of your family personally or professionally? The theft and the way it was done could be a strike at you."

Father and daughter stared. "A grudge!" Beta snorted. "That's ridiculous."

Her father shook his head. "Not ridiculous, but unlikely, I think. I'm sure I'm not universally loved but I don't know of any outright enemies. We work hard to ensure client satisfaction. Our clientele also comes from the Gage area and better parts of Highland Park, a class of people who complain to the Better Business Bureau, or sue, when they're unhappy."

"What about competitors?" Quist asked.

Shock became amusement. Janna thought Beta struggled not to laugh aloud. Her father sent her a reproachful glance. "A mortuary war...rivals stealing each other's equipment, sabotaging funeral arrangements? Come now, Officer Quist. Besides, I can't imagine any of my immediate competitors knowing enough about street gangs to imitate one so closely. I'm sorry we couldn't help, but call again if you need us and, please, you'll let us know the moment you locate Mr. Chenoweth, won't you?"

Father and daughter walked away down the corridor.

From the other direction, behind the investigators, came the group from the broadcast room, sighing in relief as they pulled off caps and shrugged out of jackets. Jerrett swaggered up, grinning. "See, I told you I was innocent. You're lucky we don't sue your badges off for false arrest and mental anguish. Then maybe you'd learn not to harass innocent citizens."

Jerrett would look good bouncing off the corridor wall, Janna reflected grimly, but she remained motionless while the Orion leader and his girlfriend strutted off down the corridor with the public defender.

Quist wore a stony mask, she noticed, and while Roos kept smiling her teddy-bear grin, a killer light glittered in her eyes. Being wrong hurt worse some times than others.

After a minute Janna eyed the others with a wry smile. "How shall we divide up Oakland?"

Janna and Mama drew the area north of Seward Avenue. Driving down the long stretch of drifts and shabby buildings, she grimaced. Some aspects of police work had not changed since officers were called cops. Legwork was one...exhausting, tedious, time-consuming. And today, when even the word *north* made her shiver—The thought broke off as a snarl in her gut reminded Janna that noon had passed some time ago. "How about lunch before we split up?" she asked Mama.

"Ten-four!"

The Oakland division station sat on Seward. She parked in the visitors' lot, where the snow had blown off to only ankle deep. Waving greetings to the officers in an incoming car, they waded to the cafe across the street.

Her ear button murmured: "Alpha Cap Ten, stalled vehicle 10-47 Kansas and Tenth Avenues. Semi down with two rear quarter fans seized up."

Seward looked like a street out of history. Janna doubted it had changed much at all in the past century. No one had added new buildings, and the only attempts at modernization were Simon cell panels on the roofs while windows not show windows had been bricked up into a series of slits or replaced with glass brick. The effort failed to look anything but shabby, however, especially with so many of the storefronts and solar panels marred by graffiti—gang names and challenges, profanities, telephone numbers with symbols which to the knowing meant unlicensed drug dealers and prostitutes—and the holo images faded or flickering.

Lazaro Wu, owner of Las Comidas Café, managed better than most businessmen along the street. His building remained clean of graffiti, though hints of color remaining in depressions on the age-darkened brick, the glass brick of his window, and the panels on the roof testified that the neatness came only at the price of effort.

The interior smelled of generations of hamburgers and french fries mixed with the odors of sweat, wet boots, and uniforms that lingered after the leos who had crowded its counter and booths at noon. Not a leo was in sight in it now, nor waitresses, only Lazaro Wu, sitting at the register frowning at the screen of his laptop computer.

Glancing up at them, he yelled, "Carita!"

An hispanic girl hurried out of the back to take their order, then vanished again.

On the small wall screen above the register, a newscanner commentator analyzed the latest stock market quotations. The name *Lanour* caught Janna's ear and she looked up to see a down symbol by the Lanour-Tenning quotation, but caught only the last part of the commentator's remark: "...that the expected proxy fight may drive stock prices even lower."

She lifted a brow. "It sounds like our company has more troubles than smugglers."

Mama shrugged. "I have a hard time working up sympathy for multinationals." He paused. "We ought to do something tonight. The Kansas City Opera is at the Civic Center for a week and this evening's performance is *Madame Butterfly*. Want to go?"

"To an opera?" Janna grimaced. That sounded no better than going home. "Besides, I have to work all day with you. Isn't that punishment enough?"

He sighed. "Bibi, there's more to life than—" He broke off, scowling. "The bastards!"

She blinked. "What?"

He pointed at the newscanner.

The screen showed a group of sign-carrying picketers. A voice-over was saying, "…at the Tellus Technics offices around the world by families of its space station employees protesting the rumored decision that the corporation will shut down the station later this year. A Tellus spokesman denied—"

"Lied through his teeth is more like it," Mama spat.

Janna frowned. "What makes you so sure?"

"I saw an interview with their new general manager. He thinks space development is a waste of time. You watch; he'll shut down that platform. No matter that the medical research there is turning out the best new allergy medications in the world—do you know I can actually pet cats now?—and that they're close to the greatest discovery of the century, a drug that keeps bone from losing calcium!"

Any moment now he would jump up on the table and start shouting. Janna said hurriedly, "What were you saying about my life should be more than this job?"

Mama blinked with the blankness of disorientation. "What? Oh. Yes…you have to do something more than work, work out at the gym, and take criminal justice classes toward Investigator III. Broaden your horizons. I had to put a wrap strap on you to get you to the ballet with me, but didn't you end up enjoying it?"

She nodded reluctantly.

"Then give opera a chance. If a semester in UMKC's theater arts curriculum can teach a Western Kansas rube like me to appreciate it, a city girl should take to it right away."

"Why don't you take Lia?"

He hesitated a moment too long before answering. "She's busy tonight."

Janna straightened. So it was woman trouble after all...again. And here she thought he had finally found a stable relationship in his current cohab. Maybe his apartment was becoming as desolate as hers. She regarded him with sympathy. "Okay, I'll—"

A stream of shrill Spanish rose in the kitchen. Something crashed.

Wu stiffened. "What the hell's going on out there!" he yelled, then glanced at Janna and Mama. "Leos, would you mind having a look?"

They headed for the kitchen door. It was only fair, quid pro quo for tolerating the leos' discharge of job tension that erupted as rowdiness at feeding time.

In the kitchen the waitress Carita stood with her back to a stainless steel table spitting at two hispanic youths planted in front of her while a third in a greasy apron fried hamburgers on an old-fashioned grill, ignoring the commotion. The two wore scarlet jackets with black bulls charging across the back and had pulled long hair into a bullfighter's pigtail at the nape of their necks.

"You ought to be nice to real people, sweet thing," one was saying in Spanish as Janna pushed open the door.

"Real people?" Carita spat at them. "You're cockroaches!"

The second one clucked mockingly. "That's not nice, little pig. What if we tell old Chopsticks you're being rude to customers? You'll lose your job. Or maybe we'll just tell Human Services that he hires slighs he can pay off in food instead of paying standard wages to real people he has to file all that paperwork on."

Janna kicked aside a pot on the floor. "What do you know, Mama. Toros. And I thought we might have trouble finding some. These cucarachas friends of yours, Julio?" she asked the cook. "You know the Department of Health requires a certain standard of hygiene in the kitchen of a public restaurant. Does Mr. Wu know how dirty you're letting his get?"

The Toros turned languidly. "It was clean until you came in, leo."

At Janna's shoulder Mama said, "Let's sit down out front and talk about that."

The two tensed and the cook's hand twitched, as though to reach for the long knife on the near-by chopping block. Janna balanced on her toes and let her hand drop down by the top of her boot, adrenaline rushing hot and cold through her.

Then the Toros shrugged and smiled mockingly. "I guess we got some time we can spare you, leo. You buying the caff?"

Mama followed them out.

Breathing again, Janna remained to eye the cook and ask the waitress, "Will you be all right?" She would never have taken the girl for a sligh, not showing that spirit and anger.

Carita tossed her head, eyes smoldering. "I am, will be, and would have been! You didn't need to interfere. They would have quit sooner or later, or I would have made them lose interest."

The first part of the sentence sounded like a sligh, but not the second, nor did the hard glitter in her eyes match a sligh. That kind of look, in Janna's experience, went with thinking of ways to get even.

"You know there are people in the legislature right now trying to characterize Unidenteds as dangerous people."

Carita grimaced. "I saw that toad on the scanner. His turn will come, too. We're not about to let anyone number and file us."

These slighs were going to ruin their own cause yet. Totally wickers, all of them. "Be careful how you avoid it," Janna said, for all the good it would do, and left the kitchen.

"Beta Oakland Nine, 1832 Division, the apartment in back. Check on a Caroline Bellman. Carephone advises she does not answer today and she is extremely elderly."

"Orions?" one of the Toros was saying as Janna sat down at the table. He laughed. "Hell, leo, who don't wish the Orions trouble? That Pluto is one arrogant bastard. We gonna mash him one of these days."

"Who hates them in particular?" Mama asked. "Anyone who might pretend to be Orions to make trouble?"

"Hey." The second Toro leaned forward. "Is this about that hearse jacking?" He grinned broadly. "Far star. But, hey, maybe it isn't anyone outside the Orions. Could be internal, a power play, someone who wants Pluto caged so he can take over."

"What's the color sequence around the Orions' eyes?" Janna asked.

The Toros blinked. "Colors? Red over their eyes, of course, then…blue and yellow? No, yellow, *then* blue." They grinned. "What prize do we win?"

Mama gave them a thin smile. "You don't have to come downtown. Where's Ladino?"

Their eyes slid away. They shrugged. "Who can say? The jefe is like smoke, like la sombra, a shadow."

"Well, you let the smoke know we want a call from him."

"Ciertamente." They pushed away from the table in a loud scrape of chairs and swaggered out of the cafe. "Adios, gatitos."

Janna frowned after them. "If Toros pulled that masquerade, I don't think those two know about it."

"No," Mama agreed. "They'd be gloating." He pushed his glasses up his nose. "I don't think any of the gangs did it. Nafsinger's idea of stealing it for a robbery has a better feel. It would explain why we haven't found the hearse, either. When we finish eating, you go west and I'll head east. Let's tap for rumors."

"Beta Oakland Fifteen, traffic assistance, East Sixth and Golden, woman in the intersection exhibiting seizure-type behavior. Complainant is a physician and suggests possible trick intoxication."

Janna grimaced in disgust. The public was so stupid! With all the legal drugs on the market, they still wanted the forbidden ones like trick and trilight, the killers. Maybe the government should legalize everything so natural selection would weed out the mental defectives.

Slogging west on Seward proved not only cold and tedious but fruitless. Everywhere she asked, stores and bars both, no one could suggest what gang might have tried to hang a Grand Theft Auto charge on the Orions. No one had heard any rumors of impending breakings or boostings that might involve the use of a hearse.

Like most of the bars, Le Play sat almost empty at this time of day, its stale air still relatively free of smoke and drug fumes. At the back of the room ran a holo of the hot new jivaqueme band Porphyry playing one of the songs from its current album. The music reached Janna almost subliminally, its rhythm and call to dance reverberating in her bones. A few girls and boys—a purely honorary term since some looked almost middle-aged—from the rooms upstairs sat wrapped in robes at one of the back tables, drinking tea while they played poker for vending tokens. They eyed Janna as she approached the table, but since they were safely ensconced in a licensed, medically-inspected house, smiled and offered her a chair.

"What can we do for you, leo?"

Nothing, it turned out. They could only shake their head when she asked her questions. "Sorry, we haven't heard of anything in the chute."

"Maybe you should ask Quicks—" one of the boys began, and broke off with a yelp. Glaring at the girl next to him, he reached under the table to rub at his leg.

"Quicksilver?" The sligh teacher. Janna knew little about his background, even less than a Documented could learn about most slighs, but his appearance suggested he came of mixed blood—causasian, afro, amerind, with possibly some oriental breeding as well—and he had once told her that he managed to educate himself by haunting public libraries and reading tirelessly. He had also perfected the art of invisibility. The Toros might call their chief smoke and shadow, but Quicksilver really *was*, conducting his school everywhere, always on the move, successfully keeping ahead of the raids that would wrap him for teaching without a license and force identation of his sligh students. In the course of it, he often managed to see and hear a great deal about things of interest to the police. "Is he holding school up in the gambling rooms here today?"

"Tongue," the girl hissed at the boy.

"If Quicksilver is here, would you ask him to come down?" Janna said. "I assure you I've never helped a raid on his school. I used to warn him when I knew they were coming. Just ask him."

They eyed her skeptically, but after a minute, one of the boys stood and padded out the back of the room. Janna sat back in her chair, careful to keep her hands away from her ear button.

A short time later the boy came back. He gave her a twitchy smile. "Sorry. I guess school let out when we weren't looking."

Janna eyed him. "He's gone you mean?"

The boy met her eyes. "You're welcome to look if you want."

That meant Quicksilver *was* gone. She stood. "Thank you for the help." Running a thumb down the pressclose of her jacket front, she stalked out of the bar.

"I don't like this," she told Mama when they rejoined an hour later and climbed into the car. "It isn't like him. Quicksilver hasn't cut cloud on me in years."

"He knows something and doesn't want to talk about it." Mama's eyes gleamed behind his glasses. "It must be something big, too, to frighten him like this. Didn't I tell you this case smells? Now all we have to figure out is what it could be. Powerful criminals? The government?"

Janna rolled her eyes. Oh, god, here they went, right into orbit. "No," she spat. "We're not speculating. I repeat, *not* guessing, and most *certainly* not dreaming up blue sky theories that take us on flying carpets to Never-Never-Land. There's some simple explanation for Quicksilver's behavior. I've used up my credit with him, maybe. What we *do* do is follow the book…gather evidence, examine it, and come to a conclusion."

Mama regarded her unperturbed. "We'll never solve it that way, bibi."

His smug sureness goaded her. "Personally, I don't care if we *ever* solve it," she snapped. "All I want to do is *clear* it, and get back to real police work…murders and assaults."

"Reports," he said.

Lord, don't let me kill him here with the Oakland division for witnesses. "Shall we just go back to headquarters?" she said through gritted teeth.

"Alpha Cap Five, will you 10-9 your last signal? Was that license number RSN 405?"

Janna sat upright. The Nafsinger hearse! She tapped her ear button. "Indian Thirty Central. Stolen vehicle RSN 405 is my case. Where has Alpha Cap Five found it?"

"Indian Thirty, Alpha Cap Five reports vehicle abandoned in the Topeka Cemetery. Advises vehicle vandalized and…" The dispatcher hesitated before continuing: "Contents, likewise."

Contents vandalized? The careful phrasing sent cold crawling up Janna's spine. She met Mama's eyes and found his mouth thinning into a grim line.

"Kick it, bibi. Get us over there."

4

Wednesday, January 24. 15:45:00 hours

The word *vandalism* hardly did credit to the hearse's damage, even viewing it a good fifteen meters back from where the vehicle sat at the end of a trail of scraped and awry early and middle Twentieth Century headstones, its front end butted into a tall gray obelisk. Doors hung open and wrenched almost off their tracks. The access covers had been ripped from the top of the airfoil skirt, windows smashed, and curtains torn down. Comments on what could be done with a corpse by someone depraved enough spread across the paint with a metallic brightness that suggested they had been written using a tube of acid paste. The vandals had even reached up on the roof to smash the solar receptors. All Janna could see for certain of the interior, however, was the outline of a shape sprawled on the floor beside an overturned stretcher.

She eyed the snow between the hearse and the drive, a pristine expanse with no recent footprints and only slight depressions left where snow had blown into those made yesterday. Nothing must disturb it until the Forensics team recorded everything. "May I borrow your hand scanner for a look at the body?"

One of the watch-car team handed her the scanner. She held it up to her eyes. With the light-enchanced mode switched on, the hearse's interior sprang into sharp visibility. Their vandals had overlooked nothing…smashing the instrument panel and slicing the side and ceiling lining to ribbons. Ribbons just about described the body, too. Janna's gut lurched. It was as though the vandals had gone into a frenzy, slashing over and over through the face and throat, chest and abdomen. Rage boiled up in her. How could any human mutilate another like that, even a dead man?

"At least we can quit worrying about the hearse being used for a robbery," Quist said.

"A cemetery." Roos grinned. "What an appropriate place to dump it. How did you happen to find it?" she asked the team from Alpha Cap Five.

"You can see the top half of the obelisk from California. We noticed it had tilted and came in to see why."

Janna thrust the scanner at Mama, who peered through it, then gave Quist and Roos their turn.

"Christ." Roos grimaced. "If Fontana was upset at his employee being lost, he's going to love learning that all the family has left to bury is cube steak." She sighed. "I wonder, though. Can we be certain the jackers did this? It's possible they dumped the hearse and someone else came along and worked it over."

Mama pushed his glasses up his nose. "Whoever it was didn't waste much time, if each of those depressions used to be a track. There aren't that many. It looks like the vandals walked around once, smashing as they went...very efficient and business-like, not like someone on a rampage at all."

A chill slid down Janna's spine. Business-like. Watching the glitter of Mama's eyes behind his glasses, she remembered his speculation about government involvement.

"Here comes Forensics," Quist said.

The van swung in through the south entrance, where tombstones gave way to flat markers and the cemetery became a rolling lawn. The van's paint matched the watch cars, white over black with a broad stripe of reflective red separating the two colors. As it hummed up the drive, the noise of its fans triggered sound-activated holos set in some of the markers, so that for a few moments as the van passed, monuments rose out of the snow, castles and mausoleums and singing choruses of angels. Above one grave the image of a nude young woman danced dreamily in the iridescent coils of a huge snake. Its timer had a long setting. The image lingered after the others had faded, turning above the snow until the Forensics van swung around an island occupied by a small, free-standing mausoleum, a real one, and settled to its parking rollers.

Side and rear doors slid open. Technicians bundled like arctic explorers swung out and began unloading their equipment: 2D and holo cameras, the video scanner and fingerprint detector's laser generator.

"Can't you people stick to finding bodies in nice weather?" one tech complained. "This isn't the optimal temperature for all these electronics."

Janna wiggled numbing toes. "Hard card."

Mama said, "I don't suppose there's any way to use all these fancy electronics to blow out the tracks so we can see what's at the bottom."

Another tech eyed the snow briefly and shook her head. "Not when the two layers are this much alike." She checked the connections between the generator, fiber-optic cable, and the minivid camera with its the monitor and video recorder.

"Then we'll be depending on you to find some useful prints with that elf-lip," Quist said.

The tech winced. "It's LVIP, officer. Laser Video Intensified Print system." She said it in the weary tone of someone used to her words making no impression. Hoisting the generator/recorder pack on her back, she trudged off toward the hearse.

"Oh my god. Poor Mr. and Mrs. Kiorpes, and Mr. Durning, and Miss Lowe!"

Janna turned to find a small, stocky man in a grease-stained jacket staring at the hearse in horror. Hair as orange as a carrot and curly as steel wool stuck out from under a stocking cap.

"What? Who are you talking about?" she asked.

"Them." The little man pointed at the obelisk and the headstones wrenched from their places by the hearse's passage.

"Who are you?" Roos asked. "How did you get past the police line?"

He drew himself up. "I'm Albert Tenpennies, the caretaker. You're going to move all that, aren't you, not just keep on walking around over the top of the Kiorpes' sons?"

Roos leaned close to Janna. "I think Mr. Tenpennies only has seven or eight left."

Quist frowned at Tenpennies. "Do you live on the grounds?"

"In the stone house by the cemetery office back on the west side."

"You didn't see this hearse drive in here yesterday?"

Pale eyes sparked. The carroty hair seemed to bush sideways even more. "I would have come up if I had, wouldn't I? Especially since there were no burials scheduled."

"You don't check the cemetery every day?"

Tenpennies stiffened. "I try to. I'm the only person who cares about some of these graves. Yesterday, though, I had to spend the whole day in the equipment barn working on the backhoe. Didn't any of your cars patrol through here?"

Now the watch car team stiffened.

Touché, Janna thought, biting back a grin. She nodded at Tenpennies. "Thank you very much for your help. We'll be out of here as soon as possible."

"Without causing any more damage for me to repair, I hope. Think about the poor people you're walking over." Tenpennies stalked off.

The investigators and watch car team rolled their eyes.

Bob Welliever, the Forensics team supervisor, beckoned to the four investigators. "Can you help us look for the access covers and side mirrors that were torn off? They might have useful prints on them."

"You mean you want *us* to paw around on the Kiorpes family, too?" Roos said. "That's disgusting."

"And cold," Janna added.

Welliever grinned. "Pretend you're a kid gathering material for a snow fort."

Pretend she was sitting beside a warm fire, Janna reflected ten minutes later as she waded in a careful spiral out from the hearse, feeling with feet and gloved hands for any foreign object under the snow.

A gust of wind lifted the top layer of snow, sending a chilly spray of it into her face and across her tracks.

Pretend she was not courting frostbite and pneumonia.

"Beta Oakland Nineteen, request you go to Sunrise Court off Croco Road. Fire department responding to alarm and requires traffic assistance."

There were worse places to be today. At least she was not a firefighter with all that water coming back in her face as ice and turning the ground to a skating rink.

Her ankle knocked against something. Digging it out, she found only a flower vase full of mummified stems. Five minutes later the snow yielded one of the access covers. The camera techs photographed its position in relation to the hearse before letting Janna deliver it to the fingerprint tech for scanning.

Under the green light of the argon laser several series of loops and arches fluoresced and were duly recorded by the minivid camera.

"I don't know if they'll do you any good, though," the tech said. "See the smears across those two? Marks like them are all over the hearse on doors and this access cover, where you'd expect the vandals to have touched it. Made by gloves, probably. It looks like your vandals weren't cooperative enough to run around bare-handed."

Which meant that the clear prints probably belonged to no one useful, just the Nafsingers and their employees. Janna sighed and returned to wading through the snow.

The searching and scanning continued until the hearse had been completely covered and all its missing pieces found. By that time the sun had set. Forensics packed up in fading twilight and left of the cemetery, following the Medical Examiner's wagon that had come for the body and the department flatbed which hauled the hearse to the police garage where it could be examined more thoroughly and in greater comfort.

"They're going back to heat," Roos said. "I hate them."

Janna refused to think about it. Shoving frozen hands into her pockets, she shrugged. "No need. When our bodies reach the ambient temperature, which should be any second now, we'll stop feeling the cold. If you two take the houses west of the cemetery, Mama and I will check those across the street north and east."

"Beta Cap Twenty-one, 10-98 crowd at 17th and Western. Religious protest blocking entrance to Fantecstacy Palace."

Janna decided that she hated canvassing houses more than she did bars. At least she could go inside the latter. No one invited her into these underground and berm houses, new and better cared for than houses farther north in Oakland. The occupants just stood in the doorways with heat and tantalizing cooking odors ebbing past them as they shook their heads and said no, they had noticed no one in the Topeka Cemetery yesterday, neither people nor vehicles, including hearses.

"I didn't even see anyone in Mount Auburn," a man in one of the berm houses added, pointing past the earth sloping up to his eaves toward the little cemetery lying across California Avenue from its larger counterpart.

Then one elderly woman just north of Mount Auburn said, "Why, yes, I saw a hearse."

The temperature suddenly became unimportant. Janna reached into her jacket to tap on her microcorder. "What can you tell me about it?"

"Not very much, I'm afraid." The woman hugged herself and backed farther into the glass-brick foyer of the underground house. "It drove in across the street about eleven o'clock and had no procession. I don't know when it left."

Eleven o'clock. The "Orions" had pushed Beta Nafsinger out of the hearse at ten forty-five. They must have driven straight here afterward. They had definitely not taken the hearse for joy riding, then. So why *had* they taken it, and who were they? "A hearse without a procession didn't strike you as odd?"

The woman shook her head. "I've seen it before." She sighed. "It's tragic, isn't it, that people can die and be buried without anyone noticing or mourning them?"

The eddy of heat from the foyer made the air at Janna's back feel all the colder. She tightened her jaw to keep her teeth from chattering. "Yes, ma'am. Did you happen to notice anyone on foot around the cemetery at that time? Or do you remember what the driver of the hearse looked like?"

The old woman shook her head.

Thanking the woman, Janna tapped off her microcorder and left, jogging to warm up.

No one beyond the old woman had seen anything, either, and after leaving the last house, she headed with relief back for the car. The very marrow of her bones must have frozen by now. She barely felt her feet as she dashed across California just ahead of a semi…and narrowly missed being hit by a Chrysler Elf beyond the truck because she slowed down, not seeing the little runabout coming through the snow kicked up by the semi's thundering fans.

Adrenaline produced a fast thaw, she discovered. Still, she was glad to see Mama already in the car and the engine running. Scrambling in, she held both hands and feet down by the heat vent.

"Bless you. Have any luck?"

He shook his head. "What about you?"

She played him the old woman's statement.

Mama straightened, eyes glittering behind his glasses. "Fifteen minutes from jacking to cemetery, and the next day we find the hearse vandalized. It's like the jackers stole it just to tear apart. Didn't I tell you this case smells, bibi?"

"I wonder if Quist and Roos learned anything useful." Their car was gone. Janna tapped her ear button. "Indian Thirty Central, what's Indian Twelve's Twenty?"

"Indian Twelve is deactivated," the dispatcher replied. "They've gone 10-19."

"Then let's head for lion country, too," Janna told Mama.

Back at headquarters they headed upstairs for Crimes Against Property. Compared to its daytime activity, the squadroom seemed deserted. A couple of investigators sat at the dictypers and another talked on the phone, scowling into its screen. Three more lounged near the caff urn. Quist and Roos stood in the doorway of Lieutenant Applegate's office watching the evening commander talk on the phone. Seeing them, Roos left the doorway and crossed the room to her desk, where she sat down on one corner and grinned at them.

"Lieutenant Yost is on the phone to Director Paget and guess what? Because of the mutilation Paget is giving the case to Crimes Against Persons." Her grin broadened. "It's all yours with my blessing, dear children."

Mama pushed his glasses up his nose. Behind them his eyes gleamed.

Janna could not share his relish. This did not look like the kind of case where solutions came easily. "Shit." She dropped into a chair. "Give us everything you have, then. What did you learn from the people in the houses behind the cemetery?"

"Nada. However—Maxwell, don't houseclean *my* desk!"

Mama pulled back from the stack of forms and printout he had started to tap into a neat stack.

Roos eyed him a moment, as though to reassure herself he would not attempt another violation of her territory, then continued, "I do have this." She produced a card from a sleeve pocket. "The telephone number for Mr. William Nafsinger. You can call and let him know his property and client have been recovered."

Janna took the card with a grimace. "May your children divorce you and your spouse cancel your marriage contract renewal in favor of a dog and a flock of sheep."

Roos grinned.

"Want me to call, bibi?"

Janna held on to the card. "Why don't you see if Vradel is still here and give him a quick oral report?" She punched the Nafsinger number.

A young female face answered the phone, another from the TV commercial. She called, "Dad!" when Janna identified herself.

The view on the screen slipped sideways as the girl swiveled the screen, giving Janna a blurred view of what looked like a moon crater…until she identified it as a three-wall TV tuned to a cineround program on the moon colony. Then William Nafsinger's face filled the screen, forehead furrowed with hope. "Thank you, Omega. Sergeant Brill, isn't it? Have you found Mr. Chenoweth?"

"Yes, and the hearse."

The furrowed forehead smoothed instantly. Nafsinger beamed. "That's wonderful. Where may I come after them?"

Janna took a breath. "I'm afraid we'll have to keep both for a bit yet. They're evidence in a felony and need to be examined for associative evidence." She hesitated. Should she tell him about the vandalism?

"Keep them? For how long? I'll be calling Mr. Fontana and I'm sure he'll want to know."

From behind the phone screen, Roos grimaced.

Janna put on her blandest mask. "I'm afraid I can't give you a definite answer just now. There was…some damage, and…" Why not tell him? He would see for himself sooner or later. "When the vandals took a knife to the interior, I'm afraid they didn't bother to differentiate between—"

"Vandals?" Nafsinger interrupted on a rising tone. "Knife? Oh, my god."

Suddenly a crowd of daughters surrounded Nafsinger against a background of mining robots boring tunnels through moon rock, all talking at once and staring in consternation at the screen. Beta's voice rose above the others. "This is unbelievable! Nothing like it has ever happened to one of our clients before. It's outrageous. Poor Mrs. Chenoweth. Do you have any estimation at all of when we can proceed with the funeral arrangements?"

Janna gave her an apologetic smile. "The Medical Examiner will examine the body in the next few days to assess and document the damage. After he's finished we—" Their stricken faces brought a surge of sympathy. "I have a friend who is an assistant M.E.," she said on impulse. "I'll check with the night attendant to see what the schedule is like. My friend might be able to do the autopsy tomorrow."

Punching the morgue on the internal line minutes later, though, she wondered if Sid would appreciate being volunteered.

The attendant who answered the phone had blue hair and painted wings sweeping up his forehead from his eyebrows. "What's Dr. Chesney's schedule like tomorrow?" Janna asked him.

"We're running slack right now. He has just two indigents, both probably hypothermia deaths."

"Then will you see if you can schedule him for the body that came in from the Topeka Cemetery this evening?"

The winged brows rose toward the blue hair. "Why? Kolb's doing the PM now."

"Now?" Janna sat bolt upright. And Sandor Kolb, the chief Medical Examiner himself? This Leon Fontana, or the Lanour Corporation, must have even more influence than she thought. Punching off, she scrambled for the door. "When Mama comes back, point him toward the morgue."

The section of headquarters Forensics and the Medical Examiner shared lay at almost the opposite end from the investigations squad rooms on the city block covered by headquarters. Janna ran most of the way through the maze of corridors, however, taking the stairs down to the morgue in the basement instead of waiting for an elevator.

The blue-haired attendant looked up in astonishment as she came pounding through. "Can I help you, officer?"

A newscanner sat on the desk behind the counter, its screen out of sight but the sound clearly audible, tuned to an interview program. "I'd like to ask the distinguished senator from Kansas why the Humanitarian Party has joined the Libertarians in their opposition to Senator Early's colonial moratorium proposal. Surely this is a strange coalition, or doesn't the senator consider that it benefits the greater good to conserve our resources?"

Janna waved the attendant back to his chair. "I know the way in."

The corridor led past the Lucite-sided shaft where corpses on gurneys could be lifted to the viewing room on the floor above and past the prep rooms and banks of storage drawers to the autopsy room at the far end with its long row of trough-like plastic tables. The sound of Senator Barbara Landon Kassebaum-Martin's thoughtful voice followed her. "Certainly it's important to conserve resources, but while my esteemed colleague in the Democratic Party foments panic over mere metal, what we're losing—to the space stations and the Moon and Mars as well as emigration—is the most vital resource of all, one that cannot be held by force...people. Space and the stars are stripping us of men and women with technical skills, the very backbone of our work force and economy. We need not a moratorium on colonization but a program to persuade these people that Earth still offers a good life. Let's stop strangling their personal liberty with laws intended—and failing—to identify and enfranchise the underprivileged portion of our society. Let's lift the crushing tax burden that our compassion has removed from the poor but political favoritism continues allowing the rich to evade."

As always, Janna had the feeling of having walked into a dreamworld in the morgue. Instead of the gleam of stainless steel that books and TV still used to characterize medical settings, these surfaces all had soft, matte finishes of pale blue...tile floor, walls, plastic countertops and cooler fronts and autopsy tables...fading into one another so that she seemed to walk through foggy twilight.

Even the dead man's gray flesh faded into invisibility on the autopsy table. By comparison, Sandor Kolb's rust jumpsuit became a blaze of color. A baggy, wrinkled blaze of color he might have been wearing and sleeping in for a week. He wore no mask or gown, just gloves and his sleeves rolled above his elbows. A tangle of gray hair stuck stiffly out from his head, almost touching the minivid camera hanging just above him like a bizarre third eye, its sensors letting it match each turn and tilt of the M.E.'s head.

Janna circled the table to stand beside the attendant assisting Kolb. "I can't believe Paget made him come back at night to do this," she whispered.

The attendant rolled her eyes. "He didn't come back. He was still here from today, asleep on one of the tables. He woke up when the body came in and said we ought to get to work."

"There's no use putting it off," Kolb said. He peered across the table. The minivid lens stared at Janna and the attendant, too, recording Kolb's interest in them for posterity along with the rest of the autopsy. "You didn't think I heard you, did you, Arrivillga? Here, put these specimens in formalin." As the attendant dropped the slices of internal organs into a container of liquid, he leaned back over the body. The camera tilted downward. "I may be a little absent-minded about minor details, but I'm not deaf, nor off my tick. Contrary to popular opinion, I do remember that I'm married, and where home is; it's just that there's so much to do here. And if I sleep on an autopsy table once in a while it's only because the High Muckies put my office way up on the fourth floor and I don't dare sleep on the gurneys. The one time I made that mistake Blue Hair out there came by so toxie on fantasy dust he couldn't hear me snoring and thought I was a new delivery, so he tagged me and shoved me in a storage drawer. A nasty piece of business, this." He patted the dead forehead, almost the only unmarked piece of flesh on the body. "Vicious. He didn't die of it, though. He's been dead for, oh, three or four days. See how the eyes are sunken? No remaining trace of rigor, either." He wiggled the jaw. "Not much putrefaction, though."

"He died Saturday on the Lanour platform and was probably in cold storage waiting for a shuttle to bring him down," Janna said.

"Platform? Ah, that explains how he died of decompression. See the petechia all over the skin? That means little hemorrhages. It's from rupturing capillaries. Petechia in the mucosa of the trachea, too, and ruptured alveoli in the lungs." He gestured toward a lung lying on the cutting board at the head of the table, sliced like a loaf of bread. "All consistent with decompression. What happened to him?"

"An accident with his pressure suit, I'm told."

"Accident." Kolb sounded vaguely disappointed. "Then it's the mutilation he's here for?"

"Yes, sir. We need it documented."

Janna stood watching while Kolb probed the seemingly hundreds of slashes, muttering up at the minivid as he worked. After a while she wondered why she stayed. It was not as though this autopsy would give them information vital to solving the crime. She had work waiting upstairs, too, crime scene and field interview reports to make out. A vague disquiet held her, an echoing memory of Mama's suspicions, and after a while Mama himself slipped into the room to join her.

"Anything you can tell us about who did it, doc?" Mama asked. "Is he left or right handed? What kind of blade did he use?"

Kolb glanced up. "Left handed. The blade was a long, thin one. Most interesting is his inconsistency, though. Outwardly, the mutilation looks uniformly vicious, but actually most of the cuts are shallow, except for a few across the abdomen in the upper left and right quadrants and across the throat. In the throat, both the trachea and esophagus have been completely severed here and here, and the trachea severed and the esophagus slightly cut in this third—" He broke off, leaning down close to the body's throat.

"What is it?" Janna asked.

Instead of answering, the Medical Examiner ran an exploratory finger along the edge of the severed tissues. "Fiberoptic."

A long cable of fiberoptic material fed down from the ceiling, followed by a cardboard-thin monitor. Kolb slid the lens into the corpse's neck and frowned at the image on the monitor for several minutes before ordering, "Retract."

Cable and monitor disappeared into the ceiling. Kolb dissected out a length of what Janna took to be esophagus. Slitting it lengthwise, he spread it open and held it up closer to the light, angling it first one way, then the other. "Arrivillga, let's look at this under the microscope."

Putting the tissue on a slide and examining it all took time, during which Kolb offered no explanations, just muttered under his breath, leaving the two investigators raising brows at each other in an agony of curiosity.

Finally Janna could stand it no longer. "Dr. Kolb, what are you looking at?"

Kolb continued to stare into the microscope. "Abrasions. I happened to notice a roughness to one end of a neck wound that could not have been produced with a knife. Something tore rather than severed the tissue. Now I find abrasions in the esophagus." He straightened and turned. "These abrasions have no leucocytic activity in the area as they would if the trauma occurred during life."

Janna heard Mama's intake of breath behind her. "Are you saying something was shoved down his throat after he died?"

"That would not be inconsistent with these findings."

Cold crawled through Janna. Something shoved down his throat, something no longer there after the vandalism and mutilation. She looked around at Mama, who said nothing, just pushed his glasses up his nose and stared past her at the corpse.

She followed his gaze. Oh, god, she hated this, but it fit. It explained. It reverberated in her bones with rightness. Now the time and crime made sense. The rest, the Orions and vandalism, were all just a masquerade to hide the fact that the jackers had been after the body, or rather, what was *in* the body.

"Did you talk to Vradel?" she asked.

"No. He'd gone home."

"I think maybe we'd better call him."

5

Wednesday, January 24. 20:00:00 hours

"Smuggling? Isn't that nice," Vradel said, grinning at Janna and Mama from the screen of their phone in Crimes Against Persons. His mustache twitched with happiness. "We can dump this on the federal boys. I'll call Customs first thing in the morning."

"What!" Mama swiveled the screen around to face him. "Who's told us we have to give the case up?"

Vradel scowled. "Good god, Maxwell. Wrap the paranoia. *No* one has ordered us give up the case; it's just what we have to do. With smuggling involved it becomes a federal matter."

"The hell with that! You know the federal boys. Give the case to them and it may never be solved, and we'll never know if it is or not. What if these people start doing to live people what they did to Chenoweth's body?"

The angled view Janna had left of the screen thinned Vradel to a sliver not much thicker than the screen. The sliver's mustache twitched again. "Maxwell, don't try pushing my serve-and-protect buttons. We can't keep the case and that's that. The perpetrators are probably long gone from our jurisdiction anyway."

"Maybe not. How could outsiders know enough about the Orions to call someone by Jerrett's name?"

Vradel hesitated before answering, then it was with a question. "What's the matter, Maxwell? Why do you really want this case so much?"

Mama leaned toward the screen. "I worry when I see people behaving cold-bloodedly. I worry about what they might do next. There's all kinds of research on the corporate platforms, some because it's too deadly to work with down here."

Vradel sucked one end of his mustache into his mouth and chewed on it. "You make a grim case, but are you sure you're not blowing the matter out of proportion simply because you hate having a puzzle taken away from you before it's solved? If there's espionage involved, it's probably just the industrial variety."

"Just!" Mama yelped. "Lieutenant, we're not talking about a new dress design or a car body improvement. We don't have any *idea* what could have come down and what effect it might have in the wrong hands."

Vradel sighed. "How do you feel about the case, Brill?"

What could she say? The treatment of the corpse enraged her as much as it did Mama, but... She swiveled the screen to face her again. "Isn't that immaterial, sir? Protocol is very clear on jurisdiction regarding smuggling across the national border, which includes from platforms and the Moon and Mars colonies."

Mama sent her a look of reproach but Vradel nodded. "You see, Maxwell? We have regulations and when we follow them our part of the world runs a trifle smoother. I think we'd be in over our heads with smuggling anyway. Have a good evening, both of you. I'll see you in the morning."

The screen went dark.

Mama slapped it face down and whirled angrily on her. "By-the-Book Brill."

"Shut up, Mama." She was exhausted. She wanted to go home, yet hated to. Maybe talking to her father would help. He would be one person glad to hear she had survived another day.

He persisted. "Sometimes I think that clearing cases really is all you care about, not solving them."

Janna sighed. How in god's name had he managed to be on the force for fourteen years and still maintain this rookie idealism? "Right now all I care about is going home."

"Do you care about Chenoweth, bibi? How can we be sure the smuggler just used his corpse? He, or she, could have arranged for it to be available."

The man was hopeless! "Space platforms are out of our jurisdiction, too," she snapped.

He grinned. "At least you recognize that murder is a possibility."

To keep from assaulting him, she buried herself in finishing the reports she had been working on this morning, dictating as fast as possible and stubbornly ignoring all suggestions for improved phrasing the dictyper's polite voice offered. Then with her share of the stack finished, she marched out.

Exhaustion sank into depression in the stretch of street between the bus stop and the steps leading up the side of the Twentieth Century stone house where she leased the second floor...no Sid to welcome her, to scrub her back while she bathed, to trade off accounts of the jokes and horrors of the day while they provided shoulders for each other to cry on.

Dropping into the molded foam easy chair beside the phone, she punched her father's number in Wichita.

But no one answered. No one answered Sid's number, either.

Around her the empty silence of the apartment reverberated like thunder. Janna slapped down the phone screen, snatched up her jacket, and headed back for the door.

The leos who took their second and unofficial debriefing in the Lion's Den on the ground floor of the sandstone, slit-windowed New Hotel Jayhawk down the street from headquarters had thinned from the crush of late afternoon by ten o'clock. Stayers and the addition of a few civilians, however, kept the bar crowded hip to hip. The noise level also remained so high, surely audible in the rooms upstairs—the New Hotel Jayhawk had *never* been a hotel, despite the sign and holographic jayhawk on the roof—and spoiling the concentration of Fleur Vientos's boys and girls, that if any but leos had been responsible for it, the Tactical Squad would have been called in with riot gear.

With the double doors hissing closed behind her, Janna surveyed the pandemonium and nodded in satisfaction. People and noise were just what she wanted, enough distraction that she could forget everything in the real world.

She shouldered toward the bar through the crowd, and through smoke and drug fumes so thick that the holo of the band Heylen's Comet playing inaudibly above the scrap of dance floor had lost all color, fading to monochromatic blues. Bumping into a she-lion still in uniform, Janna mouthed an apology, then belatedly realized that the knee boots and skin-tight gray jumpsuit had been painted on bare skin. The girl was a lion buff, here to be around leos, possibly hoping to count coup on one. Another lion buff danced on a tabletop, nude except for a g-string and tattoos...*Be safe tonight*; *sleep with a leo. Take me to TaSq. I welcome assaults with friendly weapons.*

Behind the bar, Vernon Tuckwiller, the owner, bellowed, "Tea as usual tonight, Brill?"

She never failed to marvel at his ability to make himself heard without visible effort. That voice and his bulldozer body must have struck fear into the hearts of countless deeks as Tuck came crashing through their doors back in his Vice Squad days. Janna eyed the cabinet behind the bar dispensing recreational drugs but decided against any of them. The trouble with chemical boosts was that one always had to come down afterward. "A Black Hole and vending tokens!" she shouted back.

Tuck mixed the drink and held out his hand for her Scib Card. The Card went into the register; she stared into the retinal reading plate and when the r.r. blinked confirmation of her retinal pattern, signed the screen. Moments later the register bleeped verification of her signature, too, and returned the Card. With her bank balance now smaller by the price of one drink, Janna held the tall glass high above her head and worked her way back to the bank of holo games.

Scraps of conversation reached her out of the cacophony, war stories and bitching, acid comments on the presidential candidates, debate on the Identation bill in the legislature and on the suggested colonization moratorium. Opinion seemed for the former, against the latter—let those who felt so sure they knew how to set up the perfect society do it on some other world.

Only the Deathrace game remained open, but Janna did not mind. Running down civilians suited her mood just fine. She gulped a mouthful of the Black Hole, amber on top, evilly undulating reddish/black on the bottom, and with the liquor spreading fire through her, dropped a token into the slot.

A holographic town sprang up on the board, complete with streets, houses, and people working at everyday tasks. Her car floated down the incoming highway, a blood-red Mercedes Vulcan. Janna stabbed the start button. Sailing into town she started by running down a pair of joggers and a man walking his dog, followed by a woman with a baby stroller. A second child with the stroller woman saved herself by dropping flat on the ground and an old woman in a motorized wheelchair escaped the Vulcan through a narrow space between two buildings, but Janna made up for the points lost by quick wheelwork that netted her all the contestants in a bicycle race.

By now the village had been alerted. A tank rolled out of the police station looking for her. She whipped the Vulcan down an alley, however, then through a footpath underpass in a park, which not only netted her ten more points for another jogger but eluded a vigilante civilian with a bazooka. Grinning, she spun the Vulcan in a one-eighty turn to sixty-one two leos chasing her on motorcycles.

Then the grin faded and Janna swore. Motorcycles. Quist and Roos. The hearse and body. The outside world came crashing in on her.

Her hands tightened on the game control buttons. Damn. Why did both her father and Sid choose this evening to go out?

She ran the holo Vulcan into a school yard after the children playing there.

A teacher swept up one child and dashed for the safety of a doorway. Janna sent the Vulcan after them. Suddenly the teacher set the child down and whirled, pulling an old fashioned shooter from her belt, a .45 autoloader, and fired.

"Shit!" Janna hauled desperately at the joystick.

Too late. The Vulcan's windshield shattered. From a veer, the car went into a roll and exploded in flame against the wall of the school. The holo dissolved.

Janna's fist crashed down on the empty board.

"You break it, you better have the Card to pay for it before you leave tonight, leo!" Tuck bellowed from the bar.

"You still lasted longer than I usually do," a male voice said behind her.

Lion buff, she thought, and whirled to disembowel him with some scathing comment. But the man looked familiar, even aside from that indefinable something in expression and carriage that marked him as a leo, and instead of sarcasm, she gave him a polite nod.

"Are you thawed out from this afternoon yet?" he asked.

Thawed out. Now she reconized him. "You're Alpha Cap Five."

He smiled wryly. "Dale Talavera, actually."

He had, Janna realized suddenly, a nice set of shoulders, and fine dark eyes she had to look *up* into. She smiled back. "Janna Brill. Would you like to make a contest of it?" She jerked her head toward the Deathrace board. "My token."

He shook his head. "Thanks, but I've seen you play before and you have this habit of suckering your opponent into a position where the defensive forces wipe him out while you escape. How about something less tempting to your killer instincts?" He pointed to the holo of the band.

Why not? After gulping the rest of her drink, she followed him through the crowd toward the dance floor.

The size of the floor left no room for self-indulgence or acrobatics, nothing, actually, but standing close to one's partner beneath the holo and swaying in place. As the alcohol lightened her head and the melody of an old Elric Corbin ballad rewritten into jivaqueme rhythm flowed into her bones, she and Talavera moved even closer. On the next song they wrapped their arms around each other.

Now this was what she really needed, Janna reflected, fitting herself to the length of Talavera's body. This chased the echo of the apartment much better than a dozen Black Holes or a high score at

Deathrace. He felt lean and hard and smelled pleasantly of spicy cologne and department-issue shower soap. His breath tickled her ear as he sang along with the music.

"What are you planning to do the rest of the night?" she asked.

"Sleep somewhere warm. What about you?"

His body heat soaked into her through her jumpsuit. She dug nails into his shoulders. "Where do you live?"

"Tecumseh division."

Way out on the east side of the county? "I'm on Mulvane just north of the WSU campus."

His hands slid down her back, pulling her hips hard against his. "My car is in the garage across the street."

They left without waiting for the song to end.

The landing at the top of the outside steps was freezing and the sonic lock on her door seemed to take forever to yield to the combination of tones produced by her palm-sized keypad, but eventually it clicked and the door swung open. Janna did not bother with the lights, just kicked the door closed and started peeling Talavera out of his coat and jumpsuit to the accompanying rip of pressclose seams. He returned the favor. "The bedroom is straight down the hall," she said against his mouth.

Instead of following her tug, Talavera froze. Janna felt him tense, even his breathing halting. At almost the same moment alarms shrieked in her, too. Someone else was in the room. She felt the presence, heard breathing.

It came from behind her.

Janna dropped, rolling off to her left. Her ears told her Talavera had gone the other direction to the safety of the kitchen doorway, a greater dark in the darkness. Silently cursing the entangling loose ends of the jumpsuit, she came up behind the end of the couch, reaching for the .38 Magnum shooter cached under the backrest cushion.

A dark shape filled the easy chair, vaguely silhouetted against the window behind it. She aimed for the middle. "Don't move, jon; don't even breath unless you're interested in a cardiac transplant."

"It's just me, bibi."

Relief flooded her, followed by cold fury. "Turn on the light," she snapped, and when he had touched on the table lamp, she glared at him over the sights of the shooter. "How the hell did you get in here, Maxwell?"

He pulled a sonic keypad out of his pocket. "I've had musical training, remember. I have an ear for tones and I've been home with you before. You know, you really are paranoid, bibi, programming the lock so you not only have to simultaneously punch in your birth-date and swearing-in date, but repeat the sequence twice. I about froze my nuts out there transposing the combination to my keypad."

"Hard card," she snapped. "You have to the count of five to get the hell out. One."

He grimaced. "Bibi. I have to talk to you."

"I said sail. Two."

He frowned at the shooter. "It's important."

"Three."

In the doorway of the kitchen, Talavera slid his arms back into his jumpsuit and pressed the front closed. "Maybe you ought to listen to him."

He had a shooter, too, she noticed. Interesting how off-duty weapons remained the old fashioned firearms the public had officially taken away from them.

"I've listened to him too often. Four!" She thumbed back the shooter's hammer.

"Jan, I've just talked to Leonard Fontana on the Lanour platform," Mama said hastily.

Shock choked her. "Oh, god!" She released the hammer. "For once, I hope to hell you're imagining things, partner."

He held up a microcassette. "I taped the conversation."

She opened her mouth, closed it again when she could think of nothing to say, and pulled her jumpsuit back on. At least she did not have to deal with this half naked.

Talavera eyed both of them. "Do you want me to leave?"

"We could use a referee," Mama said.

"That would also make me a witness...and I think the less I know about this the better." He picked up his coat. "Maybe we can try again sometime, Jan."

The door closed behind him.

Janna glared at Mama. "You're going to interrupt my personal life one too many times, Maxwell."

Mama pushed his glasses up his nose. "Hit-and-run sex is no kind of relationship. You need—"

"I need you to tell me about this call to Fontana!"

Mama pulled off his glasses and pressed the heels of his hands against his eyes. "Oh, yes...Fontana."

Janna arched her brows. "What's the matter? Do you admit that this time you may have gone too far?"

His hands came down. "Fontana isn't God. Why shouldn't I

talk to anyone I want who's connected with one of our cases?"

"Except it won't be our case much longer, and I wonder if the brass will appreciate you cutting them out of the communication chain." She sighed. "May I ask why you did it?"

"Well..." He sighed in turn. "I was there at the station finishing up my half of the reports and I started thinking about this Fontana's big concern over the body. I thought, what if—but maybe you should see this before I tell you what I thought."

He turned to the phone and flipping up the screen, traded his microcassette for the one already in the side of the phone.

"You called from *headquarters*?" She stared at him in horror. "Where every word is now on tape in Communications and any one of the brass can personally witness what you've done?"

He put his glasses back on, settling them in place with painstaking care. "That's where this recording came from, off their master."

She groaned and dropped onto the couch. Wickers. Totally off his tick and right over the brainbow. "I'll bet Fontana really appreciated being called in the middle of the night."

"He was still in his office. I think their schedule must be different from ours."

The screen remained blank the first couple of minutes as the telephone system connected to the satellites that relayed on to the Lanour platform, then flashed with a succession of faces representing the platform communications hierarchy, until finally the image became that of a trim man with a look of experience and authority, but almost no lines on his face and a full head of dark hair untouched by gray. Eyes as amber as a wolf's stared out of the screen above a polite smile.

"Good morning, Sergeant Maxwell. I'm Leonard Fontana. My secretary tells me you're with the Shawnee County Crimes Against Persons squad and in charge of the investigation regarding Paul Chenoweth?" He spoke with a faint drawl.

Mama's face did not appear on the screen, but the tape recorded his voice, crisply professional. "Yes, sir. I thought you'd want to know that we've found Mr. Chenoweth's body."

The smile vanished. A hard gleam made his eyes look even more lupine. "I know. I spoke to the Nafsinger Mortuary not long ago. From here, where Earth looks so peaceful and beautiful, it's difficult to believe that there are people who can be so wantonly destructive. Will it help find the gang members who did it if I arrange a reward?"

"We now doubt that any street gang was involved, sir." Briefly,

Mama told him about the autopsy, and the conclusions drawn from it.

"Watch his face, bibi," Mama whispered.

The planes of the face congealed. "Smuggling? That's impossible, sergeant."

"Isn't the platform a research facility? Some of that research must be of interest to other parties."

Fontana smiled again, but instead of reflecting humor, the gesture slammed a mask over his face. The drawl thickened. "Oh, I reckon competitors like DuPont, Astrodyne, and Mitsubishi have a yen now and then to look into our labs. Just like I wouldn't mind knowing what's going on in theirs. We don't mistreat corpses to satisfy that impulse, though. We're not working with State secrets, after all, just products we're considering manufacturing...consumer goods."

Janna frowned. Did he really expect them to believe that?

"Can you think of anything at all that someone might be interested in stealing from you?" Mama's voice asked.

"I didn't really expect him to answer," Mama said, "but I wanted his reaction."

The smile never flickered. "Sorry. I just can't think of a thing. Even if there is something, it couldn't have gone out in the body. Nothing leaves this platform, not packages or personnel, without a thorough examination, and believe me, sergeant, in the hands of my security chief, that's a thoroughness that makes Fort Knox look like it has an open door policy."

"You go to all that trouble when you have no valuable secrets?"

The grin broadened...never touching the hard shine of the wolf's eyes. "Between you and me, I reckon Geyer's a little over-zealous." He paused, glancing at something or someone out of screen range, then focused back on the screen. "I wonder if your vandals had something to do with those—abrasions you said?—in his throat. Anyone who would mutilate a corpse wouldn't stop at shoving something down its throat. Well, according to my chronometer, I'm keeping you up past your bedtime, so I'll let you go. I'd be interested in knowing when you catch the toads who did that to Chenoweth, though."

"Finding them might be easier if you could give us some idea who to look for," Mama said.

The amber eyes flickered. "Sergeant, I have no idea."

Mama punched the stop button. "Well, what do you think?"

Janna shrugged. "He evaded earlier questions but I think he was telling the truth at the last. What did you want me to see?"

He pushed his glasses up his nose. "Why do you think he evaded?"

"Oh, come on." She hugged her knees. "Do you think he's going to talk about research on a call anyone might be listening to and that he can be sure we're recording? In his place I wouldn't want to admit that anything could leak out, either. Lanour would not be pleased."

"Considering what's happening to the Tellus platform, failing security might kill Lanour's station, too...but maybe Fontana is concerned with more than his job. If security is that tight and something still leaked, someone very high up has to be involved."

She sat up straighter. "You're thinking about Fontana?"

The glasses slid down his nose as he leaned forward to rewind the tape. He peered at her over the top of them. "He certainly has to be up on the list. All his concern about the body could be just a way of keeping track of what we're doing, to see if we've fallen for the masquerade."

"So you call him up and warn him we haven't."

For once, sarcasm did not just slide off. He winced. "It was a risk I had to take to see his reaction. The smuggler doesn't have to be Fontana, though. The chief of security would be in an even better position to punch a leak."

She nodded thoughtfully. "His zeal could be just a cover." She frowned. "I don't suppose we'll ever know."

Mama sat upright, eyes gleaming. "His Earthside contacts have to be local. It isn't midnight yet and the clubs don't close until three. If we start flushing out our favorite Eyes and Ears, we might find those contacts and close this case before morning."

He tempted her. The anger she had felt in the cemetery hissed back through her again as she thought of the mutilated body and a knife slashing through the flesh looking for...something of commercial value. Her hand actually reached for her jacket before a jaw-cracking yawn brought her to her senses.

She dropped the jacket, shaking her head. "Mama, we're not going to accomplish anything tonight except contract pneumonia and maybe get ourselves killed because we're working when we're tired. Why don't you go home before Lia starts to think you're putting two with a human woman and not just Lady Justice?"

The light in his eyes died. He pushed up out of the chair. "I wonder if she'd give a damn."

It sounded like serious problems at home. Curling up alone in bed a short time later she wondered if that could be the real reason for his obsession with this case, to bury himself in his work. If that were true, could his feelings about it be trusted any longer? Perhaps it was just as well they were handing it over to someone else.

6

Thursday, January 25. 7:15:00 hours.

The temperature remained well below zero. A pewter sky and scattering of flakes drifting past the squadroom window slits threatened more snow. There were only a handful of overnights, though, complaints passed on for investigation from the evening and morning shifts: a couple of rapes, several assaults, a possible abduction, and one homicide.

"Involving our old friend Wendell Twissman," Lieutenant Vradel said, glancing around the squadroom.

Janna raised her brows. His tone sounded solemn but his mustache twitched above a mouth whose corners fought to stay straight.

Inspector Leah Calabrese grimaced. "Is he out of Lansing again already?"

"You know the compassion of the Adult Authority for the suffering caused by incarceration. Immediately after his release, Wendell apparently went hunting one of the witnesses against him. Found the man's wife instead and according to her statement, tried to attack her in her car. She pulled a shooter from under the seat and dropped Wendell in his mukluks. Cardarella and Kazakevicius, you follow up on it."

"Ten-four." Inspector Cardarella scribbled in her notebook. "Lieutenant, will silver be good enough for the medal or should I order gold?"

Raising his voice to be heard above the laughter and cheers, Vradel continued briefing them on general department activity since the day before, including faces and activity to watch for, and finished handing out the overnights.

He gave Janna an aggravated rape of a parking lot attendant. "The couple who assaulted him, one male, one female, beat him pretty badly in the process. You and Maxwell can head over to St. Francis to talk to him as soon as we've handed Customs the Chenoweth body. By the way," he added, peering around the squadroom, "where is your other half?"

She made herself shrug. "Maybe the fans on his car froze. I'm sure he'll be here soon, or call."

Inwardly, however, she could not feel so confident. Her gut had been knotting and unknotting all during briefing, wondering about him. Had he persisted in going after the jackers instead of heading home?

Behind her eyes ran visions of his body frozen under a snowdrift in some alley or vacant lot in Oakland.

Vradel eyed her with the skepticism of a commanding officer long used to partners covering for each other, but shrugged in turn. "Come on in my office while I call Customs."

Janna poured herself a cup of caff first. The spider sat waiting patiently at one edge of the web below the newscanner, she noticed. A newswoman murmured, "Port Bradbury on Mars and Port Diana on the Moon have announced an expansion of six hundred additional personnel each by this summer. NASA is taking applications now for people with technical training for Port Diana and with technical and agricultural expertise for Port Bradbury."

Janna picked a chair where she could see both the phone screen and the squadroom door.

All the activity remained on the screen, however. After a succession of secretarial faces in the Federal Building, a round face with a drooping walrus mustache regarded Vradel soberly. "Smuggling from a space platform using a dead body? There's nothing they won't try, is there. What's the contraband?"

"We don't know yet," Vradel said. "Lanour's platform director should have some idea, though, and I'm about to call him."

A mask dropped over Walrus's face. The hair rose on Janna's neck. The platform name meant something special to him. What? A glint in Vradel's eyes suggested he was asking himself the same question.

Walrus provided no answer, however, only toyed with a computer light pen. "You mean you haven't asked if anything is missing?"

"Not yet, but—what is it, Brill?"

Had she groaned aloud? Damn. She grimaced. "Well…we *have* talked to Fontana, and—"

"Just a moment, Agent Burwell," Vradel said, interrupting her. Punching off the phone sound, he tipped the screen face down and frowned narrow-eyed at her. "What do you mean, you've talked to Fontana? When? After you talked to me last night? After I told you the case was going to Customs?"

Janna resisted an urge to sink down in her chair. "Well…yes." Damn that Maxwell! *Think fast, girl.* "We thought we ought to pass on as much information as possible to Customs. But Fontana says there's nothing on the platform that anyone would find worth smuggling off. Though he also says their security is hermetically perfect even if there *were* something valuable around."

Vradel stared at her for what seemed like an eternity, chewing on his mustache, icy glints in his eyes.

Janna swore bitterly and silently…at Mama, and at herself. Why was she doing this? Why not admit the call had been his idea? "It's all on tape in Communications, sir."

Without a word Vradel flipped up the screen and punched the phone sound back on. "It seems there's been a conversation with the Lanour platform, after all. They're not sure what was taken."

Walrus's mustache performed a hula under his nose. "Do you mean you can't even be certain there's *been* smuggling?"

Vradel's smile froze. "Of course there's been smuggling. We have the abrasions in the dead man's esophagus proving something was been shoved down it."

"I hardly call that proof. It can't be impossible for those marks to have been made some other way, and even if something were put down the throat, it can be only supposition that it was contraband. Lieutenant, until it's established that there actually *has* been smuggling, and *what's* been smuggled, I don't see that this case falls within our jurisdiction."

Mama came through the squadroom door as the phone screen went dark, not exactly resplendent in the neon brightness of his chartreuse tabard-and-bodysuit, but certainly impossible to overlook.

"Maxwell!" Vradel bellowed.

Mama slouched across to the office and leaned against the side of the doorway, sighing. "I know I'm late. I'm sorry, sir."

Janna blinked. No song and dance, just an admission of fault and an apology? What had happened to him after leaving her last night? She peered more closely at him.

Vradel eyed him with the wariness of a bomb squad officer studying a strange package. "You missed hearing Customs decline the Chenoweth case. It's still yours."

Mama returned his gaze without expression. "Okay."

Janna stared. Was that all he had to say? He must be ill.

She felt sure of it when she told Mama about the call to Customs on the way down to the garage and he shrugged indifferently. "We already know someone highly placed has to be involved. Why be surprised he's pulling strings at Customs as well as here? Well, what do you want to do about looking for the jackers?"

Now he was even asking her for ideas. Unbelievable. "Find Quicksilver." The sligh's desire to avoid talking to her about the hearse was the only lead they had.

Finding him presented a problem, of course. He had not earned his reputation by being visible. This time of year, the number of places he could be holding his school became more restricted because he needed heat, but Janna did not waste energy checking the back rooms of stores or idle gambling rooms of clubs on the hope of stumbling across him. She made quick visits to businesses like Las Comidas, where she knew slighs worked. Leaving word with them that she needed to talk to Quicksilver, she headed for the hospital to visit the aggravated rape victim and wait for Quicksilver's call.

Mama came along, animated and useful as a store window mannequin.

She took the victim's statement and called the description of his attackers in to Dispatch for countywide broadcast. She also called Records. The computer reported three possible matches for the male, five for the female, and one pair when the two lists were cross-referenced.

Listening to the sultry female voice Janna reflected that maybe she should have made Mama call in. Sexy crooning in his ear might be therapeutic.

The "wanted" bulletin became much more specific.

By mid-afternoon the pair had been located and brought to headquarters. An order to look at their bank records found three transactions at locations and times in the vicinity of the assault. Janna interviewed the suspects in one of the interview rooms off Crimes Against Persons, standing so as they looked up at her, the hidden camera could record the dilation of their pupils in response to questioning. A recorder measured stress in their voices.

By sunset the victim had picked their pictures from a stack of photographs, under the watchful eye of the couple's attorney, and she formally booked the couple.

Quicksilver did not call.

They spent the evening sweeping through Oakland's clubs, catching up with known Eyes and Ears, keeping their own eyes and ears open for Quicksilver or his close associates. In vain. No one had heard anything about smuggling from the space platforms...and Quicksilver never appeared.

"It looks like he isn't going to come out," Mama said. It was his longest sentence of the day.

Janna fought the wind trying to kick the Monitor into the oncoming lane. Her jaw set. "Tomorrow I'll *make* him come out. The question is how do I make *you* come out?"

He blinked. "Me?"

She nodded grimly. "I'm not about to spend another day dragging around Mr. Catatonia. It's worse than hanging on a leash behind Brainbow Man. Do you want to talk or do I sic the professional prying of Schnauzer Venn on you?"

At first she thought he was going to ignore the question, but then he sighed and shrugged. "There's no need for that, bibi. Lia and I just spent last night discussing our relationship and deciding to terminate it. I'm moving out as soon as I find a new place to live."

They had made a decision to end the cohabitation? From the mask pulled tight over Mama's expression, Janna suspected that Lia had made the decision and he had spent the night in a fruitless effort to change her mind. "I'm so sorry. Would you like to go by the Lion's Den for a drink?"

He shook his head. "Thanks, but I just want to find a bed for the night and forget the whole world."

God, he did feel bad. Was he safe to leave alone? "Sid's bed is empty."

He blinked at her in astonishment and gratitude. "I—thanks, Jan. I really appreciate that."

She shrugged. "There's an ulterior motive. Riding home with you in your car saves me a miserably cold wait at the bus stop, and we can get an early start rounding up Quicksilver tomorrow. You just better not walk in your sleep."

"I go comatose," he promised. "I'm told I don't even snore." He paused. "Just how do you plan to round up Quicksilver?

She smiled grimly. "By being a mean bitch of a she-lion and making avoiding me infinitely worse than talking to me."

7

Friday, January 26. 8:00:00 hours

The oriental-hispanic sligh who called himself Amber smiled at Janna and Mama with a careful politeness that walked the edge of cringing anxiety. "Quicksilver? I heard you were looking for him so I'm sure he has, too. If he hasn't shown up, it must be because he isn't interested in seeing *you*."

He switched on the chip setter in his hand and resumed planting micro price-and-antitheft telltales in the labels and sleeve ends of a rack of electric-hued jumpsuits. Janna glanced at Mama. Could Teddy's Togs be where he found all those incredible ensembles of his?

She crossed the stock room to put an arm between Amber and the jumpsuits. "I don't give a damn what Quicksilver wants. He has information I need and I will see him. Today."

The sligh looked up, body quivering with an obvious effort not to retreat from her. "Excuse me, but I need to mark these suits. I can't help you find Quicksilver. He's his own master. He does as he wishes."

"Sorry?" Janna bared her teeth. "You're going to be a whole lot sorrier."

Fear and anger flashed in the dark eyes. He glanced toward the doorway, but Mama lounged there, cleaning his nails with the switch blade he had never bothered to return to Kiel Jerrett.

Janna moved closer to Amber until the tension in him told her she had violated his personal space, then decreased the distance between them still further and dropped her voice to a hiss. "For years I've declined to hunt you people. You're gutsy, if brainbent, to stick this hard by your principles. But you can all go to hell when your 'freedom' interferes with my job. I want Quicksilver and I'm going to have him or you'll suffer for it, *you* personally, Amber. If I haven't heard from Quicksilver by noon, at one o'clock Human Services and IRS representatives are going to march into this store and request the records of tax and OHS withholding on all its employees. After paying the fines for failure to file proper withholding, I doubt the manager of Teddy's Togs will ever use sligh help again. I'll point HS and the IRS at enough other businesses in this city that no owner or manager will dare hire slighs, either, and that will be the last of the inventory you're begrudged in payment for your labor. Then what will you barter for food, housing, and other necessities?"

Amber went ashen.

"You have until noon," she repeated for emphasis, and stalked out of the stock room.

Mama followed. "Christ. When you turn mean, you don't hold back, bibi."

She grimaced at the admiration in his tone. "I feel like a toad. All these people need is someone else harassing them." She sighed heavily. "Come on, let's visit our next victim before I lose my stomach for it."

The wind had died today and the sun shone in a flawless cobalt sky, but without lessening the bitter cold. The blinding glare sent Janna groping for her aviator's glasses while Mama's lenses darkened to black.

Mama started the Monitor's engine. "I don't know if this will help, but you might try remembering that Lanour-Tenning is a very big corporation which owns dozens of companies, some of them with Defense Department contracts, and all of their research that needs zero-gee—alloys and polymers and drugs—or has to be conducted in space because it's too toxic for an atmosphere, is probably done on that space platform. That includes the Defense Department work, Fontana's claims to the contrary. We *have* to know what left it in Paul Chenoweth. If you want, I'll play bad guy at the next stop."

She stopped brushing the snow from her knee boots to glance across at him and smile. Sometimes he was a very nice person. "Thanks, but everyone is used to your histrionics. If I do it, they'll take us seriously."

Thought of a Lanour-built time bomb ticking here on Earth added passion to the icy anger of half a dozen more repetitions of her act, and it helped mindset her for the most distasteful task of all, the pièce de résistance, raiding a school.

They headed the car for the Oakland division station, where Janna explained her needs to Lieutenant Nevil Enserro of division Juvenile.

He leaned back in his chair, shaking his head and sighing. "I knew it would come to this. Brill, you've been working with this black rack too long. I can't haul down a school without booking the teacher and identing the kids."

She gave him her most persuasive smile. "You can if you don't bring them back here to school right away." The division's slang still kept the old identity of the station house even half a century after the churches losing their tax-free status had forced the Sacred Heart Church to auction off the time-grimed brick school building with its worn concrete steps and empty statuary niches. "We'll hold the kids where we find them. If Quicksilver doesn't respond, we'll bring them in and follow normal procedure."

Enserro pursed his lips. "That's going to take us out in weather when we usually don't bother with schools, and tie up at least two teams all morning. What's in it for us?"

She raised her brows. "Our thanks for cooperation in resolving a major case, plus the satisfaction of knowing you're helping find a possibly dangerous object and return it to safekeeping. Also, we owe you a favor."

Lacing his fingers together behind his head, he leaned back farther in his chair. "I don't think that's enough. How about if you, personally, owe me a favor?"

"Toad," Mama muttered behind her.

Janna smiled sweetly. "Well, if we're talking personal favors, lieutenant, wouldn't this about make us even for the time Wim Kiest and I played back the tape on the interview room camera looking for footage on a breaker we'd strapped and—"

Enserro sat bolt upright. "That happened a long time ago!"

"And has gone unknown but to thee and me since Wim and I kindly erased the evidence. That earned us your undying gratitude, you said at the time." She batted her eyes at him.

The lieutenant's mouth set in a thin line. "Where's the school?"

Six of them conducted the raid: Janna, Mama, a team from Juvenile, and another from the plainjane squad, just enough to block the exits from the casino room of La Juerga. Sealed in, no one offered resistance, though the teacher, Plum Nguyen, looked up as Janna's plastic wrap strap circled her wrists, adhering to itself, and said, "Don't take the children. I'll go; I'm obviously guilty of teaching without a license, but they've done nothing, just tried to become educated the only way they can."

Janna led her out of the casino room and into the bar, where Tito Duarte, the owner, sat watching in smoldering silence. Both his eyes and Nguyen's widened in astonishment, however, when Janna pulled the little polarizer out of a thigh pocket and touched it to the wrap strap. The restraint fell away instantly.

"Maybe we won't have to take in the kids, or you, either." While she explained the price of that generosity, she reversed the polarizer, restoring the charge in the strap before carefully sliding it back into the thigh seam pocket of her jumpsuit.

Nguyen snapped to her full height, about the middle of Janna's chest. "You intend to hold the children hostage? Bitch!"

"Blame Quicksilver. He cut cloud when he knows I've always played fair with him." Janna glanced at her wrist chrono. "It's ten-oh-five."

Nguyen stared from Janna back toward the casino door, where Mama and one of the janes slouched against the wall. After a minute she pulled on her coat and hurried out the front door.

La Juerga included Deathrace among its half dozen holo games. Janna dropped a vending token in the slot and played while she waited.

"How do you leos face your mirrors?" Duarte asked.

"Believe me, I'm the lesser of several evils." But if this did not bring in Quicksilver, or it turned out he knew nothing useful, that mirror might be giving her problems for a while.

Duarte punched on the newscanner hanging over the bar.

"...despite a proposed moratorium on colonization inspired by Senator Scott Early in a campaign speech earlier this week, colonial companies continue to be formed and seek shareholders. In Kearney, Nebraska, Matthias Mankiller announced the incorporation of the Dakota Company, open to those having half or more Amerind blood, but with preference given to members of Sioux tribes."

Mama left the doorway to watch the game over Janna's shoulder. "What was on that interview room tape you and Enserro were talking about?"

"Let's just say it was a screw-up worthy of you, partner." She crashed her car through a parade, claiming points on half the band, the parade marshal, and the marshal's horse. "But you locked yourself in the back seat of that watch car with your partner, at least, not a superior officer's wife, and unlike Enserro, you didn't have a hidden camera and accidentally bump the activation button."

Nguyen reappeared shortly after eleven. "I couldn't find him. I don't have any idea where he is. Please, won't you let the children go anyway? I'll stay as your hostage."

"You all stay." Janna kept her eyes on the game. She still played her original token, though the points came slower now as the local population dwindled and she had to spend more time dodging the increasing power of the weapons carried by the survivors.

"Surely you can't expect me to be Quicksilver's keeper. No one has a right to control another's life. We are each autonomous."

"But unless we act in cooperation, we can't survive as a society," Mama said.

Acting in cooperation, the board characters finally trapped and destroyed her car. She started another game. Concentrating on it became increasingly hard, however, as the numbers on her wrist chrono advanced toward twelve noon. Nguyen and Duarte sat drinking tea and alternating between glares and anguished glances at the wall chrono above the bar.

The radio button in murmured in Janna's ear. "Alpha Oakland Nineteen, render assistance to snatcher victim, Michigan and Sardou. Loss of food and housing coupons."

Mama sighed. "I don't think he's going to make it, bibi."

She ran the playing car in through the hedge around a garden cafe to smash a lean waiter between her bumper and the building wall. The waiter reminded her of Quicksilver. Janna bit her lip. Could she have miscalculated? She always thought he had become a teacher, scraping by on the little food and clothing the parents of his pupils could spare, because he cared about children and minds, but could hiding what he knew matter even more than the welfare of other slighs?

"If he doesn't come, are you really going to go through with the school strapping and calling HS and the IRS?"

She sighed. "If we don't, what happens the next time slighs don't want to talk to us?"

The populace wiped her out again. She gave it up and turned away, glancing at her wrist chrono. And wished she had not. It read eleven fifty-four. Damn Quicksilver. Her gut knotted.

"Maybe I could play good guy and forcibly take over the operation," Mama said.

"Except you haven't objected before. It'd look like the act it would be." Eleven fifty-five. "We'd better make our calls." Double damn the man!

"Make the calls, all right, Brill. Call off your goddamn wolves!"

Janna whirled. Quicksilver stood in the doorway, as lean and sallow as ever, wrapped in a parka several sizes too large.

She kept a mask pulled tight over her relief, however. "You and the kids can go, Nguyen. Mama, would you please call the others and tell them the cavalry arrived in time?"

He headed for the phone, his grin a white blaze in the darkness of his face. Plum Nguyen hurried into the casino and reappeared with her students, leading them quickly through the bar and out the front door.

Janna beckoned to Quicksilver as the doors hissed closed behind the school. "Sit down. Want some tea?"

He dropped in the chair, eyes blazing. "What the hell are you trying to do to me? In one morning you've turned my friends into a lynch mob."

She regarded him coldly. "You wouldn't talk to me. Talk to me now."

His expression went blank. "How can I, sergeant? I don't know anything."

After all this, he intended to play *that* line? The people involved must be very dangerous indeed, or powerful. Then she cursed her own stupidity. No, of course not. How could she be so blind? Quicksilver feared no one, only *for* someone…slighs. But…how could slighs know anything about Lanour and industrial espionage?

She leaned back in her chair. "Some loyalties are dangerous, Q. These are ticklish times for slighs with that Mandatory Identation legislation in the Statehouse. Any sort of serious trouble could tip the balance toward passage."

Quicksilver regarded her steadily. "I'm aware of that."

"It's better to clean your house. Auto theft is a serious charge, not to mention the kind of attention bound to be given to what happened to the body afterward, but protecting these slighs will only make matters worse for all of you when these are caught…and eventually they will be, that I promise you. And we'll recover what they removed from that body."

"They didn't take anything." Quicksilver leaned toward her. "They didn't touch the body. They were shocked to even find it there. They're angry and light-witted but not vicious."

"Just criminal. They were willing to hire out to impersonate Orions and jack a hearse."

Quicksilver sighed. "Impersonating the Orions was their idea. They needed a disguise and picked one they hoped would also bring a little grief to some people who like to torment slighs. They never even thought of the jacking as criminal. Since no one was going to be hurt—they were just supposed to take the hearse and deliver it—it looked like a way to strike back at 'Real People'. That's all they did, took the hearse and delivered it."

"We want them," Mama said behind Janna's shoulder.

Quicksilver frowned. "They won't come in to be strapped. Not even I could talk them into that."

Janna tilted her head back to look up at Mama. Catching his eye, she raised her brows. His chin dipped in reply.

Her gaze returned to Quicksilver. "They won't be strapped. We just want to talk to them, to find out what they know. Come on, Q., you know little fish aren't important. It's the people who hired them I want."

The sligh's lips pursed. "No prosecution of any kind? You promise?"

"Since they didn't hurt Ms. Nafsinger, if they talk, they walk."

Quicksilver stood up. "I'll call you where to meet us."

Dispatch radioed them a telephone number about two o'clock at Stormont-Vail Hospital where they were interviewing the victim of a hit-and-run. By three they had parked the Monitor at the Oakland Mall and made themselves at home in The Magic Pan, sipping cups of hot chocolate. A few minutes later Quicksilver walked into the crepe shop.

None of the four with him could have been over twenty. Janna saw why they made convincing Orions. Even now they walked with the swagger of street gang members. Smoldering eyes met hers boldly as Quicksilver introduced them: a red-haired boy calling himself Titan, another boy named Mustang, a boy and girl named Havoc and Tempest, hispanic and so similar in appearance that they must be brother and sister. Was the arrogance bravado? Thinking back to the waitress at Las Comidas, Janna thought not and she wondered in dismay if this could very well *be* a street gang, a new one, and a new breed of sligh. She had never before heard slighs use names like Tempest and Havoc.

"My god," Mama breathed next to her. "What are we creating?"

So he was thinking the same thing.

The four brought plastic pseudo-wicker chairs over from another table and sat down straddling the backs.

"Buy us some hot chocolate," Mustang said. "Our memories work best when we're thawed out."

"Food would help, too. I'll take strawberry crepes," Tempest added.

Quicksilver frowned but Janna hesitated, torn between automatic hostility at the tone and a keen awareness that these four must have rarely, if ever, enjoyed such a treat. Why not, for once, let them indulge in one of the little extras that Documenteds took for granted? Only…they had demanded, not asked. "Don't push your luck, muchacha."

She did punch up more hot chocolate on the table's menu pad, though. A waitron looking like a meter-tall pillar slid up to the table minutes later with the order on its tray-top. Mama handed the steaming mugs around.

"You're welcome," the waitron intoned, and glided away on invisible rollers.

Havoc glared after it. "We shouldn't touch anything where they use those things. They take away sligh jobs."

His companions nodded grimly, but once Quicksilver gulped his chocolate with a speed that burned Janna's throat to watch and left, pleading other business, one by one the young slighs casually picked up their mugs, too.

Mama leaned back in his chair, eyeing the four. "Do you have a name for your…group?"

Red-haired Titan smirked. "You mean like a gang? No. Gangs are conformists. Like the whole damn world. Conformity is really what's behind this Identation shit, you know. Uncle's afraid of wild cards, anything that isn't analyzed, labeled, and—"

"Suppose you tell us about the people who hired you to jack the Nafsinger hearse," Janna interrupted. "Who were they?" Letting her hand drop out of sight under the table, she tapped the on the microcorder in her thigh pocket.

The sleighs exchanged glances but said nothing until Janna reminded them that their freedom depended on cooperation, then Havoc said sullenly, "There were two jons."

"Did they give you any names?" Mama asked.

They shook their heads.

"What did they look like?"

They shrugged. "Afroams."

"Try being more specific."

Tempest rolled her eyes. "One of them was about his color." She pointed at Mama. "The other one looked really black."

Janna nodded. "How tall were they? Fat? Thin?"

Havoc frowned in thought. "One was about a hundred sixty or seventy centimeters, maybe. Kind of stocky. He was the chocolate one. His hair looked kinky and bushy."

Mustang nodded. "The other one, the black one, who did most of the talking, was a rack, about like you two…real short hair, very fuzzy, and he had a couple of scars here." He drew his fingers across his cheeks. "He had an accent of some kind."

"Jamaican," Titan said.

Tempest frowned. "I thought Jamaican had more sing-song to it."

"How did they approach you?" Janna asked.

"They came up one night in the Buenas Noches," Mustang said. "Asked if they could buy us a beer. We'd been seeing them in there for a couple of nights so we said sure. If they wanted to be so generous with their Card, who were we to refuse them?"

"What night was that?"

"Last Friday," Tempest said.

"The nineteenth, then." Mama pushed his glasses up his nose. "Go on. What did they say?"

"We sat around talking about things for a while and they bought us another beer, then the tall one said he hated the way Uncle keeps claiming that everyone is free to live his own lifestyle but passes all kinds of laws that make it impossible to live decently without being Idented," Titan said.

Tempest's dark eyes smoldered. "The shorter one said if he were us, he'd be so mad he'd want to bomb the Statehouse or something. I told him that sounded like a good idea."

"So then the taller one got this big grin and said he had a idea," Havoc said. "He had someone he needed to get even with and if one of us could drive and we wouldn't mind helping him, we could not only get back at the RP's, but they would give us a hundred credits each worth of gift certificates from stores of our choice."

"I know how to drive," Titan said, "so I said what did he want us to do?"

"You never stopped to think that if he wanted to pay you, it must be illegal?" Janna asked.

His lip curled. "We're not light-witted, leo. Of course we knew, but he promised no one had to be hurt. We could handle the driver any way we wanted as long as we didn't bring him along when we delivered the hearse to the Topeka Cemetery."

"We said we'd do it and we told him what stores we wanted the certificates from," Mustang said. "He said he'd let us know where and when to go after the hearse and then they left."

"When did you see them again?" Mama asked.

"Monday night. They said the hearse would be coming north on Topeka Boulevard sometime after ten in the morning."

"It was colder than hell waiting for it, too," Havoc said.

Janna raised her brows. "You're lucky it stopped for a light near you."

They snickered. "If it hadn't, Tempest was going to run out and throw herself down in front of it so the driver would think he'd run over her and stop."

"I thought calling Mustang 'Pluto' when we pushed the driver out was a nice touch." Tempest smiled smugly. "We hear you actually strapped him for the jacking."

"What happened when you took the hearse to the cemetery?" Mama asked.

"Nothing," Titan said. "They were waiting there. We climbed out; they handed over the gift certificates and climbed in; we left."

"You didn't see them drive off?"

"Nope. They told us to sail, and waited while we did."

"Did you see any car that they might have come in?" Janna asked.

"Nope."

"What stores did the gift certificates come from, then? We're not going to cancel them," she added as the faces of the four froze into stony masks.

Once they had reluctantly recited the list, there seemed to be nothing more to be learned. Janna tapped off the microcorder and stood up. "Thank you for your help."

Tempest drained the last drop of chocolate from her cup. "If you think we helped a lot, could we have another cup?"

The little-girl tone plucked at Janna. She glanced toward Mama. His forehead creased into furrows of solicitude. Janna dug into her breast pocket for her Card.

"I'll pay for ten credits worth of merchandise on my way out. Eat it up however you want."

In the car, she grimaced. "I must be going wickers. The next time we meet that quad I'll probably be throwing wrap straps on them."

"Them and how many other angry young slighs?" Mama shook his head. "That's another time bomb ticking away among us."

Janna shook her head, too, but she was thinking of the afroams. She did not like the thoughts. "You realize that although our Genghis Four were approached last Friday about jacking the hearse, Chenoweth's fatal accident didn't occur until the next day."

"I noticed." He pushed his glasses up his nose. "It looks like our smuggler *did* arrange to have a body available."

Murder. Anger simmered in her. "Mama, let's find those deeks."

8

Friday, January 26. 16:00:00 hours

"Our jackers have expensive taste," Mama said.

"Impractical, though, if they want goods to barter with."

Just looking around the Granada Mall, without ever stepping into any of the shops, Janna estimated the prices at half again what similar items brought elsewhere in Topeka. The mall, one of the new chain of Holimalls, catered to the Cards of passengers and crews passing through the sprawl of the Forbes Aerospace Center across Highway 75. The Holiday Inn stood at the center, a luxurious tower presiding over one square mile of flanking shops, restaurants, theaters, gardens, and sport and recreational facilities, all under one transparent, almost unnoticeable roof.

"I think they're more interested in things to *have*, bibi."

She pursed her lips. "Interesting that slighs know the place so well. I suppose our Gang of Four has been riding out on the bus with transport tokens won hustling holo games."

Her ear button murmured. "Alpha Forbes Twenty, attempt to locate. A Mr. Samuel Benning. He should be driving a white over blue '78 Smith Sundowner, license number KWP 442. There is a family emergency; he needs to call home immediately."

"We should have asked them how to find this Supramodes shop," Mama said.

"Let's ask the mall."

Janna stopped at a computer terminal with a holo above it flashing DIRECTORY in all directions in glowing orange letters and typed in the shop name Tempest had given as one of those where the afroams bought gift certificates.

"Welcome to Granada Mall," a cheery female voice said. "It is a pleasure to help guide you. You will notice that each walkway is named. The names appear in the floor every twenty meters. To reach Supramodes, turn left at the next intersection onto Beta Lyrae and follow it to the red slidewalk. Ride the slidewalk across the mall to Copernicus." As the voice talked, a map appeared on the terminal screen and a line zigzagged across it, illustrating the vocal directions. The computer gave the directions twice, concluding with: "Should you have any further difficulty, please do not hesitate to consult me through another terminal. I am always at your service."

They found the slidewalk without difficulty, though Janna wondered if she would notice their exit when it came up. The walk ran through countless holographs that blocked her view of things on down the walk. Some were ads for shops in the mall...a room full of furniture to demonstrate Furniture Castle's wares, models posing in clothes obtainable at certain clothing shops, and one beautiful young women advertising Bodie Nouveau's body-painting arts by wearing only an intricate floral pattern. Other holos danced words before Janna that an audio reading reinforced...biblical quotes from a local religious organization, a public service announcement urging her to buy her narcotics from only licensed, government-approved stores and dealers. "Bargain drugs can be fatal," the announcement intoned ominously.

The Copernicus exit lay in a blessedly clear gap between holos. A voice with the solicitude of a worried mother called the name of the exit aloud, too. From there they found Supramodes without difficulty, its entrance spreading wide across from the legal offices of Bliss, Hart, and Long...whose window sign announced bargain rates for one and five-year marriage contracts for couples and groups of any sex.

A chime rang as they stepped into shop. In the open center of the store a glittering crystalline-looking sculpture beneath spotlights waved vanes like spider's legs, scattering rainbows around them.

A tall, dark-haired woman in a clinging iridescent dress floated around the sculpture toward them. "May I help you?"

Five minutes later they stood in the office section of the back room talking to the manager, trying to convince her to call up her transaction records.

With one golden brow raised skeptically above eyes painted like ladybugs and a hand held to breasts threatening to spill out of the neckline plunging to her waist, she peered from their badges and ID to Mama. Her expression clearly reflected her difficulty picturing him as a police officer. "Do you have a bank authorization?"

"We don't need one, ma'am," Janna said. "A bank authorization is required by law for examination of the financial transactions of a particular individual. To look through your shop's records, however, which are business, not personal, we need only your permission."

The manager folded her arms, accentuating her cleavage. "I really don't see what a couple of gift certificates—"

"Every scrap of information becomes vital in light of the heinous nature of the crime we're investigating," Mama said solemnly...eyes on her cleavage.

The manager's brows skipped. "Heinous crime?"

He dragged his eyes up to her face with obvious effort. "Well, I'm not in a position to give out details because of certain public figures involved, but..." He edged closer to her. "Necrophilia is involved, and activities in a graveyard too scandalous to discuss in even a society as permissive as ours."

Janna winced inwardly at the outrageous lie, but the manager's eyes lighted. "Public figure? Necrophilia? Are you sure you can't say anything?"

Mama sighed in regret. "We have orders straight from the top. Which means we're under real pressure to produce evidence. Ms. Dorn, you could really help us get the brass and political High Muckies off our rears."

"Important politicians are involved in this?" The manager almost squealed. "Oh, well...let me see what I can do." She sat down at the terminal on one edge of the transparent acrylic oval of her desk and punched in a code. "Do you want everything back to last Friday?"

"Just Saturday, Sunday, and Monday will do."

More code, then she punched the print button. In minutes, hard copy filled the catch basket.

"Use my office as long as you need to," the manager said. "I'll be on the floor if you have any questions." She paused. "Graveyard? How deliciously depraved." The word rolled around in her mouth. Still savoring it, she left.

Saturday and Sunday had been busy days, they discovered. Dividing the printout, each went through half, line by line.

"Maybe I ought to start coming out here," Mama said. "They carry Giancarlo's line. He's just starting to attract notice, but I predict that in a few years, he'll be a major fashion voice."

"He styles in fluorescent colors?" Janna asked without looking up.

Mama did not reply for a moment, then said, "You could do worse than shop here, too. You're an attractive woman who could be really flash if you'd dink up a little more."

She snickered. "That's just what I need, fashion advice from a man who wears mauve and chartreuse together."

"At least it's individual and not—here it is, bibi! Sunday, January twenty-first, fifteen thirty-seven hours, one hundred-credit gift certificate, one fifty-credit certificate. The name is Charles Emerson Andrews and the bank is the Maritime Bank of Houston."

"Houston?" She leaned over to read the printout. "I suppose we should expect them to be from out of town." She pursed her lips. "They'll have been staying in a hotel, then." She grimaced. "More legwork."

They thanked the store manager on their way out. She smiled conspiratorially. "I'm always glad to help our public servants. The case sounds terribly…interesting. Is it a Kansas political figure involved?"

Behind her, two clerks leaned forward, ears almost twitching. Obviously the manager had been passing on the lurid details.

Mama assumed a concerned face and shook his head. "A national figure, or he could be one if matters in New Hamp—I'm sorry, I'm talking too much."

"New Hampshire?" The manager's face lighted. "You mean it's one of the *presidential candidates*? Oren Travers? I've never liked that smile. You can't trust bible cultists. You just know the minute they get into power they're going to start legislating their beliefs into law. Or Senator Thayer? I'd love to see some dirt on him. Thanks to his trade protectionism bills, it's almost impossible to import those lovely African fabrics anymore. Or is someone else involved?"

Hissing, Janna grabbed the front of Mama's jacket and dragged him out of the shop. "Are you *really* brainbent? That's slander!"

"Not as defined by law, bibi. These are public figures so there has to be a malicious intent proven, and I didn't come up with the name; the manager did."

She sighed. "Never mind. Shall we start looking for our deeks at the Inn and hope we get lucky?"

She hoped in vain, of course. Although the desk clerk, and then the manager, responded to their badges more quickly than Supramodes' manager had, asking the hotel computer for a Charles Emerson Andrews registered sometime in the past two weeks brought only a polite: "I'm sorry," from the computer.

"I wonder if we can be sure that Andrews rented the room," Mama said.

Janna considered. "The shorter man could have signed the register."

"Or they work for someone powerful enough to provide them with several identities."

The manager frowned. "That's impossible. The government checks the fingerprints and retinal patterns of all applicants against the files to make sure that person hasn't already been issued a Scib Card." He paused. "Unless the government itself is doing it."

"Or a foreign government." Mama said.

Watching the manager's eyes widen, Janna said hurriedly, "Don't be paranoid. It doesn't have to be that complicated and you know it. Our jons could have a joint account, programmed to accept any number of names. Let's ask for guests with Cards on Andrews' bank."

While Mama queried the computer, Janna gave the manager descriptions of both men.

Those produced no results, either. "We serve hundreds of guests a week," one of the desk clerks complained when Janna carried the questioning to him. "How can I possibly remember one?"

Saturday and Sunday, January 27 and 28.

The sentiment was shared by most of the desk clerks they interviewed over the next two days in the course of visiting every hotel and motel in the greater Topeka area. None remembered a pair of afroams of the description the four young slighs provided. Not even the distinctive feature of the scarred cheeks helped. Nor did the name of Charles Emerson Andrews appear in any of the hotels' computer registration files. A number of other Andrewses did, though none with Scib Cards from the Maritime Bank of Houston. Each still had to be checked anyway, either with phone calls to the listed address or through tracing car license numbers back to car registrations and drivers licenses. None of them were the afroams.

By Sunday evening Janna's eyes ached from squinting at computer monitors and near-indecipherable lettering on hard copy from worn printers in cheap hotels.

Leaving the last hotel, she swung across the Monitor's airfoil skirt and dropped heavily into the passenger seat. Thanks to having sat in the sun for the past hour, the car felt almost warm. She slid the door closed against the frigid temperature outside and lay her head back against the seat. "I'm beginning to wonder what the hell we think we're doing. Those deeks are long gone, maybe even out of the country."

Mama pushed his glasses up on his forehead and rubbed his eyes. "Working is better than going home, isn't it? Even if those two don't have something we may not want loose in the world, they're our only lead to the killer on the platform."

That deek. Anger flared in Janna at the thought of him...destroying another human being just to provide himself with a messenger for his contraband. Not that they could they really do anything about him. The platform was out of their jurisdiction. Still, it would give her satisfaction to hand the deek's identity to Fontana. "Any suggestions where to go from here, then?"

"Maybe they didn't stay locally."

She frowned. That left only the little towns in the far south and far north edges of the county, where strangers created attention and memory—surely not what their afroams wanted—and places out-of-county. But the two had been at the Buenas Noches every night for several nights and must have spent some time prowling the city and Oakland area looking for just the right people to hire for the jacking. So they could not have stayed very far out of the county.

"You're thinking Lawrence?" she asked.

"It's just half an hour down the road."

Monday, January 29. 8:30:00 hours.

Mama made it to Lawrence in fifteen minutes the next morning.

Janna tightened her seatbelt as the snowy countryside blurred past the car. "You'd haul down any civilian you caught going this speed."

"Sure." He grinned. "For them it's illegal. For us it's a fringe benefit."

Their ear buttons could not pick up the highway patrol band, but Janna set the car radio for the frequency and listened with one ear while hoping the Monitor stayed on the road. The snow cover left the trees and rolling hills around them so uniformly white that contour and detail had vanished. Except for the fans of the big trailer trucks keeping the road-bed blown clear, it would have been easy for the car to miss a turn and end up wedged in a fence or between trees.

The car was still sailing and in a single piece when Mama skimmed down the west Lawrence ramp off I-70. As always when she visited Lawrence, Janna wondered why someone had chosen the one mountain in Kansas to put a university on. Anywhere on campus always seemed up from everywhere else. The University of Kansas hill with its sprawl of classroom buildings and towering dormitories dominated the skyline of the town.

They stopped at police headquarters to explain their presence to the Lawrence leos and talk a Records clerk into printing out a list of local hotels and motels. Then they began making the rounds.

With the same results as in Topeka. The name Andrews turned up on several registers, and even one Charles Andrews, though with the middle name of William, and none of the Andrewses banked in Houston. Still, Janna wrote down all the information to check out once they were back in Topeka. Their descriptions met shaking heads everywhere.

"No one of that description has stayed here in the past two weeks."

"I don't remember any black man with scars on his cheeks."

"Officer, I can't possibly remember everyone who checks in here."

Then in the record office of the Konza Motel, a geodetic-dome of bronze-colored glass, a name leaped out of the screen at Janna: Maritime Bank of Houston. The name with it was Milton Lowell, not Andrews, but the room had been a double, two beds, two persons, occupied from Tuesday, January sixteenth, to the morning of Tuesday, January twenty-third. Electricity lifted the hair all over her body. They left the day of the jacking!

"Mama!"

"I see it. It looks like you were right; they've got a joint account." He scribbled down the accompanying information. "Hamilton Lowell and friend William Solomon, 1902 Runaway Scrape Court, Richmond, Texas. That's a Missouri tag on his car, though."

"Ten to one it's a rental."

They headed out for the desk.

The two-sided newscanner screen on the counter carried an interview with the lead guitarist of Crosswhen, competing with a blaring advertisement for hallucinogens on the wall-sized TV screen across the lobby. Janna lifted a brow at the musician's thick accent. After a century, bands remained Britain's number one export.

Mama showed the desk clerk the registration information. "Do you remember these men?"

The clerk, a dapper oriental, frowned. "In 151 until Tuesday? I don't think—"

"Two black men," Janna prompted, "a smaller one who was very dark, and a taller, lean one the same color as my partner with scars across his cheeks?" She crossed her fingers.

"Oh, them. What did they do, violate someone's copyright?" The clerk snickered.

Janna blinked, nonplused. "What?"

"They were here for the seminar on Patent, Trademarks, and Copyright being held at the Law School."

"They told you that?" Mama asked.

The clerk shook his head. "I heard them talking to each other about it when they checked in. They looked like lawyers...zigzag pinstripe and green paisley jumpsuits."

"The room record says they didn't make any calls from their room, but did they receive any?" Janna asked. They would need to have been contacted about when to expect Chenoweth's body.

"We don't keep records of incoming calls."

Mama raised a brow at her. "If they called out they probably used a public phone."

No doubt called collect, sparing themselves the use of their Cards, and the attendant record of that use and number called. Janna grimaced. "Do you think it's worth trying to talk the Lawrence PD into scanning the room for prints for us?"

Mama switched the raised brow to the clerk. "Is 151 occupied now?"

"It's on its second set of occupants since Mr. Lowell and Mr. Solomon left."

"Not a chance of a snowflake on Venus, bibi."

For the sake of thoroughness, they stopped at the university, but of course no one named Charles Andrews, William Solomon, or even Hamilton Lowell had been registered for the legal seminar.

Driving back to Topeka, Mama said, "These jons are careful, finding a motel near the university instead of just off the Interstate, checking to see what was going on on campus so they could use it for cover."

"I wonder how much that's going to make this name and address worth."

A computer query to Missouri's DMV in Jefferson City brought no surprises. The license number of the car the two men drove was registered to Heartland Car Rentals at Kansas City International Airport. For grins, they tried calling Heartland, but found it had closed its desk for the evening. Another computer query, this one to Texas, came back with a notice that the Austin computer was down and could not provide information until morning.

Janna swore. "We send people to the stars and they still can't make computers that give you what you need when you need it. If we were in hot pursuit with every second counting, we'd be left wrapping nothing but air."

Mama shrugged. "Bureaucracy never changes."

Tuesday, January 30. 10:30:00 hours.

Not that the driver's license information on Hamilton Lowell proved worth waiting for when it finally arrived from Austin in the middle of the next morning: born 01/14/23, one hundred sixty-three centimeters, seventy-seven kilos, brown hair, gray eyes. The license picture showed a middle-aged caucasian male with thinning hair but a luxuriant bush of muttonchop whiskers. Obviously not one of the jons in question.

Janna spat in disgust and complained to Vradel, "So we still know nothing except that our jons also have connections that find them valid drivers license names and addresses."

"And keep their credit at the Maritime Bank of Houston." He handed her an authorization to request a bank check on account number 10 009 682419. "You want and need this, I believe. May it give you answers, because Fontana's been calling Paget almost every day and it would be nice to have something positive to report when Paget asks *me* how we're doing."

She nodded grimly.

MB of H proved stuffy but polite. As soon as their fax spit out a copy of the authorization, the bank official assigned to them, a sleek Ms. De Allende, called up the account's records.

"The name on the account is Wofford Ceramics," De Allende informed them.

Janna exchanged frowns with Mama. Ceramics might well be something Lanour was experimenting with, but could they be worth murder to smuggle? "It's a business account? Who's authorized to draw on it?"

De Allende glanced off to the side, presumably toward her computer monitor. "That varies, sergeant. Wofford maintains the account to provide non-citizen personnel with a local credit source while they're in this country."

Mama kicked Janna's ankle and grinned. She winced. Non-citizen personnel. The tall, scarred jon had had an accent. Scars! She sat upright, suddenly remembering a Nigerian boy she had known in college, and the scarring across his face that he had proudly explained proclaimed his tribal affiliation. Damn! Why had she not thought of that sooner? "Do you have a record of the current or recent Card holders?"

"I'm afraid not. Wofford has a code which gives them access to their account in the computer and they file new signatures and retinal patterns themselves."

"Is that a usual practice at the bank?" Janna asked.

Ms. De Allende sat fractionally straighter. "On request we will tailor accounts to meet very specialized needs. In this case, of course, Wofford has been required to release the bank from any liability should that code fall into other hands and fraudulent use be made of it." She paused, then said, "The account is fifteen years old. How much of its records do you need?"

Janna checked her desk calendar. "From January ninth to the present should be sufficient."

"Our computer will send them to yours immediately. If we can be of further help, please do not hesitate to call on us again."

They headed down to Records as soon as they punched off. The printout sat waiting for them when they arrived.

"I don't know what I expect to learn from it, though," Janna said.

"That they left the country Wednesday afternoon, maybe," Mama replied. "Look." He showed her the last page. "No transactions since then."

Janna's fist came down on the Records counter. "Damn! They're gone and the whatever has gone with them. We don't know who they are or where in the world they are." She chewed her lower lip. "I wonder what Wofford Ceramics makes, and since they have foreign personnel, where their branch offices are."

"Some of my buddies from law school have gone into corporate work. I'll give a few of them a call."

Her father's voice and his face on her phone screen warmed the apartment that evening. Janna met his smile. "So this year you really think you'll do it?"

"Cat says I'd better, because she's been listening to me go on for the last nine years about preferring to make jewelry full time to designing for Boeing and if I don't stop talking and *act*, she won't renew when our marriage contract is up."

"Good for her!"

He rolled his eyes. Janna saw herself in the gesture. "You're all in league to push me out of the Boeing nest. You know, I ran into your mother the other day and in the course of an actual civil conversation with her, she expressed the same opinion. She even wished me good luck. Time cools enmity, I suppose. Do you ever talk to her or your brother?"

"No." Sometimes she could barely remember her mother, except for the storm of disbelieving fury that day Janna chose to stay with her father after the marriage cancellation. "I have a faxed note from Andy once in a while. He seems happy on Mars."

"What about you, Janna honey?" His forehead creased in concern. "Are you still happy with your single leo's life? You're looking tired."

What an invitation, yet she found herself just shrugging. "Part of the job. There's a frustrating case right now. And I miss Sid. I suppose I should find another roommate."

"For the kind of mothering and fussing Sid did, you need a spouse."

She snorted. "Marriage?"

"Some people find it very enjoy—"

A bang on the door drowned him out. "Bibi, it's me."

"Just a minute, Dad." She hurried to the door and flipped back the security strip running down the edge. "Come in but be quiet. I'm talking to my father."

She hurried back to the phone.

He pushed the door closed behind him. "I have the information on Wofford Ceramics."

Wofford! She bent over the phone. "I'm sorry, Dad; the job calls. I'll talk to you later." Punching off, she whirled to face Mama. "Let's have it."

He peeled out of his jacket and fished around in a saddlebag of a thigh pocket on his jumpsuit. "One of the law school buddies is in the legal department at the Smith plant down by Wakarusa. I had him ask about Wofford through his corporate contacts." He produced a much-folded sheet of paper from the pocket, opening it as he dropped onto the couch.

Janna curled up on another section beside him where she could look over his shoulder. Not that reading the paper helped much when it was written in Mama's note-taking hieroglyphics.

"Wofford is a fair-sized company, incorporated in Texas but with offices in England, Spain, India, Taiwan, Australia, and the Republic of South Africa."

"What does it do?"

"Not much exciting, just buys up local pottery and dishes and other ceramic products at each of its offices to ship to other offices for distribution and sale. However…" He paused to grin at her.

Janna doubled a fist. "I didn't cut off my father to play games. However what?"

"Wofford is owned by Exline, Limited, in England, which actually produces ceramic products, mostly dishes and pottery. Exline, in turn, is a division of L. L. and K., in the RSA. L. L. and K. produces ceramics, too, but more interesting forms—laboratory equipment and ceramic engines for construction equipment."

Janna pursed her lips. "Could Lanour have anything in ceramics worth killing for?"

"It doesn't have to be ceramics. My friend tells me that L. L. and K. remained White-owned for a long time after South Africa became the RSA, but in the last two years, it's been bought out and all the personnel replaced with afros. And guess who bought it? Uwezo."

Janna sucked in her lower lip, remembering rumors and speculation she had heard about that corporation being a cover for afro spies. "You mean our jons could be working for an African government."

"In which case someone on the Lanour platform must be, too."

Janna took a deep breath. "Somehow, I don't think this is the kind of results that Vradel, Paget, and Leonard Fontana will be happy to learn about."

9

Wednesday, January 31. 11:30:00 hours.

The tape Mama made of his call to Leonard Fontana had not exaggerated the amber of the platform director's eyes. If anything, they looked even yellower firsthand. From where Janna sat beside the desk of SCPD director Thomas Paget with Mama and Lieutenant Vradel, the wolf gleam of them stared out of the phone screen at Thomas Paget with the intensity of lasers. "Uwezo. Well, son of a bitch. It sure looks like the African corporations have become grown-up competition all of a sudden." He smiled. "Your people have been mighty busy, director, to trace that corporate chain."

Janna frowned. That smile did not touch his eyes, and if his drawl thickened any more, he would need a matter transmitter to broadcast it. What was the good-old-boy act hiding?

Beside her, Mama pushed his glasses up his nose. "I wonder what happened to his concern about Chenoweth," he murmured. "We tell him it's murder, not just using a corpse, and he has yet to mention or react to that."

True. Why not? Janna leaned forward to see the image better, to catch any nuances of expression.

Director Paget gave Fontana an equally chummy smile. "We encourage our officers to be resourceful and imaginative, Mr. Fontana." In his serpentine-striped jumpsuit and collar-length, smoky-blond hair combed back behind his ears, he looked even more corporate than the man on the screen.

"However you did it, y'all are to be congratulated." Fontana grimaced. "Now I reckon it's up to the home office to see what we can do about recovering our property."

"Does that mean you've identified what was stolen?" Paget asked.

The smile widened fractionally. "I'm afraid I'm not at liberty to say, director."

Mama suddenly stood. Before Janna could haul him back, he reached out and swiveled the phone screen around to face him. "Excuse me, sir, but I would like to ask Mr. Fontana how he can be so confident that we're dealing with only a corporation. Or does industrial espionage often involve murder?"

Above an evaporating smile, the wolf's eyes froze. "What murder? Naturally we investigated Paul Chenoweth's death. It's important to prevent recurrences of such tragedies. My chief and assistant chief of security both examined the pressure suit and I sat in on the inquiry. Other workers in the crew with him saw the accident and they testified that his suit caught on the edge of a girder and ripped. No one else was near him. It couldn't have been murder."

"Caught and ripped?" Mama said. Janna started to reach for him but Paget waved her back. "It's my understanding that pressure suits use Kevlar in their fabric. As a law officer, I've had experience with that in body armor. Something thin and very sharp might cause a puncture, but nothing *rips* it."

Fontana hesitated. "Normally, no, but materials do fail now and then."

"That doesn't explain Uwezo's agents hiring someone to steal the hearse before your man died, though," Paget said.

The smile spread across Fontana's face again...except to his eyes. "That sure doesn't, does it. I reckon maybe I ought to look into the matter a little further. Thanks for the input. If we learn the names of the two men down there, I'll pass them on so you can swear out warrants."

Then they were staring at a blank screen. Paget turned to nod at Vradel. "We can file it, Hari."

Janna stiffened. The order did not surprise her, but her reaction to it did...anger, protest.

Mama yelped, "Close the case! We haven't solved anything." He frowned. "Are we getting pressure from somewhere in Lanour-Tenning?"

"Maxwell—" Vradel began.

But Paget waved him silent and smiled at Mama. "We *have* solved it. Semi-solved, anyway. We have john doe warrants out for those two afros and that's all the action we can take at present. The murder isn't in our jurisdiction."

Janna began, "We could check all international flights out of KCI on the twenty-third for—"

Vradel groaned. "Oh, god, not you, too."

"I admire dedication," Paget said. "To a point. Each one of us possesses only so much energy, however, and a wise person expends it on productive activity. I don't perceive any feeling of appreciation or cooperation in Mr. Fontana. So the case being on his turf, let his security personnel sweat over it. The weather bureau is predicting a warming trend this week end, and when that happens, the deeks will be out on the street in force again. Save yourselves for them. They may not appreciate us, either," he said with a thin smile, "but they're on *our* turf." He paused. "You probably missed your day off because of this case. Finish your paperwork today and take tomorrow."

"But—" Mama began.

Blue eyes narrowed to chilly cobalt chips. "Dismissed, Sergeant Maxwell."

Mama's mouth closed. He followed Janna toward the door.

The dictyper hummed as Janna talked into it, translating her words into letters on its screen, where she could inspect and edit them, sometimes to a phrase the dictyper suggested, before commanding a print. Next to her Mama silently signed the reports as they fed out the print slot.

She watched him from the corner of her eye. "Come on. We can't win them all. Paget is right; let the lend-lease leos sweat the case."

He pushed his glasses up his nose. "They're not going to solve it. They don't give a damn about Chenoweth's death, just what he smuggled out."

She raised a brow. "You were pretty concerned about that yourself, I recall."

"I wanted to know who killed Chenoweth, too."

Janna sighed. "I guess we'll never know. Don't let yourself worry about it if you want to keep your tick straight."

"Schnauzer Venn's brain training really works on you, bibi," he said bitterly.

Anger flared in her. Nice thanks he gave her for trying to help. With difficulty she held on to her temper. "Look, once we're out of here tonight let's just forget the place. Take me to the opera we missed last week."

"It's too late. The company's gone back to Kansas City."

"So...let's go to K.C. to see them. Your runabout can't make the distance but if we don't waste time leaving, we can catch a bus or the late commuter dirigible."

Mama sat up straighter. "Go to K.C.?" His eyes gleamed behind his glasses. "I think you have something there. Don't worry about the bus or dirigible, though. I'll arrange for a road car and we'll drive."

He hummed under his breath as he returned to the reports.

In fact, he appeared to be humming inwardly the rest of the day, even during debriefing while all around Janna and him uniformed officers, command officers, and investigators voiced the usual litany of complaints and frustrations.

Venn cheered everyone on, of course, twitching the Schnauzer—like mustache and eyebrows that earned the psychiatrist his nickname. It was all supposed to help them discharge job related tension, preventing breakdowns and burnout. "That's good, but not all bad happened today, did it? Don't forget, you see the worst in people, but you may also see the best in them. Any examples of that?"

Leaving the station by way of the garage when debriefing ended, Mama grinned. "What a great cheerleader he must have made in school. Well, what do you think of the car I've arranged for us?"

Janna stared at the bright red D-F Monitor. "That's our duty car. We can't—"

He held his finger to his lips. "It's all arranged with my friend in the motor pool, and perfectly legitimate. Come on, we need to dress and get going. Kansas City Society will be there, real castlerow types, so try to dink up."

Janna rolled her eyes. "In contrast to the drab rags I usually wear, I suppose?" Maybe it had been a big mistake to suggest this excursion.

Much to her surprise, however, she enjoyed the evening. The audience at the New Bartle Auditorium glittered, dinked up indeed...draped in furs and jewelry, wearing metallic fabrics and iridescent body paints, the latter under transparent thermal-plastic bodysuits. The scents of expensive perfumes and fragrant tobaccos and drugs eddied deliciously around her. Mama's scarlet and gold stripes blended in well. She saw now why he encouraged her to dress well and wished she had worn something more than a plain cobalt tabard over a black bodysuit.

Mama's whispered annotations about what was happening and who doing what to whom made *Volpone* not only understandable but entertaining. Somehow, the singing sounded less like screaming when she knew what it meant. Afterward they had caff and a snack at a top dink restaurant in the stockyards. So were a good many other members of the audience, Janna reflected, watching the furs and jewels at the other tables. Mama critiqued the production and singing while they ate.

She raised a brow. "Does all this expertise come from your single year in Theater Arts at UMKC?"

He shook his head, forehead creased in seriousness. "I may have switched my curriculum to Criminal Justice but I've never stopped being interested in the Arts. That year just introduced me to everything and whetted my appetite. I can't say that I'd never heard good music before or seen a ballet or classic play—we had television, after all—but

I never understood anything about what I was seeing, when I bothered to watch it. Then it was like suddenly gaining sight and hearing after having been blind and deaf. Opera is such *spectacle*, full of costumes and blood and grand loves and foul murder. No one in it ever has *little* problems. Sometimes I've thought, what if life were like opera? My god, how dramatic our job would be."

Janna grinned.

It was after midnight before they left the restaurant. Janna strode beside Mama, admiring the steam of their breath weaving fairy wreaths around their heads. Warmed by food and wine and amusement, she barely felt the night air biting at her face and sinking through the fabric of her long coat. Breathing deeply, she decided she had not felt this contented since Sid married.

Punching the lock combination of the car door Mama said, "Now to find a hotel."

Contentment evaporated abruptly. Janna stiffened. "Now just a minute, Maxwell!"

He looked around, frowning over the top of his glasses at her. "My god. Loosen, bibi; it's strictly business. That was the only way I could get the car. In the morning we'll drive up to Kansas City International and—"

"The hell we're going to KCI tomorrow!" She snatched at the keys, and capturing them, raced around to the driver's side. "What do you want to do, earn us more days off, but without pay?" She punched the lock combination with angry stabs. "It *isn't our case any more.* Leave it the hell alone!" Sliding open the door, Janna jumped across the airfoil. "We're going back to Topeka and pray no one finds we took a department car on personal business."

Mama climbed in the passenger side, sighing. "Just when I think you're turning into a genuine human being, you revert to By-the-Book Brill."

She started the car and lifted off with a savage leap that whipped both their necks.

She would have liked to make the drive back in stony silence, but Mama seemed determined to batter through it. "How can you just turn your back on this case, bibi?"

Was it worth trying to convince him that she hated giving up as much as he did, that she did not want Paul Chenoweth's killer to escape responsibility for the act, either? Would he even believe her? As they crossed the county line, she finally answered him. "Pragmatism, Maxwell. I have to, or how am I going to work effectively on the assaults and murders Morello will dump on us tomorrow? Do I slight those victims for the sake of—" The yelp of a siren behind them interrupted her. She glanced in the rear scanner on the dash to see a light rail flashing through the wind-driven snow. "I think we're being hauled down. Damn you, Mama. They've found out about the car."

As the Monitor settled onto its parking rollers, the watch car team approached, one on each side of the car. Janna ran down her window. "Good evening, leos."

The she-lion on her side said, "Both of them together. Once in a while we get lucky."

The voice sounded familiar. Janna peered at the face under the helmet. "Villalba? I didn't know you'd transferred to Tecumseh division. Isn't it a little cold to be playing games?"

"Not when there's a case of felony ugly like yours. Did you know there's been an Attempt To Locate on you two since six o'clock?"

Janna straightened. "What?"

The leo on Mama's side said, "Every car in the county has been watching for you. You're supposed to call Crimes Against Persons immediately."

That sounded serious. Janna glanced sideways at Mama. He looked as wary as she felt. "Thanks. Mama, we'd better find a telephone."

A thick-walled little fort of all-night convenience store up the road had one. Lieutenant Susan Drexel, the morning watch commander, came on the screen frowning, her voice crackling in exasperation and relief. "Have you two been taking invisibility lessons from slighs? Vradel says to tell you Fontana called back. There seems to have been a great deal of chatting back and forth today...Fontana with his home office, someone in the home office with the director of the State Police in New York, the New York State Police and Lanour High Muckies with our own director. The conclusion is that while jurisdiction for investigation of the murder belongs to the New York State Police—that being the state where Lanour is incorporated—since no one in that office has had prior experience with the crime in question, platform Security is to investigate, but, quote, 'in the presence of an official agency and officers with knowledge of this crime who will act as consultants and lend an appearance of authority to the investigation.' End quote."

"Presence?" Janna stared at the lieutenant, heart suddenly pounding.

Drexel smiled thinly. "Pack your bags. Frontier has a shuttle leaving from Forbes tomorrow. You and Maxwell are to be on it."

10

Sunday, February 4. 8:30:00 hours platform time.

The shuttle captain was a small, stocky woman with slavic cheekbones. "We're coming up on the Lanour," she called over her shoulder. "Do you two want to take a look at it before we start maneuvering for docking?"

Would she! Janna unclipped her seat belt and following Mama, pulled herself from her chair behind the navigator up along the cockpit to the back of the pilot's seat, where they could peer over Captain Dorrance's shoulder out the front windows.

The copilot grinned up at them. "In some ways, we never stop being kids, do we?"

"No, fortunately," Mama replied. "But some of us need to let out the kid more often."

Janna had no doubt who he meant, but she refused to answer the jibe. It would only sound defensive, and waste some of her sightseeing time.

As a freighter, the shuttle might lack the appointments for passengers that made long flights more comfortable, but it had its advantages, like sitting up with the six members of the crew and being invited forward for a pilot's view of the universe.

And what a view it was! Janna sighed happily. Stars glittered like cracked ice on black velvet and the Earth filled the sky above them, glowing the luminous blue of a star sapphire, splashed with brown continents and the white swirls of weather systems. Did colonists, looking down on it during the shuttle flight up to their ship, ever have second thoughts about leaving? As Fontana had told Mama in that first phone conversation, from here the world looked only peaceful and beautiful, a wonder with none of the evils showing.

Even more of a wonder than something like the shuttle really flying. Seeing it on the tarmac outside the Forbes terminal Friday morning, taller than a two-storey house, the upswept and inwardly-leaning tips of its delta wings giving it a wicked silhouette, Janna had been hard put to convince her gut what her intellect knew. It looked so *big* for something that expected to take off like an ordinary airplane.

Of course the shuttle had lifted without incident, and climbed toward space, first on conventional jets, then scrams, and finally, somewhere far above the ground, firing the rockets that kicked them out of the atmosphere. The navigator had given them a running commentary during the forty-five minutes from ground to parking orbit, explaining everything that happened. Lifting off was the short part. The remaining two days of the trip they spent stopping at two other platforms and chasing down Lanour's station.

"I don't see the platform," Janna said.

"There." Dorrance pointed.

Then Janna saw it, a small black silhouette floating against the glow of the planet behind. It looked nothing like a platform, of course, not even like the wheel-shaped Glenn platform the navigator pointed out to them yesterday as they passed within fifty kilometers of it. The Lanour platform bore more resemblance to a cluster of grapes, a mass of bubble shapes clumped together, though the broad wings of the solar panels spread wide between the shuttle and station blocked so much of the view of it that Janna could make out few details.

"You'd better belt in again," Dorrance said.

Janna and Mama floated back to their seats. Without a viewport of her own, she had to follow their docking progress through what she could glimpse through the front windows and the muttering of Dorrance and the copilot in response to garble from the radio.

Mama grinned across the aisle at her. "Space ship communications don't sound any better than police car radios, do they?"

The shuttle shuddered once. Moments later a muted clang reverberated through it. The shuttle crew unclipped their safety belts. Two pulled themselves aft to release the overhead hatch between the cabin and cargo bay.

Dorrance grinned at Janna and Mama and adopted the mechanical cheer of an airline attendant. "We are now at the terminal. Will all disembarking passengers please check around their seats for carry-on luggage and personal belongings? We hope you enjoyed your flight and thank you for flying Frontier."

Grinning back, Janna slung her bag across her back by the shoulder strap and pulled up the ladder after the crewmen.

It brought her into a large circular chamber where she stopped, drawing a deep breath. For a moment, she thought she smelled fresher air, but the impression faded almost immediately. Sometime in the past two days she appeared to have caught cold or an allergy that filled her sinuses; she could barely smell anything.

Half a dozen men lounged in the zero-gee of the chamber, some floating holding to metal loops on the walls of the chamber, others standing on those same walls as though on a floor, a foot through the loops to keep them in place. They wore coveralls of a variety of styles and shades—all basically yellow, however, even those with stripes or checks—and a six-sided blue-and-orange plastic badge on the left breast pocket.

"Hey, Zim. Are things starting to thaw out down there yet?" one man asked. His badge said: STORES, and under it: BREDE.

"Only New Hampshire, where the rhetoric's heating up," one of the shuttle crew replied.

"You didn't happen to stop at the Glenn this trip, did you? We heard that Taya Hollander claims to be giving up fame and fortune and the cineround to ship out with the Jubilee Company and every het jon and ho bibi in Stores is slavering to know if it's true they're going to be deprived of new views of her skin."

The crewman shrugged. "Sorry. Is there someone to show our passengers here where to go?"

"The other side of the lock." One of the receiving crew pointed up at a heavy door comprising the chamber's ceiling.

Or wall, or floor. Janna found her orientation changing just by turning in midair. Whichever, she headed the direction he pointed, pulling herself by the rings on the wall. A crewmen punched a code on a number pad to one side of the door. The intermeshing teeth across the center parted to let her and Mama through into a second chamber.

"Enjoy your stay. See you on the flight back," the crewman called as the doors clanged together again behind them.

Moments later a second set of doors on the far side of the chamber opened. Janna gulped. She stared up/down a corridor as round as a pipe and to all appearances, bottomless. Rings of light panels turned it into a sunny yellow hole, true, marked at intervals by arcs of other colors: sky blue, red, light green. Still, the appearance of infinity remained and Janna clawed across the paneling for the support of one of the railings running lengthwise down the hole. Mama grabbed it right behind her.

"Don't worry, you aren't going to fall," a voice said reassuringly.

Janna tilted back her chin. An attractive oriental woman in an abbreviated body suit and slipper socks with knee-high tops smiled at them from the top of the tube. Her badge said: ADMINISTRATION/ NAKASHIMA.

"Good morning, Sergeant Brill and Sergeant Maxwell. I'm Ginneh Nakashima, Mr. Fontana's secretary. He sends his apologies for not meeting you personally, but this is the beginning of our official day and he's tied up with some organizational details. I'll show you to your quarters. By the time you're settled Mr. Fontana should be ready to have you join him in his office. Just follow me."

"Down that?" Mama pointed at bottomlessness beneath/above them.

Sloe eyes warmed in amusement. "Technically it's down, I suppose, since it's pointed toward Earth, though without gravity, up and down are wherever you wish. Think of the corridor as horizontal, but instead of walking, you swim through it."

She gave one tug at the rail she held and sent herself sailing along the corridor, touching the rail after that only to renew her momentum. The movement looked graceful and very much as though the woman and other people Janna saw in the corridor were indeed swimming. Attempting to imitate Nakashima, however, Janna skidded into the wall almost at once, and to add injury to embarrassment, smashed her nose against the panel as her bag overtook the back of her head. Through tears of pain and rockets behind her eyes she heard Mama's voice, anxious.

"Bibi, are you all right?"

She breathed slowly, waiting for her vision to clear. "Aside from my new Pekingese profile, you mean?"

Nakashima came pulling back to them. "I'm so sorry. It's my fault. I should have warned you to be very careful until your reflexes adjust to weightlessness."

"Or pack a lighter bag." Janna resumed following the secretary but this time contented herself with moving hand-over-hand along the railing. The arcs of color, she soon discovered, marked the edges of hatches.

"For navigation reference, this is the A or core corridor," Nakashima said. "These hatches lead to the Stage One modules that have become storage space, or passages through to Stage Two pods where the greenhouses and gymnasium are located. That hatch goes to the gym. It's a gravity drum, if you feel you need to have a real 'down' for a while, or if you want to drain your sinuses. They tend to fill up without gravity."

So she had not caught cold after all. That was some comfort to know, Janna reflected. "The gym helps?"

"Quite a bit. It also stresses your bones to help maintain their calcium. Here's the C corridor where your quarters are located. It's also part of Level One, or you can remember it as the spring-green corridor. All the main branches are color coded."

C was one of four corridors joining the core at this point, Janna noted. The green paneling lasted for three meters down the corridor before yellow resumed. Openings off this corridor came in groups of three, spaced around the circumference equidistant from each other, and marked the opening of short branches whose far ends terminated in lock-type doors, most open at the moment. Nakashima swung into one with signs above and upside-down below saying: C-8 Visitors/Observation.

Beyond the lock door, Nakashima dived across a vertical shaft into a corridor opening straight ahead. It looked like a real corridor, at last, square, with a carpeted floor and lights on the ceiling. Oval doorways opened off both sides. Nakashima put her feet down and began walking, accompanied by a familiar ripping sound. Velcro on the bottom of the slipper socks?

"Your rooms are here. We've put you in singles across from each other but if that isn't satisfactory, we can arrange adjoining rooms or a double."

"No, that's fine," Janna said.

Nakashima touched a green button on a panel beside one of the oval doorways. The door split down the middle.

The room inside looked comfortingly familiar, too, except for the lack of furniture...just a sleeping bag/hammock stretched across the room above the entrance and some floor-to-ceiling wires with vests attached to the middle. That *was* the furniture, Nakashima explained. The wires were "chairs." She pointed out other features, like the closet which looked like a poster display rack, using a series of clear plastic envelopes stretched between swinging upper and lower arms. "You slip the clothes you want to hang into the envelopes to keep them flat and put everything else in the pockets on the outside."

She also explained how to use the bathroom with its dishwasher-cabinet shower and stirruped commode.

"There are book chips and a viewer in the topmost wall pocket beside the closet and others in the library in Recreation in D corridor. Oh, you'll probably want these."

Another of the wall pockets contained a pair of slipper socks to replace Janna's boots. Across the hall in Mama's room, another pair of slipper socks waited for him. Then, with baggage stowed and slipper socks on, now able to stick to the floor and walk almost normally, they followed Nakashima back toward the C corridor in a chorus of ripping sounds.

Administration lay in a pod down the blue B corridor, a honeycomb of corridors and offices with carpeting and light panels making a grid pattern on the ceiling as well as the floors, and furniture hanging above everyone like Swords of Damocles. Janna watched queasily as a secretary in an office they passed pushed away from the desk where she had been standing at a computer keyboard, and pulling her feet loose from the carpet, leaped up to the threatening bulk of files above her.

"Jesus." Janna shuddered.

Nakashima smiled. "You'll get used to it. Mr. Fontana is this way." She walked on, stepping from carpet square to carpet square.

Leonard Fontana used no chair, either. He stood at a broad desk whose top tilted like a draftsman's table. Behind him flickered a bank of monitor screens, some showing figures and letters but others clearly connected to surveillance cameras. He had a real ceiling, transparent, with a spectacular view of Earth. No, not transparent, Janna realized moments later. Unless she had completely lost her sense of direction, they were on the upper side of this pod and should be looking at stars or the solar panels. The Earthview must be a projection...on a tape loop, perhaps, because it moved.

Fontana came around the desk in a ripping of velcro, hand extended. "Sergeant Maxwell, we meet again, and you must be Sergeant Brill. This is an honor." He looked older than he had on the phone screen, Janna saw. This close, lines showed in his face, though the flesh did not sag. A benefit of weightlessness, no doubt. "I do apologize for not being in Receiving to greet you, but...executive problems. It's like being captain of one whopping big ship. I hope you had a pleasant flight and that your quarters are satisfactory."

"Top star," Janna said, trying not to wince. His handshake almost crushed her hand. "A few features in the room are a bit strange, though."

He grinned. "Well, with any luck, we can clear this problem up fast and let you return to more familiar surroundings. That's all Gin. Remind me to find a way to tell you I appreciate you taking care of our guests for me."

The sloe eyes smiled at him. "Yes, Mr. Fontana." She left in a soft ripping of Velcro.

As the halves of the oval door closed behind her, Fontana sobered. "Actually, I think we may have more than one problem and I hope y'all can help me. I don't understand this lapse in Geyer's security that allowed whatever it was to leave in Chenoweth's body...and I'll admit to you now as I couldn't on the phone that we haven't identified what that something was yet, except that considering the…storage space, it probably had to be plans or a formula rather than an object itself. Which means we may never know until a duplicate of our work here turns up in production by Uwezo. But back to Geyer. Somehow, the body slipped out without the thorough examination we use on living people leaving. Why? Of course, I don't expect my chief of security to be there personally checking every crate and person that leaves, but Ian Doubrava, my assistant chief, had been there with the body until a disturbance pulled him away to another part of the station. Was that coincidence, or did someone arrange a diversion? And why didn't the officer left examine more than just the clothing and body bag?" He hesitated, pacing in quick, short rips. "I hate to cast suspicion on my own people."

Janna's gut knotted. Was Fontana about to say what she thought he was? She glanced quickly at Mama and found him frowning slightly. He must think so, too.

"But," Fontana went on, talking somewhere past them, "the security measures had to be circumvented by someone who knew the procedures."

Anger and disgust flared in Janna. He *was* going to ask, damn him!

"So, as you aid Geyer and Doubrava and any of the others in Security, will you keep your eyes open, and without mentioning it to Geyer, pass on to me personally any thoughts you might formulate on who might be guilty? I think that if I'm given several independent opinions, then matches must be considered very good bets."

"Meaning," Mama said slowly, "that you want us to watch your Security personnel, too, including Geyer?"

You want us to spy for you, like the officers in Internal Affairs spy on us at home? Janna wanted to add. *You want us to be peeps*?

Fontana's wolf eyes flicked across them. "I want you to keep your eyes open for anything suspicious, sergeants."

If he refused to admit what he wanted, she could not spit in his eye. Janna pushed down her anger. "Yes, sir."

"Of course," Mama said.

Fontana smiled. "Then I think it's time meet with Geyer and Doubrava. Oh, but before I forget it, here are your visitor ID's. They entitle you to the same services as regular employees, though they don't admit you to restricted areas. For going those places, you'll need an escort."

He handed each of them one of the six-sided blue-and-orange plastic badges. These said only: VISITOR, but in letters brighter and twice as large as those on his badge. Janna exchanged quick glances with Mama. There would be no mistaking them for new personnel.

With the badges clipped in place, they followed Fontana out of the office. This time the trip was short, just across the corridor to the pod marked: COMMUNICATIONS AND SECURITY.

The officers and clerks in Security stood at their desks, too, uniformed in body-hugging jumpsuits of two-toned cobalt and powder blue with stylish diagonal divisions across trunk and pantlegs. For badges they wore the same six-sided ID, but in addition to section identification on the badge, Janna saw wrap strap pockets down the uniform thighs and familiar clips on the hip belt for a baton, K-12 minicanister, and needler holster. No one would mistake them for anything but Security.

As in Administration, the files here also hung from the ceiling. A holograph of the station dominated the center of the room, and surveillance monitors filled an entire wall.

Another smaller bank of screens glowed above the desk in the inner office.

And more than that glowed. Against the desk there leaned one of the most stunningly beautiful women Janna had ever seen, as tall and lithe as Janna but with fewer angles. Mixed blood, part of it afro, surely, had produced a regal face and nose, a tightly curling cap of chestnut hair, and skin that glowed luminous and tiger-tawny against the blues of her uniform. Glints of gold shone in the dark eyes, too.

"Très bueno," Mama breathed.

Fontana smiled at the golden woman. "May I present my Chief of Security, Tabanne Geyer? And my assistant chief, Captain Ian Doubrava."

The man suffered only by comparison with the goddess beside him. Reaching out to shake his hand, Janna took in a trim body, a mane of thick, dark hair, and brilliant turquoise eyes. Real, contact lenses, or cosmetically colored with one of the new tissue dyes? But who cared? A warm, firm grip met hers. "Welcome to Sky City."

Geyer shook, too, but perfunctorily.

A pocket secretary in Fontana's breast pocket murmured: "Five minutes until conference, sir."

"Well." The director looked back and forth between the four of them. "I'll leave you to get busy, then. Good luck." He ripped his slippers free of the carpet and propelled himself out of the room.

Geyer's smile faded abruptly. Janna suck in her breath. With the smile went all warmth.

"I won't waste time with polite lies," Geyer said in a voice edged with steel. "I don't want nor need you here. I may be just a lend-lease leo to you, but I'm perfectly capable of handling a murder investigation. We have several killings a year, none of which has ever gone unsolved while I've been Security chief. You're here only because the home office has panicked over this smuggling." Her mouth twisted wryly. "Personnel can always be replaced, but loss of a potential product is catastrophic. All the company's blessings and your official badges still don't put you in charge here, however. This is *my* turf and *I'll* police it. You just stand around looking pretty." She paused and her voice lowered to a hiss. "That's an order, not a suggestion, leos, because if I find myself falling over you, I promise you'll go back to Earth without waiting for the shuttle."

And wheeling in a rip of Velcro, Tabanne Geyer pushed off from the desk and sailed out of the room.

11

February 4. 10:00:00 hours.

In the strained silence left by the Security chief's exit, Janna twisted toward Doubrava, but his glance ducked hers to fasten intently on the row of monitors above the desk. Mama did not look at her, either, just stared the direction Geyer had disappeared, his jaw slack, adoration glazing his eyes. Janna's lip curled in disgust. "You're dripping saliva on the carpet." Had he heard a word Geyer said, or had he been only eyes, lost in the woman's golden glow?

Her hostility was understandable, of course. Janna had experienced the same resentment herself, as a watch car officer seeing investigators out of Capitol taking a case away from the division, and as an investigator having to tolerate federal agents using her work to finish wrapping a case and then taking all the credit. Geyer could also be aware that Fontana had asked them to spy on her. This laser blast tactic withered any sympathy Janna might have felt, however. It also raised a question: Could Geyer have more reason than territoriality for wanting them to stand clear? Might Fontana's request be justified after all? On the other hand, considering how highly placed the smuggler had to be, Fontana could be taking advantage of Geyer's natural bitchiness to make an accusation that would divert attention from himself.

Janna caught Doubrava peering at her from the corner of his eye and gave him a sardonic smile. "It's so nice to feel appreciated."

He regarded her without expression. "Would you like a tour of the platform? I'll find an officer with the time guide you."

Ah, yes, the classic ploy. Be polite to the invaders, be hospitable, entertain them...but keep them out of the way. Time to push back. "I'd rather see a transcript of the inquiry into Paul Chenoweth's death."

Doubrava arched a brow. "Brave. But foolish. Chief Geyer means what she says."

Janna bared her teeth at him. "I know how to threaten, too. Such as, can Geyer really afford to appear uncooperative? The home office and Director Fontana may feel her investigation won't bear scrutiny. I'm too nice a person to bring that up, though. I'm just one professional making a request of another who also looks like a nice person."

The turquoise eyes measured her. A corner of his mouth twitched before he pulled it back into a sober line. "But what happens to this nice person's skin if I help you? I do, after all, have to live with my chief."

Mama shook himself and, sighing, dragged his gaze from the door. "Surely the chief realizes that if we're consultants, we ought to at least appear to be involved in the investigation, and be able to answer intelligently when Fontana and other high company officials ask about it."

"Who knows...we might even have an idea or two to offer," Janna added.

Doubrava stared at them for a moment, face still expressionless. "Perhaps you have a point. There is...pressure from the home office to produce fast results. I think there's an idle desk in the outer office you can use. This way."

Like Fontana and Geyer, Doubrava pulled his slippers loose, and led the way, floating. Mama copied him. After a minute, Janna did so as well, but cautiously, keeping handholds close.

The desk stood between the wall of monitors and the station holo. Now she had time to appreciate the detail of the holo, from the sun panels around the docking bay to branching corridors and clusters of globular pods, and small tubes connecting many of the pods to each other on the same level and some on the next higher or lower level. On the middle level, some tubes ended blindly, pointed toward podless corridors on the lowest level.

"What are those?" She pointed to the tubes.

Doubrava glanced over at the holo. "Escape tunnels. In case a corridor is breached, no one will be trapped in the pods."

On the other side of her, monitors reached from floor to floor. One at Janna's eye level showed what must be the gymnasium. The camera, equipped with a fisheye lens, sat in the wall opposite the entrance. The gym spread out beneath it, circular and distorted...exercise machines, basketball court, racquet ball courts, swimming pool, and track. Other monitors, each with a letter and number designation on the lower left corner of the screen, showed corridors and pod entrances. Those with F, G, H, and I letter designations all had closed doors.

"This is quite a surveillance system." She worked her slippers into the carpet for stabilization.

Doubrava nodded. "From here we can watch any point in the station, except private rooms and offices and the labs themselves, of course." He said it with pride.

"Which of these do the monitors in Geyer's office duplicate?" Mama asked.

"She can call up any of them she wants."

But Security did not have the only monitors, Janna remembered. "What about the ones in Fontana's office?"

The turquoise eyes narrowed. "How does that relate to this case?"

She sighed inwardly. Did all the Security people have to be so damned cat-nerved? She gave Doubrava a shrug. "I don't know that it does. Sorry. Professional curiosity."

He eyed her a moment longer before replying. "A space station is very much like a ship. The director is our captain and likes to know what's going on. So the director can also call up what's on any of these monitors."

"Big Brother is watching."

Doubrava stiffened. "Everyone coming here understands that security takes precedence over privacy. We have a great deal to protect."

Guilt pricked Janna. She grimaced in apology. "I know. Sorry."

After a moment, he nodded stiffly.

"Do you record—" Mama began.

Doubrava interrupted, "I'm forgetting why I brought you out here. One minute, please."

He floated up to a file a short way across the room, and after hunting along the shelf-like drawer, came back with a stack of printouts and a file folder. He pulled himself down to the carpet. "These are the inquiry transcript and pictures of Chenoweth's pressure suit." Released from his hand, the printout remained hanging in the air by his shoulder while Doubrava opened the folder and handed Janna a number of 2-D photographs and holo plates.

The printout started to drift away. Mama reached out to capture it. Janna sorted through the photographs. Pressure suits had come a long way in refinement since the twentieth century body armor she remembered seeing with her third-grade class at the space museum in Hutchinson. A huge rent down the side from the collar ring to the left thigh spoiled the graceful lines of this suit, however.

She stared at the rip in disbelief. "How could he have done this catching it somewhere? Wouldn't he have been more careful?"

"Care isn't always enough. Occasional snagging happens to everyone. I worked in construction crews on several platforms before taking up security work and probably snagged my suit a dozen times during the course of each project. Granted I never had any damage this bad, but I've seen a few instances of neglected suits literally falling apart."

"We know this suit didn't just happen to fall apart. It had to be arranged. Why did the killer pick Chenoweth, do you suppose? Just at random?"

Mama frowned. "I'm more puzzled why anyone is even wearing pressure suits. It's my understanding that you build these pods from the outside in, spraying a balloon form with polymers to make the skin, then filling it with air so the internal construction can be done in the comfort and safety of an atmosphere."

The turquoise eyes flickered. After a moment, Doubrava said slowly, "That's how much of this station was built, yes, but it isn't the only method. We're trying something this time that requires a pipe-and-wire framework. Excuse me, but I'd better go back to my assigned job before the boss catches me fraternizing with the enemy. Of course, if you have any questions, don't hesitate to ask me."

With a nod, he floated back toward the inner office.

Mama's brows hopped. "Which doesn't necessarily mean he'll answer."

"At least he hasn't offered to bite and claw. Let's see what the inquiry had to say."

Sliding the photographs under a clip secured to the desk top, she read the transcript over Mama's shoulder. Blue jump-suited Security officers came and went from the office, eyeing them curiously and murmuring to other officers, but never speaking to Mama or her directly. Solidarity in the face of outsiders, or Geyer had them well under her thumb.

The evidence produced by the inquiry seemed straightforward enough. Eleven members of the construction crew all testified to the same thing, varying only in details. They had been putting together pipe for the framework of a new pod. Chenoweth, wearing a jetbelt, had been hauling reels of the wire used to weave between the pipes for added stability. He passed too close to the free end of one pipe. One crewmember actually saw, or thought he remembered seeing, the suit catch on the pipe end. He testified that he did not react immediately, thinking nothing of it until moments later, when he and everyone heard Chenoweth scream over his suit radio that the suit was ripping. Several people had been close enough on the sun side of him to see the particles of freezing oxygen and water vapor showering outward from his suit. They had started for him, pulling along the frame, or using jetbelts if they wore them, but his jetbelt had continued to operate, too, carrying him away from the frame, and by the time anyone could catch up, Chenoweth was dead.

Very straightforward, except for one small detail, a detail that sent electric shock through Janna.

Question, Director Fontana: Mr. Carakostas, identification in the suit indicates it was assigned not to Paul Chenoweth but to Clell Titus. How did Mr. Chenoweth happen to be wearing Mr. Titus's suit?

"Son of a bitch," Mama muttered. "Then Chenoweth's death could have been an accident after all, poor devil."

Response, Crew Chief Carakostas: Chenoweth complained to me that his suit's heating element wasn't functioning properly on checkout. I examined the suit with him, but since we couldn't find the cause of the malfunction immediately, and Clell Titus wasn't on the shift, I advised Chenoweth to borrow Titus's suit and unlocked the locker for him.

Question, Assistant Security Chief Doubrava: Did Chenoweth run a checkout on Titus's suit before leaving the locker area?

Response, Crew Chief Carakostas: To the best of my knowledge, yes; he was beginning the checkout when I left him for my briefing with the crew chief of the incoming shift.

Question, Security Chief Geyer: But you cannot testify that he finished the checkout. He could, in fact, have rushed through the checkout because of the delay caused by the other suit's malfunction, and not followed the protocol completely.

Janna grimaced. "It sounds as though she's trying to set him up for a charge of negligence, doesn't it."

"Someone set someone up, that's for certain," Mama said, "and Chenoweth had the rotten luck to fall into the trap."

Janna frowned at the transcript. "I wonder if we can arrange to see the suit."

They pulled through the office back to the inner office.

"Nice of you to tell us that Chenoweth couldn't have been the intended victim," Janna said.

Doubrava looked around from reading printout and arched his brows. "Wouldn't that have been redundant when you were going to read it in the inquiry transcript?"

Mama said, "The transcript doesn't have much detail about the suit itself, except testimony by Maintenance and Clell Titus that the suit had passed all safety checks two weeks before. May we see the suit?"

Doubrava considered and sighed, pursing his lips. "I think Chief Geyer might look on that as going beyond a mere appearance of involvement."

Mama pushed his glasses down against his nose. "What if you take a look at it and we just happen to tag along?"

Doubrava's eyebrows rose. "Why should I want to look at it again?"

Janna did not for a moment believe he could really be that light-witted, but she said, "Obviously the suit was sabotaged. It must show some evidence of that."

His mouth thinned. "You might give us credit for thinking of that already. After your conversation with the director on Wednesday, Bane—Chief Geyer sent the suit down to the labs for examination right away."

It must be handy, having the day's most sophisticated scientific facilities just down the corridor. "And?"

"And what?"

God! This was like pulling teeth. Fighting to keep exasperation out of her voice, Janna asked, "And what did you find?"

He hesitated before replying, glancing past them toward the door. "A time bomb. Someone had pulled the lining out of the suit and made long cuts several places in the inner surface, stopping just short of puncturing through, then replaced the lining."

"And waited for the suit to snag." Anger flared in Janna. Waited for a man to die so a plan or formula could go down to a buyer on Earth.

Mama took off his glasses and left them hanging in the air beside him while he rubbed his eyes. "He couldn't afford to wait too long. The ground contacts arrived in Kansas on Tuesday the sixteenth. The law seminar they were using as cover wouldn't last forever." He pulled out a group of papers shoved haphazardly under a clip on the desk and shuffled them into a neat stack, re-secured them, then recovered his glasses. "And speaking of time, sabotaging that suit doesn't sound like something that could be done in a couple of minutes while the suit storage area happened to be empty."

"Probably not," Doubrava agreed.

"Could it be that easy to take it away and bring it back hours later?"

"Obviously someone managed to."

Irritation pricked Janna. What kind of answer was that? "Why use Titus's suit? Is he the careless kind, someone the killer might feel certain would snag his suit sooner than someone else?"

Doubrava shrugged. "Not to my knowledge." He paused, then added, "Geyer wonders if maybe the smuggler wanted a double benefit, eliminating an accomplice as well as providing transportation for stolen goods."

Janna exchanged quick glances with Mama. Greed among thieves? "You've investigated Titus? What did you find?"

Doubrava shrugged again. "Nothing conclusive."

Not another round of that! "Captain Doubrava," she began angrily.

Mama pinched her under a shoulder blade. "I think we've taken enough of the captain's time for now, bibi. Let's go learn our way around the station."

"If you'll wait a moment, I'll find you a guide." Pulling loose from the carpet, Doubrava floated toward the door.

"Thank you, but we don't want to tie up any of your personnel. It'll be more fun if we get lost a few times."

Doubrava stopped in the opening and turned back to frown at them, body taut. "Not necessarily. Unauthorized personnel aren't allowed below Level One and we don't treat trespassers kindly, even those sent by the home office."

Mama spread his hands. "I have no intention of wandering anywhere much but the gym, the cafeteria, and somewhere for a drink." He paused. "You do have somewhere to drink, don't you?"

"Recreation, pod D-3." Doubrava frowned. "I hope you realize that it isn't general knowledge we're conducting a murder investigation, and certainly no one is to know we've lost any of our work."

"Understood."

Tension visibly loosened in the security officer. "Then enjoy your wanderings, and if you get lost too often, call me." He smiled at Janna. "I mean it about asking me questions. Come back any time. I'll keep the desk out there for you as long as you're on the station."

Leaving the Security offices, Mama grinned at Janna. "I think you made a conquest. Would that I were so lucky." He sighed.

"Really? I didn't realize he was your type." As Mama's eyes rolled behind his glasses, she added, "I know who you meant, and you're lucky she hates us. She'd eat you alive. Haven't you been burned bad enough by Lia?"

He sighed. "Maybe I'm looking for a cure for Lia."

Janna regretted having said anything. Hastily she changed the subject. "Are we really going to let ourselves be restricted to sight-seeing?"

His eyes focused back on her, crinkling with his grin. "If they don't want to make us part of this case, we'll just have to be clandestine."

She grinned back. "On with the tour, then."

12

February 4. 10:30:00 hours.

Finding their way around the station proved to be no problem. Specific destinations might be difficult to find, but color coding of the corridors and letter/number designations on the pod entrances constantly informed them of their location. No visitor could stray to Level Two by accident, either. Pulling along the A corridor past the Level One intersections triggered a recording, a polite feminine voice. "I'm sorry, but you are now entering a restricted portion of the station. Please return to the visitor levels."

"Shall we see what happens next?" Mama asked.

"I don't care to, no." Janna turned back.

She found a wiry man in a Mohawk haircut and the two-toned blue uniform of Security floating behind them. "Next," he said in a conversational tone, "the warning would have been stronger. 'I'm sorry, but you *must* turn back.' Then a holo image fills the corridor, a door with STOP: RESTRICTED AREA printed on it in flashing red letters, and alarms go off in Security. If you still continue, an automatic mechanism leaves you physically incapacitated and we carry you away to recover under confined conditions."

Mama cocked his head. "Physically incapacitated? Interesting. How?"

Mohawk grinned. "That we don't tell. You're welcome to find out by experimentation, however."

"Maybe we ought to look at the gym," Janna said.

The gym intrigued her, a track that sloped perceptibly upward, yet the surface always felt level. The drawback was the open structure of the drum. Working out on the impressive array of exercise machines, a person could see handball and basketball courts sitting vertically left and right, and most unnerving of all, a swimming pool directly overhead.

They peeked into the greenhouses, too, one in another gravity drum, one zero-gee, both jungle-gyms of plant racks full of grains and vegetables. A third contained a wildwood growing unrestricted from the core sphere of earth toward the skin of the bubble...except that some plants looked as though their branches and roots could not quite decide which direction to grow. A little more exploration located the cafeteria.

To her surprise, Janna found she could actually taste the food. The spices came through despite her clogged sinuses. "Can you imagine what their spice budget must run each year?"

Mama's eyes glittered behind his glasses. "No doubt it's astronomical."

He ducked the drinking bulb of caff she threatened to throw at him.

At other tables around them, station personnel stood wolfing down their food and chattering with companions, but not all anchored by slippers in the carpet, Janna noticed. A number, like the man with waist-length braids at the table next to her, had suction cups dangling from their belts and stabilized themselves by sticking the cups to the under side of the tables. Their legs did not move normally, she realized presently, just trailed along behind them as they sailed across the room. Paralyzed? This would be a good work environment for a paraplegic.

Not everyone chattered, either. Some ate with attention riveted on a six-screen cubical newscanner in the center of the cafeteria that ran stock market quotations and business news.

Mama peered at it. "Lanour is down five more points."

A woman at the same table as the man with braids hissed. "That damn board!"

Janna raised a brow toward them. "I understood it was the proxy fight that's causing the drop."

The couple stiffened, then man with the braids nodded. "It is, because certain members of the board of directors are pressuring stockholders loyal to Crispus Tenning, our president and chairman of the board, into selling their shares." His mouth set grimly. "It's the only way the board can gain enough proxies to vote old man Tenning out as chairman and pressure him into retiring from the presidency."

Mama leaned closer to Janna. "I wonder which faction sent us up here."

After lunch they drifted over to Recreation, a pod with a cylindrical central corridor whose arrangement of round doorways indicated the rooms must be arrayed like layers of spokes. Judging by the amount of noise and smoke issuing from the doorways as they irised open to admit or discharge people, and by the names written around the circumference—Siriusly Yours, Fluidics Inc., The Quark, and Damnation Alley, among others—the Lanour platform boasted more than *a* place to drink.

"Belithroche?" Mama grinned at the name around one doorway. "I have to see what that is." He tapped the control plate.

Inside they found the "floors" on the walls to their left and right, long, softly glowing surfaces with waist high tables sprouting out of them from small islands of carpet. The bar stretched out at their feet, a double bar, really, with half toward each floor. As a bar, Belithroche seemed brighter, quieter, and cleaner than most, no narcotic smoke, no holo band for music, only something mellowly twentieth century-sounding. Of course, happy hour had not started.

Even so, several dozen patrons stood at the tables and bars, slippers settled into the carpet pieces, and the patrons wore a variety of hair styles and clothes Janna would have expected to see only in the evening on Earth, more skin than cloth. Near the doorway, a couple leaned over the bar, the woman in one of the new plastic-film body suits, transparent except for glittering nebula swirls of gold and silver imbedded in it, her male companion pony-tailed and shirtless beneath a tank-topped jumpsuit. They sipped from drinking bulbs, suction cups popping each time they picked up their drinks, and loudly discussed something they illustrated to each other by sketching on the bar. The sketching reminded Janna of Lieutenant Vradel. How very far away he and Topeka and Earth seemed from here.

The bartender, dressed in a hooded red and blue costume with a web on his chest, floated along the bar toward them. "Good evening. What can I mix you?" Intensely green eyes peered out of the hood's eye holes.

Janna raised a brow. "It's just past twelve hundred hours."

The bartender shrugged. "It's evening to me, and to most of my customers."

"That's an interesting ensemble," Mama said.

The green eyes crinkled. "Spider Man, a twentieth century comic character. Classics are my bob."

"Is that the reason for the Benny Goodman music?"

"You recognize it?" The bartender sounded pleased. "I don't know if the customers like it but at least they don't complain and I figure a boss is entitled to some privileges."

Janna arched her brows. "You own the bar? The company doesn't?"

The green eyes studied them. "Obviously you're not here for one of the director's How-To-Run-A-Successful-Station tours or he would have told you that he talked the home office into letting groups of the station staff take franchises at a token cost and work the places in their off time. Anyone with a yen for the perfect watering hole can buy up a franchise and design his own. We make our liquor, too, top dink stuff, much better than we can import. Try some."

"Is Belithroche something classic, too?" Janna asked.

The eyes crinkled again. "Sort of. It's short for Better Living Through Chemistry. My group are all chemists." The eyes swept them again. "What brings you to the Lanour?"

"Death," Mama said.

Janna pinched him. "Mama!"

He ignored her to lean toward the bartender. "We work for the company that makes your pressure suits. Our bosses and your home office sent us up to look at the pressure suit that ruptured."

"Yeah? Excuse me." He moved down the bar to refill the bulbs of the sketching couple, and add a few lines and symbols to what Janna now recognized as a chemical diagram, before floating back to them. "That was a hell of a thing about Chenoweth. I thought those suits couldn't rip."

"So did we," Janna said. She might as well follow Mama's lead. "We're wondering about operator error."

The bartender sniffed. "Working for the manufacturer, I suppose you would."

"Did you know Chenoweth well? Or Clell Titus, whose suit he borrowed? Did either of them drink in here?"

"I didn't know either of them personally. We don't get many from Construction in here. They prefer the noise in Damnation Alley and Helen's Half Acre. You might try there, and the other places. Be careful going in The Quark, though. People say it's full of color and charm, but it's run by some very strange ducks."

His snicker followed them out of the bar.

The only similarity between Belithroche and Damnation Alley was the floor plan. A blast of voices and jivaqueme and a cloud of smoke enveloped them at the door. The air scubbers must really earn their way here, Janna reflected. Through the narcotic haze and the pulsing red light from the floors and band holo at the far end, she could see the place was over half full. Two bartenders worked the double bar, one a woman with her hair pulled into a topknot bound and waxed so it stood straight up. Her costume consisted of nothing more than ribbons connected to bands at her neck, wrists, ankles, and waist.

Mama sighed, watching the glimpses of flesh between her ribbons as she moved. Personally, Janna preferred the male bartender, who wore almost nothing but a huge tattooed or painted eagle. It covered his torso, wings spread out across his shoulders and upper arms, talons reaching down his hips. A moment later she realized with a shock that he had almost nothing else to clothe; his legs stopped in stumps below the hips.

Sailing up the bar toward them, he smiled genially. "What'll you have?"

He had lungs, though, and they matched Vernon Tuckwiller's for making himself heard.

Janna tapped her ID badge and shouted back, "We hear you make top star liquor. If these are good here, pour us a sample. Your choice."

The bartender grinned. "Two Mutant-makers coming up."

With a name like that she sipped cautiously from the clear plastic bulb the bartender brought back. To her pleasant surprise, the drink, dusky red in this light, slid down smooth and warm, just perceptibly cinnamon in taste. Then the fission came. Heat spread through her body like a shock wave and up her throat to the top of her head with explosive force. She gasped.

Mama tried his drink and arched his brows. "Are you sure you can dispense this without radiation safety gear?"

The bartender's grin broadened. "There's no point in drinking if you can't taste it."

"True." Mama took another sip. "Say, did you know Paul Chenoweth, the construction worker who died here a couple of weeks ago?"

The eagle's wings rippled across the bartender's shoulders. "Sure. Why?"

"We're here about the suit he wore." Janna gave him the same story Mama had told Spider Man in Belithroche. "What can you tell us about Clell Titus?"

Dark eyes went sharp as the eagle's. "What does that have to do with a suit failure?"

She smiled at him. "We have to learn all we can, like did he always check his gear carefully before and after using it? I take it you're a friend of his?"

The bartender hesitated. "I know him from serving him. Nice jon. Hard worker like almost everyone up here. He drinks and uses a few drugs, and he gambles. Has a temper, sometimes, though he never causes enough trouble to yell for Geyer's Gorillas. I knew Chenoweth a little, too. Not that I want to speak ill of the dead, but he was the kind of person I might expect to have an accident. Nice kid, for a temporary, maybe preoccupied with finishing his year out and going home. His wife had a baby just last month and that's about all he talked about. He was always showing pictures of the kid his wife faxed up. I never crewed with him—my section is Maintenance, not Construction—but I can tell you from experience that letting yourself get distracted can be fatal." He paused. "If you want information about Titus, why don't you talk to the group at that table over there?"

Following the direction of his pointing finger, they pushed off from the bar and floated toward a table with four men and two women, all remarkably similar in appearance, the men clean-shaven, both men and women with hair cropped within millimeters of their scalps and all wearing bold-patterned body suits so thin and tight that they may as well have been nude.

"Evening," Mama said.

The group looked around with broad, toxy grins, grins that quickly faded to polite smiles.

"What can we do for you visitors?"

Mama's grin never faltered. "We understand you work with Clell Titus. Our company manufactures pressure suits and in cooperation with Lanour, we've been asked to determine the reason for his suit failure."

They stiffened. One woman snarled. Color sprayed across her face at eye level gave her a mask. "In *cooperation* with? As though we don't know Seever is a subsidiary of Lanour. What are you supposed to do, prove Clell didn't take care of the suit?"

"Not at all," Janna said.

Six pairs of eyes raked her. "Sure," a man in gold-and-black zigzag stripes said. "I have this piece of alpine meadow property on Venus." He turned his back.

The woman in the painted mask said, "We heard Security sent the suit down to the labs. You look there for the cause of your suit failure." She turned away, too.

Janna grimaced at Mama. "Doesn't the outpouring of warmth remind you of home?"

"Let's try another table."

They worked their way through the bar, but met the same response everywhere. Those who knew Titus refused to say anything that might throw an unfavorable light on him.

One man insisted: "I've crewed with him off and on since he's been up here and he's a cautious jon, conscientious about suit maintenance."

"In the accident inquiry he testified that the reason he wasn't on the shift when Chenoweth borrowed his suit was because he had crashed after a week of double-shifting. How did he keep going? Amphetamines and Dreamtime?"

The man flung his head, setting his ponytail rippling. "He knew how to take them. He didn't let them make him careless!"

"He gambled. Did he have debts that could worry him, or problems with relationships? A bad enemy? Anything that might distract him?" Anything that might make him vulnerable to being sucked into industrial espionage and smuggling.

The man's mouth clamped in a thin line. "You go to hell."

Patrons in Helen's Half Acre, whose psychedelic play of lights left Janna struggling to keep down her lunch, proved no more helpful, and more political.

"Is Lanour trying to prove worker negligence so it doesn't have to pay off on the Accidental Death clause of Chenoweth's contract?" demanded the bartender, a woman in a feather bikini and cap, and wings painted on her back. Birds seemed to be a popular motif. "If you want a place to lay blame, why not ask Lanour why it decided to disregard the safety of its workers and build these new pods from inside out, so they'd have to use pressure suits in the first place instead of working in an atmosphere?"

Janna raised a brow. "Are you sure the new pod procedure wasn't your director's idea?"

The bartender's curled lip was as good as a spit. "Fontana has his faults but they don't include stupidity, and he cares about us, unlike the groundsider toads in the home office who don't have the slightest idea what it's like up here."

"What is Clell Titus like? It must be hard card, having someone else die in his suit. How's he taking it?"

"Why don't you ask him?"

Which was about the most polite response they received. After an hour of trying to draw people out on Titus, they left.

In the corridor outside they clung to a railing for support and breathed deeply to clear their lungs and heads. Janna grimaced. "It really is like home…'us' against 'them', and we're 'them'."

Mama took off his glasses, blew on the lenses, and resettled them. "Maybe there's another approach to learning about Titus. Lanour must run some kind of security check on anyone it's thinking of sending up here. Let's see if Fontana will let us look at the personnel records." He paused. "If so, we can also peek at Geyer's and Fontana's."

"Fontana." Janna pursed her lips. "What can someone with the position and power Fontana has gain by selling off company secrets anyway?"

Mama shrugged. "I'll admit, I don't know right now. Maybe there's an answer in his file."

Janna's stomach was settling back into quiescence and the narcotic haze clearing from her head. "An answer I'd like is how the killer was able to sabotage that suit. He couldn't do it on the spot, but surely he would have attracted attention carrying it away and returning it hours later."

They started pulling along the railing toward the pod entrance. Sailing pass one doorway, however, a chorus of familiar bleeps and buzzes made Janna look in...and stare. Multiple lines of arcade holo games lined both floors in one of the most impressive arrays she had ever seen. "Top star!" She grinned at a man pushing one pointed end of his ID badge into the token machine inside the door. "You must have every game on the market in here."

The man snorted. "I don't know if *any* of these are what the company sent up any more. The computer bobs keep breaking into the programming and changing it. One time I found that whole row over there wired together. When your game piece went left or right, it jumped to the next machine. Now it's Deathrace you have to be careful of." He grimaced. "Above 100,000 points, they send choppers and planes after you, and after 500,000 points, there's a killer satellite to zap you with its laser. You can't see it, just its shadow."

Janna hauled herself tight against the side of the doorway to make way for a couple leaving and three young men entering. "That's a step up in sophistication from the versions I've played before. It must give you a fat bonus when you escape."

The man snorted. "Except you can't escape. If you avoid the satellite, an alien fleet swoops down and nukes the whole village. And when you're finally hit, the machine gives you a shock that'll straighten your hair right out."

She frowned. "A shock? Someone ought to correct that."

The man smiled wryly. "Admin claims Maintenance tried, and the machine shocked the tech to protect itself, but I think another bob came instead. That has to be how they change the programming, dressing like Maintenance and pretending to service the machines."

The hair lifted on Janna's neck. Maintenance!

The man deftly caught a package of tokens the machine spit out. "I understand Fontana is offering amnesty to whoever programmed it if he, or she, will change it back."

Janna barely heard him. She whirled toward Mama, grabbing the edge of the doorway to keep from careening end over end across the corridor. "Maintenance, Mama!" She dropped her voice so no one in the corridor or arcade would hear. "Service personnel are invisible. That could be how our killer got to the suit."

"Invisible to us maybe, but not—" He pointed into the corridor, at a glass knob bulging unobtrusively between two strips of paneling.

She frowned at the lens. "I wonder if Big Brother has a camera in the EVA prep room. Let's see if Doubrava means it about answering—"

She broke off to stare at a mermaid swimming up behind Mama. It had to be a costume, of course, but it looked uncannily authentic, from the slim young woman's iridescent green tail and the sea weed draped over her breasts to green-in-green eyes and green-gold hair floating fan-like around her head.

The mermaid stopped beside them and hovered smiling, tail waving slowly to keep her in position. "Are you the people from Seever?"

Mama answered first. "What can we do for you?"

"I think I can help *you*. My name is Jenin LaCoe and I know a few things about Clell Titus. But,"—she glanced around, pushing back her hair to clear her peripheral vision—"I can't talk here." Her voice dropped to a whisper so low Janna had to read her lips to understand her. "Follow me to Pie-Eyed-In-the-Sky."

With a flip of her tail, the mermaid swam up the corridor to a door near the far end. Janna glanced at Mama with raised brows. Could this be the break they needed?

"Let's see what she has to say, bibi."

They pulled along the railing after the mermaid.

Following the tail vanishing through the bar's doorway, however, all Janna's nerves jerked taut. The light in the floors shone so dimly that the tables and bar became only shadowy shapes in the darkness. Feeling blind, and with leo-trained reflexes screaming warnings of her vulnerability, she whipped sideways out of the bright circle of the doorway. Mama dived the opposite direction. The action came automatically, almost without conscious volition, but even as she flattened against the wall to wait for her vision to accommodate, her heightened senses howled more warnings. The loud jivaqueme music sounded wrong. In a moment, she recognized why. It echoed, as sound should not in an occupied room. Adrenaline rushed icy hot through her.

In the darkness, the mermaid's voice called above the music, "Why don't you come over here?"

"10-30," Mama's voice murmured.

The code not for acknowledgment but for transmissions which failed to conform to regulation. He was signaling her that he did not like this either. "10-30," she echoed. "Signal 14?" Officer in trouble.

"We might as well have some light," another voice said from above Janna, a voice that belonged to neither Mama nor the mermaid.

The room brightened and music cut off. A man in a body suit with black-and-gold zigzag stripes slid down to plant himself in front of the door. Janna drew in a slow breath of recognition. He had been one of the group they first approached in Damnation Alley. Two other men from the group stood at the half of the bar on Mama's side of the doorway, one of them with his hand still on the control buttons of a portable music chip player. At a table with the mermaid stood a fourth man, one Janna had never seen before, square-built with short salt-and-pepper hair.

"Thanks, Jenin," he said.

"Always," she replied, and with a flip of her tail, swam for the door.

As it irised closed behind her and the guard moved back in place, the square man raked first Janna then Mama with slate gray eyes. "I understand you two have been asking a lot of questions about Clell Titus and making accusations by implication. I don't happen to think that's very polite. A person ought to make his accusations face to face." He paused. "I'm Clell Titus." And in a silence so absolute that Janna heard her pulse drumming in her ears, he floated toward Mama and her. His voice dropped to a rasp. "Now let's hear what you have to say."

13

February 4. 17:00:00 hours.

Titus had an interesting assortment of friends, Janna reflected, that mermaid and now these three: Zig-zag, a dwarf, and an afroam. She eyed them appraisingly. Zig-zag at the door did not look all that imposing, but of the others, the afroam easily made two of Mama and despite the shortness of his arms, the dwarf exhibited a powerful set of shoulders. Of course, physical strength might not be all that much of an advantage in weightlessness, but mass should. Calculating the distance to each, Janna ran through all the defensive moves she had ever learned or used, searching for one throw or punch that might work without gravity. Nothing came to her, however, except for every action, there is an opposite and equal reaction.

"Come on, ask your questions."

The rasping voice brought Janna's attention back to Titus and his granite eyes. His voice echoed in the emptiness. No one must hold a franchise for this space at the moment. Behind the bar, the enclosed shelves sat bare of bottles and drinking bulbs. Trying not to be obvious, she glanced around the room searching for the surveillance camera. Or would it be activated in an ostensibly unused room? Big Brother might *not* be watching here.

Keeping her voice carefully neutral, Janna said, "Your friends are commendably loyal, but a bit over-sensitive. We make no accusations."

"Maybe we should," Mama said. "Would a man with a clean conscience feel the need to bring extra muscle and meet in the station equivalent of an alley?"

Janna wanted to strangle him. Damn the man! Was he trying to incite assault? "Mama," she hissed.

"Clear conscience!" Titus snapped. "Are you trying to say I'd deliberately neglect my suit? You're brainbent! My life depends on that suit. Even my wife and kids don't get the coddling that suit does. If anyone mishandled it, Chenoweth did."

Mama said, "Is it normal procedure to use each other's equipment? Aren't there spare suits in case of malfunctions?"

They all stared, then glanced quickly at each other. Zig-zag growled, "Yes, but when Carakostas is in a hellfire hurry—"

"Let them ask our superiors about procedure," the afroam interrupted.

Zig-zag bit down on the rest of the sentence.

"I guess you're lucky he did give Chenoweth that suit, or you would have been in it when it ruptured," Mama said.

For a moment Titus stopped. He stared narrow-eyed at Mama. "You make it sound...inevitable."

"Perhaps," Janna said. "We'll know when we've looked over the suit itself."

The dwarf asked, "Are you checking to see if the coolant tubing could have microcracks that caused leakage inside the lining and weakened the fibers in the fabric?"

The others' smirks set off a clang of warning in Janna. Trap question! She glanced quickly toward Mama. How should they answer?

"Leaking coolant? That's preposterous," Mama said.

The group looked disappointed. Janna breathed an inward sigh of relief. Among all the clutter of trivia in that strange brain must be the plans for a pressure suit, too.

The dwarf continued to fix Mama with a gleaming stare. "Why is it preposterous?"

This time Mama did not answer immediately. Janna's mind raced, planning self-defense.

The dwarf floated closer to Mama by one table. "If you really do work for Seever, surely you know why."

Janna tensed. The wall at her back should help her fight.

Mama, however, said coolly, "What do you mean, if we really work for Seever?"

"Because I don't think you do, not after watching you come through that door. You're people who take no chances of being a target when going into dark rooms you don't know. I can think of several professions where that's standard survival technique, but a Seever trouble shooter isn't one of them. Can you answer any questions about how a suit is constructed?"

Janna swore. They were not going to talk themselves out of this. Bracing herself she said, "The home office sent us to ask questions, not answer them."

Titus floated toward her, hands reaching for the front of her jumpsuit. "You'll answer one. You'll tell us who the hell you really are and why you're here or I'll wring your groundsider neck."

The threat to lay hands on her triggered icy fury. "10-98, Mama." The code for riot or mass disturbance. Drawing both knees up, Janna kicked straight out with the soles of her slippers, straight into Titus's gut and groin.

Her back slammed into the wall with the force of her kick, but to her great satisfaction Titus tumbled backward across the room, groaning in agony.

The other three men started for her. Janna made a missile of herself, pushing off from the wall straight at the afroam. At the corner of her vision Mama went for the dwarf. Just before she hit the afroam head on in the stomach, she saw the dwarf roll aside and Mama rocket past to crash into the tables. Janna and her target flew backward together down the length of the room. She grinned. A hold on him made her fight repertoire useful again. Reaching up, she grabbed both his ears, and pulling him toward her, drove a knee into the afroam's groin.

They hit among the tables, with the afroam landing first, under her, taking most of the shock. Janna left him writhing. Pushing off from the table, she arrowed back toward Titus again, this time tucking and rolling in mid air so she would hit him feet first.

The dwarf intercepted her with a flying dive. They slammed sideways into the floor. Janna went for his eyes with her fingers and took a fast look around for Mama. He struggled with Zig-zag among the tables on the opposite floor. He had lost his glasses. Then a hand grabbed Janna's hair and jerked her head back so hard she winced in pain. Titus's granite eyes stared down into hers.

"Now I *will* break your neck!"

"You'll do nothing of the kind, Titus!" snapped a whiplash voice. "Back off right now. You, too, Janulis. Hedgecoth, let go of Maxwell."

They obeyed. Titus grinned at Geyer swinging in through the dilated door. "Hell, chief, I didn't mean it. We were just hazing the groundsiders a little."

"I know what you were doing." Her eyes glinted gold. Never had gold looked so cold, Janna reflected. "We followed the entire incident on the monitors. Now you and your friends get the hell out of here before I throw you in detention for assault."

Titus frowned. "It was self-defense. These bastard groundsiders are trying to blame me for Chenoweth's death."

For a moment Janna had the irritated feeling that Geyer wanted to laugh, but then the security chief's mouth compressed into a thin line. "Leave them to me." She glanced from Janna over to Mama, who groped among the tables looking for his glasses. "I promise they won't be bothering you again." Kicking off from the door, she sailed across to Janna. "I don't know if you're deaf or just arrogant, but I'll assume the former and warn you one more time. All inquiries here are conducted through my office, even those ordered by the home office, so if I fall over you again or find you making more trouble, *you*, not your assailants, will go into detention."

This time she deserved the look of admiration Mama gave her, Janna reflected. However blistering, the reprimand gave away nothing of their identity or mission.

"Ian," Geyer barked.

"Yo." Doubrava straightened where he hovered in the doorway with two other officers from Security.

"Leash these two. Find them something to do that's safe but productive looking to the home office."

Spinning away again, she pushed off from a table and glided out the door past Doubrava.

Across the bar Mama sighed. "Top star." He stared after her until she disappeared, then resumed hunting for his glasses.

Titus whistled. "Sometimes I can believe she actually got the job on ability."

Doubrava's head snapped around toward him. "I think the chief ordered you to sail, Titus."

The mild tone did not quite mask a flinty edge. The group left hurriedly, towing their still-groaning afroam compatriot.

With a wave of his hand, Doubrava dismissed the other officers as well, then hooking a toe on the edge of the door to stabilize himself, he folded his arms and clucked his tongue. "Naughty, naughty. She almost didn't come over here to rescue you, you know...but if you'd been hurt that would have meant trouble for Titus."

"By all means protect the home folk," Janna said.

A corner of his mouth twitched. "Now the question is, having rescued you, what do we do with you? What will keep you busy but out of trouble?"

Mama floated up off the floor, sighing with a sharp note of frustration. "Do you record from the monitors?"

The turquoise eyes gleamed. "Why?"

"Going through vids could keep us occupied for a while. How far back do you have them?"

"Twenty-eight days. Then the chips are reused. What are you interested in?"

"Whoever sabotaged that suit couldn't have done it too long before Chenoweth died. I'd like to see who opened Titus's locker besides Titus and the crew chief. Damn it," Mama added, squinting around him, "I'd like to find my glasses."

Doubrava arched a brow. "I've already seen the vid. It doesn't help, but that makes watching it busy work, I guess, so...fine, I'll show it to you. There are your glasses." He pointed toward the far end of the room, where light glinted on the lenses and frame floating toward the ventilators. "I'll catch them for you."

Coming into the Security office, Janna could see through the open door of the inner office to Geyer standing at her desk.

Doubrava glanced toward his superior, then headed for one of the outer office desks. "We'll look at the vids here." He tapped on the computer terminal clamped to the desk and punched in a code. "This turns the monitor into a video screen and accesses the chip files, which are cross-referenced by date and camera. We want to see A-2 on January fifteenth."

"The Monday before Chenoweth died," Mama said.

"Was it a Monday?" Doubrava's fingers played across the keys. "We don't keep track of days by name much. Ah, there."

A picture came up on the screen, a long tube of a room with the camera in the center giving a fisheye view in both directions and down on a double row of lockers dividing it longitudinally. A deserted room. Numbers in the lower right corner noted the date and time: 01/15/80/00:00:01.

Doubrava touched several more keys. The numbers changed in a dizzying blur. "We want you occupied, but not forever." Soon people appeared, blurs, too, hurtling themselves in and out like frenzied insects. Another touch on the keys froze the picture. The time indicator said: 07:45:47.

"Titus's locker is on the right side of the row, just about here." He touched the upper part of the screen. "Now watch for the orange Maintenance coveralls."

He tapped the terminal keys again. The picture resumed movement, but at normal speed.

Janna frowned, watching the men and women climbing into pressure suits. "You can't mean our saboteur is coming *now*. The place is full of people."

Seconds later a figure in a baggy orange coverall swung in through the oval door at the extreme bottom of the screen and sailed up the length of the locker room. Janna leaned forward, squinting at the face. It bent down, away from the camera, however.

The Maintenance tech stopped at Titus's locker. Without hesitation, he punched a combination on the push-button lock. Pulling out the pressure suit except for the helmet, he closed the locker again and started back down the room toward the door with the suit in tow.

"Gutsy bastard. I give him that," Janna said.

Mama grunted. "Smart. What could be less suspicious than walking in and taking the suit in front of a dozen or more witnesses? Can you freeze it again?"

The picture froze. Their suspect tech faced directly toward the camera but his face was too small for Janna to make out details, other than a mustache and full beard. "What about enlarging the picture?"

Doubrava grinned. "Big Brother has all the conveniences." His fingers tapped computer keys.

The tech's face spread to fill the screen. More keywork altered contrast, sharpening the picture. For all the good that did. The beard and mustache hid everything but a broad nose and dark eyes. The badge on the coverall said: SMITH.

"I don't suppose you have a Maintenance tech name Smith who looks like that," Mama said.

"Similar, but his whereabouts are accounted for at the time in question. Frustrating, isn't it, all this top dink equipment, and it doesn't solve anything? We can't even tell how the jon is built inside that coverall."

"Or even if he's male," Janna said thoughtfully. Broad nose, dark eyes, and possibly female. She glanced toward the inner office.

Geyer had left her desk to hover in the doorway, watching them without expression.

Doubrava followed Janna's line of sight and frowned thoughtfully.

Janna turned back at the screen. The tech had swarthy skin, but if he were Geyer in a false beard, the skin tone could have been altered, too.

"If the face fur is false, I wonder how genuine the eye color is," Mama said.

"So it could be anyone."

Mama took off his glasses and polished the lenses on the sleeve of his jumpsuit. "Anyone who could gain access to the labs and be thoroughly familiar with security procedures."

Doubrava grinned. "Like me. Or any number of our officers. There are people in Admin with knowledge and privilege, too, like Ginneh Nakashima. She's too small to be Smith, there, but she could have an accomplice."

"You haven't mentioned Fontana," Mama said.

Doubrava's grin faded. "Of course not. Of all the people here, he's the last person to sell the platform out."

"What happened when Chenoweth's body was being shipped out?"

The turquoise eyes narrowed. "This is—" He broke off, glancing over his shoulder toward the inner office again, where Geyer was turning away, returning to her desk, but shook his head a moment later. "No. It's wickers. She wouldn't, either. The shuttle arrived on the twenty-first. While the receiving crew from Supply help the shuttle crew off-load material for us, Officer Zachary Begay and I collected the body from A-5 where it had been stored. Before we moved it to the docking bay, we checked the bag and clothes for any contraband. I remember debating whether a dead body ought to go through the MR scanner in sick bay like living personnel have to do when leaving. Director Geyer and I hadn't discussed the matter and she'd gone off duty. Before I could make a decision Officer Keline Lowe requested a supervisor in corridor G right away. So I headed for Level Two.

"Begay says that as I left I told him to do a body cavity search. I don't remember. At that point, corpses had become the farthest thing from my mind. He didn't make a thorough search, he admits—he's Navajo and doesn't like handling a corpse—and it never occurred to him to look down its throat. I doubt if he could have pried the jaws apart in any case. The body was stiff from being in cold storage. By the time I returned, Begay had sealed the body in the transport bag and kept watch over it while the shuttle crew loaded it on the shuttle."

"Why did this Officer Lowe call for you?" Janna asked.

He grimaced. "She had had what appeared to be a false report. A man called from G-8—or what the dispatcher assumed from the voice was a man; he never came in screen range, claiming to be watching the door, through which he purported to see one of the technicians in a neighboring lab going berserk and attacking her coworkers. Lowe located no disturbance of any kind in G-8, however. She asked Dispatch for the location of the phone from which the complaint had been made, but found the lab closed and locked. Personnel in neighboring labs in the pod told her it had been closed for the past eight or ten hours while Dr. Thora Shaw, the single chemist working there, was sleeping. No one else could have opened it. The lab has a biolock programmed for only Dr. Shaw.

"I helped Lowe check every pod along G, just to be sure the automatic trace hadn't malfunctioned, but after finding nothing, decided that one of the electronics bobs had made the call as a joke and tapped into the lab's phone line to hide his real location. We have a few people here with a warped sense of humor."

Janna remembered the Deathrace game programmed to shock the player.

Doubrava pursed his lips. "Now it's obvious the call was a diversion to pull me away from Chenoweth's body, though I don't know how the person could be certain that would prevent a thorough inspection of the body. Unless you think Begay is the smuggler, or being paid off by the smuggler."

"Maybe the smuggler knew how Officer Begay would react to searching a dead body," Mama said.

"Knew Begay." The turquoise eyes went thoughtful and swung from Mama to the monitor screen. "A friend or acquaintance, you're thinking? It wouldn't necessarily have to be. He makes no secret of his blood." Doubrava paused, touching the screen. "I wonder if our perp could be someone in Maintenance after all. As Sergeant Brill has observed, service personnel do tend to be invisible, and when seen, who questions their presence?"

Even saying it and clearing the screen with a quick arpeggio across the terminal keys, Doubrava's glance slid sideways toward the inner office, Janna noticed. Could he, like her, be suddenly wondering where Tabanne Geyer had spent her off-duty time the day that Chenoweth's body left?

14

February 4. 18:30:00 hours.

Speaking of the devil.

The golden woman leaned out the door of her office and crooked a finger. "I'd like to see the three of you, please."

Janna detected no anger in Geyer's voice, no steel or acid. It sounded neutral. Still, she found herself glancing around the room, hunting the glint of a lens that would mean Security's chief could use her bank of monitors to watch, and listen to, her own outer office.

Seeing none failed to reassure Janna, nor did the way Geyer rapped the door's control plate once the three of them swam in past her. The door closed, its halves coming together with a sharp hiss.

Geyer spoke with the same abruptness. "I have an apology of sorts to make."

Janna blinked. That she had not expected. A glance sideways at Mama caught him with brows skipping in astonishment, too. Doubrava looked more thoughtful than surprised.

"Or maybe *explanation* is a better word." Geyer smiled fleetingly. "I was a bit...unfriendly when you arrived. I had reasons, and not just that even lend-lease leos can be jealous of their territory, or that I've worked too hard at this job to appreciate the implication that I'm not competent enough to handle serious trouble."

What about her boss suspecting that she might be party to the trouble, Janna reflected wryly, or did Geyer *not* know Fontana wanted them to spy on her?

"Perhaps I should have explained then," Geyer continued, "but...the home office did send you, after all." She floated back to her desk, where she set her slipper socks in the carpet and crossed her arms...not a distancing, judgmental gesture but as though she felt cold. "I had no way of knowing whether you were here as consultants or to discredit the administration of the station."

Mama asked, "Why is the station caught in the middle of the attempt to force Crispus Tenning out of the corporation presidency?"

Geyer's face froze for a moment, then her brows rose. "So you're retentive, too."

"Too?" Janna said. The rest of the remark obviously referred to their conversation at lunch with the man in the braids. Geyer must have been monitoring them from the moment they left Security this morning.

"In addition to being intelligent and persevering and a little head-strong. I just finished talking to your commanding officer. He assured me no one uses either of you." She studied Mama speculatively. "Especially not Sergeant Maxwell, whom I suspect by the lieutenant's undertone of regret, is sometimes beyond the control of even the department."

Janna blanked her face and said nothing. Mama's chin came up. He opened his mouth as though to protest...but closed it again without a sound.

Geyer went on, "The platform is Tenning's pet project and Fontana his fair-haired boy, so of course his enemies are just waiting for the chance to take over and reorganize, if not shut down the platform altogether. This smuggling and murder could provide the perfect excuse if we have to rely on outside assistance to find and plug the leak."

And as the person responsible for a security which failed, of course Geyer would be one of the first casualties of reorganization, Janna reflected. Now would she ask them to stay out so she could look good to the home office?

"I'm terrible at the art of timesliding, though," Mama said. "I want to know who killed Chenoweth."

Geyer nodded. "Since nothing short of detention is going make you take a vacation, it seems, I have another proposal, one which will hopefully not only solve the case but deprive the board of directors of ammunition against old man Tenning. You heard what the people here call Security. Geyer's Gorillas. They don't like to see my people coming any more than your city's citizens welcome you. Your citizens would prefer you to foreign troops, however, and right now everyone here sees the home office as villains."

Janna saw where Geyer was headed. Anger flared in her. "You want us to be bad guys!"

Geyer frowned. "You object? It's the same nice lion/mean lion strategy you use. Of course, encouraging people to cooperate with me means I'll have to take any credit, but which do you want, glory or the killer?"

Intellectually Janna saw the logic in it. Intellectually. She frowned.

Mama shrugged. "We might as well, bibi. Titus will be giving us bad publicity anyway."

He looked at Geyer as he said it. Was he thinking that this way he could be on friendly enough terms to have a chance at becoming friendlier? Well far be it from her to force safety and sanity on him. Janna sighed and nodded.

Mama's eyes gleamed, but he did manage to keep from grinning ear to ear.

"As long as playing bad guys lets us keep on poking around, we'd like to look over personnel records," Janna added.

A crease started between Geyer's eyes, then faded as her expression smoothed into studied indifference. "If the director gives you access to the files, I don't see how I can interfere. You'll find him in his office watching the station on his monitors. Playing spider."

Janna straightened, curiosity perking at the sudden edge in the golden woman's voice. Could there be a conflict over the monitors?

Doubrava started for the door. "Now that each side has made its deal with the Devil, anyone else who has a circadian rhythm that recognizes nineteen hundred hours as past time to eat, follow me to the cafeteria."

Janna followed.

At nineteen hundred hours the cafeteria looked as it had at when she and Mama ate lunch there…the same stream of people in and out, the same brisk disappearance of food. Was it dedication or the cheerful oranges and yellows decorating the room that stimulated diners to eat and run? The cubical newscanner still ran business news and stock quotations, but on only two faces. Other screens carried more general news, and one had weather.

"Pity. We're missing a blizzard in Colorado," Janna heard someone say sardonically.

The atmosphere had changed, though. Chilled. Conversations broke off as she and Mama floated toward the food line with Doubrava. Side glances followed them. Titus and company had been busy. Obviously the grapevine remained one plant that functioned as efficiently in zero-gee as it did on Earth.

"How early tomorrow can we see Fontana about permission to look at personnel files?" Mama asked.

"Tomorrow?" Doubrava grinned. "We'll go over to Admin right after we eat. I'll have the shish kebob," he told the attendant behind the counter, a dwarf woman, and turned to Janna. "It's the best way yet to keep vegetables and meat together and in a manageable form." He caught the tray as the attendant slid it over the counter. "Fontana is rumored to sleep five hours out of forty but I've never seen evidence of it. Sometimes I think if he does, it must be standing at his desk."

"Playing spider." Janna pointed at the shish kebob, too, when the attendant raised inquiring brows. "That doesn't appear to please Geyer."

Doubrava's smile froze for a just a moment. "You must have misunderstood. Why should we object if the boss wants surveillance capability?

Now, there's usually someone in Records twenty-four hours, so once we're authorized to look at the files, we can start any time you want."

Which closed the subject of the monitors, Janna noted. They must really be a sore point. Why? Encroachment on Security territory?

"How about eating over there?" Doubrava pushed away from the serving line to head toward one of the tables.

Mama imitated him, but pushed too hard and almost tangled in the tables overhead. Janna walked, slippers ripping along the carpet, an arm holding the cover on her tray.

As they settled at the table, Mama said, "Too bad Chief Geyer couldn't join us."

A group in orange coveralls occupied the table directly overhead. Glancing up at them, Doubrava lowered his voice. "Come on, Maxwell. How can she be seen fraternizing with the enemy?" Then his mouth twitched and the turquoise eyes crinkled at the corners. "She leaves that to me, as official leash-holder and one who is widely known for his charm, general good humor, and undiscriminating—some say tasteless—willingness to keep company with anyone, even groundsiders and corporate High Muckies." He winked at Janna.

She found herself smiling back at him. He did have charm. "If you like to be sociable, how did you ever end up in security work?"

"The uniform." He grinned. "That and a space job are a gold card lure for flash bibis."

"I can't believe how *fast* it works!" a voice cried.

Janna looked around to see a group of men and women in a rainbow of coveralls sailing noisily into the cafeteria. Snatches of their chatter carried across the room.

"Damn right. If it weren't for having to put up the framework..."

"...spraying polymers over a balloon the way we used...?"

"...forced back to spherical structures when the advantage..."

"Have you heard?" a young woman among them called to the group at a table near Janna. The light glittered on a frosty swirl of gold and silver crossing her depilated scalp and diving down her neck under the collar of her green coveralls. "That spider thing finished covering the torus pod on Level Two—a flawless skin in less than twenty-four hours!—and now it's almost done with—."

A companion hissed, tilting his head toward Janna, Mama, and Doubrava. He murmured something. Instantly the group went silent. They turned their heads to stare, frowning, then continued on to the food counter, murmuring in whispers too low to be heard.

Janna grimaced. "Our reputation is established, it would appear." She watched the group edge down the food line. "What's this spider they're talking about?"

Doubrava hesitated. "I don't know the details—that's restricted information—but it's one of the wonders from the labs. I gather it spins a skin over a framework, like a spider wrapping up a fly. The advantage of it over other methods is not only speed but the mostly non-metallic composition of the skin, which means we can build or expand space stations fast and cheap."

"Non-metallic," Mama said. "Could it build ships, too?"

"Ships?" Doubrava quirked a brow. "I suppose. I never thought—my god!" The turquoise eyes widened and his voice dropped to a whisper. "If that's what went out of here, Uwezo could produce a fleet of mining ships and send them out to the asteroids before anyone knew what was happening."

"Giving Uwezo one hell of a mineral monopoly," Mama said thoughtfully. "They have the diamond cartel as an sterling example of what to do with their power, too."

Cold slid down Janna's spine

When they saw Fontana in his office a short time later, she brought up the spider. "Have you considered that the spider might have been what Chenoweth carried out?"

Earth filled the ceiling, a fleece-swirled sapphire, serene and lovely, but across the desk, amber wolf's eyes regarded her with taut watchfulness above an easy smile. "Sure I've thought about the spider, and the implications of losing it. There's also a dozen more gadgets and processes we've been playing with that our rival corporations would give a golden Texas summer to put their paws on. That's why you're here, sergeant darlin', to help cure my ulcers by catching the traitor and sweating out of him what he stole. So of course you can look at the personnel files. Anything y'all need, you just ask for. Hear?"

Mama took off his glasses and peered myopically at Fontana while polishing the lenses with loose fabric on the torso of his jumpsuit. "Anything that will keep us occupied and out of your way, that is, isn't that right? Strange. We might just be able to help you, and while we may be here at the insistence of the board, you know we aren't its agents. If you've watched the monitors, you must have seen enough to know that whatever we accomplish isn't likely to help the board much, either. So why are you afraid of us?"

Oh, god. Janna fought an urge to stuff his glasses down his throat. What the hell was he doing…accusing Fontana? "Mama," she hissed in warning.

At the same time, she found herself watching the platform director for his response, and from the corner of her eye, she saw Doubrava doing the same.

Fontana's face petrified. The wolf's eyes chilled. Then suddenly he smiled, but a different smile from before, a wry twisting of the corners. "It isn't fear; it's resentment, the usual animosity toward one's support group, and I apologize." The drawl had disappeared from his voice. "I shouldn't take it out on you."

"*Usual* animosity?" Janna asked.

His smile became more sardonic. "Usual in isolated and stressful environments like antarctic stations, undersea research labs, submarine crews…and space stations. Wim Freeman, our station psy-in-the-sky, tells me that the stress can erupt as irrationality, like murder or the incident on one oceanographic ship where a dispute between scientists and crew over a freezer used for both soft drinks and specimens resulted in the whole freezer being thrown overboard. More often, though, it becomes hostility focused on one's support group." Pulling his slippers loose, he floated over the desk to come down beside Janna and Mama. "Undersea labs start cursing the crew of their surface ship. Astronauts snarl at ground control. There's some reason to believe that in Russia's Salyut 6 mission way back in 1980, Tyumin and Popov turned off all communication with the ground for two days. Our support group is the home office."

"But you really do have enemies there," Mama said.

Fontana hesitated. "I don't know they're *my* enemies. They disagree with the way I run the platform, true, but that may be more a reflection of their feelings toward Crispus Tenning, and the fact that they don't understand the differences between a planetary lab and an orbiting one."

"You've tried explaining?"

Doubrava snorted. "To groundsiders?"

Fontana scowled at him. "Of course I've explained, numerous times, but we disturb them. They come here on occasional visits expecting to find a weightless duplicate of one of their groundside labs, and instead they find a spherical orientation—file cabinets and tables on the ceiling—and over thirty per cent of the personnel paraplegic, amputees, or affected by some other physical condition or disease considered limiting groundside. Actually it's only limiting in a gravity field, but—I'm sorry; I tend to climb on a soapbox when it comes to defending my recruiting policies. Visiting executives meet other personnel who look like skinhead trippers or who dress as birds or fish, all qualified people but highly individual, and they find a thousand-odd people free-running according to their personal circadian rhythms. I'm sure it looks like chaos. They instinctively want to 'restore' what they perceive as 'order', never understanding that they're really trying to impose the rhythms of Earth, and never understanding that those rhythms are inappropriate to a place where up/down and day/night have lost real meaning and become merely terms of convenience. Who knows? In their place, I might feel the same."

Fontana's eyes did not match his tolerant tone, Janna noticed. A hard light made them look more lupine than ever. He obviously had stronger feelings about the home office than he chose to admit. Could it give him a motive for smuggling and murder?

"Shall I call Records and tell them you're coming over now?" Fontana asked.

Janna opened her mouth to agree but Mama spoke first. "It's been a long day for us. I think I'd like to make use of your local recreational facilities this evening and wait until tomorrow to start on the files."

For a moment Janna stared at him in astonishment—what, Mama quitting on this case before midnight?—but the surprise faded when she noticed that his eyes had focused past Fontana on the monitors behind the director's desk. Tabanne Geyer's golden glow dominated the center of a screen tuned to Recreation's central corridor. She hung with a toe hooked under a railing to stabilize herself for a conversation with another woman in a dress whose voluminous sleeves and skirts turned its wearer into a billowing cloud of chiffon.

Janna murmured to Mama too low for Doubrava to hear. "Don't you think you ought to rein in your hormones? She's one of our suspects, remember."

He just grinned and whispered back. "That's why I want to observe her closely."

She hissed in exasperation. "You're impossible. Will you try to be careful, at least?"

He sobered for a moment. "Always, bibi. Good day, Mr. Fontana." With another grin and a wave, he sailed out.

Janna followed with Doubrava. He cocked a brow at her. "You seem to have been abandoned. May I have the pleasure of your company?"

She glanced sideways at him...the pleasant face, turquoise eyes, and charming smile. She smiled back. "Why not?" With a little bit of the local liquor in him, he might be persuaded to talk about Geyer and Fontana, and about the conflict between them. "Lead on."

15

February 4. 20:30:00 hours.

A young man danced naked in the center of The Quark. He used a pole with two loops on it to anchor himself, sometimes hooking both feet through them so that he stood out at ninety degrees from the pole, sometimes putting a hand and foot through them. In that attitude, he alternated which direction his head pointed. Janna watched in fascination. Up and down became meaningless, Fontana had said. She saw what he meant. The dancer appeared equally comfortable whatever direction he faced.

Fontana had also spoken of people here developing a spherical orientation. The tables on the ceiling bore evidence of that, but Doubrava's quarters, where they had gone for him to change out of his uniform, proved an even more graphic example. While he vanished beyond a divider made of shelves and a floor-to-ceiling fish tank, Janna had stared around at the suite. Any resemblance to her room ended at the shape of the door and construction of the closet, which could be seen distortedly through the fish tank. Doubrava had decorated as though every surface were a wall, or perhaps a ceiling. Cloud murals covered what corresponded to the floor and ceiling in her room, reflected in endless progression by mirrored walls, so that she and countless ever-more-distant images of her floated in an infinity of sky. Even the oval door appeared suspended in midair.

"I'm surprised you didn't decorate with starfields," she had called.

Doubrava came around the fish tank sheathed in a shimmering body suit whose color matched his eyes. "I tried that for a while, but space is so dark, and it can cause agoraphobia in a person here and there, killing her amorous mood."

A young woman replaced the male dancer on the pole. Janna looked around for Mama, as she had watched for him when they went into Fluidics Inc. on their first stop of the evening. As nearly as she could tell in the pulsing light and peeking through a holographic molecular diagram that filled the room, he did not appear to be there. If Geyer had consented to his company, they must have gone somewhere else. Not surprisingly. From the snatches of conversation Janna caught above the wail of experimental afroasian compositions for the flute, sitar, and drum, Janna gathered that like the Belithroche and Fluidics Inc., The Quark catered to the scientific staff. The surprise was that Doubrava came here.

Or was it? Around and above her, the discussions on chemistry and physics, accompanied by illustrations scribbled on the tabletops, alternated with groups who seemed on the verge of a public orgy. Like the pair at the next table, dressed mostly in spray-on glitter and clinging together as if determined to disprove that two solids could not occupy the same space simultaneously.

But if scientists did not appear much different than the good citizens at home, their club decor was unique. Janna eyed the holographic molecule, struggling to remember her college chemistry and identify it. "I'd have expected a place called The Quark to go for sub-atomic subjects."

Doubrava shrugged. "I don't know whether quantum physics is hard to illustrate or that they think chemistry gives them more chance to attempt humor."

Janna blinked. "Humor?"

"Like using an ethanol molecule, or part of a sex hormone. Or a terrible pun. One time, I remember, they had a hydrocarbon with flowers instead of spheres representing the different atoms."

She frowned. That was a pun? Oh. Flowercarbon. Janna groaned. "You continue to come here?"

Doubrava grinned. "Between masochism and my determination to acquire higher education through osmosis—" He broke off, face blanking and head tilting. Janna identified the attitude instantly...someone listening to his ear button. She arched a brow. Was he such a rock jock he wore the button even off duty?

"You can't stand to be out of touch?" she asked.

Absently, he replied, "Not permitted to be. The curse of being a supervisor. Sometimes I think I might as well have a radio permanently implant—" He listened intently for a moment then pulled loose from the carpet under the table and pushed for the door. "Come on."

She kicked off to follow him. "Is it serious?"

He did not reply and a glimpse at the inward look in his eyes as she caught up with him told her he heard nothing but the voice murmuring in his ear.

In the core corridor Doubrava stilled the warning voice by pushing one end of his ID badge into a slot in the wall and staring into the retinal reader plate above it until the voice invited him to proceed.

As always, the corridor stretched away to the vanishing point beneath them, but Janna discovered it continued to do so even as they neared the Level Two corridors. The station must be expanding downward as well as adding to Level Two. Construction's green coveralls predominated among the colors worn by the people she could see farther down. The construction must also be very recent. She could not recall any Level Three monitors in Security.

Doubrava swung into a corridor with navy blue paneling at the junction. Whatever the nature of the problem, its location became immediately obvious. A crowd of people clustered at the entrances to the fourth group of pods, almost completely blocking the corridor...like a clot in a blood vessel, Janna mused. Past the second group of entrances, she began to hear yelling, which grew louder and more distinct every meter closer to the crowd.

Doubrava burrowed through the clot using elbows and knees. "Security. Let me past. Bendure, Ourada," he barked at two officers hovering in the hatchway. "What the hell do you think you are, spectators? Clear this corridor."

The officers flushed. "Lieutenant Paretsky wanted us to stand by in case she and Trent needed more backup."

"Backup? Guess whose back will be up if she comes and finds that human log-jam. I'll help Paretsky and Trent. You send these people sailing." Doubrava propelled himself past them through the hatchway.

Janna debated whether to offer her help, but quickly decided it would be inconsistent with her bad guy role, and would probably be resented anyway. She followed Doubrava.

A honeycomb of small labs filled the pod. The yelling did, too, accompanied by the crash of glass. "No! I won't let her have it! It's *my* project!"

It was a male voice. A female voice screamed as more glass shattered.

The noise led them straight to the source, a lab on an upper level of the pod, where the glittering splinters of glass swirled through the air like flies. A bulb beaker hurled out the door past a petite, olive-skinned female officer and a husky, blond male to smash against the opposite wall, adding more shards to the air. The woman's voice screamed again inside the lab.

"Please, Dr. Chelle," the female officer said. She pulled herself up the doorway and peered in from the top. "No one is taking the project away from you. Your year here is up and it's merely being turned over to someone else to continue."

"I'm being robbed! I applied for permanent status, but you bastards won't take me; you're just taking my project and giving it to this bitch!"

"Dr. Chelle, you know that no one owns a project. They all belong to—" Another bulb beaker hurled out the door, narrowly missing Paretsky as she pulled back. Blood spotted her face where the swarming splinters had nicked her.

"It's *mine*!" shrieked the man in the lab. "If I can't stay to finish it and can't take it back, *no* one can have it."

Doubrava cautiously warded off glass with his arms as he slid up beside Paretsky. "Who's in there with him?"

Paretsky glanced around. "Dr. Mara Xidas. Apparently he hadn't learned yet that his application for permanent assignment had been turned down and when Dr. Xidas asked him to brief her on the project, he went berserk. I can't get anything coherent out of Dr. Xidas, but from the sound of her, she's still alive."

Janna brushed at splinters floating toward her. If this were an example of Dr. Chelle's temperament, she could see why he had been turned down.

"We need a vacuum," Doubrava said.

Paretsky nodded. "I've sent for it, and for the sleeper."

More glass smashed inside the lab. Shards of it shot out to join those already in the corridor. "It's a damn plot," Chelle shouted. "I'm not some damn cripple or misfit, so you're stealing my project and throwing me out!"

"Where the hell is that sleeper?" the blond officer growled.

Janna had never heard of a sleeper. "Don't you use K-12?"

"Too much risk of it getting in the ventilation system," Doubrava said. "We don't want the whole station curled into whimpering balls of fear."

"A needler, then?"

"Do *you* want to stand in that doorway long enough to brace yourself so the recoil won't deflect the needle?"

"My god," a voice said behind them.

Janna turned to see Geyer waving away glass splinters. She had changed from her uniform into exercise shorts and tank top. Sweat darkened the chestnut hair at her temples and across the golden forehead. Mama floated along behind her in shorts and tank top, too. Borrowed? They did not seem something he would have thought to bring. Sweat tracks streaked his face and bare scalp. Janna arched a brow. He and Geyer were spending a romantic evening together in the gym?

More flying glassware snapped her attention back to the situation inside the lab. Dr. Xidas screamed again.

This time the blond officer managed to reach out and catch the beaker as it shot out the door. He grinned triumphantly.

Geyer frowned. Her voice managed to sound warm and soothing, however. "Dr. Chelle, this is Chief Geyer from Security. You know this is no way to solve your problem. Let me call Director Fontana and Doctor Freeman down here and let's all sit down and discuss your complaint like intelligent, civilized people."

"You people aren't civilized! You're goddamn thieves. I don't think you're even human any more!"

"Oh, come now, doctor. It's understandable that you're upset, but—"

"You're damn right I'm upset! Take a year contract, Fontana said. Work my own hours on any project I wanted. If I did well, I could stay and be a permanent part of the most exciting research team in the solar system. But he *lied* to me! I've done well. My critters will grow fast and fat and provide all the protein you want. But he won't let me stay!"

Janna heard more movement behind her and through the pod maze came two more officers, both with large backpacks. The hose attached to one identified it as a vacuum. The other, with wires leading to what looked like a bullhorn the officer held, had to be the sleeper.

Geyer motioned them both forward. "Are you sure? Let's ask the director about it. But first, may I have someone clean up this air so we can breathe without inhaling glass?"

"No!" More glass shattered. Dr. Xidas shrieked as though she were being murdered. "Talking's just more tricks!"

Geyer nodded to the officer with the sleeper.

The officer dived through the airborne glass to the door. Stopping himself by catching the edge with his free hand, he pointed the bullhorn into the room and pulled the trigger. On the far side of the corridor, Janna pulled herself into a position where she could see into the lab. A lean, balding man with eyes white-rimmed and face purple from fury came arrowing toward the doorway with a broken beaker. He went slack as suddenly as though a switch had been snapped off.

Momentum carried his body on, however, where the blond officer caught him. Then the officer with the vacuum went to work.

Altogether a neat, professional job. Janna nodded to Geyer. "I'm impressed."

"Me, too," Mama said. But he looked at Geyer, not the officer with the sleeper.

Geyer smiled thinly. "To think we're only lend-lease leos."

All of them but the blond officer edged into the lab past the officer with the vacuum.

Dr. Xidas, a corpulent woman with close-cropped salt-and-pepper hair, floated in a sea of shattered glass and fragmented cultures, also unconscious but apparently unharmed except for numerous nicks on her face and surprisingly slim, long-fingered hands. A medical team appeared with a stretcher to take both her and Chelle to sick bay. The officer with the sleeper unhitched the backpack to reach the control for deactivation.

Janna eyed the sleeper. "How does it work?"

The officer glanced toward Geyer.

"Sound waves," she said. "It induces a narcoleptic state."

Mama's eyes gleamed. "Is that what's in the core corridor?"

Geyer looked around the lab. "We need someone in here to clean up and see what can be salvaged."

Which probably meant one corridor did have a sleeper guarding it, Janna decided.

Mama sighed. "We could use something like that at home."

"It has its drawbacks." Doubrava said.

"Which are?"

He grimaced. "As you saw, it doesn't have all that fine a focus, and…the effect tends to persist. Dr. Xidas will be going to sleep on us every time she's excited for the next few weeks. Very inconvenient." He turned toward Janna. "Shall we finish our drink?"

She nodded. For a moment she considered asking Mama to join them, but one glance at him showed her that was pointless. Mama had eyes only for Geyer.

Coming out of the pod, Janna glanced on up the corridor, a sunny-bright tube carrying people in a rainbow of coveralls. "I don't suppose you could entertain me with a tour of this part of the station?"

Doubrava hesitated, then shook his head with a smile. "Sorry. But you can see the new pod if you like."

It lay toward the end of the corridor. Reaching it, Janna studied the four open hatchways. "Which one?"

He spread his hands. "Any of them. It's a torus, a donut shape circling the corridor. It'll give us more room when the interior is finished than a cluster of three globes does."

"This spider thing will cover any shape?"

"That's what I understand."

Janna pulled herself through one hatchway. There was little to see, however. To her disappointment, and surprise, it had no active construction, no crews, and no work lights. The only illumination came from the corridor and that showed her nothing more than radial girders stretching outward into cavernous darkness.

Doubrava floated up behind her. "It's just a shell so far, I'm afraid. On the other hand, there's no spy eye in here, either."

He was almost breathing in her ear. Janna grinned inwardly and moved out along a girder hand-over-hand. Not so fast, jon. "I'm a little surprised there's no work crew. I had the impression that every section runs twenty-four hours. Or is Construction busy on exteriors on Level Three?"

"Who cares?" Doubrava swung past her and with the faint light shimmering on his bodysuit, launched away from the girder to the next one, spun around it and arrowed back in a maneuver any gymnast on Earth would have envied. "Until they start on this interior, we have a top star playground." Grinning, he pushed away from the girder and hung in mid-air, holding out his hands. "Come space dancing with me, Brill."

The grin pulled her like a magnet. Reaching out, she took his hands. In a moment she found herself wrapped in his arms, the two of them spinning off through the air into darkness. The circles of light marking two of the hatchways shrank to peepholes.

"Are you sure Geyer intended you to keep this tight a leash?" Janna asked a little breathlessly.

The breath from his laughter tickled her ear. "She said anything that would keep you occupied. Duck!"

A girder brushed by the top of her head.

"Maybe we ought to go back to The Quark."

She did not really want to. Exhilaration bubbled up through her, and a warm pleasure that she suspected had to be attributed to Doubrava's nearness. The danger of the girders only added spice to their flight.

Doubrava began, "If we go anywhere, I'd much rather—" He broke off and let go of her with one hand to snag another girder and halt them. "No, I guess Paretsky can take care of that one without me."

His radio again. Thinking back to the incident they had just left, Janna frowned thoughtfully. "Does Geyer wear her button all the time, too?"

She felt him nod. "Of course."

"You both answer interesting or difficult calls even when you're not on duty?"

"Like this evening? Usually."

"Did Geyer come around when you and Officer Lowe were checking that false report the day Chenoweth's body left?"

He stiffened against her in the dark. "There was no need for her to."

"Wasn't that the kind of incident where you would expect her to check on what was happening and how you were doing?"

Slowly, he replied, "Yes," and she heard the soft intake of his breath. "I remember being a little surprised at the time that she didn't appear, but I never thought any more about it. That's strange. I wonder why she didn't come."

Janna smiled grimly. Why indeed.

16

February 5. 7:30:00 hours.

The scent of honeysuckle filled Records. Janna breathed deeply, surprised but pleased. A young amerind woman at a desk on the ceiling looked down at her with sooty-dark eyes. "You're the other one. Back there." She pointed toward a lattice divider partitioning off one side of the room. "I've shown the...gentleman how to access the files Mr. Fontana says to let you see."

Now Janna understood why she smelled honeysuckle. The vine and its small yellow and white flowers covered the slim plastic lathes of the lattice.

"That's a nice touch," Janna said.

"Mr. Fontana suggested plants to naturalize the environment and vines don't seem to care which direction is up." The clerk returned to her terminal.

Dismissed, Janna thought with a grimace.

On the far side of the honeysuckle, Mama stood at a terminal, too. His jumpsuit, crossing-guard-orange with a chain of large black diamonds down the side, augmented the lighting. Looking around from the screen at her, he grinned. "Vradel would never believe this, me beating you to work. Is your circadian rhythm slipping you off the clock already or did Doubrava just keep you awake too late?"

She raised her brows. "You're sun and bells this morning."

"I had a good night's sleep."

The emphasis on the pronoun and the faintly superior tone invited a come-back. Janna bared her teeth. "I'm not surprised after the way Geyer put you through your paces in the gym. Quite a game of anything-you-can-do-I-can-do-better."

Mama shrugged. "She had to appear to be trying to make me look bad so onlookers wouldn't consider her sympathetic to the home office devil. How do you know about it?"

For a moment Janna considered saying that she had overheard conversation on the topic in the cafeteria, but for all their fights and differences, she and Mama did not lie to one another. "I saw it. After the incident in the lab, Doubrava and I wondered where Geyer spent the day the body left. He suggested we look through the surveillance vids of the day and we went back to Security, only we happened to glance at the monitors and see you in the gym."

Well, maybe she lied a little, but only about *how* they found Geyer and him in the gym.

As they hovered together at the monitor wall, Doubrava had said, "While we're at it, maybe we ought to take a look at what she's doing now, too." He punched keys on a panel in the middle of the monitors. "That holo isn't just decorative. Every ID badge has a transponder built into it. By calling up the badge name, we can locate it in the holo. See, there the chief is."

A light pulsed in the pod labeled GYM in small, glowing letters.

Turning to the monitor bank, they checked the gym and found Geyer and Mama on the track. The golden woman ran like a deer. As they continued to watch, Geyer had moved on to the racquet ball courts, where she played with demonic accuracy and speed.

Thinking back to watching the game, Janna raised a brow at Mama. "She's very athletic, isn't she?"

"Very." Mama smiled at the computer screen. "She reminds me a little of you, and in more ways than that. Her job is her life, too."

Janna almost said, "I know," but bit the words off unsaid. Somehow, she could not quite bring herself to admit to him that they had watched not only the gym, but followed when Geyer and Mama left.

Doubrava's brows had arched. "They're staying together? Pairing up with a stranger isn't at all like Bane; she takes a long time to accept people. Shall we keep surveillance and see where they go?"

It felt more like peeping than surveillance to Janna, perhaps because her own partner was one of the subjects, though Doubrava's attitude stilled some of her misgivings. He watched not with the avid curiosity of the voyeur but the dispassionate remoteness of someone observing an ant colony.

He turned the sound on. Geyer said, "Come in here. I want to talk."

She had taken Mama into the jungle-like greenhouse. It had no footpaths, just hand lines. Geyer led the way along one, from one monitor to another, through a red blaze of Virginia Creepers into a tangle of sunflowers, vine-cloaked saplings, and feathery ferns.

To Janna's surprise, Mama followed, and without choking or sneezing...Mama, who was allergic to everything green or furry. Those new allergy treatments must really be working.

In the middle of the wildwood, Geyer had hooked one knee around the hand line and turned back to Mama with arms crossed. "You stuck with me. I'm impressed. Tell me, what do you hope to prove by becoming my shadow?"

From the angle of the camera, suspended high above them, Mama's expression could not be seen, but his voice sounded earnest. "What makes you think I want to prove anything but what good company I am? You're a very attractive woman."

"One of the most beautiful you've ever met, no doubt." Bitterness hardened the rich voice. "The curse of my life."

Janna stared, startled. The pause before Mama spoke indicated that he, too, had been caught by surprise. "Most women wouldn't think so."

She hissed. "They haven't been me. I've worked long and hard to get where I am. I'm damn well qualified. Yet when Fontana floats his little executive tours through the station, showing off his masterpiece, if the corporate muckies are men, nine times out of ten when they have questions about Security, it's quite obvious that they assume Doubrava really runs the section, covering for the flash bibi who was made chief probably as a reward for sexual virtuosity!" Her eyes had flashed. "Sometimes I really hate men."

Doubrava had switched off the sound, but the image of Geyer's face remained...tight-lipped and bitter.

That image came back to Janna now as she settled her feet into the carpet beside Mama and frowned at the Personnel computer. "What does Geyer's personnel file have to say?"

"I'm looking at Nakashima's right now. Interesting family. They make hand-crafted furniture. She also has a brother on Mars and one who died on Mercury in Project Sunbath. Nakashima herself is also interesting. She's picked up a Master's degree in botany by correspondence while working up here as Fontana's secretary."

Janna peered around his shoulder. "Anything to suggest that she might be involved in our—Mama, they monitor calls, too!"

On the screen had come a list headed: CALLS. Most of the entries consisted of only a date, time, and name, but one near the beginning read: "10/15/75:23:37:02: Call to Rose Nakashima Wakabayashi terminated by Communications for breach of security. Employee warned. No further action."

"And censor them." Mama grimaced. The action loosened his glasses and he pushed them back tight on his nose. "Fontana wasn't kidding about tight security."

Janna pursed her lips thoughtfully. "Those calls are probably recorded, too, which would make it hard for our smuggler to communicate with the ground contacts. Maybe the messages went by shuttle?"

Mama considered. "Possibly, but it would be more efficient to call using a code."

"I wonder who Geyer calls to groundside."

He stiffened. "Bibi, I told you, too much of her life is tied up in this job for her to act against it."

That was a defensive tone if Janna had ever heard one. She eyed him speculatively. "You sound like you're losing objectivity, partner."

He glanced sideways at her. "I wonder how objective *you* are." He punched keys. "Remember what you keep saying: look at *all* the evidence and find the person all of it fits, not look for evidence against a particular suspect? But aren't you doing exactly that with Geyer?"

Now she stiffened. "I—" Was she? Janna wondered uncomfortably. "We know it has to be someone high up. Geyer is just one possibility. Fontana is another. Let's look at his file first, then."

It came up on the screen almost before she finished speaking.

For a while, she and Mama read in silence. Janna sucked in her lip. Geyer's life might center around her job, but the facts printed on the screen added up to the station *being* Leonard Makepeace Fontana's life. Born in 2035, he had worked for Lanour since graduating from Texas A and M with a Master's in business, starting in a sales position for a subsidiary company Citadel Pharmaceuticals. Within two years, however, he had transferred to Seever Astrotechnologies and gone to work in their Houston office. From the names and titles listed as friends for a Lanour security check, he apparently spent his leisure time chumming with NASA scientists and space center personnel, though along the way he also acquired a pilot's license and a BS in psychology. In '53 he won an award for suggestions on modification of the Seever pressure suit.

"So he knows pressure suits," Mama said.

Janna nodded. A strike against him.

In '54 he wrote to Crispus Tenning with suggestions for a space station that Lanour was rumored to be thinking of building. The letter must have impressed Tenning, because within a month Fontana had been transferred to the newly-formed subsidiary Lanour Aerospace and began a rocket-driven ascension up the corporate ladder. Straight toward platform director.

A psychological evaluation by the station psychologist described Fontana as ambitious, dedicated, and a workaholic.

"I can see why he might be resented," Janna said. "It looks like the station project is as much his baby as old man Tenning's. I'd think harming it would be the equivalent of cutting out his own heart."

"Unless he's certain he's about to lose the station, bibi, then it's sweet revenge. Selling off the work here to competitors will cripple Lanour, maybe fatally."

She ran a hand through her hair. Could Fontana be certain of the proxy fight outcome so far ahead of time? "Who has he called?"

The list looked unpromising. Except for a handful of other people, none contacted more than one or twice a year, he talked only to Crispus Tenning—on a scrambled signal—and his wife and children in Beaumont, Texas.

Mama polished his glasses on his jumpsuit. "His wife would be a perfect cover for messages."

"We'll have to see if we can talk our way into a look at the tapes of their conversations. All right, now let's see Geyer's file."

Mama readjusted his glasses. "How about Doubrava?"

Janna straightened with a jerk that threatened to tear her slippers loose from the carpet. "Doubrava!"

Behind Mama's glasses, his eyes watched her keenly. "You're not excluding him, are you, bibi? Remember objectivity. After all, he knows both construction and station security."

Her jaw tightened. "There is a small matter, though, of being up near the docking bay with witnesses at the same time someone called a disturbance in from Level Two."

"An accomplice. Titus, maybe. He isn't quite what he seems, bibi."

Janna eyed him. "I take it you've already had a look at his file."

Mama nodded. His fingers moved over the keyboard.

The file that came up on the screen seemed unremarkable at first. Doubrava had washed out of shuttle pilot training but promptly applied for orbital construction work, and after ten years of that, working on various NASA and private space stations, including the Lanour platform, had applied and been accepted for a Security position on the Lanour platform. In the course of it all, he had run through five one-year marriage contracts.

Mama arched a brow at Janna. "He has as much trouble maintaining relationships as I do."

She sniffed...then the security check sent Janna's eyebrows climbing. "He's rich?"

According to investigation by Lanour's operatives, Doubrava had made a fortune speculating in the stock market, and continued to accumulate credit. All the investments were made for him by a Denver librarian named Adresina Petree, whom Doubrava had met and had an affair with while on vacation in Greece in '69. He called her once or twice a week.

"Interesting, isn't it?" Mama said.

"Except that he was speculating successfully for a year before he switched to security work and each of the stock transactions has been verified as genuine." Anger still smoldered in her. Why, she could not quite decide. Doubrava meant nothing to her beyond good company and a pleasant sexual partner. Did he? "It's perfectly possible there's nothing more involved than a friendship between two people who found something more practical than sex in each other."

"He works when he doesn't have to."

"Maybe it's for the job, not the credit. Look at his record. Every job he's tried for or held has put him up here. The psychological evaluation characterizes him as seeing space work as romantic in nature and attractive to women. If we can see those call vids, we'll find out what he and his librarian friend talk about. Now are you going to call up Geyer's file or do I ask the clerk to come in here and show me how to do it?"

With what seemed to Janna like great reluctance, Mama typed in the Security chief's name.

Janna leaned around him to read the file as it rolled up the screen. "Tabanne Uzuri Geyer. Born San Francisco, '38. She doesn't look forty-two, does she?"

Mama just grunted in reply.

Janna read on silently.

Geyer's father was a captain in the San Francisco PD...the source of her interest in security work, no doubt. She had graduated from Stanford in '56 with degrees in criminal justice and psychology, picked up a pilot's license, then attended the Fangman Academy in Abilene, Texas.

Janna's brows hopped. The Fangman Academy trained bodyguards, some of the best in the world.

After Fangman's, Geyer had joined Personal Security Services, working out of first the San Francisco office, then Houston, where she had studied electronics and economics in her spare time.

"Versatile woman," Mama murmured.

"I thought of joining PSS once," Janna said. "Wearing fancy clothes and hanging on the arm of some rich and powerful man while he went about his business or played in Las Vegas and Monaco sounded like a dream job."

Mama rolled an eye her direction. "What stopped you?"

She shrugged. "I guess it didn't fit in with some light-witted idea I had back then of ridding the world of bad guys."

In Houston, Geyer had met Thomas Hogan Holle, Lanour's Vice-president in charge of Marketing. In '70 he hired her away from PSS to be one of his full-time bodyguards, but when the Lanour platform activated in '73, Geyer had transferred to station Security.

Mama tapped the entry on the screen. "That looks like someone else wanting a particular job above all else. It had to mean a big salary cut."

Her salary would have gone up again, though. By '74 she had made assistant chief, and a year later had moved into command of Security. Still, the job could not pay what working for Holle had, Janna reflected. Something about it mattered more than financial rewards, and more than personal relationships or a family. Geyer had never married, not even for a one-year contract.

"You see?" Mama said. "Her life centers on this job, like yours does on your job. She has a trust and she wouldn't betray it any more than you'd sell out your badge."

"What if she were about to lose the job?" Janna could not forget Geyer's bitter comment on how corporate executives perceived her ability. "Doesn't that give her the same motivation as Fontana to strike back at Lanour?"

The psychological evaluation described her as single-mindedly loyal to friends and superiors she respected, but also reserved and suspicious, slow to accept new people into her circle. A security check turned up a membership in the African Heritage Association. Janna pointed that out to Mama.

He shrugged it off. "Not everyone in the AHA is radical, bibi. Several members of my family have joined, too, and you won't find more conservative, patriotic people. They even still vote Republican."

His confidence faltered when they reached the call list. Geyer made few, just to her parents, sister, and a couple of women identified as former colleagues in PSS. The pattern of calls to one of them, however, a Raine DeBrabander, had suddenly gone from twice a month to twice a week starting about Christmas.

Mama swore softly and stared at the screen, cheeks sucked in. After a long while, he sighed. "We need to see those vids, bibi. Maybe they have nothing useful on them. After all, someone here must have looked at them as soon they knew about the smuggling, but no arrests came of it. Still…"

"Still," Janna echoed. "The lack of arrests could have something to do with which of our chief suspects did the reviewing."

Mama kneaded the back of his neck, as though it ached. "I think maybe as soon as we've gone over the files for Titus and some of his friends, we might ask about the call vids."

If nothing else, Janna reflected, the reaction to their request ought to tell them something useful.

17

February 5. 12:45:00 hours.

Geyer was not in Security when they arrived at the office after lunch, only Doubrava, hanging upside-down at the monitor wall, slippers sunk in the carpet of the ceiling/floor. Like some exotic blue-furred, turquoise-eyed bat, Janna mused with an inward grin.

"You want to see the call vids?" He paused with fingers on the buttons of the panel controlling the station holo. "Of course. Does that mean you found something useful in the personnel records this morning?"

Janna searched his tone for sharp edges or anxiety, but heard none, only the same dispassionate curiosity he had shown watching Geyer on the monitors the night before. "I'm not sure. Where's your boss?"

"I'll look in a minute." His fingers played across the panel. In the holo, light flashed in a pod on Level One.

"It's in C-9," said a burly officer at a desk by the holo.

Doubrava's fingers moved again. The flashing pod swelled, replacing the station holo and turning transparent. Now the light flashed in a room in the middle of the pod.

"C-9-55, to be specific." Doubrava grinned down at Janna. "Big Brother is also useful for finding certain lost items. Dickerson," he said to the burly officer, "call Stoer and tell him where to find his badge, but since this is the second time he's mislaid it in two weeks, suggest that after this, he try: one, drinking a little less so he can retain the memory of his revels; two, taming the passion within himself long enough to undress neatly instead of shedding clothing indiscriminately; and three, picking up carefully after himself when leaving."

With a grin, the officer turned to the phone built into his desk top and punched in numbers.

Doubrava tapped keys on the wall panel, restoring the normal holo of the station. "I hope you find the calls more useful than we did. We've had two people doing nothing for the past week but reviewing them and they've found nothing, not even after running the vids through a computer cryptoanalysis program. Our killer is obviously *very* good at encoding. Where would you like to start? We have thousands of hours of calls, indexed by date and person."

"With midnight the morning of Saturday the twentieth and going through Monday the twenty-second," Mama said.

Doubrava raised a brow. "Why just those three days?"

Again, though Janna listened closely, she heard no special emphasis, nothing but normal curiosity. "Because we can be certain our killer called the ground contact sometime during them. Uwezo's agents didn't know the date and manner of delivery when they hired the slighs on Friday, but they had all that information by Monday night."

Doubrava arched his brows and smiled. "I wish we'd thought of that. Of course you realize that you'll still have hundreds of calls to watch. Half the station calls friends and family groundside during the week end period. Having given you fair warning of eyestrain to come, follow me."

He pulled loose from the floor overhead and sailed toward the door.

They met Geyer coming in. She smiled at Mama. "Hi, leo. How are you this afternoon? And where are you all going?" She glanced up toward Doubrava as she asked.

"Communications," Doubrava replied, and explained why, including the time-limit reasoning Janna had given him.

Geyer stiffened. It was difficult to tell in eyes as dark as the Security chief's but Janna thought her eyes blazed for just a moment before her face set in an expression of reproof. "And you'd load our visiting firemen with the tedium of checking those calls? Absolutely not. Put our own people on it."

Doubrava blinked. "But they *want*—"

"I said put our own people on it, captain!" Pushing off from the doorway, she sailed across the office through the middle of the holo toward her own office. In that doorway she paused to look back. "I don't mean to shut you out of the case, Mama. In a couple of minutes I'll show you the operation of the surveillance cameras and you can help me by watching Titus and his friends." She vanished inside her office.

Janna eyed the door speculatively. "Doubrava, did you ever go through the surveillance vids to see where she was when Chenoweth's body left?"

He glanced toward the office door. "She's probably popped because we wasted so much time looking through the whole month's calls. Let me talk to her. I'm sure I can fix things."

"You didn't find her, did you?" Janna said.

He hesitated. "There are no cameras in personal quarters."

"Or in the labs."

Doubrava stiffened. The turquoise eyes narrowed. "She's got nothing to hide! I'll be right back."

Not quite. He remained in Geyer's office for nearly fifteen minutes. Janna would have given a great deal to hear the conversation, but he had closed the door behind him going in.

After waiting for several minutes, Mama strolled along the monitor wall in a slow series of Velcro rips, studying the screens. "Those executives groundside are light-witted to want to replace Fontana. He has to be doing something right. Look at this place. It's as busy as an ant colony before winter but no one looks unhappy."

They did look very earnest, driven by some inner passion as they pulled and kicked along the corridors past the surveillance cameras. "I wonder where Titus is in all that."

Mama grinned. "Let's find out." He caught the burly officer's eye. "Officer Dickerson, since Chief Geyer seems to be occupied, will you help us find Clell Titus?"

The officer glanced toward the closed door. Through it came the sound of Geyer's voice, the words unintelligible but the tone furious.

"She may be occupied for a while yet, too." The officer pulled his way over to them. "Operation of the locater is really quite simple."

It was, once he showed them how.

"What if we want to track Titus back earlier?" Janna asked.

"Then you have to use a computer terminal, but that isn't difficult, either."

Janna wished she had paper to write down the codes, but at least by tapping on the microcorder in her pocket, she had vocal instructions that would hopefully recall the key combinations he pressed.

After the officer returned to his own desk, she and Mama practiced, first by finding Titus on the holo. The signal from his badge transponder flashed outside the Level Three corridors.

"Let's see what he was doing before he went out to work," Janna said.

Mama pursed his lips. "About eight hundred hours he would have been in the locker room. We can back-track him from there."

At eight hundred hours Titus and the rest of the construction crews were leaving in pressure suits for the air lock. Janna backed up the tape to watch him come into the locker room with the dwarf and afroam that accompanied him in the empty bar. Talking and laughing, they floated up the row, stopping at another locker, where Titus started to punch the combination before the afroam said sharply, "Clell, what the hell are you doing?"

Titus started and pushed away from the locker, glancing up toward the camera. "I was only going to borrow some boosters from Kirchmeier. Do either of you have any extra?"

The dwarf said, "I don't work boosted. It's a good way to end up snagged and ripped open like Chenoweth."

Shrugging, Titus went on to his own locker and climbed into his pressure suit.

Janna switched to the camera in the core corridor at a time just before Titus entered the locker room. From there, they traced him back to breakfast with the two other men and the mermaid, now minus her tail. To Janna's disappointment, the conversation contained nothing incriminating, just chatter about the torus frame they were finishing and somewhat worried speculation on the Lanour proxy fight. Janna was following Titus out of the empty bar where he left them yesterday when the door of Geyer's office hissed open. Doubrava sailed out.

Nodding at them, he headed for the door. "Let's go."

Janna cleared the computer and followed him. "You must be very persuasive."

He grinned over his shoulder. "Just remember that Security takes all the credit if this finds our killer. Agreed?"

Janna could not believe that a question of credit alone changed Geyer's mind, but at this point, how he managed it mattered less to her than that he had, giving Mama and her a chance to see the call vids. She nodded agreement.

Like every other section in the station except the visitor's quarters, Communications used the ceiling as well as the floor. As in the bars, those occupied the position of walls in relationship to the door. A long communications console with stations on both sides stretched the length of the wall/floor to the left. And here, too, where dividers semi-partitioned the right-hand floor, flowers covered them. Yellow roses this time. Fontana's preference?

Everyone in the room turned as the door divided. Most nodded greetings to Doubrava. He spoke to a dark-eyed, asian-looking young man, and in five minutes the technician had them installed at an empty station on the console with a stack of chips and a thick file folder.

Mama quirked a brow at the folder. "You mean people still write?"

Doubrava grinned. "Not much. They have to let us read all outgoing mail and calling costs less than postage. These, however, are transcripts and translations of the calls." He slipped the first chip into the console slot.

The calls began almost immediately after midnight, and as the images of both caller and callee appeared on the split screen, Janna understood the need for translations. Of the handful of calls by scientific and computer personnel, Janna could understand only the Australians'. The others to Japan and Taiwan hit her ears as unintelligible sing-song.

Janna read the translation, instead, grimacing at the syntax. Computer translations might be faster and less work than human ones, but they remained gratingly literal.

"Quite an international staff," Mama commented.

"Lanour is a multinational, but even if it weren't, I think Fontana would hire qualified personnel wherever he can find them."

For the most part the calls were tedious, recitations of personal activities unrelated to the callers' jobs and gossip about people Janna did not know. Still, she studied every word, hunting a pattern that might be a code. If it were there, though, it was too subtle for her. Mama apparently detected nothing, either. He only shrugged when she lifted her brows at him.

Activity died down after that, until about three, when two calls went to Egypt and Israel, both from computer bobs who obviously had no interest in anything beyond programming.

At four and five, the calls went to Germany, England, and Ireland, as boring as the earlier calls, though Communications had temporarily interrupted one to Germany.

As the callee's half of the screen went blank, a flat voice said: "Security breech."

The caller switched to furious English, face reddening. "What the hell do you mean, security breech? What the hell is secret about the torus design of the new pods?"

"The design employs a new and experimental process. In the future, it would be safest to avoid mention of all details concerning construction and work routine."

"Then what the hell is it I am permitted to talk about?" the caller snarled in frustration.

The Communications technician replied only: "You may resume your call."

It resumed with the caller railing against the strictness of Security and the clique-ishness of the permanent staff. The end of his assignment to the station could not come soon enough. He did not know why, Janna read in the translation, so many people seemed eager to live here permanently.

Activity stopped until noon, but then the calls became an avalanche raining on the US, Canada, and Mexico. They came so fast they must have tied up almost every one of the station's frequencies. Janna watched what seemed very much like the hundreds of calls Doubrava warned them about. At least she could understand all but those to Quebec. And familiar faces appeared.

Titus…talking to his wife, children, and co-husband in Maryland. Listening, rather. He let them do most of the talking. The co-husband asked, "Are you still finding adventure enough up there, Clell?"

On his half of the screen, Titus grinned. "Have you ever known me to stick with another job this long? I expect it to get even better, too."

Janna frowned at the transcript. "Can we read anything special into that?"

"Not off-hand, bibi, but put the transcript aside to go over again later."

Several calls later, Geyer's regal face appeared on the screen. The older woman on the other half the screen, although thinner and darker than Geyer, bore enough physical similarities that she had to be a close relative.

"Hi, Mom."

Mama leaned toward the screen, but his interest had to be Geyer, certainly not the conversation…hello, how are you, what have you been doing? Watching, though, the exchanged resonated in Janna, and after a few minutes she identified the reason. The Security chief's smile and non-committal replies that skipped the specifics of her job sounded just like Janna's conversations with her father. She felt a sudden involuntary kinship with the golden woman and swore. Sisterly feelings toward a suspect were the last thing she needed.

"Mama, what do you think?"

He frowned at the transcript, then shook his head. "I don't think so; not this call, anyway."

How could she trust Mama's judgment, or her own, now, for that matter? She set the transcript aside for closer reading later.

Fontana made two calls, one to his daughter at Texas A and M, the other to his wife in Beaumont.

As the second started, Doubrava grinned. "Dig in your slippers, children. The fun begins."

On the callee's half the screen, a slim, tanned woman with two-toned green hair and Egyptian eye makeup exercised in the nude beside a swimming pool.

"Hello, Len." Mercedes Fontana's rich voice echoed slightly. She stopped jumping jacks long enough to peer toward the screen. "You look tired, honey. Is the job runnin' you or has some sweet young companion been interferin' with your sleep?"

The wolf's eyes crinkled at the corners. "I don't have time for that much involvement. Sex has to wait for the few minutes here and there when I have nothing better to do."

The woman laughed, a rich, sensuously animal sound. "Lord don't I know that. My space man. You don't even care that I take my pleasures elsewhere, do you?" She came over to turn the phone and stretch out on a chaise the screen now faced, arching her browned body.

"As long as you don't bring them home while Drew's still living there."

She sat up, tossing her green-striped hair. "I'm lustful, not improprietous." She lay back again, smiling. "We play down in Port Arthur. Let me tell you about the last time."

"Don't you have any respect for my Communications and Security people who have to monitor this call?" The corner of Fontana's mouth twitched.

"They go through this every time," Doubrava said. "It's like a ritual."

"Len, honey, they deserve some break from the domestic drivel they're forced to hear most of the time. Y'all listenin' close now?"

The next five minutes left Janna staring at Fontana's wife in shocked admiration. What stamina and imagination! "Isn't it still illegal to say things like that over the air?"

"No, but I'm surprise the chip doesn't melt," Mama said.

"Interesting," was Fontana's only comment, however. "Can you find paper and a pencil and take down a list of errands I need to have you run for me?"

She sighed. "Don't I always? Mercedes Fontana, maturing Girl Friday, that's me."

Janna stiffened. "Mama! This might be it."

Doubrava blinked. "It's just pick up this and talk to that person. Be sure the dog has his shots. That kind of thing."

"Does the request for errands always follow the porno?"

The turquoise eyes went thoughtful. "You think the list could be code?"

"What better code, and what better timing for it than when everyone is still salivating from the latest chapter of Lady Fontana's Lover?" Mama said. "Exactly what time of day did Chenoweth die?"

Doubrava sucked in his lower lip. "Eleven hundred thirty hours. But...I still can't believe Fontana would sell out. Why don't you just put that transcript aside with Geyer's and go on?"

Nothing else looked as promising as Fontana's call, however.

"Anyone interested in eating?" Doubrava asked.

Janna looked up at a wall chronometer to see with surprise that it was past eighteen hundred hours. They had been working without a break all afternoon!

"Can we have something brought in?" Mama asked. "I'd like to get through as many of these today as possible."

Doubrava had Communications call the cafeteria. Janna and Mama moved on to Sunday's calls.

Fontana made two more calls, but neither had a transcript and both halves of the screen showed only static behind the date and time.

"Scrambled calls to Crispus Tenning and the home office," Doubrava explained.

Doubrava called his librarian friend in Denver.

"Interesting woman," he said as the tape started. "I'd considered her just a vacation playmate but when these two jons at the next table started arguing about stocks and bonds and the credit they were losing, she said, 'I don't know what's so difficult about the stock market. It just takes a wide range of reading and a little commonsense-calculation. I'll bet that I could invest a few thousand credits and triple it in six months.' Construction carried heavy hazard pay in those days so I had plenty of extra credit and I said, 'Apple, you're on.' She *quadrupled* it in *three* months."

On the screen, Doubrava and a dark-haired woman with a quiet, madonna-type beauty exchanged a few introductory pleasantries and sexual innuendoes, and then settled into a spirited but interminable and detailed discussion of Doubrava's portfolio.

Janna yawned.

"Stocks would make a good code, too," Doubrava said.

Mama peered over the top of his glasses at the assistant chief. "You're not a professional confessor, are you?"

Doubrava grinned. "If you're going to make everyone in the station suspects, you can't leave me out."

Stocks *would* make a good code, Janna reflected, and after a minute, laid the transcript with the pile of other possibles.

Geyer made her twice-weekly call to her former PSS colleague.

"Men are sons of bitches," she spat.

The bitterness raised the hair on Janna's neck.

Raine DeBrabander, who, like Geyer looked like someone who should be modeling or the darling of the castlerow set, raised golden brows. "What has who done to you this week to get you this fused?"

Abruptly, Geyer's face shuttered. She shrugged. "Nothing in particular, I guess. Sometimes I think other people aren't really people to men, just pieces in a game." She paused. "You know what certain members and would-be members of Lanour's board of directors are trying to do. Tell me, do you think they deserve anything that happens to them?"

Janna caught her breath and glanced quickly at Mama. He was biting his lip.

DeBrabander leaned toward her screen. "Does Tenning have some dirty tricks to keep power?"

Geyer's jaw tightened. "I don't think he's even going to attempt a fight. I think wants his enemies to believe he's resisting, but at the last minute he'll just walk away and let the company go to hell."

"You and the station with it? That bastard! After all the loyalty you've given him."

Geyer frowned. "I don't blame him. It's the board's fault. The consequences are theirs. If they weren't so—" She broke off, breathing deeply, and when she resumed, it was in a light tone, encouraging girl chatter.

Janna stood with a chill in her spine and knots in her gut. "She's dirty." Somehow, though, the knowledge failed to bring her the satisfaction that the nearing solution of a case usually did. "The instructions to the agents are in her conversation with her mother somewhere and now she's trying to justify her actions to herself."

"I won't believe that," Doubrava said.

"The only other explanation I can think of is almost as bad," Janna said. "She knows about the murder and is trying to justify *inaction.*"

The turquoise eyes bored into her. "I won't believe that, either."

Watching the two women on the screen gossiping about their old agency, Mama sighed heavily. "In any case, I suppose we ought to talk to her."

Doubrava drew in a deep breath. "Why don't we pull all her call vids for the past couple of months and study them first?"

Mama's mouth thinned. "Don't you think she deserves to be confronted directly, so she can defend herself?"

Doubrava frowned from Mama to the screen until the end of the call, then nodded with obvious reluctance. He tapped his ear. Janna watched his throat move as he subvocalized. He listened, spoke again, then shook his head at Mama. "She's left the office for the night and is in the Rec pod. Let me go after her. I'll meet you back in Security in fifteen minutes."

Janna watched him sail out of Communications, then turned back to Mama, who stood frowning at the console screen, rubbing the back of his neck. "I'm sorry, Mama." She meant it.

"It isn't right yet, bibi. For a moment there I thought we had it, but..." His shoulders moved irritably. "If someone had murdered some of the board of directors, we'd have motive galore. There would be reason for everyone looking guilty. They all stand to lose if Tenning does. I can't believe in any of our suspects smuggling just to hurt Lanour, though, despite Geyer's conversation. No, there's something more, something we're not seeing, a piece missing, and this won't make sense until we have that piece."

18

February 5. 20:00:00 hours.

Janna looked around Communications but did not see the young asian who had been on duty when she and Mama came in, nor anyone who looked familiar, for that matter. Not surprisingly. Even with the station's free-running schedule, the shift must have changed hours ago. Pulling her slippers loose from the carpet, Janna jumped up to the nearest desk to return the chips and transcript folder.

The thin young woman there started violently, head jerking around from her computer terminal as Janna braked by grabbing a lidded wire basket screwed to the desk top.

"Sorry," Janna apologized. She slipped the chips and folder in the basket and closed the lid to keep them from drifting away. "I didn't mean to frighten you."

A glittering swirl of nebulas surrounded the clerk's eyes, matched by metallic bronze tipping on her hair. She grimaced sheepishly. "It isn't your fault. I just can't get used to the idea that people hurtling down from the ceiling aren't falling. Sometimes I wonder how I let myself be talked into working up here. Thank god it's only a year." She peered past Janna up to where Mama drifted along the console peeking over the technicians' shoulders. "You're the trouble shooters from Seever, aren't you? Have you found out yet what made that pressure suit rupture?"

Janna arched a brow. Did some station personnel still believe that story? Temporaries must not be on the grapevine. "Not definitely, though we hope to complete our investigation soon. It was a tragic accident."

"Tragedy is in the eyes of the beholder."

Janna recognized the jolt in her head. Internal reality had just stumbled over an inconsistency. The leo in her pounced on it. Casually, she asked, "I take it you knew Mr. Chenoweth and weren't overly fond of him?" she asked casually.

The nebulas around the clerk's eyes sprang into sharp relief as she flushed. "I'm sorry; that was a snide thing to say, especially when I didn't know him, not personally. Of course his death is tragic. He has that new baby and I'm sure his wife will miss him. On the other hand, I've heard plenty *about* him." She leaned toward Janna, lowering her voice. "Not to speak ill of the dead, but it's toads like him who give us temporaries a bad reputation! He carried around a whole pocketful of 2-D's of the baby, but just for coup bait. You know...he'd be all toxy with liquor and talking about how lonely he was without his dear wife and child, and the next thing you knew he'd try to drag you off to his hammock to 'comfort' him...and bounce you off the walls if you refused. I heard that once he even tried it on our chief of Security when she was out of uniform and he was too drunk to read her badge. She bounced *him* off the walls! He didn't know how to keep his mouth shut when he was sober, either. We've had to interrupt or terminate several of his calls for security breeches."

Electricity crawled under Janna's skin, raising the hair all over her body. Inconsistency indeed. This was a very different Chenoweth than everyone else talked about. "Mama," she called, and sucked in a slow breath before quirking a brow at the clerk. "What kinds of security breeches?"

The clerk shrugged. "I'm not on the console. I just log the calls for the personnel records."

Mama appeared not to have heard Janna. He continued to hover behind one of the console techs, intent on something on a screen.

"Mama," Janna repeated in a sharper tone, and smiled at the clerk. "Do you remember the date of the last time he committed a breech? Distress or anger over being reprimanded could make a man careless."

The nebulas drew toward each other. "I don't remember an incident near his accident. He didn't always call when I was on duty, of course."

"Of course. Mama!" What the hell was so engrossing up there? Janna kept smiling. "May I see his calls for the week before he died, then?"

"Certainly." The clerk held out her hand.

Janna blinked at it.

"I need to see your authorization from Director Fontana or Chief Geyer."

Damn! Bluff time.

Mama finally responded, drifting down from the console. "You wanted me, bibi?"

What *had* he seen? His eyes glittered in excitement behind his glasses. Janna forced herself to concentrate on the clerk, however. "My authorization? Ms..."—she peered at the clerk's badge—"Ms. Kling, we've been in here most of the day reviewing call vids. Obviously we're authorized."

The clerk hesitated, then tapped the keys of her terminal. From where she stood Janna could not see the monitor, but moments later the clerk's smile became apologetic. "I'm sorry, but Captain Doubrava pulled those other chips. I can page him and ask for authorization for the new ones, though."

"What chips?" Mama asked.

Switching to Spanish, Janna explain hurriedly.

To her astonishment and irritation, however, Mama showed no interest in the information. His eyes slid away, upward, focusing on the communications console. In English he said, "We don't need to look at any more calls, bibi. I'm not sure what you thought they could tell us anyway. Come on. We have an appointment with Chief Geyer in Security." And pushing off from the desk, he sailed across the room out the door.

Damn the man! Janna followed sputtering. "Maxwell, what the hell is the matter with you? Don't you understand? There's a contradiction to how Chenoweth has been described to us. If Chenoweth isn't the sad innocent we've been led to believe—"

"It doesn't make a bit of difference," Mama tossed back over his shoulder. "He died in Titus's suit, not his own. No one could have known he would be wearing it, unless you want to postulate that someone sabotaged his suit so he would be forced to wear Titus's also-sabotaged suit." He used a corridor railing to catch himself so he could turn. "Forget Chenoweth, bibi."

Anger flared in her. Was the bastard blind? Or had whatever he saw on the console sent him blue-skying?

Fuming, Janna almost missed the words he mouthed soundlessly before turning away again: *Big Brother.*

Anger chilled instantly to caution. Her neck prickled with the feel of the cameras focused on her, and through it, watching eyes and listening ears...Geyer's, or Fontana's. For the benefit of the cameras, she continued to scowl for another minute, however, then sighed as she jerked on a railing and sent herself sailing after Mama. "Maybe you're right."

They swung through the door into Security. An hispanic officer stood at a desk just inside. Mama gave her his most disarming smile. "We're supposed to meet with Chief Geyer. Shall we wait in her office?"

The officer glanced around long enough to identify them, then nodded and returned to the sheaf of printout clipped to her desktop.

They sailed across the office through the middle of the station holo and into the inner office.

"About Chenoweth," Janna began.

"Later, bibi." He headed for the desk. "Watch for Geyer."

"What are you—" she began, and broke off, because it was obvious what he was doing.

Settling his slippers into the carpet, Mama quickly typed on the keyboard below the row of monitor screens. Communications, the reception area outside Fontana's office, the cafeteria, and two corridor scenes came up on the screens.

Janna raised her brows. "When did you learn how to work that?"

"Watching Geyer when I came back here last night after leaving you in Fontana's office."

"What do you hope to see?"

He turned on the sound for the cafeteria. "Maybe how fast the grapevine works. A message came in while I was watching the console in Communications. Crispus Tenning is on his way up for a visit."

Tenning! Coming here? For the second time that evening, she felt a jolt inside her head. "This close to the stockholder's meeting, or am I wrong in assuming it's sometime in the next couple of days?"

"You're not wrong; it's tomorrow."

She sucked in her breath. "Then Geyer was right. He *is* walking away without a fight."

In the cafeteria the P.A. came on. At the sound of Tenning's name, the clatter of utensils and roar of multiple simultaneous conversations died instantly. The announcement of the visit fell into the silence of a vacuum. Despite the distortion of the fisheye focus, Janna had no trouble reading expressions. Behind the service counter and at the tables, personnel stiffened as they listened. Faces drew taut. One young woman started to cry. Several other people crossed themselves.

Janna watched grimly. "I'm surprised he has the guts to come here to say good-bye, though."

"That isn't all that's surprising." Mama pointed at one table where men and women in green coveralls whooped and hugged each other in unbridled delight.

His fingers raced across the keyboard in letter/number combinations. One after another, the screens switched to other cameras. The same mixture of grim and gleeful faces repeated everywhere. And if the station looked like an ant colony before, it seemed even more so now...a galvanized colony. Personnel hurtled along the branch corridors and dived by the dozens down the core corridor, stopping barely long enough to shove their badges into the security slot and let the computer read their retinal patterns.

Janna shook her head. "I wonder what kind of rumors have been circulating. Even a major reorganization shouldn't affect everyone but they act like they need to squeeze in as much time on their projects as possible." She grinned. "Do you suppose there'll be a mass repeat of the Chelle incident, with the station's entire scientific staff barricading themselves in their labs and refusing to be evicted?"

Mama did not appear to hear her. He leaned across the desk toward one of the monitors, staring intently. "What the hell?"

Janna backstroked toward the door to check the outer office. All the officers there had left their normal tasks and floated in a cluster by the monitor wall, anchoring themselves by holding to the edge of the desks while they watched the screens and talked among themselves in low, rapid voices. Janna kicked off from the door to return to the desk and see what had surprised Mama so much.

The screen of interest showed her nothing unusual at first, just the Level One intersect and the personnel traffic out of the branch corridors and up and down the core. The bustle had thinned a bit, but without any lessening of the hurry. Then she noticed the panel colors in the branches and read the signs at the core intersect. Her eyes dropped to the lettering on the bottom of the screen: A-L2. Level Two!

Janna's head jolted one more time. Why were so many people heading for Level Three? Maintenance and scientific personnel among them? There was nothing down there but corridors and a few pods in the process of—

The thought broke off abruptly as details of the scene sank in, and this time her mind did not jolt. The leo in her reared back roaring. "Mama," she said slowly, "why do you suppose there's a security barrier instead of just a cautionary warning for a construction area?"

He looked around. The light from the panels in the wall behind him reflected off his scalp but left his face in silhouette, unreadable. "Good question, bibi. Here's a brother to it. Why is talking about construction details of this station a security breech?"

Mama had to be thinking of the German whose call they had seen that afternoon, and maybe Chenoweth, too. What else of a restricted nature could he know about? The sideleap of reasoning which connected the two just now in that gleaming chocolate head defeated her understanding. There was nothing to do but play straight man for him. "They're using an experimental building process."

Mama snorted. "The Construction crews can see the results, but how much could they know about *how* the spider works, and *why*? No, bibi, there has to be another reason."

A stab of his finger deactivated the row of monitors. He shoved away from the desk toward the wall where he could see the main office.

Janna stared out, too. The room had become deserted except for the hispanic officer. She floated with a toe hooked under the drawer handle on a desk, staring dreamily at the station holo in the middle of the room.

Janna heard Mama's breath catch. "That's it!" he whispered. "Jan, describe that holo. What do you see?"

She stared at him. He was obviously quite serious, but… "What do you mean? It's a three-dimensional reproduction of the station."

The wall had no carpet or handholds. Without a stabilizing grip on anything, Mama rose slowly toward the ceiling. "How do we know?"

Half a dozen thoughts collided in her head.

Drifting in mid-air, he continued: "Most of us see only the inside, and not all of that. Even the shuttle pilots can't see much. Remember how wide the solar panels are? Construction is the only group who knows the whole, true form of the station, and they aren't allowed to talk about it."

From the scramble of chaos seeking order, thought coalesced into coherence, into understanding. Janna sucked in her breath. "Level Three."

Mama nodded. The action made his whole body bob gently. "Paul Chenoweth, who tended to talk too much and was in Construction died suddenly and violently."

Janna let her breath out again. "You're blue-skying. The trap was set for Titus." Still…

Something nudged Janna, something she had heard or seen, something that almost made a connection. She groped mentally, scrambling after the half-seen thought, and cursed as it slithered out of her grasp.

"Maybe," Mama said.

The nudge came again. Janna focused all her attention on Mama, waiting for him to continue.

"I can't help but wonder why the crew chief gave Chenoweth Titus's suit instead of using one of the spares that are supposed to replace malfunctioning suits."

Another nudge, sharper this time. Janna bit her lip. Mama's concern bothered her, too, now that he mentioned it, but it was not *the* thing. "Maybe we should invite Carakostas in for a chat, too?"

Which reminded her…where were Doubrava and Geyer? They should have been here long ago. She peered around the door to check the office again.

"Actions speak louder than words, bibi." Mama frog-kicked and drove back for the desk, where he grabbed the edge to push his feet down into the carpet. Then he reached for the keyboard of the computer fastened to the slightly slanting top.

Janna grinned. Of course. That was much better than asking someone what they had done. "January twentieth." She sailed back from the door to edge in beside him. "About eight hundred hours."

The tape of the locker room at eight hundred hours showed the room filled with the crew going on duty. A pleasant-looking man in his late twenties stood at Titus's locker pulling on a pressure suit.

"Back it up, Mama."

The tape blurred. The timer jumped to fifteen minutes earlier. Slowed and sent forward again, the tape played for several minutes before Chenoweth entered the locker room. Laughing and joking with other men and women in the crew, he propelled himself down the line...straight to Titus's locker. Without hesitation, he punched the combination, pulled open the door, and lifted out the pressure suit.

The breath stuck in Janna's chest. "Mama, are you sure we have the right day?"

But the date appeared on the screen next to the time: 01/20/80.

Chenoweth slid into the suit. Still joking with the people on either side of him, he kicked off from the closed locker to sail toward the corridor door.

No thoughts collided this time. No readjustment of reality jolted Janna's mind. The memory that had eluded capture before lay down and rolled over before her...Titus coming into the locker room and going straight to one locker before prompting by his companions sent him on to the one she and Mama had been told was "his", the one Chenoweth just now opened.

Her eyes met Mama's. In them she read the same conclusions she had just reached. With icy anger seeping through her, she voiced their thoughts. "We've been skinned. It's all been a lie...the trouble with Chenoweth's suit, substituting Titus's. Even the hearing was a fake. Chenoweth *was* the intended victim."

Mama's jaw set grimly. "Everyone here has conspired to keep us from finding that out."

Including Geyer, he meant. Janna sensed that without asking. Or maybe especially Geyer. Chenoweth's behavior on that one occasion would not have given her any great fondness for him. "I wonder if we're dealing with two crimes here after all, a murder and a smuggler who made use of the death." Though toady behavior by itself hardly constituted much of a motive for murder.

"Except that the smuggler knew about the death before it happened," Mama reminded her.

There *was* that. Which left them with a problem. "Why should an entire station want to protect a smuggler and murderer?"

"An interesting question, but I hoped you'd never ask," Geyer's voice said.

They snapped around. Janna grabbed the desk for stabilization.

Geyer floated with one hand gripping the edge of the doorway, face grim.

Doubrava hovered behind her, grinning. "They're good."

Her mouth thinned. "I'm glad you find it amusing, Ian. Use Castaneda to help you take them to detention."

"Detention!" Janna hissed.

The dark eyes flicked over her. "I'm too busy to play games any longer. This way I can be sure of where you are and what you're doing without wasting manpower watching you."

She pulled aside.

Doubrava and the hispanic officer came in through the door past her. Doubrava held out a wrap strap to Janna with an apologetic smile. "I'm sorry it has to be this way. Turn around, please."

"And if I don't?"

"We'll use force," Geyer said simply.

Angrily, Janna turned, crossing her wrists behind her back. The wrap strap circled them, slick and slightly warm on her skin.

The hispanic officer wrapped Mama.

Strapped wrists handicapped movement in zero-gee more than on the ground, but the officers solved the propulsion problem by taking their captives' arms and towing them…out of the inner office and up through a door in the ceiling into a vertical corridor beyond. The door was transparent, as were all the doors opening into the corridor. It gave the detention section a deceptively open, unprisonlike appearance. The transparency made visual supervision easier, Janna knew, and judging by the badge slot and r.r. plate by the outer door, the push-button locks by the others, and the near-invisible reinforcement of monofilament mesh Janna could see inside the material of the doors themselves, the plastic was surely one of the super-impact varieties, as strong as any iron plating.

"It's too bad you're so dedicated to your job," Doubrava said. "This could have been a very pleasant visit."

"It's too bad you want to protect a murderer," Janna countered.

Doubrava hesitated only a moment before shrugging. "The greatest good for the greatest number of people. I'll put you in number Five. Maxwell will be across the corridor in Six where you can wave at each other."

Janna set her jaw. Once she went in that cell, she might never learn who the murderer was. The problem was how to stop them from putting her in. Or was it? These people might be good at their jobs here, but no lend-lease leo had the time on the street she did.

Mama pursed his lips. "We can be like Ike Garman and his friends, remember, bibi?"

So he had been thinking along the same line she was. Janna bit back a grin. "I remember, Mama."

The deek had come home from his first prison term educated in an entire repertoire of vicious tricks to help him overpower careless officers even when strapped. He had passed on his knowledge to his best friends. She and Mama had not been careless, but they wore bruises for weeks as mementos of bringing in members of that rat pack.

"Each delivering a message to the other side of the corridor," Mama said.

Doubrava and the other officer let go of their prisoners to punch the door combinations.

As the doors slid open, Janna hissed, "Now, Mama!"

She drew up her legs and kicked out against the wall. It drove her not into Doubrava, but across the corridor and headfirst into the spine of the hispanic officer, hurling both of them into the detention cell. Mama arrowed for Doubrava.

Once in the confines of the cell, Janna had six walls to use, but one was enough. Her elbow drove into the hispanic officer's throat, and while the woman writhed choking and gasping, Janna backed up to the floating form and quickly searched her for the wrap strap polarizer. Seconds later Janna stripped off the strap.

She eyed Castaneda's uniform, but decided against taking it. Too small. Janna relieved the officer of her ear button, however, and traded badges.

Eventually Geyer would know to trace her by Castaneda's badge, but in the meantime, it ought to buy some freedom. So would the radio.

She swung out of the cell to find Mama in the corridor carrying Doubrava's badge and ear button. Her conscience twinged. "I hope you didn't hurt him seriously."

Mama settled his glasses straight and worked the radio into his ear. "He'll be fine, I promise."

"Then what now? Visit Fontana? I can't think of anyone else everyone would want to protect. Or maybe we'd do better to hole up until Tenning arrives and tell him what we know."

Mama frowned. "I wonder if it's Fontana they're protecting. This station has something very odd going on and just like the murder and smuggling have to be parts of the same crime, it and the cover-up and keeping us running in circles after this suspect and the other has to be part of everything else, too."

"You mean what's on Level Three."

He nodded. "So I think that somehow, we'd better find a way to have a look down there."

19

February 5. 21:10:00 hours.

Visit Level Three. Janna sucked in her lower lip. "That isn't going to be easy."

Mama shrugged and grinned. "What are two security barriers?"

"Three." She pointed down the corridor at the closed door to the Security office. Beside it, the smoky eye of the r.r. plate mocked them above the badge slot. "That has to be unlocked from this side, too, and then there's the office to cross without being caught."

Something thudded behind Janna. She glanced around to see the hispanic officer gripping the molding of the cell door with one hand and between coughs, pounding on the plastic with the other.

"That's a problem, too," Janna added. "She might make enough noise to attract attention, and sooner or later Geyer is going to wonder why Doubrava's been gone so long. She'll come looking for him."

Mama's teeth gleamed. "Then we'd better leave." He swung into cell Five and emerged a moment later towing a wrap-strapped and limp Doubrava by the collar.

Conscience stabbed Janna again. She reached out to touch the darkening patch of a bruise on his temple and frown accusingly at Mama. "I thought you said you didn't hurt him seriously."

Mama's nostrils flared. "Don't make me the villain. You aren't wasting any concern on her, I notice." He pointed at the officer in cell Six.

Doubrava rolled his head, groaning.

"See, he'll be fine." Mama towed him on down to the door. "Watch the office, bibi."

Janna grabbed a handrail at one end of the door for stabilization and peered over the edge of the opening into the room below. It remained empty. She frowned. They needed it that way; still...where had everyone gone? The radio in her ear crackled occasionally, indicating activation, but remained otherwise silent. "It's clear."

Pushing Doubrava's badge into the slot, Mama held the security officer by the hair, then lightly slapped his face. Doubrava moaned again. His eyelids fluttered. Quickly, Mama turned him to face the retinal reading plate.

Doubrava blinked a couple of times, mumbling. His eyes opened wide. A second later, he stiffened and his eyes snapped tightly shut, but too late. The door hissed aside.

Janna grabbed the edge to keep it open. Doubrava drew a sharp breath, but before he could yell, Mama wrapped a long hand over his mouth and hauled him back toward cell Five.

Doubrava struggled, twisting and kicking. With his wrists strapped, however, it accomplished nothing. Mama shoved him in the cell. As the door slid shut behind him, Doubrava kicked his way back to it to hover inside with his lips forming words robbed of sound by the plastic barrier. *What do you think you're doing? There's nowhere here to run.*

"Room enough, captain." Mama blew him a kiss. "Let's go, bibi."

The office below remained empty. Geyer's door was open, but only someone in the doorway itself could see up into the detention section. Keeping high, then, probably gave them the best chance to stay out of sight.

"Stay close to the ceiling," she whispered over her shoulder.

Mama grinned. "I've sneaked through a lot of rooms, but never on the ceiling before."

She stared at him a moment, then grinned back as the mental image struck her. With a last glance toward the chief's door, Janna slid through the detention door. Toes digging in to the carpet strips and fingers gripping carpet nap and frames of the light panels, she held herself close to the ceiling as she pulled toward the nearest of the file cabinets.

Mama followed.

With the hiss of the detention door closing after him Janna suddenly felt very vulnerable. If anyone should come in and look up, they had no retreat, no escape. The corridor exit looked a kilometer away.

Heart pounding, she worked cautiously from one file around behind the next, keeping the metal bulk between her and Geyer's door.

The radio broke silence, simultaneously hissing in her ear and from the speaker on the communications panel outside Geyer's office. "Stech nineteen. Edward Zabokrtsky hasn't reported to the cafeteria with the other temporaries. Please locate."

Locate! Janna's heart lurched. Damn! Releasing the edge of the light panel frame she gripped, she kicked off from the file beside her and dived across the room.

"Stech nineteen," the radio repeated.

"Aurora, get that!" Geyer called from her office.

"Nineteen. Hey, wake up, muchacha!"

Janna arched in the air, reaching for a file cabinet passing above her. Her fingers met the metal…and slipped.

"Castaneda!"

Swearing silently, Janna clawed at the cabinet. Nails scraping on the metal, she hauled herself up and behind it.

Geyer's head came out of the office door, scowling. "Castaneda, why the hell—?" She broke off, looking around, then up.

Janna dug fingers into the file, slipper toes into the rim of a light panel. Her breath froze in her chest. Would Geyer notice the single eye peering around the file? Was Mama out of sight? She dared not move enough to look for him.

Then that became unimportant. Her heart slammed into her ribs. Geyer stared at the detention door. "Ian?" With frown deepening, she gathered, obviously to push off to the door.

"Hey, nineteen, is anyone there?" the radio pleaded.

Geyer hesitated, then turned for the radio. She hit the transmit button. "Nineteen here. Locating Zabokrtsky now."

A kick sent her gliding across the room to the holo controls on the monitor wall.

Janna shrank back farther behind the file cabinet until she could no longer see any of the golden woman, only the holo.

Moments later light flashed in a Level One pod. With a blink, the an enlarged pod replaced the station for a moment. Then the holo returned to normal. Could Geyer really read it that fast? Janna eased back to where she could see again.

Geyer had returned to the communications panel. "Stech. Subject is in C-7-41."

All the while she talked, however, Geyer frowned up at the detention door. Janna braced herself, doubling her legs so her slipper soles brushed against the side of the file. Sure enough, as soon as she punched off the radio, Geyer kicked upward.

The moment Geyer's badge and retinal pattern opened the door and she disappeared through it, Janna shoved off, rocketing for the corridor door.

Mama came right behind and above her.

She resumed breathing again only after they had put a turn of corridor between them and Security's door. Mama's sigh echoed her.

She did not relax, however. Any second now Geyer would be back at the holo controls, using the transponders to find them. "We'll need to dump these badges, Mama."

"I don't know if that's wise, bibi. We might attract more attention if we're not wearing any. Why not just go off the map?"

Janna grinned. Unlike many of her fellow leos, when the constant display of her whereabouts occasionally became an annoyance rather than aid, she had resisted the urge to deactivate her transponders. Now she could finally indulge herself.

Part or all of the blue border must be photocell to energize the transponder, but where was the transponder itself? Without pausing in movement toward the pod entrance, Janna pinched the badge between thumb and fingers. It thickened faintly in the acute angle of one end.

Just ahead lay the pod door. Mama pointed. "We'll use that."

Traffic continued to be heavy through the corridor beyond. Janna unclipped Castaneda's badge and holding it behind her, transponder end out, planted her feet in the narrow strip of carpet just outside the door. Mama handed her Doubrava's badge.

"Hold them a little farther away from you and one about fifteen centimeters above the other, bibi."

Smiling at people passing in the corridor, she adjusted the badges' position. At the corner of her vision inside the pod, Mama tapped the control plate.

The heavy doors hissed together, meeting with a reverberating clang that to Janna's horrified ears sounded loud enough to be audible from one end of the station to the other. She fought not to cringe or bolt for cover. Instead, she made her eyes wide and turned to stare at the doors along with surprised passers-by. "I wonder how that happened."

The doors hissed open again. Janna snatched up the badges as they floated free. Between her fingers, the transponder ends felt thinner.

"Sorry," Mama was saying to an irritated-looking man on the inside. "I hit the controls by accident." Palming Doubrava's badge as Janna slipped it to him, he muttered, "Let's get out of here, bibi."

They joined the traffic resuming its flow along the corridor.

The radio button in Janna's ear carried a stream of chatter between officers rounding up temporaries who had not obeyed an apparent earlier order over the P.A. to report to the cafeteria. She frowned. What the hell were they doing? The big problem, however, was still reaching Level Three. "Have we thought of a way through the security barriers yet?"

A brow rose above the top of his glasses. "Since forcibly using someone else the way we did Doubrava is probably impractical with this many witnesses, maybe we can slip through with a group...pretend to put our badges in the slot but keep so close behind someone else that we use their clearance."

It was worth a try.

The corridor opened into the core corridor. Janna looked around quickly for a suitable group.

"There," Mama muttered. "Coming out of the red corridor."

She saw them, three men and two women in vari-colored coveralls. Scientific personnel, probably. Pushing off, she sailed across the corridor after Mama and caught at a railing to fall in behind the scientists.

Geyer's voice cut through the other traffic on the radio, cold and sharp as a knife blade. "All officers Level One and above, code one thousand." Janna had no idea what that meant but the two familiar descriptions which followed let her take an educated guess. "The hunt is on, Mama."

Mama slipped off his glasses and shoved them into a thigh pocket. "Maybe we'd better go down with different groups. They may not recognize us as readily if we're separated."

"Will you be all right without your glasses?"

"I'm not blind. I can see form and color." He squinted noticeably, however.

The scientists unclipped their badges for the security check. Janna started to fall back, then froze, her heart lurching. A blue uniform appeared in her peripheral vision, shooting downward past them. The officer dragged herself to a halt opposite the badge slot and r.r. plate and began studying the traffic passing her.

"Mama, Security," Janna hissed in warning, and casually reversed direction.

A glance behind her found Mama doing the same. He fell in behind an upbound couple in yellow coveralls. The glance also spotted the Security officer looking her direction.

"Bertroud nineteen," the radio murmured. "I have a possible on that code one thousand, checkpoint Alpha."

Adrenaline pumped its fiery cold rush through Janna. They were reaching the Level One corridor branches again. She used the railing to swing into the nearest of them.

"Mama. Tag me."

He followed the sound of her voice.

"Code one thousand into *D*."

Janna swore. They had to get out of the corridor. Only, where to go? Those damn cameras were everywhere.

Blue flashed among the coveralls ahead. Janna swore again.

Mama caught at her sleeve. "This way."

They were in the pod before she recognized it as Recreation, and that it appeared deserted. "We're a duck shoot in here," she protested.

He pushed her toward a door. "Go. Fast."

She found herself in a restroom, mirrors with a cabinet and water pistol faucets and hot-air dryers beneath her feet, stalls overhead. Had there been restrooms on the monitors? She could not remember. No lens gleamed in here that she could see, though.

Mama opened the front of his jumpsuit with a rip of velcro.

She stared at him skeptically. "Do you think you become invisible without clothes?"

"Maybe by switching clothes we will. It'll help change our appearance."

Janna stripped, too.

"Nineteen, they're not visible in the corridor. They must have ducked into one of the pods."

She had to roll up a cuff on the sleeves and legs of Mama's jumpsuit, but otherwise it did not appear obviously too large, just made her look even thinner and more angular. The bright color, and the sash wound around hair darkened by wetting it down and skinning it back, turned her complexion muddy. In the mirrors she looked very much indeed like a different person.

Geyer's voice said, "Available officers, search *D* pod by pod. Are you listening, leos? You might as well surrender; there's nowhere for you to go."

The irregular green and brown pattern of her suit's jungle camouflage pattern changed Mama, too. Suddenly he might have been almost any middle-class businessman, albeit a bald one.

Janna grinned at him. "You look positively Establishment."

"I feel drab." He rolled up her sleeves to the elbow to disguise the fact that they ended short of his wrists. The knee-high tops of the slipper socks disguised the mid-shin end of the pants legs.

She cocked a brow. "What's the matter? Do you have a sneaking fear of being ordinary?"

He snorted, but Janna had been reading body language too long to listen to that instead of noticing the microscopic stiffening of his body. Could she have accidentally struck a nerve?

There was no time now to puzzle on Mama's psyche. She grimaced down at Doubrava's badge on her pocket. The lettering seemed printed in neon. "I wish we had a way to disguise these. If any of Geyer's Gorillas catch sight of them, we're lion meat."

"We'll go down singly, each with a different group. Realistically, only one of us needs to make it."

Janna sucked in a long breath. "You make it sound like a suicide mission."

"Who knows." He squinted gravely at her. "A man's been murdered in the course of whatever is going on here, remember."

She remembered. In her ear, officers searching pod D-1 reported their progress to Geyer. Cold bit into her spine. "Try to avoid being number two, okay?"

He grinned. "I didn't know you cared." Then he sobered. "Believe me, if I knew a way around the gauntlet, I'd take it, but we're stuck with that single corridor down."

Around? Did she really hear thunder or was it all in her head? "Mama!" She grabbed his arm. "There *is* a way around! Maybe. The escape tunnels."

He stared at her, eyes glittering. "Good thinking."

"Except...I'm not sure where the tunnels to Level Two are." Janna closed her eyes, straining to picture the station holo. The general shape etched itself clearly on the inside of her eyelids...solar panels, corridors, pods. The tunnels, however, shifted, attaching first to this pod, then that.

She hissed in exasperation at herself. A leo should be able to remember details.

"There's one from D-9," Mama said. "We're in D-3."

Janna jerked her eyes open to stare at him.

He shrugged. "Good eidetic memory. Now we just have to locate the entrance to the tunnel from this pod to D-6. As an emergency exit, it ought to be conspicuously marked."

"Still searching D-1. Negative," the radio murmured.

"Also commencing search of D-2," Doubrava's voice said.

Janna set her jaw. "We'd better find that hatch fast. They'll be in this pod any minute." Not to mention the fact that Geyer was probably watching all the monitors for this corridor.

Mama hit the door's control plate and putting on his glasses, peered out. "It's in Helen's Half Acre."

She edged in the opening above him. Sure enough, an exit sign glowed red above the entrance to the bar. "Cross your fingers no one locked up, Mama."

They dived into the corridor and with one hard pull at a railing, sent themselves rocketing toward the exit sign. Mama rapped the door plate. To Janna's relief, the opening dilated. They swung through into the darkness beyond.

As the door irised closed after them, an electronic signal beeped shrilly in Janna's ear. Geyer's voice snapped, "Code one thousand in D-3, just entering Helen's Half Acre."

Janna swore silently and swam hard for the exit sign visible at the far end of the bar. Her searching hands found no door beneath it, however, only a rough, raised, cone-shaped surface. "Damn it, Mama, where the hell is the hatch?" she hissed.

She felt him groping beside her in the darkness. "This is the volcano diorama, remember? It probably—yes, it's hinged."

The surface swung out like a door. Behind it, a dim light came on, showing them a round hatch with a wheel in the center. Janna wanted to whoop. At least there was no complicated system for opening it; it just dogged, like hatches on sea-going ships.

Mama spun the wheel. The bars withdrew smoothly. "Go on, bibi," he whispered as he pulled the door open.

She dived in. And choked. The air lay stale, dead, and cold with the lifeless chill of space. She kicked hurriedly for the far end, following a trail of small lights along the right-hand wall. Behind her the door clanged shut after Mama.

"They're using the escape tunnel to D-6," the radio hissed.

The line of lights stopped. Janna groped for the door and found a wheel like on the outside of the other door. Spinning it, however, she could only think: what if they came out into a room full of people?

"What light-wit told them about the tunnels?" Geyer demanded.

Doubrava did not answer, Janna noticed.

The door opened into a short branch corridor. Beyond lay a grid of corridors minus floors and ceilings, canyons with door-pierced cliffs that reached from the top of the pod to its bottom. Janna had followed Doubrava through identical canyons on the way to his quarters. This must be another personnel quarters pod.

"They're in D-6," the radio snapped. "Doubrava, put a guard on the entrance to the other tunnel and the pod door. Hebrera, bring up the sleeper."

Janna swore bitterly. "Mama, I don't think we're going to make it. We don't even know where the other tunnel is."

He bared his teeth. "Let's ask directions." Unlike the main corridors, the pod had no activity. The only person Janna saw was a young woman in an orange-checked coverall coming out of a door up the cliff-like wall from them. "Excuse me," Mama called up to her. "Will you come with us to the D-6/D-9 escape tunnel right away? It's very important."

She swooped down to glance at their badges. "Sure. What's happening?"

"No time to explain. We have to hurry."

Swimming rapidly, the Maintenance tech led the way down an intersecting canyon across the pod.

"Ian, damn it, hurry."

"We're almost there."

Three blue uniforms shot around a far corner. Ahead, Janna spotted the red glow of a sign and a circular hatch in the bulkhead.

Mama hurled past the Maintenance tech toward it. "Stay here," he told her, and spun the door wheel.

Janna slid by her, too. "There are three more officers coming up the corridor. Go tell them the situation is under control, will you?"

Blinking in curiosity and puzzlement, the tech turned away. Mama jerked open the tunnel door and the two of them plunged into more chilly dark and stale air.

"You think we can find the down tunnel before the gorillas head us off?" Janna panted.

His breath hissed beside her. "It's at the point where they could build the shortest possible tunnel, so it'll be on the bottom of the pod, and—"

"Any available officer, guard the D-9/D-12 tunnel."

"And since Geyer apparently hasn't guessed where we're headed," he resumed, "we may just be able to stay ahead of her, despite her monitors."

The guide lights stopped. They burst out of the far end of the tunnel into more staff quarters and dived down through deserted canyon corridors. Blue flashed above them near the entrance end of the pod. They slid into a cross-canyon out of the officer's sight.

"There," Mama whispered.

The tunnel entrance lay directly below them.

"Doubrava, twenty-one nineteen."

Janna exchanged frowns with Mama. If Geyer was using the Ten Signals, she wanted Doubrava to call the office. Because she had orders she would not risk over the radio where their quarry could hear? "We'd better hurry."

No one interfered as they opened the tunnel, however. On the chance that Geyer had somehow managed to lose track of them on her monitors, they dogged the hatch behind them.

The other end of the tunnel opened into a corridor in a laboratory pod. A young oriental woman blinked in surprise at them, but after reading their badges, nodded a greeting. They smiled back and swam past her toward the pod entrance.

Janna listened to the radio. Geyer was ordering all officers but those in D-9 back to other work. She raised at brow at Mama. Could they really have managed to escape? "Where does your eidetic memory tell you the nearest tunnel to Level Three is?"

"The pod below this one, but, bibi,"—his forehead creased—"on the holo that tunnel and the other one both end blind. If we're wrong about construction down there, we could open the far end and find ourselves breathing vacuum."

Janna's gut knotted. She sucked in a long, slow breath, debating. Should they risk it? With Geyer shaken off their tails, maybe they could go back to the core corridor. Only, traffic to Level Three had been much lighter on the monitors than that to Level Two. It would be more difficult to slip through with someone else. "Vacuum won't kill us instantly. We can just shut the hatch again."

"If we let pressure equalize first...and if the rush of air leaving the tunnel hasn't carried us out with it."

She bit her lip. "What do you think?"

"I'm thinking of a number. Is it odd or even?"

She stared. "What?"

"Am I thinking of an odd or even number?"

"What the hell does that have to do with—even." What a hell of a time to be playing games!

"Right. We go."

"I see, a decision based on cool logic." She shivered.

They left the pod cautiously, checking the corridor in both directions. No two-toned blue uniforms appeared among the thinning traffic, however. No one looked their way at all. On the radio, officers in D-9 reported a negative search of the pod. Using deliberate haste Janna and Mama dropped down into the pod entrance on the bottom of the corridor. Signs inside guided them to the tunnel.

Janna undogged the hatch and swung it open without hesitation, but once inside, following Mama and the guide lights through the suffocating air and darkness, her gut knotted. Did they dare open the far hatch?

She felt Mama hesitate ahead. In her mind's eye, his hands froze on the wheel. "Odd or even, bibi?" he asked softly.

Jesus. She swallowed. "Odd."

Metal slid against metal as he turned the wheel. "Find somewhere to anchor yourself."

Her fingers wrapped tightly around the tubing carrying the guide light wires. She held her breath.

Mama swung open the door.

Light and warmth and fresh air flooded in.

The flood of relief left Janna limp. Shakily, she released the tubing and pulled herself out of the tunnel.

"Welcome to Level Three," Geyer's voice said above them.

Janna looked up. A dozen blue uniforms hovered against the bulkhead there, one with the bullhorn-shaped sleeper pointed straight at Mama and her. It was the pod that made her stare, however. Though she had not know quite what to expect, it had not been this, the canyon corridors of living quarters. "Will you tell us what the hell's going on?"

"That's restricted information," Geyer said

"She doesn't need to tell us, bibi," Mama said. "I think the answer is obvious now. It's revolution."

20

February 5. 22:50:00 hours.

Revolution! Janna stared at Mama.

"That's absurd," Geyer said coolly, and tapped her ear. "Nineteen, tell Fontana I have them."

Absurd? Above Janna, the stiffening of several other officers belied that.

Mama said, "Is it? We have a space station actively recruiting personnel to whom Earth and gravity are frustrating and limiting, and picking very carefully, very selectively over the temporary staff members who apply for permanent assignment. The permanent staff talk about people on Earth as though speaking of another species and all have knowledge in secondary disciplines, either biological or technological. Your greenhouses are bursting with home-grown food. You're pushing your biologists to develop sources of protein. Level Three construction has restricted access. All construction is censored from calls and mail, construction that turns out to be at least partially living quarters. Add to that the company president whose pet project is this station just walking away from a proxy fight that will lose him control of the company and the station. Except that he's coming here for a visit first, and that news not only generates a great deal of activity but leads to the temporary staff being put in custody. For deportation?"

Geyer's eyes narrowed. "You're quite a creative thinker, just as Lieutenant Vradel warned me. Maybe dangerously creative. Brainbent."

Janna watched the others, particularly Doubrava, who hovered slightly behind and above his chief, grinning in delight. Mama might be brainbent, she reflected, but he was not wrong. When she added up his list, she reached the same conclusion. "Tenning isn't walking away at all, at least not from anything he cares about. You've reached the point of self-sufficiency and he's joining you for the declaration of independence."

"No doubt bringing along families of permanent personnel," Mama added. "That's who these quarters are for."

"They're both very good, Bane," Doubrava said. "Why not tell them? What harm can it do?"

She spun to look up at him. "Harm! You're a fine one to talk about harm." She turned back to Janna and Mama. "Let's go."

An officer with a Mohawk haircut, the same officer they met at the security point below Level One that first day, gestured with the sleeper toward a circle of light at the bottom of the canyon.

Janna remained clinging to the door of the escape tunnel, staring past the sleeper toward Geyer and Doubrava. "No wonder all of you seemed guilty. You are. There's one who's guiltier than the rest, though...a killer."

Doubrava looked back unflinchingly, but Geyer's mouth clamped in a grim line. "I said, let's go. Keep the sleeper on them, Hebrera."

Janna swam ahead of the officer with the sleeper, down through the pod—another torus, she saw—and into the Level Three corridor. They reached the core corridor minutes later. Personnel there took one look at the sleeper and flattened against the side of the shaft, leaving a broad path for prisoners and captors all the way to Level One, where Geyer motioned them into the blue B corridor.

"Attention," the P.A. said. "Estimated time of shuttle arrival, fifteen minutes."

The Security officers grinned in excitement. "It'll be over soon."

"Just beginning, actually," Geyer said with a thin smile

"Nineteen Chief," Janna's ear button murmured. "Director requests you bring the leos to his office."

"You come, too, Ian," Geyer said. "The rest of you go back to your stations. There'll just be two of us with you, leos, but don't try anything, or by god I swear I'll break your damn necks."

Janna believed her.

The four of them left the corridor at the Administration pod.

Fontana waited for them in his office, a questioning light in the amber wolf's eyes. Earth shone across the ceiling in majestic, dazzling beauty.

Geyer sighed. "They reached Level Three, and I'm afraid they've figured some of it out."

Fontana shrugged. "No matter. They'll be on one of the shuttles soon and out of our way."

"On a shuttle? To Earth?" Janna asked in surprise.

Fontana looked surprised in turn. "Of course. You're going back along with the temporary staff who declined our invitation to stay, or whom we haven't chosen to invite along."

"Along?" Mama said. "You're leaving orbit?"

Doubrava grinned. "They're *very* good."

Geyer frowned, but Fontana nodded. "They are. Yes, sergeant, we're leaving orbit. Part of the construction is a drive system we've developed. We're going to set up our factory and mining operations out where the resources are, the asteroid belt. This station was planned with the intention of expanding it from a research facility to include a factory/colony, but the board of directors refused to let us move on to that phase. Too much too fast, they said. Too expensive. Not cost effective."

"So you and Tenning expanded secretly," Mama said.

He nodded. "Unfortunately, certain board members became suspicious of where some of the corporation funds were being spent, and a showdown became inevitable. Crispus decided we'd better pick up our marbles and leave the game."

Ginneh Nakashima stuck her head in through the door. "Mr. Tenning's shuttle is docking, Mr. Fontana."

Fontana grinned. "The hour of liberation is at hand."

Anger boiled up through Janna. "It's a wonderful game to you, isn't it? No harm done?"

Fontana's grin faded. "I've tried to keep it to a minimum."

"Murder is an acceptable minimum?"

The wolf's eyes narrowed. "That was accidental. It wouldn't have happened if I'd known ahead of time that was how D—how the spider plans were to be smuggled out."

Cold sank into Janna's spine. In changing the sentence, Fontana had glanced quickly, almost imperceptibly, toward Ian Doubrava.

Doubrava? She stared into the turquoise eyes, her stomach jerking into a tight knot, followed by a flood of ice and fire. "You?" Her voice rasped. "*You* killed Chenoweth?"

The brilliant eyes met hers calmly, devoid of guilt or remorse. "He found out more about Level Three than temporaries are supposed to know. With his mouth it was just a matter of time before he said something in front of the wrong people and gave everything away. Besides, he wasn't much of a loss. A very unpleasant toad and insulting toward my commanding officer."

The anger burned deeper in Janna, anger against Doubrava's cold-bloodedness, anger at herself for not seeing what he was…a sociopath.

Mama's eyes narrowed. "You were part of the station plans and still spying for Uwezo?"

"I'd found out about the plans, of course, but I wasn't part of them until Bane found the secret cameras I'd planted in the labs and the director here persuaded me to join The Cause. By that time I'd already told Uwezo about the spider. I stalled as long as I could but I had to deliver it, with the smuggling looking genuine and no convenient leaks in security, to keep the bright, ambitious people who run

Uwezo from becoming suspicious and using their other sources in Lanour to poke around. The Lanour account I funneled all my credit into to help with the construction here isn't so obscure that they couldn't find it and learn what we're up to."

Then the long calls about stock were a code after all, Janna reflected angrily. How like the arrogance of a sociopath to risk suggesting that to her and Mama, sure they would never take him seriously, or break the code if they *did* suspect him. But how had Uwezo paid him? The security check on him would have found any unaccountable source of income.

A moment later the answer came to her. Of course. The stock portfolio. No doubt the first payment had been barter goods like jewelry or precious metals, to redeem for credit and start the portfolio. After that Uwezo could use its spies in other corporations to learn tips they passed on to their librarian agent, who then helped Doubrava grow rich on perfectly legitimate investments Uwezo's name could not be linked to. The African multinational had to be congratulated for setting up its agent so far ahead of time, and for finding such a good agent, too...witty and charming, and unable to look guilty because he lacked any conscience to make him feel guilt.

Janna said, "So you believe that the end justifies the means when it concerns your station colony, Mr. Fontana?"

Fontana grimaced. "Believe me, neither Chief Geyer nor I suspected how Doubrava intended to smuggle the plans out. We were shocked and enraged when you told us Chenoweth had been murdered. Up to then we thought the only trickery had been the planting of that false report recording in the phone lines with a timer so he would have an excuse for leaving Officer Begay alone to fumble the exit examination of the body."

"Yet you still did nothing after you'd learned about him."

"What *could* I do? Legally I'm an accomplice and as guilty as he is." Fontana glanced at Doubrava, who studied the image of Earth on the ceiling, ignoring the conversation. "It's better he come with us anyway, where he can't do any more harm."

"Just betray you just as he's betrayed Uwezo if it's to his own benefit," Janna said flatly. "Sociopaths are like that."

Doubrava pulled his gaze away from the ceiling to smile at her. "Sociopaths burn out. Dr. Freeman says that's happening to me, that I want to come in and join the human race. It's how Mr. Fontana recruited me, by offering me a home."

Janna ignored him to keep frowning at Fontana. "This is the kind of person you want in your colony?"

Fontana sighed. "Sometimes there's no choice. I'll be responsible for him, sergeant. If he kills again, we'll deal with it."

Nakashima looked in again. "Mr. Tenning is disembarking."

Relief swept the director's face. "I'll go right up to meet him. Chief Geyer, will you see our guests safely aboard the shuttle? I've had their luggage packed and sent up to the loading area." He smiled at Mama and Janna. "Sergeant Maxwell, Sergeant Brill, I'm sorry y'all had to be dragged into this. Have a pleasant flight back. Oh, Sergeant Maxwell, we're shipping Lanour our research results and all the catalysts and drugs we've produced, a two-year supply of some, but I'd be mighty grateful if you'd see these other items are delivered groundside?" From a compartment in his desk he brought out a shoebox-sized carton and handed it to Mama.

Then he pushed off around them, out of the office.

"Let's go, too," Geyer said.

Doubrava smiled. "Good-bye. I'm sorry about how things ended because it's really been a pleasure to meet you." He held out his hand.

Janna ignored it and sailed past him for the door.

In the core corridor they swam upward past a stream of men, women, and children coming down, eyes wide in awe. She ignored them, too, and the dazed looking temporary staff who pulled themselves into shuttle with her.

Geyer saw them to their seats and belted in. "I—I wish I could say it's been a pleasure, too, but I won't lie. I hope you'll believe me when I say I regret that we didn't meet under other circumstances. I do admire you both, despite the trouble you've caused me. You didn't let yourselves be intimidated or side-tracked. You're the kind of officers my father would have been proud to work with." She smiled at Mama. "Perhaps we'll meet again someday."

Mama sighed as the golden woman disappeared up through the hatch. "If Providence is kind..."

"They're getting away with murder, Mama," Janna said bitterly.

He turned his head to peer through his glasses at her. "Does that really upset you so much, or is it that you liked him and he betrayed you by not being what you thought he was?"

"Don't be a lightwit, Maxwell!" But the remark stung.

As though sensing that, he smiled. "Let's face it, bibi, we're both unlucky in love. We still have each other, though." He patted her hand.

She grimaced. "Is that supposed to be a consolation?"

"Casting off," a voice said from the top of the cabin.

As the shuttle slid away from the station, Janna stared out the port at it, a bubbly black silhouette floating against the blue-and-white glory of Earth.

Anger hissed through Janna. "It isn't right, Mama."

"No. Still, sometimes we've let criminals go, like the slighs who jacked that hearse, to go after bigger ones?"

She jerked around to glare at him. "My god. This isn't anything like that. What bigger crime can we possibly go after than a killer?"

"Well." His eyes glittered. "I just took a peek into this carton and there's a bunch of envelopes just about the size to hold an octodensity minidisk, each addressed to a different corporation. I don't recognize all the names, but they're international and the ones I do know are involved in aerospace."

She stared at him. Her breath caught. "The spider?"

He grinned. "I wouldn't be surprised, and maybe plans for the propulsion system, too. Uwezo will have only a couple of weeks start on them and no drive. Now if some corporation sets up a monopoly out there, it won't be by default." His grin broadened, teeth gleaming in the darkness of his face. "I think we're about to see a race, bibi, first for platform space, because I doubt the spider will work in a gravity field, and then to the asteroids, and we're elected to fire the starting gun. All the colonial moratoriums and exit tax extortion of Senators Early and Thayers' campaigns will collapse. Maybe the spider can even make colony ships affordable to slighs. I can see a host of applications for spider-woven products Earthside, too. How about for low-income housing modules? In the long run, everyone will benefit." He paused. "Is that a reasonable trade for one murderer?"

Janna debated, staring out the port at the shrinking station. "No."

"Yet you accuse *me* of clinging to idealism." Mama shook his head. "Admit it, bibi; deep down you, too, still think you can save the world from itself."

"I ought to be able to save a few people from a murderer," she said bitterly.

"Not this time, bibi. One bad guy has won and we just have to live with it." Mama cleared his throat. "Speaking of living with…it occurs to me that I still have a housing problem facing me when we land. Now you have an empty bed you let me use the other night…"

"What!" She stiffed so abruptly she strained at the seatbelt holding her. "No! Do you see me wearing a sign that says 'stupid'? I'd be over the brainbow in a week!"

"How about just until I find another place then? I'm a top star cook."

"I'm more concerned about your housekee—" she began, but broke off as she glanced out the window. The space station had shrunk to a knobby dot. Watching it vanish into the glowing blue of its Earth backdrop, she reflected that a man could have worse faults than Mama's. "All right. I'm probably wickers. I'm sure I'll regret this for years to come, but...you can stay at my place until you find an apartment."

He grinned.

"*Just* until you find another place."

"Absolutely."

"You have to promise me you won't go around straightening things all the time."

"Word of honor, bibi.

And I have this seaside property on Mercury I'll let you have cheap, Janna thought wryly. What the hell, though. She could take it for a while. Partners had to stick together.

Dragon's Teeth

1

It had to be the most tensely awaited case assignment of the year...with every investigator in the Crimes Against Persons squad praying for it to go to someone else.

Bad enough that the night before, during the cocktail hour before the Democratic Party fund-raiser dinner, seven men, six armed with needlers carrying explosive needles, had entered the Rotunda Ballroom of the Capitol Sheraton and stripped the guests of all their valuables...guests who included many of the city's richest and most influential citizens.

Worse, though, was a fact newscanner stories overlooked but which affected leos—law enforcement officers. Pass-the-Word Morello, the squad clerk, knew, however, as always, and gleefully informed the day watch as they reported for rollcall, that two of the victims had been the wife and ex-governor father-in-law of Thomas Paget, director of the Shawnee County Police Department.

Mentally counting her current cases, Sergeant Janna Brill swore. The arrests for the Maguiers rape and the Cobb hit-and-run left her with just two. Two. Lieutenant Hari Vradel, the squad commander, standing up there with a printout detailing all current cases, would know that.

"Kazakevicious and Cardarella," Vradel said.

Janna sighed in relief.

"Take Brill and Maxwell's current cases so they can concentrate on this robbery."

Janna snapped her notebook shut. "I just cut you off my Christmas card list, Lieutenant."

One corner of his mustache twitched up. "Cruz and Singer work on it, too."

Groans came from the far end of the squadroom.

He shook his head. "Such enthusiasm. Cruz, give your cases to Agosta and Yoo. Statements and stolen property lists are on the table in the first interview room. Feel free to start on them now."

Janna shoved her notebook in the stash pocket of a thigh boot and followed her colleagues to the interview room.

"I don't need this," Daniel Singer sighed as he closed the door behind them. His broad shoulders sagged. Even his rusty mustache and the yellow stripes in his jumpsuit sagged. "I've got a partner who spends our days off trying to kill me in choppers and airships, a sister so pregnant she looks like she's going to give my partner a whole litter of little Cruzes, and a cohab who's hinting she wants a marriage contract. I don't need the third floor looking over my shoulder."

His partner Emile Cruz—gray-eyed and dishwater blond despite his name—grinned. "Don't worry; these jons had to be off their ticks, riffing high muckies. Wickerticks make mistakes."

Janna hoped so. She did not need this aggravation, either, not on a day that had already begun with the April monsoons resuming in time for the weekend and her barely making roll call because her conscience would not let her leave the house until her partner was up. The man did not sleep; he went comatose. When was he going to find another place of his own? It had been almost three months since she offered him the temporary use of her other bedroom. The couple downstairs had not helped her humor, hurling insults and household objects at each other all night, and then having the balls to pound on the ceiling complaining about the noise *she* made knocking on the bedroom door that morning.

The cross in her life appeared undaunted by the assignment, however. He grinned even more broadly than Cruz, teeth bright in the dutch chocolate darkness of his face. "Look at it this way, Singer. It's our chance to mix company with castlerows instead of deeks and slimelife for a change."

Janna sighed. Yes, he would enjoy this case, Mahlon Sumner Maxwell being off his tick, too. Look at his nickname, Mama, and at *him*...standing even taller and bonier than her lanky hundred eighty-three centimeters, all arms, legs, and angles. He always had to be different. Why else would he wear the clothes he did—today a bodysuit and tabard in a harlequin pattern of fluorescent green and orange—insist on correcting his myopia with cumbersome glasses instead of practical contact lenses, and pride himself on being egg bald when almost every other leo in the department wore a conservative hair style such as a braid down the neck or a mane of tight curls like her own smoky-blonde hair.

"Jan and I are excited, right, bibi?" he asked.

She rolled her eyes. "Let's just get to work and see what we're dealing with."

"Starting with visual aids." With a flourish Mama dug under his tabard and brought out a video chip case.

The rest of them stared. "What's that?"

"A copy of one of the video chips the media videographers at the fund-raiser turned over to Criminalistics for enhancement. While you were racing up the stairs to be on time for roll call, bibi, I went by the lab and talked them into a temporary loan of this."

That explained why he came in ten minutes later than she had when they had arrived at Headquarters together.

"How'd you know there'd be chips in the lab?" Cruz asked. "And why did you want one?"

He shrugged. "Well, I glimpsed Paget's wife on the newscanner story last night and—"

Janna blinked. "You what!"

"—knowing how light our caseload is right now, I thought there might be a chance we—"

She stiffened. "You *what*!" The son of a bitch! "And you didn't *say* anything!"

Singer blocked her lunge for Mama's throat. "Take him apart in the gym after the shift."

"Meanwhile, that chip is hard to watch in your hand, Maxwell," Cruz said.

Mama grinned. "I borrowed the solution to that, too." A circle around Janna took him out the interview room door where a minute later he came back carrying a small video chip player.

She had wondered why he came into the squadroom carrying his trench coat bundled under his arm instead of draped over it in careful folds. He wanted to hide the player until the dramatic moment for producing it. Mama may have switched from theater arts to criminal justice and law in college but he had never given up Theater.

"It's showtime." He flipped up the viewscreen of the player, shook the chip out of the case labeled: *Station KADN, Wichita*, and pushed the metal edge into the chip slot in the player's front.

After an initial flurry of static, the screen cleared to reveal the camera panning a room filled with people, people glittering with jewelry and wrapped in color. Beyond them, photomuraled walls replicated one level of the statehouse rotunda...pillars, corridor entrances, statuary, and historical murals. Janna started to count the number of entrances their perpetrators had, only to realize that the photomural completely hid them.

Presently, however, doors appeared. One of the red-white-and-blue jacketed waiters slid back a panel in the middle of the wall to the camera's left, revealing a glimpse of round tables set up for the banquet. Other waiters and a number of waitrons, robotic waiters, glided in and out through a second door obviously connected to a service corridor behind the ballroom. Like the waitrons delivering orders in bars and fast food restaurants, the cylindrical service robots had broad bases, though they stood twice as tall as their cousins, nearly two meters, their brass-colored shafts pierced by a scattering of sensor openings and girdled by three shelves in place of carrying a single tray on top.

"Anyone see the main doors?" she asked.

They appeared as the camera panned, two pairs of double doors standing open to reveal a piece of lobby/corridor outside.

"So unless there are other doors we haven't seen, our jons have three ways in," Singer said.

All of which should be guarded. No one held an event like this without security.

The camera continued panning, zooming in for close-ups of notables, occasionally catching other videographers circulating through with crowd, the little cvc camera headsets down over one eye giving them the appearance of cyborgs. Janna spotted Haley Jubelt, the Director's father-in-law, and Senator Andrew Docking, home from Washington, easily identified even from the back by the prominent ears voters found so endearing.

"Quite a fashion show," Mama said.

Janna shook her head. Trust him to notice clothes...though he was right of course. For a formal occasion like this the men all wore tuxedos...breeches tucked into ankle boots and the high-necked tunics divided diagonally across the front, the upper section silver, gold, or opalescent white, the lower section the same bright color as the breeches and rest of the tunic. Scarlet or turquoise blue appeared to be the popular colors this year. The women wore a whole spectrum of colors and fabrics in all styles and lengths.

Then Janna caught herself. Damn! He had her doing it, too. "Just fastscan to where the riff starts!"

Movement became a frantic scurry. She watched, frowning. Three doors, all guarded, or supposed to be. The perpetrators must have come in as legitimate guests. The number of castlerows and public figures here could be expected to make the guards hesitant about giving anyone more than a polite patdown at the door, making it entirely possible to wear in a gun.

So did that bulge under a tunic represent a needler, or just a waistline spread by good living?

"Who's handling the security?" Mama asked.

Obviously the same thoughts had occurred to Cruz, who was scanning the reports even before Mama's question. "Beria Security has the contract to supply the hotel with security equipment and—"

"Maxwell!" Singer yelped.

On the screen the crowd had surged back from the center of the room.

Mama hit the backscan. When the recording started forward again, Cruz laid down the reports and the four of them concentrated on the screen. Janna watched hands in particular. The needlers ought to appear soon. She glanced at the counter on the player. Any second now.

The camera focused on a high-breasted woman in a shimmering lavender dress with a neckline plunging to the waist in front and a skirt slit to the hip on the side.

Cruz groaned. "Forget the bibi; we need a long shot of the entire room."

The camera lingered on the woman, however, zooming in on breasts threatening to slip out of the dress's precarious restraint.

Singer howled. "Pan, you lightwit toad! Pan!"

Too late. Above the roar of voices came the crash of breaking glass and a growing murmur of dismay. Janna swore. Now, finally, the camera pulled back its focus and swung in search of the commotion.

It found guests already in retreat, backing away from a ring of six scarlet-tuxed men braced with needlers held in two-handed grips. Except for their needlers and a gold hoop in one man's ear, the men looked conservative, unmemorable...average in height, weight, and coloring. They wore similar medium mustaches and hair short over the ears and caught in a pigtail at the nape of the neck.

In the center of their circle, oddly enough, stood a waitron. Its empty shelves and the glasses littering the carpet around it explained the breaking glass.

"Ladies and gentlemen, may I have your attention?" said a loud voice with a slight flatness of inflection. *The waitron*! "Quiet! Please."

Though less than a minute had passed since the first crash of glass, by now everyone had seen the needlers. The confused babble died into frightened silence.

The waitron's voice lowered to a more normal tone. "First, please notice that the hallway doors are closed. They are also locked. Don't attempt to leave. Mr. Salmas, the waiter in front of them, is with us. That said, I must ask that those of you with cameras shut them off and lay them on the floor."

"Clever," Mama said. "The waitron does all the talking. There are no voices to analyze and compare to suspect voices later."

A man on the front edge of the crowd scowled. "What the hell do—"

The nearest gunman aimed the long barrel of his weapon at the man's feet. Carpet exploded in a small geyser of gold fibers.

Janna ran a hand up her thigh boot, over the flat silhouette of the needler inside, and touched the Starke's butt with a stab of resentment. While the bad guys used explosive needles and old fashioned bullet shooters, the government muckies had decreed that to prevent "excessive force" and "the abuse of power" leos could carry only needles with paralyzing percurare.

Faces in the crowd went ashen. Another gunman aimed at a videographer.

"Lay the cameras down, please," the waitron repeated. "That was the only warning shot. The next needle will be aimed at someone's face or chest."

The screen went snowy.

Cruz sighed. "So much for real evidence. Now we have to rely on witnesses."

The statements all varied, sometimes wildly, but general facts remained constant. Some witnesses even managed real observations. The robbery began at 19:10 hours, according to one guest who noted the time while he still had a wrist chrono. Hotel personnel identified the waiter accomplice as one Cristo Salmas.

A statement read, "One of the waitrons started spinning around, throwing glasses everywhere. When it stopped and I looked up, there stood those men with needlers."

"After he locked the doors, the waiter handed plastic bags around," a woman's statement said. "The waitron ordered everyone to put all personal valuables into the bags and pass them forward. The waiter asked people for any vending or transport tokens we had, too."

Janna blinked. Tokens? How many tokens would there be in a room full of castlerows, who must rarely use public transport or the few other conveniences that could not be paid for with the Scib Card, that all-purpose social care/identification/bank card. Taking tokens seemed petty.

The woman's statement continued: "The waiter was a little taller than I am with slicked back auburn hair and the largest, reddest mustache I've ever seen. It looked like wings."

Another statement said, "The bags came forward. I was on the front row and when I'd dropped my chrono and a valuable sash pin in the bag, the waitron ordered me to put the bag in a hole in its side."

Still another statement read, "While the man next to me put his bag in the waitron, the gunman who moved aside for him came straight at me and stuck his needler almost in my eye. When I flinched, he grinned before backing away. Others threatened other people. They all seemed to enjoy it."

The riffers had left through the service door at the rear of the ballroom, the waiter leading, followed by the waitron, still surrounded by the gunmen. Hotel security reported that the security camera on a ground level service door out of the building malfunctioned at 19:18 hours and the door alarm had activated at 19:21 hours.

Singer looked up, frowning. "The guards claim they noticed nothing suspicious? What about the two in the service corridor? The riffers had to pass them."

Mama said, "I have their statements. 'A waiter with a huge red mustache came out of the ballroom. He tripped just after he rounded the corner past us and fell flat on his face. My partner and I helped him up and he went through the door to the stairs. Then this waitron came by and damned if *it* didn't go into the stairs, too. I never knew waitrons could use stairs. I'd have gone to watch it but just then someone came tearing out of the ballroom yelling for us."

Singer pursed his lips. "Would there be time enough for the gunmen to slip out while the guards had their backs turned helping Salmas?"

Cruz snorted. "Six men? No, the guards had to be in on it. Something else, too." He pawed through the stack of statements. "Here it is...a statement by hotel security. After the riff they played back the recordings from all the door cameras and none of them showed any men of our riffers' descriptions leaving. They had to go out that service door with the disabled camera."

"At least they made a mistake coming in. Being guests means names of some kind are on the door list."

They thumbed through the printouts. Mama came up with the guest and victim lists. He handed them to Singer. "You'd think they'd be aware of the door list and plan for it. I'm wondering how they brought guns past the guards. Did you see the poor fit of their tuxes? Obvious cheap rentals. The guards had to see that, too, and showing up at this kind of affair looking like an outsider means an automatic thorough search."

"The carry went into the waitron. Maybe the guns came out of it," Janna said.

Singer groaned.

"Found something, Dan?" Cruz asked.

"A problem. There are just five more names on the door list than on the victim list. Three are marked 'no show' and two have noted: 'left—will return.'"

Mama tapped the reports into a precise stack, folded down the VC player's screen, and returned the chip to its case. "So our riffers entered unrecorded into an area with front and rear entrances guarded. Maybe more hotel staff than Salmas are involved. We'd better check out both the hotel and security personnel."

Janna dug in the cache pocket inside her thigh boots for a vending token. "Let's flip for it."

Cruz and Singer won Beria. Janna and Mama headed for the hotel. She could hardly believe the vehicle they used, however...an Ashanti, low and broad and so aerodynamic that even crouched on its parking rollers it seemed to be hurtling toward the sound barrier. "Since when does the department own a car like this?"

Mama grinned. "It's a loaner for an undercover operation that just ended. It goes back to the dealer tomorrow, but Perera thought we'd enjoy driving it today."

Successfully defending Sergeant Angel Perera's uniformed daughter against disciplinary action last month had made the usually dour motor pool chief her partner's devoted buddy. A situation with its rewards. Department cars were Datsun-Ford and Chrysler road cars, all dependable workhorses but without flash. Unlike the Ashanti.

The Ashanti had no radio, of course. Only their ear button radios and the built-in transponders let Dispatch communicate with them and track Mama's and her positions.

Janna's ear button muttered: "Alpha Cap Eleven, see a Mr. Tarl Braman, 1314 Kansas, reference vandalism of after-hours shopper keypad."

The deluge outside did not faze the Ashanti, which sailed smoothly, even through the spray and turbulence kicked up by the big airfoil fans of the buses and trucks on Topeka Avenue. Janna did not envy the drivers of the light little runabouts around her, though. At least with this weather the bicycles lanes were almost empty.

"It's interesting," Mama said. "Historically, countries entering the world market have competed first with low-priced mass market goods. But the African nations are specializing in limited-production luxury items. I wonder if it's the example they saw set by the diamond industry when Whites had the power there."

"Capitol, Beta Cap Seven," Dispatch murmured in her ear button, "investigate report of runabout driving through yards in area from Jewell to Boswell between fifteenth and the Washburn Campus. No license number. R.P. thinks vehicle is possibly an Hitachi Bonsai or Chrysler Elf."

The arch of the skyway from the Sheraton to the grounds of the Expocentre across the avenue appeared ahead. Mama swung the Ashanti left on the turn light and set it down under covered entrance at the front doors.

Inside the hotel a plant-filled atrium made a jungle of the lobby. An attractive Afro-Asian woman commanding the register of the restaurant off the atrium gave Mama directions to the ballrooms and he started across the atrium for a broad corridor beyond it.

"Shouldn't we be asking the way to the personnel office?" Janna asked.

Mama shook his trench coat into careful folds and laid it over his arm. Where had he found one in such a brilliant shade of scarlet? It made her and her gray one fade into near invisibility. "There's something I want to check first."

The corridor stretched back through the building, flanked on the left by a sunken bar in another atrium and on the right by meeting rooms and wide stairs leading downward. At the far end, doors led to a rear parking area and another corridor intersecting on the right beyond broad double doors. Along its thickly carpeted, wood-paneled length they found a coatroom, rest rooms, and the Rotunda and Konza Ballrooms.

Mama pointed back at the double doors. "That has to be where the front guards were."

She agreed. There they could control access and check identification, yet let guests move freely once past the entry point. Call the distance fifteen to twenty meters from the ballroom doors.

"Go back to the doors," he said. "Let's see how much they could hear." When she reached the doors he spread his arms and launched into a new song by Heylen's Comet. "'You ask do I think you're beautiful...'"

Whatever else about Mama might frustrate and irritate her, his singing never did. He sang beautifully, his voice the rich, trained product of theater arts classes. However, now Janna heard little more than a whisper, even with her ear button tapped off to reduce interference.

"That's enough," she called. Her own voice fell short around her, swallowed by the carpeting and acoustical ceiling. She tapped her ear button back on and joined him by the ballroom doors. "A small bomb could have gone off in there without the guards here hearing it."

"Now let's see about the pair in back."

Janna tried the doors. Locked. They returned to the main corridor and a door marked: *Employees Only* that opened into a service hallway.

The base leg of the T-shaped hallway ran down behind the ballrooms, with the elongated crossbar servicing small meeting rooms and connecting to the service elevator, stairs, and kitchen. Tile replaced carpeting here and sprayed vinyl the wood paneling. However, the hallway had an acoustical ceiling and acoustical backing on the doors, and the tile gave under Janna's boots with a familiar resilience she felt every day in the hallways at headquarters...shock and sound absorbent semicolloidal tile.

Standing at the corner, Mama said, "This is where I'd station guards."

Janna nodded. That point controlled access to the service area behind the ballrooms and commanded an unobstructed view of all the entrances along the other leg. Like the door guards, those here had the excuse of distance and poor acoustics for not being aware what was happening in the ballroom, but the riffers should not have been able to walk unchallenged past them.

Mama headed down the service hall to the Rotunda Ballroom door. Janna followed. Together they stood studying the hallway. Mama pointed at a long, shallow alcove stretching most of the way behind both ballrooms on the rear side of the hallway. "What if the gunmen ducked in there until the guards went into the ballroom, then rabbited?"

Equipment for the ballrooms filled the greater part of the storage space: stacks of chairs and round tables with legs folded, rectangular platform sections, speaker's stands, and two idle waitrons.

Janna eyed it. "They'd be gambling the guards wouldn't look that direction."

"Not really." Mama pushed his glasses up his nose. "They knew the guards' attention would be focused on the ballroom." He frowned. "They pulled this off with split second timing. Every move had a purpose. So I wonder why they disconnected the door camera. The alarm alone would reveal which exit they used. Help me with one of these." Moving across the hall he caught one of the waitrons by its upper shelf and tipped the robot sideways.

She held the waitron at a 45 degree angle while he dropped his trench coat and knelt down to peer at the robot's bottom. It weighed less than she expected, brass-colored plastic and not metal. "What are you looking for?"

"How it moves." He prodded underneath. "Like that guard, I've never heard of a waitron using stairs."

Janna considered the idea, then shrugged. "There's no reason they couldn't. The department swatbots do."

"How many waitrons are built like swatbots?" He sat back on his heels, pushing his glasses up his nose. "This one isn't. The treads aren't flexible enough to climb anything more than a shallow riser."

She raised a brow. "Meaning they used their own custom model and didn't just reprogram one of the hotel's." That gave them another lead. "They had to bring it into the hotel somehow. We can check the hotel records to see who made what kind of deliveries this past week." She righted the waitron. "After we check on hotel per—"

"May I help you?" a steel-edged voice asked.

They turned around to face a lean man whose coppery skin and high cheekbones suggested Amerind ancestry. "I'm Captain Keleman, chief of hotel security," he said, and when they showed their identification, added, "I'm always happy to assist the police…when asked."

Mama smiled as though not hearing the reproof. "Thank you. We need directions to the personnel office. I'm also curious if anyone's determined yet how our riffers disabled the door camera."

One of the other man's brows rose. *You don't know*? his expression said. "My office sent out a service tech last night while your Criminalistics people were still here. He found a timed charge on that camera's wiring inside the hotel. What's left of the device should be at your crime lab."

His obvious satisfaction at knowing more than the "real" leos sent a flash of irritation through Janna. She pushed it aside to focus on what he said. Timed charge? First they had the waitron and now something else which needed technical know-how, and not only for building the device but familiarity with both the hotel layout and the security system to know where to plant it. Salmas might have given all the necessary information to the engineer, of course, and been given the charge and timer with instructions where and how to set it. Of the group as they knew it so far, the waiter was the one who could come and go in the hotel without arousing suspicion.

"How do employees enter?" she asked.

Keleman folded his arms. "One rear door is equipped with a biometric lock programmed to clock in employees as they enter, making it mandatory that they enter through that door. Employees insert their Scib Cards in the card slot, which activates the retinal scanner. On confirmation of the retinal pattern, the door opens and records the employee's entrance. The lock is programmed to open only for authorized personnel and only at the time of their shift."

"That sounds secure," Mama said. "How long have the guards who worked security for the fund-raiser been assigned to the hotel?"

Keleman's eyes narrowed. "You think one of them was involved in the robbery? Beria chooses its personnel carefully. We run a background check as extensive as the one your police candidates undergo. And our officers are bonded."

"Can we afford not to check them out anyway?" Mama asked.

The security chief eyed him for a moment, then said abruptly, "They aren't assigned to the hotel; they work only special assignments, such as the fund-raiser. The personnel office is up the steps by the front desk and to the left." He wheeled and strode away.

A little pouter pigeon of a woman superintended Personnel. She moved like a bird, too, in staccato steps and gestures.

Handing back their identification, she fluttered over to the computer. "You've set yourself quite a task, investigating all our employees."

"Yes, ma'am." Janna grimaced. "To make it easier, we'll start with just those on duty last night."

In her ear the radio murmured: "Capitol, Beta Cap Fourteen. Investigate 10-97 at 812 Hampton, upstairs apartment. R.P. advises one co-husband is threatening the other with a knife."

The pouter pigeon pecked at the keyboard. "I can give you the names and addresses of the hotel employees. That doesn't include anyone working up in Diversions, however. The club is independently managed. You can probably disregard its employees anyway. They're all under close surveillance, and not just the dealers and croupiers…also the barmaids and barboys."

That figured. "The club doesn't want to miss collecting its commission on any tricks the boys and girls turn."

The pouter pigeon looked up at Janna, eyes piercing as a hawk's. "Why should it, when it's paying for the house license?" She punched a key and the printer hummed to life. Frowning at the pages feeding out the top, she went on, "Mr. Salmas is not the most sterling of employees but I'm surprised that he's involved in this robbery."

Janna saw Mama regarding the woman with interest. "You know him?"

She shrugged. "I know his employment record. While it is one of intermittent lateness and absenteeism—though to his credit, Mr. Salmas is apparently efficient enough on the job—it seems to me inconsistent that he would call in sick yesterday afternoon if he were planning that robbery."

"Called in sick?" Mama frowned thoughtfully.

Janna said, "He came to work."

The plump hands fluttered impatiently. "Yes, yes. That's because he called back about fifteen minutes later and said he thought he could make it after all. Why would he make the first call if he was one of the thieves?"

"Why indeed?" Mama said. Behind his glasses his eyes gleamed. As soon as the printer stopped he scooped up the hard copy and headed for the door. "You've been very helpful. Thank you very much. Come on, bibi, we've got to go."

"Go where, and why the hurry?" She stretched her legs to keep up with him back through the hotel and out to the car.

"1930 Makepeace Road."

The Soldier Creek area? "What's there?"

"Salmas's house."

She slid the car door closed and settled back under the safety harness. "Salmas? You really expect him to be fool enough to be there?"

"Call it a hunch."

The speed of their run north had to trip every automatic speed monitor along the way, but they arrived in the Soldier Creek area in one piece. The house at 1930 Makepeace, a modest duplex, sat in a clipped, now soggy, yard. Mama did not knock at the door but walked around the house, peering through the windows. He checked the thumb latch on each.

Janna huddled in her trench coat and glanced over her shoulder. Maybe the downpour hid them. "You're considering breaking and entering in broad daylight and in front of god knows how many neighbors?"

"Of course not," he replied. "We're officers making a welfare check. Ah." A window slid sideways. He put a leg over the sill and eased through. "Come on, bibi."

Against her better judgment, she followed. Inside she stared. Lengths of glass tubing stuck up out of bins on one wall. More tubing lay on a large table beside a gas torch. In several corners tangles of glass tubing in varying colors rose glowing out of broad bases.

"Neon sculpture," Mama said. "Not bad."

Janna hissed in exasperation. "For God's sake. We're breaking and entering and you're taking the time to be an *art critic*!"

"Sorry." He glanced around. "Let's find Salmas."

They found a man answering his description sprawled fully dressed on his back on the bed in the bedroom. Under his nose spread the most spectacular mustache Janna had ever seen, a fiery set of wings indeed.

He lay very still. Too still. Janna could not hear him breathing. "Mama!"

He was already beside the bed, feeling for a pulse. "He's alive, but we'd better call an ambulance."

She eyed the limp man. "Odd he'd try suicide over a robbery."

"He didn't." Mama looked up at her. "I think he's been here since he called in sick."

She stared. "You think someone else went to work in his place? Impossible! You heard Keleman. That door takes not only a Scib Card but a retinal scan. Someone else might take his Card, but how could they pass the scan?"

"I don't know." Mama pushed his glasses up his nose. "Bibi, I have a feeling this case will be complicated."

2

Janna brooded at the foot of the emergency room bed. Salmas's breathing had improved and he moved from time to time, but...he still slept. She glanced at her wrist chrono. Two hours since they brought Salmas in.

"You're sure there's nothing we can do to wake him up?" she asked the E.R. doctor beside her.

The doctor, a young hispanic with a name tag on his cranberry scrub shirt reading: *Muñana*, shook his head. "I can't give an antagonist until the blood analysis tells me what he took. Even then I'd feel better if we also had the medical history from his Scib Card. You're sure you couldn't find it?"

"Someone stole it."

Muñana blinked. "Who'd steal a Scib Card? No one else can use it."

Supposedly. Who could be sure any longer, though? Janna grimaced. Once thumbprints had been thought to be foolproof identification with a Card purchase, then a way had been found to fake them. Now everyone believed as fervently in retinal scans, but maybe retinal patterns could be counterfeited, too. She glanced at her chrono again. "I don't want to nag, but it's important we talk to him. Would you check on the blood again?"

He sighed and headed for the door. "You do nag, sergeant, but I'll check on the blood."

The radio murmured in Janna's ear, "Ten-nine, Alpha Cap Seventeen. Your unit is where?" After a pause, the dispatcher continued in a voice leaking laughter, "Your Twenty is confirmed on the map. Do you need assistance off the roof or are you close enough to shore to swim?"

As she had many times, Janna wished Communications did not use a duplex system. Most of the car radios had been rigged to receive both bands, despite the official opinion that such a clutter of traffic distracted the ear from Dispatch calls, but the ear buttons received only signals from Dispatch at headquarters and the division stations. Too bad. The unit's side of that last exchange would certainly have been interesting to hear.

Mama strolled in. "The doctors haven't managed to wake him up yet?"

"Not without an ID on the drug from a blood analysis machine that appears to operate on the same time scale as our Records computer on a Priority Three search." She glanced sideways at Mama. "Where did you come up with that hunch about finding him at home?"

"To start with, that business of calling in sick, then calling back to say he'd be there after all." Mama polished his glasses on his tabard. "Also, we have statements by several of the other waiters saying he came and hardly said a word, just fussed with the glasses on the waitrons. It all suggested someone arranged to take his place. I just didn't know if Salmas consented or not."

Salmas twitched an arm. Janna frowned. "The other waiters swear it was Salmas."

Mama put his glasses back on. "If someone the right size and coloring and with that mustache showed up when you expected Salmas, would you give him a second look?"

Probably not. "Did you find the name of Salmas's bank and how soon will we have a warrant?" If purchase trails meant anything now. Would the bank record of Salmas's Card transactions tell them what Salmas had been doing…or only where his Card had been?

"He's at Bank One and thanks to the weight of Paget's personal interest in this case, Judge Escamilla not only processed the warrant at light speed but I've already used it." Mama pulled a printout from an inside pocket of his trenchcoat. "Here are his transactions for the last forty-eight hours."

Janna scanned them. The record showed three transactions yesterday: a roll of transport tokens from a machine at Vail and Makepeace at 12:45, a Glo-crystal pendant from Terra Crystallos at 14:17 hours, and two drinks at The Planetfall at 14:45.

"You see the drinks, bibi?" Mama pushed his glasses up his nose. "Two, purchased at the same time."

She handed back the printout. "So he had a companion."

He nodded. "After that, no more transactions. Something else…how many tokens did we find in his pockets?"

Tokens? Her neck prickled. "None." No Scib Card, no tokens. Only keys, a handkerchief, a pocket knife, and a mustache comb.

Mama nodded again. "He bought a new roll that day and I checked the phone book for the location of that shop and bar. They're both in the Granada Mall. Even two bus fares out there and back wouldn't use the whole roll. So…" He raised a brow. "Where's the rest of it?"

The waiter accomplice had a fondness for tokens. Janna eyed Salmas in frustration. "Mama, we've got to wake him up."

"Immediately, bonita," Muñana said from the doorway. He came in carrying a spray hypo. "It turns out we're not dealing with anything exotic, just Superdream on top of alcohol."

Janna frowned. Superdream, a cocktail of perfectly legal Dreamtime and nonprescription strength antihistamine…the formula recreational pilgrims claimed strengthened and extended the effect of Dreamtime, but which straddled the edge of legality since the combination had produced some fatalities. She glanced at Mama. "He could have taken it himself, after the robbery. Celebrating."

"Then what happened to his Card and the rest of his tokens?"

On the bed, Salmas sucked in a deep breath and opened his eyes. They widened in obvious disorientation. "Where am I?"

"Stormont-Vail Hospital," Muñana said. "How do you feel?"

"Stormont-Vail!" Salmas's forehead furrowed. "I must have hallucinated more than I thought. I could have sworn Kruh took me home."

"Who's Kruh?" Janna asked.

"Oh, god." Salmas's mustache vibrated like insect antennae. "I hope I didn't hallucinate calling in sick at work, too. I'm supposed to serve at a big banquet toni—" He focused on Janna. "Who are you?"

"Sergeant Brill, and this is my partner Sergeant Maxwell. We're with Crimes Against Persons."

Salmas licked his lips. "I've had some bizarre dreams. Did I…go off my tick and…do something?"

"We're trying to find out," Janna said. She reached in the breast pocket of her jumpsuit and tapped on her microcorder. "First, for the record, can you tell us your name?"

"Cristo Alexander Salmas."

Muñana straightened, touching the pager button in his ear, murmured, "I'll be right there," and left the room.

"What do you remember about yesterday?"

Salmas hesitated. "Should I be talking to you without a lawyer?"

"You're not under arrest, Mr. Salmas," Mama said.

The waiter looked anything but reassured.

Janna prompted, "You took a bus out to Granada and bought a crystal pendant."

Salmas stared. "How—oh, Kruh told you, I suppose. Shit." He sat up, mustache twitching in even more frantic semaphores. "If I didn't go home, then where's the pendant? Is it with my clothes? It's a present for my mother's birthday."

"I expect it's safe at your house. That's where we found you and decided you'd better come here. Who is this Kruh?"

"You haven't met him? Then who told you about the mall and crystal?" Without waiting for a reply he said, "Kruh is Tamas Kruh, a shuttle pilot with Frontier, waiting out the turnaround time for his bird. I ran into him outside the store where I bought the pendant." Salmas shook his head. "It was the strangest experience of my life. There I was face-to-face with someone who looked just like me…same eye color, same hair, even same mustache." He drew his fingers out along the mustache, fluffing it at the ends. "I thought I had the only one of these in the world. After staring at each other for a while, we started talking. We went and had a drink together. About then I started feeling strange. The room went weird colors and I started seeing things that couldn't possibly be there. Kruh called a cab and took me home." Salmas frowned. "I can't believe he's involved in anything serious. What is it you think he's done? Some industrial espionage? Helping smuggle corporate secrets down from the space platforms?"

"Something a little closer to home," Janna said dryly. "For starters, he appears to have stolen your Scib Card. Do you know what cab company he called?"

"I think it had a yellow flower on the door, but—my Card?" Salmas blinked. "Why?"

Janna glanced at Mama to see if he wanted to say anything. He folded his arms, their signal in this situation for: *go on; you play it*. She said, "Someone of your description reported to the hotel last night for work, and if your story is true, it had to be Kruh."

Salmas gaped. "That's impossible! The door has an r-scan—*Last* night! How long have I been out?"

"Almost twenty-four hours. If you're telling the truth," Janna said. "As you say, it's supposed to be impossible for someone else to use your Card. Also, your colleagues identify you as the waiter who helped six armed men rob the Democratic fund-raiser."

Any doubt about his innocence disappeared watching shock, horror, and terror take turns on his ashen face. Emotion could be faked; Janna had seen that often enough. However, she had yet to meet even the most accomplished actor who could go pale at will.

"Don't worry, Mr. Salmas." Mama moved in to where he could pat the waiter's shoulder. "Sergeant Brill and I believe you. That's the good news. The bad is we have to prove your story because the other waiters identified you and the hotel computer says you clocked in. So we have to hold you—as a material witness—and we need you to tell us every detail you can remember about how Tamas Kruh looked and what he did and said."

Salmas peered from one of them to the other for a long minute. Looking for some sign in their faces that they might be tricking him? As though he had any real choice but to cooperate. After a bit, he nodded.

Before they left the hospital Janna called the Sunflower Cab Company, the only one in town with a yellow flower on the door. The cab company confirmed that at 15:30 hours, they drove a double fare from the Granada Mall to 1930 Makepeace Road, and gave her the name of the driver. Punching off, she turned to Mama, "Who finds him and talks to him?"

"Perera assigned the car to me," Mama said. "Also there are a few Ears I want to visit, to see what they've heard about this riff. You check the bar, and while you're out there, visit Frontier's offices at Forbes and see if they know Kruh."

He dropped her at the Granada Mall. Clouds still hung leaden overhead as she trotted in through one set of the tall front doors, but at least the rain had stopped.

"Beta Forbes Twelve," her ear button murmured, "Granada Mall security would like to speak with an officer, reference a subject being held for attempting to buy drugs at Stambaugh's Drugs with an expired addict's card."

As always the mall awed her...one and a half square kilometers of shops, theaters, restaurants, gardens, and sport and recreational facilities beneath a single transparent roof, all presided over by the luxurious tower of the Holiday Inn with its spectacular view of the Forbes Aerospace Center across the highway. Somewhere among the maze of concourses crowded with Saturday shoppers, street performers, and display holographs lay the bar Salmas claimed to have visited.

Down the concourse to her right the word DIRECTORY glowed in midair. She wound her way to the computer terminal beneath it and punched in the name of the bar.

A cheerful female voice said, "Welcome to Granada Mall. It is a pleasure to help guide you. You will notice that each walkway is named. The names appear in the floor every twenty meters. To reach The Planetfall, follow this walkway, Sigma Draconis, to your right as far as the green slidewalk. Board the slidewalk." A map appeared on the computer screen and as the computer talked, a red line marked the route. Not a long distance...just across this corner of the mall. "If you wish a printout," the computer said at the conclusion of the directions, "push the button marked PRINTOUT, and should you have further difficulty, please do not hesitate to consult me again through another terminal. I am always at your service."

Holo ads for shops and services crowded the space along and above the slidewalk, too. One of a young man in a skin tight snakeskin-patterned bodysuit appeared to lean on the guardrail of the slidewalk, a hand reaching out as though to catch at her. For a moment Janna mistook him for a real person, but as she neared him a telltale translucency at the edges gave away his true nature. She swung her own arm through him as she passed. The engineers tried, but while holos looked three-dimensional, they never appeared quite solid.

Moments later she forgot him in the scramble to make her exit.

The Planetfall sat just inside an eastern exit of the mall, sandwiched between a luggage shop and a beauty salon whose window advertised scalp and body painting—temporary or permanent—in addition to complete hair care. The bar's circular door dilated for her, then snapped closed after she stepped through, leaving her in darkness and a fog of alcohol, tobacco, and drug fumes.

The ceiling fixtures, suspended globes painted to look like planets and moons, illuminated only themselves. All real light came from a glowing strip of something floating horizontally off to her right and similar discs clustered across the room. As her eyes accommodated to the gloom, the strip and discs proved to be the bar and tables. Music played on the threshold of perception, five flute notes endlessly repeated, with a counterpoint of ringing and tinklings.

She groped her way toward the bar and a figure behind it. "Cute door." The figure wore a stylized version of a shuttle pilot's flightsuit. Another scent reached her through the others. Hamburger? Her stomach growled, reminding her that she had eaten nothing since toast and caff this morning. "Do you serve sandwiches in here?"

The bartender held a book. She looked up from the glowing screen. "Honey, we serve anyone over eighteen."

Janna considered suggesting the bartender eat that book. "Do you serve them sandwiches?"

The bartender pushed MARK on the control pad down the side of the book's screen, closed the cover, and shoved the book in a thigh pocket of her flightsuit. "If it can be smoked, snorted, drunk, absorbed epidermally, or eaten, we serve it. We aren't licensed for anything intravenous or for sex, although..." She looked Janna over with interest. "...you and I might work out a private arrangement."

"What are the sandwich choices?"

The bartender shrugged. "Hamburger or tuna, chicken, or egg salad."

Hamburger sounded the least lethal. The bartender pulled a vacuum pack from a cupboard behind the bar, broke the seal, and popped the pack in a little microwave. Eating the result minutes later, Janna wondered what decade the hamburger had been sealed in. Her stomach welcomed it, however, and it washed down well enough with the help of excellent, slightly cinnamon-tasting caff.

While she ate, Janna glanced around the bar. Just half a dozen patrons sat scattered across the room. Or maybe eight. Two of the forms, each sitting in near-blackness at a back table, might be embracing couples. "Is this your average afternoon business?"

The bartender had returned to her book. "About. Are you interested in buying the place?" She thumbed the DN pad to advance the page.

Janna laid her ID on the bar. "I'm interested in if you remember someone who came in here yesterday afternoon."

The bartender eyed the ID calmly. "If I saw him/her." She extended an arm toward the anonymous shadows across the room.

Good point. Well, she could hope. "A jon about a hundred sixty-five centimeters tall, medium build, slicked back hair." Forget color in this light. "A mustache like wings."

"Oh, them."

Them. Janna let out her breath, and only then realized she had been holding it.

The ghostly light from the bar showed a wry smile on the other woman's face. "I had two jons in here with mustaches like that. They came together. Which one do you want to know about?"

Janna reached into her trenchcoat pocket to tap on the microcorder. "Both."

She played back the chip for the others late that afternoon in The Lion's Den. The four of them sat drinking caff and comparing information from the reports they had just finished, talking while it was still possible to carry on a normal conversation. For the moment, Vernon Tuckwiller's bar sat uncharacteristically quiet. Janna could even hear the newscanner over the bar covering presidential candidate Edward Rau's arrival at Forbes for a Humanitarian Party fund-raiser. The influx of leos coming off duty at headquarters up the street had not yet begun; they were still in debriefing, that end-of-watch session to talk out the job stress. Most of the customers at the Coruboard tables and chairs and in the colloid plastic booths remained civilians, some accompanied by half-dressed boys and girls from The Doll's House upstairs.

"They left with one leaning on the other," the bartender's voice said.

Janna tapped off the microcorder.

Cruz pursed his lips. "So it looks like Salmas is telling the truth about meeting Kruh and being sick."

"About the cab, too." Mama flipped open his notebook. "I talked to the driver and he says he couldn't forget one man with a mustache like that, let alone two. One of the men seemed near-comatose. The driver says he asked the other man if they needed to go to a hospital, but the man said his brother had only tried some designer smoke too strong for him."

"Then the conscious man paid the fare?" Singer asked hopefully. Janna could almost hear him thinking: *Scib Card.*

"Yes, but..." Mama shrugged. "...he paid in transport tokens, not by Card."

Janna blinked. Under the circumstances it would have been brainbent to use a Card. Still...pay a *cross-town cab* fare entirely with tokens? "Which explains what happened to Salmas's tokens, but his alone wouldn't be enough."

"No. If Kruh could make up the difference, it meant he brought along a good supply. Because he knew he'd need them, do you suppose?"

Cruz shook his head. "You have to admire the deek's planning."

"He scares the hell out of me." Singer tugged at his mustache. "Most of it's simple enough...track Salmas, make up to look like him, and arrange a meeting. Drug him and steal his Card. But...how did he *use* it? If he's found a way to fake an r-scan..." His voice trailed off.

"We've got wrap him as fast as we can," Cruz said grimly. "It'd help if we knew what he looks like. Has anyone checked with the lab about the enhancement of the news chips?"

Mama said, "I did. It'll be tomorrow at the earliest. I also prodded under some rocks to see if anyone's heard about something like this in the pipe." He frowned. "No one's heard a whisper."

Cruz said, "You'd think the riffers would at least have sounded out possible fences."

"Maybe they plan to wait for cool weather before cashing the carry." Singer glanced at Janna. "What did Frontier have to say?"

"That Kruh lied to Salmas about his job." Need they have asked? "Their office at Forbes checked with the main computer in Denver and it has no record of ever employing a Tamas Kruh, either as a shuttle pilot or in another capacity. What did you find out about the guards?"

Cruz answered. "Keleman told the truth. None of the four are on permanent assignment to the hotel, though they've all worked events there. Unfortunately their personnel files didn't give us anything in their lives that suggests they're vulnerable to subversion."

Bank records might, but a warrant required more probable cause than existed at this point. Oh for judges like the ones who gave TV detectives bank warrants by the fistful. Instead, she and her colleagues were stuck with talking to neighbors and friends to learn who had excessive debts or a bad gambling habit or a taste for expensive designer drugs or illegal drugs…or maybe some socially repugnant perversion one of them would do anything to hide.

Though Janna had difficulty imagining what perversion a person could be blackmailed for these days.

"Bring on the nuclear waste!" a male voice boomed from the bar's door.

A group of five men and women swept in, all talking.

"…couldn't tell the difference between the road and the river?" one woman asked.

"It was pouring," the man beside her protested. "Do you look at the road when you're chasing a speeder? You just follow, right? This deek went off the road, down a hill, and kept going over this wet looking area. How'd we know the deek was driving a damned amphib vehicle?"

The woman just snickered and called at Tuck, "Double toxins for Captain Nemo here. He needs them."

Tuck mixed drinks, his bulk sliding along behind the bar with an agility that made his thinner assistant seem sluggish by comparison.

The hour of the lion had arrived, the *real* end-of-watch therapy session. Janna watched the civilians fade toward the door.

Singer stood up. "Quitting time. Coming, Em?"

Cruz quirked a brow. "You mean, I ought to be home in case Marah goes into labor, even though she isn't due until August?" He put away his notebook and followed his partner out.

By pairs and small groups, more leos drifted in. Abandoned by the civilians, Fleur Vientos's boys and girls sidled up to them. Without missing a beat at the bar Tuck bellowed at them in a voice that still carried the authority of his Vice Squad days, "You don't peddle that down here!"

"We ought to think about going home, too, bibi," Mama said. "I'll bet you haven't eaten today. Let me fix you something."

Something? In his vocabulary, that meant a banquet. "I'm fine. I had a sandwich at The Planetfall."

He pushed his glasses up his nose, frowning. "That isn't adequate nutrition. Don't forget you have a test coming up in your Problems In Law Enforcement class next week."

Mama indeed. Call him a mother hen. Janna opened her mouth to remind him she had been of age and looking after herself for some years now, then spotted Dale Talavera, half of the Alpha Cap Five watchcar team, among a new group coming in. He beckoned to her. So she told Mama only, "I'll study later." Besides, at home the couple downstairs would likely be at it again. How could she study above a cat fight?

Without waiting to see what Mama did, she strode over to join Talavera's group. "How was the shift?"

Talavera put an arm around her shoulders and while she reflected on the pleasure of being around a man tall enough for her to fit under his arm, he said with a grin: "Aside from arresting a dog that invaded a school lunchroom, making a couple of welfare checks on people who didn't answer when Carephone called, and hunting a lost child who turned out to be hiding in the laundry hamper because he didn't want to go to school, we took the initial call on our candidate for Bizarre Murder of the Month."

From the far side of him his partner Tarla Koskow said, "This jon apparently toxy on drugs or alcohol was shouting insults and lewd suggestions at passengers waiting at the bus stop across the street from him. Just before the bus arrived, one of the passengers, a middle-aged, distinguished looking man, removed a machete from his briefcase. He crossed the street and hacked the toxy jon several times on the neck and head. When the victim went down, he returned the machete to the briefcase, recrossed the street, and boarded the bus with the other passengers. It wasn't until the bus had left that a bibi waiting for another bus thought to call us."

"Let me tell you about a call we took last week," a lion said.

That started everyone trotting out stories involving the endlessly amazing behavior of the human animal. Several drinks and sandwiches later, the subject had still not run out. The stories, however, had grown increasingly bawdier and bloodier. Then Tuck's voice boomed through the roar, "Brill! Phone!"

The supposed soundproofing of the kiosk to the side of the bar worked as long as she leaned her head close to the speaker. The face of Lieutenant Christine Candarian, night watch commander in Crimes Against Persons, looked out of the screen at her. "Brill, during this case, maybe you'd better wear your radio around the clock so we can find you fast. Get out front and wait for your partner to pick you up. Your riffers have hit another fund-raiser, the Humanitarians'. This time they've killed someone."

3

A second robbery so soon could be good strategy, Janna agreed…a strike while the police were still sorting out the first crime and before the castlerows had time to harden security in reaction.

Mama turned his MGE runabout off Gallardo Street through a crowd of media people and past a Sherwood Division watchcar guarding the gates—two gates, one ten meters inside the other—of the Lincoln Yi estate.

Why on earth had they chosen this target, though? Even if they felt confident about evading the estate's security systems, surely the riffers saw the difference in difficulty between containing and controlling victims isolated in a single room and those scattered throughout a private home.

Inside the gates a parking area spread the width of the property, featureless except for the stone block paving, still damp from the day's rain, garages at the far right end, and a massive rivet-studded wooden door in the sandstone wall ahead. A uniformed officer guarded the door, the iron gray and red sidestriping of her bodysuit vivid against the creamy tan of the stone, the white of her helmet gleaming in the light from iron-bracketed lamps on either side of the door.

Mama set the car down in front of the door between the ME's modified station wagon and Criminalistics' van—both white over black with red sidestripes like the watchcars—and climbed out grinning. "Now we see why these areas are called castlerows."

The wall did have the look of a fortress.

The she-lion at the door pushed it open for them as soon as she inspected the ID's hung on their breast pockets. "Sergeant Cruz asked me to tell you that he and Singer are already here."

A second courtyard lay beyond the door, this one much smaller, with benches and islands of vegetation in the paving.

Another uniform straightened from studying a flaming spear of blossoms. "You're Maxwell and Brill? This way."

Following him, Janna discovered that the house incorporated a series of courtyards, some covered by clear domes, some open with broad roof overhangs providing a sheltered walkway around the edge. Everywhere people dressed in the same elegant clothing Janna had seen on the news chip that morning stood in tense, bewildered clusters.

"A hell of a house," the uniform said. "It takes up the whole property except for a security corridor between the inner and outer walls. Not much furniture, though, is there? I wonder if that's to give Mrs. Yi plenty of room. She's blind."

Mama quirked a brow. "Or it could be oriental simplicity."

That matched what Mama had told her about Lincoln Yi on the drive out. Son of a banker who came to the U.S. from Indonesia in the forties to escape the Dokono regime's persecution of the Chinese minority. Owner and president of the Sunflower Federal Banks in Kansas and the Great Plains Airways. All those dirigibles flying commuter hops between small towns from North Dakota to Texas belonged to him.

While elegant, however, the house presented a major difficulty for a riffer. The spacious, spartan rooms with their white walls and open-beamed ceilings often lay between several courtyards each, and the glass panel walls pivoted open, making courtyards and rooms, in effect, a single space.

Janna frowned. "It doesn't make sense to stage a robbery here. You can't hope to control the area. Anyone who plans as carefully as our jons did the hotel robbery ought to see that."

Mama polished his glasses with a corner of his tabard. "What makes you think they didn't?"

His thoughtful tone caught her ear. She eyed him. "You have an idea?"

"Maybe." He put back on his glasses. "We'll see."

The uniform led them through a covered courtyard where buffet tables surrounded a swimming pool. Though partially depleted, plenty of food remained, and the tantalizing scents of beef and barbecued chicken filled the courtyard. Everything sat ignored now, however, avoided by guests and unattended by servants. An ice sculpture of the White House settled into a puddle.

At the far end, Dr. Anne Cordero, one of the night assistants in the ME's office, appeared out of a breezeway, a bag of sensor probes slung over her shoulder. Behind followed two blue-tunicked attendants with a stretcher.

Seeing Mama and Janna, she stopped. "You want a look at the victim before I take him away?"

"Please," Mama said.

An attendant opened the pressclose down the middle of the body bag with a rip of Velcro. Guests watching them from a huddle on the far side of the pool stared even harder, obviously curious but trying not to be obvious.

Cordero lowered her voice. "There's nothing very exciting to see. As a body, he's as tidy as they come."

Whatever the explosive needle had done to him internally, none of the damage showed outside. Not even a blood spot marred the rich perfection of the wine velvet and gold lamé of the victim's tuxedo. His face, a strong face rather than a handsome one—clean shaven, square-jawed, straight browed—stared up at them with little expression except, perhaps, disbelief. Dying had been the last thing he expected of the evening.

"Who is he?" Janna asked.

Cordero shrugged.

The uniform said, "His name's Carel Armenda."

The name sounded familiar to Janna though she could not place it. Mama evidently did. He winced.

"Was he important?" Janna asked.

Mama sighed. "Carel Luis Armenda, bibi, is president of Armenord Industries and two-time winner of the Cushinberry Award for philanthropy. His companies are known for offering minorities and handicapped people jobs and advancement opportunities they don't find in many other corporations." He glanced at Cordero. "Is Criminalistics still going over the scene?"

"Oh, yes. Measuring and sampling, photographing and recording. Headed by the King himself tonight."

Kingsley Borthwick had left his computers and everything meters to visit a crime scene personally? "What happened?" Janna asked.

"I think he heard someone sixty-oned the mayor and he came to make sure."

Janna grinned.

Mama said, "Lindersmith isn't so bad. He just isn't Libertarian. Thanks, Doc. Lead on, Macduff," he told the uniform.

The uniform headed for a sliding glass door. Through it Janna saw a man leave a seated group inside to answer their knock. Cruz.

He slid the door open, grinning. "Welcome to the party."

Singer hurried over to join them. "Lord, am I glad to see you two, though what we need is a squadron. The Sherwood Division has given us plain janes and portable dictypers to help take statements from witnesses to the actual crime, and we're having uniforms talk to the other guests, but Yi says there's almost five hundred of them. We'll be here all night. The mayor's here, too—not a witness, thank God—and a gang of media people, of course, and we've got to keep them all away from each other."

For a moment the room distracted Janna from Singer's jeremiad. Behind the group of formally-dressed civilians in deep reading chairs, shelves of printed books filled the entire length and height of the wall. The most impressive private collection Janna had ever seen. A bank of library cabinets stretching along the adjoining wall dwindled to insignificance by comparison, though the narrow drawers must hold thousands of book chips in their slots.

Cruz's voice pulled her back to business. "We also have six men in tuxedos with a waitron for the talking and a servant to collect the carry…a woman this time."

A woman? Janna frowned. A change of accomplices? Or…maybe not.

Mama must be thinking the same thing. He asked, "How tall a woman?"

Cruz blinked. "You're thinking they ran another substitution?"

"Has she been identified?"

He nodded. "Chrysanne Wald, one of the caterer's staff. We have an Attempt To Locate out on her." He paused. "If you're right, maybe we ought to try her home."

"I'll find her address," Singer said. He hurried out.

Janna asked, "Why did they kill Armenda?"

"We're just finding out." Cruz nodded toward the civilians.

Janna eyed them. "You're talking to them in small groups?"

"No…these are high muckies. Though I think Mr. Yi brought them here more to make sure they're protected from the media than to separate them from the common herd. There isn't much common herd."

Mama's eyes gleamed behind his glasses. "Were any of the videographers—"

"Not this time," Cruz sighed. "Yi had barred media from the courtyard where it happened, reserving it for off-the-record meetings between the ambassador and his supporters."

Ambassador? Janna glanced at the civilians again. Now she recognized faces among the four men and two women...the pleasant, no-nonsense features of Senator Barbara Kassebaum-Martin and a distinguished middle-aged man with a complexion several shades lighter than Mama's and a dark green tux with collar and upper diagonal of the tunic iridescent white. Edward Rau...once ambassador to China, more recently ambassador to Kenya...a leading candidate for the Humanitarian Party's nomination.

"The others, about thirty of them, are over in the game room on the far side of the pool giving statements to division janes. Except Armenda's wife. A doctor is with her in one of the bedrooms.

Cruz led the way to the civilians. "Ladies and gentlemen, sorry to keep you waiting. This is Sergeant Maxwell and Sergeant Brill. They'll also be working on the case."

He introduced the civilians: Rau, the senator, her husband Wyatt Martin, a lean man with oriental eyes that Janna knew must be Lincoln Yi even before Cruz told her, the county party chairwoman Maranne Hejtmanek, and a husky nordic blond whose watchful eyes and the needler showing inside the open front of his tux announced his profession even before Cruz introduced him as Rau's bodyguard.

"Mr. Yi," Cruz said, "please continue telling us what happened."

Yi spoke in a clear, measured voice. "As I said, the men appeared around the waitron. I don't remember seeing them before that minute. Perhaps they came into the court earlier and hid in one of the bedrooms until ready to move. The waitron instructed everyone to line up on the side of the court farthest from the breezeway. One man kept watch on the breezeway while the others covered us."

From that point on the story sounded like a repeat of the hotel robbery, including the threat displays.

"The men were very aggressive," Yi said. "They pressed forward until someone cringed, and only then backed away. The one with a gold ring in his ear evidently pulled the trigger by accident. I—"

"Why do you say by accident?" Mama asked.

"When the needler fired, he leaped backward looking very startled," Senator Kassebaum-Martin said.

Yi nodded. "I didn't understand why until Carel collapsed. It took several moments to realize he'd been shot. Needlers fire almost silently, I know, but one expects an explosive needle to…explode." His mouth quirked wryly. "An impression created by television and the cineround, no doubt."

"Then what happened?" Cruz asked.

"The waitron ordered the maid to leave immediately while the men covered her, and after she had, told the men—"

"Just a minute," Mama interrupted. "The *waitron* ordered the retreat? Not one of the men?"

The civilians exchanged glances. Rau said, "That is odd, isn't it? At the time I didn't notice, possibly because I was preoccupied with self-preservation and memorizing the appearances of the men." He smiled wryly. "I thought politics would be safer than foreign service."

"Someone obviously built an AI unit into that machine," Wyatt Martin said.

Mama pushed his glasses up his nose. "A remarkably sophisticated one to possess that level of situation recognition and reaction."

"I wish we had him working for us."

The senator's husband did something in Intelligence, Janna recalled. She sucked in her lower lip. With the waitron giving orders, it sounded more and more to her as though whoever built the waitron was not merely an accomplice but the tickman, the brains, behind all this.

She missed the next question and pulled her attention back barely in time to hear the bodyguard reply to it. "…about the men, but the maid and waitron went out the rear gate. I drew my weapon and pursued them the moment the danger to Mr. Rau appeared past. By the time I reached the pool court, they'd all disappeared, so I asked people by the buffet tables about them. The only one who remembered seeing any of them was an attendant who had asked the maid to bring another bowl of melon balls. She headed for the kitchen, he said. When I reached there, I was told she had taken the waitron to the caterer's van in the service court." The bodyguard shook his head. "I found the van, but no maid, and no waitron."

Mama eyed Yi. "I assume your security system includes a panic button. Couldn't you reach it from the courtyard?"

The banker straightened in his chair. "Of course. Our system uses remote triggers so that every member of my family and live-in staff can carry one." He pulled what looked like a pen from the inside pocket of his tux.

Most of the systems Janna had seen used hardwired buttons, but the principle here must be the same. A twist activated the trigger, sending the signal that locked all the gates and phoned an alarm to the police.

"I activated it as the thieves left the courtyard," Yi said. "I can only suppose they knew the override code for the ga—" He broke off, sighing. "My apologies. I've become absent-minded this evening. We don't have to suppose. Come with me."

He led the way to the end of the library and slid open a door. The control console for an automated security system lined one wall. While the three followed Yi in, the civilians clustered in the doorway.

Yi sat down at a computer keyboard and began typing. "The computer records all activity in the system, including the times the gates open and whether they were opened from the inside by keypad or the outside by Card and r-scan." The printer beside the computer hummed. Paper fed out. When it stopped, Yi ripped the printout free. "This is all the activity since midnight last night, and, yes, there it is." He pointed to an entry near the end of the sheet. "Here I hit the panic button and here, thirty-five seconds later, the override code was entered on the rear gate keypad. No doubt they all left then, though I'm not sure how the gunmen reached the service court without going through the kitchen."

"At least we can track them through the guest list," Hejtmanek said. "We mailed tickets out to persons requesting them and took all donations at the door by Card, so we have the names and addresses of everyone here tonight."

Cruz looked doubtful.

Mama said, "I wonder." Leaning over Yi's shoulder, he pointed at an earlier entry. "The computer records dialogue, too?"

"Whatever's said by someone pushing the call button outside either gate."

"At sixteen-thirty hours the caterers announced their arrival at the rear gate and at eighteen-thirty a keypad code opened the front gate, for the first of the guests, I assume. What's this keypad entry for the rear gate at eighteen-fifty? No one pushed the call button. Did someone leave?"

"We'll see." Keys clicked as Yi typed. "Watch the main camera monitor."

It sat at the far end of the console, surrounded by smaller screens. The image of the caterer's van appeared on it, the time and date along the bottom of the screen. The numbers raced in fastscan. Cars on the street outside sped by in a blur. Then, at eighteen-fifty, motion flashed at the edge of the camera's field. A moment later the screen went black except for the date and time.

Yi started, then frowned. "It couldn't have malfunctioned; that triggers an alarm."

From the doorway, Rau said, "Maybe the maid disabled the camera before letting in her accomplices. That's one way to avoid being on the guest list."

Mama glanced back over his shoulder at the presidential candidate. "Why disable the camera? If our perpetrators knew enough about Mr. Yi's system to have his override code, they'd know what that camera recorded wasn't likely to be played back until after the robbery, by which time what does it matter if we see them come in?"

Singer's voice spoke from behind the group in the doorway. "Maxwell, you were right about the Wald woman."

The leos slipped through the civilians in the doorway to join Singer in the library.

The red-haired investigator lowered his voice. "The apartment manager unlocked the apartment for the watchcar uniforms. They found her in bed, drugged. She's been taken to St. Francis Hospital and there's an officer with her waiting for her to wake up. Oh, and one of the Criminalistics techs just stuck his head into the pool court. He says they're finished."

Mama pushed his glasses up his nose. "Then let's take a look at the scene."

"You go," Cruz said. "I had a peek before Borthwick ran us out. On your way, will you ask one of the janes in the game room to bring a dictyper over here so I can finish with these people's statements?"

They left Cruz and Singer in the library and hailed a uniform outside. While he went after the jane and dictyper, they headed for the breezeway. The moment Janna entered the court on the far end, sidestepping the Criminalistics team loading instrument cases on their hand truck, she saw why the riffers used it. Here they had control. Only the breezeway connected the courtyard to the rest of the house, and the area had no obstacles like a swimming pool or trees. Only a few rocks, pieces of driftwood, and bonsais decorated the edges of a small fishpond near the breezeway. A chalk outline near a wooden bench in the far corner marked where Armenda had fallen. Kingsley Borthwick stood over it with his back to them, hands clasped behind him.

"Finding something interesting?" Mama called.

Borthwick turned, ramrod straight, blue striped jumpsuit impeccable, and stared down his roman nose at them. No mean feat from a height of a hundred and twenty centimeters. "You should be well aware, Sergeant Maxwell, that I never draw conclusions in the field." Ice edged every syllable. "My report, when finished, will find its way to your desk." He circled the fishpond toward them, managing a very good stalking stride for someone with such short legs. "If you have questions, I shall of course answer them as best I can without complete data." He paused. "*Do* you have questions?"

"Not at this time. Good night, sir," Mama said.

"Good evening."

They retreated through the breezeway. "Arrogant bastard," Janna said.

Mama shrugged. "Self defense. How many people would take him seriously if he were genial? Have you ever watched a new defense attorney cross-examine him? They always start by equating 'dwarf' with 'diminished capacity'. Five seconds later they're running for their lives. If there's a scrap of evidence in that courtyard, Borthwick will find it, and document it irrefutably. Let's hunt up the kitchen."

It lay beyond another courtyard or so, filled with every modern convenience, the house staff, and the caterers in their elegant black-and-silver bodysuit uniform. They all denied opening the rear gate just before seven o'clock. None of them had even gone into the service court then.

The cook said, "I think that woman who helped rob Mr. Yi did, though. She said she had to get something from the van."

That left a perfect opening. Janna turned to the catering staff. "Did Wald seem different today?" She could understand the mustache blinding people to other differences in Salmas's case, but how could no one notice the substitution for Chrysanne Wald?

"She wore more makeup than usual," a woman said, "and she had her hair down around her face."

"No, you lightwit," a man said, "they mean did she act different? Yes, she did. She hardly spoke. At the time, I thought she was just in a bad mood."

So they saw a change and ignored it. Janna sighed. "You're sure it *was* Wald?"

They blinked at her. That it might not be had obviously never occurred to them.

"She clocked in at work," the woman said. "That takes a Card, so how could it be anyone else?"

Smiling his thanks, Mama led the way out the back door. As it swung closed behind them, he said, "I wonder if we've created a trap with the Scib Card? We tell everyone it's foolproof, so they accept the Card as proof of identity no matter what they might see and hear that contradicts that."

The caterer's van sat at the back door, its sides lettered: *Holliday Catering, Holliday Square*. Beyond it sprawled the court, paved in the same stone as the front parking area, and large enough for a good sized truck to turn around. A double set of sliding barred gates, one set ten meters inside the other as the front gates were, restricted access from the street. High on one side of the inner gate, a plastic bubble housed the tiny security camera...originally copper tinted, probably, but now splattered with black paint.

"I think the motion we saw was a shooter firing a paint capsule," Mama said.

Inside the gate below the camera bubble, a metal box set in the stone opened to reveal the keypad.

Mama pointed at a plate on the inside of the door. "Beria Security installed Yi's system, too."

Janna eyed the engraved logo, address, and phone number. A link between the two crimes? Beria provided security at both scenes, security that had not worked. On the other hand, it might be coincidence. As one of the largest security firms in the city, Beria had probably installed half the systems around the neighborhood.

Closing the box, Mama turned to look up at the roof. "That roof's low enough to reach from the top of the van."

Which could explain how the riffers by-passed the kitchen, but...it still baffled her why they had bothered to rob the fund-raiser at all. "Five hundred people here and they settle for robbing a mere thirty? Why go to so much trouble for so little profit?"

"Maybe profit wasn't what they wanted."

She frowned. "What else could they be after?"

"Power." He folded his arms. "Consider: they've defeated good security to strike two political events. What if our jons are making a statement, saying: 'You politicians are vulnerable'?"

Cold ran down Janna's spine into her gut. Terrorism during the British elections last year had resulted in injuries to nearly four hundred people and the deaths of thirty, including two candidates. Was this a prelude to the same horror here?

4

Newscanner images of the British elections haunted Janna as she and Mama made their way back through the house to the game room...candidates and audience fleeing a spray of bullets from a sniper's automatic weapon, stunned faces above bloody bandages, burning cars, rubble, twisted bodies. She sucked in her breath. That must not be allowed to happen here!

Furrows in Mama's forehead suggested he had similar thoughts.

Coming into the pool court, she noticed that all but one small group of the guests previously gathered there and in the living-room opening off the far end had gone. Interviewed and released by the uniforms if they had seen nothing. Were the people left witnesses or yet-to-be-interviewed? A uniform stood talking to them.

Then she spotted the craggy face of Mayor Jordan Lindersmith among the group. At the same time, the mayor noticed Mama and her. He said something to the uniform and headed for them, followed by another man in the group.

"Inspectors? I need to speak to you." Catching up to them, he lowered his voice. "I tried stopping the red-haired detective earlier, but he claimed he didn't have time for me then. This is Mr. James Molinero, Ambassador Rau's campaign manager. He and the other members of the ambassador's staff over there need your help."

One guess what kind. Janna stiffened her back to give herself another centimeter or two of height above the polished Mr. Molinero.

Mama said, "You want to know how soon Mr. Rau can leave."

Molinero smiled. "You've read my mind..." He peered at the ID on the pocket of Mama's tabard. "...Sergeant Maxwell. While this is a tragic incident which I'm sure concerns the ambassador deeply—strengthening law enforcement is one of his aims in running—"

"Then you understand the importance of his testimony," Mama interrupted.

Molinero hesitated. "Of course, and even without having seen the ambassador I know he wants to cooperate fully. Still, there are other witnesses, at least some of them, I feel confident, who were standing closer than the ambassador to the murdered man. Theirs is much more significant testimony, while the ambassador has many other commitments important for him to keep. Surely you see that, Sergeant."

Janna saw a man less concerned about a crime and its victim than about the inconvenience that crime caused him. "Mr. Rau wouldn't be leaving here for several more hours even under normal circumstances, would he? He must have been scheduled to give a speech and then mingle some more after that."

The campaign manager frowned at her. "Yes." He sounded unhappy at having to admit it. "Under normal circumstances he would catch a nap on the plane, too. This kind of experience is very exhausting. He'll need time for more than a nap."

"I have every confidence in his strength," Mama said. "He went back into the embassy in Nairobi for staff members what, five times, after that bomb set it afire?"

Now the mayor frowned. "You're missing the point. You can't treat the ambassador like your average—" He stopped. Remembering that few of the witnesses tonight, and almost none in the library with Rau, could be considered average citizens? He resumed in a sharp voice: "We can't penalize the ambassador for being the wrong place at the wrong time."

Mama said, "Mr. Armenda was," and walked away while the two men stared speechless after him.

Janna caught up with him. "Shouldn't we warn Molinero about possible terrorists?"

"Send him into a panic before we're sure there's any danger?" Mama glanced sideways. "Once we've said the words, bibi, how long before they're on the newscanner?"

Where if they were not true already, some wickertick or extremist group would make them so. She eyed him. "If we tell anyone, we run the same risk."

He paused with his hand on the door of the game room. "So let's not say anything."

Keeping possibly vital information from other members of their team, not to mention their superiors? Hardly proper procedure. Lapses like that earned reprimands and suspensions, and did not help promote an Investigator II to Investigator III.

Yet, Mama was right. Once they said *British elections* or *terrorism* aloud, where would the reverberations stop?

He slid open the door.

The game room occupied one side of the pool court. Depressions in the carpeting running at right angles to the poolside wall indicated that the glass panels normally stood open, letting the two areas flow into one another. Now, however, the panels had been pivoted closed, making the room a world of its own. A hushed world, where the people standing or sitting in small groups spoke in whispers if at all. Janna did not count heads, but at first glance the number of people seemed almost equaled by the pieces of play equipment...TV, table and holo games, exercise equipment with holo projectors to create the illusion of other scenery around the machines. Three janes had set up portable dictypers on a large round card table and two holo boards. Janna nodded a greeting to the jane at the card table, but picked up the stack of statements already printed out without interrupting his current interview. Mama collected the statements from the janes at the holo boards. Leaning against a billiards table, the two of them read through the eyewitness versions of the theft and murder.

For the most part the accounts agreed with Yi's. Differences appeared to be no more than the normal perceptual variations. One striking similarity leaped out at Janna.

"Mama. Tokens again." The maid accomplice had demanded that each victim hand over vending and transport tokens.

Mama nodded.

None of the property reported lost was extraordinary, however, none of spectacular value...nothing to suggest greed accounted for taking so much trouble to rob these few people. Janna rubbed the prickling hairs on the back of her neck.

"Excuse me."

At the voice Janna looked up from the statements to a dark-haired bibi whose face looked vaguely familiar, and so tight it seemed ready to shatter. "How can I help you?"

"You can answer a question." Dark eyes measured Janna. "I'm Sydney Armenda. Hoards of leos have been scurrying around here talking to everyone and measuring and recording, but are any of you actually *doing* anything to find my father's killer?"

Now Janna recognized the face. The coloring, the shape of the eyes, the square jaw and firm mouth all echoed the dead man's. As her gold bodysuit and the wine velvet of her ankle length tabard echoed his tuxedo. If her presence in this room meant she had been in the courtyard and seen her father killed, no wonder she held herself with such rigid control.

Mama said, "First, we have to find out what happened and collect information that will help us identify the persons responsible."

Sydney frowned. "One of them is already identified...a maid with the caterers...about my height, a hundred seventy centimeters, medium build, honey blonde hair worn down on her shoulders. The caterer will have her name and address and if you hurry, surely you can catch her before she leaves the city. She'll know the names of the others."

Irritation pricked Janna. She loved civilians telling her her job. But she kept her voice bland. "We're hunting her now. If you've given your statement, perhaps we should ask the doctor who's with your mother to give you—"

"Step-mother," a voice interrupted. It came from a young jon fingering the controls of a skiing machine. "The houseplant is our father's fourth wife."

Sydney frowned. "C.J.!"

He gave her an insolent salute, then turned a dazzling smile on Janna. "Carel Junior at your service."

Only their father's square jaw marked them as siblings. The boy, the obvious younger of the two, was as fair as his sister was dark…a beautiful boy with golden chestnut hair pulled back in a pony tail and eyes of a turquoise blue so vivid they had to be tissue dyed.

"Is there anything either of you can tell us that might help?" Janna asked. "Anything in particular you noticed? Anything one of the thieves did or said?"

Sydney shook her head. "Nothing that isn't in our statements already. One thing, though…does Aida, our step-mother, have to give a statement tonight?"

Mama shook his head. "If the doctor think she's too upset, no. We can come by tomorrow when she's feeling better."

Sydney gave him a tight smile. "I'd appreciate that. Then will you please escort me while I collect her so the lions at the door will let us out? You'd better come, too, C.J."

Her brother frowned as though about to protest, but when she repeated his name in a sharper voice, he turned away from the ski machine and followed her.

Janna read through the rest of the statements and listened to the three janes interviewing more witnesses.

One jane pointed to four people seated down by the wall-sized TV screen. "Those are guests not at the murder scene who the watchcar teams think might know something useful."

Talking to them, Janna quickly established that their information consisted of having seen the waitron and maid leave the breezeway.

"Did you see which direction the men in tuxedos went when they came out of the breezeway?" she asked.

A bibi said, "I don't know about *men*. I saw one man, big and blond, carrying a needler. He went the same direction the maid and waitron did."

Rau's bodyguard. "You didn't see any others? They all had similar mustaches and brown hair in a braid in back."

After a hesitation, the four shook their heads. A jon said, "I wasn't paying much attention before the blond man with the needler."

The others echoed him. After taking their names and addresses, Janna let them go.

Only one witness remained when Mama reappeared.

"What did you do, escort the Armendas all the way home?" Janna asked.

"The doctors have managed to wake up Chrysanne Wald."

She arched a brow. "Ah. You stopped by St. Francis on the way back."

He grinned. "The call came for Singer while I was helping Mrs. Armenda to the car. He was still on the phone to the jane at the hospital when I stopped by the library on my way back in."

"And?"

Mama took the time to hold his glasses up to the light and start polish one lens with a corner of his tabard before answering. "It looks like a repeat of Salmas's experience. Wald told the jane that while running errands before going to work, she met another bibi who looked enough like her to be a sister. They started talking and went to have a cup of caff together. The bibi called herself Vesper Harmon. When Wald began feeling ill at the restaurant, Harmon took her home in a cab. And took her Scib Card."

A phone sat on a table near the television. Janna flipped up its screen and punched the number of the Records computer at headquarters. It answered on the first ring but murmured: "Hold, please," and kept her waiting nearly four minutes before coming on again to ask for identification and access and priority codes.

Was the computer really that busy at this time of night, she wondered, punching in her badge number and the access code, or did it have some cybernetic equivalent of a secretary putting a caller on hold and going off for coffee? "Priority two." They did not need the information tonight; on the other hand, it would be nice to have it in the foreseeable future. "Search: subject approximately one hundred seventy centimeters tall, medium build, male or female. Key words: robbery, disguises, takes tokens. End search." She punched off and folded down the screen.

"I'd like a look at the person who showed up here as Wald," Mama said. "Let's see what the media people have."

She raised a brow. "You think they'll show us after we've kept them shut away from the action?"

He smiled. "We'll win them over."

With directions from a uniform they found the group sequestered in the music room, located in another secluded courtyard.

A dozen media personnel descended on them. "What's happening? Is the group involved in the robbery and killing tonight the same one that robbed the Demos last night? Are Senator K-M and Ambassador Rau all right? How is this affecting them?"

Mama said, "Sorry. No statements yet."

The protests went up. "You can't do this to us. We have a right to report what's happening."

"We haven't been allowed to talk to anyone or see anything. We can't do anything except sit here."

Nothing, Janna reflected, except sit there with cameras on playback, reviewing the chips and planning where to edit so they could have the stories on the air minutes after they reached their stations.

"The phone's even been taken out of this room," one of the jons complained.

With good reason. She gave him a sugary smile. "You know we need to make sure the line stays free for official business. Speaking of business, we need your help."

"I can guess what kind," a female videographer said sourly. "You want our chips, just like last night."

"Not necessarily," Mama said. "We need to see what's *on* them, yes, but if you play them back for us now, you can keep them until you've turned in your stories, then send a copy of each chip to our lab."

The group hesitated, expressions thoughtful. "How about telling us what you're looking for?"

Janna ticked her tongue. "Don't push too hard."

Mama held up a hand. "It's all right, bibi. We've established that the waiter involved last night and the maid tonight are not Cristo Salmas and Chrysanne Wald, but someone posing as them. Both were drugged a few hours before reporting to work and their Cards stolen to provide the impostor with identification."

Astonishment and disbelief spread across the group's faces. One jon began, "How could their Cards—"

"We further suspect that a single individual is responsible for both masquerades," Janna interrupted. No sense letting the media know the leos had no idea how the riffers managed to use the Cards.

Mama said, "To prove or disprove that, we need images of the maid to enhance and compare to images of the waiter. We'd also like pictures of the gunmen, of course, so we'll be looking for them among the crowd, too."

After another hesitation, the group set their cameras for playback. Mama held one up to his eye. Janna peered into the eyepiece of another and pressed the scan button.

Rau dominated the chip. The videographer had concentrated on the candidate, following him as he moved through the house at Senator Kassebaum-Martin's elbow…raced through, on fastscan, smiling, shaking hands, chatting with people she introduced him to. Janna had to look past him for anyone else. No one fitting the description of Wald or the gunmen appeared in the background, however.

Rau remained central in the second chip she watched, too, though the videographer had also used some of her chip to catch other snippets of action. Such as Armenda on the receiving end of apparent angry words from an elegant, middle-aged woman.

"Who's the woman with Armenda?" Janna asked, holding out the camera to the videographer it belonged to.

The bibi peered into the eyepiece for a few seconds. "Ydra Trexler, formerly Ydra Armenda, wife number one. I had to get that scene. Every time they meet, they fight."

As Janna's parents had for years after her mother canceled their marriage contract. She concentrated on the chip to shut out memories that still left her gut knotted. After a moment she recognized Trexler's face as one of those in the game room. So Armenda's ex-wife had witnessed his death, too?

"Usually it's quite a show, with her screaming and throwing things…food, drinks, blunt objects. They had a sacramental marriage, so they had to divorce and it wasn't at all fr—"

"Bibi, I've got her!"

Janna lowered her camera to see Mama holding his out to her. She took it.

"She's in the background, almost behind a tree."

Janna saw her…a flash bibi in her black-and-silver bodysuit, honey blonde hair curtaining her face. Could that really be a man? Or had a woman played at being male last night? Janna backscanned, then ran the chip forward again, trying to see Wald's hands, which ought to reveal the sex. But intervening objects always hid them.

Someone pulled the camera away from her. "Sorry, leo, but I need that." The cameraman ejected the chip, shoved in another, and settled the camera down over his eye.

Around Janna the other videographers did the same. She quickly saw why. In the courtyard outside, Edward Rau circled the fishpond and trees toward them, flanked by his campaign manager and bodyguard. Everyone poured out of the room into the courtyard, cameras to eyes.

Rau looked at Mama and Janna, however, not at the cameras. "Sergeant Maxwell, Sergeant Brill…Sergeant Cruz is sending the senator and me on our way. I wanted you to know, though, that I've left a number with him that will let you reach me if there's anything more I can do to help you find Mr. Armenda's killers. His death is a tragedy and a great loss to Topeka. Good luck on catching his killers." He extended his hand to each of them.

Shaking it, Janna saw sincerity in the dark eyes, but could not help thinking that Rau must be as conscious as she of the cameras recording the event.

Then he was gone. Minutes later a sleek whisper-bladed heliocopter rose from a distant part of the house and glided away southeast toward Forbes.

"A Condor," Mama murmured. "Cruz has to be in lust and itching to be at its controls."

"Yi's private chopper," one of the videographers said.

As though the candidate's departure were a signal, the operation at the house folded. After a short conference with Mama and Janna, Cruz gave the media a statement and released them. Uniforms and plain janes followed. Soon Janna found herself and her three colleagues alone with the Yi's, Hejtmanek, and the servants and caterers cleaning up the pool court.

"Thank god your children weren't here," the county party chairwoman said.

Yi nodded.

Mrs. Yi touched a platter of cheeses. "So much food left. I wish it didn't have to go to waste."

"Why not send it to the East Topeka shelter?" Mama suggested.

She turned her head toward him. "Of course. Thank you."

Janna eyed her with interest. Except for the fixed focus of her eyes, the red-haired Maeve Yi hardly seemed blind. She looked straight at people talking to her, reached for objects without fumbling, and never hesitated in negotiating the obstacle course the pool court had become as the caterers packed. Since Mrs. Yi used no dog or cane, the gold filigree ear wraps curving around and into her ears must be an EchoVision system.

As though feeling Janna's gaze, Mrs. Yi turned toward her.

The fixed stare gave Janna the uneasy sensation of having her mind read. She found herself blurting out the foremost thought. "Your sonar units are beautiful."

Mrs. Yi's face lighted. "Thank you. They're an anniversary present from Lin. He had them custom made, because, as he said, there's no reason crutches can't also be objects of art." A puzzled frown crossed her face.

Mama asked, "Is something wrong?"

After a hesitation the woman shook her head. "I guess not. For a moment I had a sense of déjà vu, then I realized it's just because I said almost the same thing to a waitron earlier tonight."

Singer blinked. "To a *waitron*?"

Mrs. Yi's smile went sheepish. "Initially I didn't realize it wasn't a person. The signal came back from something tall and thin without the hard echo of dense surfaces like metal and even though the male voice sounded a little flat, he seemed to know me."

The hair rose on Janna's neck. At the corner of her vision she saw Singer and Cruz stare.

Mama drew a breath. "What did it say?"

Mrs. Yi frowned in concentration. "'You're looking top dink tonight, Mrs. Yi. I've never seen those ear wraps before. Are they new?' I gave it the same answer I did Sergeant Brill. When it left, the hum of its treads told me I'd been talking to a machine."

Cruz said, "A waitron that sophisticated had to be the one in the robbery."

Behind his glasses, Mama's eyes gleamed. "Yes…and that's our good luck."

What blue sky was he flying now? Janna wondered. "Why?"

"Because its chat with Mrs. Yi tells us the waitron isn't controlled by AI, bibi. No AI unit would be programmed to call attention to itself with un-waitronly behavior."

Hejtmanek frowned at him. "I don't understand."

The significance hit Janna, though, and from the expressions around her, she saw it occurred to her colleagues and Yi, too. If the waitron were not an AI unit, it had to be operated some other way. Janna could think of only one that explained everything the robot's behavior. "Remote control, Ms. Hejtmanek."

Mama beamed at her the way her father had when she brought A's home from school. He turned to Yi. "Did you have anyone watching the street outside tonight?"

Yi nodded. "Of course, to provide reasonable security for the cars that couldn't be parked inside the wall. I hired two off-duty officers from this division to patrol the area."

"Not the people who maintain your security system?"

The banker regarded him in surprise. "Their personnel wouldn't be familiar with who lives in the area and what they drive, nor could private security officers ask for a license check on cars they wondered about. Surely if the leos noticed anything suspicious, they'd have reported it to you."

"The person controlling the waitron would be careful not to appear suspicious. However, he had to be close. We need to know everything that team saw tonight."

"I'll get them." Yi headed for the front of the house.

Cruz and Singer moved close to Mama. Cruz said, "Even remote control doesn't explain why the waitron spoke to Mrs. Yi."

"Human error." Mama glanced toward Mrs. Yi and lowered his voice. "She said he sounded as though he knew her. Maybe he does, and when he saw her, he spoke without thinking."

Singer took a breath. "One of their friends?"

"He called her Mrs. Yi, not Maeve. But it has to be someone who's been in the house and had the opportunity to study the security system."

Janna remembered the label inside the keypad cover at the back gate. "Such as the people who installed the systems here and at the hotel?"

Cruz said, "Tomorrow someone better visit Beria again."

5

Pass-the-Word Morello burst with so much chop he had no time to build suspense before blurting it out. Director Paget had spent the night being called by anxious castlerows and politicians. This morning a commentator on KTNB hinted that the robberies might be only a taste of things to come, after which the committee setting up a Libertarian fund-raiser scheduled in several weeks called the department to beg for police protection. Paget had ordered a major case squad into operation.

"His chop runneth over," Maro Desch said, grinning.

Thinking about the KTNB commentator, Janna grimaced. She supposed she should have expected it; if Mama saw significance in two political events being victimized, other people, even those without quantum leaping minds, could, too. She could have done without hearing about it this morning, though, after spending half the night writing reports and the rest trying to sleep over shrieked accusations and crashing ballistic objects downstairs.

"Don't they ever wear out?" Mama had asked as the two of them finally reached home and heard the battle. He picked up Janna's trenchcoat from where she tossed it on the divider between the entryway and dining nook and hung it in the entry closet.

Resentment flared in Janna, fueled by exhaustion and annoyance at the neighbors. She had had enough of his compulsive neatness! "You could move; then you wouldn't hear them!"

He froze for a moment, then closed the closet door quietly. "I'm looking for a place."

The hurt in his voice pricked her conscience. Not enough to drain off her anger. "Meantime, you might try going down in uniform and telling them to be quiet."

He just sent a look over his glasses and turned away.

Janna had had to grin. Not even Mama was brainbent enough to voluntarily walk into a 10-87. "Maybe they'll kill each other."

Unfortunately, the women had not and Janna fought back yawns as Vradel reviewed the overnights.

The lieutenant, who looked as though he had not slept much, either, confirmed the major case squad. "The two teams currently assigned to the case will be joined by Weyneth, Showalter, Zavara, and Threefoxes from Crimes Against Property. The east end of the room is yours."

"Next to the caff urn, of course," Babra Cardarella whispered to Janna. "You'll probably need it."

"Cruz is senior officer and coordinator. Commander Vining in Public Information is your media liaison and will be here shortly for briefing."

After rollcall they pushed their desks to the end of the room while they waited for the other teams to arrive.

Singer sighed. "I can't believe the lions patrolling around Yi's place don't remember any vehicle our waitron operator could have been using. It had to be large enough to pick up everyone and the waitron."

"Large vehicles don't necessarily attract notice," Mama said. He plugged his phone into the wall jack beside his new desk position and swiveled the screen to precisely parallel the rear edge of the phone.

"Everyone might fit in a stretch limo, for example." He punched his phone on. "I hope the lab has those enhancements. It'll be easier finding those jons when we know what they look like."

The squad room swung open. A courier glided in on whispering wheels and threaded its way to Pass-the-Word Morello's desk. "Priority three requests: Hurtado, Roth," it intoned, its arm depositing a stack of papers on the desk. "Priority two requests: Kazakevicious, Calabrese, Cotterhill, Brill."

Her Records search.

Janna went after the printout. Not a long one, she quickly discovered. The computer had come up with three males and a female in the height/weight range who used costumes and impersonations as part of their M.O. A quick scan established that none of them habitually took tokens along with other property. Janna sighed. Maybe the tokens were a new habit. In any case, the four would have to be checked out.

She returned to her desk in time to hear Mama saying, "We need those enhancements."

"I'm sorry, Sergeant," a face on the screen said. "The program takes time to run. We'll tell you the moment we have something."

Mama sighed. "Thank you." He stabbed the disconnect button.

"We can't do anything at Beria today, either," Cruz said. "Only service technicians are at the office."

Janna dropped the printout on her desk and gave way to a yawn. "So until our colleagues show up, I think I'll have a cup of—"

A phone buzzed.

"It's for you, Maxwell," Cardarella called moments later.

Mama tapped his connect button. "Sergeant Maxwell."

Kingsley Borthwick's face appeared on the screen. Janna stared. What was he doing here at this time of day?

"Sergeant, we have a problem. Dr. Kolb and I would like you and your colleagues to join us in the morgue. Promptly," Borthwick added.

Mama snapped to his feet. "We're on our way."

"I'll wait for the others and Vining," Cruz said.

What would Borthwick consider a problem? The three of them speculated about it on their way down through the building. With Borthwick and the medical examiner himself collaborating, it must involve autopsy findings.

"We'll know soon enough," Mama said.

As always, the smell of death greeted them as the entry door slid back…pervasive, persistent, despite air scrubbers and shining cleanliness. Yet the odor bothered Janna less than the impression the monochrome blues of floors and walls, scrub suits and gurney drapes gave of having stepped into twilight.

The woman at the receiving desk pointed them toward the autopsy room and returned her attention to the newscanner behind her counter, watching an interview with the Russian jivaqueme flutist Alexei Mir. Janna eyed her as they passed. Did the M.E. choose desk personnel for their hair? At night the wild-maned orderly Kolb called Blue Hair presided. Today they had platinum and red curls in a frothy tower Janna would have thought impossible to maintain outside of zero-gee.

Blues persisted in the autopsy room…blue plastic sinks and tables, blue-gray corpses. The smells of death became more pungent and individual—putrefaction, old blood, intestinal contents—mixed with sounds whose combination had become, to Janna, forever associated with autopsies: the drone of dictating voices, a bone saw's whine, the gurgle of running water.

On Monday the weekend's crop of death would fill all the tables, but for now only two were occupied. The hiss of opening doors had distracted the assistant M.E. at the first table from opening the chest of his subject. He looked up at the investigators, causing the overhead camera slaved to him to focus on them, too, and follow them with a glassy cyclops stare as they headed toward the other occupied table.

As always Kolb looked as though he had worn his jumpsuit for a week. Uncombed hair framed his head in a wild gray halo. For all that, however, Kolb's face showed no beard stubble. He bent over the body, tall and slightly stoop-shouldered, murmuring at Borthwick, who stood on a chair beside him, and at assistant M.E. Sid Chesney across the table.

Gravity furrowed Sid's forehead, an expression that almost accomplished what his glasses and thin mustache could not, bring maturity to his baby face. Janna blew him a kiss. Until Sid married last fall, he had shared the apartment with her and though he deserved a nice guy like Treece, she missed him.

Borthwick turned on his chair. "Ah. Commendable promptness."

"What's the problem?" Mama asked.

"The angle of the entry wound," Sid said.

Borthwick turned a glacial stare on him.

Kolb said mildly, "Dr. Chesney, the man has spent most of the night at his computer and sacrificed going to bed in order to see if the autopsy findings corroborate his. Don't upstage him."

To Janna's surprise, Borthwick let pass the implication he was a prima donna and turned to them. "Dr. Cordero's initial examination of the body revealed that the needle had penetrated deep enough into the victim's thorax to leave two and a half centimeters of the tract intact after detonation."

They all nodded. Only in TV and the cinearound did needles explode on contact, spraying bystanders with blood and flesh.

"She inserted a probe and we recorded and measured the angle of entry. This morning I asked Dr. Kolb to do likewise. He has, as you can see, and verified that we were correct last night."

They crowded around the body. The probe, a piece of metal like a skinny knitting needle, jutted from between Armenda's lower right ribs.

"What's wrong with the angle?" Singer asked.

"If he were standing the probe would be almost parallel to the floor. It also angles forty degrees to his right. Consider: Armenda stood one hundred seventy-five centimeters tall. The perpetrators were a similar height, according to the statements I had the Records computer route to me as soon as you'd entered them. Also according to the statements, they held their weapons thusly." He extended both arms straight in front of him, one stubby hand clenched into a gun shape, the other supporting it. "I ran computer simulations based on information in the statements and all my entry wounds angle distinctly downward and less than fifteen degrees to the right." He lowered his arms. "I cannot fire the alleged murder weapon from its reported position and reproduce the victim's entry wound."

No one spoke, but meeting Mama's eyes, Janna knew he had to be thinking the same thing she was: if Borthwick were correct, the riffer could not have killed Armenda.

So who did?

Back in the squadroom, groans of dismay greeted Mama's briefing on the autopsy finding.

Cruz grimaced. "What do we have, then, other than double shit…one crime or two?"

Singer said, "I don't see that much difficulty. Suppose Armenda was turning to his left. That could account for the lateral angulation."

The copper beads strung in Devon Zavara's cornrow braids clicked as the CAProp investigator nodded. "He has a point."

Singer sank into his chair as though melting. A common reaction to Zavara, Janna had noticed, and today even more understandable as the other she-lion displayed her dark honey skin and hard, rippling muscles in a snug bodysuit the same color as her complexion. Small wonder Zavara's partner Trane Threefoxes wore a perpetually bemused expression.

"The lateral angulation," Mama said, "but we know how the riffers held their weapons, so how ever else killer and victim stood relative to each other, if the riffer fired the needle, it had to result in an entry wound with a downward angle. Now, I asked Borthwick to rerun his simulations and—"

"You asked the King..." Samanda Showalter began, lavender-dyed eyes wide.

"...to repeat work?" her partner Marion Weyneth rumbled.

Popular opinion held that the two from Crimes Against Property, better known as Thumbelina and Mt. Weyneth, had been partnered because averaged together they made a normal sized team. Whether the averaging required them to share sentences, or they simply liked the effect, remained a matter of debate.

Mama shrugged. "He isn't an ogre."

"More of a troll," Zavara said.

Janna bit back a grin. What a skin. Far from voicing any doubts about the simulation, Mama had put on a grave expression and said, "Sir, it would help me a great deal to visualize this if I could see those simulations. Did you by any chance also work out a range of possibilities for a source that *could* have produced that entry wound?"

Knowing that of course Borthwick would have.

Mama pushed his glasses up his nose. "He had simulations shooting from various heights and firing positions. No one taller than 145 centimeters could have fired that needle from a shooting stance."

"The entry angle falls in the range of a taller person firing from about waist level, though," Janna said.

Threefoxes' expression became thoughtful. "Someone standing to Armenda's right."

Zavara looked skeptical. "Someone who just happened to come armed? Was it even possible to bring in a weapon? We know they were verifying identification at the door, but did they search the guests?"

Cruz rubbed the back of his neck. "We need to find out. We also need to find out who stood around Armenda and who might want him dead."

The image of Armenda's ex-wife yelling at him replayed in Janna's head. Had the argument led to the ultimate violence this time? She had worked several cases where one person appeared to walk away from the argument, only to return armed some time later and attack the other combatant.

Mama nudged her. "You've thought of someone?"

She told them, adding, "Mrs. Trexler was in the courtyard at the time of the murder."

Mama pursed his lips. "I wonder if Yi kept a needler in the house, and if Mrs. Trexler knew them well enough to be familiar with that fact."

Showalter nodded. "That would be a more logical source for the weapon than..."

"...bringing it to the fund-raiser."

"So, we need to talk to the witnesses again," Cruz said. "Brill, you and Maxwell take the Trexler woman. Also check her out as a possible suspect and see who else might have a motive for killing Armenda. I'll talk to Yi and ask about needl—"

"Brass alert," Zavara interrupted.

Janna looked around. Commander Gifford Vining strode between the desks toward them. His folksy face wore the grin that had been disarming and charming the media for eight years. "Good morning, lions and she-lions. Well, Sergeant Cruz, what can we tell the media today?"

Janna lost all impulse to smile back. What could they tell the media...not how was the case going or how were they doing. That certainly made his priorities clear.

The others appeared to read his question the same way. No one moved from where they sat at or on desks, but their silence had the feel of people standing at attention.

As Cruz briefed him, the information officer's smile faded, too. "Christ! First possible political terrorists, then people who can apparently fake a retinal scan. Now this...if this *is* real, and frankly, it sounds blue sky, Borthwick's simulations or not. You're supposed to be finding answers, sergeant, not more questions."

Cruz met his gaze. "Yes, sir. We will."

"I hope so." Vining's mouth thinned. "Meanwhile I'll think of something to feed the media that won't create the circus this development would. They won't accept bullshit for long, and neither will the Director, so let me know the minute you have something I *can* report."

He walked away.

Zavara's lip curled. "Brass."

Cruz shrugged. "At least we have someone between us and the media. Let's go to work."

They divided up the chores and scattered.

After the Ashanti, their Meteor sedan felt very mundane indeed, despite its metallic blue finish. Though even the Ashanti might have seemed dull beneath the morning's threatening overcast. The light meter on the dash indicated barely enough light for the Simon cells on the car roof to run the fans on solar power.

Mama headed south rather than toward the Trexler home in the Cedar Crest area. A phone call before leaving the squadroom had already established that the Trexlers were not home.

"They're at the gallery," the maid on the screen told Mama.

He nodded and punched off, obviously knowing what she meant, but Janna asked, "What gallery?" as they slid through the light Sunday morning traffic.

"The Trexler Gallery."

She rolled her eyes. "That's a big help. I've never heard of the Trexler Gallery."

The car radio and her ear button crackled once and went silent again. Radio traffic ran light today, minutes at a time passing between messages.

"You've just never paid attention when we passed it." Mama dialed up the magnification on the dash's rear scanner. A big Aeromack closed on their rear bumper. "Naughty, naughty." Mama flipped on the emergency lights.

Janna grinned, imagining the driver's dismay at seeing flashing red, white, and blue lights come on behind the Meteor's rear grille. The big semi not only dropped back; it changed lanes. She dismissed it from notice. "Passed it where?"

"In the Expo Center Mall."

The mini-mall south of the Sheraton? She raked through her memory, trying to recall an art gallery among the gift, clothing, and sundries shops catering to guests at the Sheraton and Expocentre. Only one possibility came to mind, however, and that seemed unlikely. "You don't mean the place with the purple cow in the window?"

Mama beamed at her. "You noticed after all."

Five minutes later they passed the cow during the walk to the mall doors from the Sheraton parking lot where they left the car. It grazed in the streetside show window below glowing white letters on the combed concrete wall: *Trexler Gallery*. Painted white and royal purple in the same color pattern as a Holstein, the cow appeared to be cut from four sheets of wood, one for the body, with horns, front, and hind leg sections slotted in at right angles...like some full-sized replica of a child's homemade toy.

This was art? More incredible yet, the cow had the edge transparency betraying it as a hologram, which meant that the gallery considered the object too valuable to put the original on display outside.

"People actually pay good card for something like that?"

They pushed through the doors into the mini-mall's short, skylighted concourse.

"For a Dvorak sculpture?" Mama grinned. "Not good card. *Gold* card."

The gallery's entrance, a broad arch supported by Grecian columns, lay on their left. At the moment, however, glass closed the arch, a seamless sheet with the faint internal glitter of imbedded monofilament mesh. Peering through the door into the gallery, Janna tried not to touch the glass. Logic said it must be a heavy double thickness with the mesh sandwiched between the layers but gut reaction cautioned her to avoid even the chance of breaking it. Monofilament once snared her ankle during her patrol days and she still went cold remembering how effortlessly the fine-chain molecular structure sliced through her boot, and how easily it could have amputated her foot.

"I see someone, bibi."

Janna did, too, a woman in a baggy dark coverall and a thigh-length fall of jade green hair, disappearing behind a partition beyond what appeared to be a precariously balanced stack of metallic cubes.

Mama rapped on the glass.

The woman peered around the partition, frowned, and came toward them as far as the metallic cubes. *We're closed*, her lips mouthed. She pointed at an easel just inside the glass.

A placard there read: OPENING TODAY, GLASS FANTASIES BY LYMAN KINTICH, Hours: 1:00 p.m. to 8:00 p.m.

"Police!" Janna shouted. They pulled their badge cases from under their trenchcoats and held them up.

The bibi came to the door and studied the ID's. Though not beautiful, all rawboned angles, in fact, the woman had the most perfect complexion Janna had ever seen. The porcelain translucency of it made the jade of her hair and slanted eyes all the more striking.

She continued frowning but presently pulled a sonic key from her overall pocket and punched a combination on the keypad. Something clicked in the door. The woman slid the glass aside enough to make an opening at the left end of the arch. "How may I help you?"

Mama smiled. "We need to talk to Mrs. Trexler. About last night," he added when she did not react.

She hesitated a moment longer, then sighed. "Come in." When they had, she closed and relocked the door. "I'll get her."

"Being wanted gives me such a warm feeling," Janna murmured to Mama as the woman disappeared beyond the partition.

Off to the left of the entrance stood the original of the holo display. Janna strolled around it. In "person" it still looked like an oversized toy.

Her ear button muttered, "Alpha Cap Nine, investigate a report of a vehicle driving on the lawn of the Capitol building. Vehicle is blue, possibly an Hitachi Bonsai or Chrysler Elf."

"Sounds like the one north of the university yesterday," Mama said.

A moment later the radio continued, "Alpha Cap Nine, Beta Cap Seven advises the vehicle is a Bonsai with amphibious modifications. Do not follow it into any body of water."

Janna grinned, then noticed another sculpture and forgot the Bonsai. A metal shaft with a wide base thrust up through the middle of spiraling metal vanes. The central shape reminded her of a waitron.

She walked over to it. The vanes begged to be touched. When she ran her hand down them, they gave and sprang back, setting off vibrations that spread along the rest of the spiral in a pinging chorus.

Mama eyed her. "Don't tell me you've suddenly developed an appreciation for art."

She stroked the vanes again. "I'm appreciating the fact that we're just across a parking lot from the Sheraton and that one way to hide a waitron quickly might be to trick it up with something like this in place of its shelves."

The middle-aged woman on the video chip came around the stacked cubes. Ydra Trexler raised her brows at them. "Sergeants Maxwell and Brill?" she asked in a husky voice. "My assistant said you wanted to see me?"

Mama smiled. "Yes, ma'am. We're sorry to bother you, but we have a few more questions about last night."

Mrs. Trexler sighed. "So he might win after all."

Janna kept her face expressionless. "I beg your pardon?" Who? Armenda? Win what?

Mrs. Trexler shook her head. "Nothing. Will this take long? We're behind schedule getting ready for this showing because we had to spend much longer at the fund-raiser last night than we intended and even working since dawn hasn't caught us up."

"We can talk while you work, if that's any help," Mama said.

Mrs. Trexler nodded. "This way."

She had the carriage and good bones that maintain elegance even when age has thickened the waistline and wrinkled the skin. Not that Mrs. Trexler's skin had wrinkled. Though she must be near fifty, it remained smooth, and no gray showed in the sleek upsweep of wheat-blonde hair.

Nor did she seem alarmed by their presence. Which indicated what? A serene conscience…or supreme self-confidence?

They followed her past the stacked metal cubes and around the partition. A long, narrow room with white walls and a parquet floor stretched away on the far side, scattered with display stands. Most held an object each…a bowl or a vase, a tree, an animal…all made of glass.

A distinguished, gray-haired man looked around, frowning, from setting a fairy castle of spiral crystal towers and lacy battlements on an internally lighted stand. "Ydra, this is no time for visitors!"

Mrs. Trexler smiled at him. "They're leos, not visitors. This is my husband Loudon Trexler," she told Mama and Janna, "and you've already met Arianna Cho, my assistant."

The jade-haired woman nodded at them from where she knelt by a small crate and thumbed on a palm-sized depolarizer. She ran it down the plastic strips sealing a crate the way a wrapstrap restrained a prisoner's wrists, by the charge in the strip making it adhere to itself. With the charge neutralized, she peeled the strips loose and released the latches on the crate.

Mrs. Trexler reached into the plastic foam pellets filling the crate. "What are your questions?"

Mama said, "We need to know peoples' positions at the time of the shooting. Was Mr. Armenda facing directly at the gunman who shot him, do you recall?"

Out of the crate came what Janna at first took to be another castle, only black, then recognized it as some kind of horned animal head. Mrs. Trexler looked up with it in her hands to smile wryly. "I have no idea. The only thing in the world I saw just then were those guns. If you're interested in an opinion based on experience, however, yes, he faced the gunman. Pride would have made him stand his ground until the last possible instant of safety. Carel backed away from things but he never backed down."

Her tone did not make that a virtue.

"Where were you standing at the time? Left of him, right, behind him?" Janna asked.

Mrs. Trexler set the head on a display stand. "Left of him."

Janna kept her face expressionless and her focus on Mrs. Trexler, though she wanted to exchange glances with Mama. "About how far away?"

Mrs. Trexler opened her mouth, but Arianna Cho sat back on her heels and spoke first. "That's a strange question."

Janna gave her a bland smile. "It's just routine."

Cho's sent back a thin one. "Really? To ask where Ydra stood in relation to Carel, maybe, but…how far away?" She stood, jade eyes boring into first Janna, then Mama. "I could almost think there's doubt about who killed Carel."

Both the Trexlers started. "Arianna!"

Janna felt her smile freeze. She tried to catch Mama's eye. Did they admit the truth when their media liaison wanted to keep it quiet?

She might have known such a question would not bother Mama. He eyed Cho with a thoughtful expression. "You're very perceptive. There are facts which suggest that, yes."

Cho's lips thinned, hardening the angular face. "So you came looking for someone who might want him dead. Why do you think that's Ydra?"

Mrs. Trexler gasped. "Me!"

Janna met the woman's shocked eyes. "One of the videographers last night has a chip showing the two of you fighting not long before Mr. Armenda died. She told me that you always fought, often violently."

To Janna's astonishment, Mrs. Trexler laughed. The warm huskiness of it echoed in the gallery. "Those weren't fights, Sergeant. They were scenes, spectacles, and if they suggest anything, it's that I have every reason to want Carel alive. I threw those fits to embarrass him, which they always did. Killing him would end my fun."

"Fun?"

"Don't talk to them, Ydra," Cho said. "They'll use it against you."

Mrs. Trexler shrugged. "I have nothing to hide. Sergeant, Carel Armenda stole control of my father's company from him, then when I inherited it, he stole the whole company from me, changed the name from Nord to Armenord, and discarded me in favor of more passive houseplant consorts. Of course I hated him and attacked him. But the bitterness lasted only until I married a man who truly cares about me and wants me to share his life as well as his bed." She spread her arms to the gallery. "After that I only despised Carel, but the scenes had become a habit, and a game…a way to remind him who he really was under the facade that won him Cushinberry Awards."

Mama pushed his glasses up his nose. "He never asked for an injunction to stop you?"

"He couldn't." She smiled. "No more than he could run away from the scenes I made or cringe in front of that gunman. It would be admitting his lack of control. Carel always had to be in control, of everything…of his employees, his children, his wife. He suffered when he wasn't; he didn't feel like a man."

Understanding gleamed in Mama's eyes. "So you took control away from him."

She nodded. "He put up a calm front, pretending to patiently weather the hysterics of an unreasonable female, but I could always smell his fear that everyone around us was thinking: 'What's the matter with Armenda? Is he so weak he can't rid himself of that virago?' It was very satisfy—oh, lord, look at the time!" she wailed. "Loudon, why did you let me rattle on? We've got to get the rest of these pieces uncrated, and the crates put away. When is the Sheraton delivering the wine and cheese?" She hurried out at door at the far end of the room.

Trexler ran a hand across the top of his hair and back to the pigtail at the nape of his neck. "My wife's telling the truth; she doesn't hate Armenda enough any more to kill him. She wouldn't anyway; despite all the sound and fury when she's putting on a show, she isn't a violent person."

"Were you in the courtyard at the time of the killing?" Janna asked pointedly.

He hesitated, then shook his head. "No. We have an agreement…she can make the scenes as long as I don't have to watch."

"There's also a little problem of what she could have killed him *with*," Cho said. Anger edged her voice. "The tickets came with a statement that everyone must agree to be scanned for weapons at the door."

Well, that answered one question. Janna asked another. "How well do you know the Yi's?"

Trexler shrugged. "We've met at social functions and they're regular customers."

"Have you been in their house before?"

"Yes. To deliver and help hang paintings." He eyed the two of them. "Are you arresting Ydra?"

"Not at this time," Janna said.

"Then while I don't wish to seem hostile, I wish you'd find another time to ask your questions. We're—"

"Of course," Mama said. "In the meantime, ask your wife to see if she can remember who was near her and what their positions were. Come on, bibi.

Cho followed them to the door. Unlocking it, she said, "You want to know who else was standing by Carel when he died? When Ydra told me earlier this morning what happened, she mentioned talking to Carel's wife and children in that courtyard. So they had to be close. If you're looking for someone with a motive for killing Carel, talk to them." Cho slid the door open to let them out. "C.J. likes his pleasures and hated being on a restricted allowance. Sydney is her father's daughter, right down to wanting Armenord. Carel felt C.J. should take over but I've heard Sydney say that she intends to have Armenord, no matter what she has to do to get it."

6

Like other houses in the Lincolnshire Estates area, the Armenda house sat behind a tall wall and heavy gate, though from the bottom of the winding drive the house's low profile of buff limestone and coppery glass had struck Janna as surprisingly modest. Inside, however, modesty disappeared. Armenda had just built his sprawling house underground and down the back side of the hill, the skylighted open-beam ceilings, stone walls, and rough-plastered walls giving it an elegant cavern appearance.

"Alpha Sherwood Five," Janna's ear button murmured, "attempt to locate a loose horse on the Wrexham Road bridle trail, west of Bristol Place. Described as a gray American Warmblood gelding, wearing an English saddle and bridle."

A side glance caught Mama grinning. Janna grinned back. "The trials of working a castlerow division."

The servant they followed descended an arc of stone stairs to a room with heavy drapes on one wall partially drawn and another wall devoted to a bank of library cabinets.

Sydney Armenda stood with her back to the window, hands shoved in the pockets of a faded denim jumpsuit. "Sergeants Maxwell and Brill, isn't it? My step-mother will be down in a minute."

Beyond the drawn drapes lay a grotto-like swimming pool. Janna noticed Junior's chestnut hair showing above the edge of the steaming whirlpool.

"Interesting architecture you have," Mama said.

"My father built it for Indra, his second wife…inspired, I suspect, by the living quarters of James Bond villains."

Who?

"The movie versions of Hugo Drax and Scaramanga, you mean," Mama said.

Sydney's brows arched. "Old cinema is your bob, too? It's—" Her voice faltered. "It was my father's. We have chip copies of around six thousand movies made over the past hundred and fifty years." She waved at the library cabinets.

Janna stared. "Six thousand!"

A covetous gleam came into Mama's eyes. "Sometime I would enjoy seeing what you have."

"Be my guest."

"Unfortunately...while we wait for your step-mother, we need to ask you a few questions, too." He pushed his glasses up his nose. "Can you remember the names and exact positions of the people around your father at the time he was shot?"

A line appeared between her eyebrows. "Why do you need to know?"

Janna and Mama had discussed answers to this question on the way from the gallery, discussed it with some heat on her end. "What were you trying to do back there," she had demanded, "give the suspects a sporting head start by warning them we know what happened?" Now, as the question came, Mama looked at Janna. *Your turn*, his eyes said.

The bastard. Janna gave Armenda's daughter a bland smile. "We're just clearing up routine details."

Several seconds passed while Sydney eyed them. "Of course," she said in a flat voice. Obviously not believing Janna. "I was standing behind and a little to Dad's right. On his left was a state representative whose name I can't remember but who wanted Dad to appear at a committee meeting to support proposed state legislation easing restrictions on work permits for aliens. Aida was clinging to his right arm."

His wife had been closest? Janna sucked in her lower lip. If she had indeed been clinging, it would have been easy to put a needler against her husband's ribs and pull the trigger. The question remained of where the weapon could have come from. And what might her motive be? This many wives down the line, Armenda surely had clauses in the marriage contract that limited any material profit from the marriage. Still, it gave them questions to ask her.

"Where was your brother?" Mama asked.

Sydney hesitated before replying. "Standing to Aida's right."

"Do you remember your mother being anywhere close?"

Now the dark eyes narrowed. "Ydra? Yes…just beyond C.J. Is she the reason for your questions?"

Mama pushed his glasses up his nose. "Was her behavior unusual in any way?"

Sydney leaned back against the glass. "She followed us into the court when we went to meet Ambassador Rau. I wouldn't have expected that since she'd already made her scene for the evening." She paused. "Have you heard about those confrontations yet?"

They nodded.

"On the other hand, she loves embarrassing Dad and making another scene in front of a presidential candidate might have been too tempting to resist. She certainly had Dad sweating for fear she would. I doubt he heard half what the legislator said, he kept so busy watching her."

Which hardly upset the daughter, judging by the satisfaction in Sydney's voice, Janna reflected.

Mama said, "You find that amusing?"

Sydney's hands came out of her pockets. She pushed away from the window to stand up straight, feet braced apart, arms folded. "Suppose we stop the bullshit and come to the point. Am I a suspect, and what am I suspected of?"

Mama raised a brow at Janna. She shrugged. All right, let him do it his way.

He focused back on Sydney. "The angle the needle entered your father makes it impossible for the gunman to have shot him."

She took a minute to digest that, then gave them a thin smile. "I had my differences with my father. However, I didn't kill him. How would I have smuggled a weapon into the fund-raiser?" When they did not answer, she continued, "In any case, I'm not the only person with motive to kill him."

"You mean your mother?"

Sydney snorted. "That's an old, cold hate. Besides, she has her revenge embarrassing him."

"What about your brother?" Mama asked.

"Impossible." As though worried that she made the denial too fast, Sydney continued hurriedly, "Not that in his pleasure-loving greed he has no motive, but his style is impulsive…the blunt instrument at hand in a moment of anger…a push out a window. My brother is a creature of the moment. I was thinking of the men whose companies my father has taken over." Her gazed shifted past them. "Aida, you remember Sergeant Maxwell from last night, and this is his partner Sergeant Brill."

"I remember," a soft voice said. "Thank you for helping me to the car."

They turned. A loose black jumpsuit and cape of brilliant copper hair hid most of the woman descending the stairs. At the bottom, though, she tossed the hair back over her shoulders, revealing a face so perfect it remained beautiful even with her emerald eyes swollen and bloodshot. She looked no older than Sydney.

"Do you feel up to telling us about last night?" Mama asked gently.

Aida Armenda glanced at Sydney.

"The sooner you do it, the sooner it'll be over," Sydney said. "It's not as though you're a suspect." The comment carried the faintest emphasis on the pronoun. "If it's too upsetting, you can always stop."

The room's chairs had deep seats and high backs that curved around to enfold the sitter. Aida curled up in one, leaving little of her visible again except bare feet, eyes, and copper hair.

Sydney headed for the stairs. "You probably prefer talking to her alone, under the circumstances. Don't forget to ask her where everyone was standing."

Aida watched her step-daughter climb the stairs. When the door at the top closed, she sighed. "She's so smart. It's really a shame that—"

"That what?" Janna prompted as Aida broke off.

The red-haired woman shrugged. "Nothing. I just don't understand why my husband insisted that only a son could take over from him, especially when so many of his employees are women."

Mama said, "I'm surprised he has a daughter at all, then. You'd think he'd sex-select for sons."

"He did." Aida looked up, eyes wide. "The process isn't foolproof. What did Sydney mean about asking where everyone was standing?"

Sitting down, they gave her the story about routine details. Aida answered carefully, taking time to think, and sometimes to fight back tears. Her version of the robbery told them nothing new. She had focused so tightly on the gunman in front of her, in fact, that she saw even less than most of the other witnesses. However, she did corroborate her stepdaughter's statement about people's positions around Armenda.

Janna settled back in her chair, enjoying the velvety softness of the upholstery. That corroboration meant Sydney could not have fired the weapon that killed her father.

But Aida could have. Perhaps the marriage contract had almost expired and Armenda was not going to renew it. Aida might be bitter as being discarded. Or perhaps Armenda provided better for his widow than his ex-wives.

Or Aida could be a tool, conspiring with Sydney.

Obviously thinking the same thing, Mama asked, "If it isn't too personal a question, what happens to you now?"

Tears gleamed in the emerald eyes again. "I'll be leaving after the funeral. Carel's death voids the marriage contract. Sydney says there's no hurry and I'm sure she means it—she's always been tolerant and polite, and even kind in her way—but without Carel, I…can't be comfortable here." She huddled deeper in the chair.

"Does his Will leave you anything?"

She shook her head. "The only profit in marrying Carel is staying married to him. I leave with my clothes, jewelry, car, and the dividends from some investments Sydney's made for me with birthday checks and gambling winnings and the like."

Janna sent a glance at Mama. They ought to check that portfolio for how much "the like" Sydney had invested. Large, frequent amounts might mean payments.

The door at the top of the steps opened. Junior appeared, wrapped in a bath sheet and grinning down at them. "I feel left out. Everyone's being interrogated but me."

As though it were a game. Did he care that his father had died? "Interrogation is for suspects," Janna said. "Should you be a suspect?"

He bounded down the steps. "Isn't everyone guilty of something?"

From the corner of her eye, Janna saw Aida huddle deeper yet in her chair and recalled the red-haired woman's remark about feeling uncomfortable in the house. Now Janna suspected why. She decided she did not like Armenda's son.

Especially not the way he looked *her* over…like someone inspecting a cut of meat. He smiled. "Why don't you and I discuss it over dinner, kitty? What time do you get off?"

The toad. Janna sent back a sugary smile. "Way past your bedtime, muffin."

He stiffened, anger flashing in his eyes. For a moment Janna expected him to deliver some scathing retort, but he wheeled away, pausing in passing Mama to point at the glowing orange of the jumpsuit showing beneath Mama's scarlet trenchcoat and say, "You certainly light up a room," before focusing on Aida. "I think you've been subjected to enough questions. You look exhausted. Let me take you to your room."

"If she's tired," Sydney's voice said from the top of the stairs, "she's perfectly capable of finding her own way."

The blaze in his eyes suggested that if his sister had been within reach, Junior would probably have struck her. A crime of passion man, as his sister had said.

Aida stood. "I do have a headache. Are there any more questions?" she asked Mama.

"Not right now...though we do have a question or two for you after all, Mr. Armenda," he added when Junior took a step after Aida.

Junior turned. "I hear on the newscanner all the time about leos being hurt stepping into the middle of domestic situations."

Mama shrugged. "A risk of the job. Why don't you sit down?"

From the top of the stairs Sydney said, "Before you tell them anything, C.J., you'd better know that the gunman didn't kill Dad."

He flung himself into a chair. "Well, they certainly don't have to look far for a good suspect, do they, dear sister? Eventually you were bound to get tired of trying to please the old man and realize it doesn't matter how smart and capable you are; he was never going to forgive you for being born female." He smirked at Mama and Janna. "Even when she graduated summa cum laude from the KU law school, the old man wouldn't attend the ceremony and Edde, the houseplant in residence at the time, even got in trouble for going with our mother."

The door above them clicked shut.

Junior scowled. "You'd think just once she'd slam it when she's mad, but no, she's like the old man...no tantrums, no tears, always in iron control. Someone like that can plan and commit a murder, don't you think?"

Janna shoved her hands in her raincoat pockets to keep from grabbing the little bastard by the neck and knocking him into orbit. "You don't seem grief-stricken yourself about your father's death."

He pulled the bath sheet tighter around him. "You wouldn't be either if he were your father. Sydney would have sold her soul to make the old man notice her, but I'd have given anything to trade places with her. The bastard never let me alone. Why wasn't I getting better grades? How could I be so lazy and not want to work twenty-four hours a day? What did I mean, I wanted to go skiing; we had stock to buy up and another company to take over."

"So..." She smiled at him. "...his death frees you...and frees your finances."

The flurry of panic she hoped to see never came, however. Junior just shrugged. "You're welcome to try finding a way I could have known that robbery would happen so I could shoot my father during it. Any more questions?"

She made sure they had some, including one about people around his father. His answer matched the women's.

In the car, headed back for headquarters, Janna said, "I hope that little toad's involved."

Mama grinned. "What? Am I really hearing this from By-the-Book-Brill, the she-lion who keeps criticizing me for operating on gut feeling instead of objective facts and the rule book?"

She stared out at the traffic along Southwest Boulevard. "I'm not accusing him; I'm just saying what I'd like to be true. Hey! Those look like nice apartments." She pointed at a *Now Leasing* sign on the wall around a new complex.

Mama barely glanced its direction. "It'd make too long a drive downtown every day, even if I could afford the rent."

Too long a drive? Last week he had dismissed apartments near the Statehouse as too close to central city noise and traffic. Every place was always too something. "Just what the hell *do* you want in an apartment?"

"Let's worry about the case first. You realize that unless the Armenda gang is all lying, Aida is the only one who could fire from the right angle to have made that entry wound, and I can't see her pulling a firing button."

Neither could Janna, nor see Sydney depending on her stepmother for the task. Even less did she see Aida conspiring with Junior. "The needle had to come from somewhere, though."

Mama's expression went thoughtful. "From somewhere."

"What about Sydney's suggestion we check out the men who lost their companies to Armenda? Mama?" she prodded when he did not answer.

He glanced at her. No, she decided, not at her, just her direction. "One of my law school buddies in corporate law is an encyclopedia of corporate chop. I'll ask him what companies Armenord has absorbed."

Mama called his friend from the squadroom. Janna used the opportunity to visit the restroom. Pushing open the door, she heard sobbing, and came around the screen wall to find a woman huddled against the wall at the end of the sink row, head down on updrawn knees, her whole body shaken by the sobs. With a shock, Janna recognized the sleek dark helmet of Babra Cardarella's hair.

"Cardarella?" She dropped to her knees beside the other woman. "What's happened? What's wrong?"

Cardarella lifted her head and leaned it back again the wall, streaming eyes closed tightly. "The Gelfand boy, the missing juvenile Norm and I were assigned to last week? We found him. In neat packages in the family freezer."

Janna's gut lurched. "Dear God," she whispered. "Who—"

"His mother." Cardarella opened her eyes. They stared blindly toward the ceiling at the far end of the room. "That sweet, shy little woman who spoke barely above a whisper to us and who seemed so frantic when her son didn't come home from soccer practice." Her fists clenched. "He was eight years old. How could she do that? My Taura isn't much younger; I know how maddening kids can be, but...how could she do...*that* to her child?"

Janna put her arms around the other woman, fighting a constriction in her throat. "Have you talked to Dr. Venn?"

The head buried against Janna shook *no*. "I thought I was fine. We booked her and I came down here before I started the reports, then when I went to wash my hands..." Her shoulders shook.

"Come on." Janna pulled her to her feet. "You don't want to go home to Taura like this."

They climbed the stairs to Venn's office, avoiding civilians who might be in the elevators. Walking back down after turning her colleague over to the tick tech, Janna thought about Cardarella's sweet little butcher mother. Every once in a while someone came along to remind them that appearance had no relationship to what a person was capable of doing. Maybe she should not be so quick to discount Aida Armenda as a killer. Maybe contrary to Sydney's assessment, an artful schemer lurked inside Junior, too.

Back in the squadroom Mama sat frowning at a set of doodles. He glanced up as she dropped into her chair. "I was beginning to wonder if you'd fallen—what's wrong?"

She told him about Cardarella, then asked, "Did you reach your friend?"

He nodded. "That'll teach him to carry a phone on the golf course. He says Armenda engineered six takeovers, all small, privately-owned companies...two here in Topeka, one in Wichita, three in Kansas City." He stretched across the desks to hand her a sheet of paper, then sitting back, resumed frowning at his doodles. "Those are the companies and the ex-company heads. Several of them, male and female, were vocally bitter at the time. It's been up to ten years since some of the takeovers, though—a long time to hold a grudge."

Some people smoldered for a long time before exploding. He knew that. Why did he sound indifferent, then?

Scanning the list told her why. "I don't remember any of these names on the list of people in the courtyard." She dropped the list, sighing. Another dead end.

"They aren't. I checked. But maybe…" He drummed his fingers on the doodle. "…they just weren't there in person."

She eyed him. Excitement edged his voice now. Suddenly she realized Mama had not been indifferent, only preoccupied. She waited for him to go on.

In the corner above the caff urn, the newscanner announced that a Russian shuttle had crashed into the Sea of Japan as it attempted to land at Vladivostok.

Mama sat listening to the entire announcement before saying, "Mr. Andrew Kiffin in the list there used to own Servitron, Inc."

Janna found the names. Servitron…one of the K.C. firms.

"Servitron makes service robots, including waitrons. That started me thinking."

Always a prelude to trouble. Janna stretched her neck, trying to see the doodles. It appeared to be nothing but a group of circles.

Mama pushed his glasses up his nose. "We've been guilty of tunnel vision, saying only Aida was in the right position to produce that entry angle. There's another possible source of the shot." He shoved the doodles toward her and leaned across his desk to point. "If this circle represents Armenda, these three Aida, Sydney, and Junior, and this line of circles in front the gunmen, then if we draw a line pointing forty degrees to Armenda's right…" His finger traced a dotted line already drawn and stopped on a circle behind the gunmen, labeled: *W*.

Janna frowned at it. After a moment the meaning became clear. She stared. "The waitron? That's im—"

"Swatbots carry weaponry," he reminded her.

A tingle slid down her spine. "Mama…shooting Armenda with a needler rigged in the waitron means—"

"Someone intended Armenda to die in that riff," he finished grimly. "The robberies were just camouflage for the real objective." His eyes gleamed behind his glasses. "That's why the riffers settled for thirty people out of five hundred. And that's how Junior or Sydney could be responsible."

The theory met mixed reviews with the squad members who drifted in over the next hour.

"It explains the angle of the entry wound," Cruz agreed. "However—"

"That's a lot of trouble to go to…" Mt. Weyneth rumbled.

"…to kill someone," Showalter finished.

Cruz eyed them, frowning. "We'll get along better if you let me finish my own sentences." He turned to Mama. "These people had to circumvent two separate security setups. Very risky. One slip on the first job and they'd never have the chance to kill Armenda."

"Challenge appeals to some people," Mama said.

Cruz shook his head. "What about the risk of hiring seven people, maybe eight if your perpetrator wasn't the person controlling the waitron? That's at least seven chances for leaks, seven chances of being tied to the crime."

Showalter nodded. "It'd be much simpler to hire a..."

"...professional killer. And safer," Weyneth said. "The average person's daily routine offers..."

"...any number of opportunities for fatal accidents."

Mama pushed his glasses up his nose. "When we find who killed Armenda, maybe he, or she, will explain the rationale behind choosing such an elaborate charade. Cruz, did you find out if Yi has a needler in the house someone could have used?"

The pucker of Cruz's forehead suggested he wished Mama had not asked that question. "The only weapons Yi has are some ancient Chinese swords and stuff."

"Making it difficult for anyone in that courtyard except the riffers, and the waitron, to be armed."

Janna admired Cruz's self-possession. After a moment of eyeing Mama like someone feeling the onset of a headache, he shrugged. "You're right; at this point, we can't afford to overlook any possibilities. Have you come up with anything else today?"

Janna said, "We spent a chunk of department funding on long distant calls to locate the ex-heads of companies Armenda took over. Only Russell Brashear, who used to own Konza Holotronics, is still here in Topeka. Morgan Wiedower moved to Kansas City after Armenda took over his security firm."

Cruz's expression went thoughtful. "Someone like Wiedower knows security systems well enough to neutralize them."

Which pushed Wiedower up the suspect list next to Kiffin. Janna went on, "Also in K.C. are Andrew Kiffin; Rebecca Voelker and Miles Green, of Voelker & Green, manufacturing biometric security devices; and Lewis Pritchard, who had Videoscribe, Inc."

"Pritchard lost only ownership, however," Mama said. "He still manages the business, which transposes movies from film and videotapes to chips."

"He could still hate…"

"…Armenda's guts."

Janna looked up from her notes. "We can forget about Corelle Bruckerhoff in Wichita, at least. After losing BruckerJet, her charter air service, she bought into a colonial company. Their ramjet's been headed for the stars for the past ten years."

"That still gives us six possible suspects, if we go along with Maxwell's gunslinging waitron." Cruz pursed his lips. "Maxwell, since it's your theory, tomorrow you and Brill drive up to Kansas City and talk to the five subjects there."

Mama nodded.

"Maybe you'll get lucky and find that Wiedower and Kiffin teamed up, Weidower masquerading as the waiter and maid to take care of security and Kiffin handling the waitron."

Weyneth nodded. "And the enhancements will show the rest of the suspects…"

"…among the gunmen," Showalter continued, "the whole plot suggested…"

"…by the son and daughter," they finished in unison, and grinning, slapped each other's hands.

"Speaking of enhancements," Janna said.

Cruz nodded. "Even as Lieutenant Applegate's CAProp comedians perform, Dan is down in the lab…begging and threatening, whatever it takes to light a fire under the computer fundis."

"Fast bargain." Mama's gaze focused up the room.

They turned to see Daniel Singer coming in with a bulging manila envelope.

He threaded his way back to them and dropped into a chair, sighing. "Well, I had to promise them your firstborn children, Em, but here the enhancements are." He turned the envelope upside down. Colored computer prints spilled onto the desk. "The markings in the lower left corner of each photo are for the purpose of comparing them to the original if you want. One-A and 1-B are the waiter and maid."

They scrambled for the prints. Each showed four faces. Mama's long arms snaked by Weyneth's bulk to capture one of each print. Janna waited for him to sit down, then peered over his shoulder.

Though the frame chosen for enhancement caught the waiter at a different angle than the maid, both were the same face…androgynous…male but marginally, equally believable as female. Janna knew enough about the enhancement program to understand that the computer chose hair and eye colors according to skin tones. In their waiter's case, the computer had suggested light brown hair on both the waiter and maid photographs, but light brown eyes on one and blue eyes on the other. The face looked pleasant but unremarkable to the point of disappearing instantly from memory.

Janna grimaced. No one would ever remember seeing him.

The gunmen's enhancements seemed more promising. All were male...four of them lean, two stocky; one red-haired and freckled, one sandy blond, two of average coloring, two olive-skinned. A small gold hoop gleamed in the ear of one of the olive-skinned jons. A scar cut the eyebrow of another, gleaming white in the black hair. Another scar sprawled lividly across the back of the blond jon's hand.

"I wonder if those are real." Singer tapped the scars.

Weyneth rumbled, "Records should..."

"...tell us." Showalter raised a brow at Singer. "You did..."

"...take them by?"

Singer sighed. "Am I a rookie? I had the Criminalistics computer call the data directly into Records, Priority One, and Communications send it to NCIC. The local results should—"

Singer's phone buzzed.

Cruz pounced on it, and grinned as the Records computer's voice said, "Investigator Daniel Singer, Priority One request results." The grin faded as the enhancements ran up the screen to the computer's accompanying litany of: "Subject One-A, negative; subject One-B, negative; subject Two, negative..."

Singer stared in disbelief. "They can't all be negative."

They were. Not one photograph matched any in their files.

"Outside talent." Mama pulled off his glasses and polished them with a tissue from his desk drawer. "As long as we're going to K.C. tomorrow, we'll take a data chip of the enhancements and ask the KCPD to run it through their computer."

"Might as well," Cruz said. "NCIC won't be back by then. The FBI's computer is good but a file search for seven subjects by photograph alone is going to be a long job even for it. Meanwhile, we do have leads to follow here. We can't let the others do all the work." He picked up several copies of the prints and headed for the door

The rest of them followed.

7

No morning could have been better for traveling. Janna relaxed in her seat. The temperature remained cool enough to require a coat, but warm enough that they let their trenchcoats hang open, and the sky arched in a flawless bowl of cobalt, the last clouds cleaned away by rain last evening. Against it overhead shone the east-flying silver of a dirigible's ball-like balloon and the manta ray gondola clinging to the bottom. Turnpike stretched away across the hills in an undulating ribbon, scattered with the looming bulk of trailer trucks. The rare road cars darted like minnows among whales.

Sometimes very fleet minnows.

Janna avoided looking at the speedometer as Mama skimmed the Meteor past one behemoth after another. She made conversation instead. "Where did you disappear to yesterday evening?"

Mama shrugged. "Salmas's place."

"Salmas's place?" Janna knew the waiter had been released to house confinement under his material witness status, but what sent Mama back to talk to him again? "Did we forget to ask something?"

"I went there about his sculptures, not the case."

Janna blinked. "His sculptures? You really think they're good?"

"Absolutely." He sailed around a big Aeromac. The Meteor bucked over the turbulence of the truck's fans. "Arianna Cho thinks so, too."

"Cho?" Listening to herself, Janna grimaced. She sounded like an damned echo.

"I talked her into coming with me," Mama said. "I thought Salmas might like a professional opinion. Today she's asking the Trexlers for permission to exhibit a couple of Salmas's pieces at the gallery." He paused. "She's a bright and interesting woman. We had dinner after leaving Salmas."

At least dinner. According to the bedside clock, when Janna managed to pry one eye open to read it, he came in sometime after one in the morning.

"Did you study?" he asked.

"I tried." She grimaced again. "Witch and bitch were at it again…this time fighting over separating trash for the pickup today. Bitch accused witch of throwing recyclables in with biodegradables and witch countered that last week bitch didn't sort the recyclables correctly." She sighed. "I wonder why they ever married?"

A corner of Mama's mouth twitched down. "Sometimes, bibi, even a witch or bitch is preferable to living alone."

Janna eyed him. Maybe the reason he had not found an apartment had less to do with location and rent than with the lack of a roommate.

Surely that was nonsense. In her experience, people unable to bear solitude were insecure, and she could not imagine anyone more secure than Mama.

Belatedly she realized that he had continued talking. "What?"

He grinned. "Earth to Janna. I said the idea of everyone being guilty isn't that outré. It happened in a movie called *Murder On the Orient Express*." His eyes went thoughtful behind his glasses. "I wonder if that movie is in Armenda's collection."

Janna frowned. "You mean someone with access to the movie could have taken the idea, gone to a group of Armenda's enemies, and suggested they gang up to kill him?"

Mama smiled. "It's an interesting possibility." The toll gates appeared ahead. "Where do you want to start, after we've been polite and let the KCPD know what we're doing in town?"

She pulled their list of names and addresses out of her trenchcoat pocket. "Since you mentioned movies, why not with Pritchard at Videoscribe?"

Mama nodded. "What's the address?" Before they left Topeka, Communications had given them a Kansas City map chip but when Janna gave Mama the Broadway address, he blocked her reach for the car computer. "I can find that."

And after swinging by the Locust Street HQ building to announce their presence to the KCPD and leave the enhancement data chip at the Records section, he drove back toward I-70 and straight to Videoscribe.

The company occupied the top floor of a twentieth century brick building dark with age. Mama insisted on walking up the old fashioned open staircase but Janna took the elevator—modern despite its antique grillework car—past a party supply wholesaler, the editorial offices of a balloon enthusiasts' magazine, an architectural firm, and a colonial company outfitter. Videoscribe's reception area looked like something straight out of the building's period: leather arm chairs, potted plants, and antique movie posters in cases on the walls.

Most were unfamiliar to Janna, but Mama's eyes gleamed with enthusiasm. "*Citizen Kane*, *The Rocky Horror Picture Show*, *Icrade 16:42*, *The Dream Maze*. This is a cinema bob's paradise."

The reception desk had been built with a raised front edge to hide the word processor and communications system phone on top, and a small newscanner. Nothing, however, hid the anachronism of the incense-scented receptionist in his waist length purple ponytail and spray-fit copper bodysuit.

After examining their identification and calling Pritchard on the phone, he sent them through the double doors behind him, then returned to watching a newscanner story on whether the Russian shuttle had crashed accidentally or been shot down by the Chinese.

Beyond the doors, all antiquity vanished. The electronic equipment they glimpsed through workroom windows wore the gleam of leading edge technology.

Until they reached Lewis Pritchard's office. In it, flat metal canisters, video tape cases, and video chip cases sat stacked everywhere...around the video cassette player and video chip player on the battered L-shaped desk, filling half open drawers of metal filing cabinets, cluttering the floor, the straight wooden chairs, the window ledges, even the top of the computer on the desk ell. Long rolls of paper that might be more movie posters made a pyramid on a worn leather couch.

The tantalizing smell of coffee filled the room, coming from a steaming mug between the cassette and chip players on the desk. Real coffee. Janna savored the scent.

"Shove that stuff off the chairs," the man behind the desk said without looking up from the chip player's screen.

Mama stared at the canisters. "Shouldn't these films be in some environmentally controlled room?"

Pritchard glanced up. "What? Oh. Don't worry; the cans are all empty."

They cleared the chairs. Sitting down, Janna eyed Pritchard. A man in his late thirties or early forties, he looked pale and soft, filling his jumpsuit like marshmallow. Dark wisps stuck out all over his beard and hair. No stretch of the imagination could match him to any of the enhanced photographs.

After a minute Pritchard folded down the screen, picked up his mug, and leaned back to sip from it while he eyed them across the players with apparent puzzlement. "You're Topeka leos? What can I do for you?"

Mama said, "We'd like to talk to you about Carel Armenda."

Pritchard set the mug down. "God, wasn't that terrible? His daughter called me yesterday to tell me about him."

"You're shocked by his death?" Janna watched him.

His eyes widened. "Of course. What's going to happen to Videoscribe now? That boy doesn't give a damn about movies, let alone appreciate their historical or entertainment value. The only thing I ever saw him look at was a piece of *Dying Thunder*. That's the Paul Kendig film about the last Le Mans run with wheelers." Pritchard drank from his mug again. "Sydney would be all right. She at least appreciates what we do, even if she's not the cinema bob her father was."

"How was Armenda to work for?" Mama asked.

Pritchard shrugged. "Fine. He let me run Videoscribe the way I wanted as long as he saw the books regularly and I notified him when interesting new property came in, so he could have a copy if he wanted."

"You don't mind that he took the business away from you?"

The pale eyes narrowed. "Why do you ask that? Sydney said one of the thieves killed her father."

"We thought so at first. We were wrong," Janna said.

The marshmallow body shifted. "Well, if you're looking for suspects, you're wasting your time here. I couldn't have asked for anything better than having Armenda buy up my loan notes and foreclose. I always hated all the tax and social care paperwork. Now his accountants take care of that and I'm free to just transcribe movies and books—we also do video chip facsimile reproductions of books in danger of being lost due to paper deterioration. Corporation backing gives me more credit to negotiate for transcription rights. And Armenda provides me Colombian coffee beans that he somehow brings into the country outside the trade armistice quotas." He wrapped both hands around his coffee mug and pulled it against his chest. "I wonder if the girl knows how he did it."

Pritchard sounded anything but bitter. Though of course he could be lying. Janna asked, "You were never afraid of being fired?"

Pritchard smirked. "The licenses for access to the movies in the Turner Libraries and other depositories belong to me personally, not Videoscribe."

Mama toyed with one of the film cans. "You said Armenda liked to be kept informed of new properties in case he wanted a copy. What kind of movies did he like?"

"War movies, adventures, mysteries, thrillers. A few comedies. No heavy drama. He liked entertainment."

"What movies, specifically? How about *Murder On the Orient Express*?"

Pritchard scratched at his beard. "I expect. He collected all the movies made of Agatha Christie's books. I told you he liked mysteries and thrillers. He wanted anything with Steve McQueen or Sean Connery or David Teman. He collected directors, too, Robert Altman, Ridley Scott, Paul Kendig, Isas Cilombo."

None of the names meant anything to Janna, but Mama nodded at each. He pulled a copy of the enhancements from an inside pocket of his trenchcoat and handed them to Pritchard. "Have you ever seen these people around Armenda or either of his children?"

Pritchard studied the photos, then shook his head.

"Do you know anything about Armenda's other companies here in Kansas City?"

"Do they have to do with movies?"

Obviously he did not know. A short time later they left, leaving a copy of the enhancements and their card, in case Pritchard remembered the faces after all.

"Next stop?" Mama asked as they climbed back into the car.

She activated the car computer and recited the addresses into it. For each, the city map flashed on the dash screen and by successive enlargements, zoomed in on the block with the requested address. That gave her not only routes to the addresses but their relationship to each other. "Kiffin's office in North Kansas City looks closest."

The office, a sales and service center for IBM's robotics division, might be. Andrew Kiffin was not.

Leaving the service section, where Kiffin worked as an engineer trouble shooter, Janna shook her head. "He's been on the IBM space platform for two months? That eliminates him as a suspect."

"Maybe not."

She glanced sharply at Mama as she slid the car door closed. "Maybe not how? When you're on a platform, you don't casually drop groundside for a few hours."

Mama switched on the power. "They said he's working on the Sunbath II project."

Project Sunbath, she remembered from Modern History in college, had been a disaster. The dome over an experimental mining operation on Mercury failed, killing all four hundred people under it. It also set back for over a decade plans for any new mining projects requiring life supports, such as proposed sea bottom operations. Did this mean IBM wanted to try Mercury again? "What does this have to do with our riffers?"

"The plan," Mama said, "is to use robots this time, robots that can be controlled from the safety of a space station."

Janna took a breath. "You think Kiffin controlled the waitron from the IBM platform?"

"He has the capability."

Except it needed more than capability. "Whoever controlled the waitron knew Mrs. Yi," she reminded Mama. "Does Kiffin?"

"That's something to find out when we're home again."

Miles Green at Voelker and Green, Inc. came next on their list. Like Pritchard, he remained at the company he used to own, but as an employee. Like Pritchard, too, the small, wiry man, who talked to them in a spacious office with the title *Chief Engineer* on the door, showed no resentment of the takeover.

"Mr. Armenda's death is a tragedy. He did a lot for this company." Gadgets and electronic bits and pieces everywhere made the office look like a workshop. Green paced down a narrow path through the clutter to a windowed wall looking down on the assembly floor. "We have credit for research and development." Still talking, he paced back to the desk and picked up a caff cup. After a sip, he set it down again and headed back for the window. "We've developed three new models of our biometric locks, doubled our floor space, increased automation, and quadrupled our sales since Armenda bought us out. I only hope that before he died Armenda had the sense to leave control of the corporation to his daughter."

Another vote for Sydney.

"Junior doesn't impress you?" Mama asked.

Green grimaced. "The boy never comes except with his father, and then he's obviously bored blind." Returning to the desk, he picked up the cup again, but set it down without drinking. Janna decided that even if Green had resembled any of the enhancements, which he did not, or been tall enough to be one of the riffers, which he was not, he was incapable of standing as quietly as the riffers had. "Sydney never comes with her father but she's here several times a month…visiting with management and employees, asking intelligent questions about what we're doing, inviting suggestions for improvements."

Leaving the plant, Janna told Mama, "Sydney sounds like a campaigning politician."

Mama pursed his lips thoughtfully. "Doesn't she. Give the computer Servitron's address. Let's see if she visits there, too."

A stop at the assembly plant, located in a refurbished twentieth century brick warehouse north off I-70, and a conversation with the plant manager confirmed that Sydney did make regular visits.

"Does she go down to the assembly line?" Mama asked the manager, a stout man of apparent mixed asian/hispanic ancestry whose jumpsuit sleeves rolled above the elbows gave the impression of a willingness to work on the line, too.

The manager frowned at them. "What does that have to do with finding the thief who killed Mr. Armenda?"

"Nothing," Mama replied with an innocent smile. "We've just heard personnel in several Armenord subsidiaries express pleasure at Miss Armenda's interest in their businesses and I was curious whether that's typical of her."

The frown faded. "I don't know if it's typical, but she seems interested in not only how many service robots we produce but how we build them and if the employees are happy working here."

Back in the car, Mama said, "She's making friends and allies everywhere. Building support for taking over Armenord, do you want to bet?"

Janna nodded. "The question is, did she know when she'd have this chance?"

Their next interview, Rebecca Voelker, said, "Someone killed Carel Armenda? That's the best news I've had today." Small and wiry with burr cut platinum hair tipped lavender, she eyed them across the desk of her spice-scented office off the Plaza.

Mama leaned back in his molded foam chair and crossed his legs. "You still hate him after four years?"

Iridescent lavender nails rapped the desk top in one staccato roll. "He's a bastard." Voelker pushed to her feet. "He *was* a bastard." The lavender lips curved in a smile. "Never has the past tense sounded so sweet." She paced toward the windows overlooking the Plaza. Sunlight gleamed silkenly on the fabric of her beige bodysuit and ankle-length tabard. "If you're looking for people who wanted him dead, I'm one, but I didn't kill him." She turned to face them, smile drawn thin. "I wasn't anywhere near the scene at the time."

"We haven't mentioned where or when he died," Janna said.

The iridescent nails drummed the glass at Voelker's back. "It doesn't matter. Whenever, I was probably here." She circled the room, straightening pictures. The spicy scent eddied around Janna and Mama. "I'm almost always here. I have a business to run."

"The Meal Deal." Mama raised a brow. "Catering?"

"No." Voelker rearranged articles on a shelf of art glass. "Although it's a service we can extend to subscribers."

Subscribers. "You're a subscription meal service?" Janna asked.

Voelker swung to face them. "With a difference. We tailor our service to each subscriber's individual needs. A week's worth of one, two, or three meals a day chosen from a menu is only the start. If you're a shut-in, we can deliver every day instead, to check on your welfare. If you're diabetic or have an ulcer or are a recovering cardiac patient, or you just want to lose weight, we provide meals within your dietary limits. If you suddenly have ten people coming to dinner, a phone call provides food for all of them."

"It's an excellent concept," Mama said. "How is business?"

Voelker's smile answered the question. After a moment, the smile twisted. "I could have done as well or better with Voelker and Green, if Miles had given me a chance. But I'm afraid my cousin is a born wage slave." Voelker paced back toward the windows. "I had to talk like hell to convince him to go into business for himself and not just sell his designs to one of the companies already manufacturing biometric locks, then when Armenda came slithering into our lives, he couldn't wait to jump camps and throw away everything I'd worked to build." Her hands clenched into fists.

"What did Armenda do, buy up your loan notes and foreclose?" Janna asked.

"We didn't have any loans," Voelker said with pride. "We started small and built slowly. Armenda extorted V & G away. He started as a client, buying our locks for his security business. Then when he'd made friends with Miles, he informed my cousin that I hired slighs."

Janna straightened in her molded foam chair. Hiring slighs, unidented citizens, was in itself legal. The government urged, even pressured, citizens to be idented, but no one *had* to be...however brainbent it seemed to forfeit bank accounts, legal schooling, free medical care, and social care just because of moral objections to being numbered, digitized, and computerized. However, because unidented employees must be paid in barter, having no bank account, they turned the employer's tax and social care paperwork into hell. So most employers did not bother filing on slighs...which *was* illegal. Also, slighs usually being unskilled labor and always leery of calling official attention to themselves, employers felt safe paying them a fraction of what an idented employee earned.

As though reading Janna's thoughts, the small bibi's voice went defensive. "We needed slighs to save money. I tried to be fair, though." She paced between her desk and the window. "We provided a noon meal, and only the slighs knew they didn't pay for theirs and that I let them take home what was left each day, plus teas and caff and occasional bottles of wine when I came across something decent in bulk at a bargain price. I bought them clothes at the better quality discount houses. I arranged for visits to doctors and dentists I found who would slip slighs in among their registered patients. I located teachers willing to teach an evening or week end session to sligh children."

"Yet you didn't tell your partner what you were doing," Mama said.

Voelker spread her hands. "The more people who know a piece of information, particularly worriers like Miles, the bigger the chance of letting it slip to someone we'd rather not have know it. He certainly worried enough after Armenda told him…until Armenda said he could protect us if we'd let him become an equal partner." Her jaw tightened. "Of course, as soon as the bastard had a third, he wanted all the slighs fired. Miles voted with him. Then he bought Miles' share. I'd rather starve than be his employee, so I sold him my share, too. Only I made him pay a hell a lot more for it than he'd paid for Miles'."

But not enough. Janna eyed Voelker's hands. The slim fingers had clenched into fists. Maybe no amount of credit could be enough.

She saw Mama watching, too. He handed Voelker a copy of the enhancements. "Do you know any of these people?"

Voelker looked over the photos. "No." She could be telling the truth. Interest and curiosity showed in her face, but no flicker of eye or expression that indicated any recognition. "I take it you believe they're involved in killing Armenda?"

"Possibly."

She returned the enhancements, shaking her head. "Bad planning. That's too many people. If I were killing someone, I'd be the only one knowing my intentions."

On the sidewalk a short time later, Janna said, "The number of riffers may be the best break we have going for us."

Mama pushed his glasses up his nose. "All we have to do is find them."

Their last interview, Morgan Wiedower, worked in the Plaza area, too, as director of the Kansas City branch of Personal Security Services. The security firm occupied a floor in one of the terraced sections of the Burnham Building's twin towers. Wiedower's office opened onto the terrace itself, overlooking the Plaza and Ward Parkway. Janna admired the view beyond the open drapes as she and Mama sat down in deep, contoured chairs. Nice work, coming to that every morning.

The ruddy-haired ex-owner of Shawnee Security smiled at them across his desk. "What can I do for the Shawnee County PD this afternoon? I assume you're not here applying for a job. Although," he added, looking them over, "we could use both of you. We always need personnel who don't look like bodyguards."

He matched the gunmen in weight and height. Janna pulled the enhancements out of her trenchcoat pocket and casually glanced at them.

"If you ever think you'd like to be better paid for risking your life, let me know."

If she added his ruddy brush of a mustache to the red-haired riffer, would the two of them look more alike? "Mr. Wiedower, tell us about Carel Armenda."

He leaned back in his chair. "Depending on who you talk to, he's either a pirate or one of Topeka's sterling citizens. I favor the former, but then, I walked his plank...which you must know or you wouldn't be here."

Janna exchanged glances with Mama. Wiedower used the present tense when referring to Armenda. By design, or was he unaware of Armenda's death?

"Haven't you seen the newscanner story about him?" Mama asked.

Wiedower's eyes narrowed. "All I've seen since I got back in town last night is reports on the Russian shuttle."

"Back from where?"

"First," Wiedower said, "suppose you tell me why you're asking."

Janna handed the enhancements across the desk to him. "Saturday night Armenda died during an armed robbery perpetrated by these individuals. They didn't kill him, however."

For several seconds Wiedower sat frowning at them, then his eyes widened in comprehension, only to narrow again for a moment before crinkling at the corners in amusement. One end of his mouth quirked. "Neither did I. Aside from the fact that I gave up brooding about Armenda a good four years ago, PSS had a management meeting at the home office this week end. I was in San Francisco from Thursday night until Sunday afternoon."

Which gave him a good alibi, although he could still have hired the group, and the man controlling the waitron. Except that he struck Janna as too relaxed to be hiding the deep bitter anger Armenda's killer must feel to go to so much trouble to kill him.

"Whoever arranged the killing knows security systems," Mama said. "Could one of your former employees be so loyal to you he or she would harbor a grudge? Maybe one of them who now works for Beria Security?"

Wiedower frowned in thought. "No one comes to mind. Have you—"

The telephone on his desk buzzed.

He punched it on. "Yes, Chandra?" The phone must have focused sound. Janna caught only an indistinct murmur. "When he arrives, send him in." Punching off, he raised his brows at Mama and her. "There's a leo coming up from the lobby looking for you. While we wait for him, I started to ask if you've checked out the rumor I heard that someone in another company Armenda acquired tried to sue him for theft but never got to court because, so the accusation went, he bought off the judge."

They straightened in their chairs. "Which company?" Mama asked.

Wiedower shrugged. "I don't know. There may not even have been—"

The door slid open. Through the opening past Wiedower's elegant secretary strode a man in the gold-sidestriped turquoise bodysuit of a KCPD leo, turquoise blue helmet tucked under his arm. He headed for Mama and Janna. "Sergeants Maxwell and Brill? Did you know there's been an ATL out on you for the past three hours? Luckily I spotted your car going down into the building garage and the guard in the lobby remembered which elevator you'd taken, so I had only one tower of offices to call to locate you. You're to contact Sergeant Diosdado in Robbery."

Wiedower swiveled the phone screen toward them. "What's the number?"

A succession of lion faces on the screen stopped at one with the classical beauty of a Greek statue, albeit a statue of someone approaching middle age and with a puckish cant to his eyebrows. "Those are some interesting individuals on your data chip," the Greek statue said. "Records fed them to our computer and passed on the results to me. You're in luck, and maybe I am, too. We have a positive ID on one of your suspects."

8

Squadrooms all looked alike, Janna mused…rows of desks, many back-to-back; buzzing phones and overlapping voices; lions and she-lions talking to phone screens or civilians; dictyper screens glowing in a row against one wall. They even smelled the same, of caff, fast food, and a musty accumulation left by the decades of humanity who had sweated, fretted, and worked here.

Sergeant Diosdado leaned forward in his chair, spreading hard copy across his desk. "Your suspect is an old acquaintance of ours. Righteous name, Antony Howath Kushner. Street name, Tony Ho. Licensed in Missouri as a joyeur."

Tony Ho might actually sell his sexual favors, but he had probably bought the license to provide an easy explanation for converting large amounts of carry to credit. Even with sex being a legal commodity, many clients paid in carry to avoid having their bank records show that they paid for sex.

"Here's what we have on him locally, plus information obtained from Chicago and St. Louis the first time he was arrested here in Kansas City."

In person the puckish tilt of the sergeant's brows became even more pronounced. Give him pipes and cloven hooves, Janna decided, and he would look like the Greek god Pan. Did he share Pan's sexual appetites as well as his eyebrows?

She shoved aside the speculation to study the photograph with the hard copy. It matched the enhancements of the waiter. Janna grinned at Mama. If she had to choose just one of the riffers to identify, the waiter would have been her choice.

Mama glanced down the copy. "He cross-dresses and likes to wear disguises, bibi."

Reading over his shoulder, Janna saw that, and something else even more significant. Tony habitually took any tokens his victims had. "He sounds like our jon."

"Arrests in St. Louis for theft and fraud," Mama went on. "Two convictions, one year of community service for the first one, a year and a half at Phoenix Hill for the second." He glanced across the desk at Diosdado. "How's that project working?"

The sergeant shrugged. "It shows the lowest recidivism rate in the state. Whether that's because of its methods and the fact that it's privately run, or due to the class of prisoners sent there, I don't know."

Phoenix Hill had not rehabilitated Tony. Janna saw more arrests in Chicago for theft and fraud, none resulting in convictions. Then came a conviction for armed robbery. He had been one of five people involved in the robbery. A group effort. She pointed at the entry.

Mama nodded to indicated he saw.

Sentenced to Joliet, Tony made parole in two years. After which he moved to Kansas City, where he had been the subject of numerous field interviews as both the primary subject and a companion to the primary, had been questioned five times in relation to fraud complaints, two resulting in arrests, and been questioned half a dozen times more by Robbery, with no arrests. Charges had been dropped on both fraud arrests.

"What happened?" Janna asked.

Diosdado grimaced. "Once Tony's out of whatever role he played during the skin, he looks completely different. See the narrative info on the FIF's? He looks male; he looks female; the field interview officer wouldn't have known who he was without seeing his Scib Card. Fraud told me the witnesses in their complaints were so unsure about identification, the fraud charges wouldn't stick. The same thing happened to my partner and me." The spring on his chair squeaked as Diosdado leaned back. "We suspect Tony of being involved in two jewelry store riffs we've been investigating. Specifically, we think he's the individual who provided diversions—a pregnant woman going into labor one time, an old man having a heart attack the other—that drew security guards away from their posts long enough for his accomplices to enter the stores without resistance. Except we've had no better luck than Fraud finding a witness to positively identify him."

"Do you know who his accomplices are?" Mama asked.

"We think so, but..." Diosdado shrugged. "...so far there's nothing solid to—oh, I see what you're getting at. Our others can't be your others. We have records on several of those deeks, and none of your enhancements look like any of them. The M.O. doesn't match, either." Teeth flashed in the handsome face. "Finding Tony may give us two sets of riffers."

Something else struck Janna. Tony's record showed no indication of violence. He had never been identified as carrying a weapon, even in armed robberies. Considering that and the reported startled expression of the riffer who thought he shot Armenda, maybe none of the group expected a murder. If that were the case: "He might give them to us on a platter if we'll guarantee no prosecution for felony murder."

"What's UDMT?" Mama asked, pointing at the letter combination in a list of dates and alphanumeric designations on the first page of the hard copy.

Obviously a retrieval log. Janna presumed the KCPD's Records section did the same as the SCPD's, record the access codes of officers calling up files, in order to keep track of what criminals interested which sections. If that were the case, the access code must indicate not only the officer calling up the file but also his section. The UDMT designation, two entries before today's, stood out sharply among the succession of IVRB and IVFD codes.

"That's someone in Metro patrol." Diosdado smiled. "A uniform on an independent safari, I expect."

Possibly because Tony had victimized a friend or relative, Janna reflected, though more likely a lion or she-lion hoping for a wrap that would open the way to Investigations. City to city, leos remained the same. "May I use the phone? I'd like to call home and start warrants through the pipe."

Diosdado pushed his phone toward her.

Reaching Vradel, she reported what they had and gave him Tony Ho's name and bank. Vradel smiled out of the screen in grim satisfaction. "If you feel you're close to catching this deek, stay up there. The Russian shuttle has made most of the media forget our riffers, but the director, his father-in-law, and the mayor haven't."

Punching off, Janna sighed. "I should have brought my toothbrush along."

Mama sent her a quick sideglance, but before she could wonder at the meaning, he said, "Since we have our suspect's last known address, let's go visiting."

"You did hear me mention how different he can look, didn't you?" Diosdado asked, then he shrugged and grinned. "On the other hand, it isn't much fun here alone with my partner home on paternity leave, and we might get lucky."

One way or another, Janna mused. The grin made him look gleefully wicked. Even more attractive…more like Pan than ever. She smiled back at him.

Luck did not start, however, at Tony's home address, the second floor of a Victorian house in the Westport area. Mama volunteered to knock on the door because he looked the least lionish. Diosdado climbed out of the car around the corner to cover the back of the house while Janna waited across the street by the car, soaking up the spring sunshine. Fifteen minutes later Mama came back shaking his head. "No one's home," he said, and erupted into a string of violent sneezes.

"You all right?" she asked.

He nodded, sniffling.

She reached in through the car window and tapped the horn three times. No Tony. That hardly came as a surprise, but it was still frustrating. Missing him here meant legwork hunting for him.

When Diosdado appeared around the house to rejoin them, they gave him the bad news, too. He shrugged philosophically. "We want some challenge in the job, don't we? Are you catching cold?" he asked as Mama sniffled some more.

Mama shook his head. "Spring pollen, I think."

Or any of the other numerous plants and animals he reacted to, Janna reflected. Fortunately for him, new treatments coming down from research labs on the space platforms kept his allergies under control most of the time.

"We may not be totally out of luck, though," Mama said. "I found a little more probable cause, if we need it. I talked to a teenage girl home downstairs. According to her, Tony left Wednesday. He told the girl's mother he would be home Sunday afternoon, then came back just after midnight Sunday morning. Around Sunday noon he left again and hasn't been back since."

Diosdado grimaced. "Gone into hiding, or rabbited out of the state."

Mama reached under his glasses to rub his eyes. "Not necessarily."

The confident tone set off warning bells in Janna head. Suddenly she wondered what had Mama been doing there at the house. Fifteen minutes seemed a long time for the conversation he reported…and why should he react to spring pollen now when he'd been exposed to it all day?

When Diosdado raised a questioning brow, Mama gave them both an innocent smile. "He didn't cut cloud after your robberies, did he?"

"They didn't involve a killing, either."

"Call it a hunch, but I think he's around." Mama slid open the driver's door and swung in. "After all, he did come home, and not leave again for a number of hours. That doesn't sound like someone in a panic. We just have to hunt him without letting him know it."

Diosdado climbed into the back seat. "That won't be easy in the places he frequents, looking the way we do. On the other hand…"

Janna lost the rest of the sentence in circling the car to the passenger side, and regretted not having waited to hear it out. He must have said something amusing for Mama to be grinning that way when she slid into the car. "On the other hand what?"

"With the right clothes, I think we can make Maxwell look like mincemeat—or are you ho already?" he asked Mama. On receiving a negative shake of the head, Diosdado focused on Janna again, eyeing her appraisingly. "If you'd use more cosmetics and wear something feminine and sexy, you could pass as a female impersonator."

Janna frowned at Mama. So he found it amusing that she needed to look more feminine in order to pass as a man pretending to be female? How amusing would he find being turned into a pretzel?

Diosdado leaned his forearms on the backs of the front seats. "I have friends at Metro division. I'll see if I can talk them into giving us access to their decoy wardrobe."

Mama switched on the car. "We don't have to bother Metro; we have everything we need. I packed clothes for both of us."

Now she understood that sideglance in the Robbery squadroom. Outrage flared in Janna. "You pawed around in *my room*?"

The car rose off its parking rollers. Mama sighed. "Don't get so upset, bibi."

"Upset!" She gritted her teeth. "Who the hell's upset! You're dead, Maxwell!"

"Wait until I get out of the car so I don't have to be a witness," Diosdado said.

"Bibi," Mama said hastily, "it's just that the New York City Ballet is here this week, and I thought that as long as we were in town, it'd be a pity not to see them. There's more to life than police work. You know you enjoy these things when I drag you to them, but if I'd said anything beforehand, you'd have refused to consider it. We just need somewhere to change," he told Diosdado over his shoulder.

The K.C. detective sat back with a bemused expression. "How about Metro Division? We need photographs of Tony's friends anyway. Go south to 63rd and turn east."

They changed in the station locker room while Diosdado called Records for the photographs. Mama's bodysuit fit as though sprayed on and changed color with every shift of light, from gold to blue to a red that matched his over-the-knee boots. But why the hell had he chosen what he did for her…just because he'd talked her into buying it? She liked the metallic blue color and even the wide, latticed opening up the sides of the pantlegs, but she had never worn the jumpsuit. At home away from Mama's enthusiasm, the neckline plunging to her waist in front and back left her feeling threatened with imminent exposure. It still did.

She frowned at her reflection in the mirror above the wash basins while wiggling her feet into matching stiletto-heeled ankle boots. "What female impersonator would wear something this revealing? It'll slide off my shoulders the moment I relax, or I'll fall out of it, announcing to all the world that I'm female, and we'll be blown."

"No." Mama rolled his eyes. "In the first place, the sleeves keep it from sliding off your shoulders. In the second, what do you think double-sided tape is for?" He tossed her a roll of it and returned to painting his fingernails gold with a polish pen he had bought on the way to the division station. "A strip down each side of the décolletage will keep it flat against you and hide the fact that that's you under the fabric, not padding. Be sure to use plenty of makeup, and jewelry. I brought several necklaces. Put them all on, and the ear wraps."

She sighed and opened her cosmetics kit on the shelf under the mirrors. He would choose the most uncomfortable jewelry her father had ever designed. The support wire cut painfully into her ear with the weight of those silver leaves dangling from the lobes and curling down into the ear from the top. She began drawing on eyeliner. "This better be worth it. I'll take it out of your hide if I endure this suit and these wraps and find Tony's left town after all."

The polish pen's foam tip gilded his nails in sure, practiced strokes. "His closet and dresser drawers didn't look as though he'd packed anything, and with all night to do it, he would have if he were cutting cloud."

Closet and dresser drawers! She whirled on Mama, lowering her voice so no one coming into the locker room would hear. "I knew it! Shit. You broke into his apartment."

Mama blew on the nails. "I did not break in. The women downstairs have a key so they can feed Tony's cat when he's away."

"Cat? No wonder you were sneezing."

He continued smoothly, "I just convinced the girl that I'd heard the cat crying and we ought to go up and check on its welfare."

"And while she did, you looked around." Janna shook her head and went back to applying makeup. The man was incorrigible. "Mama, one of these days you are going to drop us in shit too deep for even you to swim out of." But as long as he had gone there… "Did you find anything interesting?"

Grinning, he capped the pen and gingerly picked up his glasses from the shelf. "The man has excellent taste. Furniture, jewelry, clothes—both men's and women's—are all top card, quality with understated elegance, nothing gaud—bibi…" As the glasses settled in place, he frowned at her. "…if you want to look like a man, you *have* to use more cosmetics than that. You're trying to cover a beard, remember." He reached for the kit on the mirror shelf. "I'd better do it for you."

She let him, and let him press on the long silver false fingernails he bought along with the nail polish pen. It made her feel like someone being made up for a play. Essentially the situation, come to think of it.

Diosdado came in while Mama fussed over her hair, frizzing and backcombing it into a bush. He held up a sheaf of paper. "Cohort photos fresh from the printer. Well." The puckish brows climbed. "You two dink up nicely. Now I don't know if I ought to let you run around the city. We don't need ho jons throwing themselves off the AT&T building in despair when after you've dazzled them, they find out you're female and you're heterosexual."

She glanced toward the mirror to see exactly how she looked, and gaped at the flash stranger staring back.

Mama smirked. "Now maybe you'll listen to your Mama's advice on how to dress."

"When your wardrobe stops being fluorescent I'll think about it. Meanwhile, let's figure out where we're going and go before these wraps amputate my ears."

They spread the hard copy of Tony's file out on a massage table and studied the FIF's for the locations he had been seen and the names of his companions on those occasions. Fraud's reports yielded a few more names as well as the locations where the skin games occurred. Diosdado had still more names in connection with the suspected robberies.

They lacked photographs of those friends without police files, however...many of whom were artists and musicians. The general impression Janna received was that fit with Tony's preferred territory, Westport to the Plaza, an area Janna knew by reputation from hearing Mama talk about his own theater and artist friends there.

"Where to first?" she asked.

Diosdado pursed his lips. "Not the clubs yet. The meat walk won't be in full parade for another couple of hours and the people we're interested in like action. Let's try some of the gallery cafes."

Topeka had none of the breed, but Janna had heard about them from Mama, who claimed Westport, rightly or not, as the birthplace of the first ones. The idea sounded pleasant...a cafe-cum-gallery, somewhere people could enjoy artwork with their food and drinks.

It sounded informal, however. She eyed Mama and herself. "Aren't we overdressed?"

Diosdado grinned. "Yes, and no. You'll see."

The Glass Dragon was their first stop. She and Mama arrived first...without Diosdado. *Too many people down there know me*, the detective had said as they planned their itinerary. *Coming in with me would tag you as lions, too.* Despite the still-chilly April temperatures, a number of fashionably dressed patrons sat at tables on the sidewalk. At their feet, or in one case, stacked in a squatty porterbot, sat bags imprinted with the names of area shops, identifying them as shoppers resting before heading home, taking the opportunity to renew their energy with a cup of caff, perhaps laced with amphetamines.

Janna envied them their jackets, wishing, shivering, she had not let Mama convince her that no female impersonator would cover this outfit with a gray trenchcoat. True he had also left his coat behind, but his bodysuit did not bare his back and chest.

A young woman at a table by the door gave them a measuring stare and began sketching on the pad in her lap.

Mama caught Janna's hand. "Get in character, bibi. Put some swing in your hips. Strut."

He himself, Janna noticed, had been strutting from the moment they parked the car. Passing the artists, he made it even more theatrical. She felt more like jogging, to keep warm.

In the Glass Dragon, the rich scents of coffee and cinnamon enveloped them. Coffee. Janna's mouth watered. It felt like an eternity since the sandwich lunch in Servitron's break room.

Mama made a pleased sound. "Solange is doing African subjects now."

He pointed at a long, oval glass panel etched with the detailed image of a Maasai warrior. It hung on the walls with paintings and other panels of stained or etched glass, above display cases containing small sculptures and pieces of art glass.

Surrounded by the art sat a diverse assortment of people that explained Diosdado's remark about being and not being overdressed. More shoppers occupied tables next to men and women in business clothes, and dancers still in the leotards and leg warmers of their practice costumes. Another artist sat sketching and glancing toward a table of young men and women wearing the baggy floral-patterned jumpsuits Janna noticed were popular with university students at home. She also spotted several male and female prostitutes, and individuals dressed much as she and Mama were.

The two of them stood inside the door looking over the room, and making no attempt to hide the fact. After all, Mama had reasoned in the car on the way, what was more natural than for someone coming in to look for familiar faces?

No one Janna saw matched any of the photographs they studied at Metro division. Unfortunately, there might be any number of people here useful to them, but she and Mama, unfamiliar with the territory, had no way of identifying them.

Mama apparently had the same thought. "Let's find a table and wait for Diosdado."

They headed for an empty one. A businessmen, catching Janna's eye as she passed, raised his brows inquiringly and tilted his head toward an empty chair at his table. She swept by him, shaking her head in disgust. Wonderful. Her reward for suffering killer jewelry and clothes that invited hypothermia was a toad who mistook her for not a female impersonator but a joyeur.

A waiter barely out of his teens materialized to hand them menu cards. "Are you looking for someone?" A white dragon crawled over the left shoulder of his hip-length green tabard, the head end of the dragon stretching across the tabard's front, its hind legs and long, elaborate tail curling down the back.

"Tony Ho," Mama replied, and when the waiter raised a brow, described their suspect, adding, "Sometimes he cross-dresses."

The waiter gave them a polite smile. "He doesn't sound familiar. What would you like?"

"Coffee," Janna said promptly. "Very hot."

"The same for me," Mama said. "Are you new? Tony comes here all the time."

"Sorry." The waiter repeated the smile, more mechanical this time. "I don't know him." He backed away from the table.

Janna grimaced. "Too bad we can't badge him. Maybe he'd try harder to help."

"Maybe he can't; Tony might prefer not drawing attention to himself."

Possibly. From the corner of her eye Janna watched the door for Diosdado. He had still not arrived by the time their order did, and Janna, savoring the coffee sip by rich, scalding sip, found herself torn between wondering what was keeping him and hoping he would not appear until she finished. She fought to keep from tearing the wraps off her ears.

Pieces of conversation drifted from the surrounding tables, fragments about classes, about dancing, an argument on the merit of a painting hanging near them. The table with the businessman who showed interest in her discussed the election as they sipped their wine. Janna listened to distract herself from the pain in her ears.

"What we need," a woman's voice said, "is another Neva McLeish."

"Another Velvet Hammer?" a jon came back. "God help us."

"Are you trying to make us think you're old enough to remember McLeish?" The woman's voice scoffed. "Lipp is charming, but what have charming Presidents brought us? A world wide trade war, near-collapse of the ecology, catastrophic pollution, and the biggest energy crisis of all time. Since we still suffer from runaway self-indulgence, we desperately need someone else with the guts to say, 'You've had enough candy; now sit up at the table and eat your spinach!'"

From the corner of eye, Janna saw Diosdado come in the door and forgot the political discussion. As she and Mama had, he looked over the patrons. Then he headed for a table to spend a minute talking to a pair of male joyeurs. After drifting on to chat with the artist, he turned and left.

Janna stiffened. "That isn't what he's supposed to do." The plan had been for him to come by their table next, to tell them what he saw and learned.

Mama frowned but shrugged. "He can do what he wants. It's his territory."

"And our suspect!" What were they supposed to do, sit with their thumbs up their noses watching him? Not her!

She gulped down her coffee and headed for the cashier. By the time the register ran her Scib Card and r-scan and she reached the street, the K.C. detective had disappeared. They could only continue down Pennsylvania to the next cafe.

No one in the Encore looked familiar, either, and it did not even have waiters; patrons placed orders electronically from the table and waitrons brought the food. When Diosdado had still not appeared after twenty minutes, they went on to Conundrum.

Etched mazes decorated the oval glass in the cafe's doors. On the wall of the entry vestibule hung a long mirror of the same oval shape. As the two of them passed, it lighted inside. A smiling face appeared in the glass. "Welcome to Conundrum," an echoing voice intoned. "This week we have five exciting new neon sculptures by Wathena Kroll. The wine list has added three new varieties from the Phoenix Hill winery. The Phoenix d'Oro is particularly excellent with tonight's special, shark fillet."

They pushed through the inner doors.

Diosdado stood across the room talking to a wizened old man with lanky hair hanging to the waist of his shapeless jumpsuit. No sooner had they spotted him, however, than he and the old man headed for the kitchen doors.

Son of a bitch! Janna clenched her fists...and quickly opened them again as the artificial nails stabbed her palms. She held up the fingers. "I always wondered why any woman encumbers herself with these talons. Now I can think of a use for them."

Mama grinned. "Come on. Let's see what he does at Downstairs at the Upstreet."

She grimaced. "What's upstairs?"

"The Upstreet Gallery, of course."

The Downstairs, too, had sidewalk tables. Janna slowed, approaching them. Diosdado's little man sat at one playing pan pipes. Appropriately enough. She nudged Mama.

"I see him."

They separated and closed in on him from two sides. Janna sat down in an adjacent chair. "You're quick on your feet. We just saw you at Conundrum."

The old man looked up from the pipes. Amusement glinted in his eyes. "I'm old, not crippled." He eyed her. "You better get a shawl or something, apple, before you catch pneumonia." He returned to playing the pipes, something slow and haunting.

Janna bared her teeth. "We saw you talking to Diosdado. We're interested in talking to him, too."

The music stopped. "He said you would be."

"What else did he say?" Mama asked.

The old man shrugged. "That he isn't trying to avoid you. If you go to The Jewel Tree and sit near the dance floor, he'll join you."

He had better be there. She was tired of being cold and in pain and not knowing what she was doing.

Oddly enough, as soon as they walked into The Jewel Tree, she felt on familiar ground again. They might have been in the Satin Rocket or the Janus Club back home. Around her milled the same patrons stirring air thick with the same smells of perfumes, alcohol, and drugs. After buying drinks at the bar, she and Mama pushed through an already thick crowd to claim the last tiny table by the dance floor. Janna remembered to swing her hips.

Around them everyone wore high dink, many with light tape inserts in the fabric of their clothing…whether men dressed as women, women as men, or straight-dressers. Lights spun and pulsed in time to jivaqueme music more felt than heard, reverberating in the bones. Though any music would be difficult to hear in the roar of voices. Clothes glittered; light tapes gleamed and twinkled; jewelry flashed. In the strobing light lovers touched each other affectionately. Singles eyed each other with measuring gazes. A few tried each other out on the dance floor, bodies glued together, hands exploring. The meat walk had begun.

Janna leaned closed to Mama's ear, shouting so he could hear her. "He sure as hell better find us, because we'll never recognize anyone here!"

"Dance?" a voice boomed.

They looked up. Above them towered a bodybuilder mountain of male with ebony skin. His suit gave them plenty of chance to see his color and muscles, too, for while it sheathed his lower trunk, right leg, and left arm in iridescent white sidestriped in blue light tape, his chest and remaining arm and leg bore only decorative spirals of twinkling blue and white light tape baring more skin than it covered.

Janna hesitated. Would the mountain take *no* for an answer?

Then she saw he looked at Mama, not her. He smiled. "Hi. I'm Marcus."

Mama smiled back, an arch, provocative smile. Playing his role to the hilt.

Neither of them could afford to leave the table until Diosdado showed up. She slipped her arm through Mama's, baring her teeth. "And he's taken. Trail time, choomba."

The mountain hesitated, then shrugged and turned away.

Mama pouted into his drink. "What a possessive bitch you are."

The lights blinked three times. The dance floor cleared. A spotlight came on and a female impersonator, gorgeous in a brief tuxedo, strutted into its circle. "Welcome, gentlefolk. It's showtime."

The show, too, consisted mostly of female impersonators, the best of which were a stripper, who took off only slightly less than he would have if he were female, and a pastel-haired trio called Raw Sugar. Janna enjoyed them despite the torture of her ear wraps and her irritation with Diosdado.

As the show ended, the dance floor filled again. Janna's impatience returned. She drummed the talons on their tabletop. Where the hell *was* the bastard?

"Dance?"

Another one? She looked up with a scowl.

Diosdado smiled down at her, his plain jumpsuit drab and out of place.

"Save my seat, Mama," she said grimly, and followed Diosdado onto the dance floor. A dozen acid comments came to mind, but she discarded them in favor of keeping the detective friendly. The object here, after all, was finding Tony. "What've you got?"

He pulled her against him. "Such impatience. Try to act like we're a normal part of the crowd." His breath tickled her ear.

The touch reminded her how much her ears hurt, short circuiting any pleasure in the contact between them and putting an edge on her voice. "If people here know you're het, should you be holding me so close?"

"You have to be able to hear me." He spun her between two other couples. "It's a necessity, strictly business."

"Then that's a gun I feel in your pocket?"

He laughed but loosened his grip. "I have a lead on our man."

For that she could forgive him everything. She pulled back to look him in the face. "What lead?"

He whirled her on across the floor. "My sources say Tony came here yesterday and went home with a friend."

"What friend?"

"One Donald Kossay, stage name Salome...the pink-wigged singer in Raw Sugar." He stopped and stepped back from Janna. She found herself at their table again.

Mama looked up, brows raised. Quickly, she repeated what Diosdado told her.

Diosdado said, "Let's go talk to Salome."

Mama pushed his glasses up his nose. "Let Jan and me go first and arrange to be invited in. Then you join us."

Janna eyed him. "Invited in?" What was he up to now?

He grinned at her. "Just follow my lead."

Five minutes later they stood in Raw Sugar's dressing room. A sandy-haired man in a bathrobe sat at the dressing table holding the slip of paper Mama had sent backstage. "I'm Jade. Which of you is Mr. Sumner Maxwell?"

Mama held out his hand. "I am, assistant manager of the Velvet Garter in St. Louis, as I say in my note. This is Hatshepsut." He touched Janna's arm. "One of our dancers."

Hatshepsut! Trust Mama to come up with a bizarre name like that.

Jade looked her over. "Wonderful legs! Once you loosen up your spine so you walk more like a woman, honey, you'll look fabulous!"

Janna put on a sugary smile. The next person making a remark like that would earn a very close view of these fancy nails!

"Your act is already fabulous." Mama strolled over to peer at a group of photographs on one wall. "Do you ever go out of town for gigs?"

Jade sat several centimeters taller. "Sometimes. Are you interested in bringing us to St. Louis?" Despite an obvious effort to keep his voice nonchalant, eagerness ran through it.

"Very. These are nice photographs of your group." Mama turned around smiling to face Jade. "Where are the others, Salome and China? I'd like to meet them."

"Down the hall in the john. I'll get them." Jade jumped up and hurried out.

Janna said, "We're in, but I don't think they'll like us when they find out we lied about being from the Velvet Garter."

"They don't have to." Mama turned back to the photographs. "I think I've found what we came for."

She blinked. "What?"

"These aren't the three people who performed tonight. The one in the blue wig is different. During the show, I kept thinking the blue-haired one looked familiar. Now I know why."

Her pulse jumped. "We couldn't be that lucky."

But he nodded.

"Here they are," Jade's voice caroled from the doorway. He stepped aside as they turned. "Salome and China. My pets, may I present—"

"Shit!" one of the two robe-clad man in the doorway yelped. "Lions!" He flung himself backward.

Janna tossed her shoulder bag to Mama and leaped in pursuit, shoving aside the second, gaping, man.

"Sic him, bibi!"

The running man raced down the narrow hallway. Janna pounded after him. "Tony! Running won't do you any good!"

He crashed through the fire door at the far end. Its alarm whooped.

Janna banged through after him. Outside a dim alley stretched two directions. The street lay up it to her left. She paused a second, breath held, listening. The slap of running bare feet faded to her right. Deeper into the alley. Janna charged that direction, too. While her reflexes carried her along, her head wondered what she was doing chasing the deek? He probably knew every a rat hole in the city. There could be dozens of traps laid this way, even monofilament. Hit that at neck height and she would slit her throat to the spine and be dead before she even felt the wire.

On the other hand, if she let Tony elude her, how long before they caught up with him? Changing his appearance and depending on friends so he did not have to use his Card could mean months before they found his tracks again.

The slapping footsteps veered left. She heard them just in time to avoid running into a wall as the alley changed direction. Seconds later they came out on a street. Spotting her quarry was easy enough...the only man in sight in a bathrobe. She stretched her stride. While she wore heels, a handicap, he was barefooted, and she had longer legs. She gained steadily.

His glance back showed her a grimace of...desperation? He dashed into the street, dodging cars. Heading toward the alley mouth she saw on the far side? She plunged after him. Fans screamed into braking mode. Drivers swore. She ignored them all; Tony could not be allowed to reach that alley. As sure as she breathed, she knew what he would do. He would reach the dark and stop running. He would pull into a hole, muffle his breath, and cut off his trail.

He reached the far sidewalk. The alley lay just strides away. But a truck bore down on her, too big, too heavy to stop in time. She dropped to the pavement, rolling. The turbulence from the truck's fans kicked at her, battering her, pushing her aside. The thin lattice on the pantslegs ripped. Pain lanced up her leg, and down her back where her bare spine scraped the pavement. Janna ignored it, rolling once more and using the momentum to somersault onto her feet and launch into a last dive after the fleeing man.

The tackle hit him at the waist just as he reached the alley. They slammed into the wall with a bruising smack of flesh against brick. The breath whoosh out of Tony. He collapsed wheezing. Almost on the sidewalk already, Janna slid the rest of the way, rolled over on her back, and lay panting beside him.

"Wasn't that...invigorating?" She no longer felt cold, she noticed. "As soon as...we catch our...breath...we'll go somewhere...more comfortable...and chat." Also, both ear wraps and half the fake nails had come off somewhere along the way. Janna grinned. Every cloud had a silver lining.

9

"Talk to us, Tony," Diosdado said. "Tell us about Friday and Saturday night."

Tony glanced from Diosdado standing over him on one side, arms folded, to Janna and Mama leaning against the interview room table on the other. Then he fixed his gaze downward. He did not, despite Janna's silent urging, look at the wall ahead, where a hidden camera focused on his face to record pupil response to their questions.

They needed that camera's information; Tony gave them no help otherwise. Fussing with the sleeves of his jumpsuit, he repeated the same apologetic answer he made to every question asked during the walk back to The Jewel Tree and the ride downtown. "I'm sorry; I have nothing to say."

Janna swore silently. That answer left them with no grip on him, nowhere to dig. If only he would say *something*, even a lie. Preferably a lie. Lies provided a good toehold for tripping him.

Diosdado sighed. "Come on, Tony. You're lion meat and you know it. You panicked and ran from these officers. No innocent man would have."

"They startled me." Tony gingerly touched the purpling swell where his forehead met the alley wall.

That reminded Janna of her own abraded leg and back, smarting under her jumpsuit.

"Jade said we were meeting nightclub people from St. Louis and would I keep on pretending to be China so we could have a gig at their club to tell the real China about when he came back from his uncle's funeral." He glanced sidelong at Janna and Mama. "I didn't expect to see the leos from a newscanner story about a riff in Topeka."

"Do you remember everyone you see on newscanner stories?" Janna asked.

Tony stared down and said nothing.

"So you realized they'd lied to Jade," Diosdado said. "That doesn't explain why you ran."

"I'm sorry; I have nothing more to say."

Diosdado's lip curled. "Tony, you certainly know your right to remain silent, but then, you've had plenty of practice. Except this isn't like being brought in for fraud, or even robbery." He unfolded his arms and leaned down until his face came within centimeters of Tony's. "This time, choomba, someone died."

Janna noted with satisfaction that sweat gleamed on Tony's upper lip. She gave him her grimmest smile. "So the charge will be felony murder. Kish? Everyone involved in commission of the crime can be tried for murder, whether or not he personally killed Armenda. In Kansas, conviction for felony murder carries a mandatory death penalty."

Mama pulled up his legs so he sat cross-legged on the table. "And it's only fair to warn you, Tony, that the legislature is now the process of passing an organ harvest law like the one in California." He pushed his glasses up his nose. "Instead of receiving a lethal injection, you're anesthetized in a surgical suite. Your blood is drained and bagged for transfusions, and every useful organ removed. That includes muscle sections, lengths of blood vessels, bone, and bone marrow, digits—whatever the organ banks need—until there's almost nothing left but brain to cremate. It's execution by disassembly." He drew out the final sentence, pronouncing every syllable separately, making the last word a long hiss.

Of all the case law and legislation they invented to bluff suspects, playing off the California law had to rank as one of Mama's best efforts. It made even her shudder.

Tony went white. They said nothing, just let him sit with his imagination working on him. At the end of the long, strained silence, however, he whispered only, "I'm sorry; I have nothing to say."

Janna shoved her hands into her pockets to keep from smacking the table in frustration.

Diosdado sighed. "I'm sorry, too, because you know, Tony, I like you. I hate thinking of you as scattered component parts."

Tony huddled in the chair. "First you have to convict me."

"You think we won't?" Janna said. "The media went to those fund-raisers. We have video chip recordings of you at both of them."

He focused on her. "Impossible."

"You were disguised, of course, but from the video chip recordings, we made these." She pulled a copy of the enhancements out of a thigh pocket and handed them to him.

He returned them after a glance. "You can't take those to court as proof. The right program can make those faces out of anyone's. Enhancements are just computerized guesswork."

Tony knew computers and the law. Did he know juries? Janna returned the enhancements to her pocket with a shrug. "We can still present the enhancements as our probable cause for arresting you, and do you think the average jury believes the computer is just guessing? Do you think they'll care, if you're the only one available to try for this premeditated murder?"

He stiffened. "Premeditated! It was—the newscanner said the killing was an accident."

Mama said, "The media hasn't been told yet that someone rigged the waitron with a needler." He unfolded his legs and slid off the table. "The killer used you and the others, Tony. The robberies were just a cover for killing Armenda. He's still using you. Do you want to stand trial and be executed for what he did?"

Tony sucked in his breath. "I want to call my lawyer."

Two hours later he sat in the interview room again, looking much happier, even smug, beneath the wing of his attorney, a plump baby doll of a woman of multiple dimples and a breezy smile. Flint glinted in her eyes and voice, however. Janna had first noticed that when the attorney negotiated with the KC and Topeka district attorneys' offices on the phone. She drove a hard bargain, too...Tony's cooperation in Diosdado's armed robberies and the Armenda murder in return for immunity in the KC robberies and a guilty plea in Topeka to robbery only, with the Topeka D.A. recommending a minimal sentence in a minimum security facility similar to Missouri's Phoenix Hill. "Ask him your questions, leos."

Janna opened her notebook. "Who are the six gunmen and the man controlling the waitron?"

The satisfied quirk at the corner of Tony's mouth vanished. "I...don't know."

So much for cooperation. Janna snapped the notebook shut, shaking her head at Mama and Diosdado.

"I don't!" Tony bounced forward onto the edge of the chair. "That's the way the tickman set it up...no names, no contact between us except during the riffs. The tickman's the only one I met!"

"Where and how?"

Tony hesitated, but it appeared to be a pause for thinking rather than reluctance to answer. He sat back in his chair. "A letter came to the house two weeks ago, not signed, no return address on the envelope. The writer said he needed someone good with disguises and I'd been recommended. He said the job paid well."

"He?" Mama asked. "The letter gave the writer's gender?"

Tony frowned. Annoyed at being interrupted? "No, but he was a jon when I met him later. The letter said if I wanted to know more, he'd phone at eight o'clock that night. Money always interests me so I waited for the call. It came exactly at 8:00."

Janna made a note of that. "What did the caller look like?"

Tony spread his hands. "He had his screen covered. He wouldn't talk about the job, either, just said to meet him at the Crown Center Hotel, room 820, within the next hour."

"And you did." Mama raised his brows. "You weren't worried about it being a sting?"

"I thought I'd look at the offer." He grinned. "A sting doesn't work if you walk away from the bait. When I knocked, this voice said come in, the door was open."

Janna poised her pen over her notebook. "Describe the man you met."

Tony licked his lips. "All I saw was a shadow by the window. The room was dark except for the light inside the door. The jon ordered me to stand under it."

A very cautious tickman. "You can't tell us *anything* about his appearance?"

"It was a tall shadow."

"What did he sound like?" Mama asked.

Tony shifted in his chair, crossing his legs. "Average…not raspy or high-pitched, nothing special to remember. No accent. He said don't bother asking his name just listen. He had two riffs planned, both political fund-raisers out of town. If I joined the team, I'd be one of seven, but I wouldn't know anyone's names and they wouldn't know mine. I wouldn't even meet them before the riffs and we'd leave separate ways afterward."

At the edge of Janna's vision, Mama started, then grinned. She glanced around in surprise. "What is it?"

"We had the wrong movie."

Tony's lawyer frowned. "I don't understand."

Mama smoothed his face. "It has to do with recognizing the M.O. is all."

Janna straightened. She saw Diosdado perk up, as well. "Who uses it?"

He sighed. "No one who can be involved here. Go on, Tony."

Tony crossed his legs the other direction. "The jon asked was I interested. My gut reaction was anyone that careful about hiding his identity wasn't a lion so I said sure. He said look in the ice bucket by the bathroom sink. I found some unset gems. Earnest money, he called it. Then he said my instructions would come by mail and had me close the door on my way out."

"You must have discussed what the job would pay sometime in there," Janna said.

Tony glanced up at his attorney.

She dimpled. "I believe that's irrelevant, Sergeant Brill. We will specify, however, that Tony was to receive half after each job."

"That was two weeks ago?" Mama asked. "What day, exactly?"

"Monday before last, the eighth."

"When did your instructions come?"

"Last Tuesday…big thick envelope with pages of instructions, a timetable, a one-month bus pass, and photographs. I was supposed to buy transport tokens and acquire some drug that could be given in a drink without the drinker realizing it and would keep him asleep the better part of twenty-four hours. The instructions also gave me a number sequence for a sonic lock and said I needed to buy a key and have a locksmith tune it to the scale the instructions gave me the code for."

Mama pursed his lips. "Do you remember the code?"

Tony grinned. "Why care when I can tell you which lock the key opens? Wednesday I took the bus to Topeka and went to an address he gave me. Apartment fourteen-forty in the Terracrest Apartments out on Lockwood." Before anyone asked, he added, "According to letters and things there, it belongs to someone named Katura Murane."

Janna wrote down the name, not bothering to exchange glances with Mama. Of course Tony searched the apartment. So would she under the circumstances. "And then?"

Tony rubbed his eyes. He winced as he touched the bruise on his forehead. "Then I stayed in the apartment studying the timetables and plans and using wigs and makeup left for me to practice making myself look like the photographs of the two people I was supposed to impersonate.

"Salmas and Wald." Mama's scalp furrowed. "You didn't follow them except on the day you approached them?"

"I didn't have to. Everything I needed to know about their habits was in the instructions." Tony shook his head, grinning. "That's one thorough tickman."

Other accomplishments bothered Janna more. "How did you use Salmas's Scib Card to clock in at the hotel?"

Still grinning, Tony shrugged. "Just the way I'd use my own, fed the Card into the slot and looked into the r-scanner. I don't know why it worked."

The attorney's dimples vanished. She stared down at her client. "You used some else's—" She bit off the rest of the sentence, mouth setting in a grim line. "Go on with your questions, Sergeant Brill."

"As the inside man, did you bring in the needlers?"

"No. I don't handle weapons, ever. The gunmen brought them in themselves."

"Did you bring in the waitron?"

"It was already at the hotel. And at the caterer's ahead of me, too."

"You had no trouble passing the scan to clock in at the caterer's, either?" Mama asked.

Tony snorted. "They didn't have an r-scanner. No real security at all." He shook his head. "I just walked in through the front door past a receptionist and back to the time clock. Can you believe that? Anyone could have come in. The time clock is just your basic shove-your-Card-in-the-cardslot type, too. Someone needs to have a serious talk with that manager about proper security!"

His disapproving tone made Janna grin.

Mama's forehead furrowed. "Do you know why someone disabled the security camera at the service door you used to leave the hotel?"

Tony blinked. "That's lightwitted. Why bother when the door alarm would tell Security which way I'd left?"

A dark eye rolled Janna's direction said: *see?*, reminding her that Mama had expressed the same thought. "After you and the others and the waitron went out the service door, what kind of vehicle picked you—"

"The others didn't follow me out," Tony interrupted. "I told you, we all left separately."

Janna frowned. They had to leave together. The security cameras had not picked them up at other exits. Unless…they had *not* left, not immediately? They wore disguises, after all. Could they have stripped off the wigs and mustaches and been drinking caff in the restaurant or enjoying gambling and sexual favors up in Diversions while the police swarmed through the hotel?

"No one picked me up outside, either. The waitron led me across the parking lot to the mini-mall there and told me I'd find my first payment in a bag taped under the biodegradables dumpster there. I collected the bag, threw my wig and mustache into the dumpster along with the waiter's coat, and took a bus back to the apartment."

"Leaving the waitron and all that carry?" Diosdado asked in a skeptical voice.

Tony grunted. "Absolutely. The instructions said the waitron was wired to defend itself with electric shock. I didn't try to see if it was true."

Wise. In light of what happened at the Yi house, electric shock might have been the least consequence of trying to rob the waitron. "Tell us about Saturday night."

He rolled his eyes. "It all fell apart. We were supposed to riff five of those courtyards, leaving one of the team behind each time to keep the group under control until we finished in the last court." He paused. "The tickman lied, didn't he? He never intended us to clean more than that first group."

"Back up," Mama said. He paced toward the door. "You arrived with the caterer's van and set up the buffet. Then at six-fifty you went into the service court, shot paint at the monitor camera lens, and opened the rear gate for the gunmen, is that right?"

Tony straightened in his chair. "How did you know—oh." He sat back, nodding. "The security system log. Mr. Yi has a top card system. I opened the gate, yes, but not for the rest of the team. They came in with the other guests, just like they did Friday night."

Janna met Mama and Diosdado's eyes. The gunmen could *not* have come in with the other guests. Either Tony lied, or there was another way through the security screen into the house.

Mama asked, "Why open the gate, then?"

Tony shrugged. "My instructions said to blind the camera and test the override code."

Across the room, Mama's face went thoughtful. "Did the others leave through the back with you?"

"No. It was just the waitron and me again. Don't know how the others got out." Tony glanced down at his wrist chrono and smothered a yawn. "It wasn't my job to worry about them."

"How did you leave the neighborhood?"

Tony grinned. "The tickman picked me up. Before you ask, it was too dark inside the car for a good look at either him or the little jon driving. The driver told me the waitron had two sections, bayonetted together. He had me break it down, put the pieces in the back of the car, and climb aboard with it. He handed me the second payment when they let me off at a bus stop about a klick away." He grimaced. "I was supposed to stay at the apartment until Sunday, but the killing scared me shitless. I wiped the place clean and headed for the bus station."

"Describe the vehicle," Janna said. How had it sat around the neighborhood all evening without Yi's leos noticing it?

"A Triton wagon in some dark color," Tony came back promptly. "Green." He paused. "Or blue, maybe. I'm not sure of the year, either, seventy-six or seventy-seven, whenever the Chryslers ended up looking like Datsun-Fords. The rear seat had been taken out and a computer desktop with a multifield screen set up in the cargo space, but without the desk, just on short legs. Probably for controlling the waitron."

Mama frowned. "A desktop? A laptop should have been..." His voice trailed off.

Janna frowned, too. Nothing about Tony's description of the car helped explain how it escaped notice.

"Since Chryslers and D-F's looked so much alike that year, how can you be sure it was a Triton and not a Monitor wagon?" Mama asked.

Their prisoner gave them a wry grin. "Because I've been FI'd in Tritons too often not to know them. The KCPD likes those wagons for its watchcars, right, Diosdado?"

After Diosdado had his turn and Tony had given the K.C. detective names from the jewelry store riffs and been sent up to the holding cells for the night, they headed for the Crown Center Hotel. Mama glanced around at the late twentieth-century decor of the lobby in obvious delight. "So they've finished the restoration. It's beautiful, don't you think, bibi?"

Janna looked it over as they leaned on the registration desk waiting for the clerk to punch off the phone...small couches and tables around a bar in a sunken center, thick columns supporting a mezzanine, a ceiling soaring three stories above them, and a waterfall tumbling down a terraced wall from high up past the registration desk. She had never seen the hotel before, but it did look nice now, if wastefully difficult to heat and cool, a restful echo of a prosperous, simpler time when life moved more slowly and resources seemed endless.

The clerk folded down the phone screen and turned toward them. "May I help you?"

Diosdado showed her his badge. "We need to know who had room 820 on April eighth."

"Just a minute." She typed on a keyboard down behind the desk.

Diosdado turned his back to the counter. "Do you suppose this will do us any good? Chances are he borrowed the room from a friend."

"Even that name will give us a place to start hunting," Janna said.

"If the friend will talk." The dark eyes followed an ascending rectangle of lights that framed the glass back of an elevator. "It's like something out of an historical movie, isn't it? And speaking of movies..." Diosdado turned to eye Mama. "...what did you mean, you had the wrong movie?"

Grinning, Mama told him about their speculation on murder à la *Murder On the Orient Express*. "But we were wrong. The M.O. for setting up these riffs comes from another movie entirely, *The Thomas Crown Affair*."

Diosdado glanced sideways at Janna. "Did anyone ever tell you you have a strange partner?"

"A strange partner?" Janna arched her brows. "Mr. Somewhere Over the Brainbow, you mean? The Wizard of Odd? How can you say he's strange?"

"*The Thomas Crown Affair*," Mama said with the slow care of someone speaking to not-too-bright children, "was made in the last century and starred an actor named Steve McQueen."

The name reverberated in Janna's head. She whipped toward Mama. "Isn't that one of the actors Pritchard said Armenda collected?"

Mama nodded. "So that movie ought to be in his collection."

Where Junior or Sydney could have seen it.

The clerk looked up. "I'm sorry, Sergeant, but 820 was unoccupied on April eighth."

They frowned at each other. "Maybe he had the date wrong," Janna said. "We can try Sunday."

"No mail deliveries that day," Mama pointed out.

"Maybe Tuesday." Diosdado leaned on the counter. "See who had it the evening of the ninth."

More keys tapped, then the clerk looked up again. "Tuesday that room was part of a block reserved for Governor Hershey's party."

Janna vaguely remembered the newscanner covering the Libertarian presidential candidate's campaign stop in Kansas City earlier in the month. Could their tickman have a friend among the governor's staff and aides?

"The party didn't check in until nearly eleven that night," the clerk went on.

Leaving the room effectively unoccupied that night, too. Janna swore under her breath.

But Mama smiled at the clerk. "What kind of locks do you have on the rooms these days?"

"Key operated, of course, to fit the decor." The clerk held one up. Instead of a serrated edge, however, the heavy key shaft carried cone-shaped indentations on the edges and sides.

As they walked away from the desk, Diosdado said, "You're thinking our jon broke into the room? You don't pick those locks without a fight, and you don't copy those keys at a hardware store."

"True," Mama agreed, "but someone who can learn a private home's override code and arrange for Tony to pass an r-scan with Salmas's Scib Card could probably manage to copy one."

Maybe he knew how to walk through walls, too. Though Janna would never admit such a thing to Mama, their killer's blithe contempt for locks and other security measures was beginning to make her feel as though they were chasing ghosts.

10

Lt. Vradel leaned back in his desk chair. "Our suspect is tucked safely away in a cell?"

Mama and Janna nodded.

"Very pleased with himself for coming out what he considers best in our deal." Janna grimaced. "He may be right. Diosdado got more concrete information than we did. Anything happening here?"

"Oh, a lot of activity." His mustache twitched. "Not much in the way of results." He leaned forward to peer at the notes and sketches covering his desk blotter. "Cruz and Singer went to the Armenda funeral this morning. A well attended affair, Cruz says, with everyone appropriately solemn but no one prostrate with grief. Junior kept leering at his step-mother. Daughter behaved very decorously, then went off with a group of company managers after leaving the cemetery.

"The FBI sent back a list of possible matches for our enhancements, though Cruz told me this morning that the first two they traced are in prison." His pencil circled a sketch of two interlocking gears. "Zavara and Threefoxes talked to the man who owned one of the local companies Armenda took over."

"Russell Brashear, Konza Holotronics," Mama said.

Vradel nodded. "He has nothing friendly to say about Armenda but doesn't appear bitter. The new company he started is doing well. Some of the employees at Konza quit after the takeover, apparently in protest. One even filed a lawsuit, but later dropped it. Brashear hired most of the protestors at the new company. Threefoxes is getting their names from Armenord to check out. Oh, yes." He tapped a sketch of a mustached face. "The Sheraton says they took delivery on a waitron Friday morning. No one thought anything about it at the time, but checking their records yesterday at Showalter and Weyneth's request, they found that none of their waitrons had been sent out for repairs. A small male with a mustache made the delivery, driving a van with the logo of G & B Cybertronics on the door. G & B normally services the hotel's waitrons and porterbots. On playback of security camera recordings for that day, they found the camera at the loading dock had caught the delivery van's license. Showalter ran the plate. The vehicle is registered to G & B but they deny sending any delivery to the hotel. They claim that particular van was on their lot out of service that day."

So the small jon with a mustache possibly 'borrowed' it to deliver the waitron? Janna exchanged glances with Mama. Could that be the same jon who drove the car picking up Tony Saturday night? "Did anyone check with Holliday Catering to ask about waitron deliveries there?"

"Cruz didn't say." Vradel checked his blotter again. "He did say that so far, our informants still have no information on the riff...not a murmur. That's about all the update I have. Nothing's turned up on Beria and hotel personnel we've checked so far. Maybe you'll have better luck. We need some results before the media loses interest in that Russian shuttle. Before you sail, however..." He looked up, tone going dry. "...I've been asked to mention that the department is not happy about receiving a traffic citation on an Ashanti 667 bearing plates assigned to the SCPD, which five separate speed monitors recorded traveling north Saturday on Topeka Boulevard at excessive speed."

Janna winced. She knew it!

Mama's eyes widened innocently behind his glasses. "That was a emergency run to check on the Salmas man's welfare."

Vradel's mustache twitched. "I explained that to Traffic. Captain Bernard reminded me in return that official vehicles, which officers are expected to use, have signals which activate with the light rail and/or siren, causing the monitors to disregard such vehicles so Traffic doesn't print out citations on them. I've been asked to urge, however strongly I think it necessary to make the point, that you do drive official vehicles hereafter." His voice hardened. "I don't know how you talked Perera into assigning you that Ashanti, Maxwell, but I'd better not hear about a stunt like that again. Ever. Kish?"

Mama stiffened. "Yes, sir."

"I'm very disappointed you went along with him, Brill," Vradel added.

Heat crawled up her neck. "Yes, sir." Damn Mama. Damn *her* for being a fool. The knot in her gut wiped out the last lingering warmth of Diosdado's lovemaking last night and his good-bye kiss this noon.

"I expect a better exercise of judgment from you. If anything happened to that vehicle, not even both your salaries for the year would cover the department's liability."

"Yes, sir." Ears burning, Janna slunk out of Vradel's office.

Mama followed. "I'm sorry, Jan."

"What do you have to apologize for?" she said bitterly. "I'm the lightwit who lets you talk her into these stunts."

He patted her shoulder. "Speaking from a vast experience in being on commanding officers' shit lists, I can assure you Vradel will forget all about this when we wrap Armenda's killer. And toward that end, let's go talk to Yi's lions."

They caught up with Martin Surowski and Sheila Inge on patrol. Lake Sherwood spread out from the overlook where the four of them leaned against their parked vehicles, soaking up the afternoon sunshine.

The radios murmured in Janna's ear and from inside the cars. "Beta Sherwood Nine. Vehicle with 10-46 or Signal 3 driver is headed south on Oakley from 31st Terrace. Vehicle has struck three parked vehicles and a power pole. R.P. reports power is out in the area."

"An unmarked car?" Inge echoed when Janna asked. "Yeah, there was one near Yi's that night."

Janna shrugged deeper into her trenchcoat, glad she had not taken out the lining yet. The sun's warmth did not quite compensate for the chill of the breeze off the lake. "Are you sure?"

Surowski snorted. "It wasn't a D-F, true, but when was the last time you couldn't recognize an unmarked car?"

"Besides," Inge said, "we approached it once to find out what was in the pipe. The black glass made it hard to see more than a vague shape on the passenger side. When I rapped on the window, this little jon wearing an ear button slides the rear door open a crack and sticks his head out. 'Get away before you blow us,' he says, then pulls back in and slams the door. We stayed clear the rest of the evening."

Janna sent Mama a glance. The little jon again. "Can you describe this jon better?"

"We didn't have much more than a glimpse of him." Surowski frowned in concentration. "You're out of luck on exact height or clothing. Slight build, brown hair short over the ears and pulled back behind them, ordinary mustache."

"Brown eyes," Inge added. "Why the interest in him and the car?"

"A dark blue or green seventy-six or seventy-seven Chrysler Triton wagon driven by a small male picked up the waitress and waitron after the robbery," Janna said.

The two watchcar officers stared at her while from inside the watchcar came a radio voice high with excitement. "Beta Sherwood Nine, Sherwood. Request backup, Oakley and Twilight Drive! That Signal 3 driver has left his vehicle and gone into a house and is throwing things out the windows at us!"

A moment later all their radios crackled to life as Dispatch broadcast the request.

Inge glanced at Surowski, brows raised.

Her partner sighed. "By the time we can get there, the fun will be over." He focused on Mama and Janna. "The car we saw was a dark green seventy-seven Triton. You mean we had two of those riffers right there and just walked away from them? Shit."

His partner expressed it more strongly. Janna sympathized with their frustration.

"I'd have done the same, under the circumstances." Mama gazed out over the lake. "When did you first notice the car?"

"It was there when we went on duty at eighteen-thirty," Inge said.

"Located where?"

"The corner of Shriver Circle, one block from the rear of the Yi house." Inge sighed. "We just let them sit there."

Surowski grinned. "We can make up for it. I remember the license number."

Mama lifted his head. Janna pushed away from the car.

"It used my wife's initials...K-J-S-five-two-six."

Janna tapped her ear button. "Indian Thirty, Capitol, requesting a 10-28 on King John Sam five two six." Then she stood chewing a knuckle waiting for the reply.

Shortly, her ear button and their car radio said, "Indian Thirty, your 10-28 shows on a 2079 Smith Sundowner..."

"A runabout!" Inge spat in disgust. "The bastard must have sto—"

Janna waved her to silence as Dispatch continued, "...registered to a Jordan or Irene Minshall, 2428 Colorado. Have you seen those plates? I have an alert on them as reported stolen."

"Hah!" Inge slapped the roof of her unit.

"When was the report filed?" Janna asked.

"Sunday, April 21st."

"The day after the riff," Surowski said.

Mama took his hands out of his trenchcoat pockets and pushed away from the car. "Let's talk to Mr. Minshall, bibi."

No one answered the bell at the Minshall house, but a neighbor working on the flower beds in her yard knew where he worked: as a law clerk for Kettering, Kettering, and Axthelm. They tracked him down at the law office. He reported he had left work around eight o'clock, as usual. The car was parked in the Sunco parking lot at 13th and Jackson, in his stall on the reserve levels.

"The tags had to be stolen there," Minshall said. "At home I keep the car in the garage."

"You didn't notice the plates missing then?" Janna asked.

He had not...not until the next morning, when the family prepared to leave for church.

Back in their own car, Mama said, "Our riffers knew Minshall's habits."

"That or they just happened to steal plates from someone who works late enough that the earliest he could report the theft would be after the riff."

So did that mean they were looking for someone with a connection to Armenda, the Sheraton, Yi, the Murane woman, *and* Minshall?

They drove back across town west to the Terracrest Apartments next.

As Mama reported to Cruz in the Gage Zoo parking lot after calling in a request to meet with him, the trip yielded only one useful fact. "Katura Murane is a behavioral psychologist at the Menninger Foundation. She's been up on one of the space platforms doing some kind of research for the past month and isn't expected back until the end of May. We have a request in to Menningers for the platform name and phone number but the manager says as far as he knows, Murane isn't in the habit of loaning her apartment to friends or giving out the tone sequence of her lock."

"So what's the useful fact?" Cruz asked.

Mama pushed his glasses up his nose. "Beria installed and services the security system at the complex."

"Someone at the agency *has* to be involved," Janna said. "They either have to know Murane or have been at the apartment complex within the last month and heard she's away."

In the distance, a lion roared, a deep, hollow sound. Cruz glanced the direction of it. "We're already checking everyone."

"Service technicians as well as guards?" Mama asked.

Cruz sighed. "Of course service technicians. Everyone. It looks as though most of the service techs, *all* the day people—five techs, four on duty at any one time—have made calls on every client sooner or later. Only some of the evening and night techs haven't. So far, though, we haven't turned up a connection between Armenda and anyone at Beria."

A peacock strutting inside the tall chain link fence around the zoo turned to peer at them and scream a high-pitched *aaah*!

"My feeling exactly," Janna told it. "Mind if we go down to Beria and poke around?"

Cruz shrugged. "*I* don't. I presume the agency people won't, either. They've been very cooperative. Naturally Beria and son are anxious to either find the rotten apple or prove their agency can't possibly be involved in robbery and murder." He paused. "Did you learn anything more from this Tony Ho on the drive back than what you phoned in to Vradel this morning?"

Janna shook her head.

"Have you found how the riffers slipped that waitron among the caterer's?"

"Maybe." Cruz pulled his notebook out of a thigh pocket. "Holliday hasn't had a waitron come back from servicing, but..." He grinned. "...Friday night around nine, workers cleaning up in the kitchen heard a sound on the loading dock. They checked and found the rear door open and a waitron halfway through it...and heard footsteps outside running away. They brought the waitron back in and relocked the door."

"'Back' in." Janna shook her head. "Sly...slip it in by pretending to be trying to steal it. Is Holliday another of Beria's clients?"

"No." Cruz slid the notebook back in a thigh pocket. "They ordered their alarms direct from a manufacturer and had a local electrical firm install them. I looked at the system. It's very basic...barrier-and-alarm, nothing tricky, nothing for recording or trapping an intruder. Anyone with some expertise in security systems could walk right through it."

Mama said, "Vradel mentioned that an employee at Konza tried to sue Armenda for taking over the company. Do we know anything more?"

"Zavara and Threefoxes are checking it out now." Cruz glanced at his wrist chrono. "If you want to do anything at Beria this afternoon, you'd better go. I'll see you at the end of the watch."

Beria's offices occupied the two floors above their security equipment store at the corner of Third and Kansas. At the top of stairs narrowed by the wheelchair lift built along one side spread a reception area as spartan as a gallery. Like a gallery, too, scattered display stands held samples of small security devices and models of larger ones.

The sleek amerasian woman behind a black glass desk raised her eyebrows at their identification. "More of you? Just a minute." She picked up a handset on a screenless phone and murmured into it. After listening, she told them, "Go on back," and pointed to the door behind her.

It slid aside at their approach, then whispered closed behind them. Before them stretched a corridor with clerical offices opening off the right side and a left-hand turn at the end.

Around that turn came a gray-haired but fit looking man in a dark green bodysuit with diagonal slashes of gold and peacock blue. "Sergeants Brill and Maxwell? I am Arkady Beria." He spoke with a faint Russian accent. "How may I help the police this time?"

Mama eyed the bodysuit. Thinking how it might look on him? "We're after more of the same, I'm afraid...still trying to find someone who knows the various security systems relevant to the crime. At the moment, it appears that individual must be must one of your service personnel."

Beria's heavy brows dipped. "I thought your colleagues already determined so, and that most of my technicians qualify in such respect."

"Now it seems likely that only one with contact in the last month is involved," Janna said.

Beria sighed. "Perhaps that helps. I hope. I would like this resolved, you understand. This way."

He led them around the corner to another sliding door. Several seconds passed before it opened, however.

"A scanner confirms I wear a transponder emitting a proper signal before opening." Beria touched a pin with the Beria logo on the turtleneck of his bodysuit. "You will need someone authorized to let you out, and out to reception area as well. Listra, we have more detectives," he said to a plump afroam woman at the computer keyboard inside. "Help them all you can."

Mama watched the door slide closed behind him. "Nice outfit. The color's a little conservative, but it's a very nice design."

The afroam woman eyed him…and the orange-and-purple diagonal striping of his jumpsuit, visible through the open front of the scarlet trenchcoat. "I'm Listra Wassman, queen of chips. What do you need, leo?"

Mama smiled at her. "Is the law firm of Kettering, Kettering, and Axthelm one of your clients?"

Wassman typed. Mama leaned on the desk, peering at the monitor.

Janna's ear button murmured, sending Beta Cap Twelve to investigate a man who had been sitting on the curb in front of a residence all day.

Wassman looked up from her screen. "Sorry. There's no file with that name on it."

"Then may we have a list of the service calls made to the Sheraton, the Lincoln Yi house, and Terracrest Apartments in the past month, and we need to know what service technician took the calls?" Mama asked.

"Terracrest? That's new." She typed in the information. Janna bent down to peer over her shoulder, too. A service log scrolled up the screen, giving the date, time, nature of the call, charge, and personnel involved. "The Sheraton's had several service calls in the past few weeks. Spring thunderstorms can play havoc with alarm systems."

Janna nodded. When she rode watchcars she had answered a number of bank alarms set off by lightning-caused power surges.

Wassman kept typing. "Mr. Yi's done better. One call to us, one initiated by us to check his system after a power outage in the area. And now, Terracrest. Lordy." A long log scrolled up. She shook her head. "Either the spring storms hit them hard or their tenants are hell on the property."

Janna read the log. Damaged window alarm circuits. More window alarm circuits damaged. Inoperable door lock due to sonic key being out of tune. A security camera out of service. Debris jammed in the cardslot of the entry gate. That must have been fun fixing in the middle of the night so tenants did not have to abandon their cars on the street. Key inoperable due to spouse changing the tone sequence. Another camera out of service.

"Which technicians have taken calls all three places?" Mama asked.

"Aschke and Spelts had the Yi calls. We can check for their names on the other service logs."

Janna watched the listings come up on the screen. Both technicians had taken Sheraton and Terracrest calls, Spelts one at the hotel, two at the apartments, Aschke one each place. "Are they male or female?"

"Both are men." Wassman's fingers played across her keyboard. "I'll call up their personnel records. I have a hard time imagining either one of them involved in something like this."

The phone chirped. The amerasian woman's face appeared on the screen. "An Officer Morello is looking for either Sergeant Maxwell or Sergeant Brill."

Janna stood closest to the phone. She moved in front of the screen. "I'll take it."

A moment later Pass-the-Word Morello's foxy face replaced the receptionist's. "Menningers called. The Murane woman is on the Russian's Mir platform. I have the phone number."

She copied it down, all sixteen digits, then with Wassman's permission, punched the numbers into the afroam woman's phone, followed by the eleven extra digits that charged the call to the department.

Wassman grinned. "You can die of old age punching in that number."

That and waiting while the screen flashed and spat, and while the cheerful female who answered, speaking Russian that switched instantly to flawless English when Janna spoke, put her on hold to contact Katura Murane. Janna sighed. "In bed? It never occurred to me they'd be on Moscow time. She's going to love us."

Wassman left the room on some errand. Janna stood staring at the phone, wondering what Earth-to-platform calls cost per minute, while Mama read through the printout of the two service technicians' personnel files.

Finally a dark-haired bibi came on the screen, groggy but apprehensive. "I'm Dr. Murane. You're from the police? What's wrong?"

No need to take time telling her about the robberies and murder. "We have in custody an individual who's admitted to entering your apartment while you've been gone."

"Broke into my apartment!" Outrage wiped away the last trace of sleepiness. "Shit! Will he, or she, tell you what was taken? It's impossible for me to come back right now and no one down there can tell—"

"Don't worry, Doctor." Janna gave her a reassuring smile. "He didn't take or damage anything. Strictly speaking, he didn't break in. He had a key."

The dark hair bounced as she flung up her head. "What! That's impossible."

"You didn't tell a friend your tuning code and tone sequence, or give someone permission to use the apartment while you were gone?"

Murane's mouth thinned. "I did not."

Mama laid down the printout to move over in the screen's range. "Do you know a Marion Spelts or a Jason Aschke?"

The doctor frowned, then shook her head. "Not by name."

"Before you left, did you have trouble with your lock that necessitated calling the security firm out to service it?"

"The lock's been just fine. However this person came by my key, I assure you *I* didn't give it to him. Talk to the manager. The office has a copy of my lock tone sequence."

"Thank you," Janna said. "That's all we needed to know." She punched off.

The door hissed open. Instead of Wassman returning, however, in trotted a small bibi with dark hair pulled up in a topknot and a Beria shoulder patch on her green jumpsuit. She stopped short. "Where's Listra?"

"Gone to the john or something," Janna replied.

Intelligent dark eyes looked them over with obvious curiosity. "I'm Karis Sandoz. That's Karis with a K." She edged toward the printout lying beside Wassman's keyboard. "Are you more detectives working on those fund-raiser robberies?"

Janna picked up the printout. "I'm afraid so."

"Good luck." Sandoz grinned. "The rumor I've heard is Republicans did it, thinking that if they take the other parties' campaign money and use it for themselves, they can become a major party again." She headed for the door. "Tell Listra I'll be back. I need to see the service log from Striker Import Auto for the past four months."

Janna read through the printout. To her disappointment, nothing in either file helped them. Both men appeared to be ideal employees. Marion Spelts, age 42, employed at Beria for fourteen years, had been chosen Beria Employee-of-the-Month three times. Jason Aschke, age 33 and employed for eight years, was awarded a bonus three years ago for devising an improvement in the security camera placement during one system installation. "I guess we need to talk to them." She glanced at her wrist chrono. Past fifteen hours. "Here, maybe, if we hurry."

The door opened again, this time for Wassman. "Did you finally get through?"

"Finally." Janna folded up the printout. "A Karis—"

"Karis with a K, remember," Mama interrupted.

"Anyway, she said she needs the Striker Import Auto service file."

Wassman grinned. "Karis with a K. Yes. God forbid we should spell it with a Ch and realize it's short for Charisma."

Janna shook her head. Another unfortunate named after Charisma Nairobi? Agosta in their squad was, too. All through her childhood, with Charismas abounding in the classes behind her, Janna had given thanks she was born before everyone went crazy over the cineround movie made from Elizabeth Chilombe's book *The Dream Maze*. "Where might we find Aschke and Spelts, if they're still here?"

"They are," Wassman said. "That's where I went, to have Mr. Beria ask them to stay. I thought you'd probably want to talk to them. I'll take you up to the service department. This way." She headed for the door.

Janna pulled her jaw back into place and followed. When Beria said help them in every way possible, he meant it. He obviously wanted very much to resolve this.

One look at Marion Spelts, however, suggested *he* would not resolve it. Janna understood Wassman's reluctance to believe his involvement. Even standing up, the rotund little jon's head barely reached her shoulder, and he wore a gold cross prominently displayed on a chain around his neck.

He sat on the edge of a plasic bucket chair in the employee lounge, feet barely touching the floor and hands folded together across his chest. "What was I doing Friday and Saturday nights? The Lord's work, Sergeant. Members of my church and I held prayer in front of The Fantasy House. Such places defile our city. We hope that publishing pictures we took of people going in will shame the citizens degrading themselves there into—"

"What time was that?" Janna did not bother giving him a smile to soften the abruptness of her voice. His group had a right to disapprove of prostitution and fight it, but not by violating other citizens' civil right to privacy.

If Spelts noticed her tone, he showed no sign of it. "From six o'clock until midnight."

"The whole time, straight through?" Mama asked. "You didn't take a break?"

"Of course not." Spelts looked offended by the idea. "We can't accomplish our mission unless we're persistent in the task."

They sent Spelts on his way and asked him to send in Jason Aschke.

A prickle ran down her spine as the second technician came into the lounge. His height equalled hers. More than that, his eyes ducked theirs when she and Mama introduced themselves. He folded into the bucket chair Spelts had vacated and slumped back.

"I already told the detectives here yesterday that I spent Friday and Saturday night at home," he muttered toward his knees. "Do you want to hear about the TV shows I watched?"

"That depends." Janna eyed him. "Do you own a video recorder?"

Aschke glanced up, then down again. He licked his lips and wiped his palms on his thighs. "I didn't have anything to do with those robberies."

Alarms rang in Janna. He had not watched TV, she would swear to that. He recorded some programs and scanned through them later.

Mama smiled at the service technician. "We have to check all the possibilities."

"But why—" He bit off the end of the sentence.

Mama eyed him. "Why what?"

Aschke shook his head. "I wouldn't do anything like that. My job is protecting people."

Janna glanced at Mama. Evasions. "Did you know Carel Armenda?"

"The man who died?" Aschke shook his head.

"Do you live with anyone?" Mama asked.

Aschke hesitated a moment before answering. "Not anymore."

"Did you see anyone at all those evenings?" Mama pushed his glasses up his nose. "Maybe someone called you?"

"No one." He scowled. "But I was home."

"Just like he was watching TV," Janna said after they let him go. She stood in the doorway of the lounge, arms folded, watching Aschke hurry down the wide central hallway of the service section.

At her shoulder, Mama shrugged. "Lying about the TV doesn't means he's lying about everything. I have a hard time seeing him as our tickman. He doesn't sound the way Tony described the hotel interview."

"He could be acting. He's hiding something, Mama. That is definitely a man with a guilty secret."

"Not the robberies," another voice said.

They looked around. Karis Sandoz stood in a doorway behind them.

She gave them a sheepish smile. "I'm sorry; I couldn't help overhearing." With a quick glance around, she moved close to them. "I know this is none of my business and that all I know about the robberies is what I've seen on the newscanner. Jason did swear me to secrecy after I accidentally found out about his project."

"But..." Mama said.

Sandoz grimaced. "But he's such a private person, and probably a little afraid of looking brainbent, I doubt he'll tell you on his own, even when it's to his advantage."

Janna frowned. "Tell us what?"

Sandoz lowered her voice. "About his robot. His passion is robots and artificial intelligence. At home he's developing a sentry robot...something that would be semi-autonomous, a hybrid of waitron and swatbot. That's usually what he's doing when he claims to be watching TV."

The hair prickled on Janna's neck. "Developing it at home?"

The small bibi nodded. "He has a workshop in his basement. I saw it once. It's beautifully equipped."

Janna glanced at Mama. A security technician with a workshop at home for building robots? Aschke might not sound to Mama like the man Tony Ho met in that Crown Center Hotel room, but he certainly deserved further investigation.

11

"You mean we finally have a suspect for the tickman?" Commander Vining asked.

Janna would have given anything for him not to have walked in on the case squad's morning discussion just as she and Mama were arguing over Aschke. Or for him to be asking Cruz. But his gaze obviously focused on her.

She settled back in her desk chair and shrugged. "Maybe." Damned if she would commit herself, no matter how much she liked Aschke for a suspect.

Vining frowned. "Do you suppose you can manage to be a little more specific, Sergeant?"

Janna told him about Aschke's connection to the two crime scenes and the Terracrest Apartments, and what Sandoz said about his home workshop. "We went to his house last night to check out the workshop. No one answered the door, so we talked to his neighbors, using the pretext of investigating reported prowlers in the area. They can't confirm or disprove the workshop. He hasn't invited anyone into the house in five years, not since his wife died. They saw lights on Friday and Saturday evening, but one neighbor's daughter, who went around Friday night selling high school band concert tickets, didn't get a response when she rang his bell."

"Which proves nothing," Mama said. "According to the neighbors, his lights can be on when he's gone, or he may not answer the door even when he's there."

"Have you checked with DMV to see if he owns a Triton wagon? Is there any connection between him and Armenda, maybe concerning his wife's death, that might give him a motive for murder?"

Did he think they were rookies? "We ran him through DMV last night. There's no vehicle of any kind registered to him. We haven't had time to hunt for a connection between him and Armenda, but there doesn't have to be one. He could have been hired for the job, in which case, maybe the tickman furnished the Triton."

"Do any of—" Vining began.

"Today we'll be cross-checking registrations of seventy-seven Triton wagons against a list of people associated with Carel Armenda." If only they had enough probable cause for a bank warrant. That would tell them if Aschke had gone to Kansas City on the eighth, a point she considered more important than Mama's concern over how the man Tony met gained access to the hotel room. After all, Aschke knew locks, and even those using drilled keys must be pickable.

Vining glanced around at other members of the squad. "Any luck finding the gunmen?"

"No," Cruz said, drawing the syllable out. "Tracing from last known addresses, we've located five more of the possibles from the FBI photo file. One is dead, three are on parole with whereabouts confirmed those nights, and one is confined to a wheelchair. We've distributed copies of the enhancements throughout the department here and sent copies to departments in major cities in the surrounding states. Brill and Maxwell left copies with the KCPD. So far, there's been no response."

The information officer shook his head. "There have to be records on these jons somewhere. They worked too smoothly to be beginners. What have you found out about the lawsuit that employee filed against Armenda?"

Zavara straightened in her chair with a sinuous ripple. "It was against the corporation, not Armenda personally, and it never reached court."

Threefoxes consulted his notebook. "May of seventy-eight, a Lesandra Santos sued for the rights to a miniaturized projector she built. Armenda claimed the projector belonged to Armenord since she was an employee and had used company research facilities for working on the projector. Apparently Santos decided they were right; she withdrew the suit."

"That doesn't mean she forgot about it. Have you talked to her?"

"No. She resigned and left the area, according to people at Konza. There's certainly no local phone listing for her. We went to Armenord's personnel department for a forwarding address but the computer had eaten Santos's file."

"In other words, we have four teams plugging away without anything to show for the time and expense?" Vining shook his head. "That won't impress the Director and the media."

Cruz stood, bringing him to eye level with the information officer. "I'm sure Paget understands these things take time. Give the media Tony Ho."

"Tony Ho." Vining shook his head again. "One small fish, who's obviously an outsider, meant to be thrown away, and no help finding the others."

Janna caught Mama's eye, thinking of his *Thomas Crown Affair* theory that made everyone an outsider. If Vining had not been there, she might have mentioned it.

"We were the subject of Hollis Dunne's eleven o'clock commentary last night." Vining glanced toward the newscanner. "'People ought to be asking what kind of security the police are providing the general public when they can't find men who rob and kill our most important citizens, even when given video recordings of the event.' He showed segments from the news chips of the Demo fund-raiser and invited viewers to call in if they have any knowledge of the crimes. 'Maybe the People can accomplish what those hired for the job appear unable to,' he said."

Zavara's lip curled. "Hollis Dunne is an asshole."

Vining turned a cold stare on her. "His four daily broadcasts are seen by better than a hundred thousand people each. If he suggests protesting trash pickup fee hikes by dumping non-recyclables on the mayor's lawn, people will. We don't need him focusing that kind of attention on us."

Janna kept her face pulled smooth over the flare of resentment in her. So honey the bastard. What did he think the department paid its Public Information section for?

At the far end of the squadroom Vradel came to the open door of his office and stood gazing their direction. "Commander, before you leave, may I see you in my office?"

"I can come now," Vining said.

Mama, who, remarkably, had not moved in several minutes, sat up on the corner of his desk. "Just a minute, sir. I think we do have something interesting for the media."

Janna grinned inwardly. Behind his glasses, Mama's eyes glinted, and for once, she waited with relish for the results of his brainbent thought processes.

Vining beamed. "Excellent, Sergeant. What?"

Mama crossed one zebra-striped leg of his jumpsuit over the other. "According to Aschke's neighbors, he became a loner after his wife died. She was one of the fatalities in the city bus that went off the Topeka Avenue bridge into the Kaw in seventy-five. I believe he's been brooding about it ever since, blaming the city government at first, and by generalization, eventually hating all government and politicians."

He believed? Janna forced herself not to roll her eyes. That had been *her* postulation in the debate last night. Allow him creative borrowing, but how did he plan to turn such a sad scenario into a punchline that would leave them laughing behind Vining's back?

Vining pursed his lips. "So you think he built a robot and set up the robberies for revenge? That might be a possibility, except for one thing…why kill Armenda?"

"You're right; he wouldn't have reason to under those circumstances. However…" Mama pushed his glasses up his nose. "What if the perpetrators are people who also hate government and merely used Aschke's feelings to recruit him to help them circumvent the security measures at those two fund-raisers? When they found out about his interest in robots, they used that, too."

Janna frowned at Mama. Political terrorism was too serious to use for a joke.

All around her, faces had gone grim, especially Vining's. He shook his head. "No. It would help explain why we can't identify the gunmen, but Armenda's death still doesn't fit. Political terrorists would have killed Rau or maybe Senator Kassebaum-Martin."

Leaning toward Vining, Mama lowered his voice. "Not necessarily. Choosing Armenda is potentially even more effective." He ticked off points on his fingers. "First, of course, the mere fact of violent death generates fear. Then as the investigation progresses, there's confusion. Is it one crime or two? Who's responsible for each and if Armenda's death is a murder, who wants him dead? We go running off in all directions. At some point the perpetrators can contact individuals like Hollis Dunne and ridicule us through them. Can't we even decide what crime we're investigating? That causes the public to lose confidence in us, which increases their terror as the perpetrators promise more violence. Killing Armenda also places control of several companies, including a jet charter service, a construction company, and a firm which manufactures locks and other security devices, in the hands of a boy susceptible to manipulation by someone who knows how to exploit his love of physical pleasure."

Janna regarded Mama with horror. Maybe he dreamed up that rationale for the information officer's benefit, but it echoed in her with the icy ring of possibility.

In Vining, too, apparently. His mouth thinned. "Thank you, but I won't give that to the media. I'll play up Tony Ho. And hope to god you're wrong, sergeant."

After he left, Janna realized that the usual voices and buzz of phones continued at the far end of the room, but everyone near the case squad's grouped desks had turned to stare at Mama. The newscanner's latest update on the Russian shuttle situation carried clearly through the near silence. Even odors seemed sharper…the scent of caff from the caff urn, the spicy sweetness of the perfume Zavara wore. Vradel marched their direction.

Cruz ran a hand through his hair. "Jesus. Why didn't you mention this before, Maxwell?"

Mama blinked at him. "Surely you didn't think I was serious?"

Now it was Cruz's turn to blink. "What?" He sounded torn between anger and relief.

"Think!" Mama slid off the desk and turned, holding out his hands to everyone. "Terrorists wouldn't need Tony. They have people just as expert as disguise. They'd also have killed Salmas and Wald and hidden the bodies so we'd be wasting time hunting them...one more thing to ridicule when the time came to reveal themselves. Vining would see that if he weren't so damned anxious to cater to the media."

"Maxwell..." Vradel said on a rising note.

Mama faced him. "Look at it this way, sir; from now on he'll be so relieved when we don't find terrorists, he'll be happy with whatever progress we make."

Vradel's mustache twitched. "Then I won't need to remind him he isn't the squad commander. But, Maxwell...while I understand your reason for this skin, I don't agree with it. Vining isn't the enemy. So if he finds out he's been skinned, you're on your own with him."

"Mama, what the hell are we doing here?" The man was incomprehensible. At the elevators he had caught her sleeve and dragged her on past to Records. "I thought we wanted to identify the owner of that Triton."

"We do. This is faster than going over to DVM. Good morning." He beamed at the clerk behind the counter. "That green looks lovely on you. Hey, Liliedahl," he called. Back beyond the counter, a thin woman with an awkward posture betraying a twisted spine looked up from her computer keyboard. Mama clasped his hands over his heart. "I need you."

Miranda Liliedahl arched a wry brow, but after a minute, pushed out of her chair and limped up to the counter. "But will you respect me in the morning?"

"Respect?" Mama said. "I am in absolute awe of your finger technique. Can you help us?" Last night they had made up a list of people involved one way or another with the crimes. He laid it and a list of Beria employees on the counter. "I need you to download a file from DMV and run these names against it."

She studied the list. "Why not have DMV do it? They have faster access to whatever file it is you need."

"Their data processing technicians are user hostile."

Liliedahl grinned. "All right." She picked up the lists. "I'll see what I can do."

By the time they went through the gate at the far end of the counter, Liliedahl had reached her terminal and was running the lists through the computer's reader. She phoned DMV. Shortly, the modem light flickered and a list of names scrolled rapidly up the screen. At the front counter, the clerk flirted with a uniformed lion. A bank of printers across the room hummed, dropping hard copy into their catch baskets.

"We want the intersects," Mama said.

Long fingers tapped keys. "Somehow I suspected that. There's the end of the file. Intersects coming up."

The screen flickered...and two words sat in the middle of the blue field: *Not Found.*

Janna stared in disbelief. "Not one of those people owns a seventy-seven Triton?"

Liliedahl shrugged. "Sorry."

Mama leaned down toward the screen, hands clasped behind his back. "Let's check the corporate registrations, too...Armenord Industries; Beria Security; BruckerJet; Custom Electronics. That's Russell Brashear's new company, bibi. Images Unlimited; Konza Holotronics; Midstates Construction; Nord Electronics; Servitron, Inc.; Shawnee Security; Videoscribe; Voelker & Green, Inc."

Liliedahl's fingers raced across the keyboard.

A clerk picked up the hard copy from the printers and began sorting it into a courier robot.

Liliedahl sat back with a last tap of a key. "Cross your fingers."

The computer's drive lights flickered. The screen blinked.

Not Found.

Janna swore. "You'd think all those companies would have at least one seventy-seven Triton in their fleets. What now?"

Mama shrugged. "We can try car rentals, or go to Armenord and ask for a list of the employees in all their companies and check those against the registrations."

She groaned.

"So I'd like a printout of the whole file, please," he told Liliedahl.

"As long as you understand I don't provide a cart for carrying it." Liliedahl resumed typing. "This may take a while."

Janna used the time to start checking out the car rental agencies by phone. Which saved them travel time, as it turned out. Only one agency handled older model cars.

Older indeed. Standing in the office of Oedipus Wrecks Rentals, Janna peered out the window to confirm what she glimpsed as they turned off Kansas Avenue onto the lot. One row of cars toward the back still had wheels.

"Do people really rent wheelers?" she asked.

The agency owner, a stocky man who had introduced himself as James Oedipus Jaax, wiped the grease from his hands and shoved the shop towel into a thigh pocket of his red coveralls. "Oh, yes...especially after some period movie with screaming-tire car chases plays on TV or at the cineround. The internal combustion models are all converted to electric, of course, but they're still fun to drive. That's why I keep them around."

"The upkeep must be difficult, though," Mama said.

From beyond a door connecting to the shop came a ring of metal and a female voice, swearing. Jaax winced. "Labor intensive. If one of those kids needs a part, I usually have to make it myself. But the challenge of seeing if you can do something is half the fun, isn't it." He pulled a printout from under the counter and laid it on top. "After you called I checked my inventory file. I have ten Tritons, three of them seventy-seven's. These are their rental logs for the past month. What are you looking for?"

Janna forgot the wheelers. Leaning on the counter beside Mama, she fastscanned the logs. "One of these vehicles may have been used in the fund-raiser robberies Friday and Saturday nights."

Jaax grinned. "One set of crooks cleans another. There is justice in the world."

Justice for Carel Armenda, too, perhaps. Janna caught Mama's eye and grinned. Two of the Tritons were wagons. One went out two weeks ago to a Leda Bondank and not been returned. The other had been delivered to the Billard airfield Friday morning, where the client, Willem Edmiston, picked it up at eight-thirty in the morning. Monday morning he left the vehicle at Billard again.

Her ear button murmured. Janna barely heard. Edmiston took over the car well before noon. Giving him plenty of time to install the desktop for controlling the waitron. Janna looked across the counter at Jaax. "How easy is it to remove the rear seat in the wagons?"

"It took us less than five minutes to pull the one out of T-seventy-seven-30 after the bibi requested it." Jaax tapped the log of the wagon rented by Leda Bondank.

Janna exchanged glances with Mama. His eyes gleamed. "May we see the contract for that vehicle?"

Jaax brought the contracts for both wagons. After reading them over, Janna carefully wrote Bondank's address and phone number her notebook.

Mama copied down the information on Willem Edmiston of Omaha, Nebraska. Who listed himself as "self-employed", Janna noticed. "May we see this vehicle?"

Jaax led them outside and down a line of parked cars, which seemed dominated by Datsun-Ford and Chrysler road cars.

"This row looks straight out of our garage at headquarters," Janna said.

Jaax grinned. "It should. Most of these used to be police cars. I buy my stock when the new-car agencies and your department auction off their old vehicles. Leo cars are a good buy if they haven't been wrecked...reinforced bodies, heavy duty fans and circuitry, Simon cells operable in very low light levels. Here's the car."

Janna eyed it. The Bondank bibi's removal of the rear seat in her vehicle made her look good as a suspect, but this wagon came in the right color. And the rental timing fit well, too.

She and Mama went over the vehicle, Mama in back checking under and behind the rear seat, she examining the front seats. Neither yielded any objects that might have been left behind by the tickman and his driver.

"We clean the cars after each rental," Jaax said.

Mama sat back in the rear seat, glancing around him. "If someone had removed this seat and replaced it, could you tell?"

Jaax frowned a moment, then pulled a mini-light from a breast pocket of his coveralls and stretched across the airfoil skirt to lay flat on the car floor. He shone his light under the seat. "There's no dust around the clamps or in the floor slots but that could be from a thorough vacuuming." He backed out and stood up. "I'd have to pull the seat completely out and take a close look before I could say for sure if it's been moved."

Janna exchanged glances with Mama. "Lab?"

He nodded and slid out of the car. "Mr. Jaax, we may want our Criminalistics people to go over the car. Please don't rent it again until you hear from us."

The car radio and Janna's ear button kept up a continuous stream of traffic while Mama drove north toward the address Bondank gave. It looked genuine, on the north fringe of the city, but was it really Bondank's, and if so, would she be there or long gone with whatever jon—husband, lover—she rented the car for?

The rural mailbox at the end of the driveway provided no help. It said: *Prairie Hill Pet Hostel.* Nor did a Triton wagon sit on the drive curving up by the brick house and low, sprawling barn. Mama set the Meteor down at the barn, by a door marked *Lobby*.

With the car's fans silent, Janna became aware of muffled barking. It became louder as they entered the "lobby".

The fragrant scent of cedar filled the room. Deep arm chairs covered in deep-pile fabric sat against walls paneled in wood and hung with inscribed photographs of dogs and cats. Janna read the inscriptions in one group, several with a pawprint in a lower corner.

Thank you for taking such good care of me, Leda and Clell.

Thank you for a wonderful visit.

Next to Max and Tori, you're my favorite human, Leda.

And on the photograph of a sleek, coppery-red dog: *To Leda and Clell. Though I'll never see you again, across the light years I will always remember you. Tsar the stardog.*

Janna pointed out Leda's name to Mama. Bondank did seem connected to this address.

A door at the far end of the room hissed open. A smiling young man with short white-blonde hair appeared through the opening. "May I help you?"

"Interesting inscription." Mama pointed at the copper dog's photograph.

The young man nodded. "Tsar was a lovely boy, amazingly mellow for a Vizsla. I don't blame Dell and Zanandra for taking him along on their colony ship, though I was surprised when they told me you have to buy pets a share in the company, too. And it costs the same as one for a person."

"Every sleeper uses a separate capsule," Mama said, "so the cost per individual is the same no matter what the age, size, or species."

One more miscellaneous fact out of that bottomless grab bag of data in Mama's head. Janna eyed him. Was there nothing he did not know something about?

Mama smiled at the young man. "Are you Clell?"

"Clell Van Hoose. Are you looking for a place to leave your pet while you're away? We pride ourselves on being a home away from home for our guests. Dogs and cats each have a large run, the cats' furnished with climbing posts and platforms and boxes for lounging and hiding. Birds enjoy the freedom of a flight cage. Reptilian and rodent pets' cages are kept in our garden atrium. We make sure all the guests are played with and petted, and dogs exercised. If they're on a training program, we continue it, as well as maintain medical and physical therapy regimes. We groom and clip, and we keep a copy of your itinerary, so you can receive regular reports of your pet's welfare. May I show you around?" He paused with an expectant smile.

Janna almost regretted having no pet to board there. "We're looking for Ms. Bondank."

"I'm sorry, she's out right now." The smile never wavered.

"When do you expect her back?" Mama asked.

"I'm afraid I don't know."

A howl rose above the barking.

"Excuse me." Van Hoose disappeared through the door.

Janna looked at Mama. "What do you think we've got…he doesn't know when she'll be back, or he doesn't expect her back?"

Mama pushed his glasses up his nose. "Doesn't know when she'll be back. He doesn't act like someone covering up her absence."

The howl stopped. Van Hoose returned carrying a small dog with a foxy face and bright eyes peering out of its fluffy reddish fur. "It's all right. Brutus here just decided he'd had enough of being alone." Van Hoose scratched the dog behind its ears. "You're a spoiled brat, you know that?" He looked up at them again. "I started to tell you that Leda's out picking up some new guests. We also provide ferry service if you're unable to bring your pet to us yourself. Are you sure I can't help you?"

Janna shook her head. "We—"

"Maybe you can," Mama interrupted. "We're from ARCA, the Association of Rental Car Agencies."

Janna grinned inside. More Theater.

"We're surveying rental customers. According to our information, Ms. Bondank is presently driving a car from…" Mama pulled his notebook out of a breast pocket and flipped through it. "…from Oedipus Wrecks Rentals? Is she satisfied with it, do you know?"

Van Hoose nodded, still petting the dog. "It's a lifesaver while her own car's being repaired."

"Very good." Mama made a note. "What kind of driving does she do? I mean, how far and where on any given day…say last Friday afternoon."

The dog squirmed so it turned over on its back in Van Hoose's arms. He rubbed its belly. "She left around noon to stop at Socrates Zupancic's vet's office for a bag of the prescription dogfood he eats, then bought some other supplies various places, then drove out to Lake Sherwood for Shogun and Samurai Gallardo, a really nice pair of Akitas." He rubbed the dog under its chin. "That must have amounted to fifty klicks or better by the time she came back here."

When she came back would have been more useful information. Janna put on a smile. "Did she go anywhere in the evening?"

Van Hoose shook his head. "We exercised dogs until dark."

That did not sound promising. "Are you the only two who drive the vehicle?"

"*She's* the only one who drives it."

Mama nodded and made another note. "What about...oh, Saturday evening?"

The dog started squirming again. Van Hoose turned it back upright. "She didn't drive anywhere at all. We worked the dogs until dark again, then played with the cats for another couple of hours."

Janna sighed. Unless blondie here were lying, and her instincts said he was not, or someone had sneaked the Triton away without him seeing it, this could not be the vehicle they wanted.

So now they checked out Mr. Edmiston of Omaha.

A call from the squadroom to the number on the rental contract reached only to a machine. A foxy face reminding Janna of Pass-the-Word Morello's appeared on the screen. "I'm sorry I'm unavailable just now. When the menu appears on your screen, please choose an option and leave a message."

The choices started with an invitation to punch in an access code, the kind which typically put the caller's message in a priority file and/or rang the phone, as the initial connection in such systems did not.

Janna raised a brow at Mama. People had any number of reasons for screening their calls. Including illegal businesses, which used possession of the access code, obtainable only through the right contacts, as an endorsement of the caller. "I wonder if the Omaha P.D. knows Edmiston."

Mama grinned. "My thought exactly."

After choosing *Urgent Message Requiring a Return Call ASAP* from among the remaining options and leaving their names and number, Mama broke the connection and called Information for the OPD's phone number.

Edmiston's name meant nothing immediately to the detective in Central Robbery who drew their call, but she promised to run him through the OPD computer and fax the information to them.

Edmiston's name came back negative from NCIC in Washington, too. How much did that mean, though, Janna wondered. NCIC had nothing on any of their riffers.

They spent the rest of the day talking to Jason Aschke's co-workers at Beria, bringing up the subject of his wife. Everyone agreed he had been devastated by her death.

"He changed completely after Corenne died," Listra Wassman said. "He never laughs or jokes anymore, never goes drinking after work with us, never attends parties. If her name happens to come up, he either looks through you or walks away."

"Do you know how he feels about politicians?" Janna still liked the theory that he blamed the city government for the accident and had been recruited for the riffs by someone playing on that bitterness.

Wassman shrugged. "He doesn't talk about politics. For that matter, he hardly talks about anything."

No one else had any more to offer on that subject. No one knew if he had gone to Kansas City on the eighth, either.

After the squad's end-of-watch debriefing, Mama dropped Janna off at Washburn University before going home to cook dinner for Arianna Cho.

"Dinner. Of course." She snickered and climbed out of his little MGE.

"There are people in this world who appreciate food, bibi," he called after her, "people to whom dining is more than an action that stops one's stomach from growling."

The comment set Janna's snarling. She headed for the student union and wolfed down a sandwich while looking over her class notes one last time before the test.

Only to have her concentration interrupted by the sound of Tony Ho's righteous name on the newscanner in one corner of the snack bar. "The case has city officials worried. Not only did armed guards and the most modern security technology fail to prevent the robberies and the death of Topeka businessman Carel Armenda, but the revelation that Kushner used the Scib card stolen from waiter Cristo Salmas to enter the Capitol Sheraton Hotel in his place has raised concerns about the accuracy of identification procedures currently employed in the use of the Cards."

Janna covered her ears to muffle the sound, but she could not shut out thoughts about the case. Even during the test, the churning questions about real problems in law enforcement kept running over the hypothetical ones on the page.

Aschke finished work early enough that on any given day he could catch a commuter dirigible from Billard to the K.C. Municipal airport. Great Plains Airways' records showed no Aschke taking any flight on Sunday the seventh or Monday the eighth, true, but that did not clear the service technician. He could have borrowed a car. Beyond that…was Edmiston involved, and if so, how had he connected with Aschke? Had Junior or Sydney gone to Edmiston and then he in turn set up the robberies? That made a long, involved chain, and long chains sprang leaks. This one showed no signs of leaks.

Janna walked home from campus still chasing questions in her head.

Which stopped abruptly at her front walk. She halted, staring. Broken furniture and shredded clothing spread across the lawn from the front porch to the street. A bookcase lay smashed at the foot of the steps, the book chips in it scattered down the walk in a spray pattern. On the porch, the front door stood wide open. Something pale fluttered on the jam. When Janna picked her way through the wreckage and up the steps, she found a marriage contract, ripped in two and spiked to the wood with a kitchen knife.

She raced up the side steps to her apartment. The garlic scent of Mama's baked marinated chicken enveloped her at the door. "What happened downstairs?"

"The final battle." Mama and Arianna Cho sat cross-legged on the living room couch, holding wine glasses and listening to a recording of something brassy and baroque. "I don't know the details—I found the same mess down there when I came home—but the ladies have lost their lease." He leaned forward to pour wine into a third glass on his round oak dinner table cut down to coffee table height. "After making sure there were no bodies downstairs, I called the landlord and invited him over for a look. Have some rosé and let's toast peace."

Amen to that. Janna tossed aside her trenchcoat and lay back in the molded-foam easy chair, sipping the wine. Warmth spread through her. So did an idea. She caught Mama's eye. "An eviction means an empty apartment…one very easy to move into from here."

Mama twirled his wine glass. "I thought about that. Unfortunately, not fast enough."

Cho shook the jade cape of her hair back over her shoulders. "I've already spoken for it." She smiled at Mama. "Meeting Mama has been a wonderful stroke of luck. In less than a week he's introduced me to a delightful new sculptor, fed me the kind of homecooked meal I love but have no time to cook, and solved the problem of the impossible escalation of my present rent."

Lucky for Arianna Cho, maybe. Janna took another swallow of wine and sighed. It left Janna Brill with Mama still in residence.

The phone chimed on the end table between the couch and easy chair. Being closest, Janna leaned sideways and flipped up the screen. "Yes?"

On the screen, puckish brows hopped. "My very favorite answer."

Diosdado! Warmth spread through her. She smiled. "To what question?

He grinned. "Several come to mind. This evening, however, it's: do these people look familiar? I had copies of your enhancements posted in all the division stations. A call came from Central a few minutes ago. A patrol officer there thinks he knows a couple of your gunmen."

12

More rain. Janna wiped the steam from the inside of the passenger window and eyed the drenched streets of Kansas City outside. With luck, though, this would keep people under cover where they could be found. She turned in her safety harness to glance back at Averill Kinderman, the Central Division patrolman Diosdado mentioned on the phone and then introduced to them in the Robbery squadroom a few minutes ago. "We really appreciate you giving up your free time to help us."

"How could I stay inside on a top card day like this? Or miss the chance to be a pretzel." The K.C. leo twisted sideways in the seat and stretched his legs by extending them toward the far door. "Sitting back here with a prisoner must be fun; you're both as leggy as I am."

Janna looked down at the enhancements in her lap, two of them circled in red: one stocky and red-haired, the other with a gold ring in his ear. "These jons call themselves Dragon and Tsunami, you said?"

He grimaced. "They sound like gangers, don't they? I remember when slighs had names like Mouse and Liberty."

Slighs. Yes. Janna sucked in her lower lip. The big surprise of the day. They had not expected to hear that about their riffers when Diosdado introduced Kinderman. If he were right, it explained the lack of records on these two. And made her wonder...if two did prove to be slighs and no records had surfaced on any of the six yet, could the other four also be?

Behind the wheel, Mama frowned. "I can't believe slighs are involved. The jons we saw on the news chips are very aggressive, and enjoy terrorizing people."

"You think slighs don't?" Kinderman grunted. "They're changing. No more silent shadows slipping away at the edge of your vision. These days when I stop them for an FI, they're so fucking full of brass I can hear their balls clank."

Janna had noticed that among some young slighs in Topeka, too.

Thunder rolled overhead. Kinderman said, "We need that mandatory identation the legislature keeps talking about but never gets around to passing."

A ripple across Mama's scalp stopped in furrows on his forehead. "We need to leave them alone. They aren't harming anyone. It's the threat against their lifestyle that's making them militant."

"Lifestyle?" Kinderman's lip curled. "Don't tell me you're one of the bleeding hearts who—

"What we need," Janna interrupted, "is to find these jons." Which alienating Kinderman with an argument would not help. "I know you said back in the Robbery squadroom that your contact with them has always been at night, but you do have some idea where they might be days, don't you? At home sleighs work places like stockrooms and in the kitchens of restaurants."

Kinderman continued eyeing Mama for a moment, then shrugged. "Here, too. Dragon and Tsunami hang around the River Quay, and since we have a few restaurants and clubs down there that manage to stay in business, I thought we'd check them out. The city market is close, too. Take a right on Main to the intersect with Delaware and follow Delaware over I-70 into the Quay."

A short time later Mama set the Meteor down on its parking rollers at the curb in front of a building Kinderman indicated.

Janna stared. Only the walls stood, a shell of blackened bricks with rubble visible through the empty arch of the doorway. "I thought you said there was a club here."

"The Levee, yes." Kinderman grinned. "The entrance is in the alley. We can shortcut through the building; most people do."

They climbed out of the car turning up the collars of their coats against the rain. Janna stared around as they followed a winding path through the dripping remains of fixtures and interior walls. She stepped over a puddle and around the pieces of a broken urinal. "Aren't the owners planning to rebuild?"

Ahead of her, Kinderman nodded. "Probably, but it usually takes four or five years and it's only been three since the fire."

"Usually?" That implied previous disasters.

Behind her Mama said, "Over the last hundred and fifty years, the clubs and restaurants in this area have all suffered periodic bombings and fires in disputes between crime families, or been the site of family leaders being gunned down. When I was at UMKC, the River Quay had been redeveloped for the umpteenth time and these were top dink places to party and eat. No longer, it appears."

"For the umpteenth time. Watch the step down." Kinderman led them into the alley.

Across it like a skyway stretched an aging holo, faded and patently transparent, of a riverboat churning up and down beside a pier. Narrow stairs beneath the near end led down between the burned building and the next one. Janna eyed them with distaste. Such daylight as existed barely penetrated the stairwell and the smell seeping up generated mental images of sewers. She followed Kinderman down holding the handrail all the way, and carefully stepped from the last tread across the murky pool below it to the raised sill of the door the K.C. leo opened. "Welcome to the Levee."

The Underground would be more appropriate. The club stretched out in a series of barrel vaults. Smoke layering the air, thick and stale and heavy with drug fumes, gave it the faded blue appearance of a cheap holo, too. Last night's smoke, Janna guessed, shaking the water from her hair and trenchcoat, since only the bartender and a woman with a pushbroom occupied the club.

The bartender glanced around from sliding glasses into overhead racks. "We don't open until noon."

"We're not customers." Kinderman pulled his badge case out of a hip pocket. "Do you know a couple of slighs calling themselves Tsunami and Dragon?"

At the corner of Janna's vision, the woman with the pushbroom stiffened.

"Who knows what their names are?" the bartender said.

Janna laid the enhancements on the bar. "Here's what they look like."

The bartender studied the pictures briefly. "Sorry. No jogs."

Mama sidled toward the woman. Her fingers tightened on the broom handle. Fighting the urge to run? Slighs tended to react that way to leos. And this was a sligh; Janna's every instinct swore to that. Mama whispered to her, bending his head to her level.

Kinderman rapped the bar with his badge case. "I've seen them here, jon." Accusation edged his voice.

"I haven't," the bartender came back calmly. "Then, I don't pay much attention unless the customer's a troublemaker or a regular."

The woman murmured something back to Mama.

"The slighs are regulars," Kinderman said.

"Not paying regulars." The bartender turned back to his glasses. "I don't know them, leo."

For a moment Janna wondered if Kinderman were going to lean across the bar and grab the bartender. His body swayed that direction. Then he turned and crooked a finger at the woman. "You. Talk to me."

Mama stepped in front of her. "I've been talking to her already. She suggests we try the city market." He headed for the door.

Janna followed. After a moment, Kinderman did, too.

Up in the alley again, he said, "She's one of them, you know."

Mama nodded.

"So you have to be careful. Slighs will say anything to protect each other."

Janna frowned. They stuck together, yes, as any minority did, but not always, and except in the case of blindly loyal friends, not when it threatened the welfare of the entire group.

Mama, however, reacted with only a mild: "It won't hurt to try the market. Besides, Jan ought to see it."

Shit. She rolled her eyes. "Mama, we came come up here to track riffers, not play tourist!"

He dried his glasses with a handkerchief. "One should never waste an opportunity to expand one's horizons, bibi."

The expansion of horizons remained to be proven, but the city market did widen her eyes. Suddenly, art studios and apartments that had probably started life as warehouses gave way to a four-block plaza. In sharp contrast to the square solidity of the surrounding brick buildings, low, interconnecting domes covered the better part of it, rising in airy grace from multiple open arches and gleaming gold even in the rain.

It looked like a piece of a fantasy city.

Reality resumed as soon as they set the car down in the perimeter parking area and hurried in through the nearest arch. Close examination showed her the domes had been constructed of Mylar, supported by air-filled ribs.

In the unbroken space beneath stretched row upon row of plastic crates and baskets sitting on the ground or in the open backs of trucks, filled with fruits and vegetables and flowers. Hand lettered signs by many of the produce stalls promised products organically or hydroponically grown, or from ground with soil and water certified free of contamination. Men and women in jeans or coveralls presided over the stalls, each with a laptop or notebook computer and Card/retinal reader for recording sales. Buyers prowled the rows towing shopping baskets or porterbots, or drove vans lettered with the names of local restaurants and hotels. The turbulence from their airfoil fans flattened Janna's trenchcoat against her legs in passing.

Kinderman made a sound of disgust as they passed a pair of winos shuffling past in the opposite direction. "Welcome to gandie land."

Janna spotted trippers, as well…thin, dressed almost uniformly in grimy clothes grown too large for them, their shaved heads decorated with blurred tattoos. Looking for a place out of the rain and, with luck, a handout of food. Except they were more likely to trade it for drugs than eat it.

Lacking a hard ceiling to reflect sound, the market seemed strangely hushed for the number of people and vehicles in it. Even the rap of rain on the dome sounded distant and muted. But scents made up for the quiet. Odors swirled around Janna in a thick tide…the sweetness of flowers and herbs, the sharp tang of citrus, fishy smells. The source of the latter became obvious when she spotted iced tanks of catfish and trout on trucks bearing fish farm logos.

Watching a brawny young man load a carton of fish into a hotel van, she also saw the potential for sligh labor. They had to love it…an environment with an informal structure but a need for laborers, where wages could be taken in food and either eaten or bartered elsewhere for clothes and housing.

Mama took a deep breath. "I always liked coming up here. Right after dawn is best, when it's bustling while the rest of the city sleeps. The commercial customers make their big buys then. There used to be an old man who showed up a couple of times a week with coffee beans. He'd take only barter and he'd be gone in half an hour with enough fruit and vegetables to feed an army. I've always wondered what he did with it all."

"Trader Jon," Kinderman said. "I think he fed slighs and gandies. I'd almost forgotten." He smiled. "It's been a while since I've been here this time of day."

"Both of you being so intimately familiar with the place, I trust one of you knows an easy way to locate those slighs in here," Janna said.

"There's only one way, bibi." Mama pushed his glasses up his nose, grinning. "The old heel-toe heel-toe."

So they walked, covering the market row by row, stall by stall, studying each face. With no luck for a long while. Then, at a wheeled truck displaying baskets of hydroponic tomatoes, the arm of a jon counting tomatoes into a bag in a porterbot set off an alarm in Janna's head. A scar crossed the back of the hand. Unfortunately, the jon stood with his back to them.

She nudged Mama. He dipped his chin to indicate he had seen.

Moving casually, Janna crossed the aisle to the tomatoes. "Excuse me. Are these vine ripened?"

Scar-hand looked around and she barely heard his answer. The lean face with its light complexion and sandy hair matched one of the enhancements. One Kinderman had not circled. Her hand slid on through the inside of her trenchcoat pocket to her thigh boot, to the wrap strap down inside it.

But rather than pull it, she thanked Scar-hand and rejoined Mama, memorizing the stall's location.

"You're going to come back later and hope he's still there?" Kinderman asked after they walked on.

"Better that than wrap him now and risk warning the other two we're after them," Mama said. "Do you know him?"

"Not really. I've just seen him around." The K.C. leo glanced back at the stall, frowning. "He's another sligh. Calls himself Rebel, I think."

Another of those names, so un-slighlike, so…Janna hunted for a word to characterize them. Aggressive? She found her hand reaching through her trenchcoat pocket again to the top of the wrap strap in her boot. Maybe Kinderman was right about slighs changing. It had to be more than coincidence that three of them with names like that appeared to match enhancements of the riffers.

If three of them worked here, what about the others?

As they kept searching the market, she watched for faces matching the remaining three enhancements.

She saw none of those, but in the next dome, approaching a stall selling cucumber and squash, Kinderman murmured, "There's Dragon."

She saw him, too…stocky, freckled, carrot-red hair pulled up in a pony tail. He might easily have been overlooked. His faded denim jumpsuit/coverall matched those worn by many of the vendors, including the middle-aged woman sitting at the front of the stall with a newspaper laid open on the computer in her lap.

Kinderman said, "Hello, Dragon."

The sligh turned from combining the squash from two baskets in one. He moved not as most slighs would, with the rigid control of someone forcing himself to stand his ground, but leisurely. An insolent smile spread across his face. "Well, you do walk around in daylight, leo. And we thought you spent it in a locker, sleeping on a bed of parking tickets and report forms."

Kinderman sent back a smile as thin as a blade. "That's only when I haven't drunk enough deek blood. Speaking of 'we', seeing you solo is new and different. Where's Tsunami?"

The vendor looked up from her newspaper. "Is there a problem, officer?"

"Not if I learn where Tsunami is." He watched Dragon as he said it.

Frowning, the woman opened her mouth as though about to respond, but Dragon snorted and spoke first. "What's the matter, leo?" He tossed the emptied basket into the airfoil pickup parked behind the stall. "You can't stand leaving the 'Companion Information' section of your FI form blank?"

"I have people who want to meet him." Kinderman gestured at Mama and Janna.

Looking them over, the sligh went still. A moment later he snorted again, but not before a hint of worry-lines showed on his forehead. "Maybe he isn't interested in meeting more lions."

Two strides took Kinderman around the produce baskets. He caught Dragon under the elbow. "Hard card. Let's find him, choomba."

The sligh's lip curled. Janna sighed. Forget a quiet wrap of the two. If Dragon had not connected this visit with the robberies and killing before, it must have occurred to him by now, and the universe could die its heat death before he led them to his friend.

Beside her, Mama shook his head. "Forget it, Kinderman. You were right; for all the swagger, around lions they turn rabbit just like other slighs. We might as well let him hop away."

Dragon stiffened. He jerked his arm out of Kinderman's grip. "Rabbit? Fuck you, puss." Putting his thumb and first finger in his mouth, he blew three shrill, rising notes. "I'll show you rabbit."

A minute later a lean, dark-haired jon came loping between stalls, the gold ring in his ear gleaming. Janna blinked. Then Dragon had not realized why they were here. Either that or he had brassier balls than even Kinderman realized.

The whistle attracted the attention of other vendors and passing citizens, who turned to look at them.

Reaching them, Tsunami grinned. "Well…if it isn't Officer Children-Man. Et al," he added, glancing across the produce baskets at Mama and Janna. "Is troikas the new fashion in lion country?"

"What's going on here?" the vendor demanded.

"Just some routine questions, ma'am." Janna moved around the baskets and behind Tsunami, where she could grab him if he tried bolting.

Mama followed. "Sergeant Brill and I are from Topeka."

Incredibly, both slighs stared back at them with no reaction except *so-what* expressions. Uncertainty stirred in Janna. She caught Mama's eye. Maybe Kinderman's identification was wrong after all.

She pulled the enhancements from her trenchcoat pocket and handed them to the slighs. "What do you think about these?"

They glanced over the pictures. Tsunami shrugged. "Someone took 2-D's of us."

"And of a sligh called Rebel," Kinderman said.

"It looks like him." The ponytail swished as Dragon pulled in his chin. "Who took these?"

Janna moved a step closer to the slighs. "First tell us about the other three. Do you know them?"

Tsunami handed the enhancements back to her. "Why do you want to know?"

He knew the others. The expression in his eyes told Janna that. He finally suspected something. That showed in his voice. She turned toward the vendor, who had stood up and was watching them with a frown. "Are you here every day?"

"Except Sunday." The woman spoke slowly. "We farm hydroponically, so we always have fresh vegetables to bring in."

"How many of those days does Dragon work for you?"

The woman hesitated before answering. "He doesn't really work for me. When I need a hand with something, I whistle. He or his friend or one of the others floating around come and help. Or sometimes one of them will stop and ask if I have any work for them."

"Was he here last Friday and Saturday?" Kinderman asked.

Her forehead furrowed in thought. "I'm sure he was. They always are."

"Do you *remember* seeing him, or his friend?"

She hesitated again, this time longer, glancing back and forth from the K.C. leo to the slighs, furrows deepening.

"Of course we were here," Dragon said in an impatient voice. "Remember the bibi who wanted two dozen squash but said they all had to be the same size and shape, so you had me go through every basket to find a matched set?"

The vendor's forehead smoothed instantly. She smiled. "Of course."

"Which day was that, ma'am?" Janna asked.

Dragon answered for her. "Friday."

The woman nodded. "Friday morning. I remember because after she left, I took a break for lunch."

"Was he here in the afternoon, too?" If they left around noon, they could have reached Topeka with time to spare before the fund-raiser.

Again a hesitation. Above them, rain thundered on the roof of the dome.

Kinderman said, "There isn't much need for them in the afternoon. Is there, ma'am? The quantity sales, the ones where you need someone to carry baskets to the buyers' vehicles, are mostly in the morning." He eyed the slighs. "Where did you go in the afternoon, and evening?"

In unison the slighs folded their arms. Tsunami said, "Where I damn well wanted to. Leo, I don't know whether you can't get enough of harassing us when you're on duty or you're just showing your country cousins how the boys in the big city do it, but I've had enough." He started to turn away.

Kinderman reached out an arm to block him.

The sligh stopped. "What're going to do, hit me? Commit police brutality in front of witnesses?"

Mama circled to where he faced Tsumani. He smiled. "We're just asking where you were Friday and Saturday night."

"I'm telling you that's none of your fucking business!"

A citizen looking over the produce at the stall across the aisle turned to stare at them.

Uncertainty nudged Janna again. She heard anger and defiance in the sligh's voice, but no defensiveness, no fear, nothing that said to her: *guilty*.

Kinderman's knife blade smile appeared again. "Oh, yes, it is, choomba." He kept his voice low. The citizens and vendors turned back to their own affairs. "Because those photos weren't taken of you here in K.C. They're from news chip recordings of six perpetrators who riffed two political fund-raisers in Topeka and killed a guest at one of them."

The slighs gaped.

Kinderman's smile widened. "So...I think we ought to continue this discussion at the station house."

Dragon started. "Wait a minute. Those 2-D's can't be us. They just look like us."

"One just happens to look like your friend Rebel, too?" Janna asked. That was too much coincidence to believe. She caught the vendor's eye. "Ma'am, we need your help." She handed the enhancements across the produce baskets to her. "Do you know the three individuals other than these two and the one with the scar on his hand?"

After a troubled glance at Dragon and Tsunami, the woman nodded. "This one with the scar through his eyebrow helps here, too. I think he's called Swift."

Four of the six. That *was* too much for coincidence.

As though reading her thoughts, Kinderman nodded. "Let's go."

"But...we haven't been out of K.C.," Dragon protested. "How would we get to Topeka? Walk? You can't pay bus fares with cucumbers."

"Someone gave you tickets."

Tsunami's eyes narrowed. "Not us." He toyed with the ring in his ear. "You asked about Friday and Saturday night so that has to be when the robberies happened. What time?"

Mama told him.

His sudden grin dripped insolence. "I don't know about the other three, but Dragon, Rebel, and I can't possibly be your perpetrators." He folded his arms. "On Friday evening at seven o'clock Officer Gariana Bondini, the lion I dream of being shut in the back of a watch car with, was FI'ing the three of us outside the Waterloo Club. Check your records. I just hope she noted under 'Narrative information' how cooperative I was, offering to let her strip search me."

From the flare in Kinderman's eyes, Janna wondered if he wanted to hit the sligh, but he only reached into a thigh pocket and pulled out an ear button. "We'll see, choomba." Without taking his eyes off the sligh, he screwed the radio into his ear and tapped it on. He murmured too softly to be heard but lip reading, Janna saw him ask for a records check.

They stood in silence, waiting for the results, while rain continued hammering the dome overhead and around them murmured vendors' and customers' voices.

Presently, Mama eyed Dragon and Tsunami. "We're going to find out the names of the other two slighs sooner or later, so why don't you tell us now and let us spend the time it would take us to find them checking out their alibis for the times of the robberies."

The two exchanged glances. Dragon smiled. "You're the detectives. Detect."

"Shit!" Kinderman swore.

They all looked at him.

He pulled the radio button out of his ear, scowling. "I don't know how you three did it, because we all know damn well that's you in those photos, not jons who look like you. I intend to find out, though, and when I do, we'll have another discussion."

"You mean they're telling the truth?" Janna asked.

He sighed. "According to Records, Officer Bondini did file an FIF on them for Friday night, just where and when they said. If we believe that, they couldn't have been in Topeka."

13

Despite a closed door, the raised voices leaked out of Lt. Vradel's office and the squadroom had fallen silent, listening. Cruz even turned off the newscanner's sound.

"They spend two days up there, and what do they come back with? Nothing...just a few names!" Commander Vining paced inside the windows. "It's been a week since Armenda was killed. What am I going to tell Paget?"

Vradel did not pace. He sat motionless behind his desk. Motionless, that is, except for the twitch of his mustache and the twirl of the pencil in his hands. "*You* don't have to tell him anything." He did not shout. Janna had to strain to hear. The biting edge on his words, however, suggested that only iron will kept the volume under control. "Facing the director is my job. You just worry about the media."

"You'd better worry, too." Vining frowned through the window toward where Janna and Mama sat on their desks. "That pair had four good suspects in their hands and they let them go! The media will be asking why."

"If they learn about it, I suggest you point out the lack of evidence. That FI report gives three of them an iron-clad alibi for one riff."

Janna sighed. Yes...although the slighs had offered it too glibly in her opinion. Rebel, whom they rounded up as soon as Records informed Kinderman about the FI, used almost the same words Tsunami had. As if they all practiced the story together.

It baffled her how they could have faked the FI, however. Certainly not by having friends pose as the three of them. When she and Mama talked to Bondini at the beginning of the evening watch, the shelion assured them she knew the trio too well to be skinned that way. Her thinly concealed contempt for slighs convinced Janna that Bondini was unlikely to have filed a false report for their benefit.

Besides, if the slighs had arranged alibis, surely Swift, whom Kinderman had located before leaving the market, would have someone more credible than other slighs to swear to his presence in Kansas City. And why had none at all been given for the last two, York and Shadow, after their pictures were identified by Central Division officers?

She and Mama found no proof the slighs took the bus to Topeka those afternoons, either. The bus line did not record who bought tickets, just the date and destination of each. Besides which, the tickets could have been bought elsewhere or days earlier, or like Tony Ho, the slighs could have been given passes. In any case, the enhancements failed to ring any bells with the drivers on those runs.

On the other hand, none of the four interviewed could prove their whereabouts Friday and Saturday afternoons. They refused to name their other jobs, claiming—probably with justification—that their employers would not only deny hiring slighs, but be so nervous at being asked that they would fire all sligh employees.

"All we have against the slighs," Vradel continued, "is their likeness to the enhancements."

York and Shadow might be the key. The inability to locate the two, even with the entire KCPD on the watch for them, made Janna wonder if they were being hidden for fear they would give something away.

"If that's all we have, we'd better come up with something more." Vining pulled the door open. "Or the heat being generated on the third floor by media crucifixions and scared high muckies will start cooking gooses down here."

Now Vradel stood, but only to follow Vining as far as the office door. From there he watched, deadpan, as the information officer stalked out of the squadroom. Then he looked over his squad, who had suddenly become very engrossed in paperwork. "All right, I hope everyone's ready for rollcall...and will continue being as attentive and quiet as you've been the past five minutes."

At the end of the briefing, Cruz gathered the case squad for their own additional briefing. He ran a hand back through his hair. "Vining's right, unfortunately. Unless we start producing results, life is going to be hell."

At the caff urn behind them, Maro Desch reached up while his mug filled and tapped the sound control on the newscanner.

"...in Beijing assured Moscow the missile firing was accidental and after expressing profound regret for the tragedy, announced his government has begun a full investigation of the incident. Campaigning in California, Humanitarian presidential candidate Earl Lincoln said—"

"So they finally admit shooting it down," Desch said, overriding the former Secretary of State's comment.

Cruz waited until Desch left before continuing. "Maxwell and Brill, the Omaha PD called. They have nothing on any Willem Edmiston. I had the lab check that Triton at Oedipus Wrecks."

Janna crossed her fingers. A little luck, please. "Had the back seat been removed?"

He shrugged. "Sometime in the past month or so, they say, based on the clean condition and smooth operation of the locks, but they can't be more exact. Taking out the seat, which was the only way to check the floor slots, put new marks over all the older ones."

Janna swore.

"It looks as though only your Mr. Edmiston can tell us if he took out that seat."

"Speaking of Edmiston." Mama pushed his glasses up his nose. "Did he ever return our call?"

"In a manner of speaking," Zavara said. She stretched in a ripple of shoulder and abdominal muscles that set several male members of the squad drooling. "I took a call from him Thursday afternoon. He claimed to be unable to say what he was doing in town last week end, but promised he'd call us back at a more…'convenient' time." She bared even, white teeth. "I advised him to find a convenient time by this week end."

Janna rubbed her forehead. The mysterious Edmiston and his rented Triton, the slighs, people with possible motives for killing Armenda, Aschke's service calls to the crime sites and apartment complex where Tony stayed…all pieces floating around but none connected to each other. They needed connections.

Mama moved around the desks to sit beside her. "I wonder how Aschke, or Sydney or Junior, would react to the enhancements and Edmiston's name."

Connections. Janna grinned. "Let's see."

After Cruz finished updating everyone on the case's progress, she and Mama headed for Beria's office.

The receptionist located Aschke in the service workshop on the building's third floor. Passing the open door of the employee lounge on their way to the workshop, they saw Listra Wassman and a young man standing on chairs hanging a computer-generated banner on the far wall. *Congratulations, Karis. Best of luck always.*

Wassman waved at them.

"Congratulations on what?" Janna called.

"Her new job. After a year of filling out forms, she's been accepted for an electrical engineering position at the American dome on Mars."

Where Janna's brother worked. Too bad Sandoz was not at work now, Janna reflected, following Mama on toward the workshop. She would have suggested Sandoz look up Andy.

In the workshop they found Aschke hunched on a stool before a computer with the face of the monitor case divided horizontally between the rectangular screen and a panel with groups of perforations. As they came in the door, he picked up one of several small circuit boards lying on the table beside and him and plugged it into the panel.

"Good morning," Janna said.

He did not look up. Long fingers continued tapping the keys. Colored lines zigzagged across the monitor, some angling up, some dropping, several stopping short of the far side. Aschke sighed…tapped more keys. A different set of lines appeared.

"We'd like to talk to you."

A new key combination, new lines. "The last time I talked to you, Mr. Beria took me off service calls."

The implication was clear: talking to them brought him trouble; he wanted no more.

Mama smiled. "We just need you to look at some pictures."

Out came the circuit board. In went another. Aschke frowned at the new lines on the monitor. "I don't...know...anything...about...those...robberies."

Janna reached out to block the monitor with her hand. She hardened her voice. "We'd like you to look at the pictures anyway."

For several moments he continued staring ahead of him, as though seeing the monitor through her hand, then his shoulders hunched still more. Sighing, he turned on the stool. "Where are they?"

Mama handed the enhancements to him.

At least he spent more time looking them over than anyone else had the past few days. Janna watched closely, waiting for a flicker or twitch, something to indicate recognition. Aschke handed back the pictures with no change of expression. "I don't know them."

That could be true even if he were involved. His part might have been only providing the information on bypassing security at the hotel and Yi's house. He must have had contact with the tickman, however...the jon from Omaha? Janna pointed at Tsunami's photo. "Have you heard the name Willem Edmiston?" He might be ready to pretend convincingly that he had not, but she hoped associating the name with the wrong person would startle him into an incriminating reaction.

Aschke only shook his head, without even a flicker of surprise.

Maybe he was telling the truth.

A twitch disturbed the smooth gleam of light on Mama's scalp. He smiled at Aschke. "What do you think about the party this afternoon? Listra Wassman says your friend Karis plans to dance nude on the table."

What! Janna gaped at Mama.

"May I go back to work?"

Then she understood the reason for the preposterous statement...to see if Aschke would react to anything they said. Since he had not, his lack of response to the enhancements and Edmiston's name proved nothing.

Time to get tough. She moved close, hopefully violating his personal space, and put a hiss in her voice. "Aschke, suppose you—"

"Go back to work," Mama finished. "Come on, bibi." He caught her sleeve and pulled her with him toward the door.

They reached the corridor before she recovered enough from surprise to jerk loose. "What the hell are you doing?"

He backed out of reach. "Saving us wasted effort. He isn't giving us anything, either because he won't, or he's innocent and he can't. Why badger him until we're sure it's a case of the former?"

Glass comprised the upper half of the partition between the workshop and corridor. She frowned through it at Aschke. "We need a bank warrant."

"Maybe Junior or Sydney will give us a connection that makes probable cause."

Provided, of course, either of them were involved...and would talk.

A phone call to the Armenda house gave them the information that Sydney had gone to Nord Electronics. They drove to the plant in the Soldier Creek division, and found her behind a copper-colored glass desk in a wood-paneled office that smelled of lemon oil and saddle soap. She waved them to leather chairs.

"You look comfortable," Mama said.

The leather squeaked as she leaned back. Her hands ran down the chair arms in a caress. "I've always loved my father's office. Now it's mine."

Janna raised a brow. "Despite the fact your brother inherits control of Armenord?"

A corner of Sydney's mouth quirked. "Correction. He inherits *Armenord*. Control is another matter. Not that he'll fight me for it. If he cared about anything except the toys our profit can buy him, he'd be asserting leadership right now. Instead, he wants to go to Rio, and being denied that until the matter of Dad's death is settled, he's consoling himself with whatever pleasures he can find in town."

"I take it he's no longer on a restricted allowance since your father died," Mama said.

She gave him a bland smile. "I want my brother to be happy. How may I help you today?"

Janna shoved the enhancements across the gleaming desk top. "Do you recognize any of these people?"

The radio button in Janna's ear murmured, "Soldier Alpha Ten, home detention unit requests enforcement aid. HDU computer locates the transponder on detainee Adara Staats at Green Hills Mall, in violation of detention limits."

Sydney studied the enhancements. "Other than these two of the man the newscanner says you have in custody, none of the faces look familiar. Are they the men who carried the needlers?"

"Possibly," Mama said. "We think the red-haired man is named Jason Aschke and the one with the earring, the one who fired at your father, is a Willem Edmiston."

Excitement shot through Janna as Sydney shook her head. "No...Edmiston's shorter than the men in that courtya—" She broke off, eyeing them. Her face congealed. "From your expressions, you already know that. What's this about?"

"Connections." Janna gave her a bland smile. "Tell us how you know Willem Edmiston."

"I don't." Sydney pushed the enhancements back across the desk at them. "My father did."

Janna collected the enhancements. "They were friends?"

"Business associates."

"Associated how?" Mama asked.

The dark eyes narrowed. "Why do you want to know? How did his name come up?"

Janna shoved the enhancements inside the top of a thigh boot. "Edmiston was in town last week end...driving the kind of car seen parked in the area of Lincoln Yi's house the night your father was killed."

The other woman went so still she might have turned to stone. She appeared even to have stopped breathing. Shocked? Or dismayed at their discovery of Edmiston's name? After a long silence, she said slowly, "You believe he's involved in my father's death?"

"It's a possibility." Mama pushed his glasses up his nose. "Unless you have information to the contrary."

Sydney leaned back in her chair. "Edmiston deals in information, not blood."

Now why did that phrase set her spine tingling again? Janna raised her brows. "What kind of information?"

"Market research."

"Also called industrial espionage," Mama said.

Janna straightened. Of course. That explained the screening on Edmiston's phone...so only bona fide clients could reach him. It suggested answers to other questions, too. That kind of "market research" often included burglary...which involved knowing how to defeat security systems. "Can you be sure there's a limit to how far he'll go to obtain information for a client?"

Sydney stared steadily back at them. "Murder isn't the same."

"Can you be sure he can't be bought for murder, too?"

Not a flicker showed in the dark eyes. "I suppose anyone can be bought if the price is high enough." Sydney stood. "If I hear from him, shall I give you a call?"

They took the hint and stood, too. "Please," Mama said. As they headed for the door, he pulled off his glasses and slipped them in his trenchcoat pocket.

Janna stared. What the hell was he up to? Without his glasses, how did he expect to find the elevator and avoid running into walls?

Outside the office door, sure enough, he tripped and went down on his knees.

The secretary caught her breath. "Are you all right?"

"Fine. I—damn!" He squinted. "I've lost a contact lens." Sighing, he groped around on the carpet.

One foot, Janna noticed, held the office door open a crack.

Understanding came. So that was his plan. Kneeling, she pretended to help with the search. In the course of it, she worked her way back to the office door.

From inside came the sound of Edmiston's recorded phone greeting, followed by Sydney's voice, reciting a number sequence, and then, steel-edged: "Mr. Edmiston, this is Sydney Armenda. We have to talk. Today."

Southbound on Topeka Avenue, a Chevy ZRX-30 tried to cut across the front of the Meteor's airfoil skirt into their lane. Pretending his vehicle was the Ashanti its body design aped? Janna shoved her steering wheel forward, revving the police-package fans into thunder. The Meteor gunned past the ZRX, clearing the vehicle by millimeters and forcing the driver to swerve back into his original lane.

Mama winced. "You accuse me of rock jock driving."

Her mouth tightened. "We should have gone back into the office, Mama."

His sigh said: *I suspected that's the problem.* "For what purpose? She didn't say anything incriminating, such as warning him to be careful because we're getting close. If we'd gone in and she claimed her intent was to ask him if he's involved, and if so, what will it cost to buy the name of the person who hired him, how do we prove otherwise?"

"We have to start pushing sometime." She dug her fingers into the wheel. "How else will we get answers that tie everyone together?"

He sighed again. "What if they aren't tied together?"

Christ. She rolled her eyes. "Mama, they *have*—"

"Do they?" His scalp furrowed. "Bibi, working this case is like catching shadows. We're riding off in all directions at once…after riffers, then political terrorists, then a murderer, now an industrial spy. Not to mention that we have a city full of suspects: the ex-wife, the current wife, the son, the daughter, Aschke, slighs, embittered corporate victims, disgruntled former employees, and Edmiston. With so little solid on any of them…just enough that we can't dismiss anyone. About the time we think we have a hold somewhere, it's gone; they were being FI'd at the time or they can't be positively identified."

Maybe that was why she longed for an excuse to throw someone, anyone, into a wall.

"Let's check out the lead Sydney gave us," he went on.

Lead? "What lead?"

He grinned. "You mean you missed it? She mentioned that Edmiston is shorter than the riffers."

So he might be the small jon involved? She waited for him to go on.

"Inge and Surowski said the small suspect spoke to them from the rear area of the Triton. That suggests he had at least part control of the waitron. Certainly the voice. I can't see Aschke being that chatty."

Nor could Janna. And the waitron had spoken to Mrs. Yi with familiarity. "So does Edmiston know the Yi's?"

Mama's grin broadened. "I think she's got it. Shall we ask them?"

They found Yi at his bank.

When they asked him about Willem Edmiston, however, the banker shook his head. "The name isn't immediately familiar. I deal with a great many people throughout the year, though. Just a minute." He tapped a key on the computer/phone console built into his desktop.

Mama nudged Janna and pointed at its screen. She nodded. It had caught her attention, too. The back side of the wafer-thin rectangle appeared to be a screen, as well, enabling Yi to display information or a phone call to both him and someone on this side of the desk simultaneously. At the moment, though, colored lines and abstract shapes chased each other around and across the screen, turning it into a piece of electronic art.

"Directory," the computer said.

"Search. Willem Edmiston."

"Visual display?"

"Yes." Yi leaned back. "If I've dealt with him, the directory should have an entry. I like to include relevant facts, also: in what capacity I've met him, names of associates, spouse, and children, that kind of thing." He smiled. "Sometimes I feel like a cyborg, with half my brain in my desktop."

Mama said, "In Roman times, important men had a slave called a *nomenclator*, whose job was to accompany him and recognize the hundreds of people the poobah knew. When they met one of those individuals, the aide whispered information about the person in his boss's ear so the poobah could sail up and say things like, 'Hail, Julius, how's your wife Olivia? Congratulations on your son Marcus being made legate in the army.'"

Yi smiled. "Really? Here I thought I was being clever and original."

The computer beeped. "Willem Edmiston not found."

Yi spread his hands. "I'm sorry."

Mama said, "Maybe you've met him using another name. May I make a long distance call on your phone if I charge it to my department?"

"If this helps find who killed Carel Armenda, I don't mind standing the cost of a call." Yi paused. "As long as it's to somewhere here on Earth."

Mama came around the desk and punched in the number. "To Omaha."

Janna grinned. She should have thought of that.

Shortly Edmiston's voice recited the message it had when they called.

Mama raised his brows at Yi. "Does the face look familiar?"

Yi studied the screen. After a moment, he shook his head. "I'm sorry, no. For something like this you'd probably do better talking to my wife; she has a wonderful memory for voices." His face went thoughtful. "It's possible, of course, that I haven't actually met him. There've been several attempts to buy my airline. Maybe he researched me looking for leverage his clients could use."

Janna considered that possibility while driving out to the Yi house. "Would ear jewelry be anything he'd be familiar with in that instance?"

"He'd certainly have learned that Yi's wife is blind. Let's just hope he didn't study them from a distance."

Maeve Yi received them in the airy living room overlooking the pool court. Not surprisingly, Edmiston's name meant nothing to her, so they called his number again, and set the phone on Record.

"Listen closely to this voice, please," Janna said.

Mrs. Yi unwrapped the sonar units on her ears and settled herself in a bucket chair with her eyes closed. Her forehead furrowed in concentration while the message played.

When the menu came on the screen, Mama punched off. "Have you heard it before?"

"Play it again, will you?"

Mama tapped the replay button.

After three replays, she said, "It isn't the waitron."

"We know that," Mama said. "The waitron's speaker was probably designed to reproduce whatever its controller said, but in a voice of its own. We need to know if the voice is one you've heard anywhere else before."

"Play it again." After listening several more times, she sighed. "I'm sorry; I don't know. It isn't one I'm familiar with. It's a very ordinary kind of voice and I could have heard it only once or twice. That wouldn't be enough to make it familiar."

"Still, you *might* have talked to him before?" Mama tone coaxed.

She slipped her sonar units back on. "I can't swear to that, but…" She shrugged. "It's *possible*, yes."

Mama grinned. "Thank you very much."

He continued grinning all the way out to the car. Janna eyed him. "What was that about? A possibility doesn't help us. It just means we can't definitely include or exclude him." Her fingers closed on empty air. "As you said…shadows."

"Maybe not." He settled back in the passenger seat. "You say bank warrants can help us. I agree. And now Mrs. Yi has said she possibly talked to Edmiston before. We can use that."

Janna switched on the Meteor, grinning. "Ten-four."

Vradel eyed them from across his desk. "This seems to be the day for bank warrants. Showalter and Weyneth just asked for one on your service technician from Beria…Aschke."

Janna caught her breath. "What did they turn up against him?"

"A ticket clerk at the bus station and a driver on the K.C. run who both ID Aschke's photo as that of a jon traveling to Kansas City several times in the past month." The outline of a bus emerged under the doodling tip of Vradel's pencil.

Janna grinned. The shadows were starting to solidify!

He looked up. "What's your probable cause for this Edmiston?"

She expected Mama to reply, but a sideglance found him staring glass-eyed past the lieutenant. Rather than drag him back from outer space, Janna answered. "As we indicate on the warrant form, he generally fits the description of the small male involved in the robberies. He was in town during the robberies, driving a car of the same make and model seen near the scene Saturday night. He arrived early enough Friday to have stolen the van from G & B Cybertronics and used it to deliver the waitron to the hotel. We learned today he's an industrial spy, which means he probably knows security systems. He's had past dealings with Armenda that have brought him into contact with one and possibly both of the Armenda offspring." She told him about the call she overheard. Encouraged by Vradel's nod, she added, "Looking at Sydney and Junior's bank records would be helpful, too."

"Bring me probable cause." He glanced over the warrant. "Good; you already have Esmiston's bank listed. From the IRS?"

Grimacing, Janna nodded. Phoning a name into the IRS computer always made her feel like someone reaching for a bone under the nose of a large dog, no matter how many times the proper access code and law enforcement identification promptly brought back the subject's bank.

Vradel scribbled his signature on the warrant. "Morello can take this over to the courthouse in a few minutes."

She reached for the paper. "We'll take it ourselves. Who's sitting? Mama…Earth calling!"

His eyes snapped back into focus.

Vradel shook his head. "Judge Kendig. Good luck."

They jogged out of the office and down the stairs to the garage. Good luck indeed. Not only did Judge Kendig have to look on them sympathetically, she had to sign the warrant soon enough for them to phone the Omaha bank before its bookkeeping department shut for the rest of the week end.

Mama halted at the edge of the garage, however. "Bibi, I have something to do here. I'll see you later." He disappeared back into the stairs before she had time to ask about his errand.

She headed for the car, sighing. Over the brainbow. She could only hope he was not up to something the brass would frown on.

At the courthouse, Janna discovered that Kendig had recessed her court at noon and was in chambers…occupied. Janna paced the corridor outside, eyeing her wrist chrono. After twenty minutes, she stopped a bailiff strolling by. "Are there any other judges around today?"

"On Saturday?" Then his expression went sly. "Pierce might be in his chambers."

She winced. So much for that idea. Experiences comparable to approaching Harlan Pierce included walking on coals and ingesting toxic waste.

Snickering, the bailiff disappeared around the corner.

Janna made herself comfortable against the wall.

An hour later the door of Kendig's chambers finally opened.

"Your client's guilty as hell, Ted," one of the men leaving said.

The other grinned. "You have to prove it, and if your arguments in there are any indication, you don't have the chance of a snowball in hell." They turned the corner out of sight. "How about a round of golf?"

Judge Kendig's bailiff invited Janna in where Her Honor insisted on reading the warrant over carefully and quizzing Janna about the case. Janna understood the necessity. Citizens' privacy must not be invaded cavalierly. Still, the judge's caution used time, and before she finally signed, three o'clock had passed.

Janna still smiled at the judge. At least this gave them a reason to look forward to Monday...and hope that then they would have some definite answers in the case, and hooks to catch those shadows.

14

At two in the morning the sound of the TV woke Janna for the third time.

"Quiet! Please," the waitron's voice commanded.

Her thought exactly. Wrapping a robe around her, she stalked out to the living room. "Mama, are you going to watch that damn chip all night?"

He sat as he had all evening, curled in one corner of the couch hugging updrawn knees and staring at the TV screen on the opposite wall. On it, gunmen surrounded the waitron. "Don't attempt to leave," the waitron told shocked guests. "Mr. Salmas, the waiter in front of them—"

"Mama!"

"Just a while longer."

Had he really heard? He never took his eyes from the screen.

This was the errand for which he sent her to the courthouse alone...talking the lab into making him a chip compiling all the news chip segments showing the gunmen. Earlier, on his third run through the chip, she had asked, "What do you hope to see?"

He had shrugged. "I don't know. A ticket agent and driver remember Aschke taking the bus. He isn't that remarkable; so why can't others recall a much more memorable group of six young men?"

"Why memorable? They're slighs," she reminded him.

He just pushed his glasses up his nose. "I can't see them trying to be invisible the way most do. At least three of them swagger, remember?"

"Maybe not this trip, considering what they planned to do."

He shrugged. "Maybe. Even so, a group of six, slighs or not, shouldn't be that invisible."

"So they boarded separately and pretended not to know each other." What was so difficult to understand…and why worry about it anyway? "They obviously managed it somehow, because there they are." She had pointed at the screen.

"And in K.C., Officer Bondini is FI'ing them." His scalp furrowed. "There must be something here that will tell us how they can be in two places at once."

His reasoning sounded brainbent then—though what else did she expect from Mama?—and at this hour of the night, even more so. "Mama, if you haven't found something by now—"

"I have."

He had not called her! "What is it?"

He frowned at the screen. "I don't know. Something wrong. It's there; I can feel it. I just haven't identified it yet."

She sighed. Blue sky. She might have known.

On the screen, the scene had switched to a section from another news chip, the only one which actually caught the beginning of the action.

The waitron, just visible at the far right, began rocking and spinning. Its shelves emptied. The videographer swung to focus on the event, only to be repeatedly jostled off target by dismayed guests scrambling away from spraying wine and flying glassware. When the camera steadied, the gunmen had planted themselves in the space that opened around the waitron.

"Damn." Mama thumbed the backscan button on the remote control. Action reversed. The waitron sucked glasses back onto its shelves. Guests closed in on it, straightening their posture and smoothing their faces. After a pause, action resumed its normal forward motion and the guests ducked away once more. The gunmen appeared from among them.

Mama backscanned again.

After several more repetitions, the scene reminded Janna of waves on a beach, rolling up across the sand then ebbing, leaving behind pieces of flotsam. In this case, sharks.

"I wish I could see where they come from." Mama slowed the action to a frame scan. The glasses floated outward in tiny jerks.

"No matter what you do," Janna said, "that camera isn't going to center on the waitron any sooner or hold any steadier."

"If I could only see them draw their needlers. Or figure out what it is I'm seeing that bothers me."

She might as well be talking to the wall. "I wish to hell you would, so you'd go to bed." She folded her arms. "If you'd spoken up faster, you could be moving downstairs, free to stay up as late as you want without disturbing anyone."

His eyes never left the screen. "You'd miss me."

"Oh, of course." Like an AIDS-C virus. "Why don't you admit the truth, Mama? You haven't seriously looked for an apartment because you can't bear the thought of living alone."

She could have sworn that he froze, but a blink later he grinned at her. "You need me here. I bring your life color."

Weariness dragged at her. Did he *ever* stop performing? She turned away. "Good night."

"Look at this place." His voice followed her to the bedroom. "The artwork and most of the furniture are mine, just as they were Sid's when he shared the place with you. You don't live here; you bivouac. Your life is the job. What kind of existence is that?"

Just what she needed in the middle of the night, advice on how to live her life! At the bedroom door she looked back. "You've successfully evaded my question. Now will you turn down your sound and the TV's and let me sleep?"

He went right on. "You're good at the job, granted...the best partner I've had. Though I wish you cared less about rules and more about people. Having all you want in life doesn't mean it's all you need. What if something happens to the job? What's left of you then?"

An icy hand squeezed her chest. She chased the cold with anger. "Just watch the goddamn chip! Watch it until you pass out. Don't come whining if I take my bicycle to work in the morning and don't wake you on the way out." For emphasis, she slammed the door.

His voice came through it, raised, yet gentler. "I care what happens to you, Jan. I don't want to see you hurt, and that doesn't mean just finishing each watch alive and whole."

She leaned her head against the door, feeling anger drain away. The bastard. Just when she had hurled a bolt of verbal abuse, he came back with something like that. And meant it, damn him.

After a minute she opened the door and padded back out to the living room. Why not humor him in this thing about the chip. Curling up on the other end of the couch, she said, "Okay, on with the show. Maybe two sets of eyes can spot whatever it is."

By morning she wanted to kill him. Not because they had watched the chip until she had memorized every scene. Not because the effort was in vain; whatever Mama had seen earlier that struck him as "wrong" defied identification. What infuriated her was that Mama showed no sign of having gone without sleep, whereas she, as one appalled glance in the mirror told her, looked like the walking dead.

In the squadroom, nearly half an hour early for a change, Mama dropped into his desk chair and sat frowning into space. Janna homed on the caff urn, praying for it to be full and hot.

"My god. I thought we were the only watch who looked like that," Lewis Albino, one of the outgoing morning watch, remarked as she passed his desk. "Would you like a waker?"

She halted. "If you have something to spare."

"Hold out your hand." He dug a blister pack out of a drawer and broke one bubble.

An oval blue-and-yellow tablet landed in her palm. She stared. "You use FTL on *duty*?"

He shrugged. "It's legal, and it keeps me awake."

"For the next week probably." Still, she needed something with kick, and FTL had that. She gulped the tablet down dry. "Thanks, Albino. I owe you."

"Brill, Maxwell."

Janna turned. Vradel stood at the door of his office with Lieutenant Susan Drexel, the morning watch commander.

"Nice to see you bright and early," Drexel said. "There's something here already for the case squad. Since you two are first in, you can tend to it."

"What is it?" Mama asked.

Vradel's mustache lifted at one end. "A gentleman from Omaha. Interview room one."

Lieutenants enjoyed dramatics, too. Awake with a jolt, Janna jogged after Mama toward the interview rooms.

At the door Mama paused. "Why don't you run the camera?"

She nodded and continued past him to the observation room. Despite the stimulant and her adrenalin rush, he still looked brighter than she felt.

Inside the observation room, the camera dangled from the ceiling, aimed through the one-way viewing panel. She switched it on. Beyond the panel, slightly mottled by the acoustic tile design that disguised it on the interview room side, their suspect paced in measured strides. His feet made almost no sound, Janna noticed. In person he resembled Pass-the-Word Morello even more than he had on the phone…small, wiry, foxy-faced.

He swung around in a fluid motion at the sound of the door opening.

"Mr. Willem Edmiston?" Mama extended a hand. "I'm Sergeant Maxwell."

"Good morning." Edmiston shook the hand. "For the record, please note that I've come in voluntarily to talk to you. I would have been here sooner except I couldn't leave the project I was involved in." He sat down in the chair facing Janna's wall.

She slipped on the headset goggles, which slaved the camera to her and fed her the image coming through the lens, giving her the same closeup view of Edmiston's facial and pupil responses.

He stared straight at the wall. "I trust your camera is recording me." The pupils showed clearly in the pale blue of his eyes. "Let me save you the trouble of playing games, sergeant. I've seen the newscanner items about Carel Armenda's death and I learned much of the rest talking to Miss Armenda yesterday afternoon…as least as much as she knows. I called her at her request. She wanted to know if her brother hired me to kill her father. I'll tell you what I told her…no, he did not. Nor, Sergeant Maxwell, did she hire me. No one did. I am not involved in Armenda's death. Assassination isn't one of the services I offer."

Janna sucked in her lower lip. Not once during the speech had his pupils dilated to indicate the stress associated with lying. Several times he glanced left, but that meant nothing until Mama asked questions with known answers to establish how Edmiston's eyes shifted during lies.

"You were here those two days," Mama's voice said.

"Yes. I freely admit that. Why not?" A thin smile flickered across his face. "A check of the hotels will establish that I stayed at the Downtown Ramada. You already know about the Triton."

"An interesting choice of vehicles."

The smile flicked again. "I always choose something that looks like an unmarked police car. It allows me to sit parked for long periods of time without the inconvenience of lions stopping to ask what I'm doing."

"But you weren't parked near the Yi house?"

"I didn't even drive through that side of town." His pupil size remained constant. "My presence had nothing to do with Carel Armenda."

"Do you know the Yi's?"

"I know their address. I made a point of asking Miss Armenda about it, on the chance that my business had accidentally taken me into the area. Your witnesses did not see *my* vehicle."

"What *was* your business here?"

For the first time he hesitated. His eyes shifted left. Remembering? Or considering a lie? "I'd rather not say. It's...ongoing."

"We have a bank warrant. Tomorrow morning we'll know everything about you, including the names of any local people who've made payments into your account."

Now his pupils dilated. "That isn't necessary. At the time of Armenda's murder, I was having dinner at the Xanadu Club as a guest of Paul Adler of Smith Automotives, Inc. He'll confirm that. So should two waitresses named Amber and Aurora." A smile accompanied his leftward eye shift. "The Xanadu offers...unique table services."

So Janna had heard. To her disappointment, he gave no details. Had that left shift indicated memory or not, then? It maddened her not to be sure.

"After dinner the waitresses accompanied us up to the whirlpools. Judging by the camera blister I spotted on the ceiling, the club monitors their rooms, so they should have a video record of our visit."

Janna groaned. Another of *those* alibis?

"If you like, I'll wait here while you check."

"He was certainly cooperative," Arianna Cho said at the apartment that evening. She picked up the platter of bones, all that remained of the rack of lamb Mama cooked, and carried it into the kitchen.

Where did the two of them put it all? Janna wondered, following with more dishes. "Too cooperative."

Mama finished cleaning off the table. "That's just a man eager to clear himself so we won't be looking over his shoulder."

Cho shook jade hair back over her own shoulders before scraping the bones into the trash. "Did he clear himself?"

"That depends which of us you ask." He raised a brow at Janna. "Adler, club personnel, and video evidence all confirm his alibi. The club does have security monitors in every room, and each frame of the recordings carries the date and time. I don't know why you refuse to accept that, bibi."

Janna set her dishes in the sink. "If he's telling the truth, then we've not only lost him but Sydney and Junior. We're back to square one."

Mama shook his head. "What kind of attitude is that, hating to give up a suspect even if he's innocent?"

"What I hate is having another alibi so similar to the slighs' when like them, he looks so good as a suspect." She frowned. "I don't know how they've pulled this rabbit trick, but—"

Mama grinned. "Thanks for reminding me." He headed out of the kitchen. "Arianna, leave everything. I want you to look at something."

Janna groaned. "Not again!"

"You don't have to watch."

She did anyway. Glancing sideways at the other two on the far end of the couch, Janna reflected that they made an interesting pair sitting next to each other…Mama in a pearlescent white bodysuit, Cho wearing a black one that emphasized the alabaster of her hands and face.

The sharp bones beneath the perfect skin showed even more clearly as Cho frowned in concentration at the screen. She pulled her legs up to sit cross-legged. "What are we looking for?"

"Inspiration…or anything that strikes you as odd," Mama said.

The familiar scenes played out. Janna found her eyes drooping. For a few minutes she fought, then surrendered to the drowsiness. Why bother watching? She knew it all by heart. The sound alone let her follow the sequences in her head.

Was Mama really watching it anyway? All he and Cho seemed to be talking about were clothes the guests wore.

She forced her eyes open. "Are we investigating a murder or attending a fashion show?"

"You could do worse than study these women, bibi. They know how to dress."

The smug bastard. "Et tu, choomba. Notice that not one of the men is wearing colors that glow in the dark?"

Cho grinned. "That's right; don't let him bully you into fuss and frills. Minimalism suits you. In fact, with your coloring, black would look—that's odd."

Suddenly Janna did not feel the least drowsy. "What?" she and Mama asked simultaneously.

Cho pushed her hair back over her shoulders. "Maybe I'm wrong. It could be just a trick of light and the artist in me. Play this part again, will you?"

"This" being what Janna had taken to calling the beach scene. Mama backscanned until the waitron appeared on the edge of the screen, then restarted forward play. Cho watched intently, leaning forward with elbows propped on her folded legs and her chin on her hands. The waitron spun. Guests retreated in a wave, leaving glassware and needler-carrying sharks behind.

"Well?" Janna prompted.

"What do you see?"

"It's what I don't see." Cho leaned back, looking from one of them to the other. "Your gunmen have no shadows."

Janna blinked at her, then the screen, disappointed. "No one does." Surely Cho saw that, and the reason why. "It's the lighting." The whole ceiling glowed, the illumination from each part cancelling out shadows thrown by other parts.

Cho shook her head. "Everyone else *does* have a shadow. It's small and immediately underneath so most of the time you don't notice it. The gunmen are different. Excuse me, Mama." She took the remote from him, backscanned, and let the chip resume forward play. "Watch their feet. See when the one with the scarred hand starts to step sideways? There!" She hit Pause.

The gunman froze with one foot elevated above the carpet. The pile under his sole remained the same gold color as that of the surrounding area.

Mama let out a happy sigh. "I love you, Arianna Cho."

Janna frowned at the screen in disbelief. "How can he not cast a shadow?"

Mama took back the remote. The images reversed, bringing guests surging back around the waitron, swallowing up the gunmen. Action froze. And remained frozen.

"Do you see something more?" Janna asked. When Mama did not answer she turned to look at him. He sat staring the direction of the screen but with his eyes glazed. "Mama?"

Cho shook his shoulder. "Mama!"

He jumped to his feet. "Let's go. There is one possibility…but we need help to prove it."

The moment Mama swung his little MGE down the ramp into Headquarters' garage, Janna realized where they were headed. She considered sending him on alone. With Cho along, though, how could she admit to being cowed by a man half her size?

She thought she even managed to look calm when they walked into Criminalistics and Kingsley Borthwick turned from peering over a technician's shoulder to impale them with his stare. The acidic scent of the lab came from reagents used in chemical tests, Janna knew, but it was easy to imagine that it emanated from the night chief.

"A bit late for you to be around here, isn't it, sergeants?"

"Yes, sir," Mama said. The respectful tone would have sent the brass who knew him into shock. "It's because we've discovered something perplexing and you may be the only person who can explain it." He held out the case containing their vid chip. "This shows scenes from the news chips recorded at the Democratic riff. The gunmen don't cast shadows."

"No shadows?" Borthwick's lips pressed into a disapproving line. "Your infamous imagination has been at work again, sergeant."

"Actually, I noticed first," Cho said.

He swung on her, eyeing her hair, her visitor's badge. "You are a friend of the sergeant, I take it? Perhaps we have mass hysteria."

Mama continued to hold out the chip case. "Why don't you see for yourself, sir?"

Borthwick stared at the case. After a moment he took it and stood turning it over in his hand. "No shadows. Intriguing." A gleam warmed the chill of his eyes. "Let's have a look."

He trotted out of the room and down the hall to a computer room. The rest of them followed.

In the computer room Borthwick climbed onto a chair and inserted the chip into a player connected to a computer. "Do you have any idea why they lack shadows, sergeant?"

"Yes, sir…but I don't want to prejudice you."

"Thank you." He tapped Play.

They stood silent behind him while the chip played on the computer screen…until the beach scene started. Then Cho began, "Watch this—

"I intend to, madam." His eyes never left the screen. "Without coaching, if you please."

Cho grinned. *He's wonderful*, she mouthed.

At the end of the recording, Borthwick leaned back, staring at the blank screen past tented fingers. "You are correct, sergeant. No shadows." He sat up again and restarted the recording. When the gunmen appeared, he froze the image. "Let's have a closer look at the gentlemen, then."

His stubby fingers raced across the computer keyboard. He boxed one figure…enlarged it to fill the screen…enhanced. He boxed one ear…enlarged…enhanced…cancelled that image for the previous one…enlarged and enhanced a hand. Edges appeared to interest him most.

After half an hour of studying first one gunmen, then another, he recalled the original image and leaned back, grunting.

Janna opened her mouth to ask if he had learned anything but Mama caught her eye and shook his head sharply.

Borthwick sighed. "The gentlemen themselves are no help. They appear quite normal. Except…they do lack shadows." He leaned forward again. "Let's examine their other interactions with the environment."

For the next hour he enlarged portions of the gunmen's feet and the carpet, first in one image, then skipping along the chip to another scene. The results apparently pleased him because he had the computer print out a number of the enlargements…of glasses lying on the carpet, of booted feet. One print documented the absence of a shadow, but Janna did not see the reason for the others.

"I could use something hot to drink," Borthwick said.

Mama looked around at Janna. She gave him the finger, then went for caff.

Only to find that the lab's urn had run dry, and the cabinet under it, which presumably contained supplies for brewing more, locked. She set off in search of someone with a key.

By the time she finally brought caff back to the computer room, Borthwick had switched his interest to the gunmen's tuxedos. A stack of new computer prints lay on the desk. All showed the same thing, the area where the diagonal front flap fastened at the shoulder, pearly white meeting scarlet. A sixth print slid out of the printer while Janna set the caff mug down by the keyboard.

Mama snatched up the print. What did it show? Mama's face had become all teeth.

She peered around his shoulder, but saw only another view of the tux shoulder.

The lab chief picked up the caff mug and swiveled his chair to face them. "You were right to come to me, sergeant."

"You can tell us why they don't have shadows?" Cho asked.

"Yes, of course." Borthwick sipped from the mug. "Is it as you anticipated, sergeant?"

"Yes, sir." Mama turned to Janna and Cho. "They don't have shadows because our riffers—"

"Sergeant," Borthwick interrupted, "this is my territory. These are my toys. Therefore, I claim the privilege of showing off here. Sergeant Brill, please pick up the prints."

She did. When Cho moved beside her, she held them so the other woman could see, too.

"Exhibit A, a wine glass lying by the foot of one perpetrator." Borthwick sipped his caff. "Notice the reflections in it."

Janna studied the print. "Of the lights, you mean?" The unbroken glow overhead turned the entire surface of the glass the color of the ceiling.

"Precisely." Another sip of caff. "Yet your perpetrator towers above it. He does not, you notice, block any of the light to the glass. Exhibit B-1, a foot planted in the middle of a carpet section soaked with red wine. Exhibit B-2; the foot has moved to an unstained section of the carpet. Exhibit B-3, the foot has moved again and the carpet where it rested moments ago remains unstained."

Janna blinked. When the riffer had stepped in the wine?

"Exhibit C-1, another glass," Borthwick continued. "Exhibit C-2, a perpetrator stepping on the glass. Exhibit C-3, the perpetrator's foot has moved and we see what remains of the glass."

The hair rose on Janna's neck. The glass remained intact. Undamaged.

"The only logical explanation is that those men have no physical substance." Borthwick set down the mug. "They're holograms."

Janna gaped at him. "That's impossible! Hundreds of people stood within meters of them, some within arm's reach. A holo can't pass as real that close, not even to people terrified by needlers in their faces."

Borthwick nodded. "I agree, sergeant; they seem perfect. I've examined them closely. Every edge is sharp and solid, without a trace of distortion or translucency. They are magnificent holos, but holos nevertheless." He peered at Mama. "Do you mind telling me how you deduced that? Surely not on the basis of the shadows. That is a quantum sideleap in thinking."

"Mama's thinking is all sideleaps," Janna said dryly.

Mama grinned. "That's the nicest thing you've ever said about me, bibi. No, sir, it wasn't just the shadows. I'd also been worrying about where they came from, because I couldn't see them in the crowd. They appeared out of nowhere. While everyone saw the gunmen, the gunmen touched no one. Only Tony Ho had physical contact with the victims. None of the gunmen ever spoke, either...not a sound." He paused. "I also remembered that one of the Armenord companies is Konza Holotronics."

Janna shook her head. "That doesn't add up to holos. I still can't believe that's the answer."

"Then consider Exhibits D-1,2,3,4,5, and 6," Borthwick said.

The tuxedo prints.

"See the stain on the upper corner, as though someone pressed it the front flap closed with a greasy thumb?"

She nodded. It showed in every print, no matter what the angle of the shot. So?

Then it struck her. She held six prints of the same stain. Six.

Janna looked up. "Each of these prints is a different riffer?" She drew in a breath. "They're all wearing the same tux?"

Mama beamed. "I knew you'd get it."

Now she believed. Janna stared past Borthwick at the image still frozen on the computer screen. Holos. That explained so much. "Christ. We're killing ourselves trying to figure how they slipped through security and they never went through. We *have* been chasing shadows."

Mama nodded. "Why were the cameras at the hotel and Yi's house disabled? To keep us from seeing how many individuals actually entered and left. Holos is also why the Triton needed a desktop…for controlling the waitron *and* six holos."

And why the slighs appeared on the news chips when they never left Kansas City. Janna straightened. "Mama, we need to talk to those slighs again."

He nodded.

Cho said, "So the waitron went into its dance to make space for projecting the holos. But…" She pushed her hair back over her shoulders. "…it seems incredible to me that one waitron could carry all the projectors and the needler and the cameras and circuitry for remote operation. We have holo projectors at the gallery and to fit even one into a waitron you'd have to aim it straight up or down."

Borthwick spun his chair back to the computer. "We can see if your Armenord company offers something smaller." He began typing again. Then clicked his light pen at the screen through a series of web pages until: "Ah, here we are."

KONZA HOLOTRONICS spread across the screen in yellow and pale blue letters. A pleasant female voice said. "Welcome. You have reached Konza Holotronics' on-line catalogue."

The sales voice offered menus of general categories of products, with the general categories broken down into lists of specific items, and then extensive information on each item.

One of those being Konza's newest holo projector, the Magus-1. "At four centimeters wide and high, and ten centimeters long," the cheerful voice said, displaying an image of the projector, "the Magus-1 is small enough to be mounted anywhere."

Even in a group of six in a waitron?

"Yet despite its size, the Magus-1 projects a image of higher quality than larger units."

High quality image. Janna drew a long breath. "I think we also need to talk to the Armendas again."

15

Mama wrapped his trenchcoat tighter around him and slid out of the MGE. Beyond the bars of the Armenda gates, the driveway curved up the hill, ground-level lights along its edge making it a glowing ribbon through the darkness of the grounds. One light showed in the portion of the house visible from the gate.

Janna frowned. "Mama, we don't have to talk to her tonight."

He leaned down to peer in through her window. "This is the best way to catch her off her guard." He headed for the call box on the gatepost.

"She could call knocking on her door in the middle of the night harassment," Janna called after him.

"It isn't that late." He pressed the bell.

She sighed. Why had she let him talk her into this?

Because, she admitted, she wanted to catch Sydney off guard, too.

A face appeared on the gatepost screen, murmuring. Mama's answer reached her faintly. "Sergeants Brill and Maxwell to see Miss Armenda."

The face vanished. A minute later it reappeared, murmuring something more. This time Janna could not make out Mama's reply. The face spoke again, then Mama. It turned into a lengthy exchange. The face vanished again, this time for several minutes. Finally it reappeared, briefly, and when the screen went blank, the gate slid aside.

As they drove through, Janna said, "Had to talk a bit to get us in, didn't you? What did you finally say?"

He shrugged. "The truth, that we have important new information about Armenda's death and that discussing it here is much more informal."

A polite version of: *We can talk here or downtown.* Janna grinned.

During the trip to the house, she found herself wondering about Armenda security. Except for the driveway, the grounds lay dark, even near the house.

Lights came on in the entryway. Before the MGE finished settling on its parking rollers, the door opened. Sydney herself stood in the opening, barefooted and wrapped in a man's robe. The warmth in the house sent a faint cloud of mist into the chilly night air.

Janna nudged Mama. "You want me to dress like the castlerows? I'll copy her."

"Don't you two ever go off duty?" The light tone of Sydney's voice did not quite hide the flinty edge on the words.

Mama slid his door closed and smiled at her. "It's a mark of our diligence, Miss Armenda. We care about finding your father's killer."

"I notice you keep looking here." She stood aside for them to come in.

After closing the door, she said loudly, "Reset house alarm."

"Alarm reset," an uninflected voice said.

She padded away down the stone-floored hallway to a set of carved double sliding doors. Inside lay what must have been Armenda's private study. A desk dominated the room, a massive antique with a top the size of a pool table, drawers everywhere, and a kneehole like a tunnel. It dwarfed the computer and stacks of wide printout on its top. Another set of doors opened in the stone of the far wall, revealing a bedroom beyond and flanked by a bookcase with drawers for several hundred chips and a newscanner tuned to a stock quotation channel.

Sydney waved them to deep, butter-soft leather chairs. She sat down behind the desk, sipped from a steaming mug—which explained the scent of coffee in the room—and frowned at the computer screen. No light show played on the back of this one. "You'll have to ask your questions while I work."

Behind her lay the outside wall, coppery glass stretching floor to ceiling, wall to wall, undraped but with blinds sandwiched between the glass layers. Janna gestured at the darkness beyond. "I notice you have no security lighting outside. Is that wise?"

Sydney looked away from the screen only to pick up some printout. "Try walking around the grounds. The motion, your body heat, and the sound of your breathing and footsteps will turn on lights around you. The idea of darkness suddenly becoming a blaze of light with the intruder caught in the middle appealed to my father." She glanced across the desk at them. "Talking to you two offers something of the same experience. What's this new information on my father's death?"

Mama crossed one pearlescently sheathed leg over the other. "It appears that the gunmen were holograms."

Printout dropped back to the desk. "What!"

Janna bit her lip. If Sydney were acting, she deserved an award. Her double take was perfect. Could she not be involved after all?

"That's impossible! The jon who fired at my father came within less than two meters of me. At that distance—"

"On the news chips from Friday night they had no shadows," Janna interrupted. "One appeared to step on a wine glass, but it didn't break. Their tuxedos all have an identical stain."

Sydney sat back looking stunned. In the silence, the newscanner reported Uwezo, the African megacorp, up by eight and a half on the Tokyo exchange.

"How high *is* the image quality of Konza's new Magus-1 projector?" Mama asked.

She shrugged, shook her head, spread her hands. "Good, but…nothing like…" Her voice trailed off. A second later, she continued in a thoughtful tone, "Its image isn't *that* good. Unfortunately." She picked up the printout and resumed reading it.

Janna leaned forward. What happened in that pause? "You've thought of something?"

"Not really." Sydney flipped through the fanfold sheets to a new section…raised a brow…turned to the computer and pushed keys. "It just occurred to me that pre-recording this action of firing at my father and jumping back in surprise proves premeditation beyond any doubt."

That might have been her thought. It sounded reasonable, except…instinct in Janna sang: *lie*! Protecting herself? Or Junior? That would fit with asking Edmiston about her brother.

"Son of a bitch!" Sydney glared at the screen. "That isn't shrinkage; that's mismanagement. Tomorrow I'll have you for lunch, you incompetent toad!" With an abrupt shift of attention, she focused back on them. "Ah…do you know who the originals of the holos are?"

A casual tone. Too casual? Janna watched her. Lines around Sydney's mouth suggested tension.

"We know," Mama said.

Sydney raised her brows. Waiting for him to go on? After a few moments, the brows came down. She picked up her coffee mug. "Then…you have some idea who made the holos?"

Definitely tension. Janna caught Mama's eye. Did he see, too? "I'm afraid we're not free to discuss that right now."

The other woman eyed them a moment, then smiled. "Meaning you don't have the slightest idea." She leaned back, sipping her coffee. Tension gone. Relieved? "There's nothing more I can do to help you, then. If I knew where to find the person responsible for those holos, I'd be out there negotiating a license to manufacture his projector."

"Or hers," Mama said.

Sydney straightened. The newscanner quoted stock prices in Manila, Beijing, and Tokyo.

Prickles ran down Janna's spine. She glanced at Mama, wishing for telepathy. What was he thinking? Something good. That comment had touched a nerve.

Sydney stood. "If you have no more questions, I'll let you out."

Mama pushed his glasses up his nose. "As a matter of fact, I do have another question or two." He smiled. "Tell us about Lesandra Santos."

The name triggered memory with a jolt. Janna swore at herself for being so slow. Of course! That lawsuit filed against Armenord...a female employee at Konza Holotronics suing over ownership of a miniaturized projector. A miniaturized holo projector, maybe?

"How good were the images from *her* projector?" Mama asked.

Sydney sat down again, mouth tight. "As I said, talking to you two is like walking in our grounds at night." She took a breath. "I don't know much about Santos. I never met her. At the time I was following the Grand Prix circuit with the Porsche team, convinced I loved Dieter Weiss. So I don't know what her projector could do, either, except that it impressed the hell out of my father."

"He'd seen a demonstration?" Janna asked.

"So to speak." Sydney arranged the stacks of printout parallel with the edge of the desk. The action reminded Janna of Mama. "One night on his way out after going over books with the new Konza company manager he noticed lights on in a workroom. When he went to investigate, he walked in on a test of the projector. C.J. told me he came home raving about it. Then he asked the company manager about the projector's production schedule and found out it didn't belong to Konza. The former owner let employees use some company space for private projects, providing they worked on their own time, paid a modest space and tool rental, and paid for all materials. In return, Konza received first refusal on production of the results, and I understand gave a good deal when it did buy." Sydney shook her head. "Dad should have done that. Look what we might have had."

Mama leaned forward. "He claimed that because she used company facilities for the work, Konza owned the projector?"

"Once in a while greed gets—" She caught herself. "—got in the way of my father's business sense. She filed suit, then later dropped it and handed over the plans. I don't know why; I think she could have made a good case. She quit her job, so she'd left before I came to my senses and left Dieter to his glitter girls."

Janna straightened in her chair. "You just said you don't have the projector."

"We don't." Sydney smiled wryly. "When we built the Magus-1 according to those plans, we had a tiny projector with only a slightly better image. My father went after the true plans, of course, but Santos had disappeared. She moved with no forwarding address. She changed banks. He couldn't bribe anyone for the name of the new bank and the courts wouldn't issue a warrant because he had no proof she'd given him altered plans. They matched the description of the projector as stated in the lawsuit. He couldn't even trace her through background information; her personnel file had vanished from the computer."

"He never found her?" Mama asked.

"He gave up the hunt. Looking only kept her in hiding, he said. If he appeared to forget about her, however, she'd surface to sell the projector somewhere else. Then..." Her hands closed.

"You didn't hunt for her on your own?" Mama gave her a teasing smile. "That would have been quite a prize to bring home to him."

Sydney frowned. "Yes." She sighed. "Only I couldn't believe the projector was as good as he thought. He'd seen it operate just once, after all, and then late at—" She broke off, stiffening. "It's late now, too. I'm tired of playing your lion games. If you believe I found her and saw her holos and then decided to arrange—"

Janna gave her a thin smile. "We were wondering about your brother. You are, aren't you?"

Sydney stood and padded for the door. "Good night, sergeants."

After letting them out the front door, she stood in the opening watching them slide into Mama's little runabout. As the MGE started, she called over the whine of the fans, "If you find Santos, let me know. I'll give her whatever she wants for the projector."

Janna shook her head in disbelief. "Santos is at least an accessory in Armenda's murder and the only thing about her that concerns his daughter is the projector." People never failed to astonish her.

Mama steered the MGE down the drive. "The priorities of business, bibi." He grinned.

Which made Janna wonder: maybe Sydney's relief a while ago had been less for her brother than because she thought she had a head start hunting Santos. Janna twisted to look back at the house. "It's too bad you didn't drop a contact lens outside the study window so we could learn if she's calling the pleasure palaces to ask Junior if he knows where to find Santos."

The car slowed. Mama glanced back at the house, too.

Considering the idea? Panic flared in her. "Mama, I'm only kidding!"

Ahead, the gate slid aside. To her relief, he sailed on through.

She sighed. "So…back to K.C. tomorrow."

"Actually," Mama said in a bright tone that sent warning reverberations through Janna, "I thought we might head that way tonight."

"Tonight!" She sat up against the safety harness. "Mama, don't you think we ought to sleep sometime? We probably can't find those slighs before morning anyway. What difference will a few hours make? Besides, we need to tell Vradel and Cruz about the holos anyway."

"I was thinking of leaving them a note when we pick up the Meteor."

She snorted. "They'd love that. 'Dear Boss, the riffers are only holos; we're taking a field trip at our own instigation and will explain everything on our return.' No, Mama; let's not do that."

Riding east on the turnpike through the starry darkness, Janna reflected that she should know better than try telling Mama *no*. At least they left a full report, with Lieutenant Candarian reading avidly over their shoulders at the dictyper. That also meant that technically a superior officer knew their whereabouts and activities, although the net effect would probably be the same as if they left only a note.

"We'd better bring home something good." She lay back and closed her eyes. Now was the time to rest. Once they reached K.C. and she swallowed one of the stimulants she'd bought at the Lion's Den on their way out of town, she would not be able to.

"Do you really think Junior's behind this, bibi?"

She sighed. Resting, unfortunately, depended on muffling the noise of Mama's mental wheels. Without opening her eyes she said, "Sydney seems to, and she knows him better than we do. He goes hunting Santos, sees the quality of the holos, and suddenly has this stroke of inspiration…he can be rid of Daddy harping at him and have even more money to play with."

"Why would he hunt Santos? I could see Sydney hoping to impress her father, but Junior didn't have that problem."

She settled deeper into her seat, lulled by the drone of the fans and rush of air past the car. "Maybe he went looking after the plot occurred to him."

"How would the idea occur unless he'd seen the quality of the holos?"

"His father told him."

"Armenda told Sydney, too, and she didn't believe they could be that good."

"So she says now."

"If she believed it, why wasn't she hunting Santos to bring the holos home to Daddy?"

Janna opened her eyes. "You don't like Junior for it?"

The glow from headlights in the westbound lanes silhouetted his shrug. "Casting him as the villain feels...weak."

What made a weak motive? People killed each other over separating the trash and forgetting to put down the toilet seat.

Exhaustion closed her eyes again. The sounds of the car and wind wrapped around her, shutting out the world and pulling her down into warm darkness.

Some time later Mama's voice broke into a dream in which she chased red-tuxedoed gunmen down winding alleys, only to have each turn to smoke as she caught him. "We're almost there, bibi."

She struggled up in her seat. They came over a hill and down around a sweeping curve. Kansas City spread out in a glittering panorama along the bottomland below and up over the hills across the river. At this time of night, almost no traffic moved. They sailed alone through the yellow glow of the lights above the highway.

In the city proper, they met little more traffic either swinging by Headquarters to leave a message with the morning watch for Diosdado, or visiting the Central Division station—a sleek structure of glass and stone replacing one leveled by a bomb fifteen years earlier. Lights shone down on deserted streets. The peace was an illusion, however, Janna knew.

After announcing their presence and business at Central's station, they headed for the River Quay. Mama circled the dark cave of the city market, then set the Meteor down on a side street. There they settled in to wait for their slighs.

Janna closed her eyes.

Mama said, "I've been thinking."

His tone of voice left Janna with no doubt he intended to discuss those thoughts. That left her with two possibilities: gag him, or let him talk.

She opened her eyes and groped in her breast pocket for the waker tablets. What did sleep matter? Sometimes his blue sky came solidly down to earth...and she did want to break this case, after all. "Thinking about what?"

"It's a who. Santos." The only working street light stood at the far end of the block. In the dim light it cast in the car, Mama frowned. "My mind keeps circling back to her. Bibi, why are we assuming she's involved because Junior or someone else dragged her and her projector in? Armenda's attempt to claim the projector gives her reason of her own to hate him, and no one knows the quality of the holos better than she does." He paused. "The height of the average woman is considered small in a man."

The last drowsiness vanished. Janna sat up straight. Santos in a mustache could be their small jon? An interesting idea...except for one fact. "Mama, Armenda didn't get the projector. She made a fool of him. From what we've heard about Armenda, that should put the most hate on his side. Or..." She turned toward him in her seat. "...do you think she'd kill him thinking that would free her to sell the projector elsewhere."

He shook his head. "There's no reason for that. In her place I'd just take the projector to another company and after showing them the holos, I'd tell the whole story and invite them to fight for the projector. Considering the facts of the case, the quality of the holos, and the free publicity the trial would bring, I'm betting they'd gamble on winning." He drummed his fingers on the steering wheel. "It's been two years, though, and in that time she apparently hasn't tried to sell the projector anywhere else. Why not?"

Janna had no trouble seeing what he thought the answer was. Another occurred to her. "Maybe she didn't think of your marketing strategy. I have a hard time imagining someone spending two years planning to kill someone she'd already made a fool of."

A watchcar passed them. At the intersection it made a U-turn. Mama ran down his window and put his arm out, badge case dangling from his hand.

The watchcar slowed to a hover beside them anyway, but as soon as he had established their reason for being there the uniform grinned—"I saw about that fund-raiser riff on the newscanner. I don't envy you with castlerows breathing down your necks. Good luck."—and drove on.

They resumed waiting, and debating. None of it led anywhere.

The stars to the east had only begun to fade when the first trucks pulled in under the domes. She and Mama strolled down to the market and stood just inside one of the archways. More trucks arrived.

Janna quickly understood Mama's collegiate fascination with the place. Silence gave way to the thrum of truck fans. Lights appeared...battery lamps set on the hoods of trucks, on chairs and stacks of crates. In the cavernous darkness the first ones looked futile, pinpoints in a void, but as more lights appeared, the darkness became mottled by pools of light. In them, shadowy figures pulled crates and baskets from the backs of the trucks. Voices called out, laughed, occasionally swore. It all felt vaguely surreal.

More figures appeared from the darkness outside to help unload.

Janna nudged Mama. Slighs.

He nodded. "Let's go."

They left the arch to head for the area where they saw their slighs on Thursday.

One of the farmers smoked a pipe while he worked. Its fragrant smoke curled around Janna as she passed. Passing another stall, she smelled hot caff. The scent set her stomach growling.

Then, ahead in a fan of light from a cordless fluorescent lamp sitting on the hood of a truck, Janna spotted carroty-red hair pulled back in a ponytail.

Mama called, "Hello, Dragon."

The sligh turned with the basket he had taken from the back of the truck behind the stall. Annoyance twisted his face. "You again?" Janna thought he also eyed the pearly white of Mama's bodysuit, visible beneath the open trenchcoat, with a touch of envy before setting down the basket and returning to the truck for another.

She leaned against the truck. "Us again. This time it's a friendly visit."

He snorted. "Just what I need. Molidor will be back in a few minutes and expects the truck to be unloaded." Another basket of cucumbers joined the four already on the ground.

"Go ahead and work. All we need to know is when the holo recording of you was made."

Dragon stacked two baskets on top of each other and brought them over with the others. "If this is 'friendly', tell me why you want to know and give me one good reason for answering."

Janna frowned. A nice problem. They could hardly appeal to their friendship or his sense of civic duty.

Mama said, "I'll give you two reasons for answering. One, it won't harm you or any other sligh. Two, talk to us and I'll give you the suit I'm wearing."

The flare of yearning in Dragon's eyes reminded Janna with a jolt of a fact so easy to forget, that although forced by necessity to dress simply, even poorly, slighs could like expensive clothes, too. "Here, this morning?"

Mama nodded. "We'll find a place and trade clothes."

Dragon eyed Mama's bodysuit. "Which recording do you want to know about?"

Janna started. There had been more than one?

A quick glance at Mama caught his scalp crinkling. Surprised, too. He recovered almost instantly, however, and smiled at the sligh. "The recording with you in a red tuxedo."

Dragon sighed. "You've seen it? I'd like to. I thought we looked top dink. We spent the whole session taking turns in it and the mustache and wig, waving the needler around. Leo said, 'Even deeks dink up. Have fun. Pretend you're facing a legislator who advocates mandatory identation.'"

Leo? Janna sent another glance at Mama. That name had not come up before. Who was he, the tall man?

Mama remained focused on the sligh. "You did appear to enjoy being menacing. When was that?"

"Last month." He continued hauling baskets from the truck.

"When did you first meet Leo?"

The sligh thought a moment. "Last summer. July sometime."

"Tell us about it."

Dragon grunted. "There isn't much to tell. Tsunami, Rebel, and I were playing Deathrace in the Waterloo Club with some vending tokens we'd gotten for collecting bottles and cans and this bibi challenged Tsunami to a game. She beat him, too, but then bought us all drinks and asked if we'd like to earn better carry than tokens. Of course we said sure. When she took us upstairs to one of the bedrooms I thought it was kinks time; she had lights and a camera and mirror set up. She explained that all we had us to was follow some commands like point an unloaded needler and pretend to be shooting someone."

Electricity shot up Janna's spine. They had not met a man after all? "You mean the bibi is Leo?"

"Yeah." The sligh's quirked brows said: *of course*.

Excitement seeped up through her. "Is Leo short for Lesandra?"

Dragon blinked. "Lesandra?" He snickered. "Hell, no. You of all people ought to know what it's short for."

The connection came almost as he finished the sentence, plunging her into confusion. "A she-lion recorded you?" How could that be?

"Yeah." Dragon shuffled the cucumber baskets into a neat grouping. "She works in research and development. That's what the holos are for, a shoot/don't shoot training course. So if you want to know about it, why ask me? You ought to be talking to your lion buddies."

16

Questions churned in Janna's head. The holos were part of a police training program? Recorded by a she-lion? Then how had they ended up being shown from Santos' projector?

She caught Mama's eye. They needed to discuss this.

Just then a black van halted in front of the stall and set down. Janna stared at the woman who slid from behind the wheel…a study in black and white…black jumpsuit and black needle-heeled boots, white hands and face, sooty eyes and lips, a flat helmet of ebony hair. She bent down to feel the cucumbers. "What's your price per bushel?"

The mundane question turned an exotic creature into a mere customer. Janna lost interest…and discovered that the distraction had cleared her head. She sighed in displeasure at herself. Stimulants and the lack of sleep must be scrambling her brain. Explaining Santos' possession of the holos presented no problem if she and Leo were the same person. This might be where she disappeared. Which could also be the reason she had not tried selling the projector anywhere; using her holos for non-commercial projects like this would avoid attracting Armenda's attention.

Too bad they had no description of Santos. When they went back to Topeka, she would make sure they obtained one.

A gray-haired man in russet coveralls hurried around the front end of the truck. Molidor, Janna guessed. He frowned at Mama and her, and at Dragon, before switching on a smile he directed at the black-and-white woman.

Mama caught Janna's eye and gestured sideways with his head. "This jon doesn't look like the kind to pay off a sligh while people are watching." He whispered something to Dragon and left the stall.

Janna followed.

They moved slowly along the row and a short time later Dragon caught up, a paper bag with the top rolled shut tucked under one arm. Seeing them, his expression went from tense to relieved. "You meant it about waiting for me." The relief stripped the cockiness from him, leaving him looking young and vulnerable.

"We haven't forgotten our deal." Janna moved to one side to let a late-arriving truck pass. "Let's talk more first. What does Leo look like?"

"Small, dark eyes, dark hair down to her shoulders. Not flash, but not dog meat, either." The swagger came back into his walk. "I wouldn't have minded putting two with her but she only cared about her project. I told you, if you want to know about her, ask the leos."

"That's hard without knowing who to ask about," Mama said. "What's her name?"

Dragon shrugged. "She never gave it. Calling her Leo was good enough, she said."

The hair prickled on Janna's neck. "You mean she never showed you any identification? She only *told* you she was with the KCPD?" Leo could very well be Santos, and not in the department at all.

"You think I'd just take someone's word for that?" Dragon's lip curled. "We already knew about her when she came up to us. She didn't tell us; we told her, and she admitted she worked in research."

Mama asked, "How did you know?"

A carrot-red brow arched. "You see someone in watchcars all the time and coming into the clubs after the shift with lions, it's obvious."

Janna exchanged glances with Mama. Someone from R & D working on patrol? That seemed unlikely.

Mama toyed with one sleeve cuff. "Think of a place we can use for trading clothes. You said she came into the clubs with other lions. Do you know any of their names?"

The sligh stopped short, forcing the driver of a restaurant van to swerve around them, shouting curses. Dragon glared at Mama. "You can keep your damn suit. I just figured out what this is about. You aren't from Topeka after all. You're from Internal Affairs!" He folded his arms around the bag of cucumbers. "She's in trouble for using slighs, isn't she? Well, you go to hell! I'm not going to help you persecute her. She treated us like human beings. All of us will swear she didn't buy us clothes or anything else; we're volunteer labor. She came to us because the department didn't believe in her idea and wouldn't give her a decent budget to develop it."

After such a passionate defense, Janna hated having to disillusion him. She handed her ID him. "Study that. We aren't KCPD and we aren't peeps."

Mama said, "I'm glad she treated you well. She may also have killed Carel Armenda and tried to make it look as though your friend Tsunami did it."

"That's a lie!" Vendors and customers turned to look at them. He lowered his voice. "I don't believe it."

Janna took back her ID. "We're looking for the person who killed Armenda. If Leo didn't, what can it hurt talking to her friends?"

"The deal for the suit still stands," Mama said.

Dragon stared back and forth from one of them to the other. More hotel and restaurant vans passed them. Gradually, his scowl gave way to uncertainty. He sighed, and with obvious reluctance, said, "I don't know their full names. All I see is what's on the name tags. The one Leo rides with more than the others is a she-lion named Hazelton."

They took the information to Diosdado.

His initial start on finding them at his desk when he came on duty turned to amusement on seeing the baggy jumpsuit Mama wore. A grin spread across the Greek-god face. "Oversized neo-pioneer ersatz homespun is a new fashion statement for you, isn't it?"

Mama sipped the caff he had poured himself from the squadroom pot. "Always expect the unexpected from me."

"It was the only thing in the used clothes stall at the city market in his sleeve and pant length," Janna said.

Lucky for them that one jon sold clothes alongside his herbs and spices. Dragon's jumpsuit had looked ridiculous, falling better than twenty centimeters short of reaching Mama's ankles and wrists. The sligh probably did not have so much to wear that he could afford to give up clothes appropriate for working in anyway.

"I hesitate to ask what happened to the clothes you presumably wore to Kansas City." Diosdado flipped up his phone screen and punched numbers on the keypad. Text rolled up the screen.

Sitting on the edge of the desk where she could look over his shoulder, Janna saw a list of cases, status, related persons and incidents, ATL's, warrants. "This is your morning briefing?"

"An anytime briefing." He tapped a number and stopped the text…made a note…let the text roll on. "The computer is constantly updating. Depending on the code I punch in, it selects for items relevant to Robbery, Homicide, or whatever, and items flagged as of general importance. Like this alert for a seventy-nine Cadillac Tracer. The vehicle, in the Denholm Body Shop for repair of damages from a hit-and-run on Friday was…" He paused, blinking, then grinned. "Breakers stole it during a burglary of the shop last night. They rammed the vehicle through the garage door and into a building and light pole across the street before escaping. I'm glad I didn't have to break the news to that owner." He cleared the screen. "So, what brings you to civilization this time?"

They told him.

The puckish brows bounced as Diosdado listened. "Tony was the only real perpetrator in the room?" He snickered. "One unarmed jon and a waitron riffed all those people?"

"And killed Armenda," Janna reminded him.

Diosdado sobered. "Right. So...you need Santos checked against our personnel file."

Mama finished his caff. "She did say she was in R & D, and development of an improved shoot/don't shoot program isn't a story you'd think would occur to the average civilian."

"You wouldn't think so." The K.C. detective punched a number into the phone. "While we don't have a research section as such, there are people attached to Information and Communications who can be considered in that category."

A female face appeared on the phone screen. "Personnel."

Diosdado talked at her. The face vanished.

He leaned back, face thoughtful. "Partying and riding along with leos isn't your typical murderer-to-be behavior, either."

Janna agreed. That part puzzled her.

"Though if you need a thief," Mama said, "what better way to locate one than make friends with people who can point them out?"

Diosdado frowned. "Maybe. Maybe the number of recordings she's made could be to ensure she had images appropriate for whatever occasion she found for killing Armenda. However, it also fits with development of this kind of program...and riding along is a logical way to collect scenarios for it. So Leo could be legitimate." He grimaced. "It would be embarrassing as hell if she were, though, and we let our program leak to a murderer."

The face reappeared. "We have a number of females named Santos, but no Lesandra Santos among either sworn or non-sworn personnel."

"Try the name Hazelton. A female officer, uniformed division, assigned to Central."

The face looked off to her right. Shortly she said, "We have a Donna Hazelton in Central."

Janna grabbed her notebook from her thigh boot and scribbled down the name. "May we have her address and phone number, too, please?"

The face read it off.

After Diosdado disconnected, Janna tapped the notebook with satisfaction. "Now maybe we'll get somewhere."

"Farther than you think," Diosdado said. "If Leo isn't with the department, she's riding along as a civilian, and that can't be done without giving a name and other verifiable information."

Janna's pulse jumped. She leaned toward him. "Then she's on record?"

He nodded. "Would someone with a guilty conscience allow that? Could she?"

Mama pushed his glasses up his nose. "Right now I think we're more interested in what happens to the information ride-alongs give about themselves. Is it in the computer?"

Diosdado grinned. "Everything's in the computer." He reached for his phone again. "There's a card the ride-along fills out that stays at the division station, but the information is fed into Records here. What do we want to know besides determining if a Lesandra Santos has been riding along?"

Mama galloped around the desk to where he could see the screen. "All the information possible on her."

When Diosdado had punched in and recited all the necessary codes, and given the computer the search instructions, the screen flashed: NO CATEGORY ONE SEARCHES IN THIS FILE. CAT TWO?

Diosdado sighed. "Shit."

Janna stared at the message in exasperation. "What's this?"

"Files containing data the administration feels is unlikely to be urgently needed are locked out of priority searches so that time can be given to more important files." He stabbed the 2 button.

THANK YOU.

Amazing how two printed words could look so smug. "What's the wait for category two?"

He grimaced. "It might be faster checking the cards at the division station. Why don't you go ahead and contact Hazelton? Check back here later. I'll make sure that if the information comes in and I'm away from my desk, it'll still be passed on to you."

Janna used the phone to punch in the number Personnel had given her.

No one answered.

"Call Central Division," Mama said. "See when she'll be on duty."

A face at Central informed them Donna Hazelton was currently on duty.

"Will you have her call Sergeant Janna Brill in Robbery, please?" Janna asked. She gave Diosdado's number. After punching off, she sighed. "Now what? I hate sitting around waiting."

"Don't we all." Diosdado pushed to his feet. "They didn't tell us how much of it there'd be when we signed up. I wouldn't mind waiting with you now, though; this case is full of surprises. However..." He plucked two folders out of his IN basket. "...the captain holds the unreasonable view that I should be working on Kansas City cases. So I'll see you later." He brushed a kiss past Janna's mouth. "We'll think of ways for you to express your gratitude for all my assistance."

She stared after him, thighs tingling.

Behind her, Mama said dryly, "Have a cup of caff and cool off, bibi."

On her way back from the squad pot, Diosdado's phone buzzed. Mama punched on. Janna scrambled to peer over his shoulder.

A pleasant afroam face with a copper complexion looked out of the screen at them. "Sergeant Brill?"

"Sergeant Maxwell," he replied. "We both want to talk to you." He held his ID to the lens at the base of the screen. "We're looking for information on a civilian woman who's ridden along with you. Small, dark hair and eyes. We believe her name may be Santos."

Janna held her breath.

Hazelton nodded. "Yes. Lesandra Santos. She's ridden with me a number of times. What do you want to know?"

Janna restrained an impulse to whoop and turn cartwheels. She did moved out of the phone's range and raise clasped hands above her head. Confirmed...Leo was Santos!

"Where we can reach her?" Mama's voice and expression remained matter-of-fact. "We'd like to talk to her."

Hazelton's voice brightened. "About her shoot/don't shoot program?"

From behind the phone, Janna tried to catch Mama's eye. So Santos used the story on everyone.

Mama kept his gaze on the phone screen. "We're interested in it, yes."

Janna straightened, frowning. Why answer that way instead of telling her the situation? "Mama," she began.

He ignored her. "What can you tell us about it?"

"That this program will null you." Enthusiasm bubbled in the she-lion's voice. "Lessa can give you all the details but basically it revolves around having a whole population of images available, any one of which may be projected from any station along the route of the shoot/don't shoot course. So the choices are infinite and never the same twice.

With the quality of these holos, holos like you've never seen before, believe me, you won't find a more realistic training exercise without using actual people."

Mama pushed his glasses up his nose. "I take it you've seen the program?"

A chuckle came from the phone. "Some of the images. One week end Lessa was staying with me and—"

"Staying with you?" Mama interrupted. "She doesn't live in the area?"

"No...in Topeka."

Topeka! Janna sucked in her lower lip. Santos had broken her trail by changing apartments and banks but never left the city? Interesting. Suggestive.

"I came home from my shift that night and a man armed with a knife lunged out of my kitchen at me. I had no time to go for a weapon, just throw my coat over the knife arm to foul it and jump aside. It was only when the coat fell through the arm to the floor that I realized he was a hologram. Even when she replayed the holo and I had time to study it, he looked real. I helped her set up similar tests on other officers." Glee crackled in her voice. Janna recognized the delight leos took in pulling practical jokes on each other. "None of them realized it was a holo until afterward, either. They each thought they had become involved in an actual situation. Can you see the potential for not just 'fun house' runs but training exercises in the field?"

What Janna saw was a terrible waste. Listening, she had found herself responding to Hazelton's enthusiasm. To remember that no such program existed, that Santos had squandered all that imagination and skill on murder, flooded Janna with disappointment and anger. Especially anger.

She scribbled: ADDRESS! on a notepad from Diosdado's desk and held the page above the phone screen. "Mama!"

This time he responded. His chin dipped. "It sounds exciting. However, it'll be difficult for us to see unless we contact Ms. Santos."

Hazelton's voice went apologetic. "Yes...sorry. I get carried away. I...can't tell you myself how to reach her. I'd think she'd be in the Topeka book."

Except Santos was not, Janna remembered. Not under her own name. Zavara and Threefoxes had already checked.

"As long as you're here, contact Frank Grauer in Metro Division. He knows her best. She usually stays with him when she's in town."

Metro provided Grauer's address and phone number, and the information that he worked the night watch. When they called his number, a square face came on the phone screen with the fixed expression typical of a recorded response. It recited a standard message. They declined to leave one of their own. Instead, they drove to his address, a brick house east of the UMKC campus, and parked across the street to wait for him.

While they waited, they checked Santos' name against the printout of seventy-seven Triton owners they had been carrying around in the car since Miranda Liliedahl in Records obtained it for them. Neither of the two Santos's listed had the name Lesandra.

Janna hissed in frustration. "Where does that damn car come from?"

"We'll find it, bibi." Mama slid down in the driver's seat until his head rested against the back. "Lord, this street brings back memories. I lived two blocks from here when I was in college. A friend of mine roomed in the basement of that house on the corner."

He launched into a story about the friend but Janna's attention wandered. Sitting here felt a bit like a stake-out…an uncomfortable sensation given that they waited for a fellow leo. She found herself brooding, too, over how to approach Grauer. Asking questions without saying why they needed the information treated him no better than an average citizen.

"Why didn't you tell Hazelton the truth?"

Mama glanced sideways at her. "You think we should have explained the situation?"

"Didn't she deserve that courtesy? She's one of us and Santos lied to her. Santos betrayed her!"

He regarded her calmly. "We don't know that for certain…and would you talk to a couple of out-of-town lions who, with no proof to give you, claimed over the phone that someone you believe in used you in planning a murder?"

He might have a point. "Are we going to tell Grauer?"

"You decide." Mama closed his eyes. "You can talk to him."

She had little time to think about it. Five minutes later a car rolled up the street and turned onto the steep driveway beside Grauer's house. She slapped Mama's shoulder on her way out of the Meteor. "A wheeler!"

He jerked upright.

Even with her head start, he managed to be on her heels by the time she reached the top of the driveway.

The coupe pulled into the garage attached to the house. Before the automatic door could close behind it, Janna called, "Good morning!"

The driver's door slid back. A broad-shouldered jon Janna's height swung out, the expression on his square face wary. That eased when she and Mama stopped well short of the garage and stood with hands at their sides, away from their trenchcoat pockets. A moment later his face relaxed. Spotting the subtle distinctions in movement and body carriage which stamped them as fellow officers?

"Good morning." Gravel rolled in his voice. He leaned back into the car to bring out a bag of groceries.

Janna strolled on toward the garage, holding out her ID. "I'm Janna Brill, Shawnee County PD. This is my partner, Mahlon Maxwell. That's quite an antique. What kind if car is it?"

"A twenty-one Dodge Kobold."

"In original condition, it looks like," Mama said.

Grauer ran his free hand back along the top, smiling at the vehicle. "Aside from an electric motor out of a fifty-seven Hurricane, yes." With a final pat on the top, he focused back on them. "What can I do for you?"

Her thoughts those last few minutes waiting for Grauer came rushing back to mind. Time to decide. Could she tell him the truth and still receive cooperation? Or was it better to be honest whatever the result? In his place, she would resent not being told.

She gave him a smile. "You might help a friend of yours. We're with our Crimes Against Persons squad. Lesandra Santos may be in trouble. If you have any information establishing her innocence, we need to know it."

Behind her, Mama murmured, "Nice approach."

Grauer's expression went wary again. "Innocence in what?"

"Murder."

Gray eyes stared into her for several seconds, expressionless, then he wheeled away. "Come inside."

Steps led up from the garage. The door at the top unlocked in response to the tones from the sonic key Grauer pulled from his jacket pocket, opening into a roomy kitchen. Another set of tones brought the garage door humming down.

"I'm home!"

A light flickered below the keypad and monitor screen on a panel built in between the refrigerator and microwave oven. A voice said, "Alarm disengaged. Shall I reset?"

"No." Grauer opened the refrigerator and began putting in items from the grocery bag. "Report."

"There have been no visitors. There was one phone call but the caller did not leave a message. The faucet in the upstairs bathroom is dripping. Shall I activate the newscanner?"

"No."

"I didn't know that house-keeper model comes with voice activation," Mama said, glancing around the kitchen.

"Les—" Grauer glanced over his shoulder at them. "I had it added."

By Lesandra Santos, Janna bet.

Grauer closed the refrigerator and turned around. "What's this about Lessa?"

A magazine called *International Horse* lay on the table. Janna pushed it to one side and sat down on the table edge. "A week ago Friday and Saturday, armed men riffed the Democratic and Humanitarian fund-raisers. A Topeka businessman, Carel Armenda, died during the second robbery."

"I heard about that." He leaned against the countertop. "How is Lessa implicated?"

"We've discovered that six of the seven men were holograms. Holograms Santos recorded—we've talked to the slighs who posed for her—and played back through a projector she developed at a company where she worked for the dead man." Briefly, Janna explained the situation with the projector.

Except for a start at mention of the holos, Grauer listened without expression, and without speaking, his arms folded. Only when Janna stopped talking did he ask, "How do you know these gunmen were holos?"

She explained the findings on the news chip. "And three of the slighs have alibis for Friday."

"Fortunately," Grauer said, "so does Lessa...for both Friday and Saturday. She spent the week end here." He crossed to a cupboard and put away the cans and cartons still in the grocery bag. "I picked her up at Municipal Airport Friday noon and put her back on the airship Sunday afternoon. In between she spent all her time with me, except during my duty shifts those nights and when she took my niece with her out making more recordings."

Mama picked up the magazine and opened it. "How did she happen to take your niece?"

"Brin asked to go along. She lives here; she adopted me after divorcing her mother, my sister."

Janna felt as though the floor had been jerked from beneath her. Santos spent those nights here? Came up by airship? She swore silently. Every good suspect in this case could produce a damn documented alibi!

Mama flipped through the magazine. "Santos always comes by airship?"

"More often by bus. She buys one-month passes." Grauer looked around. "Occasionally she indulges herself, though."

Suddenly Janna felt better. The tickman had sent Tony a one-month pass. How fortunate that Santos "indulged herself" on the one week end when the airship's passenger list and recording of boarding passengers would provide incontrovertible proof of her coming and going. Taking the girl along stuck Janna the same way...convenient. As though Santos wanted to make sure she had someone to swear to her whereabouts. Had the girl really asked to go along, or had Santos managed to make it seem that way?

Excitement rose in Janna. Suppose Santos were the tickman...had planned everything, given her accomplices—Aschke and the small jon—what they needed, and sat back safe in her alibi while they carried out the dirty work.

"How does she haul her equipment around town?" Mama laid down the magazine. "Surely not on a city bus."

"She uses my car," Grauer said.

Really. Janna exchanged glances with Mama. A car could take Santos to Topeka without the inconvenience of commercial schedules or drivers who might remember her.

The same thought obviously occurred to Grauer as well. He went on, "She never drove it to Topeka. I always check my odometer readings when I get into the car. She drove less than thirty klicks each night."

Besides which, the car was not a Triton and Santos had companionship those evenings. Allegedly. "We'll need to talk to your niece, I'm afraid...and to Santos, of course. Do you have her address and phone number?"

"Of course, but it's on the paperwork she filled out for riding along."

"We would have taken it from there," Janna said, grimacing, "except your records computer is in no hurry to tell us."

Grauer sighed and nodded. "House-keeper! Address search. Lesandra Santos."

"Searching." A short time later the house-keeper announced, "Lesandra Santos," and recited an address and phone number.

Janna wrote them in her notebook.

Grauer eyed her. "That's her home phone, best reached during the day. She works nights." Impatience flickered in his eyes and around the edges of his voice. "Look, I can see why Lessa's under suspicion, but isn't it a little difficult to believe that someone planning to use holos in a murder would spend a year and a half openly making recordings and telling everyone in sight what she's doing? Not to mention spending her days off running around with lions."

The response Mama made to Diosdado's similar comment came back to Janna. She repeated it. "If you're looking for a thief, though, don't you make friends with people who know where to find one?"

Grauer's mouth thinned. "She's never asked me to point out a thief."

Probably she never needed to. Listening to the conversation between any two or more lions as they watched the passing public would give her information enough.

"Did she ever ask about criminals who use disguises as part of their M.O.?" Mama asked.

"No!" Grauer scowled. "I think what's happened is that someone she knows here or in Topeka heard her talking and got the bright idea of using her holos."

The kitchen chair creaked as Mama leaned back, hands behind his head. "That's possible, yes. How long have you known her?"

"We met at a party in August or September two years ago." Grauer leaned against the counter, folding his arms. "She came with another Metro officer. We got to talking, liked each other, and she started coming down week ends to ride along with me."

"She's a lion buff?"

Irritation flickered across his face. "She was curious about the job. Then listening to some of us talk one night about training programs and the required annual 'fun house' run, she came up with this idea for the shoot/don't shoot program. In a way, her interest is professional since her job is private security."

Electricity shot up Janna's spine. At the corner of her vision, she saw Mama start, too. Then look thoughtful. Private security! "Did she tell you what agency?"

Grauer nodded. "Beria Security."

Beria! Janna whooped silently. Connections! Aschke had to be their tall man. Everything was starting to fall into place.

"Everything about her is on record," Grauer said.

Mama looked up. "Maybe not everything. She goes by Lesandra Santos here, is that right?"

Grauer frowned. "Yes," he said slowly.

"She uses another given name at Beria."

Grauer's shrug dismissed that. "So? There's nothing sinister in that. It's her real first name, I expect. She told me she doesn't use it because she hates it, but she might there, to keep Armenda from finding her."

"Oh, I expect so. However..." Mama pushed his glasses up his nose, and focused on Janna. "...I do wonder why a person with a clear conscience introduced herself to us—"

"To us!" Janna stared at him. They had not met Santos. The only small, dark haired bibi they met was—

"—with a different last name as well."

Sandoz.

Through the dizzy clamor of thoughts in her head she heard Mama explain his comment to Grauer, and the K.C. leo's angry, "They're almost the same. You probably just misheard."

Had they? No. Thinking back carefully, she heard the voice again. *I'm Karis Sandoz.* Sandoz, clearly with a *d* and a *z*. *Karis Sandoz. That's Karis with a K.* God forbid, Listra Wassman had said, they should think the name had a *Ch* and was short for Charisma. A name hated by a number of the girls who bore it, including this one who, Janna suddenly recalled with dismay, was quitting her job at Beria this week in preparation for leaving for Mars.

17

A fastener shaped like a stirrup held the chestnut hair back in a pony tail. A gold horse, arched in a jump with rainbow mane and tail flying, decorated one breast pocket of an otherwise plain blue shirt and breeches. Grauer's niece looked up at them from the chair beside the assistant principal's desk, hands folded in her lap, knee-booted legs crossed at the ankles and pulled back under the chair. "What did I do Friday and Saturday night the week end before last?" She glanced at her uncle.

"There's nothing to worry about, Brin," he said. "You aren't in any trouble. Just answer their questions."

Brin Terrill showed no apprehension at being pulled out of class for questioning. The glance at her uncle did not seem to be for reassurance, only confirmation that she should answer. An altogether unusually self-possessed thirteen-year-old. But, a child who demanded legal separation from her parents would hardly be the timid kind.

"Of course, Uncle Frank." She smiled up at Mama, sitting on the edge of the desk. "A friend of ours, Lessa Santos, took me with her to record holos of people. She's collecting them for—"

Mama interrupted with a nod. "We know about her program. What time did you two leave and where did you go?"

"Friday Lessa picked me up from school about three. I asked to go along with her that night. We called Uncle Frank, he said yes, and off we went. Saturday we started early, nine o'clock. Both days we ended up in Westport."

"Where in Westport?" Janna asked.

The girl hesitated, forehead puckered in thought, then shrugged. "A gallery cafe. I don't remember the name. We went in the back door. The owner or manager let Lessa set up her camera and lights and mirror in a room upstairs. Then we went for a walk up and down the street and sat downstairs drinking coffee while Lessa looked over the people. We sat at the outside tables, too, Friday night, until it got too chilly." The girl's face and voice became more animated as she talked. Her hands left her lap to gesture in illustration. "She saw three people she liked. One was a transvestite dressed all in fringe. Lessa gave him a little shooter she'd borrowed from Uncle Frank and had him pull it out of the front of his dress and point it at the camera. Then there was a bibi with hair so short she was almost a skinhead. You could see scalp tattoos through it, rainbow stripes, like her bodysuit. Another bibi was really zone, though! Her hair came down to here." The girl drew a finger across the middle of her thigh. "Peacock blue. She looked nudie, just with some blue nebulas and stars painted on her and wearing a silver cape…except it turned out she had a transparent bodysuit. I wondered how she stayed warm. The best part was this big starburst pendant on her necklace with a little dagger hidden in it. Lessa had her pull it out and lunge like she was trying to stab someone."

Behind the girl, Grauer nodded.

"What about Saturday?" Mama asked.

The girl shook her head. "She didn't see anyone she liked. There weren't too many people in the cafe. Probably because of the rain."

Rain? That day in Topeka, Janna remembered, it stopped in the latter part of the afternoon. She caught Grauer's eye and raised a brow.

He nodded again. "It rained here until the middle of the evening, maybe twenty-one hundred."

"What time did you leave?"

The girl glanced down at her wrist chrono. "I think we got home around eleven or eleven-thirty."

Mama smiled down at her. "You're sure this was the week end before last. You couldn't confuse it with some other week end?"

"No." She dimpled. "I got an A that day on my Russian test. I showed it to Lessa when she picked me up."

They let her go back to class.

Walking out to the Jacquot Middle School parking lot, Grauer said, "Brin did have a Russian test that Friday, and Lessa recorded those particular people. She showed me the holos when I came home. Saturday she complained about the rain keeping interesting people away. Now do you believe her alibi?"

Janna shoved her hands into her trenchcoat pockets. "The alibi, yes. Unfortunately, that doesn't clear her of involvement in the riffs and murder."

He rolled his eyes. "She isn't involved! I know her! Her temper is the kind that flares and is over with. She doesn't hold grudges like this killer has to."

"I hope you're right." Janna slid open the Meteor's passenger door.

Grauer stood frowning after them while they climbed in and drove away.

Glancing back as they reached the street, Janna saw him still standing by his car. "You think he's afraid we'll come back and ask the girl more questions?"

"We should," Mama said. "It was a mistake talking to her with him there. We wouldn't have allowed it if he'd been a regular citizen."

Janna straightened around in her seat, grinning. "Look who suddenly wants to go by the book." Then she sobered. "Speaking of the book, we ought to call home." If for no other reason than that Showalter and Weyneth must have been to Aschke's bank by now and learned if he had been to Kansas City on any relevant dates.

"Let's check out Crown Center Hotel first." Mama dug under his trenchcoat into a breast pocket of the jumpsuit.

When she saw the photo he brought out, Janna grinned again. Aschke. Their thoughts were tracking together.

For all the good it did them.

After introducing themselves to hotel security and being assigned someone to accompany them, they showed the photograph to staff members all over the hotel, from desk clerks and restaurant and bar personnel to maids, pool attendants, and security officers. Rather, Janna showed the photograph. Mama trailed along saying nothing, his face wearing a glassy-eyed expression he had acquired as the car set down on its parking rollers on the hotel drive. Janna considered tripping him to see if that would wake him up. Not that his participation would have changed the answers they received.

No one recognized Aschke.

"This doesn't mean he hasn't been here, of course," her escort said. Short-cropped peacock blue hair and an elegantly plain bodysuit-and-tabard made the security officer look more like a guest than a guard. "We don't remember everyone who comes through."

Janna frowned at her. "This jon had to do more than pass through. He was here at least long enough to locate a maid he could pay off to let him copy her key."

A master key made the most sense. With that in his possession, all Aschke had to do was pick an unoccupied room and invite Tony Ho to visit.

"There's no maid involved, bibi."

Both she and the security officer turned to look at Mama. So he had finally come back to Earth. "Who'd Aschke get the key from, then?"

"Aschke didn't." Mama pushed his glasses up his nose and raised a brow at the security officer. "Were you involved in the holographic recording here a short while back?"

While Janna started at the question, the security officer asked, "You mean the bibi with the leo training program?"

How did he know Santos recorded here?

The bibi said, "She used Jim Dalke and Evan March."

"May we talk to them?"

She tapped her ear button.

Five minutes later they met the two officers on the mezzanine by the waterfalls. They, too, wore civilian clothing. Only broader shoulders and a slightly more alert expression differentiated them from ordinary guests. Mama said, "Describe what happened when Ms. Santos recorded you."

The two exchanged puzzled glances. "Not much. She had us walk down halls and step out of doorways with and without weapons."

"Unlock doors?"

They shook their heads. One said, "One time she did have me hold my key up as though to put it in a lock at deadbolt height. She said that made it look almost like a small weapon, so some leo seeing the image from the corner of his eye would have to think fast to realize what it really was and not shoot."

Key! Janna grinned.

A short time later, on their way through the lower lobby, she said, "So Santos copied the key from the holo image and gave it to Aschke?"

Mama smiled. "She copied the key. She didn't give it to Aschke."

"You don't think he's the tall man?"

His smile widened. "You're forgetting, as I did until it hit me on the drive here from the middle school, who mentioned his robots and put him under suspicion. Santos. Why would she do that if he were really her accomplice? No, he isn't the tall man. There is no tall man."

Janna stopped short. What the hell had been happening in his head? "You've really gone over the brainbow, you know that, Mama? What about the man Tony met, and the one Surowsky and Inge saw in the Triton?"

"Why should she use holos for only the gunmen?"

Once the jolt from that thought subsided, it reverberated in her like a purr. Yes, of course. A holo worked perfectly in the hotel room. The figure told Tony where to find his advance payment. It never touched him. And the lighting prevented Tony from seeing that the figure did not talk. The voice was probably pre-recorded through the same electronic apparatus that changed Santos' voice into the one emerging from the waitron. The figure Surowski, Inge, and Tony Ho saw in the Triton had not spoken at all. Only the small man had. "So all we have to do is find the small man."

"I know where he is. All I have to do is prove his identity. Let's make some calls." He headed back across the lobby for the phones, digging his notebook out of a thigh pocket.

The first one was long distance, she saw. Mama charged it to the department. "Who are we calling?"

A female face appeared on the screen. "Yi house. Who may I say is calling?"

That answered Janna's question.

Mama asked for Mrs. Yi. When she came on, he asked, "Sometime within a week or so before the robbery, did someone from Beria make a night service call without you requesting one?"

Maeve Yi's forehead creased in thought. After several moments, she nodded. "Monday night. Apparently there'd been problems with the systems of some clients in the area due to power fluctuations during the storms over the week end. So they were checking everyone."

"Do you remember which technician made the service call?"

"No. I'm sure she gave her name—they always do—but I don't remember.

She. Santos?

Mama made two more calls, to the Capitol Sheraton and the Terracrest Apartments, and asked the same questions. Santos had made "service calls" at both places within a week of the riffs, using the same excuse she gave the Yi's. Calls that of course went unrecorded on Beria's service logs.

It explained a great deal. Hacking into the Yi's security system gave Santos the gate override code. Doing the same with the Terracrest records provided her with the names and lock tones of absent tenants. But it did not tell them how Tony used the waiter's Scib Card and passed the retinal scan at the hotel employee door.

They headed for the car. Coming out through the hotel doors into the covered entrance, Mama grinned. "It's so elegant. Aside from Tony, because someone had to be there for physical enforcement if necessary, there's only one person involved. Santos. She planned everything. She made the holos and controlled them. She delivered the waitron to the hotel and broke into Holliday Catering to leave it there. Simple, direct, no leaks because there's only one person who knows."

It could have been an elegant theory...except for one flaw. "Mama, there has to be someone else involved. Santos has an alibi, remember?"

"I have an idea about that." He pointed.

She turned to follow the direction of his finger. It aimed out of the covered entrance toward a large building located diagonally across the avenue intersection west of the hotel. "What's that?"

"The Pershing Equestrian Center, once the Union Station. Come on." He headed down the hotel drive.

She fell into step with him, leaning into the breeze that had stiffened since they went into the hotel. "What does a riding stable have to do with this case?"

His tongue ticked. "Kansas Citians would be insulted to have you refer to an historic landmark as a riding stable. They board horses and teaching riding, yes, but...it's more than that. Santos must have seen it when she visited the hotel." He halted at the corner to wait for the light. "Maybe it gave her the same idea for an alibi that it did me on our way in."

"Which is?"

The *Walk* signal flashed. Mama sprinted for the diagonal corner. Following him, Janna learned why he ran. The signal lasted barely two-thirds of their crossing, leaving them in a race against the wall of on-coming traffic.

On the safety of the sidewalk, Janna caught her breath, then repeated her question.

Mama just grinned and strolled up the drive to a long bank of doors leading into the building.

Inside, Janna caught her breath. More than a riding stable indeed. She stared at a broad marble-floored concourse and a ceiling soaring above them like a cathedral's. Around the concourse lay a tack shop, a club called The Stirrup Cup, and a room with snack machines and clusters of molded foam chairs around a three-sided TV in the center. Signs reading: *Veterinary Clinic* and *Exercise Room* pointed to their left.

Following Mama on into the building, Janna discovered that the concourse was only the crossbar on a huge T, and the main leg had even more of the cavernous majesty of a cathedral. Except tanbark covered the floor of this "nave", a brown plain splashed with light shafting down from the high windows and dotted with jumps and the moving figures of horses. It reminded her of pictures of the Spanish Riding School in Vienna.

A spectators' gallery rose in steep tiers, separated from the riding ring by a chest-high wooden wall. A few people, some in street clothes, most in riding boots and breeches, sat in the gallery. Others leaned on the wall.

Mama moved up the ring. As Janna joined him, a horse cantered by, nostrils flaring, neck and shoulders damply dark, its rider, a girl in her teens, murmuring and clucking. In its wake, the pungent scents of horse and sweat washed over Janna.

Another girl, slightly older, stood on the far side of Mama. "What time does the ring close?" he asked her.

"Midnight," she replied. Beneath the visor of her black velvet riding helmet, her eyes followed the cantering horse.

Suddenly Janna understood why she and Mama were here. Girls and horses. "Are you thinking what I think you are?"

He nodded. "Grauer's niece is horse-crazy. What better place than this to keep her happily occupied for a few hours?"

"A few hours? We're talking seven or eight on Friday and over twelve on Saturday." Janna shook her head. "That's a long time."

Mama grinned. "Not in horse heaven. You must be one of the few girls born not bitten by the horse bug. When my cousin Genea visited our farm, the first place she always headed was for the horses, and she'd have spent all day every day with them if she'd been allowed to."

It sounded to Janna like an affliction she was fortunate to have missed. "Now we have to establish the girl was here."

He nodded. "Let's start with the riding school office."

It lay off the concourse, a large room but crowded by the four desks in it. At the moment the chairs of three sat empty, leaving only the secretary to answer their questions.

"Do we have a Brin Terrill registered for lessons?" He swiveled to the computer on the ell of his desk, and in a few keystrokes later, replied, "Yes, she's in Tarl Byrne's low intermediate class Wednesday evenings."

Janna frowned. Of course they asked the question, but she never expected that answer. It removed the most logical reason for the girl to alibi Santos…as an exchange for something unobtainable any other way.

Mama peered over the secretary's shoulder at the computer monitor. "I remember that a few years back, helping clean stalls Saturday earned a free riding lesson later in the day. Is that still true?"

The jon grinned. "Oh, yes. And that bonus class is always filled."

"Is there a record of who rides in it?"

"Not a formal one. Jim Ledders, the head stableman, writes down the names and gives it to whoever happens to be teaching the class that day, but I've never put the list on the computer. I don't know if the instructors save the names or not."

"Who taught two Saturdays ago?"

"I don't know. You'll need to ask the instructors." The secretary grinned again. "I think they draw straws for it. Or Ledders may know."

Mama voted for asking the stableman, and led the way down a ramp spiraling from a corridor to the side of the riding ring to the stall rows below. "He should know better than anyone else who cleaned stalls."

Janna wrinkled her nose as the smells of straw, hay, and manure enveloping them. "How do you know this place so well?"

He shrugged. "Some of the other criminal justice students and I used to come down from the campus every Sunday evening to watch the P.D. mounted patrol train. The horses are stabled here. For a while I thought I wanted to be a mounted officer."

She might have known. "Is there anyplace in Kansas City you *didn't* visit regularly when you were in school here?"

He grinned.

They located the lanky head stableman overseeing the repair of an automatic water bowl in one of the stalls. "Sure I know Brin by sight." He moved to one side of the doorway as the stall's blanketed occupant stretched its head past him to investigate them. "She's one of the regular Saturday gang."

"We need to know whether or not she was here Saturday before last." Janna reached fingers through the wire netting of the stall door to touch the horse's velvet-soft muzzle. "Do you remember?"

Ledders hesitated. "I'm afraid not. You get so used to seeing some these kids, you don't notice them beyond writing down their names as they come in and keeping an eye on them to make sure they're really working. Sue Rakowski taught the bonus class that week. Maybe she remembers if Brin was in it."

When they caught the stocky instructor after the finish of a private lesson, though, she could not remember. She leaned back against the ring wall shaking her head. "The thing is, that bonus class is such a mixed bag, everything from green beginners to upper intermediates, it's impossible to run as a real class. It's mostly just an hour's ride for them—which is all they really want anyway—so I don't pay much attention to who's there. Unless one of them does something spectacularly good or bad. Brin's very average."

"Do you save the lists Ledders gives you?" Mama asked.

She shook her head. "Once the class is over, I throw them away."

Mama and Janna talked to the two other instructors, and to a number of riders and parents of riders, hoping to find someone who had been at the school that Friday and Saturday. To Janna's surprise, most had. As nearly as she could tell, they came almost every day. None of them, however, remembered whether they had seen Brin Terrill or not.

On the walk back to the hotel for their car, Janna shook her head in disbelief. "In an age when we're colonizing the stars and racing to stake mining claims on the asteroids, I can't believe there are people who do nothing but ride horses."

"Yes, it is amazing how people's entire lives can be bound up in a hobby…or a job," he added with a sideglance at her.

"As amazing as a grown man not being able to stand living alone," Janna shot back. Two could play the barb game. Then she returned to their problem. "So…we can't prove Santos left the girl at the riding school. Maybe she didn't. If the girl's there so often, why would she be willing to lie for Santos to spend more time there, and why, most of all, would she lie to her uncle for Santos?"

Mama pushed his glasses up his nose. "Let's ask her."

If talking to them without her uncle present disturbed the girl, she did not show it. She took a chair in the assistant principal's office with the same self-possession she showed earlier. "How can I help you now?"

Sitting down in a chair facing her, Janna said, "We're having trouble finding the gallery cafe where you and Lessa went." She reached into her trenchcoat pocket to tap on her microcorder. "What kind of artwork did it display?"

The girl hesitated, forehead puckering. The reaction rang an alert in Janna's head. They had seen this before when they asked where Santos took her…a deliberate kind of gesture. Practiced. "Paintings, I think. I don't really remember. We were looking at people." Her voice went carefully casual. "Why do you want to know? Is Lessa in some kind of trouble?"

Sooner or later she was bound to ask that. Janna kept smiling. "We hope not. But…" Now for the bluff. "…we can't seem to find anyone in Westport who remembers seeing the two of you that week end."

For a split second the girl stared through her, then focused and without a blink said, "I think people forget who they saw when unless they're friends or had a fight with them or something."

A fair observation, Janna agreed. Perhaps a bit mature for a child her age? Also, the average innocent person in this situation reacted with surprise at not being remembered, with disbelief and dismay, even indignation…not with excuses for being overlooked. She glanced at Mama. Time for the heavy artillery of bluff number two.

He shifted position on the edge of the desk. "People do remember people they know. Jim Ledders, for example, recalls quite clearly that you cleaned stalls that Saturday, and Sue Rakowski that you rode in the bonus class."

The girl went rigid.

Triumph crackled through Janna. Bullseye! She leaned toward the girl. "Brin, where did Lessa really go?"

The wide eyes stared through her. "I told you…we went to Westport. I didn't clean stalls or ride. They're getting confused with another week end."

Janna sighed inwardly. So the girl was going to stick with the story.

"No, Brin." Mama shook his head. "Ms. Rakowski remembers because you fell off at one of the jumps."

The girl stiffened, nostrils flaring. "That's a lie! I stayed on over every single jump, even the In and Out. I haven't fallen off in—" She broke off. Too late. The angry compression of her mouth said she realized that.

Janna let the silence stretch out for a minute, then asked, "Why did you lie for Lessa?"

The girl bit her lip. "Promise me you won't tell my uncle."

"I'm sorry, we can't do that," Mama said.

Her hands clenched. "He'll be so angry at Lessa!"

To say the least. "Brin." Janna waited for the girl to look at her before continuing. "This is a very serious matter. Your uncle will be much angrier if you don't tell us the truth."

Indecision twisted the girl's face, but finally she said, "Lessa wanted to record some people in a neighborhood where Uncle Frank told her never to go alone. She needed those images, she said, but she didn't want my uncle to know she'd gone there. So would I help her keep him from finding out by pretending I'd asked to go along and that we went to Westport together." She looked up at them, forehead creased in protest. "It was a lie, but it didn't hurt anything, just kept my uncle from worrying. I like Lessa. Why shouldn't I help her?"

Leaving the school, Mama said, "I'm sorry she'll have to find out, sooner or later."

Fortunately they did not have the dirty job of telling her. "So much for Santos' alibi. She could have gone to Topeka."

Mama nodded. "Now we have to prove she did."

18

Proof had to start with means…Santos' transportation to Topeka. Logic said it must be the Triton. "The question is where she got it, Mama. Did she buy, borrow, or rent?"

Checking their DMV list of Kansas Triton owners established that Santos had not registered one as Charisma Santos, either.

Their own car bucked in the rising wind. To the west, clouds pushed up over the horizon, heralding another spring storm.

Mama held the wheel steady. "I doubt she borrowed it."

Janna arched her brows at him.

"Whoever she borrowed it from could testify she wasn't in Westport. Let's have Diosdado run her name through DMV in Jefferson City. If that's negative, we'll try local car rental agencies. And self-storage facilities and garage rentals. In her place, I'd want a vehicle set up and ready to go so I wouldn't risk falling behind schedule if I had trouble loading and setting up the desktop."

Janna nodded. No one left a vehicle on the street if it held anything worth stealing.

When they reached Robbery, however, they found Diosdado gone. Janna swore.

An amerasian she-lion at a nearby desk looked around. "You're the Topeka detectives, aren't you? Is there anything I can help you with?"

"Thank you, yes." Mama tore a page out of his notebook and handed it to her. "We need to know if there's a car registered to either of these names in Missouri."

"That shouldn't be any problem." She glanced at the page while reaching for her phone. "Oh, before I forget, there's something from Records for you on Diosdado's desk. He asked me to be sure you got it."

Mama headed for Diosdado's desk.

"There's another message, too." The detective rummaged through the papers spread across her desk. "It came in a little after Diosdado left. I don't know now what I did with it. A Lieutenant someone in Topeka who wants you to call as soon—this is Detective Lin in Robbery," she said to the face that appeared on her phone screen. "I have a couple of names to run through DMV."

Lieutenant someone from Topeka had to be Vradel. Janna arched a brow at Mama. "Do you want to call or shall I?"

"Later." Mama passed the information from Records on to Janna.

Glancing through the pages, printouts of the information Santos gave for each ride-along request, Janna saw nothing remarkable, nothing they did not already know. Less, in fact. The ride-along requests gave her name as Lesandra Santos and listed only a personal address and phone number. If they had had only these to go by, they would never have realized she was also Charisma Santos and worked for Beria.

"I've got your registration query back," Lin called.

Janna copied the information from the detective's phone screen on the back of the Records printout. Negative for Lesandra Santos. She had no vehicle registered in the state of Missouri. Two Charisma Santos's did, but both had Missouri addresses—not near Kansas City—and neither was on a seventy-seven Triton.

That left the rental agencies.

"Thanks," Janna said. "Is there any problem with us using Diosdado's and his partner's phones for some calls?"

"Not with me. You'd better ask Captain Westfahl."

Diosdado had introduced them to his commanding officer their first trip here, a stocky lion who never quite focused on the person he talked to. As though the conversation were only one of several simultaneous thought trains in his head. They approached him in his office with the request.

He shrugged. "Use them until we need them. Charge any long distance to your own department, though."

They tossed a vending token to divide the calls. Janna won the self-storage facilities and garage rentals. Typing in the category on the alphanumeric keypad of the phone book lying on Diosdado's desk brought her the first of the self-storage listings, the first of many, a quick downscan found.

Before starting on them, then, she called Lieutenant Vradel.

He regarded her dead-pan from the screen. "Well, if it isn't one of the gypsies. How nice to hear from you."

The dry tone brought a prickle of heat up her neck, but she kept her face as expressionless as his. "I called as soon as we got your message."

"Thank you. Thank you, too, for the time bomb you left. The detonation is still echoing on the third floor." A corner of his mustache twitched. "You may hear reverberations of it yet when you come home."

No doubt. Janna sighed.

Mama left Diosdado's phone to join her. "Even when we come bearing gifts of corroboration and a possible arrestable suspect?" He outlined what they had learned today.

Vradel listened without reaction or comment until Mama finished. Then he said, "I don't know about the arrestable suspect. Everything sounds circumstantial. Though you're right about Aschke not recruiting Tony Ho. His bank records show several recent trips to Kansas City, but none that include Monday, April eighth."

Mama grinned at Janna.

"According to Weyneth," Vradel continued, "Aschke claims he made the trips to visit Servitron, trying to sell them the design for his guard robot. As long as you're up there, check it out."

"While we're doing that, oh great and wise leader, how about trying for a bank warrant on Santos?" Mama asked.

After a few moments of mustache smoothing, the lieutenant nodded. "You just bring home something more concrete on this Santos. Such as the car and a demonstrable interest in criminals using disguise as part of their M.O., and that she had knowledge of Tony Ho."

Checking Servitron was easy enough. Janna called and asked for the plant manager. Remembering her from their visit the week before, he readily answered her questions.

"Yes, I remember the jon. He's been up here several times. Has some good ideas but needs to work them out a little more."

With a few minutes' thought and checking back through his calendar, the manager worked out the dates of Aschke's visits. None of them fell on or next to Monday the eighth.

That took care of Aschke. Now for the rest of Vradel's request.

Janna sighed, punching off. "With all those evenings riding along and all the questions Santos must have asked, who'll remember her asking about riffers liking disguises? Worse, if she learned about Tony just by keeping her ears open, we'll never—Mama?"

He sat staring at the phone screen.

"What is it?"

A grin spread across the dark face. "Maybe a link, bibi." He headed for Detective Lin's desk. "Would you have time to make another call for us?"

The she-lion looked up. "To DMV?"

"To Records." He sat down in the chair beside her desk. "Last week Diosdado pulled up a file for us. Most of the officer codes on the retrieval log had IVRB and IVFD section designations."

Lin nodded. "Robbery and Fraud."

"One, though, and only one, was a UDMT…someone in Metro patrol, Diosdado said." He caught Janna's eye.

A tingle traveled up her spine. Metro patrol. Was he thinking of Grauer?

"Can we find out what officer that code belongs to?"

"I can try." Lin tapped her phone on. "First we need the code. What was the name on the record?" A short time later they had the retrieval log for Tony Ho's file on the screen. Lin jotted down the UDMT code and exited the file, then reached for the keypad again. "You can't learn other lions' codes by asking the computer for them. What I'll have to do is contact a friend of mine in records."

"Wait," Mama said. "Before you do that, will you request a search for subjects who use disguises as part of their robbery M.O.?"

"What?" Lin frowned at him. "That'll tie up my phone, and me, for god knows how long."

He smiled an apology at her. "I know. I'm sorry. We can't do it and it's very important to see the retrieval logs on those files."

Her frown deepened. "I'm willing to spend a favor finding out whose access code this is, but I don't have the time for a records search."

Charm poured out of Mama's smile. "Use Diosdado's phone. All we need is your voice reciting your code to get us into the computer, isn't that right? Or does the computer check voices all the time you're logged on?"

The she-lion hesitated, then shook her head. "Not once you're in. All right. I can do that."

Even on a category one search they had to wait almost ten minutes. It seemed like ten hours before the files began appearing on the phone screen. Then Janna quickly forgot the wait. One retrieval log after another listed the UDMT code on Sunday, April seventh. The day before Tony received his letter about the possible job.

Lin called from her desk, "My friend in Records says that access code belongs to a Sergeant Frank Grauer."

"I love you, leo!" Mama blew her a kiss. "Thank you very very much. Where would you like to go for dinner?"

She grinned. "I'd better go home or my husband will be very very pissed."

Janna sucked in her lower lip. Grauer. "Now we need to find out if it was actually Grauer who made the search."

They called him. When he came on the screen, the Metro officer frowned. "You again?"

Mama smiled in apology. "Unfortunately. We have one last question. Sunday, April seventh, did you request a records search for riffers who use disguises in their M.O.?"

Grauer's mouth thinned. "I did not. And Lessa couldn't, either. You know not even a phenomenal mimic can fool a voice recognition program."

"Someone made that search using your code. Has she been present on any occasion when you called into the computer? A microcorder fits in almost any pocket and the best ones have excellent sound reproduction."

His face tightened. With uncertainty? Janna hated what they had to do to him.

Mama sighed. "I'm sorry, Grauer, truly."

"Go to hell."

Watching the stony face fade from the screen, Janna felt anger rise in her. Armenda had been the one killed, but he was just one of the victims in this murder, and the pain of the others had only begun.

She reached for the phone book. "Let's find that damn car."

If and where Santos maintained garage space for the vehicle had to lie within a radius of fifteen klicks, to fit the odometer readings on Grauer's Kobold after Santos used it. That included a large section of the city, granted, but it eliminated storage and garage facilities in outlying areas. Janna also skipped those to the east. Santos needed to go west. It made sense for her to pick a facility in that general direction.

After washing down a sandwich from the building's bank of vending machines with a cup of caff from the squad pot, Janna planted herself at Diosdado's desk and tackled the self-storage listings. Several hours worth of calls, at a rough estimate.

As each storage facility answered, she put on a polite smile and held up her ID to the phone. "This is Sergeant Janna Brill of the Shawnee County Crimes Against Persons squad. Do you, or have you recently had, a unit rented to a Charisma Santos or Lesandra Santos?"

Of course no one at the top of the list had.

"She'll probably turn out to have rented from something called Zeke's Storage."

Mama, calling car rental agencies from the phone on Diosdado's partner's desk, grinned. "Investigation is so action packed."

"Yes," a male face on Janna's phone screen said, "I have a unit rented to a Charisma Santos."

Janna sat bolt upright. Hurriedly, she rechecked the name of the facility. Convenience Storage, Merriam. That would be on the Kansas side. Between here and Topeka. "Do you have an address for her?" Now if only this were not just someone with the same name.

The address was Santos' in Topeka. She had rented unit number 230 a month and a half ago.

"Mama!"

The whoop turned heads across the squadroom. Mama, however, only pointed at the phone book in front of her. "Save the victory celebration until we find the Triton."

An hour later he did. Thrifty Auto Leasing had rented a seventy-seven Triton to Charisma Santos five weeks ago on a month-to-month lease.

They had her! Janna grinned. If Santos were innocent, why would she lease a car and never mention it, just keep on using Grauer's Kobold?

"Does she still have the car?" Mama asked.

On the screen, the dark-haired bibi at Thrifty Auto glanced off to the left of the phone. "No. It was returned Wednesday morning."

Janna sighed. Possession had probably been too much to expect. They still had the vehicle itself, however, and the associative evidence it contained.

"Will you please hold that car until we can examine it?"

Another pause with more attention to the left, then a grimace. "I'm sorry, but it's already gone out again."

Janna swore.

"When it comes back in, hold it. It may contain evidence relating to a murder we're investigating." Disconnecting, he said, "We still have the storage space, bibi. Let's go look at it."

A tall security fence surrounded Convenience Storage. Individual units, white-painted concrete block with brightly colored doors, sat in back-to-back rows, ranging in size from overgrown closets to spaces large enough for the furnishings of an entire house. A group in the mid-range size included number 230, Santos' unit.

Janna leaned against the car watching Mama pace the distance across the blue roll-up door. "It's garage sized. Santos could have kept the Triton in it."

"And the desktop. She returned the car. What happened to the holo controls, though?" He ran his hand down the door to the lock.

The action sent a warning tingle through Janna. She pushed away from the car. "No, Mama!"

Innocent eyes turned on her. "No, what?"

The wind chased scraps of paper and other small debris down the storage row. Leaden clouds closed overhead. Janna rolled her eyes. "As if you can't guess. No...we're not going to break in. There's no point." He knew that. If they found something incriminating, they couldn't touch it. They couldn't even use seeing it as probable cause for obtaining a search warrant. "We're practically on Highway 10 here. That runs to Lawrence, where she could pick up 40 north of Clinton Lake and go straight on into Topeka. It's a perfect route for her purposes, no tolls and not as well patrolled as the Turnpike, so she could make whatever speed necessary for her timetable. We might use that to go after a warrant."

"While we're building probable cause, what if she moves whatever's left in there?" He tilted his head toward the door.

She shoved her hands in the pockets of her trenchcoat. "It's a chance we have to take. You know we can't do anything else."

"I can." He swung around and headed up the row in long strides.

Janna scrambled after him. "Mama, what the hell—" She broke off as she realized he was headed for the facility office. "Mama!" Damn the man!

He kept going.

She caught up just as he pushed through the office door. "Damn it, Mama, you—"

"I tell you I do smell it."

A jon with the face Janna had seen on the phone looked up from behind the counter. "May I help you?"

Mama pushed his glasses up his nose. "My wife and I have one of your storage spaces, and when we were down there just now, I smelled something terrible. It seemed to be coming from number 230. I thought you ought to know."

So that was the skin. She could short-circuit this. "It's your imagination. *I* didn't smell a thing."

Mama shook his head. "I don't know how you can miss a stench like that, babycheeks. It's like something died. I wonder if a rat got in there."

Babycheeks! He was a dead man. She gave him a sugary smile. "Oh, there's a rat around, but not in there."

The manager frowned. "What unit did you say?"

"Two-thirty."

"He's brainbent," Janna said.

The manager was already looking down a list behind the counter and picking up a sonic key. He headed out of the office and along the rows to two-thirty. Approaching the unit, he sniffed. "I don't smell anything."

Mama, following him, said, "Is everyone's sense of smell numb? It smells so bad I want to gag."

Frowning and still sniffing, the manager punched a combination on the key, then turned the handle and pushed up the door. Mama peered in over his shoulder.

Since he had the door open, Janna did, too.

The unit was empty. Completely. Not even dust lay on the floor.

"She's right; you're brainbent," the manager said, and hauled the door down in a rattle of vinyl-coated metal. "What's your name and what unit do you have?"

Mama never hesitated. "Keegan, number 235." He headed for the car. "Let's go, my dear."

"So," Janna said a short time later, gunning the car west down Highway 10, "what did that accomplish?"

Mama settled back in his seat with a grin. "We know to bring a vacuum with our search warrant."

"What if she never brought the desktop and waitron back with her?"

Associative evidence such as fibers from the hotel carpet or Yi's house had to come from the waitron's treads. Santos herself had no personal contact with the crime scenes.

Mama smirked. "If she disposed of them on the way back, we can look all we like without a search warrant."

The car bucked in the wind. Lightning flashed through the purple and black clouds to the west, followed by a booming roll of thunder.

He stared out the window. "In her place, I'd drop them off a bridge, and that helps us, because without a side trip, the only suitable water is the Wakarusa River or Clinton Lake."

"I'll be happy to let you out to look. I'll even tie weights to your ankles to help you dive." Janna bared her teeth at him. "Just say where…babycheeks."

Lightning chased through the clouds overhead, followed by more thunder. Farther west, the first rain appeared, scattered large drops splattering heavily on the windshield. The body of the storm hit minutes later. They reached the bridge over the Wakarusa in a deluge.

Mama sighed.

Glimpsing the river below, swift and swollen from the spring rains, Janna did, too. "Let's hope Santos dumped everything in Clinton Lake. With that current, if she chose the river, god knows how far downstream our evidence could be by this time."

"Unless we get lucky and it caught on a snag or washed up on a sandbar." He leaned back in his seat, ticking his tongue.

Some luck like that would be welcome. Janna could not help feeling that without finding the waitron and holo controls somewhere between Topeka and Kansas City, the D.A. would never consider their case against Santos. Bank records might show Santos had purchased a waitron, but building her own was safer. She could shrug off the purchase of a large number of electronic parts, and a trip to Kansas City on the eighth, as part of developing her program. They needed evidence the perpetrator had headed east after the murder, a link to Kansas City…to Santos with her false alibi and secretly rented car and storage unit. Better yet: "What we could *really* use is an eye witness placing Santos in Topeka those Friday and Saturday nights."

"If we're wishing, there's nothing better than…" His voice trailed off.

Janna glanced sideways. He sat staring ahead through the streaming windshield, lips pursed. She continued driving, letting his wheels grind, but when they reached the edge of Topeka and he had said nothing more, she asked, "Are you going to tell me what's going on in your head?"

He stretched. "Where were you planning to go now?"

"The office, to see if we have a bank warrant on Santos." She yawned. Two nights without much sleep were catching up to her, stimulants or not.

"Let's stop at Beria first."

A jolt of adrenalin short-circuited a second yawn. "To talk to Santos?"

"Don't we usually interview suspects?" He pushed his glasses up his nose. "After all, there's nothing that solves a case better than a confession."

At Beria, they had to wait for their chance at Santos. The storm was playing the usual havoc with electrical systems and she had gone out to check and readjust an alarm.

Shortly after six o'clock, however, their suspect strolled into the employee lounge, pushing escaping wet wisps of her topknot off her face. Janna studieded Santos...paying close attention for the first time. The small bibi looked no different. Janna saw the same petite stature, the same narrow face, the same intelligent dark eyes. Nothing about her suggested a killer. Seeing them in two of the chairs there, Santos' brows hopped, but without uneasiness, only surprise.

She smiled in greeting—"A wet evening, isn't it?"—and poured herself a cup of caff. "I suppose I ought to enjoy the rain while I can, though. I won't see any on Mars."

"We heard about your new job," Mama said. "When's your last day here?"

"Day after tomorrow." Santos sipped the steaming caff. "Speaking of jobs, how is your case coming?"

Janna reached into her trenchcoat pocket and tapped on her microcorder. "We know who killed Armenda."

Santos frowned. "You're not thinking it's Jason Aschke, I hope."

"No."

The relief in Santos' face surprise Janna. Mama, however, nodded, as though the comment was one he expected. "He just distracted us for a while. Which was your intention in mentioning his robots, I suspect. Only, he didn't distract us quite long enough."

Santos stiffened. "I beg your pardon? What are you talking about?"

Mama's smile broadened. "Diversion...to keep suspicion away from yourself."

The dark eyes went wary. "I still don't understand."

Janna stood so she looked down at the smaller bibi. "I think you do, Miss Charisma Lesandra Santos."

Mama stood, too. "We know the gunmen were holos, projected by projector you refused to turn over to Armenda."

Give Santos credit for being prepared, and for acting ability. Her jaw dropped. "Those gunmen were *my* holos?" No attempt to deny who she was. No attempt to deny either the projector or the existence of the holos. "You mean some of the ones I've recorded for—"

"For your alleged shoot/don't shoot program," Janna interrupted. "Yes. But you know that already. Santos, we've talked to Grauer's niece. She told us where she spent the Friday and Saturday evenings of the robberies, when the two of you claimed to be together in Westport."

Santos barely hesitated before replying. "Did she tell you why I asked her to alibi me?"

"She told us the reason you gave her," Mama said. "We don't believe it. You lied to her, just as you lied to Grauer about when you recorded those images you showed him that Friday night. Because we also know about the Triton you leased, and the storage unit in Merriam…at Convenience Storage…now carefully cleaned out. Too bad when you tossed the holo controls and waitron in the water you didn't stay around to be sure they sank. In spite of the projector holes in it, the waitron must have had some buoyancy. We found it washed up on shore. Despite it being in the water, traces of its builder and handler will still be there…a flake of skin here, a hair there. Which DNA fingerprinting will prove are yours."

Now Santos reacted. Fear slashed across her face. Janna had just time to see that and the first motion of the hand holding the cup, then scalding caff sprayed her face and eyes. She reeled back, swearing, clutching at her face.

A cup clattered to the floor, followed by the thud of feet in rapid retreat.

Pain vanished beneath a surge of apprehension, triumph, and adrenalin. "Mama!" Janna scrubbed at her eyes with her sleeve.

A blurry Mama with coffee-spattered glasses vanished through the lounge door.

Janna stumbled for the door, too. Should she follow Mama or go out the front and try to head Santos off? Then she remembered that someone would have to let her out the front. She pounded down the hallway after Mama.

A closing door showed them where Santos had left the hallway. That took them through a workshop and down back stairs, through another door into a large garage with a row of parked service vans. Two of the bays stood empty. In the far wall, the door lowered with a soft hiss of rollers down vertical tracks.

Adrenalin jolted Janna again. If it closed, they would have to backtrack to find someone to let them out! She flung herself after Mama…between vans and toward the descending door. Less than a meter of clearance remained. Eighty centimers. Sixty. Forty.

They dived for the narrowing slit…rolling. The bar on the bottom brushed Janna's shoulder, then she was underneath and in the alley outside…clear. And instantly drenched.

She ignored the rain. Nothing mattered right now except the Beria van. Racing for the nearest mouth of the alley, they were in time to see ruby and amber tail lights headed west.

They pounded up the block toward Kansas Avenue…skidded around the corner…flung themselves into their own car. It bucked up off its parking rollers, fans screaming.

"Get us some backup, bibi!"

The car heeled sharply as Mama pulled it in a U turn and around the corner after the van. Ahead, the tail lights canted as the van turned right.

Janna shoved streaming hair off her face to reach her ear, only to remember she was not wearing her radio button. She grabbed the mike of the car radio. "Indian Thirty, Capitol! In pursuit of blue Beria Security service van, bearing plates Adam Adam Union two three three, headed north on Topeka Boulevard from Third and Topeka! Female driver is a possible signal nine." Labeling her a felony suspect would bring everyone in the area running. "Unknown if signal one." Although she assaulted them with only coffee, they could not afford to ignore the chance that she still had the needler used in killing Armenda.

On the radio, Dispatch repeated Janna's information.

They swung onto Topeka, the Meteor heeling sharply. The van raced ahead of them, its tail lights reflected in blurred streaks of amber and ruby on the puddled paving.

"Vehicle is approaching the bridge."

The van shot onto the bridge over the Kaw River. Halfway across, however, the tail lights flared. Reversing fans kicked up a spray of rainwater from the paving in front of the vehicle. Lights at the far end of the bridge told Janna why. Those chasing bands of red, white, and blue could only be light rails atop watch units from the Soldier Creek Division pulled sideways in a roadblock. More light rails flashing on the Meteor's rear scanner indicated backup coming to close off this end of the bridge, too.

Janna grinned. "Now we've got her."

The van settled to the paving, its side rear door sliding open. Santos jumped out and stood half crouched, twisting to peer one direction, then the other. Distance and the rain blurred her expression but she moved like an animal at bay. For a minute she just stood, then, as the Meteor set down and Janna and Mama slid open their doors, she launched herself across the northbound lanes toward the bridge railing.

Mama bailed out of the car. "Santos! No!"

The small bibi never paused. Reaching the railing, she vaulted over it, to Janna's shocked disbelief, and vanished.

Janna reached the rail seconds behind Mama. Together they peered over. But saw no sign of Santos. Staring down with dismay knotting her gut, Janna found only rain and deepening darkness and the swift, muddy water of the river below.

19

In the first stunned moments, thought and emotion churned in Janna's head with the turbulence of the water below. Why had Santos done it? How could she be so desperate? Then footsteps pounded up behind them and lions from the watch cars crowded the rail beside Mama and her.

"Jesus! I can't believe that. She went straight over," a she-lion exclaimed.

"I can't believe it, either," Mama said. "Will someone loan me a flashlight?"

That launched the search. They started with the bridge, peering over both railings, shining flashlights down where the pilings entered the water. An exercise in futility. The rain ate the beams before they covered half the distance. When someone produced a rope, Janna tied it around her waist and went over the rail for a look at the understructure of the bridge. Santos had not tricked them by somehow scrambling to safety there.

The search spread downstream along both banks, aided by a boat and the arrival of more officers...including Cruz and Zavara. The light rails' flashing bands of color lighted up the night, reflecting off wet slickers and helmets and the puddled pavement in an incongruous air of festiveness. It drew the inevitable crowd of on-lookers and media videographers, and members of each who slipped past the watchcar barricade and had to be escorted off the bridge.

"Brill, what the hell happened?" Cruz asked.

Zavara grunted. "Looks to me like Santos saved the state the expense of prosecution."

"We talked to her, that's all," Janna said. Holding the lapel of her trenchcoat out so it sheltered the microcorder, she played back the recording of their interview with Santos.

When it ended, Zavara shook her head. "She panicked at that? But...she sounded so controlled."

Mama nodded. "She looked controlled, too." He frowned toward the van. "Too controlled to fall apart that fast."

"We all know people can look that way even when they're pulled so tight they're at the breaking point," Cruz said. "Santos has probably been living on the edge since the murder and this was more stress than she could tolerate."

"A possibility I'm sure Maxwell counted on," Lieutenant Vradel's voice said from behind them.

They spun to see his burly, umbrella-carrying form striding up the bridge.

"Right, Brill?"

With him looking straight at her, she could not side-step answering. She shoved her hands in the pockets of her trenchcoat. "We hoped she would make some incriminating statement, yes. We didn't expect…this."

"Which explains why you felt it unnecessary to confide your plans to any of your colleagues, despite the fact that this investigation is supposed to be a team effort, and didn't arrange to have anyone covering the entrances while you went in?" Vradel shook his head. "I'm disappointed in you, Brill."

Again. She bit her lip, swearing silently.

"Just a minute, sir." Mama stepped between her and the lieutenant. "All this was my idea, as usual."

"Which your partner freely chose to go along with." The umbrella twirled over Vradel's head. "Didn't you even consider seeing what the bank records showed before confronting Santos?"

Janna swore again. What had they found? Something flatly incriminating, something that would have let them arrest her and avoid this tragedy?

"We thought we knew." Mama pushed rain-streaked glasses up his nose. "It did show she's bought extensive amounts of electronic parts and was in Kansas City on the eighth, didn't it?"

Zavara said, "It also shows she's been earning extra credit making independent security installations and modifications here and in Kansas City."

Such as adding voiced recognition to house-keepers.

"The interesting find," Cruz said, "is that she also bought a large number of unset gems."

Janna exchanged glances with Mama. Gems. Tony Ho's pay for his part in the riffs? Once they could show that his carry matched the purchased gems, Santos was tied to Tony as firmly as if a witness had seen them together.

"Yet you didn't bring Santos in for questioning," Mama said.

Cruz shrugged. "We were waiting to hear if you'd found the Triton and tied it to her."

So by not pooling their information, they had arrived…here. Janna eyed the bridge railing and swore. She and Mama certainly screwed up this time.

"Sergeant Maxwell." A she-lion approached them, rain steaming from her helmet and slicker. "We can't find any sign of the body and the boat's been downstream as far as Tecumseh."

"Let's call it for tonight, then," Vradel said. He sighed. "We'll alert law enforcement agencies on downstream so they can be watching for the body."

The she-lion nodded. "Yes, sir."

They all glanced east. Zavara pulled her shoulders back in one of her fluid stretch/flexes. "Maybe it's a good thing for us she panicked. If she'd stayed iced when you talked to her, she could have cut cloud after you left and gone mole until time to catch her shuttle flight. We might have lost her."

Vradel's mustache twitched. "No, that, at least, wouldn't work. Once she disappeared, we'd be watching the—"

"Son of a bitch," Mama interrupted. He pounded the heel of his hand against his forehead. "Lieutenant, I'm a world class lightwit."

"You heard it here first, boys and girls," Cruz murmured.

Vradel frowned at him. "Zip it. Go on, Maxwell."

"If there's one distinguishing feature of Armenda's murder, it's careful planning." Mama headed for the Beria van. "Why wouldn't she plan her escape, too? The computer tech at Beria said Santos first applied for Mars a year ago." He climbed into the van, still standing open, and after switching on the dome light, began peering around the interior.

The rest of them watched from the door. Shelves with pull-out bins lined both sides. On the top shelf facing the door, half a dozen little CCD cameras sat packed in a neat row, three with their lenses peering over the edge, three equipped with cable for a remote camera head.

Mama ran his hand along the top of the cameras. "It stands to reason she'd have contingencies in case we appeared to be closing in on her." His fingers traced from them down the inside of the shelf support. "One way to ensure we wouldn't stake out bus and air terminals looking for her is to make us think she's dead."

By going off the bridge? Janna frowned. That was a hell of a risk. Too risky.

Zavara echoed the thought, shaking her head. "No. She'd have to be brainbent to do it this way. I'm a strong swimmer and *I* wouldn't gamble that I could survive the fall and swim to safety."

Cruz nodded in agreement.

"There's no risk if she didn't jump."

"But you saw—" Cruz began.

"Not exactly," Mama said. "We saw this." He pushed something behind the shelf support.

Santos appeared in the doorway. Shock jolted Janna, echoed by indrawn breath from the others. Even as reflex backed her away from the woman jumping out of the van, she understood what Santos had done. Reaching out, Janna passed an arm through the petite figure.

"Son of a bitch," Cruz breathed.

"A holo?" Zavara groped in the space occupied by the image's face. "Jesus!"

A profanity Janna felt like echoing. Even this close, her hand apparently buried in the middle of Santos' chest, the image twisting left and right still looked real. The on-lookers at the ends of the bridge certainly thought so. They gasped as the holo raced through the group for the railing. They might have screamed when it vaulted over, except Mama's hand moved again, and the holo winked out of existence short of its leap.

Vradel's brows skipped. "Then with everyone's attention focused on the river, Santos just walked away."

Mama nodded.

Or had even been escorted off the bridge. Janna recalled the civilians and videographers that watchcar officers chased away earlier.

"Then we'd better dismantle this carnival and start looking for her, hadn't we," Vradel said.

Where she hid out, they could not discover, not without revealing they knew Santos was alive, but they did learn from co-workers at Beria that she had booked her flight to the Glenn platform on the shuttle Eclipse. A call to Forbes established that the Eclipse would be lifting from there in three days. So they let the newscanner stations run the bridge story as Santos intended everyone to believe it, and when the passengers for the Eclipse gathered in the shuttle lounge of the terminal, Cruz and Singer watched from the observation window of the terminal supervisor's office, high above the concourse.

Janna and Mama sat in the snack shop, waiting for their *Go* signal to come over ear buttons set to an operations frequency that let all the team members talk to each other.

"There goes the attendant's pen into his hair," Cruz' voice said in Janna's ear. "Passenger C. L. Santos has checked in."

They stood and sauntered out of the snack bar and across the concourse. The guard admitted them to the shuttle lounge. When they caught the attendant's eye, he nodded toward a figure looking out the windows. Janna gave thanks for the attendant's cooperation.

On her own she might have been fooled by what appeared to be an adolescent boy with blue-and-orange hair that matched the colors of his tiger-striped jumpsuit.

They drifted up on either side of her. Outside sat the Eclipse, awesome in size despite its distance from them on the far side of the parking apron, white portions gleaming against the flawless cobalt of the morning sky. A beautiful sky, Janna mused, on a fine May day made perfect by wrapping this case.

"Hello, Santos," Mama said. "Guess what. We found the holo projector in the van."

Blue mirror lenses hid the small bibi's eyes but her body stiffened.

Janna smiled and pulled her wrapstrap out of her thigh boot. "You're under arrest for the murder of Carel Armenda. I don't know how many escape plans you have, but think twice before trying one of them. There are only two ways out of here. Take a look at them."

Santos turned her head the directions of both. Weyneth filled the boarding exit with Showalter tucked in beside him. Zavara and Threefoxes blocked the door back onto the concourse, showing wolfish smiles that invited her to try passing them.

After a long minute, Santos held out her wrists. "I didn't start out to kill him."

Quickly, Janna said, "You have the right to remain silent." If Santos intended to confess, Janna wanted it admissible.

While she recited the Miranda, Janna pulled Santos' hands behind her back and gave the wrapstrap a practiced flip that wrapped it around both wrists before it adhered to itself.

"Do you understand your rights?" Mama asked when Janna finished.

Santos nodded. Apparently choosing silence. She said nothing more while they led her out to the car.

There Mama and Janna sat on either side of her in the back seat. Cruz and Singer rode up front. The two Crimes Against Property teams followed in another car.

Cruz guided the car onto the highway and headed north toward downtown. Santos shifted position, grimacing. "Car seats aren't made for sitting with your hands behind you, are they." She shifted again. "Planning the murder was a game."

Janna slipped a hand into her jacket pocket and tapped on her microcorder.

Singer twisted in his seat to look back at them. "Are you giving up your right to silence?"

She did not appear to hear him. "He made me so…" Her face twisted. "Angry isn't a strong enough word. He…infuriated me, filled me with outrage." Her voice rose. "I felt so…helpless to stop him from stealing what was *mine!"*

"Helpless?" Cruz gunned the car past a dawdling Bonsai run-about. "You filed suit."

Santos snorted. "That's when I still thought Armenda played by fair rules. I was so proud of myself for not losing my temper, too. I thought, I would handle this by the book and I would win because I was in the right. You know what he did? He had me come to the manager's office there at Konza and he sneered at me. He said, 'You might as well drop this pitiful suit because you don't have a snowball's chance in hell of winning. No jury's ever going to believe you invented this projector. A young woman on her first job out of school, a young *Hispanic* woman, with her E.E. degree from a *Kansas* university, accomplishing *this* by herself?'"

Janna exchanged glances with Mama over Santos' head. She had seen this before…suspects pouring out bottle-up feelings, seemingly unable to stop themselves no matter how self-destructive and incriminating the statements.

"He said, 'They'll say it's impossible…like expecting an elephant to fly, or a crow to sing. They'll say you must have had help from the men working with you, or at the very least used research done at MIT or some other real engineering school. You'll be laughed out of court.'"

Anger flared in Janna. She could imagine how Santos felt. That insufferable son of a bitch! She would have turned Armenda into a pretzel.

Santos bit her lip. "The longer I thought about what he said, the madder I got. He had all those awards for supposedly being such a wonderful employer and then he did *that* to me? He treated my heritage as though it gave me tacos for brains? That made me angriest of all. How could he, of all people, do that!"

"You mean," Mama said, "you expected better treatment just because he's hispanic descent, too?"

"Foolish, wasn't I?" Santos laughed, a short, bitter bark of sound. "After a bit, keeping the projector away from him wasn't enough. I fantasized about killing him. At first it was very direct…run him down with a car or shoot him, or maybe go to his office and while pretending to agree to surrender the projector, poison him. Then I started seeing that it was like an engineering problem and I began working out how I might really do it, and get away with it." She paused. "It's amazing how much information you can learn about guests lists and personal records with a modem and a little patience, despite all the entry safeguards on computers."

Disbelief spread through Janna, and more anger, now directed at Santos. She wanted to slap Santos. "You killed him to *see if it could be done*!"

"No!" Santos recoiled as though she had been slapped. "I just planned it. I never meant to really *do* it. I applied for Mars. I thought, the acceptance would come and I'd leave and that would be that. It didn't come and didn't come and when it did, I'd already built the waitron and desktop. I'd learned where the fund-raisers would be and hacked into the hotel and caterer's files to find who would be serving at them that I could have someone replace. I had license plates spotted and Tony waiting for word from me."

The traffic had thickened as they neared the center of town. Cruz encroached on the bicycle lane to avoid a Peterbuilt straying out of the commercial lane. "What I want to know is how Tony passed the r-scan at the hotel."

She shrugged. "That's easy with access to the security system. I programmed the computer to ignore the retinal scan for that Scib Card on that particular evening, and afterward, forget it had ever been given any such instructions."

Just like that. No black magic. No destruction of the Scib system integrity. Janna let her breath out in relief.

Anger still washed through her, however. "You must have seen you had a wonderful thing in your shoot/don't shoot program. Why didn't you just concentrate on developing that, sell your projector to some company that could fight Armenda for the right to it, and forget about the murder?"

Santos slunk down in the seat, biting her lip. "I thought about it. I wanted to. But…the farther things went, the more they had a force of their own. It was like being on an icy hill. I couldn't stop."

"So you've wasted your creativity and intelligence, and betrayed a lot of people who thought you were their friend," Mama said.

"Yes." The word emerged as a whisper. Santos pulled in on herself. "Maybe I can finish the program in prison."

Providing the state did not execute her.

Presently they turned down the ramp into the headquarters garage, and from there, took Santos up to the holding cells on the third floor. As the elevator doors opened, however, they found themselves facing a silver-haired man in a gray paisley tunic and breeches.

Janna frowned. Why was the most expensive criminal lawyer in town meeting them?

He nodded at Santos. "Miss Santos, my name is Halian Carew. I'm your attorney."

Santos gaped at him. "What? How?"

Cruz scowled. "She hasn't called an attorney yet."

Carew smiled. "A third party contacted me and offered a retainer on her behalf."

"Sydney Armenda." Mama said.

Carew nodded. "She will be visiting you shortly, Miss Santos. She asked me to tell you she has a business proposition, one that will be with her, personally, not Armenord. She hopes you will find it much more acceptable than the one proposed by her father."

Santos's mouth still hung open.

Singer smirked. "You'll find this a tough one, Carew. She's already confessed."

The lawyer's smile never wavered. "A challenge, perhaps, but not hopeless. Being careful officers, I'm sure you have the confession recorded, so you will of course see that I'm given a copy of the microcorder chip. Now, Sergeant Cruz, may we proceed with the formalities of booking? I'd like to confer with my client as soon as possible."

He led the way up the corridor toward the cell section, followed by Santos, Cruz, and Singer.

Janna and Mama found themselves left at the elevator. She frowned after the group. "Surely not even Carew can get her off."

"But he'll keep her alive, bibi."

Janna sighed. "So Santos lives and Sydney ends up with the projector, which she'll parlay into control and probably possession of Armenord. Vining can bask in the glory of announcing *case closed* to the media. We get to file reports."

Mama smiled. "A little more than that." He headed for the stairs. "We solved the case, law enforcement agencies everywhere will soon have a wonderful training aid…and you get your fondest wish."

She ran to keep up. "What fondest wish?"

"I'm moving out." He pushed through the stair door and headed down two steps at a time.

"Out?" She followed. "To where?"

"Downstairs with Arianna." He paused at the landing to look back. "You don't have to resume paying the entire rent on your apartment, however. Arianna knows a dancer with the Topeka Ballet who's looking for a place to live. Arianna says you'll love her. She treats living quarters like a bivouac, too. Owns one trunk of possessions and a portable barre so she can practice at home. She and Arianna are coming for dinner tonight so you can meet her."

"That's nice, before you move her in."

"Arianna and I thought it was only fair." He pushed his glasses up his nose. "It's an ideal arrangement. I'll still be close enough to provide you with advice and guidance."

Janna rolled her eyes. "I knew there'd be a catch."

He grinned. "It isn't a perfect world, bibi."

"No," she agreed, sobering. Catching Santos preserved the rules, but it did not change back the lives touched and forever altered by the violence between her and Armenda. "It isn't perfect."

As though reading her mind, Mama smiled up at her. "It's all we have, Jan, so we just have to keep caring about it and doing what we can to make it better. We've accomplished at least little of that today, haven't we?"

After a moment she shrugged. Maybe. A little. In any case, it would have to do.

They continued on down the stairs to start their reports.

Lee Killough Biography

Lee Killough has been storytelling almost as long as she can remember, starting somewhere around the age of four or five with making up her own bedtime stories. In grade school the stories became episodes of her favorite radio and TV shows: Straight Arrow, Wild Bill Hickock, Sergeant Preston of the Yukon, and Dragnet, beating the episode-writing practice of Trek fans by almost two decades.

Then, in keeping with wisdom that says the golden age of science fiction is about age eleven, a pre-teen Lee discovered science fiction. Having read every horse book in the school and city libraries, and repelled by the "teenager" novels that seemed to be about nothing but high school and boyfriends, she was desperately hunting for something new to read. The science fiction being shelved next to the horse stories, she start leafing through these future/space stories and decided to try one. The book was Leigh Brackett's *The Starmen of Llyrdis* and…lightning struck. Love at first sight. But along with the pleasure of devouring this marvelous literature came fear. She lived in a small Kansas town with a small library and she could see that as with the horse books, all too soon the section would be read dry.

Lee sometimes tells people that of course she writes SF; she deals with non-human species every day in her day job radiographing animals in the Kansas State University Veterinary Medical Teaching Hospital. But she really began writing SF to make sure she never ran out of science fiction to read. And because the mystery section adjoined the SF section, leading her to discover mysteries about the same time as SF, her stories tended to combine SF with mystery.

They still do…with a noticeable fondness for cops (the influence of Dragnet, Joseph Wambaugh's books, and TV shows like Hill Street Blues). A ghost cop in "*The Existential Man*", a vampire cop in *Blood Hunt* and *Bloodlinks*, published together in the trade edition *BloodWalk*, space-going cops, werewolf cops. And the future cops Janna Brill and Mama Maxwell of *Dopplegänger Gambit*, *Spider Play*, and *Dragon's Teeth*.

Lee lives and writes in Manhattan, Kansas (notice how Kansas and plains/prairie settings do turn up in her books), where she lives with a non-human—a Miniature Schnauzer—and enjoys a committed relationship with, fittingly, a book dealer.

Michael Herring Biography

Michael Herring was born in 1947 in North Carolina. He received his art education at World Campus Afloat-Chapman College, Byam Shaw School of Drawing and Painting, London, Royal College of Art, also in London, as well as Cal State University in Long Beach, Ca.

During his twenty plus year career, he has done cover art for Science Fiction and Fantasy authors from Asimov to Zelazny. He currently lives in California with his wife, Betsy French, a photographer, and their cat, Poi-Pooh.

An excerpt from Lee Killough's *BloodWalk*

He dreamed of death, and Undeath. Inspector Garreth Mikaelian stood backed against the wall of an alley in San Francisco's North Beach, pinned by the hypnotic gaze of eyes glowing like rubies, unable to move even enough to ease the pressure where the handcuffs looped over his belt pressed into the small of his back. Red light glinted in the vampire's hair, too...not a beautiful woman, some distant part of him noticed, but she used her long, showgirl legs and mahogany hair to seem like one.

"You're going to like this, inspector." She gave him a sultry smile. "You'll feel no pain. You won't mind a bit that you're dying."

There was pleasure in the touch of her soft, cool lips, and it persisted even after the kisses moved down his jaw and became bites pinching his skin in hard, avid nips. High-heeled boots made her five-ten tower even higher above his five-eight. Lassitude held him passive while she tipped his head back to reach his throat better.

Her mouth stopped over the artery pounding there. "Lovely," she breathed. "Now, don't move." Her tongue slid out to lick his skin. She stretched her jaw. He felt fangs extend, then she bit down.

A spasm of intense pleasure lanced through him. Catching his breath, he threw his head farther back and strained up against her sucking mouth.

Presently, though, as cold and weakness spread through him, concern invaded the ecstacy, a belated recognition of something unnatural, wrong. Evil. Fear stirred. He started to twist away sideways, but to his dismay could not move. Her body slammed into his, pinning him helpless against the wall...despite the fact he outweighed her by a good fifty pounds. The fear sharpened.

Use your gun, you dumb flatfoot, a voice in his head snarled.

Her grip blocked him from reaching the weapon. He sucked in a breath to yell for help, but her hand clamped over his mouth. In desperation he sank his teeth into it. Her blood scorched his mouth and throat…liquid fire.

The vampire sprang away, ripping out his throat in her retreat.

He collapsed as though drained of bone as well as blood.

She laughed mockingly. “Goodbye, inspector. Rest in peace.”

Her footsteps faded away, leaving him face down in his blood. Leaving him to listen in helpless terror to heartbeats and breathing that gradually slowed, stumbled, and stopped.

Garreth woke shaking.

Sitting up in bed, he leaned his forehead against updrawn knees, waiting for the adrenalin rush to subside. Shit. How many times did that make for the damn dream this week?

Except that it could not be called a dream exactly. A dream was something one woke from, returning to the ordinary. For him that would be his San Francisco apartment, and joining his partner Harry Takananda in the Homicide squadroom at the SFPD’s Bryant Street station. Instead…

Garreth raised his head to look around the den-cum-efficiency above Municipal Court Clerk Helen Schoning’s garage in Baumen, Kansas…wood paneling, leather chairs, kitchenette, and closet forming one side of the corner bathroom. The uniform hanging on the open door, tan shirt with dark brown shoulder tabs and pocket flaps to match the trousers, belonged to the Baumen Police Department. Despite heavy drapes which left the room in midnight darkness, he saw every detail clearly, even to the lettering on the shirt’s shoulder patch. The daylight outside pressed down on him like a great weight. And his throat already tickled with building thirst.

He did not wake these days, merely exchanged one nightmare for another. The vampire was memory, not dream. She had existed...Lane Barber, born Madelaine Bieber seventy years ago in this little prairie town where he tracked her, where he had killed her. But not destroyed her.

Falling back against the pillow to the accompanying grit of dried earth in the air mattress beneath the sheet under him, he sighed. In all honesty, he had to agree that Bauman probably deserved better than to be called a nightmare. Everyone believed the cover story he used to justify asking questions about Lane, that his father had been her illegitimate son. They accepted him as one of the Biebers, albeit a strange one, no doubt because he came from California. The 8:00 PM to 4:00 AM shift despised by Baumen's five other officers suited his needs perfectly and the rolling hills around pastured plenty of cattle who never missed the blood he took from them.

Vampires did not *have* to drink human blood.

It was a quiet town, unnoticed by the rest of the world, a good place to hide, to bury himself—he smiled wryly—at least until someone began wondering too much about his quirks, and why he never aged.

And then? When he wanted to leave this nightmare, what did he wake up to? Where did he go?

The pressure of the unseen daylight outside shifted. Approaching sunset. *Rise and shine, my man.* Garreth swung out of bed and after folding it back into a couch, headed for the bathroom.

He shaved without turning on the light so his eyes would not reflect red. A sharp-boned face with sandy hair and grey eyes stared back at him from the mirror, boyish-looking despite the mustache he had grown and still a stranger's face even a year and half after replacing the beefier one he had grown up with. *No, boys and girls,* he mused, running the humming razor around the edges of the sandy mustache, *it isn't true vampires don't reflect.*

As he dressed, the tickle in Garreth's throat grew, flaring to full-blown thirst. Taking a thermos from the little refrigerator, he poured some of the contents into a tall glass and leaned against the counter to drink.

The cattle blood tasted flat and bland, like watered-down tomato juice, never satisfying the appetite, no matter how much he drank, but he refused to become what Lane had been, preying on people, drinking them dry whenever she felt it safe to do so and breaking her victims' necks to keep them dead. He scowled down into the glass. Since he got along on animal blood, that was all he would use! He just wished…

Garreth finished off his breakfast in a gulp and rinsed out the glass in the sink. *I just wish I could like it.*

Praise for Lee Killough's BloodWalk

Let's hear it for Meisha Merlin Publishing! Thanks to this Georgia-based publisher, Lee Killough's excellent vampire detective stories Blood Hunt and Bloodlinks, are back in print after a hiatus of some ten years...BloodWalk is strong in both police procedure and character development...BloodWalk's final resolution is a testament to Killough's skill as a writer.
—Cathy Krusbergin The Vampir's Crypt

A fine blend of mystery and the supernatural. Who says you can't do anything original with the vampire story?
—SF Chronicle

Vampirism plays a strong motivation and plotting in BloodWalk but at its heart, this is a detective story—a police story worthy of McBain or Wambaugh.
—Bayron Magazine, Dec. 97

One of the pleasures of Killough's fiction is persuasive characterization. If you're looking for a different kind of novel, this is it.
—Fantasy Review

Lee Killough's BloodWalk is a dark duet of
previously unavailable vampire novels that have been
resurrected for the enjoyment of readers of this genre or
anyone seeking a vampire story with a different slant.
Killough's writing blends supernatural elements with
fantasy and mystery to create an alluring
story with intriguing characters.
—Explorations, Oct/Nov '97

Fantasy readers should appreciate Killough's variations
on the standard form.
—Locus

Killough can be looked to for surprises in plot.
—Library Journal

Now back in print are Lee Killough's
Blood Hunt and *Bloodlinks*.

Together for the first time in one Volume:
BloodWalk

Visit our web site or write us at the address below for ordering information

Meisha Merlin Publications, Inc
PO Box 7
Decatur, GA 30031

Storm Constantine's
Grigori Trilogy volume one:
Stalking Tender Prey

The Grigori are an ancient race. Powerful people, possessing abilities and senses humans do not have. They live amoung us, their presence clear to those who have eyes to see...

Storm Constantine is a tremendously impressive novelist.
—*Locus*

She is a daring, romantic sensualist as well as a fine storyteller.
—Poppy Z. Brite

She charms the young and defiant with apocalypses of her own design.—*The Sunday Times*

This housebrick of a book is possibly the best novel I have ever read.
—Ian Read in *Chaos International* #20

Fast-paced, bright and lively entertainment from easily the most popular writer in the known universe.
—Michael Swanwick

Janet Kagan is a seductive and engaging storyteller, a first-class Science Fiction writer.
—David Hartwell

HELLSPARK

by

Janet Kagan

Kristine K. Rusch—Hugo, Locus, and World Fantasy
Award winning author of over thirty novels
teams up with
Kevin J. Anderson—X-Files, Star Wars, and the new
Dune Series co-author
to bring you a set of novels that will forever change
your dream of becoming someone else…
into a nightmare!

"Storm Constantine is a myth-making Gothic queen, I wouldn't swap her for a dozen Anne Rices."
—Neil Gaiman

"Dare I say that this is one of my favorite collections? I think I do"
—Jenny B. British Fantasy Society Newsletter

Three Heralds of the Storm,
three short stories by the peerless fabulist
Storm Constantine.

"Caitlín R. Kiernan is a origional."
—Clive Barker

"Deeply, wonderfully, magnificently nasty."
—Neil Gaiman

"Her work needs no label but the byline."
—Poppy Z. Brite

Discover her for yourself.

Caitlín R. Kiernan's

Candles for Elizabeth

Come check out our web site for details on these Meisha Merlin authors!

Kevin J. Anderson
Storm Constantine
Keith Hartman
Tanya Huff
Janet Kagan
Caitlín R. Kiernan
Lee Killough
Sharon Lee & Steve Miller
Adam Niswander
Selina Rosen
Kristine Kathryn Rusch
S. P. Somtow
Allen Steele

http://www.angelfire.com/biz/MeishaMerlin